THE

RISEN

CITY

ALSO BY ISABELLE STEIGER

The Empire's Ghost
The Rightful Queen

THE
RISEN
CITY

Book Three of the Paths of Lantistyne

———————— ⚜ ————————

ISABELLE STEIGER

ST. MARTIN'S
PRESS
NEW YORK

First published in the United States by St. Martin's Press, an imprint of St. Martin's Publishing Group

THE RISEN CITY. Copyright © 2022 by Isabelle Steiger. All rights reserved. Printed in the United States of America. For information, address St. Martin's Publishing Group, 120 Broadway, New York, NY 10271.

www.stmartins.com

Map by Karol Sowa

Library of Congress Cataloging-in-Publication Data

Names: Steiger, Isabelle, 1989– author.
Title: The risen city / Isabelle Steiger.
Description: First edition. | New York: St. Martin's Press, 2022. |
    Series: Paths of Lantistyne; book 3
Identifiers: LCCN 2022033139 | ISBN 9781250088529 (hardcover) |
    ISBN 9781250088536 (ebook)
Subjects: LCGFT: Fantasy fiction. | Novels.
Classification: LCC PS3619.T44845 R57 2022 | DDC 813/.6—dc23/eng/20220715
LC record available at https://lccn.loc.gov/2022033139

Our books may be purchased in bulk for promotional, educational, or business use. Please contact your local bookseller or the Macmillan Corporate and Premium Sales Department at 1-800-221-7945, extension 5442, or by email at MacmillanSpecialMarkets@macmillan.com.

First Edition: 2022

10 9 8 7 6 5 4 3 2 1

For my teachers and friends

DRAMATIS PERSONAE

ADORA AVESTRI: Second child of Jotun Avestri and Maribel Hahrenraith. Newly crowned queen of Issamira.

ALESSA: Kelken IV's older half-sister. Illegitimate.

AMALI SELRESHE: Wife of Dahren Selreshe and mother to Jocelyn. A skilled archer and hero of the war against Gerde Selte of Hallarnon.

AMEREI: An ancient spirit of dubious motives. Warned Marceline that her comrades were in danger during the massacre in Silkspoint, but was pronounced dangerous and untrustworthy by Yaelor.

ARIANROD MARGRAINE: Marquise of Esthrades. A powerful mage and unparalleled strategist.

BENWICK: A veteran guardsman at Stonespire Hall.

BRADDOCK: A Hallern army deserter and former mercenary. Companion to Morgan Imrick.

CADFAEL: A former arena fighter and soldier of King Eira's. Bears a scar on his face from a near-fatal wound inflicted by Talis. Brother to Rhia.

CAIUS MARGRAINE: Arianrod's father and the previous marquis of Esthrades. Died of illness.

CERISE: Marceline's older half-sister. Apprentice grocer to Halvard.

DAHREN SELRESHE: One of the foremost lords of Issamira. Husband of Amali and father to Jocelyn.

DAVEN MARGRAINE THE SIXTH: Direct ancestor of Arianrod Margraine. Allied with Talia Avestri against the Elesthenian Empire.

DAVEN MARGRAINE THE ELEVENTH: Arianrod's grandfather and a former marquis of Esthrades.

DEINOL: Bastard-born bandit. Partners with Lucius. Friend of Morgan, Roger, and Seth.

DENTON "DENT" HALLEY: Guardsman serving Arianrod Margraine. Her longtime favorite and confidant.

DIRK: One of Kelken IV's most trusted retainers. Attended Kel personally for many years. Sacrificed himself to ensure the destruction of Mist's Edge.

EDITH SELWYN: Administrator of Lanvaldis for Imperator Elgar. A commonborn scholar.

EIRA BRIONEL: King of Lanvaldis. Killed by Shinsei in the conquest of Araveil. Never married or sired children.

EIRNWIN: Adviser to Kelken III and Kelken IV. Taken prisoner after the destruction of Mist's Edge.

ELGAR: Imperator of Hallarnon, Aurnis, and Lanvaldis. A mage skilled in enchantments.

ELIN MARGRAINE: Born Elin Vandrith. A noblewoman of Lanvaldis. Mother to Arianrod Margraine. Died in childbirth.

EUVALIE VANDRITH: Head of House Vandrith, a Lanvaldian noble family. Twin sister to Elin Margraine. Aunt to Ithan Vandrith and Arianrod Margraine.

GAO SHRIKE: One of Ryo Serenin's *kaishinrian,* or royal guard. Previously a notorious drunkard and carouser, he swore off alcohol (but not mischief) after his appointment.

GERALD HOLM: Captain under King Eira and loyal to his nephews, Laen and Hywel. Uncle to Ilyn.

GERDE SELTE: Tyrannical grand duchess of Hallarnon, fond of torture and bloodshed. Died of illness. Succeeded by Norverian.

GHILAN: Former arena fighter with an insatiable lust for combat. In service to Edith Selwyn, but currently on loan to Varalen Oswhent.

GRAVIS INGRET: Captain of the guard at Stonespire Hall under both Arianrod Margraine and her father, Caius.

HALVARD: A grocer from the Fades in Valyanrend. Morgan has been his customer for many years.

HAYNE: One of Kelken IV's most trusted retainers. Protected him from an assassination attempt in his early childhood.

HEPHESTION AVESTRI: Youngest child of Jotun Avestri and Maribel Hahrenraith. Prince of Issamira. Called "Feste" by his family.

HERREN: One of Kelken IV's most trusted retainers. Killed during the journey from Second Hearth to Mist's Edge.

HYWEL MARKHAM: Younger brother of Laen Markham and legitimized nephew of King Eira. Current heir to the throne of Lanvaldis.

ILYN HOLM: Junior Lanvaldian guardswoman and niece of Gerald Holm. Tasked with escorting Laen and Hywel Markham.

ITHAN VANDRITH: A Lanvaldian nobleman. The youngest son of a youngest son. A skilled swordsman. Cousin to Arianrod Margraine. His leg was shattered during a battle with Ghilan.

JILL BRIDGER: Guardswoman patrolling the city of Stonespire. Recruited by and protégée of Denton Halley.

JOCELYN SELRESHE: An Issamiri noblewoman from a distinguished family and a mage skilled in controlling the minds of others. Subdued by Arianrod and executed by Adora after attempting to usurp the throne of Issamira.

JOTUN AVESTRI: Previous king of Issamira. Father to Landon, Adora, and Hephestion. Fatally injured when his horse threw him during a celebratory procession.

KELKEN RAYL III: Previous king of Reglay and father to Kelken IV. Assassinated by Shinsei.

KELKEN RAYL IV: Current king of Reglay. A boy of twelve. Can walk with the assistance of crutches, but only for brief periods and with difficulty.

LAEN MARKHAM: Legitimized nephew of King Eira and older brother of Hywel Markham. Killed by Edith Selwyn.

LANDON AVESTRI: Oldest child of Jotun Avestri and Maribel Hahrenraith. Former crown prince of Issamira, and believed dead by its people. In reality, exiled by his sister Adora when he refused to assume the throne.

LEN VARSTEN: Roger's cousin and greatest rival in scheming. Left Valyanrend many years ago to seek his fortune as a merchant.

LIRIEN ARVEL: A *wardrenfell*: a human who is not born a mage, but who comes to be inhabited by stray magic that is powerful but limited in scope. Possesses control over water, including unparalleled healing magic. Reviled as a witch and expelled from her hometown of Sundercliff after she healed a dying boy there.

LUCIUS AQUILA: A *shinrian* who fled Aurnis after its conquest and eventually settled in Valyanrend. Worked as a bandit alongside Deinol.

MARCELINE: A bastard child, orphan, and skilled pickpocket living in Valyanrend's Sheath Alleys. Raised by Tom Kratchet.

MARIBEL AVESTRI: Born Maribel Hahrenraith. Wife of Jotun Avestri and mother to Landon, Adora, and Hephestion.

MIKEN: A *wardrenfell* who possessed control over earth. Accidentally tortured to death by Elgar's men.

MORGAN IMRICK: Owner and proprietor of the Dragon's Head tavern in Valyanrend's Sheath Alleys. Friend of Roger, Deinol, and Lucius, companion to Braddock, and Seth's employer.

MOUSE: Sobriquet of Zackary Smith, former leader of the largest resistance group in Valyanrend. Nominally an apprentice smith. Killed in the massacre in Silkspoint.

NAISHE KADIFE: Current leader of the largest resistance group in Valyanrend. A skilled archer and hunter. Of Akozuchen descent, through both parents. Her full given name is Vanaishendi.

NASSER KADIFE: Naishe's father and an old friend of Braddock's. A mercenary and talented archer.

NORVERIAN: Gerde Selte's favorite companion and immediate successor. Incompetent and wasteful. Killed and replaced by Elgar.

QUENTIN GARDENER: Captain of Valyanrend's city guard.

RANA KORINU: One of Ryo Serenin's *kaishinrian,* or royal guard. The first woman to be appointed to that position in Aurnis's history.

RASK: A member of Valyanrend's resistance and its most talented swordsman.

RHEILA HALFEN: Aunt to Roger and mother of Len. Reverted to her former surname after outliving two husbands.

RHIA: Cadfael's sister and a refugee from Lanvaldis. Served Adora as captain of the guard in Eldren Cael.

RITSU HANAE: A young Aurnian swordsman. Compelled by Elgar's magic to believe he is Shinsei, an unquestioning and indefatigable servant of the imperator. The enchanted sword that increased his physical abilities but also perpetuated his loss of memory was lost in the destruction of Mist's Edge.

ROGER HALFEN: An exceptional swindler and thief, from a long line of famous swindlers and thieves. Friend of Morgan, Lucius, Deinol, and Seth. Half-unwilling mentor to Marceline.

RYAM OSWHENT: Varalen's young son, and Elgar's hostage to assure his father's compliance. Afflicted with the great wasting illness.

RYO SERENIN: Prince of Aurnis. A *shinrian* whose swordplay equaled that of any in his royal guard.

SEBASTIAN: Ritsu's closest friend. Ritsu killed him while under Elgar's control.

SEREN ALMASY: Arianrod Margraine's bodyguard. A fighter of formidable skill who specializes in knives. Born in Esthrades, but spent half her life in the Sahaian Empire training to be an assassin of the Inxia Morain.

SETH: Morgan's kitchen boy. Killed trying to help an injured Seren.

SHINSEI: See *Ritsu Hanae.*

TALIA AVESTRI: Issamira's Rebel Queen and founder of House Avestri. Drove the Elesthenian Empire out of Issamira.

TALIA PARNELL: Member of Valyanrend's resistance. Reports to Rask. Severely injured during the massacre in Silkspoint but stitched up by Naishe.

TALIS: A *wardrenfell* with control over wind. A peasant from the mountains of southeastern Lanvaldis. Gained her powers after jumping from a cliff to escape the men who massacred the rest of her village.

TOM KRATCHET: A thief and information broker. Raised Marceline after the death of her mother.

VARALEN OSWHENT: Elgar's chief strategist, unwillingly recruited. Rose to prominence after advising King Eira's soldiers during their war with Caius Margraine.

VESPAS HAHRENRAITH: Younger brother of Maribel Avestri. A former general of great renown, and the current lord of Shallowsend. Recently reinstated to the army by Adora.

VOLTEST: A *wardrenfell* with control over fire. An Aurnian scholar who was held in captivity after Aurnis's fall.

WREN FLETCHER: A skilled fletcher and Mouse's childhood friend. A senior member of Valyanrend's resistance.

YAELOR: An ancient spirit of valor who guided Cadfael to Adora's aid. Claims a special connection with Cadfael, but refuses to disclose its nature.

ZACKARY SMITH: See *Mouse.*

ZARA SHING: Esthradian healer of Sahaian descent. Educated in the medical arts in Sahai. Tended Arianrod Margraine's wounds after she was nearly whipped to death by her father in her youth.

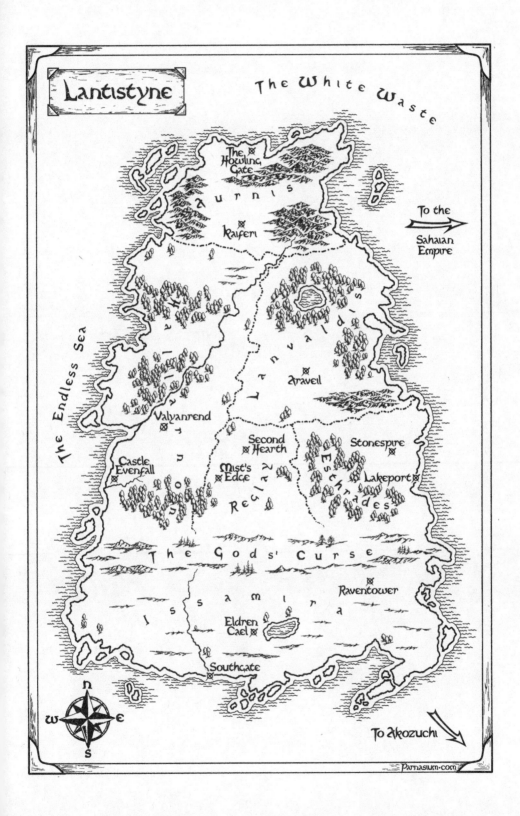

THE

RISEN

CITY

CHAPTER ONE

Valyanrend

THE MESSAGE WAS pinned with a knife to the guardhouse roof—a little melodramatic, Marceline thought, but Roger had insisted. It was just some old nearly blunt blade Morgan had only ever used to carve meat, but she had to admit it looked impressive from a distance. Almost worth the trouble she had taken to arrange it that way without being seen.

The morning sun was still gray and weak, but a crowd had already gathered, watching a couple of Imperator Elgar's men haul a ladder out to take the message down. Marceline was just another unmemorable spectator, come to gawk with everybody else. There was no chance that the soldiers would allow any civilians a look at the parchment's contents, but identical missives had been left in much more accessible locations in other neighborhoods. Roger's words would spread, she had no doubt of that.

Ever since she, Roger, Morgan, and Braddock had sworn to one another to kill Elgar and break his hold on their city or die in the attempt, it felt like they hadn't stopped moving for a moment. But all their movements until now had been in the shadows; this was the first action they had taken that was meant to draw attention. Though Roger had written the letter, they had agreed on its contents together. *To our false ruler,* it began. That would certainly raise the guards' alarm. *You must think yourself clever, but the depths of your evil designs are revealed to me. You must think yourself safe, but I can unravel the very power that protects you, just as shadow melts away at the touch of light. And soon this whole city will know the truth that you have tried so desperately to hide. You will send all the soldiers of Valyanrend in search of me, yet your eyes will never behold me—not until it is too late. I am the Fang, and your life is mine.*

"Why are you writing *I*?" Marceline had asked him. "It's from all of us, isn't it?"

"Aye, but it's more impressive if he thinks a single person is responsible for it all. And safer, if he should somehow track one of us down."

"I still think we're giving away too much," Braddock had said. "Why not hide the fact that we can undo his magic, and let him think himself invulnerable?"

"Under other circumstances, that might work," Roger said. "But if Elgar doesn't know about vardrath steel and its capabilities already, he will soon. Your aristocrat in Issamira knows, and he'll be gathering as much of it as possible to bring against Elgar in the war to come. Elgar has more than enough spies and informants to hear about that, at least. If he already knows a weapon against him exists, better to make him fear how close to him it might be."

"Fair enough," Morgan said. "My only objection is the name you've chosen. You don't think it's too . . . revealing?"

Roger had laughed. "Because dragons have fangs? That might be why I chose it, but it'll hardly lead him to the Dragon's Head. Most predators have teeth, after all."

The semicircle of civilians around the guardhouse hadn't grown any smaller, but it was still mostly silent, only a tentative question or two, and no reaction when they went unanswered. That wouldn't do. Marceline scanned the crowd, searching for a potential troublemaker, and settled on a broad middle-aged man who'd shouldered his way front and center, arms folded and eyes narrowed in the attitude of one who always thought he could do a better job than whoever was doing it.

Marceline tugged delicately at his sleeve, looking up at him with big wondering eyes. "Do you know what this is all about, sir? Why won't they let us see that paper?"

The man drew himself up, her implication that she thought he was the one to ask bolstering his own high opinion of himself. "It's a disgrace, that's what it is. Elgar's lot were so eager to assure us that ghastly slaughter in Silkspoint was necessary to destroy Valyanrend's rebels and traitors. But if the resistance has really been stamped out, what do you make of *that*? Blasted incompetence."

"There's no reason it *has* to be from the resistance," muttered a young woman at his elbow. "It could just be some fool playing a prank."

But Marceline had chosen well; the man wasn't going to allow anyone to quibble with him now that he'd put himself forward as an authority in front of an audience. "The specific author's not the point. It's some malcontent or other, after we'd been promised the malcontents were gone. It's the *principle* of the thing. And if it were a prank, would *they* be taking it so seriously?" He raised his voice. "What's it say, then? Is it from the resistance, or is it some new threat, upon the still-warm ashes of the old?"

"It's guard business," one of Elgar's men retorted. "Keep your distance."

"There." The man fluttered a dismissive hand at the guards. "It's suspicious, and it's incompetent, and it's disgraceful."

An older boy rolled his eyes. "They haven't even finished reading it, idiot. They've only just fetched it down, and you keep interrupting them."

"But they got here quick enough, didn't they?" another woman called from the middle of the crowd, shoving her way toward them. "If they're that worried about what it might be, about what'll happen if regular folk get a look at it—"

"That's what I've been saying!" the first man crowed. "We shouldn't just let them tuck it away! If it's a matter that concerns our safety, we've a right to know about it!"

A dozen voices shouted their agreement, some shouting directly at the guards themselves, who clustered more tightly around the parchment. They were about to be in the worst possible situation. If you know you can't prevent a damning piece of news from getting out, the best thing to do is act like you don't care who knows, so as not to point out your own weakness. But these guards had no notion that the parchment they had in their possession was not the only one of its kind. By the end of the day, most of Valyanrend would know not just the precise contents of the messages, but the fact that those contents had rattled Elgar's men.

All in all, a fine morning's work.

As the shouting reached a crescendo, Marceline slipped, forgotten, out of the crowd and down a narrow side street. A few more turns brought her to what seemed to be a dead end between two vacant and crumbling houses. But if you went all the way to the end and pressed against the wall and turned your head just so, you'd notice a well-concealed gap between it and the house on its left. Marceline checked to make sure she was truly alone, then squeezed into the space, holding her breath until it widened out and angled down. A few more steps, and she was beneath the ground, at the mouth of one of the labyrinthine series of tunnels stretching beneath Valyanrend; a few more after that, and she'd stepped from daylight to darkness to the flickering light of a line of torches.

In just a matter of days, the aspect of the tunnels had changed completely. As soon as Marceline and the others at the Dragon's Head had decided to take Elgar down, they knew the first thing to do was to reveal the tunnels to the leader of the resistance. Marceline had shown Naishe, and Naishe had shown Wren and Rask. All three of them agreed this was too crucial a find to reveal to the common ranks of the resistance until absolutely necessary; they still didn't believe any spies had infiltrated their ranks, but the more souls that had to keep a secret, the more perilous its survival. They had informed only Mouse's most trusted subordinates and a handful of their own, and the lot of them had set to work on the spare logs and scraps of metal Wren had obtained from his many contacts in Iron's Den. They had to be careful how much and when they brought materials down, so as not to arouse suspicion, but even with those restrictions, the work was well underway: a line of torches in hastily fashioned standing braziers, stretching down into the depths. Not everyone had Roger's sense of direction or would be able to memorize his map of the tunnels, and lugging a torch around everywhere you went would be cumbersome. So they lit up the passages, starting with the most useful:

the only one that led out of the city, and the ones that led to Iron's Den, Sheath Alleys, and a couple other convenient neighborhoods. They'd also illuminated the path to the nine statues in their underground chamber; it was the biggest room they'd found, and it served as a secure meeting place. It was there that Marceline ventured, only to find that three people had beaten her there.

Roger Halfen was no surprise; though the swindler cultivated an attitude of lazy carelessness, no one knew better than Marceline how tirelessly he could pursue a goal he'd set his eye on. Though he had long resisted the idea of striking against Elgar directly, now that he had changed his mind, he had done so wholeheartedly. He was leaning against the statue of Tethantys, perhaps trying to make up for how it had unnerved him at first. "Did you stay to see how the crowd took it?" he asked Marceline, without any preamble.

"Aye, I remember what you told me. I made sure they were stirred up."

It *was* surprising not to see Naishe; the new leader of Valyanrend's resistance worked even harder than Roger, but perhaps that was why she couldn't be spared now. Instead, Marceline looked into the perpetually sullen face of Rask, the resistance's most talented swordsman. The web of burns covering his right hand and wrist had fully scarred over, but the skin still looked raw and angry, as if his hand had been partially unmade. Marceline had known people who covered up similar unsightliness with gloves, but she would know nothing about Rask if she didn't know that was something he would never do. "And you weren't followed?"

She rolled her eyes. "No, I'm a complete idiot, so I didn't check."

Something twitched at the corner of Rask's mouth that might have been amusement—a rare sight, but not so rare as it once was. Marceline was slowly coming to terms with the idea that Rask might not completely dislike her, despite the terrible way they had started off. "Our noble leader will be busy till evening, but she sent me to speak with her voice if a question for the resistance comes up."

"How are things going with Nasser?" Marceline asked Roger. Naishe's father had come to Valyanrend to find her, but he had no idea how essential she had become to the fight against Elgar. Marceline had thought Naishe would want to have things out with him as soon as possible, but instead she had done her best to avoid him altogether. And if that was her choice, none of the rest of them dared breathe a word to him about it, even though he'd been staying under the roof of the Dragon's Head itself.

"You ought to be asking how things are going with Braddock," the proprietor of the Dragon's Head interrupted. Morgan Imrick had a sheaf of papers in one hand, and was idly twirling her vardrath steel dagger in the other. "He's been friends with Nasser for ages. I've had to do all I can to keep them apart so he doesn't crack."

Naishe might be the leader of the resistance, but Marceline thought Morgan had truly become the leader of the fight to depose Elgar. She knew most of the details of what Morgan and Braddock had gone through in Issamira, but even then, the change in Morgan was remarkable. Marceline had always respected her, as a woman who was tough, capable, and possessed of her own unshakable code. But Morgan had come back with a purpose she'd lacked before, and it had sharpened her to a perfect edge. "While you have so many of your people down here lighting pathways," she said to Rask, "I also thought we might choose some portion of the tunnels to make into a storehouse—a little food and water, things that're dried and salted, that'll last a long time. Just in case the worst should happen, and we think it's not safe to be aboveground for a while."

"I hope it doesn't come to that," Rask said, "but I can definitely see the sense in it."

"What news from your benefactor?" Roger asked, casting a glance at the dagger Morgan never went anywhere without. It had come from Vespas Hahrenraith, uncle to the queen of Issamira, as part of the deal she had made with him: her information from within Valyanrend in exchange for his knowledge of the forces gathering against it.

"He's certain Elgar must know of Queen Adora's intentions by now," Morgan said. "It's not as if she's being furtive about it—she made a speech on the day of her coronation, and her armies have already been summoned. Elgar must have received word of that, at least, but he's made no proclamation to the people. At this rate, Hallern travelers returning from Issamira may spread the news through Valyanrend before he does."

"What has Adora said about her reasons for the war?" Rask asked.

"That she moves in defense of her ally, to drive the Hallern invaders out of Esthrades. And that Elgar's ambition to possess the whole continent is clear, and they will not be subjugated by northerners again."

"I expect those reasons were popular with the people," Roger said. "We are, unfortunately, their enemies of old, just as the Esthradians were their allies. Though I thought sentiment toward Esthrades had cooled in this generation, what with the enmity between Caius Margraine and Jotun Avestri."

Morgan shook her head. "It's enmity their children didn't share, apparently. Vespas wrote that Arianrod Margraine was instrumental in defeating the mage responsible for the horrors Braddock and I witnessed in Issamira—Lord and Lady Selreshe's daughter. He wouldn't say how, precisely, but the queen must owe her a debt."

"So mages can be defeated." Roger smiled dryly. "Encouraging news, since we're trying to do just that."

"I can still hardly believe all this is true," Rask said. "A few months ago, nothing you said could've convinced me. But I saw the destruction wrought by that cursed thing with my own eyes."

They all looked to the black stone that lay in the center of the semicircle of statues. It was no bigger than a fist, but Elgar had used it to kill dozens, through the rage it had inspired in his soldiers. Though the spell that had once enchanted it had been destroyed by the knife that Morgan held, none of them had wanted to carry it on their person, or keep it in their homes. But neither could they throw it away, in case there was more to learn from it.

Roger said what they were all thinking. "He must've created more of them by now. The massacre in Silkspoint would have shown him how well it works."

Morgan spun her dagger from one hand to the other. "I won't argue that, but how *does* it work? We know vardrath steel will kill the spell, but someone would have to bring it directly to the source—no easy task, if we have to fight through a horde of enraged guardsmen to do it. Shouldn't we try to understand the spell's limits?"

"It hasn't sat well with me, either," Marceline said. "The spell didn't affect the whole district, just the area around the warehouse. And even within that area, it only worked on the guards, *and* the guards knew not to attack each other. But other than that, they made no distinction. As soon as I arrived, they tried to kill me along with the resistance, though it shouldn't have looked as if I had anything to do with them."

Roger rested his chin on his hand. "So neither truly berserk, nor truly in control of themselves. I admit I know next to nothing about magic, but can a spell that far-reaching have so many variations? So much complexity?"

"Lord Vespas doesn't seem to think so," Morgan said. "Or rather, some magical expert assisting them doesn't. I described the suppression of the resistance in my most recent letter, and he claims that, according to this mysterious person, enchantments like that should be a series of simple conditions."

"Like the condition that the stone's power would be inert until the box that contained it was closed," Marceline said. "Or that the stone Wren carried that day would make the attackers disregard him."

"Exactly. There should be some condition that explains why only those guards were affected, and the rest of you weren't. After all, if he could control you so easily, why kill you?"

"That's right," Rask said. "If we assume he didn't turn us into his ravening beasts because he couldn't, the question becomes: why *could* he do it to those guards?"

"Because they were already loyal to him?" Marceline ventured.

Rask snorted. "*That* pack of opportunists? I didn't take you for a satirist, monkey."

"You *know* my name now," Marceline muttered.

"I don't think that would work, either, Marceline," Morgan said. "If magic could read thoughts enough to detect loyalty, Elgar would have rooted out all revolutionaries years ago."

Roger had been silent for some time, wearing that expression that meant his thoughts were jumping ahead. Now he said, "You two seem to be making great progress down here, so you should stay focused on that. Marceline and I will take care of our information deficiency—just as well, perhaps, as neither of us is particularly talented at manual labor."

"What?" Marceline asked. "Me?"

"Unless there's a better thief you'd like to recommend instead." He grinned. "We need to know how that spell works, and the only ones who have actually felt its effects are Elgar's own guards. So you and I, as swindlers and pickpockets do, are going to make off with something they don't want to part with before they even realize it's gone."

Chapter Two

Eldren Cael

THE LEGIONS STRETCHED out across the plains as far as Adora's eyes could see, swords and shields and spears flashing a harsh glare in the sunlight. The humid air was filled with the clang of metal on metal, the stomp of countless feet, the brisk shouting of commands. The troops were arranged in orderly rows, but each legion was its own unit, performing its own drills at its own pace. Her uncle had told her this was customary, and no cause for concern. Even if it were possible, there would be no point to making such a great army act as one being; better to let the many strengths of diversity come to the fore, the better to combat all potential weaknesses.

Vespas Hahrenraith himself rode among their ranks astride his black courser, as in his element as Adora had ever seen him. He called encouragements or made corrections as necessary, and every soldier whose eyes he drew looked at him with the same reverence. He was a living legend, the hero who had fought at her father's side against the tyrant Gerde Selte when Adora was just a child. Only Jotun Avestri himself had won more fame in those battles, and Adora had never considered choosing anyone else to lead her armies. But she wondered what those soldiers saw when they looked at her: no hero, nor even an accomplished warrior like her brothers. Though she could boast of being as well read as anyone in the country, she had read as much of war in poetry and song as she had in texts of history and strategy, and it could be difficult to separate the two.

Vespas rode up to where she sat beneath the shade of the cloth pavilion they'd assembled at the edge of the field. He dismounted in one smooth motion, tying the horse to the nearest post. "Well, Your Grace? What do you think? An impressive showing, no?"

Adora bowed her head. Since her coronation, she had worn only a light circlet for day-to-day activities, a beautiful and intricate piece of silver twined with gold. As slender as it was, it still felt strange, and she often had to resist the urge to scratch beneath it. At least it provided an anchor for pinning her wayward curls back from her face. "The might of our people on full display would humble anyone. Though I fear that, given my inexperience in military matters, what I think of them matters far less than what you do."

He caught the implied question, taking a seat beside her. "We're in good shape. Even years after Jotun's death, his memory has kept his army's ranks full; we won't have to go recruiting, or worse, drafting. We also have your organizational skills to thank: our supplies are exactly as they should be. And then, of course, our coffers are as full as ever. Numerous, well-outfitted, and supported by their weight in gold—three very fine things for an army to be."

"But if you had to nitpick?"

He shrugged. "Not to exalt myself too highly, but since my retirement, I doubt any of my replacements have been putting the rank and file through their paces as they ought. As this country's blade, their edge has dulled a little. But I'll soon sharpen it again. To be honest, what worries me most isn't anything about the state of our army; it's the nature of our opponent. When Jotun and I took on Gerde Selte, we were fewer, poorer, and possessed of less. But Gerde Selte could not use magic."

Adora felt a chill at that, despite the heat of the day. Both she and her uncle had borne witness to the terrible things magic was capable of. But he had seen a mage's work only after the mage herself had gone, and she had fought a mage with another mage at her side. "Jocelyn Selreshe's power was so formidable because she supplemented it with the magic she stole from Lirien," she said, to remind herself as much as him. "Arianrod says that, absent that boon, Elgar's power will have harsh limits."

"Not harsh enough," her uncle said. "All the damage I saw in her parents' household was damage Jocelyn had inflicted before she ever met Lirien Arvel. And it was not inconsiderable."

They both turned to look behind them at the city of Eldren Cael, where Amali Selreshe stood beside Hephestion atop the city walls, watching the legions from on high. Perhaps he had asked her something, for she was pointing at the soldiers, head bent toward him as she made some observation or explanation.

Of all those they had taken from the Selreshes' household, Lady Amali had shown the most rapid improvement. She still flinched every time she saw a bow, but she was capable of long and complex conversations without any of the confusion or anguish that had plagued her when she first arrived. Adora had often seen her and Hephestion like this, seated in some shady spot and talking. Perhaps they leaned on each other because they had both been victims of Jocelyn's mind-altering magic, because Amali showed him how far he hadn't fallen and he showed her how high she could still rise. No matter the reason, Adora was grateful for her presence at his side, and for the even more pronounced improvement he had shown since. The fear and unease he'd felt in Adora's company at first had all evaporated by now, and he was almost like the brother she remembered, save for a touch more solemnity in his once-unerringly cheerful manner.

"Jocelyn had years to move unchecked within her own household," Adora said to Vespas.

"And Elgar has had years to move unchecked within most of this continent."

"An advantage I will be sure never to forget. But not an insurmountable one—you must not think so either, or you wouldn't be here at my side."

"You underestimate my affection for a lost cause." His smile flashed by so quickly that she couldn't tell whether he meant it as a joke or not. "I only wish that, when we march for Valyanrend, Arianrod Margraine would be at our side."

His words sank to the pit of Adora's stomach, weighing on her like lead. For days upon days, she had tried everything she could think of to change Arianrod's mind. She knew she was in the right—a rare thing when they argued—but for once it seemed to make no difference. Even though she knew as well as anyone how stubborn Arianrod could be, Adora still felt like she was failing the person who had already sacrificed so much to help her.

Watching her face, her uncle grew solemn. "I did not mean to trouble you so. A second queen would be useful, a mage even more so, but we *can* win without her."

If only that were the only issue at stake. "I'm not troubled because she is a queen, or even because she's useful," Adora said. "It's because she is my friend, and I fear that, if I let her leave, I will never see her again."

"Ah." His gaze was drawn upward, to where Amali Selreshe sat. "That's harder, then."

THOUGH ARIANROD WAS leaving on the morrow, Adora did not truly have a moment to spare for her until the afternoon. Arianrod had been spending all of *her* spare moments in the palace library, trying to make her way through as many books she hadn't read as possible. Adora wasn't surprised to find Seren Almasy standing in front of the heavy doors that marked the library entrance, every line of her body poised and alert, though Adora did not know what danger she thought lurked in these halls.

She hadn't known what to make of her at first, but now she liked Seren. Many people were awed by Arianrod's skills, but precious few genuinely liked her; to have one of them so close to her could only do her good. "How's it going in there?" she asked.

"Last I checked, there were seven books she wanted to have at least cursory knowledge of by the end of the day. I offered to help, but she said I couldn't read fast enough and wouldn't know what to look for."

Adora smiled. "I bet she also said you should come in and sit down, but you insisted on guarding this door."

Seren frowned, tense. "How did you know that?"

"It's . . . really not that difficult. I know her, and I'm at least starting to know you. You're overprotective—which I suppose is appropriate in a bodyguard—but you're also shy. You'd feel presumptuous to enjoy her company just for the sake of it, absent anything you could find to do for her."

Seren's lips pressed together, her jaw tightening and relaxing. "You see so far into people, Your Grace. It's . . . intimidating."

"Why?" Adora asked. "Don't people want to be seen as they truly are? I should hate to be misunderstood by anyone."

Seren pondered that question for some time. "When you are used to being misunderstood," she finally said, "to be suddenly perceived can feel like . . . a layer of armor has been taken away."

"Well, I hope one day you will not feel the need to arm yourself around me. Though I understand that is not a small thing to ask." She let her gaze drift to the closed doors. "I know our library better than anyone. Perhaps I can help."

"Can you not . . ." She stopped, and visibly swallowed her words. "Never mind."

"No, what is it?"

Seren bent her head. "She keeps telling me not to go with her when she leaves. I would never allow that, but if it is such a persistent wish of hers—"

"—then she must think you would be in great danger if you went," Adora said. "Which means she thinks she will be, with or without you."

Seren nodded. "The thing I fear most—" She swallowed hard again. "For most people, pain is a deterrent. You push yourself past your limits, and you learn to be more careful next time. But every time she takes her magic past its limits—every time she goes to the edge and survives—it only encourages her to push for more. It takes her longer and longer to recover, but that hasn't deterred her at all. I fear that, if she continues in this way . . . that the magic she so loves may one day take everything from her."

A chilling thought, and one Adora could imagine coming to pass all too well. Arianrod was certainly stubborn, and, despite her formidable intellect, possessed of a courage so great it sometimes tipped over into recklessness. She seemed to hate limitations by her very nature, to be unable to resist pushing on them to see if they were truly there. But mortality was a fact, not something to be outwitted—not even by her.

"I confess I would prefer it if neither of you left," she told Seren. "But if she is determined to do so, you and I both know the impossibility of stopping her." She put a hand against the doors. "Are you coming in?"

Seren stared at the floor. "I'll . . . wait out here."

"Suit yourself."

The stack of books Seren had mentioned was the first thing Adora noticed, carefully balanced on a table in the center of the library. Arianrod had another in front of her face, pacing back and forth as she flipped pages. The pallor of her skin suggested she had not eaten or slept as much as Seren or Adora would have liked.

"Did you stack them in order of priority?" Adora asked.

Arianrod barely glanced up. "Mm. Help yourself, if you're so inclined."

Adora reached for the topmost book, *Wardren Principe,* and found it to be an Old Lantian tome on the properties of spells. "Are you looking for anything in particular?"

"Anything that might help me understand why mages died out of our population, and why they have returned. Nothing in Stonespire's library ever helped me, and though my time at Mist's Edge was limited, nothing drew my eye there, either. But your library is far older."

"The Ninists controlled this place for centuries, though," Adora said. "They may have weeded out some things they found too dangerous."

"True, but there's no harm in trying, is there?" She set the book she was reading down and reached for the next one in the stack, a leather-bound journal. "This one is useless—written too early. Magic was still thriving when its writer died, it seems."

Then perhaps the one Adora held would prove useless as well, though she still wanted to make sure. "What's that one?"

"This?" She waved the journal in one hand. "It seems there used to be such things as magic instructors. This one kept a diary of his students' achievements."

"A pity I never much cared for books on magic before," Adora said. "I was so sure it was just this relic of the past, never to return as we once knew it. I didn't want to make myself sad, filling my head with thoughts of what could never be."

"One of your few scholarly oversights." A smile flitted across Arianrod's face for a moment, before she became absorbed in her reading again. "When I was a child, I thought the people around me loved nothing more than to tell me things were impossible. And over and over I learned just how wrong they were. More often than not, *you can't* just means *I couldn't*—or *I don't want you to.*" She flipped a few more pages in the journal while Adora gave up on her own find and reached for the next, this one written in modern Lantian. "Hmm. This might be something."

"What is it?"

"Near the end of a day of practice, one of his students, who'd been fine all day, suddenly had difficulty casting her spells. It's not much, but it *is* the first reference to that kind of difficulty I've ever found."

"But your difficulty is consistent, isn't it?" Adora asked. "The same spell will always take the same toll on you, right?"

"That's right, but . . . let me just see where this leads." Her nose was nearly touching the page.

Adora left her to it, and turned her attention to her own book. It soon became clear that it had been written at the height of the Elesthenian Empire, when magic was already gone, but the author had provided no clues as to the reason for its loss, just a history of its qualities and function. She put it down and took up the next—it was also called *Wardren Principe,* but it turned out to be a completely different book. It wasn't as if every writer could know the provenance of every title, she supposed.

It also took much more effort to read. About a quarter of the terms had been written in the runic alphabet, an archaic way of writing in Old Lantian in which characters were given conceptual, rather than phonetic, meanings. One rune could have multiple pronunciations, depending on the context, so though Adora was fluent in Old Lantian, it still took her time to translate.

She only looked up when Arianrod stabbed a finger into the journal, unaware of how much time had passed. "I'm sure there's something here. I keep feeling I'm a moment away from understanding it. This instructor recounts similar instances of his students having difficulty with their spells—always toward the end of the day's lessons, but never the same group of students. But he's as puzzled by it as I am. Magic has never relied on the position of the sun and stars, never waxed and waned with the moon. Why should the time of day matter?"

"I wish I could help you," Adora said. "But if you don't know the answer, I don't think my paltry knowledge of magic is going to provide any additional insight. I learned most of what I know from you, after all." She turned the page of her own book, and frowned down at a collection of three runes left alone on a single line. "Well, that's new."

"What is?"

"I've never seen this arrangement in runic before." She held the book out so Arianrod could see. "Whoever wrote this probably created it themselves."

"Lucky. It's rare to find a truly original runic configuration. I'm going to guess these two were chosen for *essence* and *turn against,* which would make this one . . . *steady? Enduring?*"

"Yes, that sounds right." Adora squinted at the sequence. "So it's a word for something that perpetually turns against itself. The closest modern equivalent would be . . . *impurity? Corruption?*"

Arianrod smirked. "Bit judgmental of you, no? What about *contradiction*?"

"That might work as well," Adora admitted. "Let me see if more context narrows it down a little." She skimmed the next few paragraphs. "It's about the ability of magic to negate or dispel other magic. I suppose that is a sort of contradiction—you can't dry something off by adding more water, but you can remove magic with magic."

"Yes, you saw me do that to Jocelyn's magic," Arianrod pointed out. "It's why the best weapon against a mage is often another mage."

"But that point does seem a bit obvious, so I wonder why . . ." She kept reading, and frowned. "Arianrod, listen to this. 'We have observed a further, somewhat disconcerting phenomenon: when two wards of great power, but opposed in intent, come to be in the same place at the same time, sometimes they do not merely dispel one another. When the two are of a sufficiently strong and virulent will, they may, upon dispelling and being dispelled in turn, still seek to work that will upon the things of this world. In such situations, in danger of losing the power that allows them to be, the wards will reach out into the living world. We have yet to find a type of matter they will not touch: stone, steel, wood, earth—all corruptible. We are not so foolish as to test it, but we believe even human flesh would not be impervious to such an assault, were the spell feeding it of sufficient strength.'"

As Adora's voice died away, they were both silent for several moments. Arianrod spoke up first. "So it's a type of spell that doesn't just negate another spell, but . . . eats away at the world somehow, changes the physical quality of objects. I wonder if that might have anything to do with whatever process creates vardrath steel?"

"I had a different thought," Adora said quietly. "It reminded me of the Curse."

Arianrod breathed in sharply through her nose, her eyes widening. "Damn, you're right. The Curse is certainly a landscape like none other on earth, and now we know it absorbs magic. Could the very soil have been altered by that method?" She frowned. "But the Curse is huge. If the results of one mage's power colliding with another's were truly so dramatic and far-reaching, I imagine most mages would fear to cast a spell at all."

Adora had gone back to the book. "You're right. From what's written here, it seems like the scale is much smaller. Square inches, not square miles. It's not enough to fully explain how the Curse was created, or why it's shrinking now."

Arianrod twirled a lock of hair around her finger. "I wonder if I could find a way to imitate that spell somehow, only with a more controlled effect. If this corruption just latches onto whatever material is closest, that's no good. But if it could be directed . . ."

Adora handed her the book. "You should be the one to finish reading this, then. I wouldn't want anything to become lost in my summary."

They paused there, each with one hand on the book. Arianrod seemed to guess that Adora wasn't finished, and, faced with that expectant look, she couldn't keep the words inside anymore.

"I wish you wouldn't go," she said, and hated how plaintive she sounded saying it. But any attempt at command would be empty: a queen could not compel another queen, and if Arianrod was truly set on returning to Esthrades, it would not be right for Adora to attempt to keep her here. "You must know you'll be safest with our armies, and I would welcome your advice even more once the war begins. Uncle is talented, of course, but I lack his skill—or at least, I lack it in matters of warfare. But you've been having skirmishes with Elgar's men for years. And that's not to mention any magical—"

"There are many things we might have accomplished together, had things unfolded differently," Arianrod said. "I had been expecting to accompany you as well, and it is unfortunate that I cannot. I'm aware it will make things much harder on you, but . . ." It was not like her to hesitate. She raked a hand through her hair. "This is still the decision that I want to make. That I think is best."

"Best for whom?" Adora asked, though she suspected she already knew the answer. "It's certainly not the best choice for *you*. If this Varalen Oswhent is as smart as you say, he'll drop everything to catch you the second you step foot in Esthrades. I can send some guardsmen to accompany you, but I can't send an army. If I could—"

"You shouldn't," Arianrod said. "The way to defeat Elgar is to force him to split his armies. It would ruin everything if we fell for the same trick."

"So the best thing for us to do is strike at Valyanrend with everything we have! I *know* that! Why does it seem like *you* don't know it?" Adora shook her head. "You're so clever, Arianrod, and so strong. But you can't take back Esthrades with only your magic, Seren, and the handful of soldiers I can spare you. That is too much, even for you."

"I know." The frank admission made something in Adora's chest tighten. "You must be the one to liberate Esthrades, after you have Valyanrend in hand. But Stonespire will not be able to hold out until then. It was not built to withstand a lengthy siege, and, as ever, we have no standing army. The militia alone will not be able to drive off the invaders. Any day now, news will come that the city has surrendered."

"They may not surrender," Adora insisted.

"They will surrender," Arianrod said, "because I instructed Gravis to do so, at whenever he judged would be the most opportune moment, in the last reply I was able to send him. Why should my people starve in a siege? Why should they be butchered and their homes razed when the Hallerns overcome Stonespire's walls and sack the city in revenge for their defiance? It accomplishes nothing. Elgar simply wants the city; if he thinks it has come to him willingly, he will not harm it."

"He wants the city," Adora said quietly, "and you."

"Yes. That's the problem. Elgar and his creatures know I am here, and they know they will never be able to reach me as long as I remain at your side. It will only be a matter of time before they use my country as a hostage."

Much as she wanted to deny it, Adora knew it was inevitable. Elgar would be a fool not to drive whatever wedge he could between the two queens fighting against him. "Tell me you are not thinking of surrendering to the Hallern army."

"Adora, can you truly picture me doing such a thing?" Arianrod smiled wryly. "That would be a very poor negotiation on my part."

"Then what are you going to do? If you aren't returning to take Esthrades back and you aren't returning to surrender, then—"

"We need to maintain chaos in the east," Arianrod said. "Now that Kelken and the Markham brothers have been captured, there is the risk that Lanvaldis will settle down, and Elgar will be able to pull his troops away from it. We cannot let that happen. But you said it yourself, Adora: the moment I step foot in Esthrades, Elgar's men will drop everything to pursue me. I don't intend to let them catch me, but I *do* intend to let them chase me. It will keep the fate of the east uncertain, and buy you the time you need to do what you must."

"Arianrod, you can't outrun an army. You won't buy any time if you're caught immediately."

"I couldn't outrun an army in *this* country, with plains as far as the eye can see. But I can certainly hide in a great forest that I know well and my enemy doesn't know at all. Not forever, but . . . perhaps for long enough."

It wouldn't be long enough. Adora was sure of that. And even then, it was nothing like the plans Arianrod usually constructed, complex and elegant and considered from all angles. "Whatever you might accomplish in the east, you could do so much more with me and Uncle and our armies. You've never had access to so many men and resources before, and think of what you were able to do with just a small fraction of that!" She bit her lip. "I know it's easy for me to say that you are more important than Esthrades, and of course I don't mean you should stop considering it entirely. But we may have reached the point in this crisis at which we simply have no better options."

"A genius would always have options," Arianrod said, as if she were quoting one of the old masters. "If you truly were one, you would know that."

"Who said that?" Adora asked.

Arianrod tilted her head, brows drawing together. "You did, of course. Have you forgotten?"

"Completely," Adora admitted. "When was this?"

"Close to fifteen years ago. You had only been to Stonespire a handful of times, but your father had already stopped bringing Hephestion with you."

"Because you terrorized him."

"Because he was a loud and overconfident idiot who was always trying to lecture me on things he knew nothing about. But *you* really did know a lot, and you weren't too shy to argue with me, even though you were shy about almost everything else. And that's when you said that to me, when we were arguing about some military strategy I thought was so clever at the time, to get out of an impossible situation. You said any fool could save their own skin by sacrificing two-thirds of their army, and it'd have to be a much more elegant solution to be worth bragging about."

Adora felt herself blush. "Well, I was a child then."

"You were, but you were also right. If I hide behind your armies while Stonespire gets dismantled piece by piece, and say I had no choice . . . that simply isn't good enough. You told me not so long ago, Adora, that no matter how much you detest war, you could never stand to be the Avestri who allowed your people to be conquered by northerners again, after all your ancestor did to break them free. Well, I know as much history as you do, and though Issamira is far older than Esthrades, House Margraine governed it for hundreds of years before Talia Avestri was ever born. In the entirety of its existence, Stonespire has never been sacked. Do you think I could stand to be the Margraine who allowed such a thing to happen?"

So that was it. This plan of hers was so flimsy because it was not truly a plan at all. It did not come from her mind, which ever analyzed situations and solved problems with a true genius's skill, but from her heart. And Arianrod, who knew so much about every subject under the sun, knew so little about her own heart that if Adora tried to explain it to her, she would deny it with genuine confusion.

You could argue with the head, but not the heart. Adora felt despair close its jaws around hers, driven by fear and concern that had nowhere to go.

"What is it?" Arianrod asked. "You look so unwell."

"If you get captured," Adora said, "you'll die. They'll kill you."

"Well, not right away; I've been such a thorn in Elgar's side for so long that I expect he'll want to make a show of it. But yes, eventually, they will kill me."

"Don't *smile* about it!" Arianrod could smile about almost everything, but this was too much. "Do you really want to die from your own arrogance?"

Arianrod tapped her chin. "Why do you count it such a tragedy that I should die arrogant? I certainly hope that I shall not die humble."

"That's not what I meant, and you know it." But how could she explain affection, friendship, sentimentality to one who had such difficulty understanding those things? "I am unwell because I cannot convince you not to go, and I will not make you stay. And I fear that means this is one of the last times I will ever see you. If that's true, the knowledge that we shall never have cause to play another game of sesquigon, to argue questions of politics or history or translation, to try to bring this continent into a brighter future together . . . I will regret it more than I could ever say, or ever explain."

At least even Arianrod could not smile at that. She stood silent, marble-still. "I am not so convinced of my death as you," she finally said. "But know that, if it does come to pass, I shall regret the same."

CHAPTER THREE

Esthrades

LIRIEN ARVEL HAD been in two countries today, and would set foot in a third before the day was out. None of them were the country she was actually trying to reach, but such was the nature of the fool's errand she had volunteered herself for. If she were free, and alone, and the erosion of her sanity were not perpetually hanging over her head like an executioner's blade, she would have found it exhilarating. This was what she lived for, after all: the vagaries of travel, the chance to always see a different horizon. But she no longer scanned the landscapes around her for wonders, only to make sure no Hallern soldiers entered her view.

It would have been safer to cross the Gods' Curse into Reglay directly. With Queen Adora preparing to march on Valyanrend, Imperator Elgar would not dare leave his city, nor send the troops he would need to defend it too far afield. His mouthpiece and makeshift substitute in the east, a man called Varalen Oswhent, did not have enough soldiers to line the northern border of the Curse, nor to mount anything but the most token defense of Reglay, a conquered nation whose king was currently imprisoned elsewhere. Instead, Oswhent had left a small portion of the forces Elgar had given him in Lanvaldis, in case further riots broke out there, and had poured all the rest into Esthrades with all haste, hoping to topple Stonespire before its mistress could return. But Rhia and Cadfael had wanted to take the measure of things in Esthrades before moving on, and they argued that there was no reason to think there'd be a robust Hallern presence in the south. With no method of hauling them after her into Reglay by force, Lirien had found herself outvoted.

She didn't mind traveling with Rhia so much. The girl had a sunny disposition, liked conversation but wasn't frivolously talkative, and was always eager to take the most difficult or disagreeable tasks on herself. But she could be impossibly stubborn the moment she felt something was a matter of morality, and her complete lack of care for her own safety made her a constant danger to herself, no matter how talented she might be. At least she was infinitely preferable to her brother. He was handsome in a boring sort of way and surprisingly good at cooking, but those were the only points Lirien had been able to find in his favor. He was dour, taciturn, irritable, suspicious, and even more cynical than Lirien herself. No wonder Talis had been so obsessed with him—he must've been the only person she could find with a personality as bad as hers. He spent every spare moment glaring at Lirien as if he found her presence a personal affront, and every one of those glances made her wish she could laugh in his face and leave him behind.

But that wasn't an option for her now. She, Talis, and Voltest were linked together by the same accident of magic that had given them their powers, that had made them what scholars called *wardrenfell*. Their mental state could influence her own, and since Talis had been captured by Edith Selwyn, all Lirien had sensed from her was anger and pain. Voltest had gone ahead of them to Lanvaldis on his own, but Lirien wasn't optimistic about his chances of rescuing Talis, not when Selwyn had stockpiled so much vardrath steel. She was used to solving all her problems with her own power, but that might not be possible this time. Better to have the sword skills of these siblings on hand, even if that meant dealing with their particular quirks.

She saw them approach through the trees—alone—and relaxed, loosening her grip on the power always coiling inside her. "Are you satisfied now?" she asked, without getting up, just leaning farther back against her tree and stretching her legs in the grass.

Cadfael scowled, which was always impressive, because it brought so much more displeasure to a face whose resting attitude already seemed displeased. "Satisfaction has nothing to do with it. It was going to be grim news regardless, but at least those in the nearby villages report no soldiers in the south, along the border or otherwise."

"So the Hallerns are stretched thin already," Lirien said. "That much is good, right?"

Cadfael shook his head. "Right now, they're all besieging Stonespire, but that won't last. Once the city falls—and it will—they'll be free to spread farther afield, to Lakeport and some of the bigger castles. Things are only going to get worse for the people here."

"Only up to a point," Lirien said. "Oswhent wants to conclude his business here so he can join his master in the west; he's not going to dally capturing every hamlet and farmhouse." She sighed. "It's a pity the marquise couldn't be here. Even with no standing army, if she could call the common people to fight, they could probably subdue the Hallerns by force of numbers. But without her presence—and her tactical intelligence—they have nothing to rally behind."

"It would be a disaster either way," Cadfael insisted. "What you're proposing might work, but you haven't seen what it's like when simple villagers go up against trained soldiers. Overwhelming the Hallerns through force of numbers just means sacrificing themselves in huge numbers to do it. Even if the marquise were here, I doubt she'd want that."

"It seems so cruel," Rhia said. "For her to be repaid like this for everything she did for Her Grace and Issamira."

"The queen's not likely to forget it," Cadfael said. "I'm sure that as soon as she's done in Valyanrend, she'll move to liberate Esthrades. That is, if the remaining troops here haven't already surrendered, which I think is more likely."

Rhia didn't look encouraged. "But by the time that happens, what will have become of the people here?"

"Well, what do you want Adora to do? She can't be everywhere at once. If she fails to defeat Elgar, she'll be failing the Esthradians, too."

"And *we* can't be everywhere at once, either, so please don't tell me you're dreaming of staying here to fight somehow," Lirien added. "I don't know what we'd be able to do here, but in Lanvaldis we can join forces with Voltest, at least. Two *wardrenfell* alongside the two of you may just be enough to rescue Talis, and with *three wardrenfell* we might even be able to keep the rebellion in Lanvaldis going singlehandedly."

Cadfael squinted down at her, brow furrowing, as if she were some puzzle for him to solve, or some enemy whose lies needed to be ferreted out. "Talis and Voltest seemed to think they were capable of handling hundreds on their own. Are you saying you couldn't?"

Lirien felt her mouth twist, and did her best to push aside the throb of anger that always pointed to where Voltest was. "Don't say *handling,* say *murdering.* Talis and Voltest, you see, are very fond of the idea that they could murder hundreds at a stroke if they wanted, so I'm not surprised they insisted on talking about it. I probably *could* do as much, but only if I could focus on them as a mass; if there were innocents or allies mixed in with those I wanted to kill, I'd never manage it. We did something like that once before, at Mist's Edge—we knew it was only full of Elgar's soldiers, and no one else—so they do have some grounds to back up their boasting. Here's what might be difficult for you to understand: I don't *like* to kill people. What happened at Mist's Edge . . ." She gritted her teeth, and felt the strain in her jaw. "It was horrible. I only went along because I thought I'd be able to temper those two, but the reverse happened. They completely overwhelmed me—their anger, their grief, their desire for vengeance. I forgot which parts were me, and which were them."

Rhia was looking at her with those big eyes, so full of sorrow and sympathy. She tugged at her brother's sleeve. "You could show a little more consideration." To Lirien, she said, "You don't have to talk about it if you don't want to."

"I don't want to talk about it, but he needs to understand how things are. *I* won't claim to understand why he cares about Talis so much, since I know she tried to kill him on at least one occasion. But just because Talis hates me, that doesn't make her morally superior to me. Or whatever else she told him to get him to distrust me so much."

"Who says she told me anything about you?"

"Oh, so you just treat people who helped save your life and your sister's life with distrust and disdain as a matter of principle?"

Cadfael looked about to retort, but then he rubbed his jaw, with a sideways glance at Rhia. "I wasn't actually suggesting that you try to destroy the Hallern army around Stonespire all by yourself."

"I know. You were testing me. Again. What I still don't know is why, or when you'll be satisfied."

"That makes two of us," Cadfael said. "Shall we set up camp for the night? The sun's going down."

A transparent evasion, but Lirien was too enticed by the prospect of getting out of his presence to delay it by arguing. "The two of you can set up camp if you like, but I'll be leaving after dinner; I'll catch the fish, as usual. I feel like sleeping in a bed tonight, and you said there was a village nearby."

"There is," Cadfael said, "but I'm not sparing you any coin for an inn. It's a wasted expense."

"How fortuitous, as I don't require any coin, for an inn or anything else."

"Then what bed do you propose to sleep in?"

Lirien smiled sweetly. "Someone's, I'm sure. These things have a way of working out for me." And she headed for the river, to freeze herself some fish.

"ALL I'M SAYING is that she insists on being deliberately disagreeable and troublesome, and it's tedious," Cadfael complained, watching their second round of fish slowly crisp over the fire. Lirien had barely stayed for the first, but he and Rhia needed more than that to fill their bellies. "Of course traveling together was always going to have its sacrifices, but she seems determined not to make any."

It didn't bother him as much as he let on. How could it, when his sister had been returned to him, after he'd believed her dead for three years? He was like a man who, having stumbled into paradise, discovered he had to share it with a particularly persistent gnat.

But, taken another way, that was precisely the problem. Now that he'd been given a second chance, he was terrified that he might ruin this one, too. If there was even the smallest possibility someone or something posed a threat to Rhia, he could never relax. And Yaelor had outright warned him to be careful of Lirien. Cadfael still didn't know who or what Yaelor truly was—or whether what Adora had told him about Yaelor being the name of an Old Lantian spirit of courage had any truth to it—but he'd kept his word to Cadfael in the past. He, not Talis, was the reason Cadfael was so wary of Lirien, but he couldn't tell her or Rhia that.

"She's made sacrifices," Rhia said, brushing her hands over her bent knees. "Sometimes it's difficult for her to be near the other two at all, but she's still doing it, to help them *and* us. And I can't say you've been especially agreeable to her, either."

"Talis told me she was capricious," Cadfael said. "As capricious as water."

"Everyone at the palace in Eldren Cael told me she couldn't be trusted, too." Rhia's voice had sharpened to an edge. "And then when I was in danger, she did more to help me than anyone. If someone's going to doubt her again, it isn't going to be me."

"Then I guess it'll have to be me," Cadfael said. "See how well we work together?"

She laughed, that laugh that he loved, fond and carefree. "I know it'll be all right, Cadfael. We've both made it this far alone. I can't imagine we'll fail now we're together."

"I'll make sure of that, no matter what. I promise you that." He took the fish off the fire and set it aside to cool, gently slapping Rhia's hand away when she tried to steal a piece too soon. "I just . . . I know you, so I'm worried. If it were up to me, I'd help Talis, and I'd go home—to our old home, if it's still standing, or else to whatever one we can make. But that's not going to be enough for you, is it?"

"I could turn that question on you. I can't help but be curious about someone you'd go so far to save, especially because she almost killed you once. If it were someone else, I'd think they wanted to make up for the wrong they did her, but I know you better than that."

"You're right, of course. It's entirely selfish, as all my decisions are. But I wonder if I can explain it to you. I . . . find most people tedious, and I can't wait to quit their company. But I didn't feel that way about her. Even though she had contempt for me, I didn't mind it, or our time together. I felt there was some way in which we were the same."

Rhia rolled her eyes at him. "You can just say you liked her, you know. I'm sure such things do happen, even to those as determined not to like people as you are."

Cadfael shook his head. "If I told you I liked her, you'd misunderstand. It's a tenuous thing, not at all like you're imagining." He started cutting the fish into chunks, and they each swallowed a few mouthfuls before he continued. "Your turn. Supposing we are successful with Talis, what would you do next?"

She tucked her hair behind her ear, a sheepish gesture he knew by heart. "I'm sure you already know what I'm going to say."

"I probably do. But let's hear it anyway."

One hand clenched reflexively around the hilt of her sword. "Once we know Talis is safe, I'd kick this Administrator Selwyn and her lot out of our country, if I could. I'd want it to *be* a country again. I've no patriotic pride toward Lanvaldis, and I don't think Eira was doing such a good job of things before he was killed. But that doesn't mean I want her in the palace making things even worse." She frowned. "In the end, though, Selwyn's just a symptom. The root of all this discord is . . ."

"Elgar," Cadfael finished. "I knew it. You want to topple Elgar."

"With any luck," Rhia said, "the *queen* is going to topple Elgar. I just want to *help*." She tapped her fingers against the hilt. "We've been given these, and we know how to use them. And I know you'll scold me for saying so, but I can't help feeling that, because we have these gifts—our skills with a sword as much as the swords themselves—we have a responsibility to use them. You've made a difference already, with Adora; if you hadn't decided to protect her, even though you didn't have to, she might not have been able to reclaim her throne. Why shouldn't we continue to make a difference?"

Cadfael felt a stab of guilt at that; he had helped Adora as part of a deal with Yaelor, not out of his own goodness. "Look, it's not that I object to the idea. Honestly, if I could be sure of success, I'd love to kill Elgar. By telling me you were dead, the bastard precipitated three years of suffering for both of us, and I'd happily pay him back in blood. But more than that, more than anything, I just don't want to lose you. If we did nothing, and the continent fell to Elgar, you'd never forgive yourself; I know that. But if we *did* do something, and we saved the continent, but you lost your life in exchange, doing some stupid heroic thing like you're always dreaming about—that's what *I* couldn't live with."

Rhia draped her arms around him, hanging heavily on his neck the way she had as a child when she wanted to get his attention. "You're a little bit important to me, too, you know."

"Just a little bit, eh?" It was both strange and achingly familiar to feel the way smiles kept creeping up on him, cracking the harshness of his face. It had been so long since it had happened, and yet, even after only a few weeks, he was returning to his well-worn habits of living with her as if they had never been interrupted.

"Let's agree on this for now," Rhia said. "Rescuing Talis is our first priority, before all other concerns. And once she's free, I think we both want to make sure she and Lirien and Voltest can live peacefully, without any of the difficulties that have plagued them so far. I doubt that's going to happen without some kind of intervention, magical or otherwise. So we'll follow that thread to its end, before picking up any others. How's that for a compromise?"

Cadfael smirked, preparing to dodge a swat. "You know how to compromise now? Perhaps you learned something in the years we were apart after all."

LIRIEN WOKE JUST before dawn, and had slipped into her dress and out the window of the tiny cottage before three minutes had passed. It was a routine she was quite familiar with, and her erstwhile bedmate—nice man, good with his hands, surprisingly decent mattress—didn't even stir in his sleep. She had learned long ago that it was easier to take her leave this way; when you were someone who would not stay, it was best to prevent the possibility of being asked.

The small field between the village and the forest where Rhia and Cadfael were probably still sleeping was wet with dew, an overnight fog slowly burning away in the first light of morning, drifting across the grass like a giant's breath. These were the sights she had wanted to see always, the ever-changing, ever-wondrous landscape of the traveler. But the peace she felt at seeing them was only momentary, and would remain so until she and Talis and Voltest repaired the tangled knot of disordered emotions that tied them to one another. She knew there was no avoiding that anymore.

She took one last look back at the little village, the sun straining to rise above its roofs. She had been expecting only stillness and silence, all the inhabitants either still sleeping or only just beginning their morning rituals. But standing at the far end of the well-worn track between houses that could only generously be called a street, there was a single figure, a woman whose long hair blew freely in the breeze, as if the wind itself wanted to caress her face. She met Lirien's eyes, even over so much distance, and smiled.

Lirien took a step back, irritated at having her morning disturbed, and unnerved at the knowing edge to the woman's smile. And in just the space of that moment, the figure was gone.

CHAPTER FOUR

Araveil

IT WAS SUNSET when Deinol returned to their camp by the little river outside Araveil's walls. Lucius was still in the city, on some errand or other he had insisted Deinol didn't need to accompany him for. Another time, Deinol might have tried to push his luck, but he was worried about Ritsu, and the earlier he got back, the earlier the two of them could start on the food he'd brought.

He found Ritsu sitting cross-legged on the riverbank, eyelids fluttering as if he were in a doze. His face was serene enough, but Deinol thought the grass looked disturbed around him, as if he'd torn it up. "Everything all right?" he asked.

Ritsu's eyes opened slowly, without any disorientation; he clearly hadn't been sleeping after all. "Yes," he said. "I mean, everything's all right that can be, considering our situation."

Something was different about the way he spoke. It was the kind of vacillating answer Deinol was used to hearing from him, but there was nothing dazed or dreamy in his tone. "Did something happen while I was gone?"

"Yes," Ritsu said. "I finally recalled the memory that had eluded me. It was as the swordsman suggested: I was a prisoner in Serenin Palace once—five years ago, when the Hallerns took the city."

It took Deinol a moment to realize that *the swordsman* must have meant Lucius. He scratched the back of his neck. "I don't mean to sound judgmental, but doesn't it worry you to have forgotten something that important, even if only for a while?"

Ritsu made an expression he had never seen on his face before; Deinol might almost have called it pitying. "If only a faulty memory were the extent of it. But the truth is far worse. I have been cursed."

He said the words with unshakable certainty, but as calmly as if they were discussing the positions of the stars. Deinol couldn't feel the same. "You've . . . what?"

"My memories were stolen from me," Ritsu said. "They were locked away, and replaced with false and empty convictions. I'm sure that must be hard to believe, but I have to try. You've shown me nothing but kindness; I'm only sorry I couldn't remember the full extent of it until now. If there's a chance I could be a danger to you, you deserve to know."

Deinol sat down across from him. "I don't know much about magic and curses, but it seems I've come close to those who believe in them more and more often lately. I don't think that's a coincidence. Why don't you just tell me what you can, and I'll try my best to keep my mind open to it?"

Ritsu nodded, brushing his hair back from his forehead. "I've been thinking about it, and the only way it makes sense is if there are two separate spells. You remember that sword I used to carry?"

"Aye, how could I forget? Did you lose it?"

"I did. I wouldn't be able to recover it now even if I wanted to, and I certainly don't. But before I lost it, I used to carry it with me everywhere—except for one time when it was taken from me. Right before you met me, when I was held prisoner in that village and my weapon was confiscated. Back then, when I traveled with you and Seth, and now—those were the times when I've been able to think most clearly. When, at least, I knew who I was."

"But I can't help thinking there's a great difference between you then and now," Deinol said.

Ritsu nodded again. "Yes, which is why I think the curse must be twofold. One on the sword, and one on my very person. Now that the sword is lost, that part of it is irrelevant, but whatever was done to me isn't gone. I can only hold on to so many of my memories at once. If I let one slip from my consciousness, I have to struggle to get it back. So before I say anything else . . ."

He rested his hands on his knees, growing, if possible, even more grave. "There is something I must warn you about, while I can still remember. That swordsman, the man you call your friend—he's lying to you. I can't think of a reason he would mean you harm, but you should still be careful around him."

The words fell on Deinol so heavily not because they seemed unthinkable, but because they coincided so well with his own doubts. Hadn't he already thought that the story Lucius had told him about his life in Kaiferi and his search for his prince didn't all fit together the way it should? Hadn't he already thought that Lucius was lying to him about something?

But years of friendship were not something to be thrown away on a hunch and a nebulous warning. He owed Lucius the benefit of the doubt, at least. "You'll have to explain what you mean by that."

Ritsu winced. "As to that, if he wishes to lie, it isn't my place to expose him. I can't imagine how far he must have fallen to be as he is now, but in Kaiferi he was exalted as few swordsmen in a generation are. Not just his skill—his honor, his entire being was held beyond reproach, so far above someone like me as to exist in a different world. If I didn't owe you, I wouldn't have said even this much about him."

"Then why must he have fallen?" Deinol asked. "Why couldn't he have simply left?"

"Because his prince is dead, and he is still alive," Ritsu said. "The only way he could survive that with his honor intact would be if Ryo had sent him on some mission. Would he be dallying here with us if that were true?"

Ryo might not be dead, but Lucius had asked him not to say anything about that to Ritsu. Still, it was clear Lucius had believed his prince dead for five long years. "Can I ask you another question about your . . . curse? Who would do such a thing to you, and why?"

Ritsu bit his lip. "If a vessel is empty, you can fill it with whatever you like. For a long time, I acted as a servant with no will of my own. Forgive me, but I think that's all I should say about it. If your friend should learn all I have done, he might view me as unworthy to live." His mouth twisted. "No matter how hypocritical that might be."

Deinol rubbed a hand over his face, trying to come to terms with all he had heard. "Do you have any idea how a curse like that might be removed? Broken?"

"I do, because it was broken once before." He nodded in the direction of Araveil. "In that very city, more than three years ago. There was a young woman—a girl, really—who defeated me. I thought I had killed her, but that must have been just another manipulation of my memory. In reality, she touched her sword to mine, and its power melted away. She touched it to my bare skin, and I suddenly remembered everything. It didn't last—the man who did this to me must have found me and cast his curses anew. But they never worked as well the second time. That's the only reason I'm able to talk to you like this now."

Deinol's head was still spinning, but he tried to focus. "That's better than no leads at all, at least. What else can you remember about them? The girl or the sword?"

"She was small, with pale hair and green eyes. A few years younger than I was, so she'd be about twenty now. As for the sword . . . it was strange. I was incapable of noting it at the time, but it was a *tsunshin*—my people's blade. I'm not used to seeing them south of Aurnis, but perhaps the style has gained more popularity than I'd thought. And the metal was strange, too—brighter than steel should be, somehow, and as perfectly clear and reflective as a mirror. I've never seen anything like it, before or since."

"The metal you're talking about is vardrath steel," Lucius said from behind Deinol, making him jerk in surprise. He hadn't even noticed Lucius's footsteps. "It's native to this land, but the method used to create it has been lost. The blades

it creates are unparalleled in sharpness and durability, so they're quite valuable."
He glanced down at Deinol, his usual enigmatic smile firmly in place. "Am I interrupting something?"

"Not at all," Ritsu said. His face had never changed, so he must have been aware of Lucius's approach over Deinol's shoulder. "But if it's so rare, that poses quite a problem for me. I was hoping to obtain some of it for myself, or at least to examine a blade forged from the stuff. Are you saying that's unlikely?"

Lucius shrugged. "Actually, if it's vardrath steel you're after, you're sitting just outside the greatest stockpile of it on the continent. In Araveil they say Administrator Selwyn has been confiscating vardrath steel blades from noble houses all over Lanvaldis."

"Ah. That is certainly curious, but I doubt the administrator would allow me access to any of them, even for a moment. And I'm afraid I have no talents as a thief."

"It's so important to you just to behold one of those blades?" Lucius, who cared for his sword like a lover, cast a skeptical glance over Ritsu's weaponless state. "I hadn't thought you much of a swordsman."

"Indeed I am not," Ritsu said. "But even one so much lower than your exalted self might still have a use for something so rare and wondrous."

Before this moment, Deinol hadn't known Ritsu to ever infuse his statements with any bite, or even to understand facetiousness at all. But though Lucius had been so unusually irritable with Ritsu's dreaminess and ponderous respect, this new sharpness made him bow his head solemnly. "It must be clear that I'm not exalted anymore. I'm as low as you, if not lower. If I ever seemed to imply otherwise, the fault is mine, and I apologize for it." When Ritsu said nothing, he added, "I did encounter one other person with a vardrath steel blade, but I'm afraid I lost track of him in Stonespire, and I have no idea where he might be now. Still searching for Commander Shinsei, probably."

At the sound of Shinsei's name, Ritsu recoiled, as if Lucius had stung him. "Why are Shinsei's whereabouts a concern to him?"

"Because Shinsei killed his sister, and he wants revenge. That's about the only thing he wants anymore, from what I could see."

"Ah," Ritsu said, though his lower lip trembled a little. "Then I don't know that that's a promising idea, either."

Lucius collapsed on the grassy bank beside them, leaning on his hands. "So how important *is* this to you? Important enough to compel you to part ways with us? If locating a vardrath steel blade were something that could be done quickly, I wouldn't mind helping, but there are things we have to do, too. And precious little coin to last us until then."

Ritsu frowned, uncertain. "I would prefer not to abandon Deinol, but I don't want to be an inconvenience to him, either. It would help if you two would just tell me where it is you're planning to go."

"The thing is, we don't know yet ourselves," Deinol said. "We're looking"—Lucius glared at him—"that is, we're in search of—I'm helping Lucius find . . . something. We managed to track . . . it . . . to Lanvaldis, but we seem to have lost the trail."

"And what will you do if you never find it again?" Ritsu asked.

"That's not an option." Lucius was as calm as ever, but his tone brooked no argument. "Perhaps under different circumstances I'd be willing to say more, but since *you* have yet to say why you were working, even as an errand boy, for the army that destroyed our home, I think it's best if I keep my silence."

Ritsu nodded. "That, at least, I understand. Even so, without a promising lead on the steel, I think I ought to stay with Deinol. I'll be safest that way. And if you think I am ever not safe for him, I trust you have the skill to act on that conviction."

Lucius's shoulders twitched, as if he sought to shrug off such a weighty responsibility. "What makes you so safe with Deinol?"

Ritsu's eyes flicked to Deinol's face, and stayed there. "Because he knows who I am. The right answer. The true answer. And he will remember it, even if I forget." He smiled sadly. "If only you could say the same."

CHAPTER FIVE

Araveil

KEL NO LONGER had even the ghost of an inkling of how long it had been. Perhaps if Hywel's face had been better suited to a beard, they might have marked the passage of time with the growth of his stubble. But all his face produced was the finest silvery down on his cheeks, barely perceptible from more than a foot away. They had counted meals at first, but soon began to suspect their captors had been bringing them at irregular intervals in order to disorient them. The odious Administrator Selwyn had returned several times to question them, though her colossal manservant, Ghilan, had never again been with her. Kel and Hywel had adopted the personae of two green boys out of their depth, offering up information in a desperate plea not to be harmed, and under that guise had wasted hours of the administrator's time with a feast of entirely useless details. But it had been so long since they had seen her that they suspected she had given up. Still, they were both alive, so they must have possessed some value as hostages, at least.

If Kel had had to endure this ordeal entirely on his own, he might have gone mad by now. But he and Hywel filled all their time alone with talking, as if despair could only stalk them in silence. They talked about their childhoods, their families, the subjects they had studied. Kel now knew that, despite being raised as a commoner, Hywel was surprisingly well read, especially when it came to the history of his own country. And, for all the good it did them, they talked about what they could possibly do next.

That was what they were doing when their latest meal arrived; as soon as they heard the scraping of the key in the lock, they seamlessly changed topics to guesses about the current date. Since they'd proven themselves such mild-mannered prisoners, Hywel was loosely chained ankle to ankle and wrist to wrist, bindings that weighed him down more than they restricted his movement. And though Kel's arms were bound tightly to the arms of the chair on which he sat with ropes so thick a knife would struggle to saw through them, his legs were now left free. His captors probably figured they were useless anyway, he thought. For all he knew, his crutches had been burned, or were sitting in a rubbish heap somewhere.

Two guards entered the cell on either side of a servant from the kitchens, a nervous young woman with her hair in plaits. She carried a tray with two bowls of the thin soup they'd eaten most often in here. She placed one on the ground in front of Hywel, then balanced the tray with the other atop Kel's thighs. "It's not too hot?" she asked, eyeing the thin wooden plank supporting the steaming bowl.

Kel felt a stab of gratitude. He did have feeling in his legs, and he appreciated her understanding of that fact. "It's fine. Thank you."

She ducked her head to avoid making eye contact, then glanced at the two guards. One nodded, and she reached for the ropes binding his right arm, struggling with the elaborate knots.

Hywel was already eating, slumped over on his side on the floor so his weighted wrist would only have to lift the wooden spoon a little to get it to his mouth. Kel wouldn't be so lucky. Once the girl was done, he'd have to balance the bowl on his knees so he had his only unbound hand free to hold the spoon. The first time he tried it, he had knocked the bowl over, and he wasn't given a replacement. That had helped him learn well enough.

The girl finally got his arm free, backing up quickly as soon as the ropes dropped. But then she realized she'd forgotten to give him the spoon, and she stretched her arm out without moving her feet any closer, just managing to put the handle into his hand without making him lean out so far he spilled the soup.

One of the guards laughed. "What do you think the boy's going to do? He can't even support his own weight, let alone drag that chair after him."

Actually, Kel's arms were quite strong, and he and Hywel had practiced a movement in which he swept the chair around with his bound hand hard enough to hopefully knock down someone who'd ventured within his range. It needed some work, as it always ended with him flat on the floor, but he could get a single solid hit in, if they truly had no other options. He would never have used it on this poor girl, though; he doubted she was happy with her new employers.

The guards let the girl go out ahead of them before locking Kel and Hywel in once more; experience told them they wouldn't have long to finish eating. But Kel let the spoon dangle limply in his hand, closing his eyes and counting imaginary footsteps in his head.

"Kelken?" Hywel asked. "Are you all right?"

He opened his eyes—that was probably far enough away—and shook out his right arm, but nothing happened. "You'll have to reach up my sleeve," he told Hywel. "Don't spill my soup."

"And what exactly is up your sleeve? Besides your arm?"

"Whatever that girl just put up there while she was fumbling with my ropes," Kel said. "But I think it's parchment."

Hywel carefully unwound himself from around his bowl, dragging his chains across the floor. It was difficult for him to rummage around in Kel's sleeve with so much weight hanging from his arms, but eventually he worked something free, holding it up triumphantly between two fingers. It was, indeed, a folded-up piece of parchment.

Hywel read it through while Kel shoveled spoonfuls of soup into his mouth as quickly as was safe; he'd arouse suspicion if he left his food unfinished. "It's from Gerald," he said. "That is, Gerald Holm, Ilyn's uncle. He was a captain in Eira's army. It's written in a cipher he taught me and Laen before we left. It says he knows that you're with me, and that . . . Laen is dead."

Kel gave him a moment to compose himself. "What about the others?" Hywel's brother's death had thinned their number from six to five: Kel and Hywel; Ilyn Holm, a junior guardswoman who'd accompanied Hywel and Laen; Ithan Vandrith, a Lanvaldian nobleman who was Arianrod's cousin; and Talis, the mysterious *wardrenfell* who'd agreed to use her power over wind to help their cause. They hadn't seen the other three since their capture.

"It says Ilyn and Lord Ithan are alive, but there's no mention of Talis either way. He tells us not to give up hope. It's true that many of the rioters were arrested— some even died during the riot, trampled or outright cut down. But the mob was made up of civilians only—those we hoped to one day turn to our cause, but hadn't yet. No one under Gerald's command was in the streets, and they remain safe."

Kel felt the relief sink into his bones. "So there's still a chance. The rebellion Arianrod needs us to cause can still happen."

Hywel smiled wryly. "Leave it to you to be more concerned for the cause than for yourself. *I'm* hoping this means they'll find a way to get us out of here."

"Well, does he say anything about that?"

"He says they're working on it. They've clearly infiltrated the palace already, at least in some capacity. But I bet he's worried about Ilyn—and Lord Ithan, to a lesser extent. If they were to rescue us but leave those two be, Selwyn might have them killed in retaliation. But rescuing four prisoners is significantly harder than rescuing two, especially given that we aren't all in the same place."

"Five prisoners," Kel said. "This only happened to Talis because she wanted to help you and Laen. We can't leave her to die, either."

"I don't want to leave anyone to die," Hywel said. "But it may not be up to us. Gerald can send messages to us through that girl, but without ink, there's no way for us to reply. If he comes up with a plan, we may have no choice but to go along with it."

That made Kel grit his teeth. Since his conflict with Elgar had started, it sometimes seemed as if he did nothing but sacrifice others to save himself, over and over, with never anything to show for it. "Aren't you tired of letting other people make you the center of the world?"

"You forget," Hywel said, "until now, it was always my brother they made the center of the world. But to answer your question, yes, I'm already tired of it."

"Does he say anything about their plans so far?"

"Not in any great detail. He urges caution for now, keeping our heads down, avoiding suspicion. He hopes to be in contact again soon."

"If things are moving quickly, perhaps it's worth appealing to Selwyn sooner rather than later," Kel said.

Hywel blinked at him. "Appeal to her for what?"

"For a chance to see the others, of course. We know Talis isn't with the other two, so even if we succeed at negotiations, we might not get a chance to see all three. But even one would be worth it."

"Why on earth would she agree to that?"

"Maybe she won't," Kel said, "but I don't see the harm in asking—respectfully, always in deference to her authority. It wouldn't seem odd, I don't think—on the contrary, it would imply we imagine that the five of us will be here for a long time. And then, if it did happen, any information we could exchange while we were with them could only help us."

Hywel nodded. "It's a good idea. You're right, I don't see a downside."

Kel reflected, a little guiltily, on how much easier it was to work with Hywel than it had been with his brother, who was too obsessed with pride and self-importance to engage in a bit of harmless begging if it would lead to a good end. But that just made him think of his own sibling, somewhere out there in the wide world with only Hayne and the proof of Hywel's claim to the throne for company. He wondered where she was now, and what she was thinking of. But no matter her situation, he knew she hadn't given up. He hadn't, and Alessa was at least as strong as he was.

He glanced back at Hywel to find him staring the letter down, as if a gigantic insect had landed in his palm. "What is it?"

"It's just . . . Gerald writes that I should destroy this after reading it, but it's not as if we've got a stray fire lying around." Hywel swallowed hard. "Should I . . . eat it?"

Kel couldn't help the laugh that bubbled from his throat, a bit rusty after having gone so long unused. "If nothing else, it's clear that you and I have read some of the same books about daring prison escapes. I suppose the better question is, can you possibly stomach it?"

CHAPTER SIX

Valyanrend

ROGER'S MIND WAS always in flight these days, darting from one subject to the next, swooping down in an instant upon sighting a new target. He'd made his livelihood by planning a dozen moves ahead, by understanding people's most essential natures—above all, by never getting caught unless it was already too late to matter. If he succeeded in toppling Elgar, he definitely wanted his name in the history books; it just wouldn't do for anyone to catch wind of it before then. But he'd also made his livelihood by working alone, and the need to work in concert with others was constantly niggling at him, like a loose tooth.

At least loosening up a target with a drink was something he knew how to do in his sleep, and the man in front of him looked like he could desperately use one. Londret Wapps had bags under his bloodshot eyes, dark and puffy, making him look bruised and swollen at once. In a bit of irony that Roger doubtless found more amusing than Morgan would have, the Sheath-born Londret avoided her tavern due to her too-virtuous reputation, even though he was literally employed as an upholder of the imperator's law. That much would have been clear from the sigil-less blue-black he wore, the particular hue that Elgar had chosen to denote his men. Roger could scarcely believe he had the gall to wear it in Sheath, but since no one here was giving him any trouble over it, they were probably too afraid of his fists. Good thing Roger hadn't come to brawl.

He didn't do much more than nod at Londret at first, taking a stool beside his at the bar (he couldn't help noticing both were empty, despite the sizable crowd indoors). He ordered ale and sipped at it slowly, letting his gaze wander around the room and linger on whatever it would: a group of drunken singers toward the back, a nervous young man in the corner spying on either a rival or an infatuation, some bizarre stain on one wall he didn't want to examine too closely. Then, as if reluctantly, and only after having searched for amusement in everything else, he brought his gaze back to Londret Wapps. "Gods, man, wolves wouldn't sniff at your sorry carcass. If honest work so takes it out of a man, I'm fortunate never to have spent a day at it."

He didn't know Londret well—he was the older brother of one of Morgan's infrequent patrons, and that was as far as their circles converged—but he did know him as a growler, a bristler, quick to take offense and quicker to act on it. So he was taken aback when Londret's head sagged forward, as if it was too heavy for him to hold up. "Honest work," he muttered into his drink. "Is that what it is?"

Roger actually felt a stab of pity for him in that moment; he had such a lost look in his eyes. But he wasn't here to comfort the man, he was here to steal whatever it was he knew—and more besides, if his and Marceline's hunch was right. Londret was the only guard whose identity he knew and who he knew had been at the Silkspoint massacre. If this didn't work, he didn't have another candidate.

So he suppressed the instincts of one human being toward another, and focused on those of a swindler toward his mark. And a swindler could never show too much interest in what he wanted. "That bad, eh? I admit I'd never dream of taking orders from anyone in the Citadel, but I thought it would at least be simple."

"It was. It used to be." He shook himself, but if he'd hoped to grasp some shred of alertness, he failed, only sagging back into the same weary pose.

Too early to ask him to elaborate, no matter how much Roger wanted to. "Tell you what. I don't do this often, but you *really* look like you could use it. I'll buy you *one* drink, but it had better be a cheap one."

Londret laughed weakly. "You're the definition of cheap, Halfen. Good to know you haven't changed." But he signaled the tavern keeper to pour him another, watching pointedly until Roger set down the coin for it.

They drank alongside each other, Roger forcing himself to draw the silence out, second by second, until whatever was weighing so hard on Londret snapped the fragile thread of it. Finally, the other man set his tankard down with a trembling hand. "I suppose you've heard the rumors about me."

"Rumors?" Roger didn't have to feign surprise for that one.

"That I'm a murderer."

Still no need to feign surprise. "So's a third of Sheath, I'd wager—in battle, if nothing else. If they'd judge you for that, they're hypocrites."

"But that's just it!" His shaking fingers clenched into a fist. "If I could've been sure it was a part of my duty . . . that they were all . . . that they intended ill . . ." He let his hand fall to the bartop. "You must've at least heard about what happened in Silkspoint. And that I was there."

Let nothing slip, Roger told himself. No lean toward him, no quickening of breath, no quirk of the lips or gleam in the eyes. "I suppose everybody knows about Silkspoint by now. I can't say for sure that anybody told me you were there, but it's not surprising that you might've been."

Londret brought the tankard to his lips and threw his head back, draining it in a single gulp. When he set it down, he whispered into its emptiness: "It's so much worse than everyone thinks. They have no idea what it was really like."

You'd have to be dead not to be curious about *that,* so Roger didn't fight to keep it off his face. "I did hear a lot of people died. But . . . wasn't that the plan?"

"No," Londret said firmly. "We were expecting an attack, but we were only told to guard His Eminence's property. Stay where we were assigned, and don't break formation. We didn't know how many would be standing against us, but we had reason to believe they would be numerous, so my superiors took great pains to ensure our position was solid—that we could dig in and hold off even several times our number. And the attack came just as we predicted, but *we* didn't act the way we practiced. No one held position, no one kept any discipline, and no one gave a thought to His Eminence's property. Instead, we turned the whole thing back on them. We didn't just fight them out of the warehouse, we chased them into the street and cut them down there, even as they fled. It was chaos. Utter chaos. And it was monstrous."

Now Roger feigned a look of surprise. "But if you'd never practiced or discussed an all-out assault, how could everyone have seemingly decided on it together? How did *you* decide on it?"

"That's just it! I don't *know!*" Londret drove a fist into the meat of his thigh. "I know panic can be contagious, sometimes, even among soldiers that are well-trained. And bloodlust can be contagious, too, though no one likes to admit it. But that's not what it felt like. It seemed . . . rational. I thought I knew what I was doing, that it made sense, that it was . . . gods, that it was *right*." He knocked his forehead against the wood of the bar, but then his eyes slid suspiciously to Roger. "You're going to tell me I'm mad, aren't you, Halfen?"

Roger shook his head. "It sounds like if I called you that, I'd have to say the same for every guardsman who was there that day. Did your opinion of your enemy change? Did they suddenly seem more threatening? More despicable?"

Londret scrubbed a hand down his face. "I . . . didn't truly think about them, not as separate individuals. As a mass, they were His Eminence's enemies, and so also mine. And I wanted to get rid of them, so I could be safe."

"And what about your fellow guards? Did they seem less capable, or did you worry you wouldn't be able to fulfill your orders for some reason?"

"No, it was nothing like that. If anything, I stopped considering them altogether."

"Hmm." Roger tapped his tankard with one fingernail. "I don't consider myself the advice-giving sort, but if *I* had had such an experience as one of Elgar's guardsmen, I'd find a way not to be one anymore, as quickly as possible."

"And do what else? There's no job I'm qualified for that pays as well."

"But there are plenty of jobs less likely to get you killed," Roger said. "And certainly those that'll blacken your conscience less severely."

Londret snorted, but his eyes were shifty. "This from a swindler?"

"A swindler who's never killed anyone," Roger corrected him, wagging one finger in the air. *Though I'm certainly trying,* he thought. "And swindlers know better than anyone the importance of knowing exactly what you're purchasing before you make a deal. When you accepted that uniform you're wearing, surely you didn't intend to end up like this?"

Londret mopped at his forehead. "Ugh, I should've known not to share drinks and woes with a man who lives and dies by his words. Listening to you is like suffering an itch I can't scratch." But Roger thought he saw half a smile slip across the man's face, one corner of his mouth twitching persistently upward.

Londret yawned and stretched, getting to his feet. "This isn't a good place to collapse, so I'll be on my way. Thanks for the drink, Halfen."

"But not the company?" Roger clapped a hand to his heart in mock-injury.

Londret gave a gravelly laugh. "Perhaps for that, too. I suppose the future will tell."

Roger stayed seated as Londret walked out, but he kept his eyes on the other man's retreating form, waiting for what was supposed to happen next. He heard it when Londret stumbled out the door—the impact as he collided with someone who was heading straight down the street, and then something he was too far away to hear over the indoor conversations, but that, from the tone, sounded like Londret's apology.

All according to plan, then.

After finishing his drink, Roger left, too, taking Sheath's meandering ways back toward the Dragon's Head. About halfway there, he slid around the corner into an alley, leaning against the brick. Marceline was already there, little more than a shadow at the far end. She drifted within whispering distance.

"Well?" Roger asked.

Marceline shook her head. "Nothing. And I'm sure I went through every bit of pocket on him."

Roger swore. It had seemed such a promising idea when he and the monkey had first hit upon it. They needed to figure out why the guards at the massacre had ignored each other but killed indiscriminately otherwise, and they realized they already had an example of such a phenomenon: the white stone Marceline had unknowingly stolen from Elgar, that Wren had had on his person when the guards spared him in Silkspoint. They had originally thought Elgar had made the white stone only for himself, but if each of his soldiers had been carrying one, too, wouldn't that explain it?

"Maybe it would've been too suspicious," Marceline said. "Telling your men they each have to carry a stone like that, but without any explanation for why . . . that's bound to raise eyebrows, or even just give rise to those who don't take it seriously."

"And Wren himself wasn't subject to any kind of killing frenzy, after all."

"That's true, but the stone he carried was one Elgar originally made for himself, so it stands to reason it'd be different." She frowned. "Speaking of Wren, have you heard anything in Iron's Den about Elgar's people buying up more plate?"

Roger shook his head. "Mail has always been for cavalry officers, or else the elite of the elite, or else those so rich they don't know what to do with it. As far as I know, that hasn't changed. Why?"

She chewed her lip contemplatively. "There was something odd about Londret's chest. When I brushed against it, it felt harder than it should've been. Like there was something solid under his shirt."

"Could you make out a shape?"

"Aye, thin and flat. That's why I asked you about plate mail. But now that I think on it, it couldn't have been a breastplate. Whatever it was, it was definitely too small for that. It didn't cover the whole chest, just the center or thereabouts."

Before Roger could answer, a shout split the night, the pitch and forcefulness of it making them both tense to flee before the content had a chance to sink into their minds. The accompanying sound of a truly godsforsaken horn blast announced it as a herald, but heralds almost never ventured into Sheath. Whatever the news, it must have been of great import.

So he and Marceline did not laugh, but remained perfectly silent, craning their heads toward the noise. "Danger!" the herald shouted, a man's booming voice resounding off the walls of every house. "Danger and treachery! Despite the imperator's efforts toward neutrality and peace, Adora Avestri no sooner seized the crown than she declared her intent to invade our borders and sack this very city. Beware Issamiri treachery! Defend your country and your homes!" His voice started to fade; he must have passed them.

Roger spat into the street. "So that's the tale he's weaving them. We knew he'd have to do *something* with the news from Issamira, but . . ."

"To be fair," Marceline said, "the Issamiri *are* the ones who declared war first, so he doesn't have to lie about that part."

"The Issamiri declared war because Elgar invaded Esthrades, *after* invading every other country on the continent," Roger said. "Perhaps the first or second times might have been passed off as legitimate disputes, but he doesn't even share a fucking border with Esthrades. And our history with Issamira only involves *us* provoking *them,* over and over. Can anyone here really be fooled anymore?"

Marceline bit her lip. "I don't think that's what it's going to be about, Roger. He's trying to make people afraid that the Issamiri will hurt them—will kill their friends and neighbors and destroy their homes. Even people who don't want war won't just sit idly by while they're being invaded, and the invaders' reasons won't do anything to lessen the horror of their actions. If someone you'd swindled out of a week's wages came around hoping to bash your face in, would you let him, simply because his grievance was legitimate?"

Roger groaned. "You're the one who recruited me for this noble resistance business. Is it a surprise a thief isn't naturally suited for it? But even thieves ought to have lines they won't cross. You can't resist taking a stroll through other people's pockets, but I don't see you prying the last copper out of the callused fingers of an old beggar woman. And I've never swindled anyone out of a week's wages, just so you know. I target those with money to burn."

"So what you're saying is, perhaps you're better suited for this noble resistance business I recruited you for than you thought?"

"You'll never hear me say *that,*" Roger insisted.

She peered out into the street. "What now? Did you hear anything when you were working him over that could point us in a new direction? Because we need one."

"Not when I was talking to him," Roger said. "When I was talking to you. I think you've pinpointed our next move, in fact."

"I have? When? What did I say?"

"That Londret Wapps was in possession of something strange. It just wasn't in his pockets." He smirked. "Noble or not, you and I are still thieves. So let's steal ourselves that clue you brushed up against earlier, and see precisely how our imperator's been outfitting these troops of his."

Chapter Seven

Lanvaldis

LIRIEN HAD SPENT an absolutely miserable night sleeping in the rockiest field she'd ever encountered, so the following morning, the instant a village appeared on the horizon, she breezed past all of Cadfael's tedious objections and insisted on having *one* meal in a godsdamned inn. Cadfael had scowled for all he was worth, but relented at a single beseeching look from Rhia, nearly throwing the coin at Lirien's head but refusing to enter town with them. She could only presume he was stalking off to brood in some woods somewhere, but that only meant her meal would be that much more pleasant without him.

Poor gentle Rhia was doing her best to please both sides, saving room in her stomach for Cadfael's cooking but keeping Lirien company at the inn. She couldn't resist nibbling a little once the plate of eggs, sausages, fruit, and fresh bread arrived in front of them, but otherwise she kept her hunger admirably restrained. "You *did* do this on purpose to annoy him," she mumbled, with that pitiably hurt look that always reminded Lirien of Miken.

She dipped the bread in the egg and swallowed a huge bite before speaking. "Your brother's a talented cook. I'm just not used to having so many meals in a row all from the same person. And the money the queen gave him was meant to be *ours*. I don't begrudge him the right to hold on to it, but I'd like to use it for my own purposes at least once." She chewed on a grape, relishing the moment when the firm skin burst between her teeth. "It doesn't bother you? That he dislikes people so much? You seem to admire them, more often than not."

"Of course it bothers me," Rhia said—a much more direct answer than Lirien had expected. "He's always done so much for me, and did all he could for our father. It's the great pity of his life that he has so much potential for love, and spends it among so few people."

"Perhaps his love has such depth precisely because it is spent on so few. If you have but a handful of coins, every one is precious, but given thousands, 'twould be hard to care about any one in particular."

Rhia tilted her head, frowning. "There's that habit of yours come out again. What's wrong? It only happens when you're nervous."

Lirien had never told her that, and was both impressed and irritated that she'd discovered it on her own. "I've felt odd since we sat down. Like someone is looking at me, or the way they say it feels when someone steps on your shadow."

"Well, some people *are* looking at you," Rhia said, blushing. "You're . . . used to that, surely?"

Lirien took her time with the next handful of grapes to delay having to answer that, examining each one as if they had words written on them. Oh, that poor guileless creature. As difficult to handle as her brother, in a way, but only because Lirien feared bruising such a delicate sensibility.

She had found that many people were attracted to her, and that she was attracted to many people, overlapping often enough that her interactions with other humans tended to be pleasant, if fleeting. Rhia was pretty and kind and upright and seemed the type to take to instruction *very* well, and under different circumstances, Lirien would have been more than happy to relieve her of this flustered, girlish infatuated state and suggest that they simply do something about it. But just as his impetuousness and immaturity, made more dangerous by the power he wielded as a prince, had made her loath to become entangled with Hephestion, no matter how beautiful he was, so she sensed that Rhia's affections, however trivially they might first be engaged, would prove painfully deep and abiding. And while Lirien viewed deep and abiding connections as more trouble than they were worth, she did not wish to be a liar, nor a reckless breaker of hearts. No doubt Rhia's heart would eventually be broken by *someone,* given the nature of the world. But Lirien didn't want to be the one to do it, if she could possibly help it.

She wasn't sure Rhia was even aware of the nature of her feelings in the first place. She seemed utterly bereft of any kind of romantic experience, and her head was so stuffed with honor and justice and duty that there probably wasn't much room for her to think about it, either. At least she'd been born in an eastern city, which gave her upbringing an advantage over Lirien's. Though Ninism was centuries dead, it had pervaded the continent for generations upon generations. And the Ninists had had all sorts of rules about what bodies were supposed to do and look like, who you were supposed to desire, who you were supposed to marry, even what desire and marriage were *for.* Those proscriptions had all died out, but in some cultural enclaves there remained faint scars. Lirien had grown up surrounded by an increasing haze of uneasy questions she never asked aloud, like whether it was strange that she found the Clarkes' daughter more fascinating to daydream about than their son. No one had ever told her she couldn't, that it was wrong, but no one had ever told her she *could,* either. She wouldn't know the answer for sure until she'd left Sundercliff entirely.

But she couldn't very well ask Rhia, *Are you aware that you're attracted to me,* because, at worst, she'd embarrass the girl so severely that Cadfael would probably try to kill her. He wouldn't succeed, but it would be annoying all the same.

Instead, she decided to just answer the question Rhia had asked, and no more. "People who stare at me don't always do so with harmless intent, so it's safer if I don't get used to it." She relented a little. "Probably more likely to get that kind of trouble when I'm traveling alone, though, I suppose."

Rhia's expression darkened. "If there's anyone who causes you concern, I'll sort them out for you."

Lirien felt her lips twitch in amusement. "I'm perfectly capable of sorting them out myself, but if you insist on providing me with the entertainment of watching you do it, I'll not say no."

But as her eyes swept over the bustling ground floor of the inn, the mirth curdled in her stomach. There was a single person sitting at an otherwise empty table, the only corner where shadow fell in the entire bright room. It was the same woman who'd grinned at her early that morning in Esthrades, when they were the only ones awake in the whole village. Her eyes were flitting here and there, a slight smile on her lips as she watched the occupants of the other tables eating and drinking, laughing and singing and trading tales. But as Lirien stared at her, the woman's eyes met hers. Her smile widened, that same knowing, infuriating smile.

Under the table, her left hand clenched in her lap. Such an unnerving coincidence had several explanations, none of them particularly comforting, but she hoped to rule out the worst of them first. "Rhia," she said quietly. "Do you see that woman over there? The one sitting alone?"

Rhia squinted. "The one in the far corner? What about her?"

Lirien tried not to show her relief. "I saw the same woman in that village in Esthrades. The one where I stopped for the night."

"But we've made such good time, and we never saw her along our way. For her to take a different route and still get here so quickly . . . or do you think she's following us? Spying on us?"

"I don't know," Lirien said. She normally kept the magic coiled tightly within her, especially when among other people, but now she released it, using it to expand her senses beyond eyes and ears. She concentrated on the lone woman, seeking her out through the sea of bodies. "She doesn't—"

She broke off when someone stepped between her and the woman, and she was annoyed to recognize the chest as Cadfael's. The face, too, when she reluctantly looked up. "I was bored," he said to Rhia with a shrug and a half-smile, ignoring Lirien entirely.

Lirien had a dozen biting rejoinders for that—did he mean to say that solitary forest brooding was *not* a riveting leisure activity? Shocking!—but for Rhia's sake, she choked them all back down, simply ignoring him in her turn. He took a seat at their table, and Lirien shot him a look that said, *Just* try *to remove a single crumb from that plate,* and he did not. "Why do you both look so serious?" he asked Rhia, instead.

Rhia looked at Lirien uncertainly. "It's that woman at the table in the far corner. Lirien thinks she saw her before, in Esthrades."

Cadfael, of course, leaned forward immediately, his face going even more insufferable, all tension, suspicion, accusation yearning for a target. "Where in Esthrades?"

"In the village where I stopped for the night," Lirien said, "though I barely exchanged a glance with her there. And no, I don't know how she got here so quickly. That's why I brought it up."

"And you're certain it's the same woman?"

"I'm certain." She was, and she only now considered that that was odd. She'd only seen the woman for a few moments in Esthrades, from much farther away than she was now. Yet there was no doubt in her mind. It wasn't about a particular feature, her hair or the curve of her mouth or the eyes Lirien was still too far away to see clearly. It was the woman's essence that was the same.

Speaking of essences, however . . . "There's one more odd thing about her," she said, lowering her voice even further. "Because I have this power, I can sense water, even when I can't see it with my eyes—even when it's in a strange form, like the bits of it in the air even when it's not raining. Every person carries a large amount of water in their bodies, much more than they could hold in their stomachs alone. Since, unlike Talis and Voltest, I actually like to be around people, I've learned how to more or less ignore it—it would be overwhelming to be constantly focusing on water coming from so many different directions in a crowd this big. But that woman . . . it's not that she feels completely inert, like a stone; when I reach out to her with my magic, I do feel . . . something. But it isn't water. Somehow, there's no water in her body at all."

Cadfael went pale, his knuckles whitening as he gripped the edge of the table. Lirien had mentioned it more as a way of thinking out loud than anything else, but now she went back over her own words in her mind, trying to come to whatever epiphany Cadfael had. And when she looked toward her again, to confirm what she had felt, she realized the woman was gone.

TALIS FLOATED INFINITELY in a sea of pain.

She could no longer remember what it was like not to hurt everywhere at once, not to feel like every secret place in her mind had been broken open. And yet no

matter how long the pain endured, how thoroughly it had ransacked her, somehow it always found just one more drop of blood to draw, one more angle from
which to strike. It was like being so tired you felt you were coming apart at the
seams, and finally, finally, being about to drift off, only to be drenched in ice water
at the last moment.

The view from the top of that infernal cliff had assailed her eyes so many times,
and yet there was no way to shut it out, no way not to inhale the bitter scent of
pine, to feel her breath steam in the chill air. She *knew* it wasn't real. But it had been
real, once, and the sharpness of those memories mocked her with how little she had
been able to forget. How little she would ever be able to forget.

She was just about to plunge into thin air again when she felt the cuffs removed
from her wrists, the instant, shuddering shift in reality that left her sprawling and
chained to the floor. Her eyes were closed, and she finally saw only darkness behind them, after so long. But then she opened them, and beheld the face she was
growing to hate above all else.

"If you keep this up for much longer," Talis said, "I won't be coherent enough
to answer any of your godsdamned questions."

"That is a concern," Edith Selwyn admitted. She'd taken to having a stool
brought in for her on these visits, and Talis hated the ease that implied, that Selwyn knew she was never in any danger. She was sitting there, one leg crossed
over the other, a notebook open on her lap. *Observations on the creature,* perhaps, or
something like that. "But I've already reduced the time you spend under the steel's
influence twice in the past three days. If I make it much shorter, there will hardly
be anything to observe."

Talis felt her face tighten as she struggled to remember. "Have you?"

Selwyn clicked her tongue. "Yes, precisely because of these increasing lapses in
memory you seem to be afflicted with. Though your body recovers from exposure
almost immediately, it seems your mind is faring worse."

Talis spat at her feet. "You really need *observation* to deduce that torture is not
beneficial to a person's mental state?"

"And yet the nature of this torture you claim to feel remains elusive. If it were
not, all this observation would not be necessary."

"You claim to be a scholar. Wouldn't a scholar more than anyone know that—"

"I *am* a scholar," Selwyn snapped, her icy gray eyes narrowing.

"And yet you don't seem to realize that an experiment that continually pro-
duces no results ought to have some part of it changed. That's obvious to me, and
I hadn't read a dozen books in my life before I met Voltest."

"Who is Voltest?" Selwyn asked, leaning forward.

But Talis did not fear for him; Voltest was a name he had made up himself, and there wasn't a score of people on the continent who had heard it. Searching for that name would get Selwyn nowhere. "He's the one who's probably going to kill you," she said. "Probably fairly soon. If you think to have as easy a time capturing him as you did me . . . well, I'll enjoy the results."

"Why? Is he more powerful than you are?"

"How would I measure it?" Talis asked. "But he's more *violent* than I am, and he won't have a group of princes to protect."

Selwyn sat back on her stool, stroking the edge of her jaw. "So there *are* more of you. I suspected you couldn't be the only one."

"There might be hundreds of us, for all I know. I wonder if you have enough of that blasted steel to handle that many."

"We certainly have enough for one," Selwyn said. "I wonder if he'll prove a better subject than you are."

"WELL, THAT'S BRILLIANT," Lirien said, setting her pack down in the grass. Cadfael had insisted on keeping away from any roads, despite Lirien's objection that that would only make it harder to spot the woman if she followed them. He led them to a river he claimed to have crossed on his way to Araveil before, but a recent rainfall had swollen its banks, the meandering silver streak he remembered now bloated and treacherous, swirling with conflicting currents. "And no bridge in sight. I don't suppose you remember one?"

Cadfael shook his head. "I don't remember needing one. And I'd think we wouldn't need one now, either. Can't you get us across this?"

"That depends. What did you have in mind?"

He waved a hand across the divide. "With your control over water, you wouldn't even need to freeze it, right? You could just part it enough to create a path, and then close it up again behind us."

"And what do you think would happen if any other traveler happened by while I was doing that? With a current this strong, if I released the river mid-crossing, we'd all be swept away. And if I didn't, our witness would chase me down for a witch. Again."

"So, what, you really want to walk all the way around? I don't even remember how far it goes."

"Lirien knows her own limits better than we do," Rhia reminded him. "If she says it's not going to work, it's not going to work."

Lirien paced along the bank, staring at the water. "It's too risky to part it, but perhaps I could just calm the currents. That wouldn't be visible from the shore, so no one would be able to tell I was doing it. But it could take the peril out of our crossing, though it would mean drenching our clothes and supplies."

"If there's no current, I can hold my pack above my head," Cadfael said. "I don't care about my clothes, but there's food in here I can't get wet."

"I'm not carrying anything that would be harmed by a bit of water," Rhia added. "I say we try it."

Lirien still didn't like it, but it did seem like the best option. "If you're sure. But it's safest if you two go ahead of me, so I can see it if you slip."

"Rhia, I'll go first," Cadfael said immediately. "You stay between me and Lirien, all right?"

Rhia rolled her eyes, but didn't argue. Lirien closed her own eyes, reaching out to the river. She let her mind drift along the currents, tracing their intricate patterns beneath the surface. And then she coaxed them gently awry, diverting them temporarily down milder channels. The rush of water quieted slightly, and she opened her eyes. "All right. It's deep, but it should be easy to wade through."

Cadfael strode into the water as if trying to shoulder his way through a crowd, holding his pack above his head as promised. He seemed surprised, in the first few instants, at how little resistance he met, but then he set a confident pace, as if he had flowing water up to his shoulders all the time.

Rhia was next, and Lirien was a little more worried about her: she was significantly shorter than her brother, though not too short to stand upright in the river. But Rhia herself was cheerful and unhurried, marveling at her surroundings as she entered the water. With a glance back behind them to make sure no one was coming, Lirien plunged in after them, the water cool and welcoming against her skin, licking at the hollow of her throat as if trying to get her attention. She'd learned from experience that it was much easier for her to dry out her clothes; she could convince the water to dissolve itself into the air faster than it would normally. The three of them would squelch a bit at first, but on the whole, perhaps this idea wasn't terrible.

Then, out of nowhere, the space at the edge of her consciousness Talis usually occupied was suddenly filled up, seething with so much rage and suffering that it hit Lirien like a physical blow.

In the beginning her magic had been comforting, empowering, a fullness beneath her skin, constant proof that she was just a little bit *more*. After Miken's death reduced them to three and threw their magic out of balance, it became harder to hold on to that feeling, but especially without Talis or Voltest around, Lirien was still able to capture it again, moment by moment, if she really tried.

This felt like the magic was trying to claw out of her, like a blind beast had burrowed into her flesh and didn't know how to get free. Feelings crashed over her in waves, each one worse than the last: fear, anger, despair. And pain. Always pain, the brutal deadening echo of it, the knowledge that, somewhere not so very far away anymore, Talis was feeling something even worse than this. Talis was being torn apart, picked clean, unmade by this, and if she ever got free of it, the only thing she had left was revenge.

Lirien tried to send something back, calm or stability, even just the absence of pain, but it was as if Talis's feelings overflowed their connection, forcing it only one way, the way a river cannot flow upstream. The pain bent her forward, and she held her breath to avoid inhaling water. But she couldn't see, and something deafening rushed in her ears, air or water, she couldn't tell. She couldn't feel the pulse of power until it was too late.

The surface of the river exploded, erupting like a geyser from one bank to the other. Lirien's entire field of vision was filled with water, too much to tell which way was up and which down. For a moment it was so wild it felt like the sea that she had left behind in Sundercliff, always ready to dash the unwary to death. But there were no rocks here, and it was shallow enough to stand. She had to remember that, had to bend the current back to her will.

Talis faded past the point of perception, cut off from her again. Lirien calmed the water around her, found the bottom with her feet, and blinked her vision clear enough to take stock of her surroundings. Cadfael was standing a bit forward and to her left, his feet just barely touching the bottom, thrashing about as the rough current tried to force water into his mouth.

But she couldn't see Rhia at all.

CADFAEL FORCED HIS head above water, sputtering and spitting, head spinning, desperately searching for the patch of shore on the other side. It seemed so close, yet every time he tried to move his limbs, they felt three times as heavy as they should be, waterlogged and battered by the current. He needed to catch sight of the bank, and he needed to catch sight of Rhia. But at first all he could see was water, and then only Lirien.

"What the hell happened?" he yelled, trying to wade over to her—still damnably difficult. "Where is my sister?"

"I'm trying to find her!" she yelled back. "And don't come toward me! Get to shore where you'll be safe!"

"Not without Rhia!" He kept struggling toward her; Rhia had been between them, after all. His pack was soaked through already anyway, so he shifted it onto his back and kept going.

"I'm a better swimmer than you are, idiot!" Lirien snapped. "And I can sense her beneath the surface. If you stay here, you'll just get in the way."

"I'm not leaving this to you! You're the reason this happened in the first place! I'm going to—" He saw Lirien take a deep breath to yell something back at him again, but then she abruptly closed her mouth. Instead, she raised a hand as if to call for silence, and a great wave formed in the middle of the river, breaking directly over Cadfael's head and forcing him back toward the far bank. When it receded, he was left sprawled damply in the shallows, coughing up water and collecting mud.

He pushed himself to his knees and scanned the water for Rhia again, or even Lirien, but he saw nothing, just the roiling surface. Then Lirien burst into the air, with Rhia tucked under one arm like a sack of supplies. Cadfael met her in knee-high water, reaching out to take Rhia's weight so Lirien wouldn't collapse.

Gasping, shivering, they gained the bank, struggling up the slope in clothes that were drenched, and laid Rhia out on the grass. Her skin was pale and cold. He couldn't tell if she was breathing.

"You can fix this, right?" he demanded. "I've seen you close all sorts of wounds. Tell me you can fix this!"

"I'll fix it a lot faster if you stop screaming in my ear," Lirien muttered, sliding a hand over the side of Rhia's face. "Too much water in her lungs. I can sense it."

"Then just pull it out! That should be easy for you!"

Lirien gritted her teeth. "Do you have any idea how much water is in a body? If I pull it all out, I promise you won't like the results. I've got to get only the water that's not supposed to be there, and for that I need to *focus*. If you say one more unsolicited word to me I will freeze your lips together."

Cadfael knew when someone wasn't bluffing, and clamped his lips together voluntarily. Lirien closed her eyes, hand still pressed against the side of Rhia's face. She breathed deeply in and out several times, and on the next exhale, Rhia breathed out as well—only she breathed out water, hacking and coughing until her lungs were empty.

Cadfael sagged in relief, and saw Lirien do the same. It took a couple more rounds of coughing before Rhia could speak, her voice hoarse and raspy. "S—sorry for the trouble. What . . . what happened?"

"It was Talis," Lirien said grimly. "She's beyond my reach more often than not, whatever's confining her interfering with our connection. But every so often she breaks through, and this time was . . . particularly bad. I think she's deteriorating. Not physically, but . . . as the pain persists, her anger at it grows. If she continues like this, it will blot everything out."

"That's not unreasonable," Cadfael said. "Isn't everyone angry when someone's hurting them?"

"You don't understand." Her braid was in ruins, and she scraped back the wet hair that had gotten stuck to her forehead. "I know Talis told you there were originally four of us: earth, fire, water, and wind. Balanced. I know she told you we've found our magic harder to control since Miken died, and that we even started acting in ways that were strange to ourselves. We each have emotions that touch us more deeply than they should, but they aren't the same emotions. It's Voltest who's weak to anger—the anger that he felt at being imprisoned, perhaps. It's what makes him so touchy, but it also means he's used to it. Talis isn't, not in the same way. She feels rage, and she's susceptible to Voltest's rage, but that's not what truly drives her."

"No," Cadfael agreed. He knew what lay at the bottom of her; he had seen it, back when she had told him about falling from the cliff to escape the pillaging of her hometown. "It's despair."

"So you know even that much." She wiped off the back of her neck, looking away from Cadfael. "If she submerges herself in this anger and revenge to escape it, I wonder if it would even be possible to pull her out again. And with her adding so much fuel to Voltest's inner fire, what might *he* not be capable of? I can't fight both of them. On the field, or in my head. It would be beyond disastrous."

It wasn't that Cadfael didn't understand her dread; indeed, he shared it. But he felt frustration, too, so much of it, with nowhere to go. Until he'd met Talis three years ago, he hadn't known magic existed. He'd been so confident in his skill with a sword to protect his family, but Talis's power had overwhelmed him. Now magic seemed to come from everywhere: Lirien and Voltest were *wardrenfell,* too, Elgar and Arianrod Margraine were mages, the very sword his father had left him could cut through spells, and Yaelor, an incorporeal being who claimed full knowledge of the past and present, had warned him of the machinations of a similar being, Amerei, whom Cadfael knew nothing else about. He no longer knew how to protect himself and those he cared about, what direction danger might come from or what form it might take. And his simple life had been replaced with an indecipherable spiderweb. It had become so hard to figure out, moment by moment, what he was supposed to do, and the feeling that possibilities might be slipping through his fingers even now grated on his very bones.

He looked at Rhia, small and shivering, lips still nearly blue. And then he looked at Lirien.

"Our situation is too precarious for games and coyness," he said. "I need everything out in the open, and I need it before we go another step farther. What are you hiding, and what is your connection to Amerei?"

He'd hoped his knowledge of the name might shock her into a reaction, but Lirien just stared at him blankly. "Who is Amerei?"

"Unless I'm very much mistaken, she's the one who's been following you," Cadfael said. "Do you really expect me to believe you don't know that?"

Lirien took her hair in both hands, wringing the water roughly out of it. "Do you expect *me* to believe that *I'm* the one with a connection to this mysterious woman, when *you're* the one who somehow knows her name?"

"When I was warned about Amerei," Cadfael said, "I was also warned about you."

"Me?" Lirien shouted, her normally immaculate complexion flushed and blotchy. "I have a rather significant secret, yes, but you already know what it is! Can you honestly think I'm hiding something even bigger behind that? My life has been so simple you could sum it up on a single page. I was born in a small and closed-minded town, and exiled from it when I used my powers to heal another villager. Since then, all I have done is wander the continent at my own whim, doing odd jobs on the rare occasion I required a few coins, until Jocelyn Selreshe stole my magic. You helped kill her, and here we all are. If there was anything else to say, even if it was shameful, I would have said it, if only to get you off my back! But there just *isn't*!"

"She's telling the truth, Cadfael," Rhia said quietly.

"Rhia, I know you want to believe—"

"No. Listen." She sliced a hand through the air. "Through all of that, she didn't say *'tis* or *'twas* once. So she's angry, but she's not nervous. She lied to me when we first met, to hide her magic from me, and she was nervous then. But this indignation is real, not summoned to mask her guilt. And I believe it's justified. So apologize, and let this suspicion go."

"I don't want an apology," Lirien said. "I want you to do as you have just bid me, Cadfael, and reveal *your* secret."

"What secret?" Rhia asked, before Cadfael could say anything.

Lirien smiled at her sadly. "Have you truly not thought it odd? How much he seems to know, and how little explanation there is for how he knows it? He said his theory that Talis was being held captive by Edith Selwyn in Araveil was just that, a theory, cobbled together from things he had heard about Selwyn's fascination with magic and collection of vardrath steel. And it does make sense, especially now that I'm this close to the city—the ability I have to feel for where Talis and Voltest are does seem to put her in the direction of Araveil. But he made his conjecture before he knew that, and he has not once acted like it is only conjecture. I believe he has treated it as a certainty because he *is* certain of it."

"But how could he be? Before he was with us at Eldren Cael, he was traveling with the queen. He couldn't have been anywhere near Talis when she was captured, and he couldn't have seen her imprisoned."

"Precisely," Lirien said. "So if he knows where she is and why, it must be because someone told him. And I think it's high time he told us who this someone is. As well as one other thing." She turned back to Cadfael. "I saw the way you reacted when I mentioned that I had felt no water in that woman's body. That meant something to you, or else you figured something out. Since this woman mostly seems to be bothering *me,* I have a right to know. Was that what made you think she might be this Amerei?"

Well, this had turned around on him spectacularly. Lirien wasn't like Rhia— someone he could just ask to trust him. Which was fair, since he hadn't trusted her. But now even Rhia was looking at him expectantly, and he felt his options dwindling. Yaelor had never strictly forbidden him from telling anyone, and if he didn't now, he had no idea what on earth he would say instead.

"You're right," he said. "You're right. I'll warn you it's hard to believe, but I'll tell you everything."

And he did. He told them how Yaelor had first appeared to him in Lanvaldis, claiming that if Cadfael didn't help Adora Avestri secure her throne, he would suffer a grievous loss—something he now knew meant Rhia's life, since she had been alive in Eldren Cael and might have been killed by Jocelyn if he hadn't helped stop her. He told them how Yaelor had seemed to know everything about him, how he had claimed to know all that was past and all that was present, to use that knowledge to see the paths the future might take. He told them how Yaelor had been able to mimic the appearance of a human, but that Cadfael's hand had gone right through him. And he told them Yaelor had claimed there were other beings like him, that his actions were limited by an agreement he had made with them.

By the time he had finished, their clothes had dried in the sun. Rhia had stopped being able to close her mouth about twenty minutes back, and Lirien was flicking the end of the braid she'd unknotted and rewound as he spoke. "Well. I feel like I should be less surprised. I thought I was comfortable with magic. But this isn't a person who has magic, this is a magical *being,* a . . . spirit or something. And they can just drop in on us whenever they like?"

"Yaelor said they made a bargain with one another not to interfere," Cadfael reminded her.

"And how good are they at keeping to it? Because it seems to me that they *are* interfering."

"It seems to *me,*" Rhia said, "that if he truly wanted you to shun your own traveling companion, he should have given you his reasons. Like this, we don't even know if the trouble is something he thinks Lirien's going to cause, or something that might just . . . follow her, become attached to her in some way. We might need to be afraid *for* her, not *of* her."

"That's true," Cadfael admitted. "I had assumed she and Amerei were on the same side in some fashion. But perhaps our troublesome spirit simply has designs on her, whether or not she's willing."

"I'm decidedly not," Lirien put in.

"Have you tried to talk to Yaelor again?" Rhia asked. "To ask him for more details?"

"I have, but nothing's come of it, nor did I really expect it to. At the palace in Eldren Cael, I told him to come to me again after we had rescued Talis, and that seemed to please him. But I doubt any of us will see him before then."

"Do you think Amerei is going to try to prevent us from accomplishing that goal?" Lirien asked.

"I'm not sure." He rubbed his jaw. "I don't think she could, and Yaelor didn't make it sound like she wanted to. It was more as if he thought she would try to direct our aims, not thwart them."

"Adora mentioned that Yaelor was the name of a spirit of courage," Lirien said. "That makes sense, given his personality. So it stands to reason Amerei is a spirit of something else, something opposed to him. Cowardice? Selfishness?"

"No," Cadfael said. "Adora told me the ancient Lantians gave names to virtues specifically. Not vices."

"Well, that's harder. Is cunning a virtue? Is pragmatism a virtue?"

"I don't think we have enough information to narrow it down yet," Cadfael said. "Yaelor told me she has the ability to lie, and that she wants everyone to be hers, but falsity and greed aren't virtues, either."

Rhia spoke up again. "I didn't think that woman at the inn felt sinister. But looking at her made me sad. As if . . . as if I had remembered something." She looked at Lirien. "I only felt that way one other time. At the lake, when I first woke up after you healed me—though I didn't know that then. I felt as if I had lost something, something I could almost remember. I don't know what it means, but . . . surely it must mean something."

Chapter Eight

Valyanrend

NAISHE'S MORNING, AS seemed to happen more often than not these days, began with a persistent shudder from beside her, stirring her into wakefulness.

As her eyes fluttered open, she noted the sight of sunlight streaming through the window of the second-floor room in Edgewise she'd been renting since she got to Valyanrend. At least it was time to get up anyway. She rolled over in bed, stroking her fingers down Wren's bare arms and resting her chin on his still-trembling shoulder. "You're safe," she murmured. "You're only dreaming."

His eyes shot open—one brown, one green, both transfixed in a moment of terror that gave way to softness when he recognized her. "Ah. Sorry. I did it again, didn't I?"

It wasn't as if Naishe had never had any nightmares after the Silkspoint massacre, had never woken with Wren's arms around her. But perhaps because she had not seen her best friend hacked to pieces beside her, or because there was something delicate about Wren that had nothing to do with physical strength, she had been able to shake it off more easily than he had. "Do you want to talk about it?"

"No, that's all right. It hasn't changed. But thank you." He turned to face her fully, holding her tight. She felt him smile against her neck. "Good morning."

"Good morning yourself. I wish we could spend more of it in here."

He laughed. "I won't tell your adoring followers you said that. They believe you're incapable of laziness."

"Who said I wanted to stay in to be lazy? I'm sure you and I could be extremely productive, if we only had the time." But they didn't, so she disentangled her limbs from his, stifling a yawn as she padded over to the basin to wash. "They need you at the shop today, right?"

"Till dinnertime at least. Will that interfere with your plans?"

"Your help is always welcome, but I'll manage." At least in his father's workshop Wren was a step removed from warfare; he made the tools, but he didn't have to use them. "And I'm sure your parents miss you."

He blushed. "I haven't heard the end of it from them. I wonder if I ever will." He took Naishe's place at the basin as she started struggling into her clothes.

"They'd have you over for dinner every night this week if you'd let them. Probably to thank you for condescending to return my feelings, or something."

Naishe laughed. "I don't know why they take that attitude about it. I know how proud they are of you."

"It's because they like you," Wren said, with one leg in his pants.

"Well, I'll pay them back by showing up for dinner *one* night this week, at least." Before Wren could respond, they were interrupted by a clamor from the floor below, raised voices and some sort of banging. One voice was Mr. Redding's, her landlord and a purveyor of odd trinkets that he sold on the floor below during the day. The other she had not heard in far longer, but it was too familiar for her to ever mistake.

Naishe clapped a hand to her forehead. "Gods, if he thinks he's just going to barge into this room like he owns it, I swear I'll kill him."

Wren frowned. "Mr. Redding? He does own it."

"No, not—" She shoved her feet into her boots; there wasn't time for explanations. "Put your shirt on as fast as you can."

Wren obediently snatched it up, but he also asked, "Why?"

"Because I assume you want to be wearing a shirt the first time you meet my father?"

Wren forced his hands through the sleeves so haphazardly it was a miracle he didn't tear right through them, but he'd still only just gotten the last button done when someone who definitely wasn't Mr. Redding started hammering on the door. Naishe had half a mind to ignore him, but that door was her only dignified way out; even if she wanted to chance a second-story window, it would only look like she was afraid of him.

So she unlatched the door and flung it wide, only barely resisting the urge to scream at the man on the other side.

Nasser Kadife was just as tall as she remembered, though perhaps a bit grayer around the temples. At the first sight of her, he actually went perfectly still, fist still raised for another attempt at punching through the wood. "Vanaishendi. So this is where you've hidden yourself all this time."

Getting angry would only weaken her position. *She* knew she was a woman grown, but insisting on it aloud would hardly make her appear mature. So Naishe took a deep breath, and willed her face to remain calm. "Father, Mr. Redding has a shop to run on the ground floor. You're causing a disturbance."

He folded his arms, glaring down at her from his annoyingly superior height. "That's all you have to say to me? After all this time, and all I've been through to find you? I thought you were dead!"

"Then that's an assumption you made entirely without my assistance," Naishe said. Internally, she did feel a bit bad about it—she'd known from Marceline that her father feared she was likelier dead than alive, and she could have allayed that fear at any point during the last several weeks and had chosen not to. But any resentment she might have felt at how deeply he had underestimated her aside, the leader of Valyanrend's resistance had a never-ending list of goals to accomplish and duties to attend to. She had known that, as soon as she revealed herself to her father, he would quickly discover everything, and just as quickly disapprove. Whatever disagreements they may have had, Nasser Kadife was an immensely capable individual, and she had not wanted to find out just how thoroughly such an individual could hamper her plans. So she had tried to delay their meeting—not forever, but simply until she was in a stronger position, less vulnerable to his disruptions. Leave it to her father to refuse to act according to her schedule.

"You must have heard of the massacre that took place in this city," he insisted, as if he were not speaking to two people who had fought their way out of it. "With all you wrote your mother about your fascination with Valyanrend's resistance, what was I supposed to think when I heard of its fate?"

"Valyanrend's resistance is alive and well," Naishe said, trying to keep the bite out of her voice, "and I *still* know more about it than you most likely ever will."

"Yet all this knowledge has not dissuaded you from trying to win yourself a place that would only bring you danger and hardship! I taught you the bow so you could *protect* yourself, not think yourself invulnerable!"

"And who the hell is *this*?" he demanded, rounding on Wren, as if a man who couldn't make eye contact with most humans were some sort of nefarious seducer, and not someone who'd sworn his life in defense of Naishe and their cause.

Naishe linked her arm through Wren's. "*This* happens to be the man I love. He has a name. Perhaps you might ask him?"

Poor Wren. Rarely had she seen him look so anxiously unhappy. "Sir, I apologize about the circumstances—"

"Well, at least you have that level of awareness," her father snapped. "Vanaishendi, we are *leaving* this city—"

And there it was. Naishe was able to rein in her outrage only because she'd known it was coming. "I'd be delighted if you left this city, Father. But *we* are not doing anything."

He acted like she hadn't spoken. "—if I have to drag you all the way back—"

"With all due respect, I wouldn't do that if I were you, sir."

The quiet words landed with the force of a trumpet blast. Naishe couldn't quite keep the grin off her face. So Wren had decided to fight today.

Her father turned his head toward Wren slowly, as if begrudging him the attention. "You wouldn't, would you? Why, because *you'll* stop me?"

Wren smiled wryly. "If Naishe wanted me to, I'd certainly try, though I'm much better at making arrows than shooting them. But the problem is much larger than just me, sir. Hundreds have sworn to Naishe, and hundreds will rise to defend her, should you try to take her away from them. Even you might experience some difficulty then."

If she hadn't already known she loved Wren, the look on her father's face would have pitched her headlong into infatuation. His jaw dropped open like it had ceased its proper function, his eyes opening as wide as she had ever seen them. "Explain," he managed.

Naishe threaded her fingers between Wren's. "For this," she said, "I'll be happy to oblige."

In theory, Morgan Imrick still had a tavern to run.

She had more or less the same collection of evening drinkers as always, and the odd traveler looking for a room, even with the looming prospect of war keeping people closer to home. That business had, once, seemed like work enough to fill a life: coin to earn, ledgers to maintain, an existence to ensure, one transaction at a time. It was surprising, and not a little unnerving, to realize how much of it she could still perform in the background, while her heart and mind were fully engaged with another goal, another life.

Braddock had been invaluable, of course—in every way. He manned the bar on nights Morgan simply couldn't, learned all her shorthand and filled in the blanks in all her records. More than that, he kept her grounded and sane, reassured her that she wasn't taking on more than she could handle (and pulled her back when she was). If someone like her could really do this, it would be, more than any other singular thing, more even than Lord Vespas's support, because of him.

She might have gotten the better end of the deal with Lord Vespas, too. She had tidbits about the resistance to share, and had written about the massacre in Silkspoint and their efforts to determine how Elgar had ensorcelled his men. But beyond that, all her information was confined to things any average citizen of Valyanrend would know. He, on the other hand, controlled the queen's armies and served as her right hand. Morgan wasn't fool enough to imagine he told her more than a fraction of what he might have, but even that was significant. Still, she knew how clever that man could be. If he was convinced this arrangement was to his advantage, she didn't want to bet against him. He and his army remained a ways off yet, still massing on the Gods' Curse as of his last letter. Perhaps her true usefulness to him would be revealed the closer he got to Valyanrend's walls.

She must have been pondering it more deeply than she realized, for she looked

up from the bar to discover someone was in the process of shoving a large and inde-
terminate object through the Dragon's Head's front door. "Watch it!" she snapped.
"Those hinges are old! Do I even know you?"

"No, ma'am," came someone's voice from behind the object, "but I'm making
a delivery on behalf of—"

"Morning, Miss Imrick!" came a voice from behind the first voice, bright and
cheerful where the first had been heavy and phlegmatic. And that voice, at least,
Morgan knew. "Sorry for the interruption. Marcus and I won't be a moment."

Marcus, a broad, dour-looking youth, had finally gotten his cargo through
the door, and Morgan saw that it was a tightly sealed wooden barrel, about the
height of her waist. Without him blocking the door, she could make out the young
woman behind him: Talia, one of Naishe's favored companions within the resistance, and Rask's student in the sword. She was the one who had retrieved the
proof of Elgar's sorcery during the Silkspoint massacre, though she had taken a
slash to the abdomen that nearly killed her. "Thank you so much, Marcus; I know
it was quite a ways. I ought to have been able to do it myself, but . . ." She trailed
off, one hand clenching over her stomach.

She didn't want to tell him the true reason she couldn't lift it, Morgan realized.
She opened her mouth to help distract from the issue, but then realized it wasn't
necessary; the young man simply bobbed his head obligingly. "Of course, Miss
Parnell. Wherever you needed it, Mr. Parnell said. I just hope you're sure about
this. This neighborhood is . . . unsafe."

"Now, Marcus, that's uncharitable of you," Talia said, leaning against Morgan's bar as if she'd been drinking there for years. "There's plenty of honest folk
in Sheath, and Miss Imrick is chief among them. I'll be as safe with her as I am in
my own home."

Marcus's skepticism at that, Morgan had to admit, was fair. "I should at least
escort you back to the shop."

"Oh, don't be silly. Father shouldn't have to spare you any longer, and should
worse come to worst, I'll remind you that my swordsmanship instructor remains
thoroughly impressed with my progress."

Damn, but even Morgan would've found it difficult to push back against the
iron certainty beneath that silken cheerfulness. Talia's companion ducked his head,
half a shrug. "I'll tell Mr. Parnell that's what you said, then. See you at the shop,
Miss Parnell."

The door had barely shut behind him when Talia sagged into a stool, wiping a
hand across her brow. "Whew! He's a nice enough fellow, but I couldn't have him
underfoot, obviously."

"Talia," Morgan said, summoning the most patient tone she possessed, "what precisely is this?"

"Why, what you asked for, of course! Supplies to keep in the tunnels, lest any of our people should be stuck there. Sorry to bring them round to the Dragon's Head instead, but I needed Marcus's help to carry them, and I couldn't very well take him through the passages. Naishe still says no lifting anything heavier than my arm; I feel entirely well, but she says these things can be more fragile underneath than they appear."

"Ah." Well, she *had* asked for that. "Sorry. I just didn't realize you'd be bringing them, or so soon. I can keep them here until Braddock's around to move them."

Talia tilted her head. "Who else would they ask for supplies? Anyone else would have to pay, but I just asked my father."

"What does your father . . . wait." Morgan repeated the conversation in her head. *Miss Parnell.* "But you can't be *that* Parnell, can you?"

Talia beamed, her spine straightening. "So you've heard of us! Parnell Grocers and Sundry, finest raw ingredients in all of Valyanrend."

She wasn't exaggerating. The Parnell grocery was nothing like Halvard's modest shop in the Fades, where Morgan purchased her supplies. It was a sprawling indoor and outdoor market a stone's throw from Goldhalls, the richest district in the city, and it worked to satisfy every craving those gluttons could dream up—with prices to match. "I can't possibly afford this," Morgan said.

"Oh no, you don't have to pay! My father doesn't even know who you are. I just asked him for a favor."

Morgan raised an eyebrow. "I don't know what's in there, but for him to give you a barrel that size full of even the cheapest foodstuffs he sells as a *favor* is . . . quite generous."

"Well, my father's quite a generous man! And my mother's quite a smart woman, who tells him when not to ask questions." Talia ran a hand over her stomach. "I couldn't be moved for *days* after I got this, you know. Naishe had to let them know what had happened to me, which meant letting them know what I'd been up to. So, since then . . ."

"Since then, they understand it's safer for them not to know certain things," Morgan finished. "Fair enough. Do you need to rest for a bit before you head back?"

"I will, thanks." Though she'd said she was well, she leaned her head all the way down against the wood of the bar. "I'm just tired. So much to—"

"All right, Morgan, we've got it this time. We're sure of it." That was Roger, throwing the door open as if he owned the building, a sack over his shoulder and

Marceline trotting at his heels. "Just shy of a dozen, from all over the city. We haven't cut them open yet, but we didn't want to risk that until we knew we were safely away."

Morgan felt a headache starting between her eyes. "And just what are you doing?"

"Had a night of thieving." He threw the sack down off his shoulder and stretched out the kinks in his neck. "Bit refreshing, I must say; a swindler's schemes are done with words, and it's not often I get to exercise the old fingers as well."

"I'm delighted for you," Morgan said, "but then why the hell didn't you bring this shit to the underground? I know it's morning, but business *does* still come through here."

"It's because you're here," Marceline said. "Or rather, because the dagger's here."

"This *has* to be a wide enough net to catch our target." Roger dumped the sack's contents right onto the floor, revealing what, to Morgan's eyes, was no more than a heap of laundry. "And there you have it."

"If you're expecting me to be impressed, you've definitely missed the mark," Morgan said. "What is all this, and what do you expect me to do with it?"

"We have another theory about how Elgar's capturing the minds of his soldiers." Marceline prodded the pile of clothing with her foot. "If he can transfer his will into a relatively small object—and we've already proven he can—then he could sew it into the lining of his guards' uniforms. They'd never even know it was there. And then all he'd have to do to get new recruits is get them to put it on. So we're going to cut these open, to see if there's anything hidden in the lining. And if we do find anything, we need you to test it for magic."

"Ooh, I've never seen the famed vardrath steel at work. Can I stay and watch?" Though the enthusiasm in Talia's voice was sincere, she truly must have been tired; she simply turned her head to the side, resting her cheek on the bar instead of her forehead.

"I don't mind," Morgan said, "but if we're doing it in here, one of you two jokers is going to have to watch the street in case someone approaches before we're finished." As Roger wordlessly took up a place by the window, she moved the pile of shirts behind the bar, so they'd be out of sight if someone came in quickly. Then she glanced at Marceline. "Do you want to start cutting them open?"

"Actually, now that I'm thinking about it, do we need to? I thought that knife of yours just had to get close to feel cold, not actually touch the magic."

"That is what Lord Vespas said. Pass them up here, then. One at a time."

For a while, they didn't need to say anything. Roger watched the street, Talia remained slumped on the bar, and Marceline sat on the floor behind it, keeping the uniforms out of sight. She passed them up to Morgan one by one, Morgan ran the knife over them as thoroughly as she could, and when she didn't feel the temperature change, she dropped each piece on her other side and reached for the next. She was most of the way through the pile when she got her first twinge of cold—fainter than the chill she had felt the first time, when she touched the knife to the black stone Talia had found in the warehouse in Silkspoint, but still a clear sign. "Well, what do you know. Your ransacking of the city's laundry lines may have come to some good after all."

She made to cut into the cloth, but Talia stopped her, putting a gentle hand on her arm. "Wait. If there's something magic in there, and you touch it with the knife directly, you'll destroy it, right?"

Morgan set the knife down. "Isn't that the point?"

"I thought the point was to ascertain whether the magic existed," Talia said. "If you already know it does, wouldn't it be more useful to keep it? Just in case?"

Morgan glared down at the uniform. "If we're right, whatever Elgar's put in here can turn the wearer into a mindless murderer. And you think we should *keep* it?"

Talia shrugged. "It'd be the work of a moment to destroy it later, if you ever changed your mind. But once you do destroy it, it can't be undone."

"Why don't you finish going through the pile first, Morgan," Roger spoke up. "Don't want to leave any potentially active ones in there that we don't know about."

Morgan did as he'd suggested, but only one other uniform drew any reaction from the dagger. "Surely there can be no arguments if I cut into this one, since we already have a spare." Without waiting for verbal confirmation, she started running her hands over the fabric, searching for any lumps. At first she thought there was nothing, but a second search revealed something hard, about the size of a fingertip, tucked into the seam of one armpit. Morgan sliced around it, shaking it out, and a sliver of stone tumbled onto the bar. She touched the dagger to it, and a curl of cold air wafted into the room, slowly dissipating.

"Finally," Roger breathed. "An end to dead ends."

"And an answer that's only going to lead to more questions," Morgan said. "And more trouble."

CHAPTER NINE

Araveil

FOR THE FIRST time since their imprisonment began, the door of Kel and Hywel's cell opened to admit someone other than Administrator Selwyn and her underlings. They glanced at each other, and Kel saw his own nervousness reflected in Hywel's face. This was hardly a position they wanted to be in, but they'd talked over all their options. Poor as it might be, this was the best one.

Still, Kel could never have been prepared for the woman who walked through the door.

Euvalie Vandrith, the head of one of Lanvaldis's most influential noble houses, was also Arianrod's aunt; he'd known that from the beginning. But even so, the resemblance was startling, even unnerving. Her long pale hair, gold streaked with white, the blue-gray color of her eyes, the pensive brow and unyielding jaw—she looked like nothing so much as a vision of the future, what Arianrod herself might look like in thirty years. She was even dressed with the same elegant simplicity, the same preference for pale, faded colors. Her dress was blue trimmed with silver, her necklace silver with a single sapphire; her only other adornment was some kind of hair ornament at the back of her head, also silver, long and thin, holding a complicated knot of hair in place like a pin.

She caught him staring and gave a wry smile—an expression he knew well, though not with the flicker of distant warmth he thought he saw in her eyes. "Well, that answers one of my questions."

"Which one might that be, my lady?" Hywel asked.

She reached up and tugged at the end of her hair ornament as she answered, but it must have been very firmly fixed, for it hardly moved. "Though I have long wished to lay eyes upon my sister's child, her father made that impossible. He refused to let the girl leave the country while he lived, nor would he allow me to visit. Then after his death, Lanvaldis had already been conquered by Elgar; it would not have been safe for Arianrod to come here, nor was I free to cross to Esthrades and back. But they tell me the child is an image of her mother, even more so now that she is grown. And Elin and I were born twins, identical in features, though our personalities so diverged that no one would ever have mistaken one of us for the other."

"She is quite tall, my lady," Kel said. "Taller than you are. But aside from that, the rumors that have reached you have not overstated things."

"Caius's influence, no doubt," she said. "I seem to recall the man was quite overgrown."

The guards had let her enter alone, since she was smart enough not to say anything of import in their presence. But they had set down a simple wooden chair, and Lady Euvalie sank into it gratefully, that wry smile flickering over her features again. "At least they can still show this much courtesy. I'm afraid my knees are not what they once were." Her posture, at least, was nothing short of perfect—another difference, as Arianrod liked to drape herself over chairs. "Now. I assume you've been given your orders, and I won't stand in the way of them. Why don't you say whatever you have to say to me?"

That, as she'd guessed, was the crux of it. They were not here to make idle chatter, but for something much more unpleasant. As Kel had predicted, Selwyn had agreed to entertain their request to meet with Ilyn and Lord Ithan, and had offered more nebulous assurances regarding Talis. But she had demanded a heavy price in return. Lady Euvalie, too, was here to ascertain the condition of Lord Ithan, her younger brother's child, and Selwyn had charged Kel and Hywel with attempting to persuade her ladyship to admit that Lord Ithan had acted with the full sanction of House Vandrith when he took up his family's vardrath steel sword and left to fight on behalf of Laen and Hywel's cause. Doubtless Selwyn had believed that fear for Ithan's life would cause the Vandriths to bargain for his protection, but that had not come to pass; while they requested leniency, they claimed no responsibility for his actions, even when Selwyn had threatened to execute him. But Hywel was Lady Euvalie's king, and Kel was certainly *a* king. He wondered if that would make a difference, though part of him hoped not.

Hywel was clearly choosing his words carefully. "My lady. Your nephew comported himself as well as you could have hoped—"

"As well as someone who flouted the administrator's orders twice over, I suppose you mean," she said.

"As well as someone who defended me with his life, at great cost to himself," Hywel finished quietly.

She bowed her head. "I am sorry indeed for such an injury. They tell me it is still uncertain whether he will ever walk again, but they might have only said that to scare me. He certainly put up a brave front when I saw him, though perhaps that is all it was."

Kel's flimsy chair quivered as he rocked back into it. "You've already seen Ithan?"

"I take it you have not, then. He is comfortable—surprisingly so. I suppose if they threw him in some dungeon, and the poor treatment made his injury worse, or prevented him from healing . . . well." She pressed her lips together. "It is heartening to see that Selwyn still fears displeasing House Vandrith to that extent. He is housed far better than you are, that's for sure—in chambers I know well, that used to be for only the most important guests when Eira was alive. The young lady is there, too, but only so that she might more easily do the work of nursing him back to what health he can still manage."

Whatever the reason, it was a relief to know Ilyn was being treated better than they were. Hywel's voice was stronger when he spoke again. "Lady Euvalie. May I ask what you plan to do about your nephew?"

She cocked an eyebrow in bemusement. "It is my understanding, young man, that you are the king of Lanvaldis, and thus that it is your prerogative to ask me anything in the world you wish. Perhaps you had better work on your comportment, if you still have an eye to the future." There was both a question and a sly declaration in there, though Kel did not know if Hywel had caught either.

"Then, my lady, although I have yet to be crowned, I must repeat my question, with whatever amount of regal authority I can claim to possess in this state."

"What am I going to do about my nephew?" She fiddled with her hair again. "Ithan is a good boy, but I have other nieces and nephews to consider, whose safety and well-being matter no less than his. He knew what he was doing when he left, what he was risking; he knew we could not defend his actions if he was forced to answer for them. Indeed, if I were to throw even only myself on the sword for his sake, I would still put the very legacy of our house in danger. He is a prize for Selwyn only because she believes she can use him to unmake House Vandrith at the root, but, as always, that young upstart has overreached. We have not survived for generations by haphazardly throwing ourselves into the hands of our enemies for the sake of sentiment."

"You consider Edith Selwyn your enemy, then?" Kel asked.

"I did not say that, Your Grace." She had, though, even if she had not used those precise words; Kel was getting used to her manner of saying things without saying them. Although Administrator Selwyn wielded absolute power in Lanvaldis, she was ultimately subject to Elgar; under her, Lanvaldis would only ever be a province, not a country. That meant the Lanvaldian aristocrats would see their influence dwindle, so it was no wonder many of them had sought to support Laen and Hywel behind the scenes, even though they were only the children of Eira's half-sister. The written proof that Eira had wanted his sister and her children to succeed him should still be in Alessa's hands—the price of their current imprisonment—and that would certainly help Hywel's cause. But Kel sensed that more than a preoccupation with bloodlines or a sense of her own importance was behind Euvalie Vandrith's allegiances.

She had turned back to Hywel. "Did you know that, in our youth, your uncle and I were actually great friends? Eira was intelligent and well read, but had little patience for those who could not hold their own in a conversation with him. Thus most people found him icy, caustic, difficult. But he seemed to appreciate my wit no less than I his, and so I often found myself invited to those same chambers my nephew is forced to occupy now, whiling away evenings in private conversation. Those nights had stopped many years before he died, but I still cherish their memory."

"Stopped for what reason?" Hywel said, and Kel saw him bite his lip to prevent adding something like, *if I may ask.*

Lady Euvalie's face was grave. "Our disagreements, by that point, had gone far beyond the simply academic, and he was less willing to debate when it came to his own rule. One of the hazards of being a king, I suspect; you don't truly *have* to listen to anyone."

Another hidden question. But this one Hywel definitely heard, because he answered it. "I was not raised as a prince. Even when my brother and I learned of our birthright, he was the elder; I always viewed it as something that had to do with him, not with me. I fear I will need the assistance of a great many people if I am to have a hope of thriving in the role. What I have learned from Kelken, even within the confines of this room, has shown me how far I have to go, but also the ways I can change, with the right help."

Lady Euvalie scrutinized Kel's face more closely, as if she could discern the advice he had given Hywel written there. "An impressive feat, that you should already be teaching at an age at which most people are only learning."

"I have plenty of that to do as well, but thank you," Kel said. "If you had enough wit to tangle with Eira—something my own father did not think he possessed—I wonder if it is not a waste for us to make our case to you. You must already know what we would say and why, and it seems we will not move you."

"Would you truly wish to move me?" she asked—but before they could answer, she tugged at her hair ornament again, and this time she pulled it out. "Oh, drat. A moment while I fix this stupid thing." Kel couldn't have said why, but it somehow seemed a private matter for her to wind that piece of hair up at the back of her head and stab the pin through it, as if he were witnessing her getting dressed in the morning. He dropped his gaze to his lap, and saw out of the corner of his eye that Hywel had done the same.

Lady Euvalie fixed her hair with impressive speed, given that she could not see the back of her head, and resettled her hands in her lap. "Apologies, Your Graces. Where was I? Ah, yes—your request. Though I suspect it is not truly *yours* at all. Either way, I must decline. I am needed too much to allow myself to waste away in some dungeon just for Ithan's sake."

"I wonder, in that case, that you trusted Selwyn's word on this arrangement," Hywel said. "You are in a dungeon right now—what if she refuses to let you leave it?"

Euvalie Vandrith actually laughed, the smile still curving across her face even after she had fallen silent. "Oh my, I hope she attempts it! That would raise the ire of the people even faster. But I suspect she will not dare that far. She is arrogant, but no fool. Was that all the two of you had to say to me?"

"There is much I wish to say to you, my lady," Hywel said. "But I fear this is not the time or place. I can only hope that you and yours are well, and that you remain so."

Kel was impressed; Hywel had asked an indirect question of his own. Lady Euvalie's slightly raised eyebrow said she shared his sentiment. "These are trying times indeed, for me and mine as much as anyone in Lanvaldis. We are bruised a bit, but well enough. Well enough, Your Grace, never fear that." She reached down and clasped his chained hand in both of hers, the links clinking slightly. "I will bring news of you back home with me. I suspect my family will be dreadfully curious. If there is anything I might ask in return . . . what did you think of her? Elin's daughter?"

It was clear from the way she asked that she did not mean as a marquise, but simply as a person. Hywel looked to Kel. "Kelken has spent much more time with her than I ever did. I have never been alone in her presence, but those two were cloistering themselves even when I visited."

With Lady Euvalie's hungry gaze turned on him, Kel chose his words carefully, searching for a description both true and fair. "She is a formidable person, my lady—more so than anyone I have met, perhaps. But I sensed that she . . . understood me." He slapped his thigh. "These legs of mine have caused others to view me as deformed, an object of pity. They have put me on the outside, looking in. But when I was with her, I felt she stood outside with me, rather than within."

"And why is that?" she asked.

"Perhaps because there are those who see in her mind and my legs the same kind of deformity. A disservice to us both."

"I think I am beginning to see what you meant," Lady Euvalie said to Hywel. "What a frightfully precocious child."

"I am told your niece was much the same," Kel said.

"Yes, I was told that as well. A shame Caius did not allow anyone else to aid in her upbringing. Perhaps if Elin had lived, she would have been able to pass more of herself to her daughter than simply her appearance."

"I think it would be difficult for Arianrod to be any other way," Kel said. "But I am sorry for your loss, Lady Euvalie. The thought of losing my own sister is bad enough."

"It is an immense grief," she admitted. "But, after all this time, a far distant one. I will keep your sister in my thoughts, but if she is even half of what you are, I would not fear for her." This time, Kel couldn't read beneath her words: had there been a message there as well, or had he only wanted to hear one?

Lady Euvalie got heavily to her feet. "I regret to say it, Your Graces, but I think our time has passed. Any more would not benefit either of us. I hope you will not judge me too harshly when I remain firm in my convictions."

If they ended things like this, would Selwyn still keep her end of the deal? Kel started, "But—"

Hywel shook his head. "It's all right, Kelken. We did what we could. If Selwyn denies our request, at least we may be comforted that someone has seen Ilyn and Ithan well."

Lady Euvalie left their cell without a backward glance, one of the guards poked his head in to say that Selwyn would be in to see them after her ladyship had been escorted off the premises, and Kel was left to wonder if he and Hywel had bungled that or not. It was good to have news of their fellow prisoners, and heartening to hear, through Lady Euvalie's coded assurances, that the resistance was alive and well. Still . . . "Was that really as much as we could get out of her?" he muttered to Hywel.

"Well, there's *one* other thing," Hywel whispered back. "But you'll have to tell me where you think I should hide it."

He uncurled his fist, and stretched out his hand to show Kel what lay in his palm: a long, thin metal rod with a blunt and oddly shaped end, as if there were small but deep grooves carved into it.

"What is it?" Kel asked.

"I don't know," Hywel said. "Lady Euvalie passed it to me when she took my hand. I think it's a piece of that hair ornament of hers."

"That makes sense, I suppose. The guards probably wouldn't have thought to examine it when they searched her. It still doesn't explain what it *is*, though."

They searched every flap and seam of their clothing for the best hiding place, but the riddle of the rod's true nature was solved more quickly than they could have believed. Selwyn did return to see them, and decreed that their efforts, while futile, had been obedient, and thus deserved reward, to encourage similar obedience in the future. She would let them speak with Ilyn and Ithan, but not privately, and for a quarter of an hour only. Afterward, while they would not be permitted to speak with Talis, they could see for themselves that she still lived.

And as Selwyn approached the door to what Lady Euvalie had called the rooms for Eira's most important guests—Hywel shuffling along in his chains behind her, Kel carried, chair and all, by a pair of guardsmen—they noticed that the lock was of very peculiar make. It was smaller than any lock Kel could remember seeing, a circle within a circle, the inner ring a ridged hole.

As one, the guards all looked to Selwyn, who produced her own ring of keys, thumbing through it until she found a metal rod identical to the one Lady Euvalie had given Hywel. She inserted it into the inner ring of the lock, twisted her wrist, and the door to their friends' prison sprang open.

Chapter Ten

Stonespire

THE SUN ROSE over the spire, painting the far-off clouds in rosy and golden hues. The three of them stood upon what passed for battlements at Stonespire Hall, the narrow curtain wall stretching between the front gate and the bulk of the hall itself. Their collective mood, as they looked down at the city spread out below them, was as far distant from that glorious sunrise in spirit as their bodies were in the flesh.

Gravis, as captain of the guard and leader of the quarter-court Lady Margraine had appointed in her absence, had the task of deciding whether the city would surrender to the invading Hallern army or attempt to hold out. Dent had been assigned to the quarter-court as well, but perhaps it was because he was her most trusted guardsman that she had not given him this role. And Jill Bridger was technically not supposed to be at the hall in the first place, as her post was down in the city proper. But she had still come up every morning seeking the latest news and commiserating with Dent, her mentor and greatest advocate.

Someone had to break such a terrible silence. But Dent and Bridger did not seem obliging, so Gravis put himself forward. "Today will be the day for sure. We'll have their terms for our surrender delivered to the hall before midday, I'd bet anything."

Bridger braced one foot against the parapet, her face twisting in distaste. "Pft. I'd be surprised if they offered terms at all, besides an order to open our gates."

"They can't think us so beaten down as that already," Dent objected. "If they decide to wait us out, we can last for weeks yet. And if they come over those walls instead, we have enough strength to make them pay for it, even if we can't defeat them. It's in their best interest to court us a bit."

Gravis clenched one mailed fist. "If I were acting only under my own advisement, I would not have us surrender for anything. But you both know those were not my orders."

That was the heavier gloom that lay over them, like one weight added to another. Lady Margraine had ordered him to delay at first, which he had done. And she had ordered him to strike no surrender that did not guarantee the safety of all civilian persons and property. But if those terms *were* offered, she had forbidden Gravis from refusing, even though he wanted to do nothing more.

Bridger shook her head. "For once Captain Ingret and I are in agreement. Her ladyship cannot truly mean for us to abandon a fight we can win before a single blow can be struck. It goes against everything I thought I knew of her."

She and Gravis both looked to Dent, who knew the marquise the best of all of them—better than he did, Gravis was forced to admit, though they had known her the same amount of time. "No," Dent agreed. "It isn't like her to abandon a battle she can win. But it is like her to avoid a battle that does not have to be fought. More than anything else, it is like her to fight a battle of her own rather than let that task fall to those around her."

"But we *do* have to fight," Bridger insisted. "It's fight, or be conquered. Fight, or cease to exist as Esthrades, to become nothing more than a piece of Elgar's empire. Can she accept that fate? For I cannot, sir."

Dent smiled sadly, bowing his head in deference to Bridger's passion, which so rarely showed itself. "Rest assured, Bridger—however far you would go to avoid such a fate, she would go twice that length."

"But—"

"He's right," Gravis said. "I have faith Esthrades will endure, one way or another. I just . . . would prefer to fight for it in a different way."

"I don't like it, either, but her reasoning is as sound as ever," Dent said. "As important as Esthrades is to *us,* the decisive battles of the war won't be fought here. Even if we were to fight the Hallerns and win, if the Issamiri lose, we'll end up falling eventually as well. But if we fight here and lose and the Issamiri win, the fragment of the Hallern army that's outside those walls right now will never be able to hold this city. Under those conditions, why shouldn't we surrender, and wait out the end of the war in peace? It's the difference between losing thousands and losing no one."

Bridger sighed. "Your words speak perfectly to my logic, sir, just not to my honor."

"Well, as to that, you must know the woman you serve has no more understanding of honor than these stones we stand upon have of the movements of the stars. Only worldly realities can possibly move the scales by which she judges things."

Bridger scuffed the toe of her boot against the wall. "You well know, sir, how that normally makes it easier for me to serve her. And you know why it is so difficult now."

"And do you think it is not even more difficult for me?" Dent asked gently. "Before Seren came here, I would've said no one had a higher claim to stand at her side than I did. To be one of the lives she's risking her own to save . . . how did I become so helpless?"

"Whatever our differences, this is not what any of us first took up our swords for," Gravis said. "I swore an oath to her father—"

"You swore an oath to *her*," Bridger said, her irritation betrayed in the hitch in her voice more than in her impassive face.

In the past, that might have led them to an argument. But enough had happened to give Gravis the distance to see that she was right, and the calmness to admit to it. "Yes," he said. "You're right. That is the oath that matters now." Not the oath he had sworn to Lord Caius, to defend his daughter above all else. No matter how much the man had meant to him, that oath had been superseded long ago. "She was never one to demand unthinking obedience, but rather considered trust. So you know what I must do, if the demand comes to me in appropriate terms."

"I wouldn't ask you not to," Dent said.

"No," Bridger agreed. "I would do the same, in your place. But still, is there not something else we can do? Not *instead of*, but *in addition to*?"

"Something she did not order?" Gravis asked, raising an eyebrow.

"Well," Bridger said. "Not anything she expressly ordered us *not* to do, certainly."

She had expressly ordered them not to do quite a few things, no doubt because she knew all three of them too well. "Let's see, then. We aren't permitted to flee the city in search of her. We aren't permitted to stir up rebellion or disobedience, whether among the common people or our own fellow guardsmen. If and when we are occupied, we are not permitted to plan assassinations of our occupiers, or to martyr ourselves, as she puts it, toward that end. And Bridger, she says you're to leave your post in the city for the time being, to be stationed at the hall with me and Dent."

"So you can't get into trouble in the streets without us, I expect," Dent said, with a wry smile.

Bridger leaned against the parapet, folding her arms thoughtfully. She was a champion at taking things narrowly when it suited her—when she was still a newly minted guardswoman under Lord Caius, only eighteen or nineteen, she had let more than a dozen child thieves escape on technicalities—and if there was a loophole to be found, Gravis didn't doubt she would find it.

Finally, she drew her foot through the dust between them. "She doesn't forbid us—or any other guard—from leaving the city? Just from leaving in search of her?"

"In search of her, to aid her directly . . . that sort of thing. But yes, you're correct."

"Small problem," Dent said. "We're under siege. No matter what Lady Margraine would or wouldn't allow, none of us are getting past the army at our gates."

"Not now," Bridger agreed. "But if and when Captain Ingret is compelled to give our surrender, the gates will open back up. At the very least, our occupiers will have to eat."

"Aye, they'll have to let civilians out, or go out themselves, if they hope to do any hunting or fetch any supplies. But they certainly will not let any Esthradian guards out of the city, no matter how much time passes."

"How will they know?" Bridger asked. "I suppose Captain Ingret gives himself away through his insistence on wearing full plate all the time, but as for the rest of us, if we're not garbed for duty, who's to say we aren't civilians?"

"They're smarter than that," Gravis said. "The moment they take the city, the first thing they'll do is check the hall roster and round up everyone on it. And it's a lot more detailed now, after the trick that little weasel Kern was able to pull with it." Gravis's traitorous former protégé had forged names on the roster in order to sneak Varalen Oswhent's minions into the hall, a hole in security Gravis had thoroughly plugged.

"But they haven't taken the city, sir," Bridger said. "As of this moment, that roster remains in our hands."

In spite of himself, Gravis tried to let his mind imagine a little more freely. It was something Lady Margraine liked to say, that to a closed mind, even the most achievable option would seem impossible. "We can't just rip pages out of the book, or cross names out. Any half-competent person would see through that immediately, and hoping our enemies will be stupid won't get us anywhere."

"Well said." Bridger's face remained impassive, giving him no clues. "Marking guardsmen as dead would be too easy to find out, and if we mark them discharged, our foes might decide to imprison them anyway, just to be safe. But there is another reason why guardsmen on the roster might not be present at Stonespire."

"Because they've been sent to another town or village," Dent finished. "Just as Caius used to send Gravis all the time, to settle disputes with more authority."

"Precisely. It is, as Guardsman Halley says, entirely common. And because we know our enemies could barely scrape together enough soldiers to besiege this city, they'll have no way of checking the roster's accuracy, especially if we spread our targets out to as many far-flung villages as possible."

It was conceivable, Gravis had to admit. They could keep the truth from becoming known to all but the hall guard, and he would have vouched for all of their loyalty; only torture would have gotten them to spill the secret, and if torture were not forbidden by the terms of surrender, Gravis wouldn't have to agree to it. And the city guards and common people could hardly divulge what they did not know.

"All right, I'm with you so far," he said. "It's a way of making the enemy think some of our own aren't in the city. But they *will* be in the city. What do you mean them to do there?"

"She's just said, Gravis," Dent spoke up. "They'll pose as civilians—the Hallerns can hardly take an inventory of every soul in Stonespire. And as civilians, once our foes are confident they hold the city, they can leave."

"Leave for where?"

"For aid," Bridger said. "Not for her ladyship, since that's not allowed. But for *us*. For this city."

Gravis shook his head. "No one is coming to aid this city. If they were, her ladyship would have called upon them already."

"In her current position, she doesn't have the ability to call upon her debts in the north," Bridger pointed out. "But we can, on her behalf."

"Kelken and those brothers do seem the sort to care about debts, and honor them," Dent said. "But they are all captured, or killed. They can no more dispense debts than she can ask for them."

"Then I'll do both." Bridger raised her chin defiantly. "I'll bring our people north, and aid theirs one more time. And when we have done that, I will demand that they finally give us our due. Just give me enough people to do it. Everyone we can spare without drawing too much suspicion."

Gravis met Dent's eyes. After a friendship that had lasted so long, they did not always need to speak to know when they were in agreement. And he knew that Dent believed in Bridger as much as he believed in anyone.

"We can hardly lose more than we stand to lose already," he said. "But if we're going to do this in time, we'd better start now."

CHAPTER ELEVEN

Araveil

CADFAEL HAD NOT set foot in the city of his youth for three years. As soon as he had recovered from the wound on his forehead enough to travel, he had locked the door of the house where he and Rhia had lived with their father, and left it and Araveil behind, for what he had thought would be forever. A home bereft of the people who had made it what it was had been too painful to dwell in.

But now he was standing among streets he knew, with his sister by his side. When Cadfael had left, Elgar and his men had only just occupied the city, and he was surprised how little it had changed. Perhaps it was silly to think some pall would have lain over it, that the color and vibrancy would have been drained from it somehow.

"I don't know how to feel," he confessed to Rhia. "Should I be relieved? Dejected? It's like nothing that happened matters to everyday life."

Though he had not spoken to her, Lirien shrugged. "Well, it doesn't really, does it? I know you served him, but Eira wasn't known as a king who cared overmuch about the well-being of his people. In that sense, Selwyn's quite in line with him, isn't she?"

"That sounds like something a Hallern would say," Cadfael scoffed. "I wasn't Eira's soldier because I liked him. It was a job."

"That led to you trying to kidnap Talis," Lirien said. "Yes, I'm aware. And if you'll recall, I had someone very close to me murdered by Elgar's people, which is more than he's ever affected you personally. Being born in Hallarnon has nothing to do with it—in my village, we could no more conceive of him than we could the gods. The local tax collector was the greatest authority we could comprehend. Perhaps there are people here who feel the same about Selwyn."

That was fair. Cadfael still remembered what Talis had told him about the boy—Miken—who had died because of Elgar. It was true that the three *wardrenfell* had more cause to hate him than Cadfael did, now that he knew Shinsei had not taken Rhia's life after all.

In an effort at being more conciliatory, he said, "Now that we've finally arrived, I have to admit I don't know what to do next. It would be a pity to attempt to rescue Talis alone when we theoretically have scores of allies in this city. I just have no idea how we're to go about finding them."

"We could look for Voltest," Lirien offered. "I doubt going around asking where the resistance is will get us anything but thrown in jail, but we know Voltest beat us here, and he can't hide from me. He'll at least know more about the situation than we do, and if he hasn't charged into the palace and gotten captured yet, we might as well ensure he doesn't start."

She closed her eyes, reached beneath the collar of her dress, and pulled out a pendant with a small blue stone, a sister to the diamond-set one Talis had shown him once. Lirien only needed to consult it for a moment. "He's quite close! And not particularly enraged, either. We shouldn't waste this chance. Follow me."

They found Voltest at the meat market on Lantern Street, haggling over a pile of bacon that could have fed three of him—an action so astoundingly normal that Cadfael was shocked. Perhaps Adora's influence had rubbed off on him; the first time Cadfael had met him, he had taken to smearing his face with soot, as if to be closer to his element, but the queen had convinced him to dispense with the habit while they traveled together, and it seemed he had not resumed it. Was it that Adora had that effect on people, or simply that Voltest had finally come to his senses enough to admit that wearing grime on one's face was excessive?

He wasn't wearing that tattered, bright-red cloak of his, either; he had traded it for a nondescript brown one, tear-free. His black hair was still long and unkempt, his face still set in a severe frown. But without Lirien to guide them, Cadfael could not say for sure whether he would have known Voltest on the street, had they passed each other.

He must have known that Lirien, at least, was coming; he could sense her as she sensed him, and this close, she could not possibly be missed. But he waited to speak to them until after his business was concluded and the merchant was wrapping up his meat. Then he turned halfway toward them, sparing them one eye. "I see you finally decided to show up," he said to Lirien. Now *that* was typical Voltest.

"It isn't as if you sought my company," Lirien said. "You couldn't have left the palace faster if you'd tried. *Someone* had to let Queen Adora know what had happened, so you're lucky I was there to do it."

"And these two?" he asked, nodding at Cadfael and Rhia.

"They wanted to help. Surely you aren't going to begrudge them that, now that we know what they can do?"

Before he could reply, Rhia slipped in front of Cadfael, extending her hand to Voltest with a slight bow. "We were never properly introduced in Eldren Cael, but I owe you my thanks for all the assistance you gave the queen and my brother. We're ready to do whatever we can to aid you and Talis in return."

Voltest was struck silent by such forthright friendliness, but the reappearance of his parcel of bacon gave him a momentary reprieve. With a nod to the butcher, he slung it under one arm and turned back to Rhia reluctantly. "Well . . . we shall see how things unfold. Perhaps there will be a need for your skills before this is over." He moved away from the line of stalls. "Shall we go somewhere we will have more space to talk?"

They fell into step with him, and Lirien poked his parcel with one finger. "If that's what you've been eating, I wonder why you're still as gangly as ever."

"It's not for me," Voltest said. "Or rather, not only for me. But I'll explain the rest when we get inside."

"Inside where?" Cadfael asked.

"The place I've been staying. How much do you know of the situation in this city?"

Cadfael considered what they had heard so far. "That it remains firmly under Selwyn's control, though she has yet to fully stamp out those still loyal to the blood of King Eira. Unfortunately, we heard that she has captured the prince—or princes, the stories vary—that Eira named his heirs. That can't have put the rebels in a good position."

"There is only one heir left alive," Voltest said, "yet the administrator does have two royal prisoners. The second is Kelken the Fourth, of Reglay."

That put Cadfael off his stride, and he felt the blood drain from his face. "Kelken?"

"I believe I spoke perfectly clearly," Voltest said, and gods, Cadfael had forgotten what an insufferable prick he was. Lirien was looking more and more like a paragon of every virtue by comparison. "There are also one aristocrat and one relative of a rebel leader. And Talis, of course."

"What about Kelken's sister?" Cadfael asked, half-dreading the answer. The boy king had been so brave in defense of his sister, but he was so young, and neither of them were fighters. Cadfael couldn't regret parting ways with him, because if he hadn't, he most likely would never have reunited with Rhia, helped the queen, or even met Talis again. But if Kelken and Alessa had been shattered in this conflict, it would be a far crueler fate than either of them deserved.

"She's not at the palace," Voltest said. "Beyond that, I know nothing of her. My information only goes so far."

He had led them to a neighborhood Cadfael vaguely knew, about half an hour's walk from where he'd lived with Rhia, and with residents of comparably modest income. Voltest approached a slate-roofed house at the end of a narrow street, pressed his palm against the door, then hesitated. "Before we enter, I should probably correct you on one thing. You referred to Eira's nephew as a prince, but though he has been kept from his crowning, in the eyes of Lanvaldis's rebel host, he is a king. If you call him otherwise, you may unthinkingly arouse their ire."

"And how would you know that?" Cadfael asked. "I doubt that kind of information is just floating around."

"You are correct," Voltest said smugly. "I know it because some of the rebels told me."

"Then—"

"*No,*" Lirien insisted, before Cadfael could even ask the question.

"Yes," Voltest said. "When I first arrived and took stock of the situation here, I was able to make contact with enough rebels to make it worth my while. Most of them are not in the city, because they cannot afford to be seen here. As for those who are"—he lifted his parcel—"I am content to run errands for them from time to time."

"You found the resistance?" Lirien repeated. "*You?*"

Voltest drew himself up in a huff. "I don't see why you're so shocked. I've always been good at tracking down information, and I . . . can be subtle when I need to be."

"Can you?" Lirien asked. "Because it would have been wonderful if you'd made use of that skill even once in all the time I've known you."

Still very visibly put out, Voltest waved his free hand up and down his body, taking in everything from his clothes to his scrupulously washed face. "Well, I'm doing it now, aren't I?"

"Yes," Lirien admitted, "I suppose you do look less like a small child's nightmare. Perhaps being cut off from Talis most of the time has actually been good for you."

Possibly proving her point, Voltest didn't snap out an instinctive retort, but actually considered her words. "There may be some truth to that. You and Miken always possessed calm natures, Talis and I agitated ones. With her magic cut off, we're in equal balance again."

"But a couple days ago, she threw me off terribly," Lirien said. "Did you feel that?"

"I did, but it was as if you absorbed most of it. Nothing happened on my end that was any cause for alarm." He tapped the doorpost. "Let's get inside. It isn't good to linger over these topics out here."

With a soft but complex series of knocks on the door, he pushed it open and walked into one big, dimly lit room, the shutters pulled closed. He lifted his parcel high. "I was more successful than I thought, as it turned out. I found some old comrades of mine at the market."

The room contained two men, youngish, who were sitting at the room's single table and debating a piece of writing one was working on, and a woman leaning against the far wall, whose features were largely obscured by shadow. And standing at the stove, stirring a pot of simmering vegetables with a wooden spoon, was a girl Cadfael knew. She had put off her fine clothing in favor of a simple wool shirt and trousers, but he could never have forgotten the golden hair that had so reminded him of Rhia's. He did not know if it was safe to call her by name—if the people here knew who she was—but he couldn't stop himself from saying, "It's you."

Alessa fumbled the spoon at the edge of the pot, only just managing to keep from burning her fingers. "Cadfael! My goodness. I would never have expected to see you here."

"I thought that was my line. I spent most of my life in this city."

"I meant"—she gestured around the room—"here. You do know what this place is, don't you?"

"The very place I've been looking for," Cadfael assured her. "I wasn't looking to find you in it, but I'm glad of it. I was sorry to hear of your brother's predicament, but I hope there may be something I can do for him."

She frowned, exchanging a glance with the woman by the far wall, who stepped forward into the light, revealing herself as one of the guards who'd attended Kelken on his way to Mist's Edge. "I'm . . . surprised to hear you say that. When last we spoke, you were quite insistent about parting ways. What changed?"

"So many things, but let me start with the most important. The story I told you of my family turned out to be nowhere near as accurate as I had thought. So, however shocking it may seem, please allow me to introduce you to Rhia, my sister."

He watched the rapid movements of Alessa's eyes: widening at the sight of Rhia, then roving over her, taking all of her in, and finally a spreading warmth as she smiled. "That certainly is different. So you've been restored to life, is that it?"

Cadfael knew she was not speaking to Rhia but to him. "Something like that. I'm still determined never to follow a king's orders again. But I can help one, if you'll let me."

"I can do you one better. If we succeed, you'll have helped two." She extended her hand to Rhia. "Glad to meet you as well. Your brother was a great help to us when we needed it."

"Yes, he told me all about it, though I think he's a little embarrassed," Rhia said, taking her hand. "And Lirien is Voltest's . . . associate."

"We can discuss that later," Lirien said. "We heard about the riot. Has that set your plans back a great deal?"

Alessa shook her head. "We thought it would, but our recruitment efforts since have more than made up for it."

"Forgive me," Cadfael said, "but I would've imagined that your liege's capture would put spirits and recruitment efforts at a low."

"Perhaps that might have been the case under normal circumstances. But Kel and Hywel weren't merely captured; they sacrificed themselves to save something priceless, something Laen never had. His claim."

Cadfael inhaled sharply. "The proof of their lineage?"

"*And* proof that Eira wanted them to succeed him, all in a single official document. That document was entrusted to me and Hayne—and, as soon as we found the rebels, to Gerald Holm. He has used its existence to swell our ranks to a size greater than they have ever been, or so he tells me. We haven't been able to communicate with Kel and Hywel very much, but we have hope they'll be ready to respond, once we get to them."

"Get to them?"

"And capture Selwyn, all at a single stroke," Alessa confirmed. "We're going to assault the palace."

Chapter Twelve

Esthrades

THE TENT WAS small and low to the ground—big enough to sit up in, but not to stand. It shuddered in the unrelenting rain, but the tarp held fast. Beneath it, atop several blankets spread over the damp grass, there was barely enough room for Seren, Arianrod, and their meager belongings. Under normal circumstances, the marquise of Esthrades would never be quartered in such shoddy accommodations, but even Seren couldn't object this time. The smaller and less conspicuous they could make themselves, the better.

The dozen soldiers Queen Adora had insisted on sending with them had set up a couple tents near theirs, and had taken the job of alternating watches through the night. Seren was grateful for that, for it meant she could spend the night at Arianrod's side—literally, in this case, since the tent's size forced them to remain close together.

"I know it's been quite the circuitous route," Arianrod said, "but we *are* drawing nearer to Lakeport. It's conceivable that we might be able to slip inside within the next few days."

Despite its name, Lakeport was a seaport—the biggest and most significant commercial port in all of Lantistyne, and a major source of Esthrades's wealth. It wasn't a fortified town, so they could hardly dig in there and make an extended stand against the Hallern forces. But it was still the destination Arianrod had had in mind since the beginning.

She smiled wryly, as if sensing Seren's doubts. "I don't intend to simply sit there. As their marquise, I should be able to commandeer at least one ship. And with a ship, I become much more difficult for Lord Oswhent to capture. The war might well be over before he manages it."

"If the war ends that quickly, I don't believe it will be to our advantage, my lady," Seren said.

Arianrod frowned. "What makes you so sure of that?"

"Because you will not be at Queen Adora's side, helping her win it."

That brought the smile back. "You don't think I've done enough?"

"Always," Seren said. "And yet this struggle always seems to have greater need of you, and demand more of you."

A third expression, one Seren saw rarely: pensive hesitation, as if she had to ponder what to say. "I don't mean to cause you more worry over me. But I'd rather know my actions have weight, power, than to simply be helpless. Whatever you may think, I have done my part in this conflict, at least as far as I can see. Whatever happens to me now, Stonespire is safe."

"I don't understand."

"It's about the order of events. I needed to return *before* Stonespire surrendered. If I had still been behind Issamiri lines at that point, I suspect Lord Oswhent would either have started executing guardsmen or destroying neighborhoods, to bait me into returning. Now that I'm here, that's no longer necessary."

"But it is," Seren said. "It's not as if you've delivered yourself directly into his hands. If he could use the threat of damage to Stonespire and its people to get you to return to Esthrades, why not use it to force your surrender outright?"

"Because while I remained with Adora, that was his only choice. He could never have gotten to me if he had to go through the entire Issamiri army; it's simply impossible. If I were a ruler of lesser intellect, he could just take the territory and leave me be. But he doesn't want me using my strategies to aid Adora, and I suspect Elgar wants his mage rival handled personally. He would do anything to get to me, even take a great risk. But now that he can send his men to hunt me through the woods, that same risk will seem . . . riskier."

"What risk do you mean?"

"Angering the people of Stonespire, of course." She smiled. "When Stonespire was first gifted to my ancestor, it was nothing—a tiny village around the base of some ruins on a hill. He built himself a very beautiful hall upon that hill, but I don't have to tell you it's hardly a fortress. The city around it grew and grew, and today it boasts walls befitting a country's capital. But the hall is much the same as it was in my ancestor's day; it could never withstand any great attack. That is why the ruling Margraines always told their children: if you lose the trust of your people, those towering city walls will become the bars of a cage, trapping you in here with them. The same is true for Lord Oswhent. He may occupy Stonespire now, but there is nowhere in my city secure enough to keep him safe from the wrath of its people, should he inflame it."

"Which he would do if he executed them or destroyed their homes after they had surrendered," Seren finished. "And he's too cautious to resort to that as long as he believes he can get to you without it. I see."

A brief silence stretched out between them, and then Arianrod nudged her shoulder. "You're holding back. You aren't going to say the rest?"

"There are so many things I could say, my lady. I can't even begin to guess which you're referring to."

"I suspect you're being charitable, but I'll let it go." She shifted in the small space, and Seren caught her breath: Arianrod had turned slightly, and rested her head against Seren's abdomen. She was so focused on remaining as still as possible that she almost missed Arianrod's next words. "To be frank, it's troubled even me. I can't seem to stop thinking about how . . . strange it is."

"What is?"

She didn't hear Arianrod sigh, but she felt it against her skin. "When Kelken was at the hall, he told me about plans he'd made to destroy Mist's Edge after him, so that no one on the other side would be able to use it. He told me that the decision to leave Reglay had troubled his heart, but that he had made it for the good of the continent. And he told me that he assumed I was an old hand at such choices, and that they no longer troubled me.

"And yet . . . look at me. I had the opportunity to make the same choice Kelken did—to abandon my country for the sake of the continent. To stand at Adora's side as she crushed Elgar, as Kelken resolved to stand at Laen's when he regained his throne. But I did not make the choice that Kelken made. What I'm doing now is for the good of Esthrades alone. And in that sense, I wonder if it's . . . illogical."

Seren had wondered that, too. "Normally, it wouldn't be like you to make such a choice—one whose logic you could possibly doubt. But you definitely don't do things for no reason, so there must have been one, logical or not."

Arianrod laughed softly; Seren could feel that, too. "It was no more nor less than this: what is Lantistyne to me without Esthrades? These are *my* people—no one else's. They are my responsibility. Anything I did for the continent, I would do partly for myself—because Esthrades will thrive most in a stable peace—but mostly for the sake of others. So it seems I am unable to choose others over myself."

"My lady," Seren said, "are you trying to make me angry?"

That got her a much more enthusiastic laugh. "In fact, I was not aware I could. If I had been, I would have tried much earlier."

"You choose others over yourself all the time," Seren said. "Because you understand that most people are weak, but you're strong, and you can do things they can't. This time is no different; you're simply choosing to put yourself over one group of people rather than another. Kelken's sister is only one person, but he would put her above himself more easily than he would the entire rest of the continent." *And I would put you above everyone else,* she thought, *even if I had to damn the rest.* "The people of Esthrades may never know it, but you're risking your life for them. True selfishness would be running away across the sea."

"Bah. What would I do across the sea?" But she looked brighter, her expression smoothing out. "Even if we do manage to reach Lakeport and get that ship, I wouldn't go far with it. Just north up the coast, most likely."

"My lady," Seren said. "Do you truly believe that we will get there?"

Even though she wasn't expecting to see it, part of her still hoped that Arianrod would give her that confident smile and chastise her for her lack of faith. But she only sighed. "I think that we *may* get there. If I thought there was no chance, I would have tried some other scheme instead. But it is far from certain—I don't know that it's even probable. Why do you think I did everything I could to get you to stay behind?"

"And why do you think I was that much more determined to go? The more danger you are in, the more I do not wish to leave your side."

"I thought you did not wish to leave it regardless," Arianrod muttered, with an expression Seren could not read.

"That's . . . true." She had admitted as much, and would not go back on it now. "I sought to make a duty out of my own selfishness. But, selfish or not, I *am* your bodyguard, and I don't wish to fail in that, either."

"You say *selfish* like it's such a bad thing. It cannot have escaped your notice that I am quite vain. If you so prefer my company to that of others, surely you can't believe it will upset me?"

Seren couldn't help smiling at that. "Not upset, but . . . it's true I didn't wish to burden you. To presume beyond my place."

"It would never have been that." Her face was serious, her usual dry humor gone. "I simply don't want you to be disappointed. Many people, from my father onward, have sought some other version of me, or believed they could bring it forth— someone who would speak and behave in ways they found . . . approachable. Acceptable. Whatever they were looking for. But there is no other person beneath my surface. I am who I am, all the way down."

Seren turned those words over in her mind, trying to answer them with the honesty they deserved. "On the contrary, I've always felt that it's easier to be around you than other people. You know the extent of my skills, but you aren't afraid of me. You make an effort to understand me even though I'm not very good at talking. You . . . it's hard to explain. You make me feel like I'm not alone. I know that doesn't matter to you, but it does to me. And I'm . . ."

"Oh gods, *don't* say grateful." Arianrod groaned. "How unbearably dismal."

All right. Perhaps that wasn't the best word anyway. She tried to think of a better one. ". . . Happy, then. I'm happy, even now. Even with only this. Because you're here, and because you trusted me enough to let me be here with you."

Arianrod reached up and brushed Seren's hair back from her face. She let her fingers linger there, against Seren's forehead, twining across her scalp. "And that weakness of yours, combined with your stubbornness, is going to hurt you terribly.

With all my skill at planning, you were too stubborn to allow me to save you from that."

If only I had figured out how to be stubborn enough to save you, Seren thought. Out loud, she said, "My old teacher used to say that if someone can no longer be hurt, it means they're no longer alive. So often our weaknesses are the things that bring us joy. And what is strength, even perfect strength, with no joy?"

She had thought it a trifling thing to say, but Arianrod's body relaxed completely, all the tension going out of her in something like relief. "Ah. Of course. That's what it was."

"What?"

"The difference between me and Kelken. I was worried that this might mean his determination was stronger than mine. But though he wants to do right by it, he has never loved Reglay, or had any joy of it. That is why it was possible for him to leave it." She yawned, her eyes flickering closed. "I'll take this back if anything happens to you on this journey, but . . . I'm glad you're here, too."

CHAPTER THIRTEEN

Hallarnon

ADORA HAD READ about scores of battles in the lines of Valter Lisianthus, her favorite Old Lantian epic poet. While he loved to exalt the courage and skill of individual warriors, sparing no detail in his vivid accounts of how they struck down foe after foe, he had nothing but sorrow and solemnity for the aftermath of a battle, the field strewn with corpses, the injured struggling back to camp, bowed under the knowledge that they would have to do it all again all too soon. Adora could not fight, so she hadn't taken the field with her uncle and the others, just watched everything unfold from a safe distance away. And still, she felt that Lisianthus had failed to do the tragedy of it justice.

From up on her hill, she had heard the great clamor of the fighting, but the vividness of the wounds, the blood, had been kept too far away from her. She could see where the bodies lay, and where they were being dragged away for burial or to be stripped of valuables, but those corpses had none of the immediacy of the first man she had killed with her own hands, his drowned and bloated face. Even so, those wounded and dead were just as much her fault, created by her orders if not her blade.

Her uncle had fought the Hallerns before, back when Gerde Selte ruled them, when Adora's father was still new to the throne. That war was spoken of in such glowing terms back home, those who fought in it raised to the stature of heroes, none more so than her father himself. Adora could understand why: the Hallerns had tried to conquer them, to steal the freedom and the way of life their ancestors had fought so hard for. By driving them back, her father and the rest had proven that Issamira would not be subjugated again, that they would endure on their terms and theirs alone. And even though Adora had technically started the hostilities this time, she knew her people understood that she was fighting for the same reasons. Still, she wondered if her uncle had been able to feel any sense of pride or accomplishment in the aftermath of his battles back then, or if he could possibly do so now.

Her soldiers had pitched her tent upon a rocky hill not far from the one where she'd watched the battle. Adora waited outside it, scanning the still-hectic ranks for signs of her uncle. She might not know swordplay, but she did know strategy, enough to give her consent to the plan he had proposed: to take the Hallerns head-on on flat land rather than fight through the trees that were a mile off on either side. There were few forests in Issamira, and they couldn't risk the chance that the Hallerns might know these well. Better to fight under familiar conditions if they could.

There was Vespas, his horse further trampling the flattened grass. He handed it off to one of his subordinates at the foot of the hill, and began the remaining trek on foot. Adora ducked her head inside the tent, telling the figure who sat within, "He's here."

Amali Selreshe met them outside as Vespas gained the summit, and all three of them surveyed the field together. Amali had been a last-minute addition: they had not dreamed she would feel well enough to travel with them, but in the end it was she who had begged leave to go. Though Hephestion was in better shape than she was, and though he wanted to fight, Adora had commanded him to remain in Eldren Cael with their mother, so that one Avestri would still dwell in the capital. But Amali had fought in the same war as Vespas and her father, and Adora didn't doubt her insight would prove valuable. And, though she would never have asked about it, she suspected Amali had sought relief from the pain of being in Eldren Cael with her husband without being able to help him. As much as she'd improved, Lord Dahren's condition had never changed: he did not speak, and ate barely enough to keep from starving. There was no telling if he would pull through one day, or if he would simply waste away.

Vespas was streaked with dirt and sweat, spattered with blood not his own, but he smiled as he approached them, inclining his head to Adora. "A fine performance from our side, Your Grace. The foe took heavy losses, and they'll have to pull back at least ten miles to the north, perhaps more. We made the right decision."

"So I see," Adora said. "I am relieved to hear it." She was sure she didn't look it, but though her uncle surely noticed, he did not mention it.

"You led them well, Vespas," Amali said. Though she had once been one of the foremost archers in Issamira, holding a bow was the one thing she was still reluctant to do, so she had not fought in the battle herself. "I'd advise against pursuing the Hallerns further tonight, though, even simply to do reconnaissance. The forest and the dark combined gives them too great an advantage."

"Yes, yes, you're right. I won't ask, even though part of me wants to."

"I understand," Adora said. "As well fought as this battle was, it was intended to delay us by any means necessary, and in that sense it succeeded. It's frustrating to be unable to do anything but play into Elgar's hands in that way."

Thanks to one of her ever-resourceful uncle's contacts in Valyanrend, they now knew the horrible truth of how Elgar intended to get an army big enough to conquer and hold the whole continent: by using magic to bend his own subjects to his will. Adora had experienced that type of magic briefly herself, at the hands of Jocelyn Selreshe. Arianrod had theorized that it might be possible to control hundreds or even thousands in such a way, if Elgar could create enough enchantments to do it—enchantments her uncle's contact said he had already begun distributing among his guards. Eventually, Elgar might use such a net to ensnare every able-bodied fighter in Valyanrend, but he'd need time to prepare so many spells. He needed to stall the approaching Issamiri army so they couldn't surround Valyanrend before he was ready for them. But even knowing that, they couldn't afford to be impetuous, or they'd risk the lives of their own soldiers.

"At least we know such a plot exists," Amali said. "Can you imagine if we had pressed on to Valyanrend unawares, thinking the campaign was going so well, that the war was nearly over before we'd even reached the city? I thank the gods for these informants of yours, Vespas, though I can't say how it is you manage to find them so easily."

Her uncle laughed. "In this case, actually, it was Hephestion who found them. If he hadn't sent them on an errand and paid ten times what it was worth, their path and mine would never have crossed. But that is a story for another time." He put a hand on Adora's shoulder. "What thoughts so occupy that head of yours, Your Grace?"

Adora had been struggling to put those very thoughts in order, to calm the racing of her heart. How she wished, for the thousandth time, that Arianrod had not left! Magic was her purview, and she could have advised them about Elgar's capabilities as she had once advised them about Jocelyn's. Without her, Adora was forced to rely on general principles Arianrod had explained before she left and what scant reading she'd been able to do back in Eldren Cael. "Trying to imagine the results of this plan of Elgar's, even if he does succeed at it. Just because he wants an overwhelming supply of elite warriors, that doesn't mean that's what he's going to get."

"You're correct there," Amali said, with a wince she almost covered. "My memories from when Jocelyn held sway over our household are confused, but I do remember she was not able to command anyone to do something they could not do under their own power. If Elgar controls someone with no fighting skill, the spell alone shouldn't be enough to give it to them."

Vespas frowned. "So he might end up with an overwhelming supply of cannon fodder—which would be ghastly to have to cut through, especially knowing they weren't doing it willingly, but not, potentially, insurmountable."

"At a certain point, numbers are numbers," Adora said. "You're the finest warrior we have, Uncle, but even you couldn't fight fifty men at once, even fifty civilians. And an offensive war is always harder to fight than a defensive one. Valyanrend will be difficult enough to overcome even if it's only protected by an army of normal size."

It was the same problem that had plagued Adora's ancestor, Talia Avestri. As far as anyone knew, Valyanrend's formidable walls were perfect, and no invading army had ever taken the city from the outside. In the end, the Rebel Queen had not needed to take the city at all: a rebellion had erupted from within that had destroyed the remaining leadership in Valyanrend, and she had turned back, leaving the survivors to piece a new government together on their own. Arianrod had had much news of a robust resistance within Valyanrend now, and Vespas's mysterious informant said much the same. But part of that resistance had already been slaughtered by Elgar's forces once. If they had to contend with ranks of guardsmen swollen by those drafted in by magic, would they truly be able to overthrow him? And if they failed, how would Adora manage to take the city without them?

"There's something else the marquise said, if I recall," Vespas said. "That in order to function, enchantments must be very simple in nature."

"And enchantments are what Elgar seems to be using to control his soldiers," Adora said. "Jocelyn controlled people directly, but that meant she had to focus on one at a time. You'd never build an army that way."

"Yes, but my point is that these soldiers of his shouldn't be capable of complex strategy. My informant says all the ones in Valyanrend did was kill mindlessly— not just their targets, but anyone, save one another."

Adora shuddered. "They wouldn't be able to surrender, no matter how terribly the battle turned against them. We'd have to wipe them out to a man."

"Not necessarily. Enchantments have to reside in physical objects, and if we destroy the magic within those objects with vardrath steel, those controlled will be set free."

"I'm sure Elgar wouldn't make such objects easy to reach," Amali said grimly. "We don't even know how far away they can be from their targets."

"The one my contact discovered in Valyanrend was quite close."

"But that doesn't mean it *has* to be. And Elgar might have made refinements since then."

So many variables. So many things they still didn't know, despite all the information they'd gained. Adora bit her lip. "I'm . . . nervous for them. For our people, our soldiers. I'm nervous all the time. That I'll cause them to lose their lives through my own mistakes. I try not to let them see it, but I always feel it."

Vespas and Amali glanced at each other. "Your father said almost the same thing to me," Vespas said. "More than once, during that war."

"My father won every battle he ever commanded himself," Adora argued.

"So have you, Your Grace."

"Because I've only fought three battles!"

"There was a time when your father had not fought any," Vespas said. "When he wasn't even sure he could. He was not born the man that he became. He built himself one piece at a time, just as you're doing now."

"I know. And I decided long before now that I would never run from my duty, no matter how difficult or unpleasant it might become. Far worse for me to force those decisions on someone else."

"It doesn't mean you can't have help making those decisions," Vespas said. "That's why we're here."

"I suppose that means there's something you wish to say. You know you don't need permission to say it, Uncle, whatever it is."

Vespas sliced a hand through the air, as if gesturing at an imaginary map. "When we reach Valyanrend, the Hallerns will expect us to besiege it, as Talia Avestri did. But I suggest we don't take that route. As you know, they have an endless supply of fresh water pouring over the walls through their aqueducts, and even without the prodigious amount of food in the city proper, the Citadel has carried dried and salted provisions in its lower levels for hundreds of years to prepare for just such an event. We wouldn't truly be wearing them down by circling their walls; they'd be wearing us down."

Adora folded her arms, trying to clear her head. "I see your point. What alternative would you propose?"

"Once we near the city, we don't venture past the edge of the trees. Let the forest obscure our numbers, take out anyone they send in there after us, but don't allow ourselves to be drawn out onto the plains beneath the city walls."

"But if we cluster up there, we'll have to remain in the south," Adora said. "We run the risk of being surrounded ourselves."

"Only if they deduce our formation *and* send a very large army pouring out of the gates very quickly. They wouldn't be able to hide it, because *we'd* already have taken up all the closest available hiding spots. We'd have enough warning to meet them in the open field, and in the open field we'd crush them. As for our formation, I have a plan I can draw out for you, a series of scout camps placed so as to confuse the foe about our lines."

"Let me look at it as well," Amali said. "Scouts have always been my purview."

"Certainly," Vespas said, smiling, "if you'll hold your criticisms at least until I've finished drawing it."

"I don't object to any of this in theory," Adora said. "But, ringing the city or clustered in the forest, we're still only waiting. We need a plan to get *in* the city, or else to somehow render the need to get there moot—lure Elgar out or something. I don't see how your plan gets us any closer to that."

Her uncle ran his thumb beneath his chin, fiddling with his beard. "As to that, I'm afraid I must beg your indulgence. The Valyanrend problem is going to be onerous no matter what, but I believe the formation I've proposed will buy us the most time while I . . . hopefully come up with a solution. There are reports I've received from my informant that are most promising in that regard, but I'm still unfortunately far from a complete plan, or even one worth presenting to you."

Adora wasn't sure how she felt about that. She knew her uncle well enough to know that, if it was something he didn't want to tell her, it was because he was sure she'd object to his plan in its current state, and he wanted to shore up his case before taking the risk of presenting it to her. On the other hand, she did trust him, and demanding that he tell her now would only fray that relationship for no good reason. In the end, she nodded. "Keep it to yourself for the moment, then. But it's Elgar who wants to take his time, not us. I trust you won't forget that."

Vespas bowed his head gravely. "It is ever uppermost in my thoughts, Your Grace."

CHAPTER FOURTEEN

Valyanrend

THE GLASSWAY WAS a dream for young thieves, Tom liked to say. The most expensive wares in Valyanrend were bought and sold there, books with no known copies, weapons once wielded by the world's greatest fighters, paintings and sculptures crafted by the most celebrated artists, and ornaments comprised of so many jewels it was a wonder their wearers could stand up under their weight. In the Glassway, it was possible to steal one thing and be set for life—theoretically possible, anyway. That was why Tom put the emphasis on *young* thieves—those too naïve and undisciplined to properly weigh risk and reward. In Sheath, the names of those who had successfully stolen from the Glassway in the last hundred years could be counted on the fingers of one hand. Those who had tried and failed were as common as grass in a meadow.

Roger, on the other hand, believed that glory, not coin, was the greatest calling for a thief, and a harder challenge only represented a more meaningful target. But Roger had never stolen anything from the Glassway, either.

In this particular case, Marceline hewed more closely to Tom's thinking than Roger's, but for once she was not planning on stealing anything today. Ironically, it was legitimate business that had called her to the Glassway.

The district got its name from a massive pane of glass hung horizontally over the length and breadth of its widest avenue. The glass was stained all manner of colors, and held flecks of gold leaf suspended within it, so that as you walked past the storefronts you were awash in fantastical light. From beneath it, the glass seemed to be floating impossibly in the air, but Marceline knew it was anchored to the buildings on either side of the avenue by hundreds of slender wires, almost too small to see.

"This makes me nervous," she muttered to the others. "I don't like having certain death constantly hovering over me."

Talia shook her head. "The way it's balanced, you'd have to do more than cut a wire or two to bring it down. More than half would do it—maybe. They didn't take any chances with its construction—it's a demonstration of the quality of the Glassway's craft, after all."

Along with Marceline, Talia, Naishe, and Rask had been chosen for this particular mission. Naishe, because the potential expenditure of this much coin needed the approval of no less than the resistance's leader herself; Rask, because the furtive transfers of coin he received from his aristocratic Lanvaldian relatives made him not only the resistance's best swordsman but also its fattest purse; and Talia, because the Parnells had connections with two dozen merchants in the Glassway, including this one. As for Marceline, you could trust a thief to know how valuable a treasure was or wasn't, and Roger wasn't particularly keen on traveling around with members of Valyanrend's resistance.

Rask was predictably sour, and predictably complaining. "I don't even want to think about what else this much coin could have been used for. This bloody merchant must think we're idiots."

"This bloody merchant hasn't even met us yet," Marceline said. "The figure was just an estimate we got from having others poke around on our behalf. If we end up paying *that* price in full, we should be ashamed of ourselves."

"Besides, aren't you the rich lordling?" Talia asked. "You should be the last of us to worry about money."

"I told you, my cousin married into that family. I'm not noble by blood, any more than I'm a Lanvald. And when it comes to my personal accounts, I'm much poorer than you, *Miss* Parnell."

"Settle down," Naishe said. "If we plan to haggle, it won't do to come in looking already agitated."

Rask jerked his chin at Marceline. "I still can't believe *that* one is supposed to be our champion haggler."

Marceline frowned. "I may have learned at Tom's elbow, but remember, it can't come from me. I'm a child in a group of adults; no merchant is going to take me seriously. So you lot had better have memorized your roles."

"But of course." Talia curtsied. "I'm the helpful fellow tradesperson, bringing business to my family's good friend. I don't even look like I want to buy anything—I'm just showing my friends around the Glassway, nothing more."

"I'll wait for your signal, Marceline," Naishe said. "You'll pick out a piece that looks about the price of the mark, and I'll set my interest on it. Then Rask will—"

"Will do what he does best, and throw cold water on everything," Talia said.

"Will bring the proceedings back down out of the clouds, and point out we can't spend that kind of money," Rask corrected.

"After that, you have to remember to take your time," Marceline said. "Really sell your disappointment over the decoy piece. Then, just when he's sure you're about to leave empty-handed, you let your eye happen to fall on the real mark. And then the true challenge begins."

The four of them nodded at one another, and then pushed through the double doors below an elaborate sign advertising JESPENSON FINE JEWELRY.

None of her companions were born actors, but they performed better than she'd expected. Talia was the most brilliant, letting her natural cheerfulness and charm shine through, her delight at being able to introduce her friends to such a trusted and exceptional jeweler never edging into overenthusiasm or falseness. Naishe was more stoic and remote—as was her nature, after all—but that made her supposed pleasure at the garnet necklace Marceline surreptitiously indicated all the more striking. And while Rask excelled at acting skeptical and discontented, he even managed to just barely pretend to be a couple with Naishe without being laughed out of the store. Wren would have been better at that part, of course, since he wouldn't have had to act, but just the thought of deceit and haggling together had made him practically beg to be excluded.

At last the preamble came to a close: on her way to the door, Naishe paused, eyes alighting upon a heavy metal pendant strung on a silver chain. It was a square with a slightly scalloped edge, and within the square, a ring of tiny emeralds surrounded an opal.

As Naishe and Rask fussed over it and Talia murmured encouragement, Marceline hung back, waiting for her cue. She had to force her mouth shut during the haggling, trusting the others to remember what she'd taught them. As she predicted, the merchant's first offer was lower than the estimate they'd been given: Naishe and Rask had already rejected a piece they supposedly liked better at that price, all his prices were inflated anyway, and he *did* want to make a sale, especially to friends of the Parnells. When at last the arguing was done and Rask reached for his purse, they'd knocked him to 70 percent of the estimate—not bad for amateurs. But before Rask could hand over the coin, Naishe put a hand on his arm. "Wait, let's have Marceline look at it first."

The merchant looked at Marceline with raised brows; he, like most people, had forgotten she was there. "Marceline is our young apprentice friend," Naishe said. "We thought we'd let her get some practice in."

Marceline pulled out a glass Tom had lent her, inspecting the gems carefully. They weren't the most crucial part of the piece, but it would definitely help if they were real. She also kept one eye on the merchant, and noted no increase in nerves, which also implied the gems were real, as well as that he'd assumed *apprentice* meant she was an apprentice appraiser.

She put the lens away and passed the pendant back to Naishe. "Lovely work. All's as it should be here." She smiled at the merchant. "Thank you for letting me look at it. Where did you find it?"

He smiled back, wider as Rask finally paid him. "Oh, this is an old one, inherited from my mother—she ran the shop before me. But it gleams like new, doesn't it?"

"It certainly does," Rask said, helping Naishe get the pendant over her head so it didn't get caught on her hair. He let himself show just the tiniest little smile.

The three of them didn't immediately break character after they left the shop, strolling down the avenue and gawking at storefronts like any other group just here to browse the Glassway. But after a few minutes, Marceline felt the tension leave them collectively as they relaxed into their natural attitudes.

"Thank the gods those gems were real," she muttered. "Roger could probably still manage to sell false ones, but like this they'll be a lot easier to fence."

Talia glanced longingly at the pendant, still hanging around Naishe's neck. "Pity to pry them out, though."

"We damned well better pry them out," Rask said. "I only just scraped together the money for that thing, and we can't afford not to get any of it back. Can't sink that much of our capital on any one thing, even if it is vardrath steel."

For that was the true prize: not the gems themselves, but the steel setting in which they were placed. It gleamed like new indeed; most likely it had never had to be polished. If the merchant had inherited it from his mother, he might not even have known the setting had any value in itself; he certainly hadn't mentioned it, and vardrath steel would be known to weaponsmiths, not jewelers. That was the most important reason for Marceline to lay hands on it: while putting on that show with the lens, she had also slipped one of the stones they had taken from the soldiers' uniforms into her hand, waiting for the telltale coolness as the steel dissolved the spell.

"So now, with Morgan's dagger, we have two," Naishe said, stroking the edge of the pendant with her thumb. "Though this one unfortunately can't double as a conventional weapon. What do you think we should do with it?"

"It should stay right where it is," Rask said. "We know our enemy can alter minds, and our leader is the last person we'd want affected by such a spell. That's probably why the thing was made in the first place: not as a weapon, but to protect someone important from malign influence."

"Though you'll probably want to hide it," Marceline said. "It'll look valuable before the gems come off, and suspicious after."

Naishe pursed her lips. "Well, if you insist. Though it does feel a bit awkward to accept."

"You'd best get over that," Rask said. "Now that we've got your father to deal with on top of everything else, you can't have too many advantages."

"My father to 'deal with'? I thought *I* was the one dealing with him. He may be an irritant, but it's not as if he's going to betray me to Elgar."

"No, but he doesn't want you leading the resistance, and he doesn't want it very badly. That makes him unpredictable, and unlikely to make things better for our side if he does get involved. We should—"

They were cut off by a scream.

The street was so densely packed that at first Marceline couldn't figure out where it had come from. But then three men broke through the crowd about twenty yards ahead of them, swords waving, one of the three blades already coated in blood. "For the rebellion!" one yelled.

The four of them looked at one another in bewilderment. "What the hell?" Rask asked no one in particular.

But they didn't have time for anything more, because the men weren't done. They started hacking their way through the crowd, wounding anyone who got too close, then seeking fresh targets once a circle of empty space had formed around them. "The rebellion!" another one shouted. "Glory to Issamira!"

"You've got to be fucking joking." Rask strode forward, then abruptly pulled up short, probably remembering the rest of them were weaponless. His sword was the only one they'd brought to the Glassway, because they hadn't wanted Talia to have to explain to the merchant why she and her good friends, a young couple who'd come to buy jewelry, were armed to the teeth. Rask, Naishe, and Talia together could definitely have made short work of those three, but now Rask was the only one with the means to fight.

He held out his hand to Naishe. "Let me borrow the vardrath steel. It won't be like last time, I swear it."

Last time. Marceline would never be able to forget the massacre in Silkspoint, where she and Talia had nearly lost their lives. But they couldn't let the ghost of that day obscure the truth.

Rask slashed a hand through the air. "Come on! Last time the stone was nearby, right? This time we know how to destroy it! We've got to find it before this gets worse!"

"No," Marceline said. "Look at them, Rask. They're weaving through the crowd, choosing targets with purpose instead of just attacking whoever's closest. They're speaking aloud, showing emotions more complex than blind rage. This isn't a spell. These people are acting of their own free will."

"But—" She saw his eyes rake frantically over the attackers, confirming that everything she'd said was true. "They're . . . doing this on purpose? Are they soldiers of Elgar's in disguise?"

"Or else people he's paid to do this, I'd guess," Naishe said. "Less chance of them being recognized that way."

For a moment Rask was still, and then his burned hand clenched hard on the hilt of his sword. "Well. Even better, then. If they're doing this of their own will, I don't have to feel guilty about running the lot of them through."

"Rask, wai—" Naishe started, but he had already surged forward, forcing his way through the crowd with his sword drawn.

He didn't meet much resistance—the crowd was already skittish of naked blades, and they were all trying to go in the other direction. They parted around him, rushing past on either side, further opening a corridor between him and his targets.

Once he got within range, he didn't hesitate. The first man was beheaded before he could even look in Rask's direction. The other two tried to flank him, but he feinted and stabbed the one on his off-side through the stomach. The third barely managed to exchange three parries with him before Rask had disarmed and stabbed him through the throat.

By the time the rest of them reached him, the crowd was tentatively surrounding him; it was over so fast they weren't quite sure their savior was real. But as they gained confidence, they pressed in close, taking his hand, clapping him on the back. Rask took all the praise with a stiff grimace, but Marceline knew him well enough by now to understand why: to a member of the actual resistance, this kind of attention was nothing good.

He gave a minuscule shake of the head when he saw the three of them: a warning not to reveal they were together. They edged as close to him as they dared, but they couldn't draw right alongside without dislodging the people congratulating him most profusely.

Now that they were sure the danger had passed, chatter proliferated among the onlookers, as if they were gossiping at a grand ball. And as she listened, Marceline felt her insides twist.

"I knew the rebels were desperate after Silkspoint, but to stoop to an alliance with our adversaries . . ."

"Why are you so shocked? Don't they both want the same thing? Mark my words, if they had their way, they'd be more than happy to divide this city up between them."

"But are the guards really stretched so thin? Have things gotten so bad that young people have to come to our rescue in the street, in broad daylight, in the Glassway itself?"

"If it were just an army, it wouldn't matter. Elgar's undefeated against armies. But these Issamiri have no honor. He's got to contend with spies everywhere." As that last remark left its owner's lips, he took a step toward Talia, looking her contemptuously up and down as half the crowd turned to stare with him.

Rask forced himself between the man and Talia before he could say more. "She had nothing to do with this. I killed the ones responsible, and I didn't see you helping."

The man held his hands up and backed away, but many in the crowd were still staring. Talia shrank back against Naishe's side, and Naishe put a hand on her shoulder, glaring at the crowd on her behalf. Marceline wanted to punch someone. Didn't this lot of babbling fools know the *real* resistance was the only thing standing between them and a terrible fate?

Suddenly, the crowd parted again, and this time, soldiers clad in Elgar's blue-black strode through. Rask rolled his eyes. "Of course. *Now* they show up."

Two knelt by the corpses, rifling through their pockets. The other two flanked Rask. "Are you the one who took down the rebels?" one asked.

Rask glowered, no doubt straining under the weight of all the things he wanted to say but couldn't. "I don't know anything about rebels. They were cutting into civilians, so I put a stop to it. You can ask anyone here."

The chorus from the crowd was immediately obliging. "He cut them down in a matter of moments! We might all be dead without him."

"They claimed they were fighting for Issamira! Does the imperator know about this? We should have been warned!"

"How are you going to ensure this doesn't happen again? Armed insurgents in the Glassway itself, and our supposed protectors nowhere to be found!"

Three of the soldiers moved to pacify the crowd, but the fourth stayed on Rask. "You'll be coming with me."

"What the hell for? I helped, you heard them! Is it illegal to resist the slaughter of your neighbors now?"

"You aren't being arrested," the guard said calmly. "You're being commended. A young man of such skill and bravery ought to be brought to the notice of His Eminence himself."

But for Rask, being brought to Elgar's notice was no honor, only a disaster waiting to happen. Talia started toward him, but Naishe laid a surreptitious hand on her wrist; at the same time, without turning to look at them, Rask gave another slight shake of his head. It would only look more suspicious if he tried to avoid this; all the rest of them could do now was keep themselves from getting wrapped up in it, too.

So they did nothing as he followed the soldier out of the Glassway, though Marceline saw her own glum spirits reflected in Naishe's and Talia's faces. "At least the mission was a success," she muttered.

"And he wasn't carrying anything that could draw suspicion," Naishe said. "Thank the gods he gave the necklace to me after all. I expect we'll see him back before we know it."

Instead of Talia chiming in, there was a heavy silence. Marceline turned to see her biting her lip, one hand twisting against her side. "Talia, you all right?"

Talia flinched, and then caught herself, smiling sadly. "Sorry. Just thinking it's probably a bad time to be named after Issamira's Rebel Queen."

"Only with the ignorant," Naishe said firmly. "If you ever think you need more protection from our people, you have only to say the word."

"I'll be fine. I'm just worried about my mother. She *is* Issamiri, though she's lived here for decades. And I hope the shop doesn't suffer—not that it's worth more than her safety."

"Eh, rich people would have their luxuries even if they had to buy them from demons and fiends," Marceline said. "I bet Parnell's will still flourish. But I'll ask for Roger's help, too. No one knows how to move the soul of a crowd like him."

Talia shook herself, as if trying to leave her gloomy thoughts behind. "Thank you. I'm grateful to have friends who know the truth, at least."

"But many more have to know it if we are to succeed." Naishe squinted at the crowd. "I suppose, if nothing else, this was a window into what challenges await us on that road." She glanced down at the pendant, still hanging from her neck, then tucked it beneath her shirt as Marceline had suggested. "I know I won't rest easy until Rask is returned to us."

Chapter Fifteen

Esthrades

LAKEPORT DIDN'T LOOK like much from far away: a dark smudge on the horizon, far less compelling than the glittering ocean surrounding it. Even when you got a bit closer, it was easy to mistake it for just a coastal village, bereft of walls or castles. But then the land beneath your feet dipped, the land before you opened up, and the size and splendor of that sprawling port was revealed. Then it was easy to understand how Lakeport had changed the fortunes of House Margraine forever: it had been just another trifling lordship until the second Daven Margraine had successfully argued for the inclusion of Lakeport, then a newly established settlement, in Esthradian territory. As stewards of what eventually became the largest port on the continent, the Margraines had become fabulously wealthy through import and export tariffs alone.

Until now, they'd been able to take an indirect route to their destination, hiding out where the forest was thickest and any path all but disappeared. But they had no choice but to make the final approach to Lakeport straight on; you could only reach it by land from one side. And once the approach started sloping downward in earnest, the forest went from thinning out to all but disappearing, only a lone tree cropping up here and there like an abandoned sentinel.

Seren's heart had been in her throat from the moment she'd heard that today would be the day they made for Lakeport. Three days ago, they'd been spotted by a Hallern patrol that had fled before Seren and Adora's guards could pursue them, which meant the Hallerns knew they were in this area. Arianrod was certain the enemy couldn't block the entrance to Lakeport, at least; their main force was still besieging Stonespire, and if they tried to close the port without a proper army, they'd be overrun. Lakeport's citizens were an often-rowdy lot, but they tended to hold passionate loyalty for two causes: trade, and House Margraine, which had championed their rights for generations in the face of the Ninists' attempts to strip them. Putting a chokehold on trade would be bad enough, but if the port dwellers found out it was meant to capture the current marquise, the Hallern soldiers would have a full-blown riot on their hands.

The forest had been tranquil since they awoke, with no sounds but the calling of birds, their own soft footsteps, and a snapping twig that had turned out to be a lone doe. When they reached the edge of the trees, they had an unobstructed view all the way down the slope to the port, without anywhere for a group of people to hide. The enemy couldn't be lying in wait for them, but at the same time, once they started the walk to the port, they'd be exposed until they finished it.

"I don't think there's going to be a better time," Arianrod said. "Not now that they know we're here. And this is the only route."

Seren was about to agree, but then she saw a flash of color out of the corner of her eye, a dark blue that looked out of place in the forest in the early morning. Pretending to scratch her leg, she worked her smallest knife out of her boot. She could tell Arianrod had noticed by the way her eyes stayed on her, but she knew enough to let Seren work.

When the flash of color grew larger, Seren flicked her wrist, and a body hit the carpet of leaves with a soft thump.

One of the Issamiri made a slight startled noise, but another touched her wrist, and she choked it off. The rest were as silent as Arianrod. Seren walked over to the body, and pulled her knife from its throat. But from that vantage point, she saw another shape, a person half-hidden behind a tree. Before she could so much as raise her hand, the second interloper had jerked back, disappearing into the forest.

Seren ran back to Arianrod, barely bothering to pitch her voice low. "We need to go *now*."

But before Arianrod could reply, a dozen people slid into view at once. They were all armed in some fashion, though none with bows, just swords and a spear or two. And they wore the blue-black she knew too well, the color that marked out soldiers of Hallarnon.

"I think there are more of them behind," she said to Arianrod. "We're outnumbered—impossible to say by how much. We should—" Then she realized Arianrod wasn't looking at the soldiers. Her gaze flicked around the forest and away, taking in the ground where they stood and the approach behind them.

At first Seren didn't understand what calculation she was trying to make; if the Hallerns hadn't brought archers, all they had to do was outrun them, and in a straight line across a downward slope, they had a good chance of making it to Lakeport. But then, heart clenching in her chest, she realized her mistake. *She* had a good chance of making it to Lakeport. Any of Adora's soldiers might, too. But Arianrod had never sprinted that distance in her entire life, and could not possibly do it faster than a trained soldier. She wasn't wondering whether she could make it; she knew she couldn't. She was wondering where to make her final stand.

She cast one more glance at the sparkling port, no more attainable for them than a desert mirage, and gave a composed little sigh. "Ah well. It was worth trying."

She turned to the Issamiri. "You lot ought to make for the port regardless. You can write to Adora, tell her what happened here. You'll be more use doing that than staying." They wouldn't be of much use either way, but Seren knew Arianrod was trying to give them permission to run away without thinking themselves cowards.

Most of them did run, pelting down the slope with a speed Seren envied. But three stayed where they were, bravely or foolishly determined to share in whatever fate Arianrod and Seren had brought on themselves. And even though Seren had known it would happen, it still hurt when Arianrod turned to her next. "Seren—"

"No." She took a step closer, drawing the knife from her sleeve. "Don't you dare even ask."

"All right." She took a deep breath, bending and straightening her fingers as if they'd gone stiff. "Then I'll just have to protect you, too."

There was no time for them to exchange any more words, no matter how much Seren wanted to. The frontmost Hallern soldiers had begun to filter out of the trees, coming within striking distance. From this point forward, any moment could be the last. But Seren was determined to take as many of them down with her as she could.

When he first started teaching her to fight, Gan Senrian had told her that it was hopeless for her to try to become the strongest assassin of the Inxia Morain. So she hadn't trained to be the strongest. She hadn't trained to be the fastest. She had trained to be the best at not getting hit. As long as she had the space to move, she was confident that her opponents would make a mistake before she did, and any member of the Inxia Morain worth their blade could turn a single mistake into a fatality.

She let the three Issamiri form a wall in front of Arianrod, and made her targets anyone who tried to go around them rather than engaging. At first it was only one or two at a time, and that was easy, twisting out of the way of their pathetic slashes and getting in close enough to end them with a single cut. But as the enemy soldiers kept coming, the Issamiri bulwark splintered and broke, its members succumbing to their wounds. And without them to cover her, Seren was faced with five, eight, ten at once.

Arianrod did what she could to help, setting soldiers alight or turning swords molten. But though she had once killed more than fifty men at a stroke, that single spell had felled her, and however many she dispatched now, there always seemed to be more behind them. Seren could tell she was trying to conserve her strength, but if she kept casting, it would give out eventually. How many soldiers did the enemy have?

She danced out of reach of her foes; she didn't make a mistake, over and over.

And her opponents did, and one by one they died. If any slipped through, Arianrod found some way to destroy them. It was so tempting to pretend they could keep this up forever, that they would be able to stand over the body of their final foe and move forward again together. That this wouldn't have to end, this journey Seren had been lucky to make at Arianrod's side all this time. That they would live long enough that perhaps one day Seren would be able to say all the things she truly wanted to say to her.

But Arianrod was already looking pale and weak, and Seren's opponents only seemed to breed more of themselves; wherever she struck, someone else immediately moved in to fill the space. And then there were just too many. They hemmed her in, and when she killed one, others pressed against her from all sides, and bore her to the ground.

She ought to have died years ago, executed on Arianrod's tenth birthday. She had cheated death so many times since then, through all her training, through the missions she'd undertaken on Arianrod's behalf. When the boy Seth had unknowingly traded his life for hers, and when Arianrod had healed her infection with magic. Even the best of the best could not evade death forever. There wasn't a soul in the Inxia Morain who did not know that.

But the final cut never came. Instead, a vaguely familiar voice shouted, "What did I say? Don't squander a golden opportunity!"

Seren was hauled to her feet, a man gripping each of her arms with both hands. A third person stood behind her, one arm locked around her chest, the other holding a knife to her throat. A twitch in the wrong direction, and she'd cut herself open on that blade, without the soldiers having to do anything at all.

She had no room to turn her head, but she could see Arianrod standing alone, frozen with one hand still outstretched, and the soldiers crowded a distance away, wary of getting any closer. Then two people she knew crossed into her field of vision, two people she'd never thought to see together. The first was that obnoxious giant, Ghilan, Edith Selwyn's lackey, the glee in his beady little eyes even more irritating than she remembered. She had to think further back to recognize the second one, but the red robes sparked her memory: Varalen Oswhent, chief strategist to Elgar himself. He was somber, at least outwardly, but he carried himself with confidence—much more than she remembered seeing from him at Mist's Edge.

"None of your options here look especially promising, Your Grace," he said, "but I still recommend you consider them carefully. His Eminence will prefer I bring you back to Valyanrend alive, but that doesn't mean I won't kill you if I must."

For a moment Arianrod just stared at him, as if there had been some riddle in his words. But when she spoke, all she said was, "What makes you think *I* would prefer to be killed in Valyanrend?"

"Perhaps you'd appreciate the chance to live that much longer. But even if not, there's something else I can offer you." He nodded at Seren. "Come with me back to Valyanrend, without any more attempts at magic, and I'll let that one go."

In the first instant, Seren wondered how he even knew enough to make that offer. In the second, she wanted to laugh in his face. *Surrender and I'll spare the others* was a tactic so hoary that the words Lord Oswhent spoke were practically covered in cobwebs. And sure enough, Arianrod rolled her eyes. "You must be wandering in your wits if you think I believe that. At this point, you don't need my surrender to kill me."

"But I'll almost certainly need it to get you to submit to the vardrath steel I intend to bind you with before I take you to Valyanrend." His eyes narrowed. "I won't claim to understand all that lies between you, but I saw enough at Mist's Edge to know that this one means something to you. To me, she means much less than the men you might be able to kill before we can defeat you. So leave me their lives, and I'll leave you hers."

That hardly changed things. Having her magic bound would restrict Arianrod's available options far too severely, and like this, Seren was no longer any use to her. It would be a terrible trade. Surely she had seen that for herself already. No one was better at calculating odds, at finding a way forward no matter what, than Arianrod was.

But she didn't see Arianrod roll her eyes again, or hear her contemptuous rebuttal. She heard nothing at all, nothing loud enough to penetrate the sound of her heart beating in her ears. And she saw Arianrod with no smile on her face. Saw her take a breath, and hesitate.

With a nauseating lurch, all Seren's certainty flipped.

And then she began to struggle.

VARALEN OSWHENT WAS sweating, dirt-stained, possessed of at least three leaves tangled up in his hair, and, finally, on the verge of a triumph he'd awaited for weeks, or perhaps even longer than that. He hadn't needed to remain to oversee the siege of Stonespire, because it didn't truly matter how the siege went. Once you cut off the head, the snake's body became no more than a corpse. All that mattered was that the siege had acted as the bait he knew it would be. She had made herself conquerable out of concern for her city. And now, he was sure, she would do it again, for the sake of this one person.

Well, that was if his soldiers didn't kill Seren Almasy with their incompetence first. "Watch her bloody neck!" he snapped at the group restraining her, as her sudden thrashing nearly sliced it open on the soldier's knife. The three of them struggled, but eventually they got Almasy pinned without killing her, though she looked as furious as Varalen had ever seen her. And that made him even more certain he was right, because he had never seen her look furious before at all.

"My lady," Almasy said, "you can't be so—"

Arianrod Margraine talked over her, directing her words at Varalen. "You'd have to let her run away—to Lakeport at least. Otherwise, what would stop you from killing her the moment I was chained? And that's if I can even convince her to run in the first place."

She couldn't, if Almasy's face was any indication. "I couldn't let her run regardless," Varalen said. "She's simply too talented, and too determined. She'd be trying to kill me all the way back to Valyanrend, and I doubt a head start would help me much. I'll only spare her if certain . . . steps are taken to ensure she no longer poses any threat to us. And if she poses no threat, why should I bother breaking my word to kill her?"

Lady Margraine frowned. "Nothing permanent."

"It would have to be, or else it would be meaningless."

"No." Still outstretched, the fingers of her extended hand clenched tight. "I won't allow that."

"You can't prevent it," Varalen told her. "I'm giving you the opportunity to decide whether she lives or dies, but that's all."

She shut her eyes, and he saw a shudder pass through her, like a gust of wind shaking a tree to the roots, but he couldn't tell its meaning. Anger? Apprehension? Uncertainty? "Nothing severed," she said at last, eyes still closed. "And nothing she's likely to die from anyway."

He supposed that much didn't matter. "Fine. But only if you decide *now*."

"There's nothing to decide!" Almasy snapped. "My lady, you're smarter than this."

Varalen would have expected that to irritate her if anything did, but Lady Margraine just stared at Lakeport on the horizon. "I'm not sure what you think I'm giving up. A shred more dignity, perhaps, but everything else I've lost already."

"Well," Varalen said. "You might count it a bit more than a shred, I'm afraid." He gestured to Ghilan, and the big man handed him the vardrath steel that had once comprised the blade of Ithan Vandrith's sword, reforged back in Araveil. Multiple fetters would have been ideal, but they only had the one blade to work with—Varalen hadn't wanted to test his luck by pressing Selwyn for more. There would have been enough steel to encircle each of her wrists, but not to chain them together, and since he had no way of taking her measurements beforehand, he couldn't make sure she wouldn't be able to slip out. So he'd come up with something different.

Lady Margraine's eyebrows lifted when she saw the collar. "Oh, dear. My lord, this is . . . *truly* embarrassing."

Varalen smiled grimly. "That's the idea."

"Oh no," she said, "I mean it's truly embarrassing for you. Are you that afraid of me?"

He wouldn't rise to that bait. "Say what you like. You know my terms."

Almasy would have kept struggling if she could, but the three soldiers on her were now holding her so tightly she barely had room to fill her lungs with air. Lady Margraine looked at her, as composed as ever, but perhaps there was a little wistfulness in her voice. "Seren, you can't give up," she said. "Not like last time. No matter what happens, you have to keep fighting. When you want to, no one can fight for life harder than you."

"What for?" Almasy asked. "What would be left for me to do? *I'm* supposed to be *your* shield!"

"And my weapon, and my tool, and so many other *things*. Imagine how much you could do if you allowed yourself to be a person." She sighed. "Either way, a bodyguard was never what *I* wanted. I wanted to be entertained, by someone who had seen and done things I never could. You could hardly have succeeded more brilliantly at that." To Varalen, she said, "You won't touch me with that steel until you're finished with her. And if you go too far, I'll turn the blood in your veins to poison before I make your men kill me."

"So long as you understand what we have to—"

"I understand, damn it." Her eyes burned into his. "I won't stop you from doing that much."

Whatever she thought, he wasn't going to enjoy this, either. But it was necessary. He had to be thorough, lest His Eminence fear that any of his enemies might still be able to cause him harm. "Ghilan." He nodded at the big man. "Make her irrelevant."

Ghilan clicked his tongue, but Varalen could see the eager glint in his eyes, like a child's at the prospect of sweets. "A pity I'll never get the chance to have a proper fight with her. But orders are orders."

He ripped Seren Almasy from the grasp of the three men who held her as if she could have fit in the palm of his hand. She tried to twist away, but even one as nimble as she simply didn't have the time or space to maneuver. He'd thrown her to the ground in half an instant, and in another he'd swept one foot beneath her stomach, kicking her right arm out from underneath her body.

With the ball of one foot, Ghilan pinned her arm to the ground at the elbow.

He raised the other foot, held it for just a breath, then brought it down with all his strength on the exposed fingers of her hand.

Varalen had been bracing himself for the cry of pain, the sound of bones snapping, but he flinched anyway. Ghilan did not, just raised his foot for another strike, and another. Though Varalen gritted his teeth, his body still jerked backward with each impact, as if trying to escape. He could not calm the racing of his heart, not even when the big man was satisfied with his work and switched his attentions to the other hand.

He'd assumed Lady Margraine would look away. But through it all, she stood there like a statue, eyes wide open, mouth flat, hands still at her sides. And she did not say a word.

When Ghilan had finished crushing both hands, he raised his eyes to Varalen, a silent question. "And one of the legs, I think," Varalen said. "Just one break, just to be safe. Knowing that one, she might try to follow us even if she can't fight."

The sound of it made bile rise in his throat, but Varalen swallowed it down, and then the thing was done. Almasy had fainted from the pain, which, given her sorry condition, was probably for the best. Lady Margraine's eyes lingered on her, but she moved toward the cart without having to be dragged. And when the rest of the soldiers had taken up positions within and around it, she stood still as Varalen fastened the collar shut around her throat.

He'd been waiting, half dread and half anticipation, for the reaction Edith Selwyn had described, when she had first admitted to him what vardrath steel could do. He had never seen it with his own eyes—he had never wanted to—but he didn't doubt she'd told the truth: the steel had not only caused her test subject tremendous pain, it had rendered her oblivious to the world around her, unable to see or hear. But Arianrod Margraine did not scream, or fall to the ground. Her face wrinkled with discomfort, and her shoulders twisted as if she could not help herself, struggling in vain to find a contortion that would shift the metal away from her bare skin. But that was all. It was clear from the way her eyes focused that she hadn't lost sight of him, either.

Selwyn *had* warned him that the effects of vardrath steel might not be consistent between her test subject and a true mage, but she had seemed to suspect the effects would be more severe, not less. Still, as long as it suppressed magic, that was all he needed—in fact, it would be a relief to make the journey back to Valyanrend without listening to Lady Margraine scream the whole way. And Selwyn had assured him that the steel's magic-suppressing power was well-documented even among true mages.

She seemed to catch his uncertainty, and smiled thinly. "Were you expecting something else?"

"I'm certainly happy with what I got," Varalen said. "Are you?" Her silence was all the answer he needed.

Before he could help hand her up into the cart, Ghilan cleared his throat. "I believe that's all our business with each other, my lord."

Varalen caught his foot before he could stumble. "What do you mean?"

"I mean you told me that I could return to Lanvaldis when this errand of yours was done," the big man said. "I played my part, just as you wanted. I can't imagine the lady's going to give you any more trouble now. So I would like to leave, without the hassle of going all the way to Valyanrend and back."

Was he serious? Varalen passed a hand over his brow. "If this is an attempt to weasel more coin out of me, it won't work. I'm sure that when we return to the imperator, he'll be in a good enough mood upon seeing our results to grant you quite a boon. That's the time to ask for coin, not now."

"You mistake me, my lord," Ghilan said cheerfully. "I've always been paid very well by the administrator, and I'm sure I'll continue to be once I return, His Eminence's mood notwithstanding. If what I wanted was coin, I'd simply have asked for it. I'm quite good at asking for what I want, you see."

"You're not seriously telling me you want to return for loyalty's sake? I'll never believe it. What do you think that woman can give you that her master can't?"

"Well, that's up to him, isn't it? But *until* he offers me something she can't, my lord, I'm going back north. And I'm leaving now."

Varalen thought about commanding him to stay, but one look at that smiling, cold-eyed face, so far above his own, was enough to make him hesitate. Ghilan must have taken it as acquiescence, because he nodded to Varalen and turned away, lumbering off into the forest like some armored bear.

"Good riddance, I suppose," Varalen muttered under his breath. Men that talented were in short supply, but he suspected men that arrogant were also rather rare. Better to wash his hands of Ghilan before he caused more trouble than he solved.

Still, as he watched Arianrod Margraine climb into the back of the covered cart ahead of him, he found it difficult to be truly irritable. This was the latest scheme in a string of them that had gone exactly as he'd hoped—ever since his abysmal failure at Mist's Edge—and it was perhaps the most important yet.

She took a seat with enviable posture, barely swaying as the cart started to move, though he could see the marks of fatigue in her face. Varalen sat across from her, waiting to see if she would speak, but though she normally loved the practice, Lady Margraine remained silent, face smooth and blank and telling him nothing. Her eyes faced forward, but they weren't quite in focus, as if part of her attention was somewhere far away.

"Badly done, Your Grace," he said.

"Funny." Her face remained composed, but she could not do the same for her voice, so much venom poured into that little word. "I was just thinking the same about you."

"I don't blame you, but our meanings are different. You doubtless find my methods brutish, distasteful, any of a hundred insults that could justifiably be applied to them. None of that matters, of course, because they were also successful. But *you* . . . what a sad end to your grand plans. I admit the woman was useful, but putting the servant's well-being above the master's undoes the very purpose of a bodyguard. She was meant to die for you; you should have let her."

"I should have traded her life for a few more moments of freedom?" she asked. "You and I both know you outplayed me this time. Once your people spotted us, I could never have changed the outcome."

"So you simply chose to give up?"

"Far from it. When I escape this snare, there will be more value in having her alive to witness it. A value I do not expect you to understand." She smiled coldly. "Though there is something *I* would certainly like to understand. What was your price, Lord Oswhent?"

"I beg your pardon?" But he didn't, not really. He knew what she meant.

"There was a time when you refused to call that man *His Eminence*—even a little man could only be pushed so far, you told me. There was a time when you would not have labored on his behalf so assiduously, or showed such shameful pride in bringing his enemies low. So how did he buy you? What was the offer?"

"Why, are you going to try to make me a better one?"

She threw back her head and laughed. "Lord Oswhent, there is only one thing you will ever get from me. I believed, when last we met, that you were a pawn unhappily used. As such, even when your schemes caused great trouble for me—as when you conspired with that boy Kern to smuggle soldiers into my very hall—I bore you no anger for it. You were simply doing what you had no choice but to do, and I am sure you derived no more joy in devising it than I did in falling victim to it. But this is different. You have caused incalculable damage, incalculable suffering, to one of my very own, and you have mocked me in doing it. For that, I will obliterate you along with your master."

She said it as if her wish to do it and its occurrence in reality were one and the same, as if she were not bound and helpless in the back of a cart. "You'll forgive me, Your Grace, if I don't quake with fear quite as much as you wish."

"Ah, but you are afraid of me, Lord Oswhent." Her tone was confident as ever, but with something sharp and bitter in it he hadn't heard before. "It's what you've been afraid of all this time, isn't it? That I'm smarter than you? Well, let me put your uncertainty to rest: I am smarter than you, and you haven't put my wits in chains. Already the gears are turning and turning in my head, and you cannot stop them. They will not rest until you are in an agony to surpass that of my poor Seren, an agony that burns you to your very soul. And when it has you in its grip, you will remember that I told you it would come to pass, and you did not believe me."

Varalen shook his head. "You are formidably talented, Your Grace—as talented as that man Ghilan, whom I had to let slip through my fingers. But just like him, you are also formidably arrogant. Someone like you will believe they will end up the victor until the very moment they lose their head. And before that moment comes, no amount of persuasion can convince them of their folly. You would do better to recognize you are finally out of options than to attempt to conjure them from clouds and air. That is an impossible feat, even for a mage."

Arianrod Margraine tipped her head back against the side of the cart, closing her eyes. "A genius always has options, Lord Oswhent," she said. "If you truly were one, you would know that."

Chapter Sixteen

Valyanrend

The moment Rask was through the door of the Ashencourt house, three people tackled him to the floor, one sitting on his legs, one pinning his arms behind his back, and one carefully holding his head still. "What the hell?" he sputtered, as angry as a wet cat. "I've not been gone twenty-four hours! Surely it's not so long you've all forgotten what I look like!"

"Sorry, Rask." Naishe crouched before him, digging the pendant out from beneath her shirt. She pressed the edge to his forehead, and felt no chill. Good. She nodded to the others. "Strip him."

"Wait! Wait, damn it! You can't just—"

"We'll protect your modesty." Naishe held up a sheet, then passed it to the others, who had not heeded Rask's plea to wait. In another minute, everything he had been wearing was lying in a heap in the center of the room, and he was trussed up in the sheet like meat in a pastry.

His glare could have cut stone. "You'd best explain yourself, Kadife."

"Of course. This is hardly the time for pranks." She lifted his sword and its belted sheath first, running the pendant over them. "It's as you said when you gave me this: our enemy can alter minds. You just spent the night in the very depths of his territory. We've got to make sure he didn't get to you, and unfortunately, we can't trust your word. You might not know, or be compelled to tell us otherwise if you do."

"And *this* was the least embarrassing way you could find to accomplish that?"

"If it had been anyone else, you know you'd be the loudest voice insisting on it," Naishe reminded him, reaching for his shirt next.

He hid his face in the floorboards, voice muffled. "I know. That's why I'm not saying anything now."

Once she was done with the shirt, she threw it over to him, and he slipped it on gratefully, cinching the sheet around his waist. "Was there anything unusual about your time there?"

"Not that I can think of. They acted like the whole thing was some reward for bravery or mark of distinction, but it was clear I wasn't allowed to refuse any of it. Which might have meant nothing: they could have just wanted Elgar to look better by connecting himself to me and what I did to those murderers. I did think that, since he almost definitely hired them, he wanted to make sure I didn't suspect that was the case, so I was careful not to even hint I thought they were anything but rebels. I never saw Elgar himself beyond his initial greeting, his thanks, shaking my hand, all that. But that was done in a minute."

"And if he'd enchanted you then, the pendant would have dispelled it when it touched you." Naishe spread his cloak out flat on the floor, running the pendant just above it in tight, careful swerves. At first she felt nothing, but then, as she neared the bottom, there was the telltale prick of cold at her fingertips. "And here we are."

She dropped the pendant back under her shirt and started searching the cloak for anything that seemed odd or different. Finally, she found what she was looking for: on the inside of the cloak, at the back, about an inch shy of the bottom hem, she felt a change of texture, and brought it close to reveal a little spot of dark metal, smaller than a fingerprint and flatter than a coin. It was attached to the fabric with tiny thorns, like a burr, and she had to pry it loose with a knife. She brought the pendant close, but didn't quite touch it, and the cold sprang up again in confirmation. She waved it at Rask. "This is it."

Rask squinted at it, frowning. "When the hell did he do that? They confiscated the sword, but I never took the cloak off once the whole time I was there—I'm not an idiot."

"If that's the case, they probably insisted on searching you, to make sure you weren't hiding any more weapons under it," Naishe said. "The one doing it must have been particularly nimble-fingered—Elgar's version of our monkey."

Rask smiled wryly. "Now, don't sell the monkey short—I'm sure if she were here, she'd call this an amateur job. Here's the more troubling question: how did they know to target me with this? They shouldn't have been able to tie me back to the resistance—I was captured alone, I wasn't doing or carrying anything suspicious, it wasn't odd for me to be in the Glassway or at all unreasonable that I attacked those men. And ironically, I wasn't carrying a lot of coin on me, since I'd just given almost all of it to that merchant. If they could make the connection regardless, that's . . . very bad for us."

"I doubt it had anything to do with the resistance, actually," Naishe said. "I'm willing to bet it's your much more obvious value. As you're always reminding everyone, Rask, you're an incredible swordsman. You made that clear to everyone who saw you fight in the Glassway, and Elgar must have received reports of it, too. He must have wanted to exploit your abilities for his own gain."

Rask extended his hand, and Naishe placed the little speck of metal into it.

He turned it over between his fingers, watching the dull way it caught the light. "Pity vardrath steel can only kill magic, not make it give up its secrets. Aren't you curious what sort of plans the bastard had for me?"

"I'm incredibly curious," Naishe said. "But I don't know how we can find out. The only one with that information is likely to be Elgar himself."

Rask brushed his thumb against the flat part. "But you didn't actually break the spell yet, right?"

"No, not yet. But Rask, you can't be thinking—"

"It could be a window into his plans. If he's using me as a test case, and we find out what for, we'll be better able to take steps to counter it before it happens on a larger scale."

Naishe shook her head. "Rask, I don't like to do this, but as your leader, I'm ordering you not to have any further contact with that thing. The one thing we *know* Elgar has used these devices for is to turn ordinary people into murderers. Your conscience aside, you're the best swordsman we have. If Elgar turned you against us without warning—or worse, against civilians—I don't know how many you might kill before you could be stopped. It's just too dangerous."

Rask still had his eyes on the metal object, but he nodded slowly. "I don't disagree. Just the thought of having to walk around knowing my mind could be stolen from me at any time makes me ill. And you're right: I'm too valuable, and I'm too close to you and other key members of the resistance. Even if Elgar never intended to use me as a weapon, if there were any way for him to interrogate me, ask me about what I've seen, I might give the whole resistance away. But remember what happened when Wren kept hold of that little white stone Marceline lifted off Elgar? He'd clearly made it for himself, but it was no less effective in Wren's pocket than it would have been in his. It seems these things can be switched from one person to another and still work."

"So you want us to pin it on someone else and watch them?"

"It'd need to be someone whose permission we could ask, of course," Rask said. "But someone a lot less deadly than I am—or preferably, not deadly at all. Now, my choice would be Wren, because he's not much of a fighter *and* he's so timid that any aggression from him would give the game away immediately, but—"

"Absolutely not," Naishe said.

"But you'd never agree to it. Exactly. Besides, he does know where you sleep, so there's still the potential for some rather unfortunate outcomes."

Naishe fiddled with the pendant's chain. "The trouble is, everyone who knows enough for us to ask their permission is someone who knows too much. Marceline is small and doesn't have much combat ability, but she has plenty of other skills, and Elgar's seen her before. Talia is a much better fighter than she looks—"

"—thanks mostly to me—"

"—and she'll be exposed enough as it is, if this anti-Issamiri sentiment grows any greater. As for the others . . ." She clicked her tongue, frustrated. "I'll think on it. I promise I'll think on it. But until I reach a decision, let's lock that thing in a box somewhere, rather than leaving it on anyone's person."

"Agreed," Rask said. He glanced at the remainder of his clothes. "Can I have those back now, please?"

Naishe waved the pendant at him. "Should probably do them, too, just to make sure there wasn't a second one."

He groaned. "Let me do them, at least. I'd like to get out of this with *some* semblance of my dignity intact."

CHAPTER SEVENTEEN

Araveil

THEY HAD GONE over the plan so many times that Cadfael could have recited, word for word, how Gerald Holm had delivered it. He had the palace plans memorized, every route they could possibly take in or out. He had actually begun to feel something like optimism toward the idea, as risky as it was. And now, on the eve of their planned assault, came a piece of news that held the power to throw everything off balance—or, at least, so he gathered from the captain's reaction. To Cadfael himself, the news meant absolutely nothing.

"Ghilan?" he repeated. "Can so much have changed in three years? When I was considered the best among Eira's soldiers, I knew nothing of him."

He had known Gerald Holm, though not very well; though they were soldiers together, the captain viewed his job as an honor and a duty, while Cadfael had only ever seen it as a way to earn more coin, and so they had avoided each other. Of Holm's captured niece he knew nothing at all; she was even younger than Rhia, and had barely been in training when Cadfael left Araveil. "Was he some prodigious young recruit or something?"

Holm shook his head. "No, he took your path. He's about your age, too, or perhaps a bit older. He made his name in the arena before Selwyn snapped him up. I must entreat you not to underestimate him. I know your skills well, but his are no worse. It was our one stroke of good fortune that Lord Oswhent insisted on taking him out of Lanvaldis."

"Yet now he has returned," Cadfael said, riffling through his memory of the arena combatants he'd known back when he fought there. Ghilan, Ghilan . . . it didn't sound familiar, but then he supposed he'd never been keen on getting to know those he might have had to kill on the morrow. "Does that mean we can hope something went awry with Oswhent's plans?"

"It doesn't seem that way." Holm paced back over to his table of maps, tracing absentminded patterns on the parchment. "If anything, it means the opposite. My sources in the palace claim he was discharged after completing whatever mission Oswhent had for him, but they couldn't find out what that mission was."

"The news is even worse than that," Alessa said quietly. Holm had wanted her to limit the number of people who knew her true identity as much as possible, but she and Voltest had both taken such an active role in their planning that she'd eventually revealed herself to him, at least. "Ghilan is the one who captured the others, while I waited with the cart like my brother had asked. He's the one who defeated Talis, and stopped her magic. I didn't see it, but Hayne can testify to it."

Hayne, who normally preferred to stand silently at Alessa's side, spoke up at her cue. "Selwyn's people will have access to vardrath steel regardless, but that Ghilan wielded it especially well. I agree with the captain; his involvement isn't something we should take lightly."

"I understand that," Cadfael said, "but how much bloody longer can we delay? Lirien and Voltest have told you that Talis's condition is deteriorating by the day—even by the moment. If Ghilan finished Lord Oswhent's task, but Lord Oswhent did not return to Araveil with him, he's likely here to stay, and I suspect the chances of drawing him too far from Selwyn's side are slim. If you need someone to fight him, I'll volunteer, but it's madness to let all our plans fall to ruin for the sake of one man."

"I'll also volunteer to fight him, if it comes to that," Rhia said. "Cadfael's right: we've waited long enough. Elgar and Selwyn aren't fools; they know as well as we do that there is greater unrest in Araveil than in Valyanrend, and that its leader is less well protected. The moment she sees an opening to do so, Selwyn will send her prisoners to Valyanrend, out of our reach, and our momentum will fade. I say we don't delay the plan."

Holm looked to the two *wardrenfell,* who shrugged, unusually in step with each other. "You know we wish to free Talis from this confinement as soon as possible, for our own sake as well as hers," Voltest said. "This man doesn't scare me."

"Perhaps not, but you shouldn't fight him, not if Selwyn has granted him use of vardrath steel," Lirien said. "I, on the other hand, can still heal our people, so I'll tag along with the siblings over there. Though you'll both have to put your swords down if you need healing."

Holm sighed, scrubbing at his face. "I should count myself fortunate to have so many exceptional individuals at my back. If you're all so willing, I won't be the one who prevents the plan from going forward. Gods know I've waited long enough for a king already."

RHIA WASN'T SURE if she was supposed to be nervous.

Her brother had long called her reckless, and she had to admit he knew her better than anyone. But he was the one who had been the most impatient through Captain Holm's endless explanations and practice runs, his insistence on absolute perfection before they started anything. Was it arrogant to think they were simply well prepared, that they were a match for the task they had set themselves?

The majority of their recruits were engaged in another riot that would engulf the city—a much larger and more determined one, and with a fixed purpose: distraction. Voltest would be with them, using his magic to set enough well-controlled but persistent fires to keep Selwyn's people occupied. Between that and the sheer number of rioters, they expected Selwyn would have to send reinforcements from within the palace, especially now that Lord Oswhent's men would not be returning to support her a second time. If they were lucky, this Ghilan fellow might even be drawn out, but Rhia wasn't betting on it.

The captain knew more about the palace than Rhia could have imagined, much more than Cadfael could remember from his time serving there. *Sinthil Vlin,* it was called in Old Lantian: *Star Castle,* though no one could remember why. It certainly wasn't star-shaped, more of a rough square. And it had been altered and rebuilt so many times that more than the name had fallen by the wayside; little more than the original foundation remained. The curtain wall no longer existed, but the towers it had once connected did, now welded to the castle proper by narrow corridors. The captain said there had once been a series of passages one floor beneath ground level, used most often for servants to get from place to place with minimal disturbance to their masters. But thieves and other rogues had made such use of them that they'd been collapsed and filled in more than a century ago, and now any servants who worked at Sinthil Vlin had to use the western-facing gate, a modest entranceway that led straight to the kitchens. It was guarded, of course, but they were always going to have enough men to overwhelm their initial opponents with strength of numbers. The more pressing issue was making sure the door was not shut on them from the inside as they approached.

Just before the western wall of the castle came into view, Lirien muttered to the captain, "You're *sure* the girl knows the plan?"

"Backward and forward. She won't dare to approach the entryway until she's sure your work is done."

"Good, then." She did not look it; Rhia could see her tongue swiping restlessly against the inside of her cheek, as if trying to dislodge a bad taste. She would have volunteered to do it herself, if it were within her power. But none of them could hit multiple targets faster or more accurately than Lirien could.

They didn't even have to get close. When Lirien saw the guards arrayed before the gate, she didn't even break her stride. And the guards did not fall; they barely moved. One moment they were living, breathing humans, and the next they were frozen solid where they stood—a spell Rhia had seen only once before, and was no less disconcerted by now.

They crowded by the entrance and waited, until the heavy door opened to reveal a scrawny serving girl who winched the gate up for them. As they passed inside, Rhia saw three more guards standing near the doorway, as frozen as their comrades.

"That's five," Lirien said to Captain Holm. "I'd prefer not to add to that number."

"So would we all," he said, "but these traitors made their choice. I anticipate having to slay far more than five before I reach my king."

"But you've done enough in that regard," Rhia said, trying to reassure Lirien. "Even if you only stay to heal those on our side, it would be valuable enough."

The captain nodded stiffly, veiling whatever reluctance he might have felt. "Just make sure to keep yourself out of danger."

Hayne and her group broke off from theirs almost immediately, headed for the tower cell where they'd learned the two boy kings were being kept. But Captain Holm was leading the group charged with freeing his niece and Ithan Vandrith, and they were locked not in cells but in a series of rooms intended for honored guests. Selwyn's own chambers were not far from theirs, so if all went well, the captain and his companions would press on in hopes of taking her hostage. And if Rhia and Cadfael couldn't find Ghilan, they were free to go wherever they judged their help would be most needed.

Most of those they passed were servants or messengers, who threw up their hands and pressed themselves against the walls as their group forced its way out of the kitchens and into the corridors beyond. The first wave of armed soldiers was scattered out of any formation, clearly taken by surprise and scrambling to compensate. Captain Holm, at the front, was as good as his word, he and the companions flanking him cutting down their enemies before Lirien could reach them.

"Perhaps you and your sister should take up positions in the courtyard," he said to Cadfael. "We'll have to pass through anyway to get me to Ilyn, and you won't have a better vantage of the palace's interior anywhere else."

Cadfael shook his head. "The courtyard's too exposed. In a tighter space, numbers matter less than skill, but if we're swarmed—"

He fell silent as the courtyard itself loomed before them, the sudden bright light of late morning making Rhia squint. There was a circle of cracked and weathered stone tile within a square of overgrown shrubbery, perhaps an herb garden used by servants. Some of those very servants were still fleeing the courtyard, while others tentatively gawked from the open passages on the second and third floors before running off to report what they had seen.

There were few actual soldiers in the courtyard, but perhaps there didn't need to be. All eyes were drawn to only one.

Though she had longed to be tall as a child, fate had seen fit to make Rhia shorter and slighter than the average adult, and she had long had to resign herself to being towered over. But *tall* did not begin to describe the man standing in the center of the courtyard, a steel warhammer in his huge hands that was nearly as long as she was high. His broad back and oxlike shoulders heaved with each breath, and even his head was massive, though somewhat masked by the helm he wore. The rest of his armor was patchy, as if he'd had to put it together from whatever scraps he could find. His chest and back had the most protection, with noticeable gaps down his arms and only leather below his thighs. And on his hands, two gauntlets gleamed as bright as Rhia's sword ever had. Vardrath steel.

Cadfael glanced at the captain; if he felt any trace of nerves, even Rhia could not detect it. "I suppose this is where we part ways, then. As promised, we'll buy time for you to succeed, if nothing else."

"I'll stay with the two of you," Lirien said. "I know I won't be able to harm him, but you're putting yourselves in the most danger, and we can't afford to lose either of you."

"Are you sure?" Cadfael asked. "If Hywel or Kelken—"

"Hywel and Kelken will have a score of men defending them," Lirien said. "You two will be fighting alone."

"She's right," the captain said. "Ghilan's already ruined things for us once before. We can't risk failing to keep him occupied."

"Oh, I'll do more than occupy him." Cadfael cracked his neck, and turned to Rhia. "Listen, I'm taking the lead on this. Even though I don't remember him from my arena days, if he fought there, he might have picked up some habits or techniques I recognize—or maybe I'll remember something when I see him fight. Besides, I'm older, so I have seniority." A joke, even if he didn't smile. "You back me up, and if I falter, it's your turn. Agreed?"

Arguing would only throw them into disarray, so Rhia swallowed her objections and nodded. "Grudgingly."

"I'll take it." He drew his sword, and Rhia let him step ahead of her, keeping her own sword sheathed. It was not out of overconfidence; a *tsunshin* was just as effective in either position. If this man was truly so powerful, let him think her unprepared.

"Don't stay to watch us," Cadfael told the captain. "Take your men, and do what you came to do." He leaned the flat of his sword against his shoulder, a cavalier display that was unusual for him. But as he strode into the circle of broken tile, Rhia saw why: the vardrath steel blade caught the sunlight, gleaming like a beacon to draw every eye.

The big man could hardly have failed to notice. Though the rest of him was oversized, Ghilan's eyes were comparably small, a pale and watery blue, gleaming with amusement or excitement or greed. "Well now, what's this? You've already lost your head by forcing your way in here, but I'm quite sure the administrator confiscated all the vardrath steel in Lanvaldis."

"You're welcome to try to take it from me," Cadfael said. "Though I don't promise your safety if you do."

Ghilan laughed, loud and carrying. "Such confidence! I like it. There's no fun in a fight when your opponent's trembling before you've even touched him. You're someone important in this little resistance of Holm's, I take it?" Those beady eyes roved over Cadfael, and then his head cocked to the side. "Wait. I know you."

"From the arena?" Cadfael asked. "I don't believe we ever fought."

"No, but I watched you enough times. You were everyone's darling back then, weren't you?" He laughed again; the sound already grated on Rhia's ears. "It seems someone got the better of you after all. I almost didn't recognize you with that gash on your face. What would the ladies of Araveil say, I wonder?"

"You of all people should know that any injury that doesn't affect a warrior's skill is immaterial. Though I'm happy to let you grieve over my face, if you think you can afford the distraction."

"Now, now, what's the hurry? I've wanted to fight you for years, but Eira kept you too protected. Give me a chance to savor the moment."

Cadfael shrugged. "It's all the same to me, but would your mistress look kindly on this savoring?"

"Ah, you're right." He lifted the hammer onto one shoulder. "Best regain her favor by ending this quickly, then."

Though neither of them had ever seen him fight, Rhia had a general idea of how this contest had to go, and she was sure Cadfael did, too. True, Ghilan wasn't in full plate, and he must surely be immensely strong, but someone wearing that much metal on his body and carrying that much metal in his hands simply wasn't going to be able to move at great speed. He'd seek to make up for that with the sheer reach the hammer afforded him. To wound him, Cadfael would have to get within and back out of that reach without being struck, but Ghilan wouldn't have to get close to strike. And judging by the size of the hammer, even a single hit would prove very grievous indeed.

But Cadfael looked as untroubled as ever, slicing his blade through the air as if making an idle practice swing. "Oh, it'll end quickly all right."

KEL WAS SO nervous his hands hadn't been able to stay still since he'd jerked into consciousness in what he hoped was the morning. Two meals ago, there had been another smuggled letter with their food, only the second one they had ever received. It had contained a brief, perhaps purposely vague description of Gerald Holm's plan to storm the castle on the following day. If all went accordingly, they would take Administrator Selwyn hostage, and install Hywel as the rightful king as soon as possible. But even if that much was beyond them, they hoped to at least rescue Kel, Hywel, and the other prisoners, disappearing into the forest with them if need be. He had written a code phrase for Kel to say at the next meal, about the tray being hot, if he and Hywel were amenable to the plan, and a different one if they knew of some reason why it should not go forward.

Kel and Hywel had assumed the captain knew more about the risks involved in his plan than they did, so they had given their permission for it to proceed. But there was still no way to tell the passage of time in this room. They had fallen into a fitful, uncomfortable sleep eventually, because they had thought it best to be rested for what was to come. But now, awake, they had no way of knowing whether they'd been sleeping for two hours or ten. They had no way of knowing whether anything had gone wrong.

"You can go back to sleep if you like," Hywel said. "I'll keep watch. There's no point in both of us fretting ourselves to the bone for nothing."

"No force on earth could get me to sleep now," Kel said. "If only these walls weren't so thick."

"Well, the door's heavy enough that it's impossible to open without making enough noise to wake the dead. No one's going to surprise us, at least. And Gerald made it quite clear in his letter that they didn't need our help, and all we had to do was be ready to leave when his people arrive."

"He probably said that to comfort us, or perhaps that's what he hopes for. If things go wrong, they may end up needing us—needing anyone who could possibly turn the tide back in their favor."

Hywel smiled gently. "Kelken, you've kept my spirits up when I would've thought it impossible. Let me do the same for you now. Gerald is staking everything on this, and I know him: he's as thorough and methodical as anyone you're likely to meet. If he says the most important thing for us to do is to be rested and ready, then that's what we'll do."

They waited and waited, for minutes or hours, with not even a breath of wind to disturb the silence. Kel sighed. "Of course my body picks *now* to remind me I'm hungry. But there's no way to tell if they're late with our meal or not."

Hywel was seated in his customary spot on the floor, knees drawn up to his chest, rocking his feet back and forth. "If they are late, it's probably a good sign. Gerald and his people might be holding them up."

"Or I could just be hungry too soon."

"No need to puncture our hopes before due time, Kelken."

Still they waited, an errant noise twice causing them both to pitch forward before they realized it was just the sound of the building settling around them. But then, at last, came the sound they'd been straining to hear all this time: the heavy door rattling in its frame.

"This has to be them," Kel said.

"Or the guards trying to stop them."

"Or that. Either way, we've got to be ready."

"Leave it to me." Hywel shuffled over beside the door and raised his manacled wrists, ready to choke the first person through with the chain strung between them. Kel held his breath. All that scratching and fumbling at the door could be good—if the people outside were trying to pick the lock, they were probably on their side. Then again, they could just be nervous and slow with the key.

The door finally swung open, and Hywel started forward—only to jerk immediately back, lowering his hands completely. The couple of seconds before Kel could see around him were the longest of his life, but at least his payment for them was worth it: a familiar solemn face, wreathed in dark hair. *"Hayne?"*

"Good to see you, Your Grace." She wasted no further time on reunions, but swiftly closed the distance between them and cut him free, swinging him onto her back. "Apologies, but this is the fastest way to get you out of here."

"You'll hear no argument from me," Kel said. "If you're here, does that mean Alessa—"

"With great difficulty, we persuaded your sister to remain behind, as she cannot fight," Hayne said. "But she awaits your return."

As good a report as he could possibly have hoped for. "Do you know that Lord Ithan—"

"Aye. Captain Holm's group is on their way to rescue his niece and the lordling."

"They'll get them out faster with our help," Hywel said. While Hayne had been assisting Kel, her companions had set to work on the chains binding his wrists and ankles, cracking them with the same facility they'd used on the door. "The lock on those chambers is intricate, special, and we have reason to believe that Selwyn keeps the only other key on her person. But Lady Euvalie entrusted us with hers. If we aren't able to meet all our goals today, and we have to flee—"

"And Talis," Kel broke in. "Who's going to go get Talis?"

"We have a third group on that," Hayne said, "but it's the group that'll probably take the longest. Our informants pinpointed your location and the others', but all we know is that Talis is in the underground cells somewhere, not one of the towers like you. They'll have to search until they find her."

"They'll have to do more than that," Kel said. "She isn't just cuffed with vardrath steel, she's also chained to the floor. They'll need to remove both to get her out, and that'll take even more time."

"Time we don't have, you seem to be suggesting," Hayne said. "But you can't truly mean to leave her?"

"He doesn't," Hywel said. "Kelken and I know Talis's cell. With me at their side—"

"No, not you, Hywel," Kel interrupted. "I need to be the one to go."

"Kelken—"

"No, listen. There's no time for extended debate." Kel slapped his leg. "We already know Ithan is lame, at least for now. We shouldn't have both prisoners who can't walk in one group, and if you go instead of me, you can help him along. But I'm small enough to be carried, and once Talis's powers come into play, I doubt our speed will matter. Don't stop to argue with me. Just help them get to the others."

Hywel hissed through his teeth, but he didn't waste any more time. "I'll see you outside," he said over his shoulder, the firmness of his tone allowing no more dissent than Kel's had. "Who's going with me?"

"I'll take Hayne," Kel said. "You keep the other two; you'll be escorting more people." He squeezed Hayne's shoulder. "I'm sorry to impose on you like this, but do you think you can carry me until we get there?"

"The only imposition is that I can't hold a sword and you at once, Your Grace," Hayne said. "If we run into combat, I may have to put you down."

THE FIGHT HAD not ended quickly.

They had sparred and practiced together on the road, but this was the first time Rhia had truly seen her brother fight in three years. It was clear that time had not dulled his edge in the slightest. His strikes were beautifully precise, his footwork flawless; if Ghilan had come close to hitting him, it was only ever part of a feint on Cadfael's part. But that didn't mean that Ghilan wasn't talented, or that the captain had overstated his skill. He couldn't move anywhere near as fast as Cadfael, but he still moved faster in all that armor than Rhia would have believed possible. And he swung that hammer around like it was half its weight. Cadfael had scored some shallow hits on him, most of them in the gaps of the armor covering his arms and one on his left thigh that was still dripping, but they weren't severe enough to slow him down. As eager as the big man seemed with those hammer blows, he was surprisingly good at defending himself, and Cadfael hadn't managed to penetrate his reach for more than an instant before having to dodge away again.

At Rhia's side, Lirien tilted her head, as if listening for something. "Voltest is still in the city proper. He's steady—an undercurrent of anger, as usual, but he's managing it. Things must be going as he expected, which is good for us. I still can't feel Talis at all, though. They must not have reached her yet."

Rhia winced. "That's bad, isn't it?"

"Hard to say. We always knew she'd be the most challenging to get to. And if the captain's team can take Selwyn hostage, she might become a moot point anyway."

But with their limited manpower, they might need Talis's magic to get to Selwyn in time. If they didn't have her captive before the soldiers in the streets realized the mob was a diversion and returned to the palace, the odds would be stacked against them.

Ghilan wound his hammer up and back, and Cadfael circled him warily, waiting to see where the blow would fall. Her brother was sweating faintly, but she had seen what he looked like winded, and knew he had plenty of stamina left in him. It was harder to see whether the big man was tiring or not underneath his armor.

Lirien followed her gaze. "Do you think you should step in? I know honor is a sticking point for you, but . . ."

"It's not about that," Rhia said. "If we both tried to fight him at the same time, we'd just get in each other's way. With that hammer, having enough space to evade is essential."

"Then shouldn't you leave him? They look like they can go at it for a while yet. It seems a waste for you to be idling here when you could be assisting some other group. And I can stay in case he gets injured."

Her words made sense, but Rhia wondered if that was truly best. Cadfael had been the one who led them here, whose determination to rescue Talis had never wavered. Rhia didn't know the true nature of the unfinished business that lay between them, but she knew it was important to her brother as few things had ever been. And yet he had sacrificed that desire, at least for the time being, in order to let everyone else have a greater chance of succeeding at their own missions. As for Rhia . . . why had she truly come here? What had she hoped to do?

Gripping the hilt of her sword, she made a decision.

"Cadfael," she said. "This isn't where you should be. Like this, we aren't keeping him occupied, he's keeping *us* occupied. A quick victory would have been good for our pride and our strategy, but this is taking too long. You need to do what you came here to do."

Cadfael took her meaning immediately, though he didn't look happy about it. "I can't leave you here. Even with Lirien—"

"No, you should take Lirien. We don't know what'll happen to her when Talis is set free. If her power explodes again, it could have bad consequences for my fight. Better to remove the distraction."

That didn't make Lirien look happy, either. "Rhia, if the two of us both leave you, you'll have no support at all. If reinforcements decide to swarm the court-yard—or if you get injured and I'm not here—"

"There's nothing here that's important enough for them to send reinforce-ments," Rhia said. "There's only him, and if he needed reinforcements, he wouldn't be so dangerous. I'm not about to lose to my brother. If I can't keep this one busy at least as long as he did, I'd never be able to face you two again."

Lirien gritted her teeth, but then, surprisingly, she looked to Cadfael. She trusted him to know her, Rhia realized—to know if this was something she could or could not do. She found herself holding her breath, waiting for his judgment just as much as Lirien.

He stepped away from Ghilan. "You won't lose to me—I'll hold you to that, you hear me? Lirien, let's go."

Ghilan started to lumber after them. "Oh, I don't think so. I'm not letting one like you get away."

But he couldn't possibly catch up to them, not with armor on and Rhia in his path. "Sorry," she said. "Unless you can get rid of me, you're staying here."

He just looked bored. "And what are you, little one?"

"Didn't you hear? I'm his sister."

"Aye, but it's a pity you don't share his size. You've got to understand, orders are orders, but I've no pleasure in crushing weaklings. Better that you run along, instead of denying me the chance for a real fight."

"Don't be hasty," Rhia said. "My brother's overprotective, that's all. I let him face you first out of courtesy, but I'm at least as much a match for you as he is."

"Is that right?" Amusement danced in his pale eyes, but the brows above them lifted in skepticism. "Why did I never see you in the arena then, I wonder?" He tapped his fingers against the shaft of his hammer. "Then again, I suppose you might've been too young."

"If I'd been a hundred, you would never have seen me there," Rhia said. "I don't treat swordplay as a game, or a sport, or an occupation. I only fight when lives and honor are at stake. So it's a rare chance you've been given to face me now."

Ghilan shrugged his massive shoulders. "If you wish to rush to your death, I won't stop you. But be quick about it; I oughtn't let that brother of yours get too far away from me."

Little did he know just how quick Rhia could be. And being small had one key advantage: less surface area for your enemies to aim at. She kept her hand on the hilt of her sword, and waited for him to raise the hammer.

She'd never fought anyone who wielded that particular weapon before. But she had watched the care Cadfael took, the movements he made, how close he dared and when he chose to retreat. And she knew very precisely how fast he was, and that she was faster.

But Ghilan did not know that, so when she stepped into his range to meet him and he swung the hammer down, he had every expectation that he would hit his target. Instead, Rhia ducked, and dodged forward instead of back. The hammer came down behind her and slightly to one side, splitting the stone tile of the court-yard. He had missed, and the hammer was so long that she was now too close for him to strike without moving.

He would have been a fool to do anything but step back, but before he had the chance, Rhia drew her sword directly into a strike, aiming as far up as she could. Though she failed to sever the artery, her sword struck flesh in the gap between his helm and the metal plate across his shoulder, a spot he'd probably thought her too short to reach. Blood beaded at his throat, rolling slowly down the curve of his neck.

She'd expected him to look dismayed, or at least wary. But instead, Ghilan's smile sharpened and grew teeth, as if he were a predator and the blood he scented was his prey's, rather than his own. "Well, well. It seems I have to beg your pardon after all. What a travesty that he's been hiding you all this time. You might prove to be even more entertaining than he was."

"There's only one way to find out," Rhia said, raising her sword between them.

CHAPTER EIGHTEEN

Araveil

"THAT'S THE THIRD fire I've seen so far this morning," Deinol shouted, struggling against the tide of people. "Has the whole city gone mad?"

The riots had started a couple hours after dawn, though he still didn't know precisely *why* they had started. One moment, he, Lucius, and Ritsu had been moving through a dilapidated market in search of information; the next, stalls were being turned over, their wares used to pelt the faces of the guards who arrived in force to restore order. Just about everyone was yelling something, there was no longer a single upright stall in his entire field of vision, and he still couldn't understand where all these fires were coming from.

"There were riots right before we arrived in Araveil, remember?" Lucius shouted back. "Apparently the people got their second wind."

"Aye, but what for? One heir's captured and another's killed, right?" He ducked, and a flying cabbage sailed over his head. "Are you trying to tell me this is just pent-up rage?"

"It isn't," Ritsu said, so softly Deinol moved his head closer to hear better. "There's no impulse behind this. It's coordinated. Keep your eyes on any of the rioters for long enough, and you'll see it."

Deinol wasn't sure what he was supposed to see, but after surveying the crowd, Lucius muttered, "He's right. Watch the moves they make, what they throw and where. Anger would make them try to attack the guards, but that's only incidental. They're trying to create the most chaos."

Deinol watched as a merchant tried to set his stall upright, only to have it snatched from his hands and dashed back to the ground. A basket of fruit was thrown into the street, where stampeding feet quickly smashed it into wet pulp, slicking the uneven stones. There was *another* bloody fire. "Then there can only be one reason for this," he said. "It's a distraction."

"That was my thought as well." Lucius smiled. "Whatever they're distracting the guards for, it would be a pity if it didn't succeed, no? Shall we join in?"

"Wait." Ritsu caught him by the sleeve. "You're not a civilian. You're strong. And Deinol isn't bad with a blade, either; I've seen him."

"All true," Lucius said. "What's your point?"

"If you want to help this effort, throwing a few things here would be a waste of your talents. While this is going on, the rebels must be sending their best people to do battle somewhere else. Shouldn't you find wherever that is, and help *those* people fight?"

Lucius looked to Deinol. "A fair argument. What do you think?"

"I think even if we knew exactly where this battle was taking place, we'd have a hell of a time getting there through this crowd," Deinol said. "But I'm game to try if you are. Just give me a direction, at least."

"Well, the most obvious direction would be Sinthil Vlin."

"The palace? You don't think that's *too* obvious?"

Ritsu was still staring at the crowd. "Even if the palace sends a third of their guards into the city, they should still have enough to hold the entrances. So if an attack on the palace is happening, and it has any hope of succeeding, the attackers must know something Selwyn's people don't. That they have compatriots on the inside, or . . . some other advantage. It could be a hundred things." Damn. He was a decent strategist when he was lucid.

"All right, let's head for the palace, then," Deinol said. "If there's an assault on it, they shouldn't be able to hide it once we get close."

But as he'd predicted, even with a clear intention, it wasn't easy to do. The guards didn't seem to want anyone to go anywhere, whether they were part of the riot or not, and whether by accident or design, the debris caused by the rioting itself created further obstructions. Every other person he tried to shove past seemed to think he was looking for a fight, and soon the three of them were hopelessly tangled in a knot of people, and he couldn't even see enough to find the direction he wanted to go.

"How do we get out of this?" he panted to Ritsu, who was closer.

"You're asking me? This is the first time I've—no." He squeezed his eyes shut, pressing a hand to his forehead. "I've been here before. When I . . ."

He swayed on his feet, but Deinol had seen him like this before, and he knew what to do. He gripped Ritsu's shoulder gently but firmly. "Ritsu, it's all right. I know you. You remember me, right?"

Ritsu's dazed expression gradually cleared, his eyes coming back into focus. "Oh. I did it again. Thank you."

Deinol didn't understand the details, but apparently the curse Ritsu had yet to fully shake off interfered with his knowledge of who he was. When he remembered things he had done under its influence, sometimes he forgot himself. But having someone there to remind him, to call him by name, seemed to be enough. It was another reason Deinol was reluctant to part ways with him; what would happen if one of these episodes came upon him while he was traveling alone, with no one to anchor him in reality?

He realized he'd forgotten all about Lucius, and cast about for him in the crowd, anxious that they shouldn't be separated. But when he found him, Lucius was standing stock still, oblivious to the chaos erupting all around him. His face was ashen, frozen, but his unblinking eyes weren't horrified; they were shining with what might have been tears.

Deinol followed his gaze, and saw someone he dimly recognized—someone he'd seen once before, while he was in a drunken stupor in an Esthradian tavern. An Aurnian woman with short black hair and a wiry build, who wore a *tsunshin* on her left side. Her right arm hung lifelessly at her other side in the same odd way he remembered, but once again, just as he started to wonder if she couldn't move it, she lifted it above her head, letting a tiny clay drinking cup bounce off her outstretched arm before it could hit her in the face.

"Lucius, who is that?" he hissed, trying to break him out of his trance.

But it was Ritsu who answered, looking almost as stunned as Lucius. "That's Rana Korinu, the most talented swordswoman of her generation in all of Aurnis, and our first female *kaishinrian*. But she died in Kaiferi. For her to be here . . ."

"It's her," Lucius said softly, as if the words were coming from far away. "I didn't dare to believe it, but . . ."

Deinol turned back to Ritsu, and dropped his voice. "Can we really be sure of that? I know you both say you recognize her, but it's been five years since either of you saw her, and at this distance—"

"If it were only me, there might be room for doubt," Ritsu said. "But if he says it's her, it's her. He spent more time with her than anyone, save the prince she served and her closest friend. He could no more forget her than you could forget him."

Deinol wondered how that could possibly be, and what precisely Lucius's relationship with Rana Korinu had been, if even a bystander to their existence like Ritsu had known about it. But before he could ask, the woman turned her head, and finally saw Lucius staring at her. She pulled up short, head bending toward him as if to make sure her eyes weren't playing tricks on her, though her feet stayed rooted to the ground. Deinol could read shock in her face, but couldn't interpret anything else, not even whether she was happy or displeased. And then she turned away and melted back into the crowd, which swallowed her up like the sea.

Lucius moved after her, but Ritsu grabbed him by the arm. "If she'd wanted to speak to you, she would have."

"Unhand me," Lucius snapped, his voice unusually thick.

Ritsu ignored him. "Now I understand. The thing you were searching so desperately for, that you didn't want me to know of. As impossible as it seems, our prince must be alive, for it would be more impossible still for his most dedicated *kaishinrian* to outlive him."

"I didn't trust you to keep it a secret," Lucius said.

"I know. I wouldn't have trusted me, either. Elgar and his people must never know of this; they believe Aurnis has been subdued for good."

"Agreed. Can you let go of me now?"

"Not if you're going to chase after her," Ritsu said. "She knows you're here now, and she and the prince can find you if they want to. But inflicting your presence on them is selfish, especially in the midst of such chaos."

Lucius shook off Ritsu's hand, but he didn't move. "I still have one last duty to perform. If the prince doesn't wish it of me, that's his decision. But I have to at least offer."

"They're not going to forgive you," Ritsu said quietly.

"I don't seek their forgiveness," Lucius replied.

"I don't believe you."

"It's the truth. Of course I *want* their forgiveness, more than anything. But I know I have no right to it."

"Are either of you going to tell me what they aren't going to forgive him for?" Deinol asked.

Lucius and Ritsu exchanged a glance, and then Ritsu looked at the ground, a sign that he would defer to Lucius's answer. Lucius ran his thumb along the hilt of his sword, taking his time. "I suppose, more than anything, it's that I didn't die. I've already told you that my fame as a swordsman was largely a result of Ryo's favor. Being as close to him as I was offered certain tangible benefits—benefits I never asked for, but that I can't deny were given to me. And then, after the way I acted the day Kaiferi was taken, the cowardice I showed, I wouldn't be surprised if they believed I was a spineless sycophant the whole time, faking friendship and admiration for Ryo for no other reason than to improve my own lot in life. You wouldn't forgive someone who had done that to you, would you?"

He said it like a rhetorical question, but his eyes searched Deinol's face, seeking out an answer. And Deinol himself was torn. On the one hand, while he certainly hoped for loyalty from his friends, asking them to die for him was a bit much. Perhaps it was different if you were a prince, but he didn't think it should be. If Ryo and Rana's gripe with Lucius was that he hadn't stayed to fight a doomed battle with them, then perhaps they didn't really deserve him.

On the other hand, he couldn't ignore the way Ritsu was looking away from him, biting his bottom lip. Was Lucius telling him the truth?

Finally, Lucius turned away without an answer, and Deinol felt relief and regret in equal measure. "Ritsu is right about one thing: now that they know I'm here, they'll let me know if they want to see me. Until then, let's see what we can do for the people of this city."

Chapter Nineteen

Araveil

KEL CLUNG TO Hayne's neck, cursing the long weeks of his confinement. His legs would've had trouble gripping her hips in the best of circumstances, but now even his arms had weakened, leaving him barely able to hold on as she ran. But he couldn't afford to slow her down any more than he was already.

"This must be it," Hayne panted, finding the double oaken doors to the underground cells already standing ajar; the other group must have beaten them here. "What's our plan?"

"Ideally, we find three keys," Kel said. "The one to Talis's cell, the one to the vardrath steel cuffs, and the one to the other set, that's keeping her chained to the floor. I know where the door keys are kept, and I know which one it is—there are numbers etched into the handles to help the guards know which one is for which door, and when Selwyn took me and Hywel down here, I made a note of the number. But we weren't allowed past the threshold, and they didn't unlock any of her chains. I didn't get to examine the ring of keys in detail, but I suspect all the keys pertaining to one cell are on a single ring. The only rub is the vardrath steel. The key might be in a separate place, or, in the worst case, Selwyn might have the only copy. We'll just have to see what we can find."

He couldn't see Hayne's face, but he felt the smile in her voice. "Well done, Your Grace. Now we just have to hope enough of Captain Holm's men have made it here."

But when they reached the corridor of cells, they were faced with a grim development. Gerald's men were here all right, but so was a swarm of guards, more than Kel would ever have expected—much more than he'd seen when he and Hywel had last been here. "Damn," he muttered. "I should've anticipated this. Selwyn has such a fanatical obsession with studying Talis, but I never thought she'd compromise her own security to keep her. And she must have, to pack the halls like this even with so many of her people out in the city."

"This isn't safe for you, Your Grace," Hayne insisted. "If I try to take you into that mob, you'll be sliced to pieces."

She wasn't wrong. All told, there weren't more than fifteen people still alive and in combat, with a handful more wounded or dying, but the corridor was so narrow and the fighting so furious that Kel could hardly make out where one body ended and another began, or who was on which side. Still, they couldn't just stand there and wait for a victor to be decided. "The keys are kept in that room," he said, pushing Hayne's cheek so she looked in the right direction. "We can grab them, at least."

The rings of keys were hung on metal spikes that had been driven into the far wall, taking up its whole surface. "Look for number sixteen," Kel said. "The key to the vardrath steel looked different, newer—it must have just been made recently. As for the keys to her other chains, your guess is as good as mine."

Hayne set him down in one corner of the room and did a quick inventory. She found the vardrath steel key first, all by itself on a separate hook, and then lifted the ring for cell sixteen on one finger, showing him that there were several different keys hanging there. "I don't want to hope for too much, but could these be the door and the chains?"

"I don't see anything else that looks promising, so let's hope so. Even if we can't unchain Talis completely, we can at least enable her to use her magic."

Hayne handed him both sets of keys, then hauled him onto her back again. But when she turned to face the doorway, she stopped dead. "What is it?" Kel asked, craning his neck to try to see around the doorframe.

Hayne jerked back as several figures raced by, just a series of blurs in Kel's vision. More blurs followed, and he heard shouts layered all on top of each other, too garbled to make out. "It looks like Selwyn's guards are retreating, and our allies are giving chase."

"Then we're winning," Kel said, his already weary limbs sagging with relief. "And the way to Talis should be clear. Let's hurry."

Though Hayne did her best to obey, Kel could tell that carrying him was taking its toll. As they headed down the corridor in search of cell sixteen, he was struck by the sudden quiet, hollow and empty after so much chaos. Shouldn't he at least be able to hear Talis? Or was he still too far away?

They were passing door number thirteen when they finally heard something, but not from the direction of the cells. It was coming from behind them, a clatter of footsteps that weren't their own.

Hayne turned, and Kel saw two men run into view, both with swords drawn. Two of Selwyn's men—they must have doubled back after their companions had been chased away. They'd had plenty of allies just a few minutes ago, but now Kel and Hayne were the only ones here.

"Your Grace," Hayne said, and he felt her whole body tense beneath him, "I think I may have to put you down, or run."

Kel couldn't leave Talis, not when they were this close. "Do you think you have a chance against them?"

"Perhaps. Should be able to occupy them, at least."

"Then I'll do the rest. Put me down."

Hayne set him behind her and ran the rest of the way forward, slashing wildly at both men to keep them from edging around her. The clang of steel on steel made Kel wince, but he couldn't afford to watch the fight. That would only waste the time Hayne was risking her life to provide him.

It would have gone so much faster if he only had his crutches. But he wouldn't fail. Not here. Not mere yards from his destination. Kel put the keys between his teeth, extended both arms in front of him, and began to pull himself forward, inches at a time.

Normally, his arms were quite strong, since they worked with the crutches to support his weight. But in their newly weakened state, they protested against the sudden return to heavy exertion. His neck protested, too, from being craned at such a sharp angle so he could count the doors as he dragged himself along. He just needed to get the door open. Once Talis was free, everything else would be fine.

The cell number was sixteen, the same as the engraving that marked the key. He could hear nothing from within, not even the faintest sound through the heavy wood, and that terrified him. The last time he'd been here, Talis had been screaming so loudly the door barely muffled it at all. Selwyn wouldn't possibly be so careless as to kill her, would she?

It felt like he was tearing a muscle in his abdomen, but he managed to haul his upper body up against the door and fit the key in the lock. The door swung into the cell, and Kel fell after it, landing hard on the stone floor. When he got his breath back and lifted his head, at first Talis was no more than a dark shape, hunched on the floor in a mass of chains.

His whole body ached by now, but this was the last step. He dragged himself toward her, fumbling for the keys. Better to get the vardrath steel cuffs open first, since those were the ones causing her pain.

As he drew nearer in the dim light, he could see that Talis was lying on her side, curled in on herself, her hands open and limp, sweat lining her all over. She was very obviously breathing, harsh, heavy panting that rattled in her chest, but that was the only sign of life that he could see. Most unnervingly, though her eyes were open and unblinking, they seemed somehow opaque, as if a film lay over them.

She didn't stir when Kel reached for her chains, when he called her name, when he touched her shoulder. She didn't even stir when he fit the key into the lock and opened the vardrath steel cuffs from around her wrists. But as he drew them away, letting them clatter to the floor, she groaned softly, turning herself onto her stomach, her eyes blinking slowly and then more fitfully, as if to clear grit out of her vision. She braced herself on both forearms, using them to push herself to her knees. And then one hand shot out, and she grabbed Kel by the throat, pinning him to the stone under the heavy weight of her chained arm.

Kel struggled to choke out words. "Talis, it's me. Kelken. I came to—"

"The keys." Gods, her voice sounded terrible, like rusted metal against stone. "Give me the keys if you want to live."

"That's w-why I came," Kel gasped. "Don't you—recognize me? I came to free you—I took off the vardrath—"

Talis's grip on his neck didn't ease, but for the first time, she took stock of her surroundings: the open cuffs on the floor, the keys lying between them, the cell door standing ajar. "To free me," she repeated, without any emotion Kel could detect. "Good, then. I'll spare you. Get these off."

For the first time, Kel felt a stab of doubt. He had fought so hard to reach Talis, but he had never expected that *this* was what he would find. But having come this far, what could he do? He could never put those manacles back on Talis again, to force her to be in such pain. And if he didn't get the rest of the chains off, she might really choke the life out of him.

She was chained in two more places, one around each forearm, and Kel had two more keys. It took trial and error to find the right one for each lock, but it couldn't have been much longer than another minute before she was completely free. She pulled herself to her feet oddly, as if she'd forgotten how her body worked, but at least she let go of his neck. "Please hurry," Kel said. "Hayne's still in the hall—she's fighting alone to buy us t—"

He wasn't sure if Talis even heard him. She grabbed him by the scruff of the neck like a cat and dragged him over the threshold, where he could see that Hayne had already dispatched one of Selwyn's two guards and was in the midst of cutting down the second. So she hadn't needed their help after all. "Where is Selwyn?" Talis asked.

"Somewhere in the palace, but I don't know more than that," Kel said. "Can you at least let Hayne carry me?"

"Your Grace?" Hayne took a step toward him, lowering her sword, head tilted slightly in confusion at the sight of him and Talis.

Talis didn't speak a word. She didn't hesitate. She simply raised a hand, and the air tore into Hayne, blood welling up in her arm, her thigh, her abdomen, the side of her neck—too many wounds to track, but enough to stagger her in seconds, her clothes drenched with red. "No!" Kel shouted. "What are you doing?"

Talis didn't look at either of them again, just walked past Hayne as she sagged against the wall, one hand pressed uselessly against the side of her neck, the other flailing with too many wounds to cover. Kel tried to crawl to her, but his battered body was barely moving.

For so long, he had stayed pragmatic, clear-headed, focused. Even before his weeks of imprisonment, when Laen had been killed, when he'd left Dirk and the others behind to die, all the way back to his father's assassination, he had pushed away despair and self-pity, and kept his mind on the future. He had held fast to what he could do in the moment, because he had believed that was the kind of king his people deserved. And he had believed anyone could do that much, even him.

But in this moment, the result of all his waiting and planning and hoping, he could do nothing at all. Hayne was going to die before he could even reach her. And it would be his fault, because he was the one who had set Talis free. Was that what he did all this for? To have the last of his most loyal friends cut down in a needless act of betrayal he didn't even understand?

He willed his mind to persevere, to find him a way out of this. But all he felt within himself was grief, and fury at his own impotence. What was the point of surviving so long just to keep watching the people you cared about die, over and over, and knowing you could do nothing for them?

"No!" he shouted, feebly beating his fists against the stone floor. "Why? Why?" He felt as if everything he'd ever been given, his throne and his title and his father's legacy, had all been stripped away from him, all meaningless. He was just a little boy, crying.

He must have squeezed his eyes shut, because when he felt hands turn him onto his back, he flinched away, startled. But it couldn't have been Selwyn's men come to haul him back; the touch was gentle, and an accompanying voice said, "It's all right. You're all right now." Kel's eyes snapped open. He knew that voice, though he had never expected to hear it again.

It was Cadfael who lifted Kel in his arms as he stood back up, supporting his head and legs carefully. His severe, scarred visage was the same, but perhaps something had melted in the depths of his blue eyes. "Cadfael, you have to help— Hayne is—"

"It's all right," Cadfael repeated, moving Kel with him as he turned. "Look."

A woman Kel didn't know had gone to her knees by Hayne's side—a woman not garbed like a warrior, but wearing a simple faded dress, her long braid lashing the air. She reached for Hayne, but she didn't try to prop her up, or put pressure on her wounds. Instead, she placed both hands on the bare skin of Hayne's face.

Hayne had time for one harsh, rasping breath. By the time she breathed again, the edges of her wounds had lined up, melting seamlessly into unmarred skin. A miracle.

"Hayne." Kel's voice was trembling. "Are you . . . ?"

"She'll be fine," the woman said, but Kel wanted to hear it in Hayne's own voice. She stretched her limbs out cautiously, and then Kel saw her frown, pulling up one sleeve. He knew the long scar that stretched from her forearm to her elbow, sustained when she had put herself between him and an assassin's blade. But the cuts Talis had inflicted had sliced across the scar in several places, and where the woman had healed them, the skin was now perfectly smooth. Instead of one long scar, Hayne was left with several fragments, as if she'd been cut multiple times.

"That will take some getting used to," she said. "But I believe I am otherwise unchanged, Your Grace."

The horrible tightness in Kel's chest finally started to ease, relief making him feel lightheaded and weak. "Cadfael, what are you doing here? Who is this?"

"Questions we'll have to save for later, I'm afraid. Talis did this, didn't she?" He glanced down at the woman with the braid. "Can you tell me where she went?"

"If she was set free of her bonds, I should have been able to sense her presence in that same instant. But . . ." She closed her eyes, inhaling deeply. When she opened them, they were dark with worry. "This is very strange. I can't feel Talis at all—not muted, not distorted, not far distant, nothing. The only other time this has ever happened was with Miken, and that was because he was . . ."

"Dead?" Kel felt Cadfael stiffen around him. "Is that what you think? She's already dead?"

"She wasn't dead when she left here," Kel said. "I freed her myself. She attacked Hayne, and then she made to go aboveground. She wouldn't listen to me at all. I don't know why."

"Then there's no reason to think she's dead," the woman said. "If she was alive and free for that long, and I couldn't feel her, there's a greater chance that something's wrong with our connection. At least that means I should be able to approach her without being affected by her, but it also means I have no insight into what she's feeling right now, or why she would have done such a thing."

"Leave all those matters to me," Cadfael said. "Will you—"

The woman jerked her head at Hayne. "I'll guard the king and this one. Go."

Cadfael put Kel gently into Hayne's arms. "I'm sorry for such a poor reintroduction, Your Grace. I hope you'll give me the chance to amend it the next time we meet." And then he was gone, running back up to the surface, one hand on his sword.

"Are you hurt anywhere?" the woman asked, brushing her fingertips against Kel's forehead. "Just some scrapes and bruises. I can get those for you." And he did feel immediately better, every ache and sting smoothed away. It felt like even the swelling in his legs had gone down, though he was still exhausted.

Even so, they couldn't afford to just lie here. "Hayne, can you walk?"

"I think so." She stood, pulling him up with her. "We should get somewhere safe, Your Grace."

"No, we should find Hywel. He might need us."

"I'll go with you, then," the woman said. "I won't be able to help subdue Selwyn if she's carrying vardrath steel, but I can offer aid to those fighting her."

"No," Kel said again, shaking his head. "If you would protect us until we reach Hywel, I would be grateful. But then you must help Cadfael, not us. If he's following Talis, he'll need it more than anyone."

NOT THAT SHE was counting, but Rhia had definitely marred Ghilan's exposed skin with more wounds than her brother had by now. It was as if the big man were made of stronger stuff than mortal flesh; though his own blood still dripped from his neck and now down his arms as well, he acted as if he couldn't feel the pain. It certainly didn't seem to have weakened or slowed him; he was clearly growing tired, but so was Rhia herself.

Instead of swinging the hammer, he'd taken to thrusting it forward, like a spear. It was a movement he could do a lot faster, though he had to sacrifice the wide arcs of his swings. Rhia was still figuring out how to get around it; she could feel the burn in her muscles, and didn't want to overestimate herself. Ghilan had stopped taunting her, saving all his energy for the fight, but his eager expression hadn't flagged once. It was irritating how much he was enjoying this.

"This *has* been fun," he said, as if reading her thoughts. "A true pleasure for me. But if you want to live, now's the time for you to retreat. You're talented, but young, and you've overextended yourself. You're too tired to keep up the speed you'll need to defeat me."

"So you say."

"So I can *see*. You can't hide it from me. But if you'll only learn from experience, I'm happy to provide."

As if his words had been prophetic, Rhia's muscles screamed in protest at his next thrust, seizing up just when she most needed them to be limber. She stumbled, moving only half the distance she intended to, and not far enough to keep her out of the way.

Suddenly, there was a dark shape between her and the hammer, too big to be Cadfael, and a hand pushing her aside. Rhia still flinched, expecting someone else to be hit, but the only sound was a metallic skittering as a blade brushed against the side of the hammer. It belonged to a *tsunshin*: the same sword Rhia herself wielded, so uncommon outside of Aurnis. And the man who carried it had come off without a scratch.

Rhia had received very little formal training, and used a style largely invented from her earlier lessons and supplemented with more basic and reliable maneuvers her brother had devised. But though she could never have duplicated it, she knew enough to know that this was the true style, passed down through the first school in Aurnis. Whoever this man was, he must be much more than a simple wandering swordsman like her teacher.

Though nowhere near as broad across the body, he was but a couple inches shorter than Ghilan, though he moved so lightly that he seemed somehow smaller than he was. His worn and travel-stained clothes were black and dark blue, a long coat and simple shirt that she suspected hid leather underneath. And he wore a patch covering one eye, an unadorned bit of dark leather with cloth padding sewn into the underside.

He tucked his sword lazily back into its sheath. "Far be it from me to interfere with a duel, but this one seems a little lopsided, no?"

Rhia struggled to catch her breath, to answer him without visibly panting. "If you're making that judgment based on my size, then you're underestimating me more than he is."

"Oh, I wouldn't dream of it," the man said. "I was referring to the fact that he's wearing armor and you aren't."

"You don't need to worry about that," Rhia said. "It would only slow me down."

"Fatigue will do that, too," he replied. "Did your allies leave you here alone?"

She jerked her chin at Ghilan, who looked to still be getting his bearings, hefting the hammer again experimentally. "I've been a match for him so far. And I don't see any allies with you, either."

"Unfortunately, we were separated in the rioting. I thought they'd ventured into the palace, but perhaps—" He stepped forward, making himself the target of Ghilan's next thrust, then sidestepped it and drew his sword in the same movement. "Either way, this is a more pressing problem. I trust them to handle themselves for a few minutes."

"I'm in no need of protection," Rhia insisted, trying to get out from behind him.

"Are you a *shinrian*?"

The question caught her off guard enough that she answered it without thinking. "No, I never—"

"Then you're my junior in the art, and I'm perfectly within my rights to look out for you. One might even say that honor demands it, if you care about such things."

"I suspect I care far more about it than you do," Rhia said.

He grinned. "I suspect you're right."

"Are you quite finished?" Ghilan asked. "I'll fight the both of you at once if you insist on it."

"Admirable ambition," the man said. "But in your current state, a single fresh fighter of competence should be more than enough to—"

He didn't stop talking; Rhia simply ceased to be able to hear his words, as they were drowned out by the unnaturally sudden gale that descended on the courtyard. She raised her arm to keep the loose sticks and leaves from striking her in the face, and when she lowered it again, she saw a woman descending from the heart of the storm, with tattered clothes and matted brown-blond hair. Though the wind seemed to shake the very walls of the castle, it set her down on her feet so gently that it made no sound. Her face was haggard and pale, her feet bare and filthy, but it was her eyes that concerned Rhia most: an empty gray, the pupils wide and unfocused, as if she were looking at some other scene entirely. Her voice was rasping, and devoid of any emotion. "You," she said, and Rhia realized she was speaking to Ghilan. "Finally. You can tell me where she is before I end you."

She could only be Talis, but this was nothing like the way things had been supposed to go, or how Cadfael had described the woman he'd been so desperate to free. Rhia's stomach sank. She couldn't guess the details, but something must have gone very wrong.

She stepped in front of the man, drawing her sword; against this foe, there was no advantage to keeping it sheathed. "Sir, you must trust me to protect you now. Ordinary blades will do you no good in this fight."

She saw no fear in his face, just a smile that reached the one eye she could see. "It's been quite some time since someone has protected me. I shall attempt to enjoy the experience."

FINALLY, SHE HAD reached the open sky, and the wind descended to welcome her, tearing shrubs from the ground by the root, hurling stone tiles through the air like leaves. She had thought it would feel better to be outside and aboveground, that it would give her enough power to drown out the pounding memory at the back of her mind, but it was as if the surface of her skin had turned to ice, or stone. She felt things only at a great remove, or as if they were happening to someone else. The sun hurt her eyes, even from behind a veil of cloud. The scents of grass and metal and blood and fresh earth had lost all their vividness, as if the damp of her cell had permanently stained her senses. The wind roared all around her, but not loud enough.

Once, long ago, she had wanted many things. Now only two were left. She wanted to forget everything, every reason for pain and regret, everything she could feel like spikes in her chest every time she breathed. But before that, she wanted revenge on the ones who had hurt her.

The second one, at least, she knew she could do.

She recognized the big man, Ghilan, and the bright gauntlets he wore, that hateful steel. She did not know the two beside him, a tall man and a smaller girl, but the girl bore the same metal, a slender blade quivering slightly in the gale. If they were of Selwyn's party, then they would die, too. They would all die, every last wretch who had aided that woman in even the smallest way. She would scatter their ashes to the ends of the earth.

The tall man tried to shout something to the girl, but her wind snatched his words away, rendering them unintelligible over its howling. She was so tired of listening to them speak, but there was one thing of value they might know. Selwyn, she remembered. Selwyn was the one she wanted to kill most of all. Ghilan might have been the one who captured her, but it was Selwyn who had tormented her for weeks, who had looked upon her suffering only with dispassionate interest. She let the wind carry her words to them. "Where is the administrator?"

"You've no need to know that," Ghilan said, his little eyes glittering as he tightened his grip on his hammer. "I don't know who let you out, or where you found such bravery, given what I did to you last time. But I subdued you once, and I'll do it again."

Last time, three things had been true that were not true now. The big man had had a squadron of soldiers with him. He had possessed cuffs of the steel to keep her bound. And she had been hampered because there were others there that she had been trying to protect. But she did not need to waste her breath to tell him that. He would learn the difference soon enough.

Ghilan raised the hammer—and dropped it immediately as a hail of broken tile blew at his head, aimed through the gaps of his helmet at his eyes and mouth. He held the gauntlets before his face, and the fragments of stone fell to the ground before they could touch him.

The girl stretched up as tall as she could, and the man beside her bent his head so she could speak right into his ear. He must have agreed with whatever she said, for they moved as one, standing over Ghilan's hammer so he couldn't pick it up without going through them.

So they weren't his compatriots after all—or else they sought mercy from her by betraying him. Either way, they were no longer any concern of hers. As long as Ghilan wore his gauntlets, she couldn't touch him with her wind directly, couldn't slice open his flesh or hurl him into the air. But she could throw almost anything else, and she sent gales whipping through the courtyard in search of possibilities, clods of earth and shards of stone, saplings torn out by the roots, all pulling together at the center, waiting to be sent in whatever direction she wished.

They were all afraid, even Ghilan—she could see it in their eyes. But the girl planted her feet, standing squarely in front of the other man, and raised her sword to the level of her eyes, while he placed a hand on her shoulder to steady her. And Ghilan started moving forward, step by heavy step, fists held tightly in front of his face.

The wind itself couldn't touch him without dissipating, but the objects it carried were solid enough, and she hurled them at him again and again, picking up anything that struck the ground. Most of him was armored, but she slashed at his arms and legs with fragments of hurled stone, adding to the copious cuts she could already see there. She waited for him to get close, to think he could lay a hand on her with those hateful gauntlets. And then she rose into the air above his head, impossibly out of his reach, and battered him anew, bringing every stray scrap of matter in the courtyard against him.

She must have unknowingly sliced some essential strap in two, for the next thing she knew, the metal plate that covered his chest had slipped out of position, bending forward with a groan and taking some of the surrounding pieces with it. If he wanted to readjust it, he'd have to lower his hands from his face, and she wasn't about to waste the opportunity to hit him there.

But Ghilan did neither. First, he stepped out of the armor almost entirely, shedding the plate from his torso and ripping the leather-and-steel patchwork from his arms. And then he ran, still wearing the gauntlets, but leaving the rest behind, even the hammer. She sent as many projectiles as she could after him, but though a couple scraped across his back, none even slowed him down.

Part of her wanted to pursue him—she hated being denied her prey. But he'd be hard to bring to ground with the gauntlets still on, and if she gave chase now, she risked letting Selwyn slip away. And it was Selwyn, above all, that she must destroy. There'd be time for the lackey later, if she even still cared by then.

She turned to the tall man and the girl, still guarding the hammer. "Where is the administrator?"

"Where are the others who went to free you?" the girl asked, in lieu of a reply. "Where's Lirien? Where's my brother?"

At the name *Lirien,* something twinged in her head, some vague recollection of absence. Something had been there before that was gone now. But perhaps that was for the best. She wanted to forget everything, and no doubt that person, whoever they were, would only interfere.

She drew the wind in closer, letting it howl around the other two. "I won't ask you again. Where is the administrator?"

"You can ask as many times as you like," the girl called back, struggling to be heard. "We don't know where she is. It's not my place to go after her. And if you intend to go back inside, you've got to control that wind of yours a lot more than you are right now. Like this, you're a danger to everyone."

She didn't *have* to do anything. She was beyond all that. "You think you can defy me just because you're holding that metal twig, little girl?"

"I think I can defy you because you're not some queen," the girl snapped. "Gods, what did Cadfael ever see in you that made him so desperate to attempt this rescue?"

Another name, another painful twist in her head. She knew that at some point, before she lost so much, the knowledge that Cadfael had cared so deeply about her rescue would have meant something to her. Would have made her feel . . . something. More pain, perhaps, and she was done with pain. From now on, pain was something that would happen only to others.

She drove her wind more fiercely against the pair of them, and the girl lifted her sword, slicing through it and forcing it to dissipate on either side of her. But unlike Ghilan, she wasn't wearing any armor, and the tall man had no protection at all. She could shred the girl bit by bit, or she could focus on him first, to teach the brat a lesson.

But before she could do either, a persistent noise filtered into her consciousness. Shouting. A single word, repeated over and over, as if the shouter sought some specific response, and would continue until he got it.

She turned, and saw a man with a drawn sword, running toward her from the courtyard entrance. Sweat had stuck his brown hair to his forehead, but it couldn't hide the scar that ran down the center of it, ending at the bridge of his nose. His features were handsome, but realizing that irked her, as if she had caught herself admiring a mortal enemy. Was that what he was?

"Talis!" he shouted again, as he drew near to her. She wanted to forget that word, too, more than any other. "Talis, wait!"

She forgot about the girl instantly. She didn't know the girl, but she was absolutely certain she knew *him*. He had . . . done something, something that she hated. Abandoned her, or else come for her when she had wanted to be abandoned. He had made her feel pain, though she was also suddenly sure that he had never physically harmed her. And she had wanted something from him, too. More than one thing, or things that had contradicted each other.

She tried to slash at him, but her wind skirted around his blade as harmlessly as it had the girl's. More of that steel. "Talis," he said, "you've got to stop this."

That again. When would they learn? "I don't have to do anything."

"You do, or there'll be nothing left of you. This isn't who you are. I don't know what Selwyn did to you, but—"

Yes. Selwyn. She'd been in danger of losing focus. "I'm going to destroy her. Where is she?"

"Gerald Holm and his people are handling her. If all goes well, she'll be subdued before you can even reach her. She—"

"*No.*" Again she tried to cut him, but again the sword deflected it. "She's mine, and all her soldiers. I won't let anyone steal her from me. I'll bring down this whole castle if that's what it takes."

"No," Cadfael echoed, but with none of her anger. "You've killed before, when others brought the fight to you, or in return for wrongs they inflicted on you. But even if you could, you wouldn't bring this castle down on all the innocents within."

Where did he find such confidence, to speak as if he knew her better than she knew herself? "Why, are you going to stop me?"

"You're going to stop yourself," he said. "I'm just here to remind you."

"You're here to cage me, with that hateful steel you bear. But I'll never let it touch me again. If you come near me, it won't save you; I promise you that."

He stared at the sword, as if he'd forgotten he held it. For a moment he was frozen, and then he lowered his arm, his wrist turning so the sword hung horizontal in the air.

The girl said, "Cadfael, don't—"

But he did. He swung his arm, and the sword spun away across the courtyard, landing with a definitive clang on the stone.

Now he had no defense against her, and she could have tossed him over the castle walls with a thought. But when that sword hit the ground, a memory invaded her mind: the first time he had thrown it away, that day in the forest, even though she had known what it meant to him. The way he had tried to shield her body with his own, even though a tree could have fallen on them at any moment—even though she was the one who had let the wind slip from her control. She had always thought it was so foolish of him, and yet, at the same time . . .

He took a step toward her, and she snapped out of her thoughts. "Talis, please. Remember how you came here, and what you were trying to do. We're on the verge of succeeding. You don't have to fight anymore."

"No, I . . . I don't believe you." If she didn't need to fight, then what was left? This power was the only gift she'd ever been given, the only thing she had.

"Look around you. There's no enemies left."

"There's you."

"Then fight me if you must, Talis," he said, drawing closer still. "But I never want to fight you again."

As he moved, she raised her hand, meaning to summon a wind that would fling him to the far side of the courtyard. But though it whipped through her hair, it sputtered out around him, fluttering harmlessly against his face. That wasn't the steel, wasn't any trick or theft of her magic; she had simply let it slip through her fingers without meaning to. It had raged without her consent before, but this was the first time it had refused to do so when she wanted it to.

He must have guessed what had happened, for he stretched out his hand to her. But she jerked back out of reach, and finally a blade of wind tore free at her command, slicing through his side just below the ribs.

He slowed, staunching the blood with one hand, but still pressed forward. She cut him again, and then again, shallow wounds to his shoulder and across one cheek. The girl started toward him, but he shook his head. "Rhia, don't. Not with the steel."

Unlike him, she was unwilling to let it go. But she obeyed him, and stayed where she was, shielding the other man from the wind.

Then it was just the two of them, at the center of the storm, so close that no other sounds could reach them. "You cut me once before," Cadfael said. "You remember that, right?"

She could have, probably, if she let herself. But she didn't want to. Memories had been used to torture her for so long.

"You said you intended to kill me, that you thought I had died. But if you truly wanted that, you could have made sure of it, without ever letting me leave that meadow. As small as it might have been, you still left me a chance to live." Even dripping blood, he was calm, extending his hand one more time. "I told you I owed you my death, if you wanted it. That shouldn't change just because I found what I was looking for. If killing me has the power to exhaust your rage, to bring you back to yourself, then do it. But don't lose who you are over this."

Her vision swam and burned, as if she'd stared too hard at a bright light. She felt sick, exhausted, but for the first time since she'd been released from her chains, she wanted to remember who she was. She wanted to know what precious thing he had seen in that person that made him so unwilling to lose her, even at the cost of his life.

As soon as she allowed it, it all came back to her, everything that had happened to bring her to this moment. The choice she had made—twice—to help the Markham brothers. How Ghilan had captured her, and the questions she had never been able to answer to Selwyn's satisfaction. How the boy king had shouted at her helplessly, and the wounds she'd inflicted on Cadfael—and the first wound, the morning after they met, years ago.

She stumbled, her legs suddenly too weak to support her, but Cadfael caught her in the crook of his arm, letting her fall against his body so she stayed upright. She could feel the way his chest heaved, the rapid beating of his heart.

He winced, and she put her hand to his side. "You're bleeding. I—I'm sorry."

"Don't be. Lirien is coming, anyway."

Was she? She wanted to turn her head to look, but her muscles wouldn't obey her. "I'm . . . just so tired."

"It's all right." She could still see his face, devoid of any doubt. "You held fast to yourself through all of this. You'll only get better now."

Talis wanted to say something cutting to pay him back for such overconfidence, but then the whole world started spinning, and she blacked out.

EVERYTHING WENT SMOOTHLY until they found Selwyn. By the time Kel reunited with Hywel and Lirien left in search of Talis, they had already freed Ilyn and Ithan, and Hywel was helping Ithan down the hallway on his one good leg while Gerald gave orders to his men. There was a final cluster of guards in front of the administrator's chambers, but Gerald's people fought through them. Hayne would have, too, but Kel insisted she stay back with him; he couldn't risk her again, not so soon. And then Selwyn was dragged out, each arm in the grip of a Lanvaldian loyalist.

Still holding tight to Hayne, Kel managed to nudge Hywel in the shoulder with his elbow. "They'll probably have you address the people soon. Best think about what you want to say."

"Gods, don't remind me. Any chance they'd let me sneak a quick nap first?" He grinned. "Oh, I should've asked. Are kings allowed to nap?"

"I'll champion the cause if you will. I'm just glad you can joke about it."

"Rather than becoming ill, you mean? I promised you I'd be the king. This is far from the hardest thing that will entail. And don't worry, I'll have some more crutches made for you as fast as the woodcarvers can carve."

"Thanks. Would you believe that being carried everywhere isn't as fun as it sounds?"

"Pardon the interruption, Your Graces," Hayne said, "but it seems the people are in need of guidance sooner than you might have hoped."

Kel and Hywel immediately turned their attention to the front of the crowd, where Gerald was still delegating tasks to his soldiers, Selwyn's vardrath steel rapier clutched in one fist. "We may not be able to organize an execution until tomorrow—I want to give priority to the king's coronation. Survey the cells downstairs; make sure there aren't any security weaknesses I should know about."

Ilyn had been standing at his elbow, but now she spoke up. "We should kill her here and now. This particular battle is over, but those loyal to her are still fighting our people elsewhere in the palace, and probably elsewhere in the city. If we show the remaining traitors her head, they'll know all is lost, and precisely what fate awaits them. If we show them she's been taken captive, we'll only invigorate them with the hope of rescuing her."

Hywel fidgeted under Ithan's arm. "No," he said, "we—"

"Our priority is the safety of the royals, as well as yours and Lord Ithan's," Gerald said. "If we keep her alive, we can use her as a hostage. Perhaps we can get the rest of her forces to surrender."

"To *surrender*? Uncle, you can't possibly accept that. Is there even space enough in the dungeons for all of them? This woman killed her rightful king while he was chained and helpless, and everyone who served her is either a foreign infiltrator or a complicit citizen. They may not be fully as guilty as she is, but not a one of them is innocent. She ought to serve as an example to them."

"No," Hywel said again, louder. "We'll expel any members of the Hallern army from Lanvaldis, and hear any charges that the people of Araveil have to bring against the rest. And Selwyn must live to stand trial, before the whole country, that they may understand all she's done."

Gerald and Ilyn had to squint at him over the distance that separated them, and Ithan disentangled himself from Hywel. "I can stand on this leg, as long as I don't move. You should be with them for this."

Hywel struggled to the front, and without being asked, Hayne moved up a bit, too, so Kel had an unobstructed view. "Your Grace," Gerald said, "a trial could take months to prepare. If she lives that long, those months will see her supporters trying relentlessly to free her. Letting that storm break over us when we don't have to is tempting the good fortune that granted us this slender victory."

"I'm afraid we do have to, Captain," Hywel said. "If I were an anointed king residing in this palace, and she entered it with an army to slay me, her treason would be clear. But we are the ones who stormed this place today, and in the eyes of many, I will be an even less legitimate ruler than she is. She must be brought before the people, alive and in accordance with every proper law."

Kel could see the sense in that, but before he could speak in support, he was drowned out by the metallic scrape as Ilyn drew her uncle's sword from its sheath and laid it against Selwyn's throat, seizing her hair in her other hand. "How could you say that? How could you of all people say that, after what she has done?"

"Ilyn, stand down," Hywel said.

She looked to her uncle. "You know I'm right."

"Tell her to stand down."

Gerald took a deep breath. "You're making a mistake."

"It's his to make," Kel said.

"And it's my job to protect him."

"No." Hywel's fingers twitched. "Either I'm your king, or I'm not. If I'm not, there's no reason for me to be here. But if I am, I won't be some figurehead that you can stop listening to the moment you disagree. Stand down, and tell her to stand down. Or tell me I'm false, or that you're a traitor. But you've got to do one of them."

Gerald sighed. "Ilyn, give me the sword."

"I won't." She could barely hold it steady. "I can't forgive it. What she did to the king—"

"I am the king!" Hywel shouted. His whole body shook as he spoke, as if it was too fragile for the noise that had erupted from it. "He was my brother, Ilyn. Are you going to tell me you feel more at his death than I did, when I saw it with my own eyes? If you betray me now, then you betray him, too!"

For one anxious moment, they were both frozen; even Gerald seemed afraid to move, with the administrator's life so completely in Ilyn's hands. But then she lowered the sword, and he snatched it away, as if to keep her from changing her mind. "I wasn't—I didn't mean—of course you're right, Your Grace. Please, forgive everything that I—"

"You're forgiven, Ilyn. Imprisonment has been hard on us all. The important thing is that you did not do anything you could not undo." Hywel smiled, but his shoulders sagged, and the breath went out of him, leaving him looking tired and small. "Please don't make me raise my voice like that again," he said. "I . . . I don't like it."

THEY FOUND THE courtyard a mess, storm-tossed from Talis's power. But Talis herself was safe, sleeping peacefully in one of the clean patches of grass, and Lirien had closed Cadfael's wounds. Kel was about to ask Hayne if he could retire for the day, too, when the best surprise of all shouted to him from across the open space.

Hayne barely had time to put him down before Alessa had run to his side, throwing her arms around him. Kel buried his face in her shoulder, holding her as tightly as she did him. "What are you doing here? Tell me you didn't sneak in to fight after all."

"No, I promised Hayne I wouldn't. But I got tired of waiting outside the palace. Once a couple of Gerald's people came out to tell us things had gone our way, *then* I snuck in." She grinned sheepishly. "Or forced my way in, more like."

"And you've been all right? You and Hayne weren't hurt after I left you?"

"You mean after you were *captured*?" She shook her head. "I should be asking you that. When we heard Laen had been killed . . ."

"I won't say it was easy," Kel said, because she would see through any attempt at bravado. "But I'm unharmed, and I'm here. At least they kept me and Hywel together."

"I definitely agree," Hywel said, and Kel and Alessa looked up to see him standing a bit awkwardly beside them. "Sorry. I hope I'm not interrupting."

"Of course not." Alessa stood to offer him her hand, though she kept the other on Kel's shoulder. "It's good to see you well. Thank you for protecting my brother."

"Not at all," Hywel said, blushing a little. "In truth, he is the one who protected me. I hope to possess even half of his strength someday. I'll certainly need it, if I am to step into my brother's shoes."

Alessa nodded solemnly. "I'm sure you have many trying days ahead, but if it helps, Hayne and I brought your claim directly to the captain ourselves. Even if it were to be destroyed tomorrow—which I am sure he would never allow—there are hundreds of people who can now say they've seen it with their own eyes. Those who would seek to question your legitimacy will have a difficult fight."

"So I've heard. I owe you more for that than I can express." He rested his other hand over hers, so that it was folded between them. "It's not unfair to say that that piece of paper cost my brother his life, so it provides me solace to know it was able to do some good in the end." He kept her hand in his, but turned his body to admit Kel into their little circle. "Now that I've seen you two reunited, I wonder if I might ask you for one last favor before I set myself to repaying all the ones I already owe. And, hopefully, before I'm summoned to speak to the people."

Kel and Lessa exchanged a look. "What is it?" he asked.

Hywel put one hand to his side, and for the first time, Kel noticed he was wearing a knife there; he must have picked it up from one of his soldiers. "It's . . . well, it sounds a bit silly to say aloud, but it's the matter of my hair. There was a tradition among my people that I read about, from before the Ninists ever conquered Selindwyr. Children used to wear their hair long from infancy, and cut it off when they entered into adulthood. According to those customs, I would've been considered a man grown long ago, from the moment my parents died. But I didn't feel grown, and I wondered if I had lost something, from not being able to participate in such a tradition when I was young. So I grew my hair long anyway, and figured that when I was man enough to cut it, I would know."

He held his braid out with both hands, as if making an offering. "There is no time, anymore, for me to be a child. And so I want to ask the two of you to do me the honor of removing this final indulgence."

Kel looked at Lessa again, and then they shrugged—and laughed at their own casualness. "If it means something to you," Lessa said, "I can't think why we would possibly refuse."

So Hywel sat before them on the grass, and Kel held the braid steady while Lessa sawed it off at the base of Hywel's neck until the whole length of it came away in Kel's hands. She brushed the rest of his hair back from his face, doing her best to shape it into something presentable for the people. "There you are, Your Grace."

"What do you think?" he asked.

Kel hadn't expected to, but he did notice a difference. Without all that hair, Hywel's face looked older, sharper, more severe, the lines of his cheekbones and jaw more clearly visible, as was his gauntness from weeks in captivity. "Not bad," he said. "Could use a good wash, though."

Then all three of them laughed, as if they could still be children for a moment, one final moment on the precipice of something more. And Kel knew he would remember it forever.

Chapter Twenty

Valyanrend

VARALEN WAS, TECHNICALLY, returning to Valyanrend in triumph, but though he had been born in this city, and lived most of his life there, he felt as if he was returning to it as a stranger. The majestic walls, the sprawling districts, the forbidding Citadel . . . they felt somehow novel to him, as if he'd only ever seen pictures to compare to the real thing. He didn't *feel* triumphant, or even as relieved as he would've thought. Despite his bravado with Lady Margraine, he'd spent the whole trip back waiting for something to go wrong.

If anything had, he couldn't see it. She had been a quiet and well-behaved prisoner—so quiet, in fact, that she'd barely said a word the entire journey. If the gears of her mind were truly turning as assiduously as she'd claimed, her scheming had come to nothing; she hadn't tried to escape once. And now they were at the Citadel, where her confinement would be reinforced by another mage, as well as a small army. If she hadn't been able to come up with a plan before, her chances were even worse now.

Varalen had expected an order to take her down to the dungeons, but instead the guards at the Citadel gate claimed Elgar wanted the marquise brought directly to him. And so Varalen found himself once again in the room that had once seated the Council in the days of Elesthene, surrounded by Elgar's maps, with the very subject of so many of their strategy meetings beside him.

She was not cowed, of course—Varalen was beginning to wonder if that was possible for her—but the journey had not done her any favors. Her long hair was tangled, her clothes sweat-stained, and there was a wan cast to her face, no doubt the result of perpetual exposure to the steel collar that Varalen had not dared remove.

Before saying a word, Elgar looked her up and down, taking her in to his satisfaction. "It seems you've had a bit of a fall in standing since last we met, Your Grace."

Lady Margraine blew a strand of hair out of her face. "Was that truly the best you could come up with? You've had *days* to practice, and that wasn't clever *or* humorous."

"And yet I find myself quite entertained."

She groaned. "Oh gods, tell me I'm not going to have to sit through all of *your* gloating after already suffering your little lapdog's. Don't either of you have any dignity? If I'd captured you, I would just kill you and move on."

"Wise advice," Elgar said. "And I'd normally be happy to follow it, but it turns out I have one more use for you before you die. Or perhaps I should say your death itself will be of use to me, if I can achieve it under the right circumstances."

Her eyes narrowed. "*What* circumstances?"

"Ah, it seems I'm capable of holding your interest after all. We'll get to that in due time, but it's bad form to ignore my chief strategist, especially since he's been so busy on my behalf." He held out his hand, and it took Varalen a moment to realize Elgar wanted to clasp his. "A magnificent showing, in Lanvaldis and afterward. I always knew you had such greatness in you."

Perhaps the praise was meant to make Varalen feel important, or accomplished. Perhaps it should have. But all he felt was tired to the bone. "Can I leave her to you, then, Your Eminence?"

"In a few moments. You'll be part of our coming performance, too, so it's only fitting that you should be present to hear of it."

"What do you mean?"

"I'm not sure how much news reached you on the way here, but the Issamiri are forcing their way north at an annoyingly rapid pace," Elgar said. "Which means I'll have to speed up my own plans if I'm to have a hope of defeating them. To do that, I need a way to inspire fear. Not of me, but of what might happen *without* me—of the great and pernicious strength of our foes, and of my ability to bring them low, to keep us safe. Those in the villages of Hallarnon fear the Issamiri, but those within Valyanrend's walls less so—our southern neighbors have never breached them, after all. But now I have something that has terrified our people for centuries, a newly risen threat, long thought extinct. I have a mage."

"Oh, you little *fool*," Arianrod Margraine spat, muscles flexing taut against her bonds for the first time.

Varalen blinked at him, wondering if fatigue from the journey had dulled his senses. "But . . . but you yourself are a mage."

"But my people don't know that," Elgar said. "Why, were you going to tell them?"

Lady Margraine was still seething, and that was so unusual for her that Varalen couldn't help questioning it. "Does the manner of your death truly matter so much to you? Or do you find it some insult to be publicly named as a mage?"

"Mages are returning to this world, Lord Oswhent," she snapped. "Your master and I are hardly the only ones, and I don't doubt more will be born, in greater numbers than in the past. If he follows through with this contemptible plan, empire won't be the only thing he'll restore. Even before magic died on this continent, mages were persecuted nearly out of existence by the same hysterical fears he would so blithely resurrect." She glared at Elgar. "Surely you can see what will happen? Mages will be beaten to death, hanged, cast out even by their families. The younger and less experienced they are, the less adeptly they'll be able to hide their gifts, and the more easily they'll become targets, cut down before they even have a chance to learn or become anything. All the research, the advancements and discoveries magic might bring to this world—all will be snuffed out in service to your selfishness."

Elgar rolled his eyes. "Of all people, you were the last I would've expected to be so melodramatic. Currents that are encouraged one day can be just as easily curbed the next."

"Oh, can they? You think that fanaticism can just be put back in the box when you're done with it? I'm told this building houses four separate libraries, yet you seem to have made no use of any of them."

"It's not as if you'll live to see what comes of your execution anyway." Elgar gave an expansive shrug. "If I were you, I'd try to enjoy your final days while I set the stage for your death. Not that I intend to make them easily enjoyable, especially for someone of your . . . former rank. At least you'll be kept out of the dungeons—I had a peculiar escape from the lower levels not so very long ago, and I can't risk having it repeated. But I'll try my best to replicate the experience of a cell for you, even aboveground."

"Charming. If only you could put that much effort into competent decision-making—you didn't use to have a problem with that." She swayed slightly, off-balance with her hands bound, but soon steadied again. "I don't suspect we'll see each other much after this. So perhaps you can humor my curiosity for a few moments."

Elgar folded his hands, his mouth quirking to one side in a not-quite smile. "If you're saying there's a question you've wanted to ask me, consider me curious enough to hear it."

Her face took on that intent look that meant she was pursuing something with all her focus. "You're the most talented ruler Hallarnon's had in decades. You aren't deranged and bloodthirsty like Gerde Selte, or a vain idiot like your former master. And you're more than simply skilled at maintaining order or capable of leading an army to victory; you actually administrate. You have the care and attention necessary to improve conditions within your territories, and you know how to speak to the people—it's why you've only had trouble with rebellions in the past several years, as the strain of your many wars has taken its toll on the improvements you began with. You have no other rampant desire that I can see—not for money, finery, decadence, pleasure, nothing. So why this one? Why this dream of empire? If all these wars prove too much for you, it will be that dream, and that alone, that caused your ruin. I have tried to see the logic in it, and yet I have found nothing."

Elgar remained very still, yet he did not seem tense. His mouth tugged to the side again, bemused. "Have you yourself never dreamed of expanding your territory?"

"No," she said. "When my father ruled, he fought King Eira for years in a bid to do just that—he had some foolish belief that a scrap of Lanvaldis was ours by right, and Eira was disinclined to give it up. My father never succeeded in winning it, only in getting his own people slaughtered. Yet even if he had won it, the land was rocky and barren, its people poor and unlearned. I never understood what he thought he would have gained."

Elgar stroked his beard. "Well, Esthrades has always been small, I suppose. A dream of holding the whole continent would be even harder to realize from there. But to answer your question, I have, actually, read some history. The great Elesthenian Empire, spoken of with such awe in the Hallarnon of today . . . its leaders might have lived in splendor and magnificence, but on the whole, the place was a riot of mismanagement and excess. So much money to the Ninist leaders, and for what? Their Lord of Heaven had no need for coin. And the Council seats were given to the families of oldest rank, each of the seven only concerned with surpassing the other six, while the lands went to rot around them, ungoverned."

"All true," Lady Margraine said, "and yet it seems to me that only strengthens my point."

"Then you fail to see *my* point. That flawed and broken creation lasted unchallenged for hundreds of years, and left a legacy that will never fade from this continent, not completely. If that's the case, imagine what would come of an empire ruled with competence and efficiency, that cared nothing for gods or bloodlines but only progress, the refinement of a way of life. The kind of pathetic conflict your father had with Eira would be no more, because this entire map of little territories endlessly butting heads would be wiped clean, replaced with one territory working only for itself. It would change the shape of more than this continent. It would change the entire world."

Though he had projected an air of confidence and certainty, Varalen did not miss how closely Elgar watched her, searching for a reaction to his words. She swayed again, mouth twisting in concentration. "The lesson I always took from Elesthene," she said at last, "was not that such an empire should be perfected, but rather that it should never have come to exist in the first place, and should never exist again. It would grow bloated and myopic as a matter of course, not by some accident of governance. And the people of this land are too varied in dreams and desires to ever dedicate themselves willingly to a single way of life."

"For any great undertaking to exist, it must weather the scorn and skepticism of those who believe it can never be," Elgar said.

"You're right, of course. Yet I wonder how much of this land and its people will be left to make up this glorious new world of yours, after you're done tearing them apart to reach it."

"Enough," Elgar said, and it took Varalen a moment to realize he was not telling her to be silent. Enough people, he meant, would be left when he was finished. And Varalen did not doubt that was true, because he did not doubt that if only a dozen people were left in Lantistyne after Elgar's wars finally came to an end, even that would be worth it to him, in exchange for the future he dreamed of.

"Other matters command my attention henceforward," he continued. "But there is one more thing I need from you." His eyes flicked to Varalen, as if he'd momentarily forgotten he was there. "Varalen, roll up one of her sleeves for me, if you would."

It was a little difficult to do with her arms bound, but by the time Varalen had gotten one of her sleeves rucked up past the elbow, he saw that Elgar had produced a small glass bottle and placed it, unstoppered, on the table. He handed it to Varalen, and drew the dagger he always wore at his belt. "You don't have to fill it to the brim, but at least try to get it most of the way."

And why should that, after everything, make him feel queasy? He had maintained his composure while watching Ghilan splinter Seren Almasy's bones, and now he was troubled by a little blood? *I really must be tired,* he thought.

Elgar sliced into the fleshy part of the marquise's arm, just below the elbow, and Varalen held the little bottle to the lip of the cut to catch the blood, wincing when it splashed onto his fingers. Once he was satisfied, Elgar sealed the stopper back in place, turning the bottle to the light as if it contained some rare vintage, or liquid gold. He left the marquise to bleed, and it was up to Varalen to press a corner of his robes to the cut until he was sure it had clotted. She was staring at the bottle, brows drawing together. "That's not very wise."

"I think you'll be surprised at how wise it is." He smiled. "Let me show you what a true enchanter can do with the blood of his foes." To Varalen, he added, "Take her to the room we've prepared. The guards can show you the way."

"If they know the way, they can take her themselves," Varalen said. "If that's all, I'd really like to go see Ryam. You know as well as anyone how long it's been, and I'll feel better once I'm able to make note of his condition with my own eyes."

"I've had my healers examine him very carefully, and they tell me his condition is unchanged since you left. But by all means, go to him if you like." He paced over to his maps, ignoring them completely, and once again, it was left to Varalen to take Lady Margraine by the arm and lead her from the room.

"How much time does Ryam have without Elgar's help, then?" she asked.

"Shut your mouth and go to your cage," Varalen replied.

Chapter Twenty-one

Araveil

As it turned out, Ritsu was right: the prince and his associates could find Lucius if they wanted to. Three days after the riots, the owner of one of the taverns where Lucius regularly went to ask for information came back with a letter for him—by description, not by name. So not only had the people he'd been tracking also been tracking him, they were also apparently much better at it, which was more than a little worrying. Then again, Deinol supposed Lucius hadn't exactly been trying not to be found.

He wouldn't let Ritsu or Deinol have a single glimpse of the letter's contents, just slumped into a chair in the corner of the tavern and hunched over the parchment. It couldn't have been that long a letter, but he just sat there staring at it as the minutes passed, as if it contained a riddle he needed to solve.

Deinol was about to stalk over there and wave a hand in his face when he felt a gentle tug on his sleeve. "Deinol," Ritsu said. "Can I talk to you? Outside?"

Deinol glanced back at Lucius, who seemed not to even have noticed the exchange, still staring at the letter as if it were the only thing in the world. "All right," he said. "Let's go."

They walked across the street from the tavern, and Deinol leaned against the side of the opposite building. "I still want to keep an eye on the door. Have to make sure he doesn't slip away when I'm not looking, and try to meet with them on his own."

"Why are you so determined to go with him?" Ritsu asked.

"Because it seems like it'll be dangerous, and he should have someone there to watch his back."

"It will be dangerous," Ritsu said. "For you, in particular. That's why I want you *not* to go." He pressed his hands together, as if to keep from reaching out. "Please, Deinol, don't go."

It was hard to resist such a sincere entreaty, from such a guileless face. But he couldn't just abandon Lucius, either. "Why will it be dangerous for me in particular?"

"Because you're impetuous, and . . . loud. And you don't seem to have a lot of respect for the way things are done. I'm not saying that's a bad thing, but you'd be walking into a meeting with three of the deadliest *shinrian* in Aurnis. If you have a disagreement that comes to blows, you won't win."

"Well, three on two is bad odds to begin with," Deinol admitted. "But I thought these particular *shinrian* were known for being all honorable. Lucius talks about them like they're the most morally fastidious trio in the world. You really think they'll be so eager to hurt me?"

Ritsu shrugged unhappily. "I never knew them personally—not the way he did. They were respected in Aurnis, but . . . so was he, once. It's clear that people change, or reveal depths of a different color than their surface. There's one thing I know for sure: if he keeps seeking them out, he'll only try their patience."

"Why?"

"Because he betrayed them." There wasn't a shred of uncertainty in that answer. "I don't know the details, but it's clear from everything he said that, however he ran, it was a cowardly act. Perhaps it is different among Hallerns, but I was raised not to pay the insult of showing my face to anyone I had offended in such a way."

Deinol frowned. "Then how can you ever apologize?"

"Unsolicited apologies are for family, lovers, close friends. Not those above you in rank, and definitely not your prince. If that letter were an invitation to come and explain himself, that'd be one thing. But if that were the case, he'd be ecstatic. Did he look ecstatic?"

"I think we both know he didn't," Deinol said. He held onto his head with both hands. "What the hell was the letter about, then? A warning for him to stay away?"

"As to that, your guess is as good as mine."

"Is there any way we can convince him not to go after them?"

"As to *that,* your guess is probably better than mine, since you know him better."

Deinol did know him better, and no, they couldn't. "Do you remember Seth?"

Ritsu bowed his head. ". . . Yes."

"If he'd survived all that somehow—if I found him again, but he blamed me for what happened, and he couldn't forgive me . . . at first I thought I'd never stop trying to earn that forgiveness. That I wouldn't give up even if he ordered me to. But then I thought, that's selfish. That's just for my own sake. If I could know he was happy, and well, even if he never wanted to see me again . . . that would be enough for me. Maybe that's what Lucius wants, too."

Ritsu was still looking at the ground, his whole body tense. "How much is he willing to pay for that knowledge? How much are you?"

"How much would I pay to ascertain the well-being of people who, you're implying, would kill him and me just for showing our faces—"

"They *might* kill him for showing his face," Ritsu corrected. "They'd kill you for defending him."

"Either way, I wish I could understand what Lucius sees in them, if they're willing to treat him like that. If it were me, I'd be content with the knowledge that they lived, and go about my own life without them. I would've thought he'd do that, too."

Ritsu shrugged. "He lost more honor than some people gain in a lifetime. I was never one to care very much about that, but the person he was did. Whatever he says, I'm sure he believes he can gain at least some of it back."

Deinol scoffed. "Oh, please. It's a concept, not some currency to be doled out."

"As I said, I agree with you. I don't hope to understand a person like that."

He kept saying that. "What kind of person was he, back then?"

Ritsu's mouth twisted fretfully—he might not believe in honor, but he seemed to believe in rank, because he still thought he owed Lucius the right to keep quiet about something. "It wasn't just that he was strong—many *shinrian* are strong and still lazy, selfish, reprehensible in any way you could name. Back then, his reputation was of one who worked tirelessly in pursuit of justice. He apprehended criminals for the crown—those who were so violent or otherwise dangerous that no one else dared seek them."

"Criminals?" Deinol frowned, trying to picture Lucius as Ritsu had described him. "That . . . doesn't fit with what I know of him. After all, he *is* a criminal—or at least he was." Was that what he had meant by telling Deinol, back in Esthrades, that he remembered too much of his old life to steal anymore?

"It's true," Ritsu said. "My memories are still muddled in many areas, but I remember him clearly. Sebastian idolized him, more than anyone save the prince. Though I wish I could tell him what a waste that would turn out to be."

"Hey." Deinol folded his arms. "Lucius might not be perfect, and he might not be what you thought, but he's risked his life for me more times than I can count. I bet he never asked for anyone's adoration, and he definitely doesn't deserve your hatred."

"I don't hate him," Ritsu said. "I just don't want either of us to die for him. And if you're determined to keep following him, as much as I don't want to, I . . . I have to part ways with you, Deinol."

The sadness in his face was no less than Deinol felt himself. "But why? Do you think even you will be in danger from the prince?"

"Yes. For the same reason I don't want to tell other Aurnians about the full extent of my curse. The prince will still consider me a citizen of his land, subject to his judgment. And because the things I did undoubtedly resulted in harm to my people and aid to our enemies, he may decide my life is a fitting price for them. I would never raise a hand against my own prince, but that means it is better that I avoid him entirely, even though I would dearly like to see proof that he lives."

He was pensive for a moment, looking down at his feet. "Your friend must know the prince might want to fight him. But I don't think he has fallen so far that he would be willing to kill him, even if they came to blows."

"Kill Ryo?" Deinol asked. "No, I can't imagine that, either."

"Then he must tell himself that his death is an acceptable possibility. He risks his life for his own reasons, for honor or justice or repentance. Reasons that I can't agree with.

"For so long, I didn't get to choose. I thought I knew who I was, why I acted as I did, but it was all a lie. Now that I'm truly able to make decisions for myself again, it can be overwhelming sometimes. But I know I have a chance to make a difference. I'm not going to throw that chance away on some symbolic gesture. You understand that, don't you?"

"Of course," Deinol said.

"And you . . . you won't make the same mistake, will you? If he's going to die, you won't try to save him for the sake of friendship, even though you know you won't succeed?"

"Well, that's . . . ugh." He raked a hand through his hair. "That's harder. Are you saying you wouldn't have done that for Sebastian?"

"Died for him for no reason?"

"No, fought for him because you had to try, even if it seemed hopeless. That's how Seth died, but he *did* save Seren. I don't know if he would've chosen that if he'd known the consequences, but I'm sure he would've done it to save me. I can't show less courage than he did. Do *you* understand that?"

Ritsu gnawed on his lip, but he nodded. "In a way, I suppose that's what I'm doing, too. Trying to show courage because of Sebastian's courage." He extended his hand, palm up, and smiled a sad smile. "Goodbye, Deinol. Thank you for everything."

"Not at all. I'm glad we could help each other." He clasped Ritsu's hand, and dug around in his pocket with the other. "Oh, and . . . you don't have to keep this, but I saw a scribe writing away in the tavern a few days ago and bothered him until he let me borrow his materials for a bit. Thought it might help. Forgive the penmanship."

Ritsu unfolded the parchment, and saw what Deinol had written: Ritsu's name, and as many details as he could remember from the memories Ritsu had shared with him over the past couple weeks. "Ah. Thank you. I'll have to hope I remember to check my pocket if I need it, but it's a good idea." He folded up the bottom flap, and frowned when he saw more writing there. "What is this?"

"We're parting ways now, but it might not be forever. Or even if it is, if you're ever in Valyanrend, and you need help, or a place to stay, you can go there. The Dragon's Head tavern, in Sheath Alleys. Just ask for Morgan Imrick, and tell her I sent you. You can trust her. If Lucius and I survive this, I expect we'll make our way back there eventually, too."

"The Dragon's Head," Ritsu repeated slowly. "Is that where he was from as well?"

"Seth? Aye, he lived there with Morgan."

"Then I hope I get to see it someday. It's probably foolish for someone like me to attempt to plan, but . . . I may get there, with a bit of luck."

"We could certainly use a bit of that, couldn't we?" Deinol clapped him on the shoulder and turned aside, because if he lingered there any longer, he wasn't sure he'd make it back to Lucius. "Let's both try to stay alive till you get there, then. First drink's on me."

Chapter Twenty-two

Araveil

GERALD HOLM HAD insisted on a formal coronation, to ensure the people of the legitimacy of their new king. It had to be done in all haste, and so could hardly have been as festive an affair as some would have liked. But it was still done, and Hywel Markham had become King Hywel Markham Brionel, sole ruler of all of Lanvaldis. And he didn't drop his eyes or blush once during the ceremony, though Kel was sure he must have wanted to.

According to the new king's wishes, Edith Selwyn still lived, though she would languish in a dungeon for the immediate future; they were still mustering up the resources and precautions necessary to hold a trial. Ithan Vandrith had been restored to his family with honor, but though the palace had been thoroughly turned over in search of it, the vardrath steel blade he had once wielded with such pride could not be located. Gerald Holm had been promoted to captain of the Araveil city guard, and took his responsibility for His Grace's safety, if possible, even more seriously; his niece Ilyn had been removed from duty, at Hywel's insistence, until she had been given sufficient time and space to begin to recover from all that had happened. And as for Kel, he found himself cheered and celebrated as he had never been in Reglay. Everywhere Hywel went, he wanted Kel and Lessa at his side, and everywhere he went, he praised their courage, and the friendship they had offered him during such a dark time, to all the crowds that had turned out to hear him speak. "I'm a little worried about what will happen if I become more popular here than I am at home," he had confided to his sister.

But Lessa had taken the opposite view. "There were many in Reglay who were set against you from the start, because our mother was unpopular and they viewed you as an extension of her. This can only improve things. When our people hear your deeds and your bravery being praised here, they will want to claim you for their own, to share in even a small fraction of what you are and what you have done."

And Hywel was giving him the chance to do even more. The moment he was crowned, the nobles of Lanvaldis had descended like a murder of crows, jostling for power and influence in the new king's administration. But Hywel did not want to be beholden to noble houses alone, and had kept debate over his potential decisions confined to an informal and unofficial council consisting of Kel, Gerald, Euvalie Vandrith, the heads of two more noble houses who had contributed the most toward the rebellion, and representatives from four guilds of merchants and craftspeople within the city. Kel was grateful for the recognition, but he had no talent for shouting others down, so he had remained a passive observer through most of the debates.

That changed on the tenth day after Hywel's coronation, when a very tall and very thin woman calling herself Jill Bridger was admitted to speak to the council, and delivered very grave news.

The surrender of Stonespire they had known; even before its citizens were allowed to come and go as they pleased again, those outside the city had seen the Hallern armies entering and passed the message along. But Jill Bridger claimed that something far worse had happened.

"The marquise has been captured?" Gerald repeated. "In Esthrades? But the last news we have of her put her at Adora's side in Issamira. Why would she leave it for a home already under siege?"

"To protect Esthrades," Bridger said. "Or so I can only assume, for her ladyship does nothing without a reason."

Kel was so sick to his stomach with worry that he forgot to be too nervous to speak up. "How did you come by this information? We've heard nothing of it, from the Hallerns or otherwise. If they'd captured someone so crucial to their enemies' cause, wouldn't they want the whole continent to know of it?"

"As to that, I couldn't say, Your Grace. I am not within the mind of the imperator, and never hope to understand him. But I know what I say is true because after I left Stonespire I went directly to Lakeport, hoping to find more allies willing to fight for our country. I found them, but I also found some Issamiri soldiers who were there when her ladyship was taken. They were overwhelmed, and she told them to flee to the port to save their lives."

Gods, that was even worse. "So you don't even know if she's alive? If these soldiers fled before she was taken, how do they know she wasn't simply slaughtered?"

"I asked that as well," Bridger said solemnly. "Not all of their number retreated, and those who lived returned to the spot in the days that followed to try to recover their fallen comrades' bodies. They succeeded in this, and their failure to find her ladyship's body is not conclusive; the Hallerns could have kept it as a trophy, or proof to bring back to their master. But the Issamiri did not find Seren Almasy's body, either, and she would have defended her ladyship to the last. If Miss Almasy lives, I am sure my lady does also."

Kel couldn't say he knew Seren Almasy all that well, but she had seemed to take her duties very seriously, and if Bridger, who must know her much better, was so certain, it was probably all right to hope. But before he could ask another question, Hywel stepped in. "I thank you for coming so far to bring us this news, as sad as I am to hear it. But I imagine you did not come here for that reason alone."

"Indeed." Bridger bowed her head. "I came here to ask for your aid—and now that I know the king of Reglay is here, for his as well. My lady helped you both when you needed it, and without her generosity, you would never have been crowned. I ask that you repay the kindness that was given to you, and help liberate my lady's city from our mutual foes."

Gerald raised a hand. "Now, hold a moment. Arianrod Margraine gave us her aid freely, in exchange for a price we paid, with no other conditions attached. No formal alliance was struck, and we certainly never promised her any of our soldiers—just as we were never given any of hers."

"If I believed you had entered into such an agreement, sir," Bridger said stiffly, "I would have come here to demand your help, not to ask for it. Helping us is the right thing, but many in your position fail to do the right thing every day. There is no reason for you to be any different, save my own hopes."

Euvalie Vandrith laughed, not relenting in the slightest when the captain shot her a wounded look. "I think I like this one, Gerald."

"Well, you would; she speaks on behalf of your own niece. Forgive me for saying so, my lady, but you can hardly be objective in this matter."

"An imperiled niece. That certainly sounds familiar." Lady Euvalie rested her chin on her hand, eyes glittering. "Ah yes, it seems to me that you yourself recently had an imperiled niece—imprisoned with my imperiled nephew, as a matter of fact. And yet, strangely, in that situation you neither viewed yourself as unobjective, nor argued that I was."

"I value your judgment no less than Gerald's, my lady, in this as in everything," Hywel said. "But both of you, please allow me to finish questioning this woman before we start debating the matter." He turned back to the woman in question. "Miss Bridger, can you explain to me why the aid you are requesting is for the city of Stonespire? It's been protected from ransack and slaughter by the terms of your surrender, but even if it weren't, taking it back won't do anything to help Lady Margraine. Shouldn't your aid be primarily for her?"

"Exactly," Gerald said. "And through that logic, if we send soldiers anywhere, it should be to Hallarnon, not Esthrades. We can be that much more certain of defeating Elgar and rescuing her."

"You'll never do *that* in time," Bridger said, as if talking to a child.

Before Gerald had time to be affronted, one of the other nobles spoke up. "Even if we could, our own position is still tenuous. We can't send our soldiers so far west, lest we're retaken."

"*I* know that," Gerald said. "But then I wonder what the young lady would have us do."

"You can't send troops that far west," Bridger repeated. "But Stonespire is much closer, and it's the only major territory the Hallerns hold in Esthrades. We could take it back easily, without any kind of siege. Members of her ladyship's guard are disguised as civilians within the city; they could open the gates for us. I've organized volunteers from Lakeport. I've alerted the militias in a dozen villages, and they'll alert more. Even a few hundred more soldiers could—"

"Could still weaken our own position," Gerald said—to Hywel, not to Bridger. "And I repeat, taking Stonespire back does nothing to help Lady Margraine. Why such urgency? Once the battle in the west is won, she'll have all the soldiers she could possibly want."

"I'll tell you what it does to help her," Bridger said, also to Hywel. "The Hallerns used the siege of Stonespire to lure her ladyship back to Esthrades. She knew that if she didn't give them an opportunity to get at her, they would sack the city in retaliation. And even now that they have her, the city still serves as a hostage." Her eyes flicked to Kel, then back to Hywel. "I'll be frank with you: I expect Lady Margraine has already been taken beyond the reach of armies. At this point, the person most likely to save her ladyship is herself. If she knew her city was safe, she would be free to . . . to do what she can do. It is difficult to speak of, but I suspect you know what I mean."

"Well, *I* don't," the head of the smithing guild said. "I've heard she's a brilliant strategist, but she isn't a fighter. And a strategist can only use their talents when they have men to command."

Kel had, indeed, long suspected what Bridger must be hinting at. The last time he saw her, Arianrod had told him that she had unlocked some of the secrets of magic. She had been purposefully vague about what that meant, but he'd be willing to bet it wasn't some arcane technique, but rather an innate power within Arianrod herself, like the mages of old. But no one else in this room would have an inkling of that, so he cleared his throat. "I've spent enough time with Arianrod to vouch for what Bridger says. I think it's worth it to ensure she's able to use every tool at her disposal." He shot Hywel a look that he hoped successfully conveyed, *I'll explain it to you later, in private.*

"She has been better at fighting Elgar, with fewer soldiers and resources, than anyone could have believed," Lady Euvalie said. "That would be true whether she was Elin's daughter or not. She's worth fighting for, Gerald."

"Everyone is worth fighting for," he replied. "That doesn't mean we can fight for them all. My loyalty is to this ruler, and this country."

"This ruler and this country would do well to help their neighbor," Kel said. "Because of his origins, the continent knows little of Hywel, but leaders and commoners alike will soon form their first impressions. Do you want him to achieve a reputation as a king too weak or callous to help those who have helped him in turn? Who would want to become his ally then?"

"He's certainly helped *you*," the last noble said, "though it remains unclear to me precisely how you have helped him. You're a king without a kingdom, a green boy—"

"Kelken is a king of courage and principle, and he helps me by the example he sets and the counsel he provides, which is reasoned well beyond what his years might suggest," Hywel said, while Kel tried not to look embarrassed. "And it is that counsel I want to hear now. I know what Lady Euvalie thinks; I know what my captain thinks. Allow him to finish without interrupting him."

Kel already knew what he wanted to say, so he could face so many eyes turned toward him without faltering. "It's as Bridger says. Arianrod helped me when I had nothing and nowhere else to turn. She's been shouldering the burdens of this whole continent much longer than Hywel or I, and her wisdom makes my own seem truly that of a child. In this matter, I don't see any conflict between the right thing and the smart thing. Both my head and my heart have come to the same conclusion."

Hywel nodded. "Your mind in this is as my own, Kelken. 'A king without a kingdom, a green boy . . .' So Laen and I were when we first came to her. If she had dismissed us as such, none of this would have been possible. So if the rest of this continent is waiting to see what kind of king I'll be, I'm prepared to show them my own courage, and my loyalty."

"They may also take you for naïve, and easily swayed," Gerald warned.

"Then let them underestimate me, and be surprised. Selwyn did, after all." He turned back to Jill Bridger. "Miss, in the coming days, please present us with a thorough list of everywhere we may pick up Esthradian allies, and every place you know Hallern soldiers to be."

"And I'll come up with a list of candidates to lead this offensive," Gerald said, loyal even in his disappointment.

"I'm happy to review them," Hywel said, "but they can only be second in command. It's only right for me to lead this offensive myself."

Amid the uproar in the council chamber, only Kel and Hywel remained calm. Their eyes met, and perhaps it was all the time they'd spent alone in a cell together, but Kel knew they understood each other perfectly.

"In that case," he said, "please allow me to come with you."

Hywel smiled. "I wouldn't have it any other way."

THOUGH SHE WAS free to move around it as she pleased, the protectors of the new king had insisted that Talis remain in a cell for three days, until they were sure she was fully in control of herself. She was furious about it, and more furious still because she couldn't truly blame them. So she had spent the entire three days brooding, left the cell after the allotted time feeling no better, missed Hywel's coronation entirely, avoided as many people as she could since, and been, if she was honest, afraid to use even a little of her power, and afraid to tell Lirien and Voltest that.

She should've known that Cadfael would interfere. Again.

He cornered her on one of her walks around the city, as she attempted to reaccustom herself to so many people and so much noise. He fell into step with her as she turned down a side street, so naturally and unobtrusively that Talis would have felt like a truly pathetic coward if she had tried to run. So there was nothing for it but to walk beside him, and wait for him to tell her what he wanted.

"My sister's alive," he said at last. "Elgar lied about her death."

"We've met," Talis said. Did he think she'd been too addled to remember? "I can see the resemblance."

That made him smile, a sincere and open smile. Like she'd complimented him. Like it *mattered* to him that she'd complimented him. "Really? Most people say we look nothing alike."

"You don't," Talis said. "I was referring to the stubbornness. And the insistence on getting involved in things that aren't your business."

"Trust me, when it comes to that, I learned from her."

He was silent after that, and stayed silent until Talis grew so irritated she broke it herself. "Well? There's no point in pretending you just happened to catch sight of me. What business of mine are you here to get into now?"

"I haven't decided yet. I don't suppose you'd do me a favor and tell me what business of yours there is to get into?"

Talis groaned. "Did you just make a joke?" When he didn't take the bait, she waved a hand through the air, as if to dispel the seriousness from what she was about to say. "You were there. You saw the mess I made of things. Is it any surprise that I don't want to face any of the people I might have hurt, or present them with my utter lack of excuses?"

"It seems to me you have plenty of excuses," Cadfael said. "Long imprisonment; torture the likes of which most of us can barely conceive; the burden of even having this power in the first place, that you've had to live with for so long. But if those excuses—what I would just call *reasons*—aren't enough to satisfy you, then they probably aren't worth very much. Yours is the opinion that matters, after all."

She snorted. "My opinion isn't the one that determines whether or not I get locked up again."

"But it is the one that determines whether or not you can live with yourself," Cadfael said. "Prisons can come in many forms."

"Oh, no. What the hell happened to make *you* talk like this?"

"If you're asking what's on my mind, I'm happy to tell you. I have no secrets from you." He drooped a little. "I asked Yaelor to appear to me again after I freed you, and to decide then whether I was worthy of some secret he knows about me, something he's always refused to tell me. Even if his mind remains unchanged, I thought he'd at least say so to my face. I thought . . . it sounds foolish, but I thought we had a deal. An understanding."

Despite all the evidence that Cadfael was telling the truth, Talis still wished she could disbelieve the existence of this Yaelor, simply because she didn't like it. There didn't seem to be any way to prevent these beings from observing them, from knowing *everything,* and though Cadfael seemed to have reconciled himself to being judged by Yaelor at every turn, Talis couldn't think of anything she'd like less. "So you haven't seen him since leaving Eldren Cael?"

"Exactly. It's strange. He seemed to approve of the idea, and he's definitely someone who prides himself on keeping his word. I know I shouldn't claim to have grasped the personality of someone who isn't even a person, but in some ways I think these spirits—if that's truly what they are—are even more rigid than humans. We can be many things mixed together, but they are only one thing, repeated forever."

"Well, he can't die, and he can't be harmed, and he can be anywhere he wants to be, at any time," Talis said. "If he wanted to appear to you, what could possibly stop him?"

"As far as I know, only the rules he's set for himself—the deal he made with the others like him. But if my proposal violated those rules, I think he would've told me at the time." He shrugged. "It's useless to obsess over it. If he's washed his hands of me, I should attempt to do the same."

Talis agreed, but his phrasing brought to mind another question, one *she* had tried in vain not to obsess over. "Why haven't you washed your hands of me?"

"What do you mean?" Cadfael asked.

"You tried to take me captive, unjustly, and I know you regret it. But we must surely be even by now. I dealt you a wound that nearly killed you, but even after that, you wanted to travel with me, to help me. You came to Araveil to free me, and you let me nearly kill you a second time in the process. And after all that, here you *still* are, trying to understand me. I can't be worth this much guilt."

Cadfael looked down, and though he didn't blush, she realized that he was embarrassed. "No, I . . . it wasn't about guilt, and I never even thought about . . . evening the score between us, or anything like that." He hesitated. "Well. Only in one way. It's selfish, but I didn't want you to hate me."

Talis curled her nails into her palms. She didn't want to be affected by his words, and tried to stifle the emotions they raised. But he was looking at her, waiting for an answer, and she was too rattled to come up with a good lie. "I don't hate you. I . . . haven't hated you for a long time. I still think you're annoying in multiple ways, but you're not the person that you were. I'd have to be an idiot not to see that."

Cadfael smiled. That kept unbalancing her, too, that she could make him smile when she was trying to do the opposite. "What's annoying about me?"

"You want the whole list?"

"Why not? Or is it so long that you have to set aside time to go through it with me?"

"You really have to stop trying to make jokes." She gave a put-upon sigh so he would know she was doing this reluctantly, and started counting on her fingers. "You're rude, you're dour, you're stubborn, you have no idea how to talk to anyone—"

"Wait, wait. Aren't those all things that are also true about you?"

"What's your point? If you wanted me to limit the list solely to flaws you have that I don't, you should have said." She started counting from the beginning again. "You disdain most people, but you're still so nosy. You're selfish until you suddenly *aren't,* and then you're willing to put yourself in danger almost endlessly. You try to shut yourself off from feelings, and yet you seem to want me to feel all of mine—"

"I don't try to shut myself off from feelings," Cadfael said. "I just don't have a lot of them, most of the time. I try not to *act* on my feelings, or at least not to act without making sure I've thought it through, because my sister always acts on her feelings and never thinks it through, and it always gets her in trouble, and one of us has to be responsible. But I feel all kinds of things when I'm around you. Maybe that's why I want you to feel yours, so we can be the same."

"You feel things like what?"

He touched his face, not closed off, just thinking. As silly as it seemed to believe it, maybe he really didn't have secrets from her. "That we're similar. That perhaps you could understand me. That I *want* someone to understand me, when I didn't think that mattered to me. That I want to understand you—all the things you're not telling me. That we could help each other be more . . . something. I'm not sure yet. Better, maybe."

"I'd like to believe that," Talis said. "I just don't know if I do."

"Well, we could try, at least. If you'd agree to be around me a little more. If you'd open up to me."

"To be around you more? But you aren't staying here, are you?"

"It doesn't seem that way. I thought Rhia might want to protect Hywel, or help liberate Esthrades, but she's set her sights on taking the fight to Elgar directly. We'll be heading west—to Valyanrend, if it hasn't been besieged by the time we get there. But couldn't you come with us? You don't have to fight anymore if you don't want to, but you could still travel with us. Or is there something else you wanted to do?"

The truth was, Talis hadn't had the faintest idea where she was going or what she wanted to do. She didn't like the idea of trotting around after him like a faithful dog, but neither did she like the idea of letting him walk away, and all their business remaining unfinished. "I was planning on taking advantage of finally having my freedom again, knowing I'm owed a favor by my new king. Traveling with you doesn't preclude that, as long as I'm free to leave whenever I wish."

"Of course. I can't promise I won't ask you to stay, but I would never force you to."

"And your sister won't be disagreeable to me?"

He laughed. "No, I should think it far more likely that you'll be disagreeable to her. But I expect she'll take it well. Rhia has a very cheerful disposition, so long as you don't offend her honor."

"And then . . ." She sighed. "Lirien. That's the bigger problem. Lirien will be coming, too, won't she?"

"Lirien?" He obviously hadn't thought about her until now. "I honestly couldn't tell you what she'll decide to do. But if she does come along, it'll be for Rhia, not me."

LIRIEN ARVEL WASN'T sure what she wanted to do.

Normally, that was the opposite of a problem. She used to go wherever her whims led her, the world a blank canvas perpetually unfurling before her. Jocelyn Selreshe and Edith Selwyn had brought a halt to those days, but now the two of them had finally been rendered harmless, to *wardrenfell* and everyone else. Now that Talis was free, the immediate danger she, Voltest, and Lirien might have posed, to others or themselves, had been taken care of. They still had to coexist with their magic out of balance, as they had since Miken's death, but perhaps coming together in pursuit of a single goal had helped, for Lirien hadn't felt any irregular emotions since Talis had been freed, and even her awareness of the other two felt a bit dimmer.

She could continue fighting the threat her home country posed to the rest of the continent, whether by accompanying Rhia and Cadfael or striking out on her own—or perhaps even alongside Talis and Voltest, depending on how they felt about the matter. But she didn't *have* to do that. Although the fight against Elgar could use her power, it was also important for her to retain control of herself, and that meant avoiding situations that would cause her too much anger or pain. Killing even those few soldiers in the retaking of the palace had made her feel awful enough, but she also wanted to hold on to that awfulness, to keep from sinking into that state where she couldn't feel that anything was awful at all. If she decided that it would be safest for her to go back to her old nomadic life, who could stop her? She could see the world at her own pace again, adventure and explore the way she hadn't for months, feel the peace that came from living solely for herself.

She could do any of those things. And that was the problem. Each path had its own advantages, and its own drawbacks. And she'd been sitting in this meadow outside Araveil for half an hour, but the quiet had not, as she'd hoped, made it easier to think, only easier to doze off in the sun, devoid of resolutions.

"You know, when people have a weighty decision to make, they often talk it over with others."

Lirien jerked up to a sitting position, only to find someone else already sitting beside her. Someone else, but not a person, for this was the same woman who'd been haunting her steps since that little village in Esthrades. The wind rustled her long hair about her face, but when Lirien reached for it, her fingers passed right through the strands. Her eyes were green, and smug, and she hated them immediately.

"Go away," Lirien said.

The woman—or spirit, or whatever she was—pouted prettily, as if she were posing for some bizarre portrait. "I don't know what I could possibly have done to merit such coldness. All I did was make a suggestion."

"I heard. Small problem: I don't trust anyone else's opinion as much as I trust my own. And that goes double for you. If you really are this Amerei, then you're the reason Rhia's stupid brother made my life a constant irritation on the way up here."

"No, Yaelor's the reason for that. *I* never told Cadfael to be wary of you. I never told him anything at all, in fact."

"So you're going to say Yaelor lied? Cadfael claims he isn't capable of that."

"Oh, he isn't," the spirit said. "The oceans would boil before that sanctimonious oaf would condescend to bend the truth even a little. But it's just as you told Cadfael: just because he's fond of Talis, and Talis disapproves of you, that doesn't necessarily mean she's right and you're wrong."

"Ah. So Yaelor doesn't like or trust you, but it's a terrible misunderstanding, and you've been unfairly insulted? Or *you're* the hero, and he's the villain?"

"Neither of us is anything of the kind, or ever could be," Amerei said. "We can only be what we are. My being encompasses lies, but his does not, and he cannot see the value in what I am any more than I could for him. Lies can spare others pain, or win over those you admire, or become necessary in pursuit of a long-desired goal. Sometimes you don't mean to lie at all, but delude yourself: because the truth hurts too much, or because you are too dazzled to see it. I can be all these things, though I am also the truth that shatters such illusions beyond repair, the truth that seeps through the cracks of every wall built to keep it out."

"And that all sounds very grandiose," Lirien said, "but it doesn't make me trust you a whit more. Why have you been following me all this time?"

"Dearest, I follow everyone. It's unavoidable, when you exist everywhere at once. I was simply letting you *know* I was following you. Consider it a courtesy."

"I won't consider it anything of the kind." Lirien pushed to her feet and paced a circle in the grass, while the spirit watched her with amusement flickering in those infuriating eyes. "You want something. Tell me what."

The reply was immediate and shameless: "I want you to do me a favor."

"No."

Amerei clapped a hand over her heart, with a deep and dramatic sigh, but Lirien knew she wasn't put off in the slightest. "You don't even wish to *hear* it?"

"I don't even wish to be speaking to you. If you had any solidity, I'd have struck you by now."

Amerei clicked her tongue. "That really isn't wise, dearest. You distrust me because you've heard I am selfish, but I know you're selfish, too. It's one of the reasons I like you. You've simply assumed that if I gain, that means you must lose. In reality, if you lose, it is very likely I will lose as well. Shouldn't that make us friends?"

"Name one single benefit I will obtain by doing as you ask," Lirien said. "Ten words or less."

Amerei tapped her chin; she actually seemed to be poring over her ten words with some enthusiasm. "The chance to influence the fate of this continent," she said at last. Then she smiled, taking all the gravity away from that statement. "Nine words. I just made it."

The tenth word forced its way past Lirien's clenched teeth: "How?"

"I could direct you to a certain individual, currently suffering from wounds only your gift is strong enough to heal—an individual whose heart's desire is impossible to achieve as they are now. You could choose to change that. And if you did, I believe the continent itself would ultimately change."

"From what? To what?"

Amerei shook her head. "That is more than I can tell you."

"Why am I not surprised?" Lirien threw up her hands. "If that much is forbidden, how is everything you've said already not forbidden? How is your request itself not forbidden?"

"Because, while we agreed not to try to steer events to suit our own whims, we *can* intervene on behalf of another of our number, provided no others object. In doing this favor for me, you would actually be helping me help Asariel."

"And what does Asariel want?"

"The same thing we all want," Amerei said. "To find ourselves in the hearts of mortals. To make them burn with the same flame that gives us life. One of Asariel's favorites is probably going to die, and if that happens, her influence will be weakened, and much that might have been learned will be lost. That is something she cannot abide."

"So you want me to save this favorite?"

"No, that would be impossible for you. And even if you could, that particular mortal means no more to me than any other."

"But the one you want me to heal does?" Lirien guessed. "And accomplishing that will somehow help you and Asariel both?"

"I don't bother with favorites, you understand," Amerei said. "Why would I, when I want everyone? But I will confess a weakness for those who have done much in my name, and this one will do much, much more, if only given the chance. I would be greatly discontented to see that chance snuffed out, along with all the glory it would bring me. Surely that is understandable, and not overly contemptible? At least one life is saved, possibly two, Asariel gets a way to bring knowledge that was lost centuries ago back into the world, and you and I get to feel important. Oh, and your tyrant's dreams of empire might die. But that's secondary, and not guaranteed. That man does have a great deal of advantages, after all."

"It would weaken Elgar? Why the hell didn't you mention that to start with?"

"Because that's not what you really care about," Amerei said, with a poisonously sweet smile. "Or have you traveled with that girl so long that you've confused her goals for your own? I'm sure Yaelor will be thrilled."

"I haven't confused anything," Lirien snapped. "If you know me, then you know what I want most. My freedom, the chance to explore this world and all its beauty as I wish. A world soaked in blood and covered in ash has no beauty to offer me. And a world in chains would confine me as much as anyone." She glared at the spirit. "What about you? Old Lantian virtues, Adora said. Yaelor stands for courage, and if this Asariel cares about knowledge and learning . . . wisdom, or something like it. But what does that make you?"

"You really haven't guessed?" Amerei laughed. "Then I couldn't possibly tell you. But if you do as I've asked, perhaps you'll be able to figure it out." She stood up, closing the distance between them, those green eyes glittering. Yaelor had told Cadfael that a spirit's appearance was determined by the person looking at it. So why did this one have eyes so disconcertingly similar to Lirien's own?

"Don't flatter yourself," she said. "I don't have anywhere near that much curiosity about you, but if saving this person for you will damage Elgar's prospects, then I'll do it. Not for you and your *glory,* but for myself."

Amerei opened her mouth, but Lirien held up a hand. "One moment." She curled her fingers into a fist, and lashed out with all her might, aiming right at the center of Amerei's face.

Her hand passed through air, without even the sensation of a breath of wind against her skin. The spirit was still standing in front of her, just a little bit more to the left, with a disapproving frown on her immaculate face.

"Just checking," Lirien said.

TALIS GROANED, RESTING her chin on her folded arms. "I can't believe you're actually going to do it. I know we disagree on almost everything, but I thought you'd want to play the servant as little as I do."

"That's as true as it ever was," Lirien said. "I don't want to do it at her request, but I suspect it might still need to be done. And if I didn't suspect I might need help to do it, I wouldn't have mentioned it to any of you in the first place."

She looked around the rickety table, the most out-of-the-way spot they could find in the tiny tavern. Talis, Lirien, Cadfael, Rhia, and Voltest only just managed to fit around it. "I'll come with you, of course," Rhia said. "If someone's in pain, we should try to help them, no matter who they are. Well, as long as they won't pose a danger to you if you heal them, but this spirit didn't make it sound that way."

"From a being that lies, that means very little," Voltest said, beating Talis to it. "Of course she wants to make her errand look appealing to you. We don't even know if this person truly exists, not to mention whether healing them won't just cause more trouble, for us and the world."

"If we go there and we don't want to heal this person, for whatever reason, I just won't heal them," Lirien said. "All I'm saying right now is that I think it's worth investigating. I know it's something of a detour for those who were headed directly to Valyanrend, but it's not terribly far out of the way, and you know how fast I can heal. We might actually do some good, and even if we don't, I don't see how it's a huge inconvenience."

"I agree," Rhia said firmly. "And I'm going either way."

Cadfael met Talis's eyes, and spread his hands helplessly. "If your mind can't be changed, I'll go, too."

"Wonderful," Lirien said, rolling her eyes.

"*My* mind can't be changed, and I'll be staying far away from it," Voltest said. "Talis?"

No doubt he thought he already knew her answer, and asking was just a formality. But Talis herself didn't know her answer. She was stuck looking at Cadfael, and remembering all he had said—and all it had made her feel, the good and the bad.

"It's not for me," she said at last. "Lirien should have enough support if something goes wrong, and I just . . . want to stay as far removed from these spirits as I can." Cadfael ducked his head, trying to hide his disappointment, and she bit her lip. "But mark the place out on a map for me," she blurted, "and I'll meet up with you after it's done, one way or another. We can head for Valyanrend together, assuming you're still going."

Lirien's and Voltest's raised eyebrows were predictably annoying, but Cadfael's obvious relief drowned them both out. So maybe she had decided, after all.

Chapter Twenty-three

Valyanrend

IT WAS ONE of the few days Morgan had intended to spend actually tending the bar, and nothing else. She'd even assured Braddock he could take the full day to do whatever he wished, anywhere in the city, with no need to ensure he could be contacted instantly. So of course, to punish her for daring to show consideration to a man who'd worked so hard on her behalf, she'd only gotten as far as breakfast when Marceline burst through the door, red-faced and breathing hard.

Roger, her only customer at that hour, popped the end of a slice of bacon into his mouth, licking his thumb. "See what you get for giving your man the day off?"

"My thoughts exactly," Morgan grumbled. "What's the trouble, monkey?"

Marceline leaned her hands on her knees, struggling to draw breath. "'S . . . a swindle."

Roger bent his head toward her. "Did you say a swindle? You can find a dozen of those within walking distance every hour of every day—most of 'em originated from right here in Sheath. That can't be what's got you so agitated, can it?"

"Aye," Marceline croaked, noisily drawing air into her lungs. "It's Elgar— Elgar's swindle. We've found out how he's going to disseminate the enchantments. You've got to come quick—they're setting up in the Fades now. We can make it if you hurry."

Morgan pinched her nose. "I can't leave the tavern. I've got to—"

"I'll mind it," Roger said. "I've done it before, and this time won't be for long."

"You wouldn't rather just go in my place?"

"I wouldn't, actually. Unless you'd like to lend me that dagger?"

"Point taken." She practically vaulted over the bar. "We'll report back. Come on, Marceline."

It didn't take ten minutes to reach the Fades, where a robust crowd was forming a ring around a little wooden table that had been planted in the middle of the street, with one of Elgar's soldiers standing self-importantly on either side of it and a man in blue-black robes behind, waving a glass vial of something Morgan couldn't make out.

"His Eminence long held his suspicions," the man in the robes was saying.

"The devastation the marquise inflicted upon our armies, no matter their skill, their courage, their numbers . . . it didn't seem natural. He had no way to prove it before, but he passed the intervening time with research, turning over the great libraries of the Citadel from top to bottom. And now that Lord Oswhent's cleverness has delivered Arianrod Margraine into our hands at last, His Eminence has the proof he sought."

"Talia said a couple of her parents' apprentices saw the first performance in Speaker's Square this morning," Marceline whispered. "Elgar did the speechifying at that one, but not the demonstration. If it stays the same, you'll see why."

The man in the robes bowed his head. "His Eminence pondered long on what to say to his people. He did not want to induce panic, especially not when he remains confident that our victory against even the most wily and nefarious of our foes is at hand. And, after all, the threat the marquise of Esthrades once posed has now been quelled; she is confined in the Citadel, where she will remain until her execution, to which you may all bear witness. But then he considered that it is unlikely that woman is the only one of her kind. Better that our people know the danger now, that they may be prepared against future threats."

"One of *what* kind?" someone in the crowd demanded.

"One of what kind indeed, my friend," the man said, nodding sagely. "I'm sure you've all heard the stories, just as I have. Centuries past, there lived those who possessed more power than any one human ought to have. And they could use that power in secret, to kill or influence from the shadows. Magic, they called it. We all believed magic was dead for good, so His Eminence knew this city would be full of skeptics. Arianrod Margraine, a mage? Impossible. So I'm here to show you the proof His Eminence found, just as he found it. First, behold an invaluable artifact: vardrath steel."

He took a piece of metal out of his pocket and held it up for the crowd to see: a flat circle, like a coin with no insignia. It gleamed in the morning light, bright enough to see your reflection in it.

Morgan caught her breath. "I think that's real vardrath steel."

"If there are any scholars among you," the man continued, "you may have read that vardrath steel was used as the best weapon against mages. It could identify them, no matter how they tried to hide. A mage cannot bear the touch of the steel against their bare skin—a sight you will witness for yourselves soon enough. But in the meantime, this vial of the sorceress's blood will have to suffice."

Morgan watched as the man laid the circle of metal flat on the table and carefully unstoppered the vial. He let a single drop fall—and when it struck the steel, it hissed into steam, dark and faintly acrid.

Some in the crowd gasped, but many others frowned in confusion, or simply stood there, stoic and unconvinced. But the man in the robes did not wait for their approval. "His Eminence's research did not stop at this. He could not rest, knowing such a threat existed, without finding a way to combat it. And he is on the very brink of success. The fruits of his experimentation have already been tested to perfection on His Eminence himself and a select few volunteers, and he is working tirelessly so that one day, soon, protection against arcane influence will be available to every Hallern citizen who wants it. He wishes his people to take heart, and wait just a little longer. But be vigilant, for the truth is clear: magic is once again in our midst."

He and his assistants packed up their little table and moved on, brushing away the onlookers and their questions. Left alone, the crowd began asking those questions of one another, firing theories back and forth. But while they were busy debating, Morgan and Marceline slipped away—straight back to the Dragon's Head, to describe the scene for Roger.

After they had finished, he sat for a while, twirling a stray silver coin between his fingers. "He's playing a risky game here. He wants to stoke the people's fear of mages to make them more dependent on him to protect them, but he's a mage himself. He must be quite confident that knowledge will never get out. He even revealed the truth about vardrath steel to the whole city—it *can* be used to identify mages, including him."

"He has every reason to believe we—that is, the Fang—know about vardrath steel already," Marceline pointed out. "For all he knows, we're on the cusp of telling everybody how it works anyway—which we probably would have done, after securing as much of it as possible for ourselves before the price went up. If he thought it was unavoidable, it makes sense to reveal it himself; it protects his identity as a mage precisely *because* it doesn't seem to make sense for a mage to reveal it."

"There's a lot that doesn't make sense to me about this, I admit," Morgan said. "But one thing stands out to me in particular. That trick with the blood and the steel—do we think that was genuine? Lord Vespas never said anything to me about a reaction to the blood of a mage when he sent me the dagger. And we've seen the steel cause smoke before, but only because of the intense cold it can emit. That smoke looked different. Like it burned."

"Aye, I'd be willing to bet it was a trick," Roger said. "Remember, the charlatan is a mage himself. He has access to as much of her blood as he wants, and I'm sure he can enchant it in a thousand different ways."

"But we can't prove that to the people," Marceline said.

"Aye, and he doesn't need all of them to be afraid, or to believe. Only enough." Morgan drew her dagger, staring at the blade. "It was bad enough when we thought he was going to restrict his influence to those he'd recruited. Now he's preying on the whole population." She tested the blade's sharpness against her thumb. "Or its most capable members, at least. If he's going to offer his 'protection' even to babes, he's truly depraved."

She sheathed the dagger, and Marceline slumped against the bar. "We were hoping we could convince people of what Elgar was doing, but with this muddying the waters . . . this is bad, isn't it?"

But Roger stayed calm and composed, a grim smile on his lips. "Not at all. He's just made the worst mistake he could make, as far as I'm concerned. He doesn't know it, but he's challenged me to a swindling contest—his product against mine. And if there's one arena in which I refuse to lose to him, it's in what I do best."

Chapter Twenty-four

Hallarnon

At the first strategy meeting of the morning, Adora assumed she'd heard the worst news of the day. They were close to the position her uncle had wished them to take up, but they still needed to draw closer to Valyanrend before he deemed it wise to disperse into the forest. They were a score of miles distant . . . and had been so for days. Elgar had mustered up his largest army yet to attack them—using soldiers he'd pulled out of the east, Amali suspected—and they'd had time to erect a series of wooden palisades, blocking the Issamiri advance. They couldn't burn the things—they'd reduce the whole forest to ash—but they hadn't been able to successfully fight around them, either. Neither Adora nor Vespas was content to simply throw their people at the walls until they overcame them. But if they'd been stymied by wooden constructions a handful of feet high, what would they do when they encountered the massive stone walls of the Hallerns' capital city?

"Well," Vespas joked at the meeting, "I suppose we can have a little bit of sympathy for the Hallerns now. Turns out an offensive war *is* harder to fight than a defensive one."

"When we chased them off under your father, we didn't go far beyond the boundaries of the Curse," Amali said, as if trying to console her. "We didn't need to. Our army has already gone farther now than Jotun ever ventured."

"But not farther than Talia Avestri," Adora said. "We know it *can* be done. And we know we need to do it."

"We'll do it," Vespas insisted. "I didn't accept commandership of this army only to give up at the first sign of difficulty. Just give me some time to think it through. Even if we could burn down only part of the forest, or clear it out, we wouldn't want to. We need that same forest to conceal us once we surmount this obstacle. So it's imperative that we don't damage anything but the palisades themselves."

Amali tilted her head back, trying to get a good view of the sky. "It's looked for some time like there will be a bad storm soon. That might be our best opportunity. The Hallerns have relied on firing at us from behind the palisades, picking us off while denying our own archers targets. It would be a stroke of luck if they don't have enough wax for all their bows, but even if they do, in a true downpour even the greatest archer would suffer a loss of accuracy. It's not much, but it would give us an advantage."

Vespas sighed, massaging his temples. His eyes slid sideways, meeting Adora's almost unwillingly. "I hate to say it, but . . ."

Adora's chest ached, squeezing tight. "I know. I've been thinking it, too. This is exactly the kind of problem Arianrod could have solved better than anyone. She could've used magical fire to destroy the palisades without harming the rest of the forest, or snapped the archers' bowstrings from afar—or even used no magic at all, just that mind of hers, to come up with a solution none of us have thought of." She shook her head. "It's useless to rely on aid we know can't come to us. Let's try to build on Amali's idea. There may be a way we can widen our advantage in those weather conditions."

The worse tidings came after the meeting had adjourned, around noon, while Adora was poring over maps and eating rations in her tent. The messenger reported news that had overflowed from Valyanrend, trickling down through the surrounding villages and spreading ever outward, until it met a similar flow coming from the east. Arianrod Margraine, both sources of information confirmed, had been captured by the Hallern army in Esthrades, and taken back to Valyanrend. In that city, they said Elgar had already announced her forthcoming execution—for, among many other things, the crimes of being a mage and using that magic against others. And he had advised his people to beware, lest they also fall victim to such dark influences.

It was only because Adora was so used to devastating news that she had learned to bear it with outward equanimity. She had watched her father take the fall that had eventually killed him, and witnessed his last moments. She had received the message that her brother Landon could not be located, and was most likely dead. And she had heard and seen, from Voltest's lips and in his flames, that her throne had been stolen, her brother's mind warped, her mother held captive, and her most loyal friend tortured. If she had survived all those blows intact, she could bear this one without breaking.

That didn't mean it did not hurt.

She had seen this outcome so clearly, back in Eldren Cael. She had seen it, and known it, and feared it, and yet she had been able to do nothing to prevent it. *How* had she been able to do nothing to prevent it? Or had she merely been too timid, too afraid of overstepping, when another, bolder person in her place might have saved Arianrod's life?

Was this the frustration Arianrod had felt, when she urged Adora to fully assume the throne after Landon's disappearance, and warned of what would happen if she did not? Events had unfolded exactly as she had predicted, just as, in this case, Adora had been the one to see too clearly. Yet back then, Adora had not taken her old friend's advice, not because it had not seemed sound—quite the contrary. She had not taken it because she felt she simply had to do what she was doing, even if it was not the wisest choice. And she had known in Eldren Cael that, unusual as it might seem, Arianrod was following her heart. Perhaps there had never been any way to stop either of them from making the mistakes they had made. Perhaps they were both just too stubborn.

An impromptu meeting began in a matter of minutes, their faces even grimmer than they had been in the morning. "It . . . is dispiriting news," Amali began. "And it must fall hardest on you, Your Grace, since you've known her for so long. But we ought to ensure this report does not distract us from our true goal. Arianrod Margraine was an asset we already assumed we would not be able to use, so the confirmation of that fact does not actually weaken our own position any. It shouldn't cause harm in the east, either, from what I can tell."

Not was, Adora thought. *She isn't dead yet.* But such a comment would only make them more certain she couldn't be clearheaded, so she kept silent.

"Forgive me," Vespas added, "but I must also say . . . you know, Adora, that if Elgar tries to use her as a hostage to get us to halt or delay our advance, or make other concessions . . . you know you can't accept."

"He's not going to do that," Adora said flatly. "If that were his goal, he would have opened negotiations with us before exposing her as a mage and announcing her execution to the world. Even if we offered him everything, he couldn't hand her over to us now without losing face with his people. But to answer the question you implicitly asked, Uncle, yes, I am aware I could not accept those terms. And I wouldn't, not least because I know she wouldn't want me to." She pretended not to see their looks of relief.

"At least there's an easy way to strike back at this," Vespas said. "If Elgar's a mage—and I'm sure that he is—we can simply make that truth known. We might be able to find some proof of it, but even if we can't, the rumor alone could harm his standing with the very people he's trying to stir up."

"No," Adora said firmly. "That's exactly what we can't do."

Vespas's eyebrows rose, his head tilting slightly. "We can't? Why on earth not?"

"We can't inflame the fears of the people any further. It'll be hard enough to combat the damage he's already doing."

"But Adora, it's not as if we'd be saying something that isn't true. He *is* a mage. He *does* mean to use that power on his own people, with the most malign intent possible. Simply to say that aloud isn't the equivalent of—"

"No, it isn't," Adora agreed. "But your goal isn't only to tell people the truth, Uncle. You wish to stir up their fear and suspicion. You wish to turn them against the idea of magic, and mages, and one mage in particular. The only difference is the particular mage you've chosen."

"Against one mage in particular, I admit," Vespas said. "I wouldn't encourage fear of all magic, though I suppose that might become an inadvertent result. But the benefits of—"

"No, Uncle, listen." Adora stood up. "When Arianrod told me how to defeat Jocelyn, she knew that she was putting herself and other, future mages at risk by releasing that information into the world. But she did it anyway, because she believed Jocelyn had to be stopped—and because she trusted me with that knowledge. I promised her that I would never allow mages to be feared as long as I rule. And it's a promise I will keep, whether or not . . ." She swallowed hard, standing strong. "Whether or not she ever lives to see it."

Vespas sighed, fiddling with his beard. "If that's what you've decided, Your Grace, then that's how it must be. I will think more on this problem, in addition to the points brought up by Amali earlier."

And then, for the moment, there was nothing more to say. Vespas and Amali left her to herself, and Adora sat alone in her tent, conscious of the loudness of her breathing in the enclosed space. *Know that, if it does come to pass,* Arianrod had said, *I shall regret the same.*

They had both made mistakes, but Arianrod had helped save her from the consequences of hers. If Adora could not do the same for her, how could she ever hope to be the queen that Arianrod was?

CHAPTER TWENTY-FIVE

Lanvaldis

FOR THE BETTER part of an hour, they picked their way through the forest in silence. The wind grew stronger as they walked up a gradual slope, blowing directly in their faces as if trying to push them back. But Deinol knew Lucius would never turn back, so neither would he.

The trees grew closer together here, towering, ancient oaks and elms casting grave shadows over them. Deinol had never known a forest until a few months ago, but now he felt sufficiently studied in them to detect small differences. This forest, for example, though dense and old, did not make him feel the back-of-the-neck chill the forests of Esthrades had, as if absolutely anything could come lumbering or gliding or shrieking out of the trees in the next moment. The only thing he expected to see here, besides the three people they were looking for, were calling birds and the occasional hare.

As they neared the top of the slope and the ground started to even out, Lucius turned abruptly toward him. "You can still turn back, but only just. This is probably your last chance."

Was he really still on that? "If I didn't take any of the other ones, why would I suddenly be keen on this one?"

Lucius smiled, genuine despite his melancholy. "Then I have to ask you for a favor. Well, a couple of favors."

"Seems like you've been asking me for a lot of those lately, but I'll hear you out."

Lucius nodded, and took a deep breath, gathering himself. "I know Ryo isn't your prince, and that you've never had anyone be to you what he was and is to me and the others who believed in him. But even if you can't respect him, please don't get in his way, or trouble him at all if you can help it. He must live and thrive— that's what I want most. If I'm allowed to help in that, I will, but I would never want a friend of mine to hinder it."

Deinol waved him off. "Aye, understood. I'll leave His Royal Importance be."

"Then, there's only . . ." His hands shook, muscles tightening in his arms. "Deinol, there are things I haven't been truthful about, important things I was too cowardly to say. I'd tell you now, but it may be that in a little while you no longer care.

That you can't forgive me for the things I've done, and no amount of truth, no apologies, will change that. If there's anything you want to know, after this, I promise I'll tell you everything. But if not, if you could believe that I've never lied about our friendship . . . if you believed only that of me, and nothing else, I'd be content."

"How could I doubt that, after everything you've done?" Deinol shook his head firmly. "It's our friendship that means the most to me, Lucius, not your past. Since I've known you, you've done nothing I could reproach you for, and I'm not interested in blaming you for things you did before we ever met. Is that good enough for you?"

"It will be if you feel that way in an hour," Lucius said. "But thank you."

From there, the rest of the way felt too short. The slope evened out, the trees opened up, and Deinol knew they must be nearing the spot Lucius said Ryo had written of in his letter. In the gray light of late morning, three silhouettes were visible even from far off, unmoving as Lucius and Deinol drew closer, even when they could not possibly have failed to see them approach.

Then there they were at last, the same three Deinol had encountered that night in Esthrades. On his left, the woman they'd seen in Araveil, hands hanging slack and empty at her sides, face smooth and composed but dark eyes troubled. On his right, the tall man with the patch he'd bumped into in the tavern, hands curled into loose fists, face stormy and severe. And sitting between them, arms over his knees, was a man whose lip curled in contempt, but whose eyes were just as Deinol had remembered them: constantly burning, full of intensity.

Lucius put a hand on Deinol's shoulder—telling him, *No farther.* Then, with nothing more than a nod, he walked past him, and faced the three ghosts of his past. He said nothing; he did not even kneel, as Deinol would have expected. He just stood there, as if trying to fill his eyes with the image before him, to burn it into his consciousness.

Finally, the seated man spoke. "I was sure you'd run."

Lucius almost staggered at hearing that voice, but caught himself. "No."

"It must be foolish of you, then," the man said, "for I am sure it can't be brave."

The insult visibly wounded him, but Lucius only replied, "Perhaps."

"Why did you come?"

Lucius's eyes flicked up, taking in the three of them together. "Am I permitted to speak to Gao and Rana?"

The prince glanced at his comrades. "I'm not sure what you think they have to say to you, but I don't hold their tongues in thrall any more than I ever did yours. Gao, Rana, would you answer this traitor?"

The woman shook her head once, her mouth twisting as if in pain. But the tall man smiled, and it was such a bright and amiable expression that at first Deinol did not see that his eyes were cold. "So you've grown out your hair after all, just as you were always threatening to do back in Kaiferi. It looks fine enough, but I suppose it's true what they say—cowards *do* stay pretty. Funny how I don't like your face as much as I used to."

Those words clearly cut deeper, but though pain glimmered in Lucius's eyes, his mouth bent in something that was almost a smile.

The prince caught it, too. "Why the hell are you smiling?"

"Forgive me," Lucius said haltingly. "I just . . . he sounds just the same."

"Even *you* sound the same, although you shouldn't. You should be cowering before me like the wretch you are." He finally pushed to his feet, bending forward to peer into Lucius's face. "You haven't answered my question. Why didn't you run again? Why face me, after all this time?"

"If I had known you lived, I would have faced you much sooner," Lucius said. "But I didn't come to face you—any of you. I just . . . wanted to see that you lived."

For a moment the prince stood frozen, those burning eyes fixed on Lucius, and Deinol tensed, certain he was going to lash out. But then he laughed, full of bitterness and resentment and the flash of teeth. "You mean after all you had done to ensure the opposite?"

Lucius swallowed hard. *"Kaihen—"*

"Don't *kaihen* me!" He paced in a half circle before him, back and forth, hands slashing impotently at the air, as if he held more energy than he could contain. "You're standing there with such emotion in your face, as if we're loyal friends reunited at last. But my loyalty was never returned, Kaitan. If my life was so precious to you, perhaps you shouldn't have left me to die!"

The last four words were shocking enough, but it was a different word Deinol focused on, that forced itself out of his mouth unbidden: "Kaitan?"

All four of them looked at him, the prince as if he had only just realized he was there. If he or either of his sworn swords remembered meeting Deinol before, they gave no sign of it. "Who is this?"

"An associate of mine from Valyanrend," Lucius said, too quickly. "We were traveling together when I saw Rana, and when I received your message. I tried to shake him off, but his curiosity would not be sated."

Curiosity. A fine thing to call Deinol's friendship, but if Lucius did so, it could only be to protect him. He kept his mouth shut.

But Ryo seemed no more satisfied with that than he was. For the first time, he spoke to Deinol directly. "What name did he give you, then, that you are so shocked to hear his true one?"

"His name is Lucius." Both the words and the force behind them came out before Deinol could stop them, ringing too clearly in the suddenly silent air.

"Ah." The prince's eyebrows rose, a mocking facsimile of surprise, but Deinol couldn't tell if it was directed at him or Lucius. "Fascinating. And who is this Lucius? He has not thrown away his sword, so perhaps he still knows how to fight, or has causes for which he would draw his blade. A respectable sort, is he? Courageous? Loyal?" When he was met with silence, he scowled at Deinol. "Answer me. Do you fear to speak?"

"Not at all," Deinol said, "but it doesn't please me to speak when ordered. Where I come from, we don't have princes."

"Aha." Ryo slapped his thigh. "Not an associate at all, then, but a confidant, if he's already told you who I am. Why hide it, Kaitan? Did you think I would visit harm on your friend, merely for the crime of being taken in just as I was? If anything, I should commiserate with him."

"There's no need." Deinol hadn't meant to interfere, but it seemed Ryo was determined to hear from him, and would keep going until he did. He tried to keep his voice level. "I have never counted myself anything but fortunate to know him. If you feel differently, perhaps the problem lies with—"

"Deinol, shut up," Lucius snapped, the angriest three words he had directed at Deinol in their entire acquaintance.

The prince had gone very still, not even a twitch in his face. Was it a handsome face? Hard to say, when the eyes exerted such a pull it was hard to look anywhere else. "Is that what you came to say to me, Kaitan? That it is some deficiency in me that caused you to betray our friendship?"

"No. Never." Lucius took a step toward him, then abruptly stopped, as if an invisible barrier lay between them. "*Kaihen,* he doesn't know you. He speaks out of blind loyalty, he doesn't understand . . ."

Deinol was only half listening, preoccupied with struggling to dredge up a memory from the depths of his mind. The name *Kaitan* sounded familiar. Where had he heard it before?

It was a common name, Lucius had said to him once, without much interest; he had known two or three of them back home. But that wasn't it.

Then it struck him. It had been at the end of a list. Lucius had talked for years about the *kaishinrian* of Aurnis, the royal guard, spinning tales mostly for Seth that made them out to be living legends. But he had only said their names once. And the last name on that list . . .

"That was you?" he asked, heedless of interrupting again. "All this time, *you* were Kaitan Enrei, the *kaishinrian*?"

So that was what Ritsu had been too forbearing to say. Deinol had been expecting the lie to be some small but pivotal detail, but Ritsu had known all along that Lucius had been lying about the very essence of who he was. No wonder he had never wanted to call him by name, not to be complicit in the lie. Lucius hadn't just walked away from a war in which he knew his benefactor was bound to fight, he'd abandoned the liege he had sworn to protect. Vowing to put your life before someone else's as a matter of duty wasn't something Deinol could ever imagine doing, but at least the prince's anger made sense now.

"That man is no *kaishinrian*," Ryo said. "Comparing him to those who died in Aurnis, to those who stand at my side now, would be to insult them beyond forgiveness."

"So Gao and Rana really are the only ones left." Lucius shook his head. "I don't understand. I heard the report of your deaths myself."

The tall man, Gao, scoffed, flicking at the base of his eyepatch with his thumb. "A premature report, and an insult to my skill. Rana had grand ideas about holding the outer corridor to buy the rest of us time, but she must have forgotten to consult me. We were both a mess by the time we fought our way back out, but 'dead' was overselling it a bit. Didn't you make the same mistake yourself, Kaitan? Or did you flee even before our liege was injured?"

"He knows I didn't."

"I know no such thing," Ryo said. "When I fell, all I knew was that I could not see you. I was hardly lying there a minute, but when Gao and Rana arrived, you seemed to be long gone."

"I saw it," Lucius said. "I could never forget it. You were struck right in the chest—you were lucky your body didn't cleave in two at such a blow. I couldn't imagine that any man could withstand that. I still can't imagine it."

"Then you underestimate me, Kaitan." He put a hand to his chest, clenching his fingers in the layers of cloth there. "I could not move under my own strength. Had I been alone, I would surely have bled to death. But I had friends more stalwart than you. It was a near thing, and painful beyond measure, but I survived. And though I could not take up the sword again for months, I am now as whole as I can hope to be. But I will not leave you with such a timid explanation. I will show you, so you know that I am not some ghost or illusion or imposter."

Beneath his faded coat, he wore a simple linen shirt whose buttons he quickly unfastened, throwing both layers to the ground together. And when he finally stood before them, stripped bare to the waist, even Deinol sucked in a breath in shock.

It was the most brutal scar he had ever seen, starting in the middle of Ryo's chest, near the base of his collarbone, and shearing away to the left in a gradual curve, so that by the time it reached the end of his ribs it had moved all the way to his left side. One single, devastating stroke, encompassing almost his entire torso. Deinol couldn't imagine how much damage it had done when it was fresh; as Lucius said, Ryo was lucky he hadn't been cut in half. Perhaps the cut was shallower than it seemed, though how shallow could it have been, to leave such a mark?

When it seemed he could stare no longer, Lucius put his head in his hands. "So all this time . . . all this time, if I had remained with you, I could have known the truth. Thinking you were dead was just . . . fitting recompense for my cowardice."

Ryo scoffed. "Fitting recompense? Ha! You let yourself off far too easily, Kaitan."

"I don't," Lucius said. "I know I can never understand your pain, and everything you had to do to survive all these years, the pride and the ideals you must have had to set aside. But you had each other. I was cast out and alone—alone, I believed, in the entire world. Among the rest of you, I had valued my life so highly, but once I escaped, I realized I had left everything I lived for behind. I knew I had made the worst possible choice, but I was doomed to live on knowing I couldn't change it. I have no one to blame for my suffering but myself, but it was not nothing."

"Is that truly what you came to say to us?" It was Rana who spoke, stepping up to stand beside her prince. "To tell us how you've suffered? You don't even know what suffering is."

They were the first words she had said to him, and they struck him like a physical blow; he seemed to shrink before her, to stand slumped where he had been tall. "Rana." Not a question, or a plea. Just an acknowledgment.

She let her left hand trail gently up and down her sword, fingertips just brushing its sheath. "How many duels did we have, Kaitan, over the years? Can you even remember? They said we were so splendidly matched, each the perfect whetstone on which to hone the other's skills. And we did, didn't we? We grew together, we rose together . . . we reached the very pinnacle together, one right after the other. I thought it would always be that way, that there must be so many remaining heights left for us to reach, side by side. And now we have both fallen, but not in the same way."

She used her left hand to pull up her right sleeve, revealing a scar much simpler than her prince's, a single silver cut across the inside of her forearm. "This is the wound I sustained holding the outer corridor. A meager price to pay, I thought at first, when I had thought to give my life. How wrong I was. The price, indeed, was far worse. For though the wound is healed, it seems I never shall."

She closed her eyes, as if holding back tears, but when she looked at him again, her face was steely and resolute. "Shall you and I have another duel, Kaitan? Shall we see, after all these years, how we compare to each other?"

She reached for her sword, and Deinol wondered if she really did plan to fight him. But as her fingers neared the hilt, they did not clutch it; they bent inward a little, into a clumsy clawlike shape, but no more. Rana gritted her teeth, face taut with strain, yet though her fingers shook, they did not clench even a little tighter. Finally, the mystery of the hand she still possessed, yet never fully used, was revealed. That was as much as she could do. She could not make a fist, could not grasp objects tightly. And she could not possibly fight, because mastery of the *tsunshin* required two working hands. "And now you see. I, who was once one of the foremost swords of Aurnis, will never take another step toward those heights we dreamed of. Our prince still calls me one of his *kaishinrian,* but in truth I am no more fit to serve in that role than you. How can you stand there, still wearing your sword so proudly, and say you've suffered, when I can't even draw mine to face you?"

Out of everything they had seen since arriving here, nothing had shattered Lucius like this. The tears flowed freely and silently down his cheeks, and he made no attempt to wipe them away. "No," he whispered. "Oh, Rana, no."

"She misspoke in one respect," Ryo said. "No one is worthier to stand at my side. I don't care about her arm, or Gao's eye. How could I, when those wounds were sustained in my service? But because of those wounds, I can't allow either of them to face you in my name. The only one who can answer your dishonor is me."

Gao balked, taking a step forward. "*Kaihen,* he doesn't deserve to face you, or any of us."

"Perhaps not. But he defeated me once. He proved, in his way, that he deserved a place among us then. And his service was not entirely free of noble deeds. I wish to see if his cowardice has blunted his blade." He drew his own, and pointed it at Lucius. "This time, I challenge you, Kaitan. Let this rematch wipe out the memory of our old one."

Tears were still tracing a path down Lucius's cheeks, but now he finally wiped them away. His voice was steady, almost calm. "I refuse."

Ryo glowered. "This is how you would answer me? Stop cringing and fight!"

"No. Not against you, *kaihen.*" Lucius shook his head. "Never against you."

Ryo sheathed his sword with hands that trembled. "I—I offered you an honorable duel, a chance to reclaim even a scrap of the valor that you lost—which is more than you deserve—and you cannot even do that much? You would truly show this much cowardice?"

"If I have no honor," Lucius said, "I have no more to lose. And if I'm already a coward, I can't become one again. Besides, *kaihen,* the memory of our previous duel is precious to me. I have no wish to wipe it out."

Ryo froze where he stood, and stared at him. There was something exposed in his face, some vulnerability that made him look younger. "Are . . . are you mocking me?"

"I would never do that, least of all about such a sacred subject. That duel is a reminder of the debt I owe you—the great kindness you once bestowed on me. Whether you won or lost that fight was meaningless compared to the valor you showed in accepting my challenge at all. Did Gao not know the same, when he accepted Rana's challenge? That a truly brave *shinrian* does not begrudge another the ability to surpass him?"

"And yet you would begrudge me the same," Ryo said. "You fought me once—"

"With blunted swords! Because I knew no harm would come to you! I may have forsaken my vow to protect you, but even I would never fall so far as to risk doing you injury. Please, *kaihen*. Show me this much mercy. Don't ask me to do such a thing." Lucius bowed his head. "But even if you do, I will not. There is nothing you can do to make me."

Ryo looked him over, hands sliding fretfully down his hips, as if he longed to draw his sword again. "Nothing I can do? You're bluffing, Kaitan. You know there's no glory in dueling someone who won't fight back, so you assume you're safe from me as long as you refuse. But you're more than just a swordsman now. You're an oathbreaker, and a deserter, too. Anyone can bring such a criminal to answer for their crimes, by force or no."

Lucius shook his head sadly. "Now who's bluffing? You no longer have any court to try me in. Yours has been taken from you by that vulture in the Citadel. Are you going to drag me after you in chains until the day you win Aurnis back again? I doubt you'd want to endure my company for so long."

Ryo turned to his sworn swords. "You see? That's as much as to say he knows he's safe from us."

"*Kaihen,*" Gao said, "let me—"

"I won't fight you either, Gao," Lucius said. "I wouldn't even fight Rana, if she were well. You can't make me a challenge that I'll accept."

"Stubborn bastard." Gao fiddled with the strap of his patch. "In this case, *kaihen,* the coward serves best as his own punishment. Let him be banished from Aurnis, even when we have retaken it—especially then. And let him be banished from your presence, to wander the world away from his true home and wallow in his own faults."

Sheath is his home, Deinol thought, even though he knew, now, that it wasn't true.

"That's no punishment for him," Ryo said. "That's what he's been doing already. He looks well enough to you, doesn't he?"

Rana bit the corner of her mouth. "*Kaihen,* for you to act simply to hurt him would be beneath you. If he accepts his punishment, it means he still possesses a scrap of shame, that's all."

"It's not simply to hurt him," Ryo insisted. "You're right, that would be contemptible. It's because the injustice of it grates on me. Gao says his cowardice should be his punishment, yet you have suffered so much more. How is that fair? How is it that I, your prince as much as his, can do nothing to correct it?"

He drew his sword again, pointing it at Lucius. "I won't even hurt you, Kaitan. I just want you to admit it. If I truly made you fight for your life, you wouldn't just stand there peacefully. You and I both know it."

Lucius didn't move. "I'll say that I'm a coward as many times as you like. But I won't fight you."

"Because you think that protects you!" He thrust the point of his sword beneath Lucius's chin. "Defend yourself, damn it! Draw your sword!"

Deinol dearly wanted to draw his, and settled for putting a hand on the hilt. But Lucius grabbed his arm in the same instant that Gao reached for his own blade. "Deinol, don't. This isn't like a brawl in Sheath, where the one who's better at posturing can win. If you draw, they'll take you seriously. And they won't back down."

"That prince of yours already isn't backing down!"

"He's just trying to provoke me," Lucius said. "But I won't be moved so—"

He grunted as Ryo's sword fell across his shoulder, tearing the fabric there. Gao did draw his sword then, stepping to his prince's side. "*Kaihen,* you mustn't—"

"Why? Why should he be allowed to walk free?" Ryo thrust his hand angrily at Lucius's shoulder. "Calm down. I barely touched him."

"*Kaihen—*"

Deinol had seen enough. If the two of them had both drawn already, he didn't see what he was supposed to gain by keeping his sword sheathed. But as he tried to pull it free, he was brought up short by a tug at the crook of his right elbow. He hadn't even noticed her approach, but Rana had hooked her arm through his, trying with limited success to draw him backward. "Don't get involved. You'll make it worse."

"He's my friend," Deinol said.

"Then you'll make it doubly worse. Let Gao calm the prince."

"I would, if he seemed to be succeeding!" He tugged again, but just dragged her with him for a few inches. He called out to Lucius. "Look, if it'll satisfy him, just admit to it! Even if it isn't true, just say it!"

Lucius glanced at Deinol for only a moment, and then back at Ryo, who had furiously sidestepped Gao's efforts to get between them. "Tell him I would willingly harm him, for any reason? No. Let him kill me, if that is the only way to prove I speak the truth."

Rana swore under her breath. "Why is Kaitan being such a fool?"

"*He's* being a fool?" Deinol sputtered. "What about your prince?"

Said prince was still swinging his sword angrily but carefully at Lucius; Lucius took the blow on the forearm, where it scarcely produced a single drop of blood. "You're this confident I won't harm you? Don't tempt me, Kaitan."

"Do it, then!" Without hesitation, Lucius unbuckled his sword, and threw it all, belt, sword, and sheath together, at Ryo's feet. "You could kill me for a traitor if you wished. So do it, if that's the justice you prefer! I came here because I was ready for it!"

More than ready, Deinol realized. This was the outcome Lucius had expected— wanted, even. He had known he would never be forgiven, and could think of no other way to balance the scales.

Ryo lunged forward again, and Deinol moved without thinking, putting himself between Lucius and the prince. But he couldn't get his sword free, because Rana still had half a grip on his right arm. Instead, his left hand came up by reflex, as he used his body to push Lucius behind him.

The next thing Deinol knew, he was staring at an abbreviated hand. There were his wrist and palm; there was even his thumb, twitching slightly all by itself. But instead of the rest of his fingers, there were stumps of varying lengths, made uneven by Ryo's diagonal cut.

He had just enough time to take in Ryo's wide-eyed stare. Gone was the visage of the vengeful prince; he looked, if anything, like a child who's accidentally broken his own toy, that guileless and confused. And then Lucius was between them, his back to Deinol and front facing Ryo, arms spread as wide as he could. "No, no, leave him out of it," he begged, though Ryo looked as shocked as he did. "Kill me, that's your right, but don't touch him."

Ryo stared at the blood on his sword, and then dropped it, as if it had burned him. "You would die for this man, but not for me?"

Lucius met his gaze. "If I could do it over again, *kaihen,* I would die for you a hundred times."

There was something Deinol wanted to say, even if only to distract from the terrible pain in his hand. But the words crumbled in his mouth as he tried to form them, and soon his vision was crumbling, too, everything bleeding into black.

Chapter Twenty-six

Valyanrend

WHEN VARALEN HAD first returned to the Citadel, he'd thought presenting Elgar with Lady Margraine's capture heralded some great shift in the way the war would unfold. But at least in the first handful of days, things felt much the same as they had before he and Elgar had left for Reglay all those weeks ago. They still spent long hours reading reports and debating strategies, Elgar's collection of maps ever spread out before them. Varalen still spent sleepless nights nursing headaches, adding up numbers in his head, calculating the likelihood of possible outcomes. And more often than not, he feared that the task his master had set him was simply impossible.

The most significant difference was that, instead of fretting over the machinations of his greatest foe, Elgar joked about how she must be faring in captivity, or that he must ask her opinion on some fresh bit of news he was well aware she knew nothing about. He was in much better spirits than Varalen: he'd survived a disastrous siege at Mist's Edge, curbed a riot in Araveil, and captured a monarch in Esthrades, but after all those twists and turns, he'd returned home to find just as many foes sprung up again, like a tree whose fruits were ever-renewing. And while no foe they would encounter was likely to be as cunning or capable as Arianrod Margraine, they had never faced an army as large, well-funded, or rigorously trained as Issamira's. Many Hallerns remembered the last time their two nations had come to blows: a supposedly simple invasion by Gerde Selte's much larger army turned into nightmare after nightmare as the new king outmaneuvered her in every battle. Jotun Avestri was dead, but Hallern soldiers' fear of his country, his family, and the army he'd commanded was as robust as ever. That would have been plenty to deal with even without taking the rebellion at home into account, and now they were grappling with even worse news. Araveil had rioted again, this time with much more success, knocking Varalen's triumphs down to one victory out of three.

"It seems Selwyn completely failed to hold Lanvaldis in even the barest sense," Elgar said. "She's currently in prison awaiting trial, and the entire country is now singing the praises of Lantistyne's *second* boy king. As if Kelken wasn't bad enough."

Varalen sighed. "I knew I should've left more men with her. The situation in Araveil was clearly unstable."

"If you'd left more men with her, your gambit in Esthrades might not have come off so well," Elgar said. "You did as you ought to have done."

"I'm surprised you can be so cavalier about it, Your Eminence. It took six months of hard fighting to capture Araveil the first time. Now all that work's been undone."

"I wouldn't say that. We now hold Reglay and Stonespire, neither of which we were even close to having the last time Araveil fell."

"But the Lanvalds are probably going to attempt to retake Stonespire—it's what I would do. And if you look at the numbers, they have a good chance of succeeding. Despite all our efforts, this city is still in revolt, and you've got an army of Issamiri marching ever closer to your doorstep!"

Elgar sat down beside him, folding his hands over each other. "You seem rather agitated."

"Of course I'm agitated! You know what I have riding on this!" He couldn't bear to say it aloud. He hated that Elgar had such an inescapable grip on his deepest vulnerability.

"I do know," Elgar said quietly. "But *you* should know by now that if I were displeased, you would know it. What I promised you is not reliant on a single battle, a single enemy, a single piece of territory—it will come when I have achieved my ultimate victory. And the path to that victory is still wide open."

Varalen felt his breathing slow. No matter what, it wouldn't do to lose his composure. "Perhaps you'd care to enlighten me as to your thinking on this matter, Your Eminence?"

"With pleasure." He spread his hands wide. "You've already taken care of the greatest obstacle in my way—she's as jailed and helpless as Edith Selwyn. Now Arianrod's strategic mind is useless, and she cannot use her magic to counter mine. And with my magic unopposed, I have access to more resources and opportunities than even you could guess.

"Our second largest obstacle is the Issamiri army. That's why I couldn't afford to give Selwyn more men, even though she clearly needed them—if any weakness at home caused us to lose Valyanrend, it would all be over. But if and when we crush the Issamiri, the hopes of our boy kings will die as well. They can't defeat me even at our most generous estimates of their numbers, so however long they hold out, it will only be a matter of time." He smiled sardonically. "Have I assuaged your fears somewhat?"

"And the resistance in Valyanrend?" Varalen asked. "What are you doing about that?"

"I'm glad you asked. That, my tireless strategist, is where you come in."

He reached into his pocket, and set a folded piece of parchment down between them. "You've been away, so you haven't had a chance to read the latest missive from our rebels, though I doubt you'll decide you missed much. I always knew the Silkspoint business hadn't eradicated all of them, but there's something different about this Fang character. I think they might be someone new—or several someones—rather than part of an existing group. But you know Valyanrend better than I do, so I'm putting you in charge of investigating this. Find this Fang, and find out whether they're connected to the group we defeated in Silkspoint or not."

Once Varalen had gotten the letter unfolded, he only half listened to Elgar's words, devoting the rest of his faculties toward masking any reaction that wanted to appear on his face. The content of the letter was useless, ridiculous—typical revolutionary posturing meant to recruit admirers or instill doubt in Elgar and his people. What so shocked him was the penmanship, an uneven scrawl made painstakingly legible, as if the writer had been practicing lines with his non-dominant hand. Which, in fact, was precisely what he had done, in order to disguise his natural handwriting. It had been years since Varalen had seen it, but he'd seen it enough not to forget it. And the grandiose prose . . . well, that was familiar, too.

"I'll start right away," he told Elgar, stashing the letter in the pocket of his robes.

IT HAD TAKEN Roger time to make any headway with the Halfen clan, but by now he figured he had convinced a good percentage of them to aid his plans in one way or another, given that they were a family of thieves, not freedom fighters. It was hard not to imagine what Gran might have done better or differently—she was the last true leader the family had had. She had wanted Roger's father to succeed her, but he had gone straight in a vow to his wife before they married, and kept it until the grave came for them both. His father's brother was a rakish good-for-nothing who had brawled himself to an early death, which left his sister, Roger's aunt Rheila, as Gran's only living child. But Rheila had always been nervous and shy—still a fine thief, not as fine a speaker. Roger had done little more than tip her off out of courtesy, assuming she'd want to stay out of any revolutionary activities, so he was caught utterly by surprise when she said she'd found a contact who wanted to speak with him regarding just that. Whoever it was, it was someone whose trust she didn't want to break, because she wouldn't give him any more details until he'd met this mysterious man in person.

Roger loved his aunt, eccentricities and all, and he'd never believe that any Halfen could sell out another to the law. But he'd still worn a hooded cloak to the tavern for this meeting—a Fades tavern, just out of Sheath proper, and half as full as a Sheath tavern would have been around the same time. His aunt's contact must have had the same idea, for the thin man half in shadow at the table in the far corner had his hood up, too, his back to the wall. Roger ordered an ale at the bar, took a sip, grimaced, and made his way to the back.

He had barely sat down when the man dropped something on the table, a sheet of parchment that he pressed against the wood with his fingertips, as if afraid of sustained contact with it. *"I am the Fang, and your life is mine?"* he hissed. "Really? Where did *you* find the balls to write something like that?"

Roger swore he could feel the blood draining from his face. "How the hell did you get that?"

"So it is true." The man leaned forward, his other hand disappearing beneath the hood to press against his forehead. "Gods, I should just let them arrest you. If the years have made you this stupid, you're clearly a liability I can't afford. Do you have any idea the position this puts me in?"

He doubtless could have continued, but by then Roger's apprehension had been fully replaced by anger. He knew that voice. Or rather, more than the sound of it, which was rougher and deeper than the one in his memories, he remembered the endlessly condescending things it had always said to him.

Before the man had time to react, he reached out, sweeping the hood back from his face. And there he was: more than a decade older, but still the same pinched and put-upon expression, the same faint sheen of Halfen red in his long brown hair. "I don't believe it," Roger said. "*Len*? You pick *now* to come back?"

His cousin rolled his eyes and gritted his teeth in a way Roger knew well, but hadn't missed in the slightest. "I have told you over and over to dispense with that stupid nickname. We aren't boys in Sheath anymore. My name is *Varalen*."

"I don't care how old you bloody are, or what airs you put on," Roger said. "You're Len Varsten of Sheath, and you'll never be able to change that."

Len gave a thin smile. "Wrong again, I'm afraid. I left the Varsten name behind with the rest of the refuse we grew up mired in. No one I run with now has known me by any name but Varalen Oswhent."

Despite himself, Roger had to stifle a noise of surprise. "You spat on your own father's memory for the sake of that parsimonious old merchant?"

"*That parsimonious old merchant* was more of a father to me than Irius Varsten ever was," Len said. "Not to mention a better husband to my mother."

Oh, Roger definitely hadn't forgotten *her*. "So Rheila wouldn't sell me out to the law, but she made an exception for her son, is that it?"

"My mother didn't sell you out to anyone," Len snapped. "She doesn't know I have this letter, and all I told her was that I wanted to meet with you."

"I don't know why you needed to involve her for that. I've never liked you, Len, but I'd have at least spared you the time of day now that you've finally come back west after all these years. In fact, I'm hurt that you *didn't* tell me."

Len had the decency to look embarrassed, staring down at where his fingertips were still pressed to the parchment. "Actually . . . I've been back in Valyanrend for some time now. Just . . . not in Sheath. I—"

And perhaps Roger should have put it together earlier, but that was the moment it finally dawned on him. Len had gotten hold of the letter on his own, without using any family contacts. Len was living in Valyanrend, but not in Sheath, and he didn't want anyone who'd known him as Len Varsten to know he was here. Morgan and the others had told him a story once, when they had gone to rescue Seth from Elgar's dungeons, about a clever sort of strategist who worked for the imperator, a man who had a title but claimed not to be a noble, a man they'd called—

"*Lord* Oswhent," he spat. "It's been you all along, hasn't it? Chief lickspittle to Elgar himself. No wonder you were so careful not to let me catch you back here before now."

Len's face flushed red. "I'm not afraid of *you*. And even if I were, it's not what you think. I left Valyanrend with my stepfather just like I said, and worked as a merchant under him until he died. But then I got a chance to work as a strategist instead, helping King Eira drive off Caius Margraine for good. That's what caught His Eminence's eye in the first—"

The title was more than Roger could stomach. "Gran always said you were no true Halfen. She knew you were no good, from the very beginning."

Len scowled. "That old woman was just sour that I wanted an honest living and wouldn't let her make me one of her pathetic little family of thieves."

"An honest living?" Roger laughed in his face. "An *honest living*? Shall I give you a list of the crimes committed by your master? Or, hell, I should probably be asking *you* for a list of *your* crimes. What do you want to bet it outstrips mine?"

"Roger—"

"All that incessant posturing about how you were so far *above* swindling and thievery," Roger continued, barreling right over him. "And now it comes out that it wasn't the immorality you objected to, just the risk of capture. Lot easier to transgress when the guards are on your side, eh?"

"It wasn't *like* that!" Len's fist clenched on the table, but he caught it quickly, careful not to tear the parchment. "I never *wanted* to work for him, but he wouldn't take no for an answer! I tried to refuse him a dozen times!"

"For a captive, you seem remarkably free to come and go," Roger said, but if Len truly meant it, he ought to at least check. "I shouldn't have to tell you that if you really were in that kind of trouble, the family would never forsake you, and we'd call on every favor owed us in Sheath if we had to. We could get you out, and I think you know it."

"It doesn't matter." Len's eyes were dull, the fire behind them burned to ash. "He has my son." A tiny spark of anger rekindled itself. "Not that you thought to ask if I had any family."

"Oh, please. I could have twenty sons, and you'd never care a thing about it. Why couldn't we get your son out as well as you?"

"He's . . . sick." His voice was heavy with old pain. "He can't run, he can't be moved roughly—it's dangerous even for him to be agitated. He might not survive an escape, and he could never live the life of a fugitive. But it's more than that, Roger. That's why I'm here, to warn you to stop this before they find you even without my help. Elgar isn't a conventional foe, and no matter what advantages you think you have, you won't be able to beat him. I know this must be hard to believe, but Elgar is—"

"What, a mage?" He could see in Len's face that he'd guessed right. "I'd say you've got to stop underestimating me, cousin, but after nearly thirty years of it, I doubt you're going to change now. Did you truly think I'd move against him this aggressively if I wasn't sure I knew enough about him?"

"I never thought you the sort to move against *anyone* aggressively," Len said. "Apparently that's one thing that has changed. But if you can be so cavalier about his power—"

"You let me worry about his power. You've no idea what *I* might have at my disposal—and I'm certainly not going to enlighten the lackey of the man I'm trying to kill. But there's nothing cavalier about it, Len. I'm moving against him in deadly earnest—as seriously as I've ever done anything. I'm doing it because staying out of things won't save me, or anyone else."

"Of course it will," Len said, as if talking to a child. "Elgar has no interest in citizens who aren't in revolt. He's not some capricious torturer like Gerde Selte."

"That's not what I mean, and you—" He caught himself. "Or could it be that you really *don't* know what your own master is planning?"

He couldn't explain how he knew what he knew. Even if he were willing to reveal the identities of Morgan and Marceline and the others, or admit he knew the resistance's leadership and had connections to a noble of Issamira, there was no way he could have brought whatever Tethantys and Asariel were into the discussion. But even if Len didn't believe him without the how, he could at least explain *what* he knew.

And Len, who had been a relentless skeptic every day Roger had known him, listened to everything he said without any outward disbelief. Spending years working for a mage had to have some effect, Roger supposed. "It's difficult to give you total credence when you leave so much of your story untold . . . yet you do seem certain of what you say."

"Even if you weren't part of the planning for what happened in Silkspoint, you must have at least heard about it," Roger said. "I'm telling you, massacres like that will continue all across Lantistyne if your master has his way."

Len scratched his jaw. "I suppose if he truly had his way, he'd recruit enough people into this army of his that there'd be no massacres. But I take your point."

How could he stay so calm about this? Len didn't like to be in the dark, or other people knowing things he didn't, or wasting time—he'd never have let Roger go through that whole explanation unless he really didn't know Elgar's plans. But shouldn't someone who hadn't known be more surprised than this? "Are you going to tell me I don't know what I'm talking about?"

"No. It sounds like something he would do. As to whether it's something he *could* do, I trust him to know that better than I could. And I don't know how to explain this Silkspoint business otherwise."

"But if you believe me, you know why I'm doing this," Roger insisted. "You know why I *have* to do this."

"It certainly makes more sense, yes," Len said, still so infuriatingly calm. "But it doesn't change what *I* have to do."

"What do you mean?"

"Roger, listen. However this unfolds, it won't be as bad as you think. From what you've told me, he can control minds only in the simplest sense—an indiscriminate kill command that can be called upon or not, and when it's not, the subjects' minds are their own. He couldn't keep it active all the time, or even most of the time. There'd be chaos. So he'll use it to win the war, and then possibly to put down any truly large-scale rebellions in the future. And otherwise, he'll put it away. It won't matter."

Roger didn't slam both hands down on the table, but only because he didn't want to draw attention. Instead, he curled them into fists, and set them down as delicately as if they were made of glass. "It *won't matter* if Elgar has the power to force people to commit murder whenever he likes, against their will and their conscience?"

"Well," Len said. "Perhaps that was an ill choice of words. I meant it won't matter to *you*. Atrocities happen all the time that you've done nothing about—cared nothing about, because you weren't affected. You said yourself that you only got involved in this because you felt there was no neutral ground left. So don't fight Elgar, don't rebel after he wins, and lay low in the meantime so you don't get drafted, and you'll be fine."

"Or I can kill him," Roger said, through gritted teeth, "and then I'll be better than fine. I'll be free of him."

Len sat back in his chair, shaking his head slightly. "You aren't going to kill him, Roger. I won't let you."

Roger hated that he was the one who was surprised, showing all the shock and horror that Len hadn't. "You want to protect him? After everything I've said? After everything *you've* said?"

"I've already mentioned my son," Len said. "His illness has no cure, save one born of magic. Without it, he'll die a terrible death. That's the price I've exacted from Elgar—the reward I *will* reap, for everything I've done. And I won't let you or anyone else interfere."

"Gods," Roger breathed. "You're so fucking selfish."

"Selfish?" Len snapped. "You wouldn't say that if you ever had a child, or were even capable of feeling a father's love."

"I have plenty of people that I love. People I might not be bound to by blood, but people I've fought through adversity beside—people I've sworn to live or die with, as we do what has to be done."

"Then tell those people what I'm telling you." Len leaned forward again. "I'm giving you one chance, Roger, because we *are* bound by blood. I haven't told Elgar I know who you are—and I won't, if you stop now. Convince your friends if you can, but if not, at least withdraw yourself. Because the next time I hear of the Fang's activities, I'll lead the soldiers to your door myself."

"Fine." Roger pushed his chair out abruptly. "I'll talk it over with them. And I'll be sure to tell Aunt Rheila to be wary of her son. I hope I never see you in Sheath. Are we done?"

He was lying, of course. He had no intention of stopping, and nothing Len could say would make him. But now that he knew Len had the imperator's power behind him, he couldn't be sure that, if he said that, Len wouldn't have men lying in wait to bring him in immediately. He had to warn Morgan and the others; Len might not know them, but he knew how Sheath worked. With just a few words to a few people, Roger could and would have all of Sheath closed to Varalen Oswhent forever, but that would only affect things going forward, not anything Len had already heard or might already know. They were all suddenly a lot less anonymous than he had assumed.

But by the time he had said those few words to those few people, and paid an exceedingly unpleasant visit to his aunt, Roger had realized things were even worse than that. He couldn't warn Morgan and the others. Len might have let him leave, but that didn't mean he didn't have men tailing him, waiting to see exactly who he would run to. Len wasn't bound to them by blood, and might want to get rid of them anyway, just in case. Roger couldn't take that risk. He couldn't be the loose brick that brought the entire edifice of their rebellion crashing down.

So after leaving his aunt's, Roger left Sheath entirely. He left every neighborhood he knew well, pacing down streets where he had rarely ventured, whose
buildings only featured in some distant memory. And then he went where he had
no memories at all, where Roger Halfen had never been: through the eastern gate
and out of Valyanrend entirely, onto plains that seemed so empty and desolate,
despite the smell of flowers in the air, the strange feeling of grass trying to spring
up beneath his feet.

He felt naked without his city all around him, armoring him in its familiarity.
But he had to stay here, where he couldn't reveal anyone, until he was sure any
spies on him had lost interest, and he couldn't say how long that would be.

Gran had always told him he was the cleverest Halfen, but always, always save
one. True Halfen or no, Len was always the smarter one in her eyes, those eyes
that had seen so much. But Roger had to outwit his cousin anyway, even if he had
never done it before. He had to prove that Len was right, and Gran hadn't known
everything.

CHAPTER TWENTY-SEVEN

Esthrades

THEY FOUND THE cottage just where Amerei had said, and though they stopped in the nearest village first, its residents knew only that the old couple who lived there had taken in some injured person they'd found in the woods. It was smaller than the barn that lay half a field away from it, but light glowed merrily from within, a curl of smoke twisting up from the slender chimney. Lirien had to knock several times to get anyone's attention, but when the door did swing open, the man and woman who appeared on the other side smiled genuinely enough.

It was a good beginning, but before Lirien could speak, the couple saw that she was not alone. They shrank back, and, too late, Cadfael remembered the swords he and Rhia carried. But Lirien stepped easily forward, smiling the most disarming smile he'd ever seen.

"Good evening," she said. "I heard the two of you have been kind enough to nurse some poor unfortunate, even without the training for it. Though it's honest more than humble to say so, I am a healer of some skill, and I meant to offer my services. I see my friends have made you uneasy, but since I know nothing of swordplay myself, I am grateful for their protection on the road. They will not enter the house if you don't wish it—nor will I, of course, though I assure you it is not the healer's way to charge a fee."

By the time she had finished, the couple looked completely at ease; surely it wasn't right for one person to possess such a supply of charm. "My word, has news traveled as far as the village?" the woman said. "We'd be only too grateful for your help; we're at our wits' end for what to do."

"You wouldn't be entering the house, though," her husband said. "We had her there to start with, but after such trouble as she caused us, we only felt safe with her in the barn."

That raised Cadfael's hackles, but he thought it best to leave the speaking to Lirien. "Such trouble, sir?"

The couple exchanged a worried glance. "I hope you won't think ill of us, miss," the woman said. "We did it for her own sake, but . . . we had to tie her down. She would not rest, and her attempts to leave only ensured more damage to herself. Yet all our efforts to reason with her were to no avail; she has shown us no more understanding than a wild beast."

Lirien's eyebrows were thoroughly raised, and Cadfael couldn't blame her. Just what sort of person had they been sent to save? "The situation is even more dire than I had heard, then. Do you have any objection to my seeing her straightaway?"

The couple claimed they kept a lantern in the barn for their unfortunate guest, but they provided Lirien with a candlestick all the same. The three of them approached the barn as if they were besieging a castle, peering in the dim light for all possible entries and exits. There was only the faintest glow spilling out from within, but at least the lantern was still lit. Cadfael took the edge of the door in both hands, nodded to the other two, and hauled it open, noting that Rhia kept one hand on her sword.

In the silence after he let go, they could hear a faint noise: thick, labored breathing. Then they stepped over the threshold, and all three of them saw her, laid out on a hay bale with a blanket spread over it, brutally clear in the light of the lantern.

Rhia gasped, Lirien hissed between her teeth, and even Cadfael felt like he was going to be sick. The injuries were bad enough—not the most severe he had ever seen, but certainly the cruelest. But in all the time he had spent wondering about this person Lirien had been sent after, he had always pictured some stranger. He had never expected that they would know her.

He opened his mouth, to apologize for what she had suffered, to assure her they could help, but what came out was: "Who did this to you?"

Whoever it had been, the violence had been precise and purposeful. Her face was completely untouched, and though he couldn't swear there wasn't any bruising or fractures to her ribs, it was nothing that had swollen enough to be noticeable. But the angle of her leg was grotesque, and as for her hands, they were hardly recognizable as such. The bones looked to have been broken so many times, they were little more than splinters wrapped in skin.

Seren Almasy's eyes were glassy, dull, full of wrung-out fatigue that could only be the result of days and days of unrelenting pain. But when they focused on Cadfael, she shifted on the hay bale, and he noticed for the first time that one wrist and one ankle were very loosely tied to the wooden posts that held up the barn's rafters. "You . . . how did you . . . get here? You were headed for Lanvaldis . . . but this can't be . . ."

Before Cadfael could answer, Lirien stepped in front of him. "Hello. Remember me? You must know what I can do for you, but I'm *not* going to do it unless you prove that you can calm down, keep your knives sheathed, and not inconvenience these people any more than you already have."

Seren slumped back, and even that clearly hurt her, jostling her twisted leg. "I would never have . . . hurt them. I just don't want to be confined. They wouldn't let me leave."

"They probably saved your life," Lirien said. "Now hold still."

She traced her fingertips down Seren's bandaged hands, then curled them gently around each wrist. Seren flinched as her bones began to reassemble themselves, catching a cry of pain between her teeth. It was a testament to how badly they must have been shattered that it took so long for them to heal, their shape inching closer and closer to what proper hands should look like until they were finally whole. Lirien stepped away. "They'll be tender, and weak. If you start fighting or training right away you could damage them again, so don't. Do you understand?"

"Are you going to fix my leg?"

"Do you understand."

"I can't afford to stay here," Seren said, not irritable or stoic but pleading. "They've taken her to Valyanrend. There's no telling what they might do to her there, and no way for me to hear news of her. But whatever they have planned, sooner or later, it must surely end in her death. Knowing that, how can I waste even a moment?"

Cadfael was shocked by the revelation that Lady Margraine had been captured—for she was the only person Seren would talk about in such a way—but Lirien drew back for a different reason, with a sharp intake of breath. "So that's it," she muttered. "She was right; I really should have guessed. *That's* what that bitch is after."

"Who else knows about her ladyship's capture?" Cadfael asked Seren. "Does Adora know?"

Seren shook her head helplessly. "I know nothing of the outside world since she was taken. They left me like this, and I couldn't walk, or . . ." She wet her cracked lips. "I don't even know how long I've been here. These people found me, and they wouldn't let me leave."

"Because you'd have killed yourself," Lirien repeated.

"All the same, this village has no healer, and they didn't know what to do with me." She shuddered. "Though someone with the proper knowledge could probably have set my leg, I doubt anyone but you could have done a single thing for my hands. How did you even know I was here?"

"That's a complicated story," Cadfael said. "Do you know who specifically took her ladyship? Or anything else that might be helpful?"

"Is she going to heal my leg?" Seren asked again, looking at Lirien.

Lirien folded her arms. "Of course, eventually. But I'm well aware that as soon as you no longer need us, you'll burst out of here like a stampeding horse, and we'll lose our chance to learn anything more from you. So stop being in such a hurry, and answer his questions."

"I'll answer them," Seren said quietly. "But it's . . . very painful." Even without the clear evidence of his eyes, he'd have known that was true—Seren would never have admitted to that much weakness if she could help it.

"Lirien," he said. "I know you don't trust her, but she must have been in constant pain for days. It'll be hard enough for her to focus on our questions even without a broken leg."

Rhia had hung back behind them, but she nodded at Cadfael's words, speaking up for the first time. "She's helped you and the queen before. She risked her life with the rest of them to defeat Jocelyn and restore your magic."

"All right, all right. It's not as if I enjoy taking someone so wounded to task." Ever so gently, she worked off Seren's boot, spreading one hand out above her ankle and running the other across the surface of her foot. "Try to relax. This one will be brief."

When the leg snapped back into alignment with an audible crack, Rhia and Cadfael both winced. Lirien just kept hold of the foot, soothing the skin with the pads of her thumbs until she was satisfied the damage had been fully eradicated. "There. How does that feel?"

But Seren had passed out completely. "Didn't take her for the squeamish sort," Rhia said.

Lirien shook her head. "It isn't squeamishness, it's exhaustion. We should let her rest for now; she definitely needs it." She rubbed a hand across her brow. "But ugh, what a mess. The marquise captured? That's the last thing we need."

"Do you think Elgar plans to use her as a hostage?" Rhia bit her lip. "To force Her Grace to turn her army aside?"

"I doubt it," Cadfael said. "You haven't met the man, Rhia. Even if he knows of the friendship between the queen and the marquise, I doubt he would believe in it enough to think he could change Adora's mind that way. Arianrod is not a hostage but a prize for him. She humbled him so many times, foiled so many of his plans. That'll be uppermost in his mind. He has the pride for it."

"A surprisingly clever assessment," Lirien said. "But you know what that means, don't you? If she's not a hostage, she can't be ransomed. If she's a prize, he won't release her for anything. I don't like her chances then."

"But . . ." Rhia glanced down at Seren. "Where does that leave her? She can't simply abandon the one she serves."

"She won't," Lirien said flatly, "but not for that reason. Amerei would have no interest in that—in loyalty, duty, even self-sacrifice. Whether there's a way to rescue the marquise or not, that one will do it or die in the attempt. And nothing we say to her will change her mind."

Rhia was still looking at Seren's sleeping face, as if she could read some deeper truth in it. "I don't really understand her, and I can't say much for her personality, but . . . isn't there anything else we can do to help her?"

"Of course there is," Cadfael said. "We can do what we're already doing, and make our way to Valyanrend to bring down Elgar."

Lirien tugged at the end of her braid, brow furrowed. "That'll help some people, but not the marquise, I don't think. She must be held at the Citadel by now—if she hasn't been killed already. And even if Elgar were to be overthrown tomorrow, he would never depart this world without taking his most hated foe with him."

"Kelken and Hywel were captured, too, and we saved them."

Lirien smiled sadly. "Have you seen the Citadel? Don't mistake this for anything resembling national pride, but it's an entirely different breed from your little pile of stones in Araveil. It can house hundreds upon hundreds of soldiers, and unlike Selwyn, Elgar isn't suffering a shortage of them. Do you really think he's going to take any more chances with her security than he would with his own?"

"Well, if you're determined to be defeatist, there's nothing I can say to you." Cadfael folded his arms. "Surely the marquise is the second life Amerei spoke of, that might be saved if Seren survives. If a being with that much knowledge thinks there's a chance—"

"Do you really not understand yet?" Lirien snapped. "Amerei doesn't *care* about the marquise's life. If Seren rushes to Valyanrend and gets herself spectacularly killed fighting through Elgar's army single-handedly, that'll suit her just as well—better, perhaps. These spirits aren't concerned with our survival, with our happiness; all they want is their own glory. That's the truth behind the warning Yaelor gave you about Amerei. She never posed any danger to you at all. The danger was to *him*."

"What do you mean? A spirit can't be—"

"Killed, I know. I'm talking about their interests, not their lives. They want to see themselves in humans, Amerei said. Yaelor wanted you to go to Araveil, to fight Selwyn's people, but he wanted you to do it for *his* reasons, not hers."

"I don't even know what her reasons are," Cadfael said.

"I do. What can be selfish and remain a virtue?" She pointed at Seren. "What is that, if not a profoundly selfish and unselfish person? She'd run herself into the ground without complaint—and drag the rest of us down with her. You're like that, too, aren't you, about the people that you love?"

There is much of her in you already, Yaelor had said. For what had Cadfael wished to live for, if not to protect his family?

"Do you see now?" Lirien asked. "You were worthwhile to him only when he thought he could mold you in his image. But what you did at Sinthil Vlin wasn't an act of bravery. You risked your life like that because you didn't want Talis to die. And now he has abandoned you."

Cadfael opened his mouth to argue further, to say that he had always seen genuine pain on Yaelor's face where Rhia was concerned, but then Rhia herself stepped between them. "That's enough for now; we don't have enough information to make a decision yet anyway. Let's just wait for Seren to wake up, and hear what she has to say."

The morning light had streaked the sky before that time came. The elderly couple brought them breakfast out of gratitude to Lirien, and any doubts they might have had about her status as a healer disappeared when they saw Seren's condition. They couldn't let the couple know just how talented Lirien truly was, of course, but the bandages still largely obscured the state of Seren's hands, and Lirien claimed all she had done was set her leg. The couple didn't seem to have any medical knowledge of their own, and they accepted her explanation readily enough—perhaps they were so relieved at having the problem Seren posed taken care of that they would have believed anything.

Seren awoke before the bowl of porridge they'd reserved for her had gotten cold. They let her eat first, which she did ravenously, almost spilling it. And then, when they were sure she was done, Cadfael said, "Seren, we want to help. Just tell us what happened, or anything else you know."

And Seren did, detailing the full account of their capture at Lord Oswhent's hands, even the deal that Lady Margraine had struck for her safety. Cadfael swore when he heard that Ghilan had been responsible for her injuries. "Damn it, I can't believe we let him get away. If I'd known, I would've hunted him down myself."

"That one is mine to kill," Seren said. "And I will, no matter where he runs. I'm used to waiting for my vengeance."

Cadfael frowned. "Don't overextend yourself in pursuit of him. He's already defeated you once."

"Three people held me down before he even *touched* me," Seren snapped.

"I don't mean any insult to you as a warrior. I fought him myself, in Araveil, and found him a more challenging opponent than I had expected. We were essentially at a stalemate."

"I don't mean any insult to you as a warrior, either," Seren said, "but you and I were trained in different ways, for different purposes. I was not taught to fight in wars, to hack through armies on the field; I was taught to choose a target and end them, no matter how they might try to evade me. And I've chosen one." She twitched one shoulder. "Well, presuming it doesn't interfere with freeing my lady from Elgar. But Ghilan must have gone to Valyanrend by now, if what you've told me about the retaking of Araveil is true."

"Wait, what makes you so sure Ghilan is in Valyanrend?" Cadfael asked.

Seren rolled her eyes. "That man is *obsessed* with fighting—the first time I met him, he tried to pick one with me, solely on the strength of my reputation, even though he had nothing to gain from it beyond the fight itself. But he's not some ascetic duelist. He likes to live comfortably; you can tell that just by looking at him. So if you're someone who loves to fight and loves to get paid, and the Lanvaldian arenas are closed—"

"—you attach yourself to powerful people, and fight their enemies for coin," Cadfael finished. "But with Selwyn's defeat, those who have power in Lanvaldis now would kill him before they hired him. Esthrades is in chaos; Reglay's been captured; he and Adora would . . . not get along. Hallarnon is all that's left. And Oswhent already took him on once. Ghilan's either pursuing him again, or going after Elgar himself."

"And it doesn't really matter to me which," Seren said. "Either way, it puts him in the same place: Valyanrend, where I need to go anyway. For all I know, I might go up against him as a matter of course, without any extra effort at all."

Seren was one of the few people Cadfael liked, and he knew enough to appreciate her skills. But he had just watched Lirien literally put her back together after her last encounter with the people she was so eager to find, and taking on the Citadel's defenses added a whole other layer of difficulty to the endeavor. He glanced at Rhia and Lirien, unsure whether they would support what he had to say, but he still decided to try. "Seren, we don't have the attachment to the marquise that you do, but her importance to the war should be obvious to anyone. We were planning to go to Valyanrend anyway, to do whatever we can to help against Elgar. Why not come with us? There are two others we plan to meet up with first—Voltest you already know, and Talis is a *wardrenfell,* just like him and Lirien. I won't lie to you: saving the marquise from whatever death Elgar has planned is going to be difficult, no matter who's on our side. But with all of us assisting, it'll at least be easier than if you tried to do it alone."

Seren's gaze drifted away from his. Her expression was closed, and he couldn't tell what she was thinking. But whatever it was, it didn't take long. "I'm sorry," she said, in her usual flat tone. "But I'm going ahead to Valyanrend alone."

"Why?" Cadfael asked, before he could help himself. "Are you so disdainful of other people's abilities? Or are you just insisting on doing everything yourself out of pride?"

"That's not it at all." He was surprised at her surprise, so evident and undisguised. "Is that really what you think?"

"Then explain it to me."

She looked down at her still-bandaged hands, clenching and relaxing her fingers experimentally. Cadfael saw her wince, so they must have been as tender as Lirien had warned her they would be. "Cadfael, I . . . I *am* grateful. For your coming here, and your offer. Under different circumstances, I might even have accepted it. But I can compromise on no detours, not even for a moment. If I delayed, and that delay proved the difference between her life and death . . . I could suffer no worse fate. So let me go ahead of you, and I'll wait for you if I can. If Elgar—" Her face twisted, and she choked on the words before regaining her composure. "If he'd killed her immediately, enough time has passed that the wider world would have heard of her death by now. I think he must be waiting for something. In that case, I might be able to wait, too. And you're right that any of you, or all of you, could only help me."

Cadfael knew better than to argue with that. Wouldn't he be the same, if he thought he only had the narrowest chance to rescue Rhia? "I understand. I'm sorry for assuming. I just want you to be careful. Lirien's right that you're not at full strength yet, and you won't save anyone if you get killed before you have the chance to truly try."

"I understand that, too," Seren said. "I already told you what happened—the choice Oswhent forced my lady to make to save my life. After all that, if I just threw it away . . . I'd never make her sacrifice so meaningless. So I can promise you this: I'll make my life count, one way or another."

Cadfael nodded slowly, letting his gaze wander over to the other two. "I suppose that's all any of us can hope for."

Chapter Twenty-eight

Lanvaldis

It took days before Deinol was well enough to do anything but bleed.

They had carried him, the four of them—even Rana, with her bad hand. There had been a village close by, but, wary after what had happened with Seren's wound not so long ago, Lucius had interrogated the healer who came to dress Deinol's hand until he was satisfied they were doing enough to prevent infection. But there was nothing they could do about the pain, for all they had was snow's down, which could not be ingested or used on open wounds. So he had just lain there, on the bed, in the dark—it must have been the prince's coin that paid for the room, for he and Lucius had barely any left.

It had been terrible for Deinol once before, to be forced to be alone with his own thoughts. But it had been terrible because all the thinking in the world changed nothing: Seth was still dead, and it was still his fault. This time, though his thoughts remained unpleasant, they changed, his understanding of everything that had transpired slowly filling in with new detail.

He had not seen Ryo and the other two since their arrival; perhaps they had already left. Lucius had looked in on him once or twice, but had not questioned his silence or his exhaustion. After that it had just been the healer, and the servant boy at the inn who brought his food. It was always something he could eat with one hand.

After a span of days he could not have numbered, the pain, though still constant, began to lessen. Deinol could sit up and look at the bandages, though they did nothing to disguise the truth. He had two knuckles left on his first finger, one on his middle finger, an odd little nub on the fourth, and his little finger was gone entirely. He was fortunate to still have the thumb, the healer had said, and that the injury wasn't on his dominant side. He'd have less to relearn how to do. Though her hand looked prettier, it had probably been more of an adjustment for Rana, even if you left out the swordsmanship. Perhaps he'd talk to her about it, if she was still here.

If only I could have sustained such wounds for Seth, he thought. *Then they would mean something.*

As if on cue, Lucius poked his head into the room. "Oh. You're up."

"Half up," Deinol said. He had to get this over with at some point, he supposed.

Lucius sidled into the room, nudging the door shut behind him. "It's . . . dark in here."

"I think they expect it will help me rest."

"Oh," Lucius said again. "Should I . . . let you?"

"No," Deinol said. "You promised to tell me everything."

For a moment Lucius looked blank, but then he must have remembered when he'd said that, right before they had encountered Ryo and the others. He'd probably assumed he was likelier to die than have to fulfill it, Deinol thought.

Lucius moved toward the bed, but didn't actually sit, just kept fidgeting awkwardly. "Where do you want me to start?"

"You were a swordsman from Kaiferi named Kaitan Enrei," Deinol said, "and you became a *shinrian* because your prince accepted your challenge and you beat him. Then he appointed you to his royal guard, where you apprehended criminals, as well as serving as his shield. But when Elgar's army invaded Kaiferi and stormed Serenin Palace, Ryo was gravely wounded, and you fled the palace, and the city, and the country, rather than stick to the terms of your oath."

Lucius bowed his head. "I thought he had died, but yes."

"You did . . . whatever you did . . . and eventually you came to Valyanrend. To Sheath Alleys, the home of criminals." Deinol's voice began to shake, and he fought to steady it. "I won't ask why you came to reside in the capital city of your greatest foe. But why Sheath? Anyone could have told you what kind of people lived there, and you could have lived anywhere else."

Lucius raked a hand through his long hair. "Sheath was the best place to disappear, to pass anonymously among people who knew not to ask questions."

"No," Deinol said. "The truth, Lucius."

Lucius trembled, pressing his lips tightly together. But then he nodded. "I . . . after what I had done in Kaiferi—the betrayal of all I had ever claimed to stand for—I felt that I was a criminal already, and that it would be even more contemptible to pretend otherwise. But I've never liked to be alone. I thought, rather than troubling people of honor with my company again, I should seek out those who would be more suited—"

"What, to your new life as a criminal?" Deinol asked. "But it's more than that. When you approached us back then—me, Roger, even Morgan, though she'd never committed any crime—it wasn't in friendship. Was it? You wanted to be among people where you wouldn't feel ashamed, but that was only possible because you felt *we* should be just as ashamed of ourselves as you. Because you felt you were at least no worse than we were, and probably better, given the good you did once. Or am I wrong?"

The words were squeezed from Lucius's throat as if they had to be dragged out. "You aren't . . . wrong, but . . . it was only like that at the beginning. I wasn't sure how close I even wanted to be with anyone again. The idea was to be among people, but not to let myself get truly involved with them." He smiled hesitantly. "But when I met the lot of you, I couldn't keep to that goal. As time passed, and I saw more of you, I found myself wanting to be more than just another face in the background of Morgan's bar. It surprised me, too. I hadn't thought I could ever feel such kinship with—"

He bit off the end of the sentence, but Deinol finished it for him. "With thieves and liars. With the dregs of society. That's all we were to you." He had figured it out already, but to hear it aloud stirred anew the anger he'd thought he was too exhausted to feel. "And yet we've never failed one another. Not like you failed those comrades of yours."

Lucius stared at him, surprised more than hurt, though the hurt was there. "You said you didn't care about my past—"

"*You* told me you never lied about our friendship! But the whole thing was *founded* on lies! I was minding my own business in Sheath, just trying to get by, and you came around with that friendly fucking smile, drinking Morgan's ale, listening to Roger's stories, telling me we should be partners and run jobs together, and behind it, all the while you were thinking, *I suppose I belong in the muck with these other pigs.* We were never your equals, just the ones you ran with because you wanted to debase yourself, to forget this glorious past of yours. Isn't that right?"

"You were—you *are*—my friends," Lucius said. "And I would give my life for you, then as now. I'm sorry for how I began it, truly. All of you deserved better. But it ended in the same place you always thought. Isn't that the important thing?"

"It's not what I thought. It still isn't. I saw how you were with them—how you'd never been with us, not even me. They're the people who mean the most to you in the whole world. And I thought . . . I suppose it was arrogant of me, but I thought that was *us*." Deinol shook his head, angry with himself, too, for still being so upset. "We were just . . . the next best thing. The people you settled for because you couldn't be with them. And if that prince of yours had truly tried to kill me, you wouldn't have stopped him. Would you?"

"He would never have tried to kill you," Lucius said, as if ill at the very thought.

"That's not an answer. If he had, would you have stopped him? I know that if I'd raised my sword against him, you would have done whatever it took to protect him, even if that meant you had to kill me. But what about the reverse? Would you have hurt him to protect me? To save my life? Would you have, Lucius? Or . . . whatever I should call you?"

Lucius stood there, face twisted in pain, jaw working as if he had so much to say. But no words came out. Deinol waited, cursing himself for hoping. But eventually he had to accept that Lucius would not, could not, give him an answer. Which, of course, was an answer all its own.

"Fine, then," he said. "I think you and I both know, anyway."

"Deinol—"

"Look at my hand!" Deinol shouted, waving it in his face. "Look at what I did for a liar and a fraud! It wouldn't have mattered if you'd just been who I thought you were. But you made a fool out of me!"

"I—" Lucius stood there impotently, staring at his feet. "I'm so sorry."

"Aye, that's what you said to him, too, isn't it? He may be a prince, but I understand one thing about him perfectly. It's the pain of knowing you'd do something for someone that they wouldn't return. It's having you make a fool out of him, and all you can offer is your regret."

He curled himself up, turning to face the wall. "I have nothing more to say to you. And I don't want to see you here again."

He kept his eyes shut until Lucius left.

KAITAN ENREI SHUT the front door of the house behind him and walked around its side, out of the way of the main street. There, half-masked by the building's shadow, he could sag against the wall in peace, sliding down it until he was slumped in a heap. He put his hands over his face, listening to how muffled his breathing sounded when he exhaled into them. Fitful spots of light broke through the cracks between his fingers, and he squeezed his eyes shut.

He had always prided himself on being master of his emotions' outward seeming, no matter how he was truly feeling within. It was essential for one who was strong to have control of himself, so he did not act impulsively in ways he'd regret. And it was something to cling to, when he had nothing else. How fitting that, now that he'd lost so much, even that seemed to want to leave him.

He felt a presence settle next to him. "Has his condition deteriorated that much?"

That voice. Gods, that voice. It had taken him so long to convince himself he would never hear it again, and almost as long to reconcile himself to the fact that its owner might still be alive. Yet he could not hear it, still, without struggling against a wave of emotion that threatened to pull him under.

Ryo was still speaking to him, albeit for a terrible reason. That was most unbelievable of all.

"It's not that," Kaitan told him. "The healer says he's recovering as well as can be expected, and there's no sign of infection. He just . . . doesn't want to see me. In any way whatsoever."

Ryo could have responded cuttingly to that, giving voice to any one of a hundred condemnations flickering through Kaitan's own thoughts. Instead, he sat beside him in silence. This close, it was all Kaitan could do not to pore over every aspect of his face, searching for similarities or differences, expressions made harsher by time. In the past, a silence like this between them would have been companionable, safe. Now it was an abyss with no bottom, the far side too distant to make out.

"I thought you were dead," he said, because he had absolutely nothing left to lose. "There's no way I can prove it, but I truly did."

"I believe you thought so," Ryo said. "But I also know you could've checked, and didn't. You were running too fast for that."

"I know I could have. I know I ought to have. That I didn't will haunt me every day, every day for as long as I live."

Ryo said nothing. Kaitan searched his face, but it didn't answer him, either. He just sat there next to him. But even though they were at such odds, still it did Kaitan's heart such good to see him. He was older, rougher, scarred, yet he was the same man. He threw his vengeance aside to help a stranger harmed inadvertently. And he wouldn't strike at Kaitan now, not without announcing it. Such were his principles—not the hollow things Kaitan had pretended to, but immutable laws of his universe.

Finally, Ryo spoke. "When I offered you the chance to join my *kaishinrian*, why did you accept?"

"Why?" Kaitan repeated, incredulous. "Why wouldn't I have? It's what I wanted most."

"No. I don't think it was." He said the words without anger. "It was what Rana wanted most, which is why she met every misfortune with equanimity except the one that robbed her of her fighting skill. It wasn't what Gao wanted most, but he chose it freely, which is why he never tried to escape it. But you're different."

Yes, he was. He always had been, no matter how he had tried to be otherwise. "You're right that the position itself meant nothing to me. I've never cared about honor, though I grew adept at faking it. I suppose I do care about skill, about strength; I genuinely enjoyed learning the sword. It was my skill that led me to Rana, and she . . . changed everything for me. She was exactly the kind of person I wanted to be like, that I wanted to be close to. But no matter how many times we sparred, it never made me feel important to her the way I wanted to be. Then, while I was too cautious to try to make *shinrian* until I knew I was ready, she issued an impetuous challenge, defeated Gao after a week of matches, and forged a friendship stronger than steel. And then, while I scarcely had time to covet that, you came along and made them *kaishinrian*. But you didn't just want servants— you wanted friends, fellow warriors on the same path with you. I wanted a bond that tied me to someone else that tightly. No, not just someone else—someone as magnificent as the three of you were."

"Ah." Just that much, that little crumb, and no more. Kaitan searched his face again, that face whose moods he had once read so easily. No, he was done. That was all he meant to say.

So Kaitan spoke instead. "What about you, *kaihen*? Why did you choose me?"

Ryo sighed. "Because I thought you were like me. It was so hard for me to prove myself as a swordsman, to find someone willing to challenge me who could forget I was a prince and stop holding back. And you faced difficulties, too. Because you'd almost won once, and against such a talented opponent, no one wanted to give you another chance to surpass them. So I did it myself. And then, when you beat me—when you didn't hold back, and came at me with everything—I thought you understood. I thought you believed we were the same, too." He shook his head. "I was too naïve, and too self-important. I just vainly saw myself in you, like a dandy so obsessed with his own reflection he sees it in every shop window."

"I wanted to be like you," Kaitan said. "But I was never capable of reaching your heights. Eventually, I had to admit that to myself."

Ryo shook his head again. "Anyone could be like me if they wanted."

"No," Kaitan said. "No. You are the only one I've ever met who is like you."

Silence, again. He knew it was selfish, to want to know everything Ryo thought and felt about him. He had always wanted that, from the moment they first spoke. But he couldn't keep himself from asking, "Do you hate me? I wouldn't blame you if you did. I just . . . want to know."

Ryo pressed a fist to his chest, where Kaitan knew that horrible scar lay. "Hating you would be much simpler, though probably just as exhausting. I'm *angry* at you, but that's not the same thing. And . . . I feel that I'm finally starting to understand you, after all these years. It didn't make sense to think that everything about you had been a lie from the start, but what you're saying now *does* make sense—so much so that it can only be the truth I sought in vain in my memories of you. The fact that still matters to me . . . I suppose it proves I haven't been able to cut you from my consciousness cleanly, as much as I'd like to say I have."

He stood up, and brushed himself off. But then he lingered, his head turning slightly toward where Kaitan sat, as if against his will. "I know you're sorry, Kaitan," he said. "I know you've suffered—in a different way than we've suffered, and in a way you brought upon yourself, but still. You have suffered. Perhaps you always will." He looked away, though he didn't truly seem to see the village houses, or even the open sky. "But I can't forgive you, Kaitan. And I don't think I ever will."

It would have been better, Kaitan thought, to die at his hand. Deinol would never have been harmed, and he could have departed this world wrapped in some fantasy that he was balancing the scales. That he was giving his life for Ryo, the way he always ought to have.

But he had already spent five years knowing that it would have been better never to have run. He knew how immutable the past was, how pointless to go over it again and again, as if it were some work in progress that could be changed.

They said nothing to each other, but neither moved, as if conscious of a thread that still pulled taut between them. And then Ryo broke it, and walked away.

Kaitan remembered a time, years and years ago, deep in the snows of Aurnis. They had been set upon suddenly, a group of bandits in the night, who had melted away into the darkness after their initial assault was repelled. As the youngest and newest *kaishinrian,* Kaitan had been left to guard the prince personally while the rest of them spread out to track their foes.

Ryo had been so charmingly naïve back then, unable to retreat or show caution when he could attempt to fight through a situation instead. He believed there was nothing that could not be achieved through sufficient valor and force of will—and so, when arrows started flying in their direction from out of the darkness, Kaitan had to tackle him to the ground to keep him from being hit, covering him with his own body.

He could still remember those moments so clearly, Ryo flopping helplessly in the snow like a beached fish, trying to slip out of his hold. "Damn it, Kaitan, this is too undignified. Just let me up! I can fight them!"

"Kaihen," he had begged, "please stay down, please just stay down until the others get back . . ."

Where had he found such courage back then? He remembered being sick with fear, but only at the thought that a stray arrow might slip under his arm or through some other gap and strike Ryo despite his best efforts. It barely occurred to him that he might die himself, and he felt no concern at the thought. Perhaps it was the closest he had ever come to being the person he wanted to be.

It felt like it took an hour, but finally the others had arrived—Gao first, with Rana trailing not far behind. "It's all clear," she called.

Kaitan had finally let go of Ryo, but that didn't do anything to save them from Gao's significantly raised eyebrow. There he had been, larger than life as always, both eyes glimmering with mirth. "Ah, so that's how it is, eh? The rest of us do all the hard work while the two of you roll around in the snow?"

"Gao, don't add to my humiliation." Ryo had punched both fists into the snow, sending up flurries. "I ordered Kaitan to let me fight, but he ignored me."

"Well, that's your own fault, isn't it, *kaihen*? You're the one who gave us permission to disobey your orders if we felt it was a matter of principle."

"Subjecting me to this embarrassment was a matter of principle?"

"If you'd listened to him, there wouldn't have been anything embarrassing about it," Rana said. "He probably saved your life."

She was always like that—unfailingly polite when she felt honor dictated it, but never too timid to say what she thought was right. Of the three of them, she looked the least different now, but Kaitan knew what a cruel joke that was.

Subdued and chastised, Ryo had sat up, resting his hands on his knees. "That's . . . true, I'm sure. Sorry, Kaitan. You know I get carried away sometimes, but rashness is unbecoming in one who would ask others to defend him."

Kaitan ducked his head. "Oh, no, it's not for you to apologize to me, *kaihen* . . ."

Gao laughed, leaning down to slap him on the shoulder so hard he was nearly knocked flat into the snow. "Look at this one, still stuck on ceremony! You'll learn to leave that behind soon enough."

Rana rolled her eyes, but the fondness in her face was unmistakable. "No one's thrown off more ceremony than you, Gao. You could stand to take on a little more once in a while." She smiled. "Well done, Kaitan."

"Aye, not easy to subdue this one when he's in a mood."

"Yes, yes, I'm so very difficult a charge." Ryo stood, shaking off the snow, then extended a hand down to Kaitan. When they were all standing, he looked them over. "I know how lucky I am to have you," he said, any trace of joking gone. "All of you."

Kaitan didn't notice at first that he'd closed his eyes again, or dropped his head back into his hands. He just tried to hold very still, as if to keep from flying apart. But then a familiar boisterous voice said, "See, here he is," and he looked up, blinking until his vision stopped swimming.

Gao and Rana took Ryo's place, sitting on either side of him. "Well," Gao said calmly, "this sure is a rotten mess, isn't it."

"You must have learned to expect that, where I'm concerned," Kaitan said.

"Oh, I have. But this one, at least, isn't completely your fault."

"It is," Kaitan insisted. "Deinol . . . I should've tried harder to lose him. I should have ordered him not to follow me, for the sake of our friendship. I should have just told him everything beforehand, so that if he was going to end up hating me anyway, he wouldn't have had to get hurt first."

"Do you really think that would've worked?" Gao asked.

"I don't know! But I should've *tried*!" He raked both hands through his hair, trying to find his usual steadiness. But what was the point? These two had always been able to read him.

"Ryo says he won't ever forgive me," he told them. "I suppose you feel the same?"

"Well, I can't exactly say I'm proud of you for it." Gao tilted his head back, catching the meager rays of sun on his face. "On the other hand, you never swore an oath to me. I might be spitting mad at you, but it's not for me to forgive you or not. Only Ryo can do that."

Rana was quiet for longer, staring at her right hand. "I knew you longer than anyone, Kaitan. Longer, and, I thought, better. When Ryo determined to make you *kaishinrian,* he asked me what I thought, since you and I had been such famous rivals at the first and second schools. I said I didn't think being *kaishinrian* was what you wanted. Then you seemed to flourish in the role, and I regretted what I had said. But I was right all along, wasn't I?"

"In a way," Kaitan admitted. "I did want it, but not for the right reasons. I thought achieving it would make me equal to the three of you. But you're right. Someone with those motives should never have received the honor."

"Still," she said, as if musing to herself. "You were good at it, for a time."

"It was easy, as long as you all were with me. Because you were the true reason I did it. Once I believed everyone I had cared for was gone, I became a coward. But if I had known the truth . . . if I had known I could've been with you this whole time . . ."

"And never met your friend?" Rana asked. "Is that really what you want?"

"It would've been doubly better," Kaitan said. "If he had never met me, he wouldn't be in this pain."

"Perhaps. But I asked if that is what you *want,* Kaitan. It's clear you fight for him, too."

What had she called them? Each the other's perfect whetstone. She forced him to sharpen even against his will, refused to let him linger in any kind of dullness or obfuscation. So, then. What did he really want? On the one hand, the chance never to have been separated from Ryo, never to have failed him—never to know the pain of thinking him dead, or the pain of the words, *I can't forgive you, Kaitan.* The things they might have done together, these past five years—the closeness that only grows between those who have survived such things together. The pain Kaitan might have eased for them, the burdens he could have shared. It was an alternate history he would never know, but that was beyond price.

But what price, then, could he put on those he had known in Sheath? He had been terrible to them in the beginning, though they had never known it. Deinol was right. He had hidden his feelings of superiority behind a smile and an air of courtesy, but underneath, despite his knowledge of all he had done, he still thought he had the right to judge them, even if he never said the words aloud. He had thought they were little people, crude, who had never striven or longed for anything noble or beautiful.

But over time, so gradually he hadn't even noticed at first, his views had changed. *He* had changed. He had seen the unobtrusive ways they helped each other, with no talk of scores or debts. Deinol would take it upon himself to patch a leak in the Dragon's Head's roof, and Morgan would give him a hot meal even when she knew he lacked the coin, despite all her talk of business. Roger would overpay her for something after he'd had a windfall and invent a reason for it, and she would drive off some belligerent victim of his schemes who'd shown up at the tavern looking to settle the score. And when Seth had come to Valyanrend, a penniless farm boy, no great nobles or soldiers or swordsmen had taken any notice of his plight; if it had been up to them, he would have starved to death. It was Deinol and Morgan, a bastard thief and a tavern owner, who had fed him, sheltered him, given him sanctuary. And Kaitan had wanted to be a part of that, as much as he had ever wanted to be noticed by the prince of Aurnis.

"So that's it," he said. "I want two things, and I can't have both."

"Eh," Gao said. "From where I'm sitting, it looks like you can't have either."

"Gao, enough." Rana flicked him on the shoulder. "These little swipes are a childish way to express your anger."

"Right as always. And I intend to continue them." He grinned at Kaitan, that same coldness in his single eye. "If he objects, he can always fight me over it."

"You'll hear no objections from me," Kaitan said. "Just answer me one thing, Gao. How did the three of you escape Serenin Palace alive?"

"I don't know why you're so surprised. We went the same way you did: through the hidden entrance to Kaiferi's underground river. Providing royals an escape is the whole point of its existence."

"But we already tried that," Kaitan insisted. "Ryo refused to leave. He was determined to make his damned last stand at the palace."

"Aye, so he was," Gao said. "But with a wound that severe, he was no longer in a state to refuse anything. Rana and I were the only ones left, so we took the liberty of changing his plans." He showed a flash of his teeth. "We did waste some time looking for you, out of, oh, loyalty, or some such, but we couldn't find you. So we carried Ryo to the passage, meaning to use the river to escape. And what did we discover, Kaitan, but that you'd already taken the bloody boat, and left us stranded? Gods' sakes, if you'd run that fast in competition, you'd have beaten the best sprinters in Aurnis."

Of course it hurt. How could it not, to have such evidence of how far he'd fallen in Gao's esteem? But it was no less than Kaitan deserved. "That only makes your survival more impossible to understand."

"Because you'd fucked us so thoroughly, you mean? Well, don't worry, you definitely had. Thank the gods for Rana's quick thinking. The passage to the underground river, you'll recall, starts in the throne room, but wends its way past the kitchens' largest pantry, with a second entrance there. And everyone else in the throne room was dead, our people and Elgar's both—though we knew Hallern reinforcements would be upon us any minute. So we stripped Ryo of his cloak and sword—the only fancy things he wore—and put them on the body of the soldier who looked the most like him, then dragged Ryo himself down the passage and out into the kitchens through the pantry entrance. The kitchen servants kept him there, in the guise of one of their own who'd been attacked too aggressively by the invading army.

"Elgar's people were much more timid in those days, so eager to prove themselves reasonable and merciful overlords so the people wouldn't rebel. If they'd gone through the palace with fire and sword, we'd have been lost. Instead, they allowed the healers full access to every wounded civilian. They gave our prince no worse care than we'd have given him ourselves, but only because they thought he was a commoner."

"But he must have woken up eventually. How would his honor stand for such a deception?"

"Rana guessed it," Gao said. "By the time he regained consciousness, every servant in the palace had signed onto the lie—that the prince was dead, and Ryo just a servant. If he'd revealed himself after that, who could say what vengeance the Hallerns would have wreaked on those servants?"

Of course. Ryo might be willing to die for his principles, but he'd never take others down with him. And of course Rana had seen that.

"But Rana and I couldn't disguise ourselves as servants," Gao continued. He gestured to himself. "This form was simply too well known, and for good reason."

"What he means to say," Rana interrupted, "was that a dozen Hallerns got a good look at us and our fresh wounds when we abandoned the outer corridor. They would have recognized us if we attempted to hide who we were, so we had to hide ourselves entirely. We fled back into the passage to the river with as much food as we could carry, and rationed it while we waited."

"Once Ryo's condition had improved enough," Gao finished, "one of the other servants was able to get word out of the castle, to her brother. Using directions Ryo had provided, he found the place where the underground river breaks the surface once more. Apparently, you'd even left the boat tied up there, Kaitan. This fellow took it back upstream to me and Rana, Ryo slipped away through the pantry entrance, and the four of us followed the river back out and away. In the wider world, everyone thought we were dead, so no one was looking for us. We had no coin and no resources, and don't have much now, but we've been able to live the last five years without being hunted."

"Though not without the shame of being unable to liberate our home," Rana said.

"Aye, of course, can't forget that. And that's the story, Kaitan."

"I still can't believe it was such a near thing," Kaitan said. "I . . . almost didn't lose you."

"If you hadn't chosen to run from us to begin with, you wouldn't have needed to rely on luck to keep us close," Rana said, her words bearing the same sting of truth as always. "It's not fate, but your own choices that separated us."

It had always been his own choices, over and over. He might change his name, but he would never be able to throw off who he was. Someone who had come so close to his dream, then dashed it to pieces with his own hands.

"Even so," he said, "it's good to see you again."

They were silent. Perhaps he deserved that, too. And yet they could have told him the opposite was true, and they didn't. He would hold on to that.

It SEEMED DEINOL was still not to be left alone, for the door to his room creaked open and closed once more. He knew from the tread that it wasn't Lucius, but he was still surprised when he looked up and saw Ryo standing over him. "Sorry," Deinol said, "you can't frighten me. If you were going to finish me off, you'd have done it already. And if you've come to complain some more, that's fine, too; I was hoping to get some sleep in."

Ryo betrayed no reaction, just stood there like a statue. Was he . . . awkward? "I don't wish to disturb you any more than necessary. I simply did not want to appear as if I was hiding from my responsibility toward you."

Deinol shrugged. "You're paying for the room, aren't you? You're not a healer, so I don't know what else you could do."

"There is . . . one more thing."

"Oh? If you have coin left over that you don't know what to do with, I'll happily take it off your hands."

Ryo drew a knife, and Deinol tensed despite his earlier bravado; the prince was just so hard to read. But as Ryo extended his arm, it was the knife's handle that he pointed toward Deinol. "Kaitan was right about one thing: I had no quarrel with you. To let such an accident occur, with all the skill as a *shinrian* and judgment as a prince I claimed to possess, is simply inexcusable. But such an apology does nothing to change your circumstances. If I still had the resources of a prince, I could offer you more proper restitution, but I have long had to make peace with the fact that I lack the ability to take back what's mine. Instead, all I can offer you is my blood. My suffering, to pay for yours."

The knife hung there between them, neither of them moving an inch. Then Deinol shook his head in disbelief. "Is that really the best you can do? For a prince, your solutions are so childish. Killing Lucius won't do anything to lessen the pain you feel at his betrayal, or turn him into the person you thought he was. And what the hell do you think a few of your fingers are going to do for me? I can't sell them, I'd prefer not to eat them, and I certainly can't use them in place of the ones I lost. If that's your idea of recompense, I'm not interested."

He'd thought Ryo might be angry, but he just stood there, considering Deinol's words. "You tell me, then. What price would you have me pay?"

Deinol took a moment to arrange his words, but he already knew the gist of what he wanted to say. "There's someone I wish you could've met. A young boy of no rank, who worked at a tavern. He gave his life to save a woman I thought was my enemy, and she wanted to pay him back. But I have to admit she knew him well, because she knew he was too wise to ever care for vengeance. Instead, she risked her own life to save me and Lucius, even though we meant nothing to her, because she knew we were people Seth had loved. That was her recompense, and that was worth something. You want to pay me back? Do it by helping the people I care about."

"And who do you care about?" Ryo asked. "Kaitan?"

"No," Deinol said. "Not him. Not anymore."

Whatever the prince felt at those words, he kept it hidden, at least from Deinol's eyes. "Who, then?"

"The ones I left behind in Sheath," Deinol said. "Sheath Alleys, in Valyanrend. Morgan Imrick. Roger Halfen. And aye, I suppose even that layabout Braddock, too. If you count it knuckle by knuckle, I've essentially lost three fingers. So let's say one of my friends for each of my fingers, and we'll be even."

"Fair enough. I accept those terms. Will you return to Valyanrend?"

"Aye, as soon as I'm well enough to travel."

"Then I and the remains of my *kaishinrian* will go with you." Deinol didn't know what else there was to say, but Ryo remained where he was. "It is a good price," he said at last. "A better one than mine. I . . . understand what he saw in you."

"Is that supposed to make me happy?"

"I couldn't say. It would not make me happy, if you said the same to me. But it's the truth."

THE RISEN CITY   223

Deinol slumped back down on the bed, cradling his wounded hand against his side. "What are you going to do about him? Do you still want to kill him?"

"Gao and Rana have asked that I do not draw my sword against him again, so long as he refuses to fight me," Ryo said. "And they're right, of course. That is how I should've handled it from the beginning. And he will never fight me. I know that now."

"He may try to follow you," Deinol insisted. "He'll *probably* try to follow you."

"Well, I'm returning with you to the place that is his home now. I can't forbid him from going there, too. But I have nothing to say to him, and that will not change."

"Huh," Deinol said. "Then I guess we have something in common after all."

Chapter Twenty-nine

Valyanrend

Ritsu had known it would be worse once he was inside Valyanrend proper, but he hadn't counted on just how much worse it would be. There were so many sensations: the differences between districts, temporary marketplaces that spilled over into the streets, the marble Citadel with its black walls in the distance, the sound of blacksmiths' hammers, merchants hawking their wares, the scent of smoke, the feel of his boots on stone. Things that Ritsu Hanae had never experienced before, or not in this specific way. He had never been to this city, but Shinsei had known it like the back of his hand, and that discrepancy, the constant assault of things he *did* remember, made it so much more difficult to hold on to who he was. Who he wanted to be? No, who he *was*. He rustled the parchment in his pocket; he'd taken to using the sound to remind him it was there. Even if he forgot what his hand was doing in his pocket and tried to take it out, the sound always set him straight again.

He pulled the parchment free and unfolded it, taking comfort from the untidy scrawl that helped him remember Deinol. Morgan Imrick, at the Dragon's Head, in Sheath Alleys. Shinsei knew where Sheath Alleys was. Should he . . . no, dangerous to rely on that knowledge. Better to ask someone. Sheath Alleys. Sheath Alleys.

The people he asked gave him strange looks, but he was fairly certain it wasn't because of how he looked or how he asked, and more because they couldn't imagine why a traveler would want to go there.

The parchment went back in his pocket, clutched in his clenched fist, and he walked on. It got a bit better once he arrived in the neighborhood itself; perhaps Shinsei knew of its existence, but had not spent much time there, because there were no streets or buildings that raised any uncomfortable memories. But then, rounding a corner ahead of him, he saw . . . that color. Two men in blue-black uniforms, the color that Shinsei had worn for five years. That *he* had been wearing when Deinol had found him, because . . .

The next thing he knew, he was kneeling in the street, one hand covering his face. The other was stuck in his pocket, but he had forgotten why. What was he doing here?

Someone prodded him with a foot, as if trying to turn him over. But before he could lash out, a high, sharp voice said, "Hey, leave him alone. He's not a corpse for you to loot."

"Rich hearing that from Tom Kratchet's monkey," another voice said—the owner of the foot—but he obligingly walked off. Someone else crouched beside him, peering into his face, and he tilted his head up so he could see her. It was a scrawny girl with reddish-brown hair, face screwed up in a frown that felt more puzzled than accusatory. Neither Shinsei nor Ritsu Hanae had any memory of her. It made him feel, for a moment, like he was one person, and not two.

"You all right?" she asked. "Do you feel sick?"

"I'm . . . not sure. I . . ." He tried to pull his hand out of his pocket, and heard the rasp of paper. "I have it written down. I'm trying to get—"

He didn't feel the girl rifling through his pockets, but somehow the parchment was in her hand anyway. Her frown deepened as she read it over. "What's all this? Information on some person you're looking for?"

"No, it's . . ." He winced. "It's me. I think."

"You wrote down information about yourself?"

"No, my . . . friend wrote it." He couldn't remember his friend's name, not without seeing the handwriting.

"Why would—you know what, never mind. Let's just get this sorted. You're Ritsu Hanae?"

"Yes." It was such a relief to hear it aloud, even as a question and not a statement. "Ritsu. That's right."

"And you're . . . shit." She bit her lip. "Morgan Imrick, at the Dragon's Head? That's where you're trying to go?"

"Yes," Ritsu said, remembering that, too. "He told me I could trust her. I need someone to remind me to be myself, until I can break the curse."

"I've no idea what that means, but I'm about to make you Morgan's problem instead of mine. I can take you there. Come on." She helped him to his feet, then threaded her arm through his, pulling him along with her. It was nice, because he didn't have to look at anything too much. And when they got to the tavern, he didn't recognize it, either.

The girl pulled him inside, where it was cooler and darker. There was a woman with long black hair standing on the other side of the bar. "Thank the gods you're here today instead of Braddock," the girl said. "I wouldn't want to have to wait with this one for you to get back."

Ritsu didn't recognize the woman, but there was something about her that was familiar. Like he'd heard about her from someone, once. "Is he hurt?" she asked the girl.

"He's definitely confused. But he was carrying this."

She handed the woman the sheet of parchment, and she'd only taken a glance at it when she hissed a breath out through her teeth. "Deinol. I'd know this pathetic attempt at handwriting anywhere. Good to know he's still alive, I suppose. And still sending confused young men to my doorstep." She waved the parchment at him. "You're Ritsu Hanae? Why did he send you to me?"

"He said I could trust you. He said if I needed a place to stay . . ."

She clicked her tongue. "And let me guess, you've no money."

"No," Ritsu admitted, "but I can work. That's how I got here—I worked for meals, and places on carts. I'm stronger than I look."

"Well, you look to me like you're very ill."

"That's just the curse," Ritsu insisted. "It's gotten worse since I've come here. I've been looking for the steel so I can break it, but I can't find it anywhere."

He expected them to look at him in bewilderment—everyone else had—but instead they both caught their breath, and the woman leaned down toward him over the bar. "The steel?" she repeated.

"Someone used it on me once. It broke the curse then. But I don't know where she is." He sighed. "I shouldn't expect you to understand."

The girl tilted her head toward the woman. "Shouldn't you . . . ?"

"We just met him," the woman said. "You want to let him know so easily? What if he tells someone?"

"Would anyone believe him? Is there . . . some other way to help him? Without telling him?"

Ritsu was used to not understanding what people were talking about, so he waited patiently for them to finish. The woman frowned at him, pinching the bridge of her nose. "All right. Here's what we're going to do. Ritsu, if you really are cursed, I might be able to break it. Can you think of anything you're carrying that might be the cause?"

Ritsu shook his head. "There used to be a similar curse on my sword, but I lost it. This one is just on me."

"Cast on your body directly? Is that possible?" She looked deeply troubled at the thought. "Either way, I'll try to help you, but I have two conditions. One: once the curse is gone, you tell me absolutely everything about it, everything you can remember."

Ritsu would have preferred to avoid that if he could have—he didn't want anyone knowing about his connection to Shinsei—but if it was the only way, he'd take it. "All right. I promise. What's the second condition?"

"That you sit on that stool right in front of me, close your eyes, and don't open them until I tell you."

"That's it?" What a strange request. But he did as she'd asked, squeezing his eyes firmly shut. "Are you going to do it now?"

"Yes." He heard a slight metallic scrape, and then something was pressed to his forehead: cool, then freezing, and then—

He remembered everything.

It was as if his vision had been blurred until now, and he could finally, finally see. Memories were no longer revealed to him only a few at a time, constantly slipping through his fingers even as he struggled to hold on to them. They were simply there, waiting to be combed through at his leisure: the faces of his parents and friends, every nook and cranny of his former home. He could remember the time his father had taken him beyond the Howling Gate to the northern coast, all that silver-white ice stretching infinitely off into the distance. He had thought, back then, that he would remember that sight forever, and now here it was. It wasn't lost. It hadn't been destroyed. It was all here, right where he had left it—all the things that had ever made him real.

And the man called Shinsei was only a phantom, a bad dream, burning away in the sun like a wisp of fog. How ridiculous, how laughable to think that he had ever been Shinsei. He could remember so clearly who he was.

He heard someone say, "Are you all right? You can open your eyes now," and realized that they were still closed. He opened them, but he no longer saw figures that he only half understood. He was whole again, and could make solid new memories now, as well as recalling old ones. This woman behind the bar was Morgan Imrick, the friend of Deinol, whose kindness had brought him to this moment. And the girl with the reddish-brown hair had been called *Tom Kratchet's monkey,* though that was a riddle he had yet to solve.

He leaned forward and took Morgan's hands in his. "It's finally over. Thank you. Thank you so much."

She fidgeted a bit, not meeting his eyes, but didn't pull her hands away. "Ah, well, it's not as if it was any great effort. It's more important that you keep your silence about it."

"*And* that you keep up your end of the deal," the girl piped up.

"Of course. If you had the power to break the curse, you must possess vardrath steel. I would never repay your kindness by revealing it to anyone. And I am in your debt, far beyond simply relating my story. But I must ask . . . I told some of it to Deinol, but it greatly surprised him. You seem to know much more of magic than he does. Is that true?"

"When the two of us parted, neither of us knew anything about it at all," she said. "But we've been on different paths since then. He's probably learned things on his that I could never dream of, but here's where mine has brought me: the one who cursed you was the imperator, wasn't it?"

"So you know even that much." He picked up the parchment Deinol had written him, which Morgan had left on the bar. "What a twist of fate. When Deinol sent me to you, it was for no more than shelter. If only we had both known earlier that you held the answer to my dilemma all along."

"And here I thought he'd only sent me more trouble, not just the person I ought to speak to. Then again, I suppose that rogue's always had the gift of being lucky when it counts." She squinted at Ritsu's forehead, where she'd touched him with the steel, as if she expected a mark to be left behind. "Elgar truly cast the spell on your body itself, without any kind of intermediary? We didn't know he could do that."

"We?" Ritsu repeated.

She pressed her lips together. "Those who wish to stop such foul magic."

"Well, you can certainly count me among that number, though I won't press you for more than you want to say. I didn't know this was something he had done to others. So in your experience, people are controlled with objects?"

"Aye, but not swords, like you said. Tiny things, like stones."

"But I don't understand," the girl said. "If he doesn't need intermediaries, why use them?"

"I believe I am the answer to that," Ritsu said. "I was first cursed five years ago, in a process that killed dozens before me. As far as I know, I am the only one to survive it. He must have been experimenting with his powers back then. But creating one successful soldier for every fifty or sixty deaths is a terrible rate of return, and the more of those experiments he performed, the less likely he could keep it a secret. Also, I think I'm . . . different from the others. He erased my memories—all of them, even my own name. But that only worked because he found me when I was a prisoner in Aurnis, and he brought me to Hallarnon afterward—a new country, where no one knew the person I truly was, and there was nothing to stir the memories he had suppressed. He couldn't do any of that here. An epidemic of memory loss, or of people disappearing, would be as suspicious as a rash of deaths."

Morgan leaned heavily on the bar. "But it sounds like his control over you wasn't temporary, or only limited to a simple command or two. He controlled you completely, all the time?"

"Not exactly," Ritsu said. "He made me believe I was someone else, who trusted him completely and would do anything for him. But within those beliefs, my will remained my own. Perhaps you've heard of the man I thought I was. Elgar called him Shinsei."

Both women balked, momentarily stunned. "*You're* Shinsei?" the girl said. "Damn, you weren't lying about being stronger than you look."

"My superior strength and speed were gifted to me by the enchantment Elgar put on my sword." He smiled. "But I am still stronger than I look, yes."

Morgan nodded slowly. "I think I'm starting to understand. Shinsei had a reputation for behaving erratically that trickled down even to us commoners, who had never seen him. Elgar expended so much effort on you, and you were still . . . not a failed experiment by any means, but perhaps not as reliable as he could have hoped. So he decided he didn't want an army of Shinseis, and that must have been what started his experiments down the path they've arrived at today. Simple, temporary commands, but greater control over his victims' will while they're in effect."

"And it doesn't seem like they carry any risk of killing the people they're cast on," the girl pointed out.

Ritsu slumped down in his stool, running a hand through his hair. After the coldness of the steel against his skin, now he was sweating, the hair over his forehead already damp. There was so much to take in. He had been afraid to examine Shinsei's memories too deeply before, lest he lose his grip on who he really was, but now that danger had passed. He had lost so many years, committed so many atrocities. Nothing could ever change that.

"Hey." The girl put a hand on his shoulder. "I don't know anything about how you must be feeling, but you should know it's not your fault. I've seen people affected by his magic before, people he used to kill. As merciless as they were then, they only felt more grief when it was over. It's not a reflection of who you are."

It's not your fault. That was what Sebastian had wanted him to know, too.

"Thank you." He put his hand over hers. Here was another thing that had almost been taken from him: the ability to forge new connections with people and remember them. He turned to Morgan Imrick. "I meant what I said, you know. I can work to earn my keep here. And if there's anything else I can do, to repay you or to help bring him down, you have only to ask."

She pressed her fingertips to her temple. "That's certainly a puzzle. What should we do with you? We can't have you walking the streets, that's for damned sure. As far as the wider world is concerned, you're Shinsei. If you're out and about in Valyanrend too much, *someone* is bound to recognize you. And that'll create a whole mess of trouble we don't need."

"But wait," the girl said. "If he's Shinsei, isn't that good for us? He's a commander. He could get access to all sorts of things easily, couldn't he?"

"In theory," Ritsu said. "But as Shinsei, I'm afraid I developed quite the reputation. If I reappear now acting . . . well . . . like a normal person, I'll raise their suspicions immediately. And it's difficult to pretend that you're wandering in your wits, so I don't think I'd make a very good actor." He winced. "And if Elgar him-self suspects me . . ."

"Then he'll just cast the same spell on you, and you'll be right back where you started," Morgan finished. "None of that, then. You'll stay at the tavern, and out of the public eye."

"I do think it might be possible for me to acquire something or do something as Shinsei, as long as I could get in and out quickly and we could be sure Elgar wouldn't be there," Ritsu said. "But let's save it for a last resort. I suspect it's the kind of thing I'd only be able to pull off once."

"In the meantime," the girl said, "what about putting him to work in the tun-nels? It'd keep him out of sight, and you were saying we ought to have more people down there patrolling anyway. He can help lay out the braziers, too; they've got the most essential routes lit by now, but they're still not done. And even if Naishe or Rask happened to recognize him, though I don't think they've ever seen Shin-sei, at least they know enough that we could explain the truth."

"That's a good idea," Morgan said, though her gaze had gone hazy, turned in-ward. "Do you have any objections to that, Ritsu? There's already food down there, and you can alternate between the tunnels and the Dragon's Head as you prefer."

Ritsu wasn't sure what specific tunnels they meant, but he was surprised to find the idea of underground spaces didn't bother him. Although he and Sebastian had been confined beneath Serenin Palace in Kaiferi, these tunnels would probably feel very different. "That's fine, but what are you thinking about?"

Her gaze snapped back to him in surprise. "Oh, just . . . a friend of ours has been difficult to find for the past couple days. It's not like him. I was just thinking that the work of marking out the different routes has been going more slowly without him."

"It is unusual," the girl agreed. "I can ask Tom if he's heard anything; he doesn't like to admit it, but Roger's doings always interest him. You all right if I leave you with him?"

"Wait," Ritsu said, reaching out a hand toward her, but when she turned back, he felt a bit embarrassed. "I just . . . you never told me your name."

She laughed, and then he wasn't embarrassed at all. "It's Marceline, but most people don't call me that. Still, where you're concerned, I think it will fit best."

And then she was gone, with a jaunty tap to his shoulder that was so light and quick he almost thought he'd imagined it. Morgan glanced over at the door with an amused little half-smile. "All right, let's get you fed before we discuss anything else. You can start earning your keep tomorrow."

CHAPTER THIRTY

Hallarnon

"Damn," Voltest said. "What happened here?"

"I think it's still happening," Talis replied. The forest ahead of them was filled with wooden barricades, most of which had been at least partially hacked apart. The ground was littered with arrows, spears, and the corpses of soldiers.

"I suppose we didn't manage to beat the Issamiri army here," Voltest said. "But see, it's deserted. There's no one alive left."

"Not quite." Talis held up a hand for silence, letting the wind carry sounds to her from farther away. "There's still a battle raging farther in. If you want to press on, we should be prepared."

"Hmm. These corpses aren't fresh, so this particular skirmish is old. That means there's no telling what the current battle looks like." He shrugged. "Shall we give the Issamiri our assistance? We might as well."

"Is that really wise? If they even want our assistance to begin with, they might not let us leave afterward. After being the prisoner of one nation for so long, I'm not keen on leaping right into the clutches of another."

"You were Selwyn's prisoner," Voltest objected.

"Aye, and nearly Eira's before that. These grasping rulers are all the same."

"I've met Adora. You know that."

"You told me you weren't that impressed with her."

"That's very different from telling you she was the same as Eira, or even Elgar. And I also remember telling you she was as good a monarch as we were likely to get."

"Ah, I see. So you actually liked her after all, you were just being your usual patronizing self. This is why it's so hard to converse with you, you know."

Voltest ignored that. "So can we help them or not?"

"*You* can. I suppose I'll come along to rescue you in case your new allies turn on you."

"That *would* make us even, since I just rescued you," Voltest said, with one delicately raised eyebrow.

"Gods, you really are insufferable today." Talis rolled her eyes. "Hurry up and lead the way before I change my mind."

"You're the one with the enhanced hearing, but as you wish."

He was as good as his word, gliding easily between the trees with little sound. Talis followed in his wake, still tensed to attack or flee, no matter what he said.

The trees made it hard to see the full scope of the fight, but the problem the Issamiri were facing became crystal clear: after all the hard-fought effort they had poured into overcoming the previous array of barricades, here was a second one fifty yards behind the first, obscured from their view by the forest. They couldn't retreat, or they'd give their opponents time to repair the first line, and everything they'd done would be for nothing. But they couldn't simply rest and wait, either, because they were caught within firing range. What a nightmare.

At least there was one issue Talis could solve immediately. She pulled on the wind, and blew the newest volley of arrows off course, scattering them harmlessly to the forest floor. "What now?" she muttered to Voltest.

"I've got to find Adora. She's one of the only people here who will recognize me. If you and I just jump in, we risk being attacked by both sides."

They ran behind the front lines of the Issamiri, but since Voltest was the only one who had seen the queen before, Talis couldn't help him find her, and had to stick to keeping arrows out of their way. Luckily, while the soldiers all around her certainly looked confused, they had no way of connecting their sudden good fortune to her. And then Voltest grabbed her arm, pointing ahead of them to a dense knot of soldiers forming a semicircle in front of a young woman with black curly hair. "That's her. Just . . . don't look threatening."

Talis couldn't see how she was more threatening than he was, given that there wasn't a visible weapon between them, but she let him do the work of hailing the company. "Adora!" The authoritative tone and the lack of title made all the queen's subordinates bristle, but it also turned her head immediately. "We need to speak with you at once."

"Can you not see she's in danger? Who the hell are you?" Talis hadn't noticed anyone approach, but suddenly there was a drawn sword sliding between Voltest and Adora's group, wielded by a tall man with a small pointed beard. "If you're content to use words, they'll work well enough from where you are."

Voltest drew back with a hiss; Talis was too far away to feel anything, but she knew by the sheen of that blade what it was made of. Hadn't she warned him about this very thing? Hadn't she said these people were all the same?

But before she could turn to run, she heard a shout. "Uncle, wait!" Adora hauled the steel-bearer back with both hands. "I recognize that man. He wouldn't be here to help Elgar."

"I certainly wouldn't," Voltest said primly, smoothing down his cloak like a bird whose feathers had been ruffled. "This is Talis—I know you've heard me mention her. We came to offer our assistance, if we can do so without being harassed by your people."

"Talis?" The queen's eyes roved over her face, and Talis shrank a little under the weight of that gaze. "Cadfael and Rhia were successful, then. Thank the gods. They aren't with you?"

"They're on another errand with Lirien, but we can discuss that later," Talis said. "I'm keeping the arrows off you, but how else can we help? What's your goal here?"

"We've got to destroy those barricades," the queen's uncle said. "But we can't burn the forest, and we can't just throw our people at them to be slaughtered."

"Then it seems that, together, we may be able to help you." Voltest squinted at the barricades. "What do you think? Can you manipulate the supply of air to my flames enough to hold them back if they get out of control?"

"It depends how big a blaze you're thinking of. And I won't be able to do that and hold off the arrows at once, so her side will have to weather them until we're done."

"The barricades are the problem," the queen said. "If you can handle only that, we're capable of reckoning with the rest."

"But there might be a third row behind," her uncle added. "Be careful."

They didn't have Lirien with them, Talis reminded herself. When she was around, all they had to worry about was avoiding instant death, and anything else would just be healed. But though Voltest could burn anyone or anything that stood in his way to ash, and Talis could use the wind to toss people aside or float herself out of danger, they were both vulnerable to attacks they might not see coming. The greater the numbers set against them, the more dangerous a situation became.

"Let's try one at a time," Voltest said, and Talis gritted her teeth, even though she knew he was right. It would be much more dangerous this way, to bring down the walls only bit by bit. But they wouldn't burn the forest down. . . . Probably not, anyway.

She reached out to the wind again, only this time, instead of stirring it into a frenzy strong enough to deflect arrows, she drew it in close to her, coiled and waiting. The air around her grew breathlessly still, while Voltest poured his flames upon the nearest wall of wood, singeing any soldiers who had gotten too close to it.

Talis kept hold of the stillness as the flames spread, as more soldiers surged toward them. She watched the edges of the blaze, and when they caught the roots of a nearby tree, she pressed the stillness down directly on top of the nascent fire, stifling and suffocating it.

So they moved down the line of structures, one by one, and the Issamiri troops rushed in to fill the gaps they created, taking down the archers and leaving Talis and Voltest more space to work. The queen's uncle hung back to protect her at first, but once he was confident there were not enough enemy soldiers nearby to threaten her, he too joined the fray, and was soon leading the charge. But Talis only perceived these things as if from a long way off; too much of her concentration was devoted to controlling the wind, coaxing the fire one way and barring it from all others, over and over.

Perhaps if she'd been able to expand her view, she would have seen the arrow. Or perhaps, seeing the last of the barricades fall, she would have dropped her guard anyway. As it was, she didn't even see the archer, just heard the thrum of the bow-string, and then the arrow was in the air, flying too fast for her eyes to track. But she heard the impact clearly, and snapped her head toward it, only to see the shaft buried in the meat of Voltest's side.

Perhaps she should have used her wind to strike down the archer, or attempted to pull Voltest back. But instead, she was so shocked at the sight of his sudden wound that she did nothing at all, inadvertently letting the wind she'd gathered slip from her control.

It lasted only an instant, but in that instant Voltest's flames exploded outward, fed on the force of his anger and pain. Talis staggered and almost slipped on the dead leaves, but she righted herself at the last moment, and summoned the wind again, trying to corral his flames just as before. But this time, something was different.

All four of them had observed that their magic was reluctant to combine; when they tried, their power slipped past and through one another's, as if trying to wriggle free. Lirien and Voltest, in particular, had powers so opposed to each other that they could barely cast spells in close proximity. But Talis and Voltest had always been able to get their magic to work in concert, if not to truly combine; it just took a great deal of effort.

This time, when her magic struck Voltest's, it went wrong. Or perhaps it was his magic that had gone wrong, and the contact made that wrongness bleed into hers. His flames were still dying down, just as she'd intended, but somewhere beneath that, the magic was warping, doubling her over with a wave of pain and nausea. Why was this happening? Her magic had caused her difficulty in half a hundred ways, but never like this.

She turned her eyes to Voltest, but he was running ahead of her at an angle, away from both armies, into the woods. Talis glanced behind her, wondering if he or the Issamiri needed her help more. The barricades were more or less demolished, and without them, Adora's people clearly had the advantage. So she left them to win the day on their own, and ran into the forest after Voltest.

Though he'd had a head start, it wasn't hard to find him. It wasn't just that the power that connected them had been magnified; it was as if, when she had tried to restrain his fire, their magic had tangled together, and now his was pulling at hers every time he moved. It was still making her slightly sick to draw close to him, but at least she wasn't in danger of losing him. "Voltest!" she shouted, and he pulled up short, whirling to face her as if she were a stranger. He was breathing heavily, one hand pressed to his side, where the cloth around the arrow was stained a brighter red than the tattered cloak he was so fond of. "Voltest, you're hurt. Running won't fix it."

"That's not why," he panted, wincing as each deep breath pained him. "Can't you feel it? Something has happened."

"I know." They'd all lost control of their magic before, but it tended to erupt in a quick burst, over in a handful of minutes. A great deal of damage could still take place in a handful of minutes, of course, but that wasn't the point. Voltest's flames had stopped spreading, but the magic was still wrong. His anger wasn't raging out of control, either, as it usually did when his element got the better of him. Talis didn't feel her mind pulled in any direction; she just felt sick, and a little short of breath.

"I'm . . . trying to hold it in," Voltest said. "But it wants to burn everything, everything I can see. I had to get away from the armies. But I . . . don't understand. I've been hurt before—"

"You've never been hurt like this. We have to get out of the forest, in case you start a fire again. And we have to treat that wound as soon as possible."

He shook his head, not saying no, just in confusion. "I don't understand why it's different. I thought . . . didn't we all feel better after we freed you from Selwyn?"

Talis froze in the middle of offering him her arm, her thoughts returning to that horrible time. It had kept taking her back to the destruction of her village, over and over, endlessly. The magic often forced her to recall that on its own, but always as a memory. Never as something that felt like it was actually happening. "Voltest, are you thinking of anything right now? Remembering anything?"

"Not now. For a moment when the arrow hit, I thought—" He pressed a hand to his forehead, where sweat was breaking out. "Nothing good. But I'm fine now." He smiled wryly. "Aside from the warped magic and all the blood, of course."

But Talis couldn't smile about it. She had thought what had happened to her in Araveil had remained cut off from the other two, and that it was in the past. But she had the creeping fear that what Voltest was experiencing now was some echo of what she'd felt then—some watered-down version, perhaps only brought on by the intense pain he'd experienced, but it could grow. It could get worse. And this time there would be no vardrath steel to remove, no Cadfael to bring him back to himself if he should lose his way.

"Come on," she said, finishing the movement she'd started, and letting him put his weight on her shoulder, trying to hide her misgivings for now. "We can discuss this more once our surroundings are less flammable."

CHAPTER THIRTY-ONE

Valyanrend

NAISHE ALMOST NEVER saw Morgan and Braddock together outside the Dragon's Head, because one of them was always behind the bar. "Tavern's closed for the day," Morgan said, as if seeing the question in her face.

"Then this must be important. Is it about my father?"

"What? Oh. No, it's not that. I don't see Nasser much anymore." She shot the quickest of glances at Braddock. "He . . . figured out we knew you were leading the resistance. It was probably inevitable."

Naishe had distant memories of Braddock from her youth, when he and her father had served in the same mercenary company. After that company's ignominious end, he'd still come around to visit every so often, and Naishe knew he had helped her father out on his travels more than once. "I'm sorry for asking you to keep my identity a secret from him. It must have put a strain on your friendship."

"He was pretty spitting mad at me," Braddock admitted, "even though Morgan tried to sacrifice herself to take the blame for it. But I think he'll realize eventually that I was just doing what I thought was best for both of you."

"I wouldn't hold your breath," Naishe said. "He's so damned stubborn."

"Aye." Braddock smiled slightly. "Seem to recall him saying the same about you."

"Well, if you didn't come about him, I can only imagine what the matter is, and I expect it can't wait." She swung the door of the house wide. "Come in."

At the time of the massacre in Silkspoint, the house in Ashencourt was a new acquisition for the resistance, an abandoned shop owned by the family of one of their members that had yet to be restored in any way. The sign over it was so old and faded it was hard to make out whatever it had once said, and the mortar holding the building together was cracked and drafty, but it had fast become a favorite of Naishe's, out of all the refuges they had left. They hadn't wanted to dress it up too much on the outside, so as not to draw suspicion, but the inside had changed since she'd first fled here with Wren and Talia and Marceline, rugs set down and cushions piled up. Wren had even spent an afternoon repairing the only two chairs in the place, and Naishe gestured to them as Morgan made sure the front door was latched.

She and Morgan sat down, and Braddock leaned against the wall by the door. "The trouble is Roger," Morgan said. "He's gone."

Naishe didn't know Roger Halfen well, but she knew Marceline held his talents in high esteem. She had a natural aversion toward thieves, but Marceline was one, and had proved a true friend, so Naishe had tried to reserve judgment where he was concerned. "Can you be more specific? Who was the last person to see him, and when?"

"As far as I can tell, six days ago. I turned up a handful of people who spoke to him briefly then, but he didn't tarry with any of them. He just mentioned something about his cousin—I've been wondering if that was supposed to be code for something else, but I haven't come up with anything. And this is unlike him. Roger might disappear for a day or two while he's in the thick of some scheme, but six days without a word to me, especially now? It's much more likely that something is wrong."

"And by something you mean you think he's been arrested? Attacked?"

"We couldn't find any evidence of either," Braddock said, "and Elgar's people aren't known for their discretion. If he had been taken, I bet someone would have heard. But the timing is suspicious. We need the swindler to unveil this plan of his to dissuade people from trusting Elgar's protective talismans. We can't start without him."

Naishe certainly hadn't had any better ideas. Her specialty—besides archery—was motivating others with the truth. When they refused to believe it, her rhetorical skills faltered. So she needed Roger Halfen as much as Morgan and Braddock did. "Can you tell me more about this cousin of his? Perhaps it wasn't a code after all."

Morgan shut her eyes. "Gods, what do I even remember about Len Varsten? He was a few years older than Roger and I, so I suppose I grew up with him, too, but it seems I hardly ever saw him. Roger was always in the streets, getting into trouble. I was usually trying to stay *out* of trouble, which should've endeared me more to Len, but . . . there was something about him that was hard to like. This air of superiority. Then after Len's father died, his mother married this merchant, and he and Len went east by themselves to seek their fortunes. I don't think he ever came back, and I don't know why Roger would have mentioned him all of a sudden."

"None of the people you spoke to could tell you?"

"They said it was just the barest bit of procedure. Wanting to make sure that

Sheath remained closed to a Halfen who was no true Halfen. It makes sense—honestly, I'd assumed the rest of the Halfens had done that years ago—but it doesn't help me find Roger. I've only come to you because I'm at my wits' end. I know you don't know him anywhere near as well as I do, but you have resources I don't, and I only have influence in Sheath. If you could help me spread the search to other districts . . ."

Naishe held up a hand. "Let's be absolutely certain we've thought it through before I do that. If Roger's absence is voluntary—because he needed to hide, say—stirring up the city in search of him may be counterproductive, even if only my people know of it."

"If he needed to hide, why wouldn't he use the tunnels?" Braddock asked. "He knows them better than anyone."

"Perhaps he was being followed, or thought he might be."

Morgan raked her hands through her hair. "But if that's the case, how could he outrun someone who's been actively following him for six days? It would be much more likely that he was already . . ." She trailed off—unwilling to finish the sentence, Naishe thought at first. But then she frowned, and drew the dagger at her side. "Do you have something magic in here? The blade's carrying a bit of a chill."

Naishe opened her mouth to say no, and then she remembered. "Oh, just one of those little charms like the ones you found on Elgar's soldiers. Rask had it pinned to him when he came back from the Citadel. We talked about what we might do with it, but we couldn't decide, and in the end I just kept the thing here."

But that didn't clear the clouds from Morgan's expression. "That's it?"

"That's definitely it. Why?"

"Where is it?"

"In that box on the table by your elbow. I didn't want someone to touch it by accident." When Morgan said nothing, she repeated, "Why?"

Morgan opened the box carefully, squinting at the contents as if they might come alive. "I've detected those charms before. I know how close I have to get before the steel starts reacting. If this is just more of the same, I shouldn't have been able to feel it from that far away."

That was right. When Naishe had first found the little metal burr on Rask's cloak, she'd had to get very close to it; just standing next to him while wearing the necklace hadn't been enough. She clutched the pendant in her fist, but all she felt was a faint warmth from her skin. But as she took two strides toward Morgan, that warmth ebbed away, replaced with a dull chill. "This is different," she said. "The aura coming off that thing wasn't as large before."

They stared at the charm, lying there all by itself in a box much too big for it, but to the naked eye, it looked just the same. Morgan inched a fingertip close to it, careful not to touch, and shook her head. "Nothing. No heat or cold or anything."

"But something must have changed. If the steel is reacting more strongly, perhaps the charm started using more magic for some reason?" She cast around for something to prod it with. "It's been inert all this time—at least, it hadn't changed Rask's behavior at all when we found it. What if it's finally being put to use?"

They stared at one another, the possible ramifications of Naishe's guess unfolding in the silence between them. "Would Elgar know where Rask lives?" Braddock asked. "Or where he's likely to be at this day and time?"

"You think Elgar might have called on more than one of these things?"

"I'm sure of it. One killer might be a madman; several together is an enemy faction."

Naishe searched her memory of Rask's time with Elgar, as he'd recounted it. "He lives a few streets away from Draven's Square, but I can't recall if he told Elgar that or not. He couldn't have mentioned any occupation—his only occupation these days is helping the resistance, managing the money that comes from his wealthy relatives in Lanvaldis. So there's nowhere else Elgar could be sure he'd be, unless he summoned him somewhere again. But I think Rask would find a way to send word if that had happened."

"If you were going to stir up trouble, Draven's Square at this time is a good choice," Braddock said. "The Night Market will have mostly dispersed, but this early in the morning there'll still be some stragglers. Enough victims for any potential attack, but not so many as to cut into the reserves for his future army."

Naishe was already moving, heading for the door. "Let's go."

Ashencourt was adjacent to the neighborhood of Draven's Square, so they arrived in a handful of minutes. Even so, the attack was already unfolding. Stalls had been overturned, their contents spilling out across the cobblestones. People were screaming, most in flight down whatever side streets they could reach, though some, weapons drawn, were wading carefully into the center of the carnage. And at that center, a group of people carried bloody swords, hacking at anyone they could reach. None of them wore armor, or any uniforms, and there weren't any obvious commonalities between them. One might almost have thought they'd all decided, independently of one another, to turn to murder on a whim.

Morgan's brow furrowed. "This again? Didn't they already try this when you lot went to the Glassway?"

"No, this is different." Naishe's blood ran cold, for she recognized it. "These people haven't been paid to sow propaganda; they've truly been touched by magic. They'll kill until they're destroyed, or until Elgar takes the magic away. But I don't think he's going to, this time. If they come to their senses and live to dispute his narrative of their actions, he'll have done all this for nothing."

"But we might still be able to save them, if we're fast enough," Morgan said. "The steel should be able to restore them to themselves, no matter what Elgar does."

"You'd have to get too close for that, Morgan," Braddock said. "They'll kill you before you can break the spell."

"But we've got to do *something*."

"We will," Naishe said. "I'll get between them and their victims, you let Braddock cover you, and we'll both wait for an opportunity to use the steel. We can't save them all, but we might get through to some."

They joined the shifting knot of people, but without any uniforms, it was difficult to tell who was enchanted and who was an ordinary person trying to strike back at the attackers. Naishe was less confident in her sword skills than her archery, so she fought defensively, taking hits on the flat of her blade and buying time to examine the combatants more closely, to see which made an effort to lash out at her and whose behavior was most similar to her own. The other unenchanted people were probably doing the same thing, and as they recognized one another, they slowly drew together in a rough line, closing in on the aggressors. But by that time, Naishe had noticed a different problem. Those who were technically on her side were going to cut down the attackers before she and Morgan got a chance to disenchant them. And how could she tell them to stop? Even if she explained what she knew, would they believe her? In magic, perhaps, after all Elgar had said, but in magic that came from Elgar himself?

She did what she could to protect those who fought beside her, to reduce the total number of dead even if she couldn't stop the carnage completely. They slowly pushed the attackers back, and one by one they started to fall. But just as Naishe began to hope that the last few might be successfully restrained, that she and Morgan might be able to touch them with the steel surreptitiously, Morgan grabbed her arm. "Wait," she said. "Look."

Naishe followed her gaze, and saw a line of soldiers in Elgar's blue-black filing into the square, drawing their swords and shouting orders to the civilians who were left. "The guards are here," Morgan said. "We've got to go."

"But we can take the rest alive!"

"It doesn't matter! If we're caught here with the steel, they'll do more than take us to Elgar for congratulations. It'll expose everything we've been doing. We'll be killed, the steel will be confiscated, and then they'll start tracking all our associates! Everything would be over!"

Naishe gripped the pendant so hard that it bit into her flesh, but she knew Morgan was right. It was the Silkspoint massacre all over again, when she had made the decision to flee with those she could, because the rest could not be saved. If the three of them were taken here, she would sacrifice much more than a few lives.

So she let herself be led away, and they retreated. They remained on the fringes of the square, and watched as the guards stormed upon the remaining killers, cutting them all down. And Naishe winced at every stroke, because she knew none of those being slain had taken up swords by choice. Elgar's soldiers might very well have been ignorant of it, but they were killing those their master had unleashed.

It didn't take long for that very master to send more of his pawns to address them—only a couple hours, which Naishe would have deemed so soon as to be suspicious, but Elgar evidently felt differently. She, Morgan, and Braddock had continued waiting in the square to watch the official response: no interviewing the witnesses, or making any attempt to understand what had happened. Elgar already understood perfectly, after all. Instead, the surrogates who came to the square offered another speech—and then something much worse.

After the first third of it—empty commiseration and insincere condolences—Naishe almost left in disgust. But just as she turned away, Morgan yanked on her arm again. "Impotent and widespread fear," Elgar's orator said, "does no one any good. His Eminence told you what he did, when he did, because he had the confidence that it was a problem he could solve. You already know how tirelessly he has been working, testing his cures on himself and those of us in his retinue who have volunteered. The art of combating magic is still in its infancy, and there is much more work to be done, but he could not look upon such tragedy without doing all he can to prevent the next. So he has given us leave to announce that, in the days to come, the talismans he has been crafting will become—*provisionally*—available."

There was a rush of chatter, firmly silenced by the orator and his fellows. Naishe glanced at Morgan and Braddock, and saw in their faces the same certainty that she felt. They knew what was coming next.

And sure enough, the orator raised a dull metal pendant, set with a shiny black stone.

"Again," the orator said, raising his voice to be heard above the crowd, "these are still being tested within the Citadel. They're subject to much further refinement, which they will undoubtedly need in the days to come. And they are in limited supply, so at this time they will only be made available to able-bodied adults from the ages of twenty to forty-nine. These people would be able to cause the most damage if they were enchanted as those you see before you were today. Perhaps in the future the list of candidates can be expanded, but that is not possible for now. The talismans will be distributed beginning the day after tomorrow, and each of you must come in person to claim one, in order to prove that you meet the requirements. But if you do, it is in your best interests, and that of your family and friends within this city, that you claim the protection the imperator is offering you."

The "candidates" he had mentioned were indeed the ones likely to cause the most damage if enchanted, which was surely why they had been picked. And judging from the mood of the crowd all around her, there would be far more takers than not. Like this, Elgar's future army was limited only by the number of these charms he could produce at once. But even a conservative estimate would be far more than the resistance could hope to combat in their wildest dreams.

Morgan must have read her thoughts in her face. "Come on," she said. "*Now* we can get out of here."

They walked back to the Ashencourt house in silence.

As soon as Naishe was sure they were alone, she let out the noise that had been trapped in her throat, frustration and anger and helplessness. "What are we going to do now? He's making them faster than we can possibly destroy them, and we're still no closer to knowing where he's hidden the hub stones that control them! At this point . . . at this point we'll have no choice but to try to convince the people of what he really is, to just reveal everything we know. What other option is there?"

"Definitely not that one," Braddock said. "If we tried it, the guards would find out, and they'd remove us from the streets, one way or another."

"But we have to at least *try*!"

"No, we have to get Roger back," Morgan said. "This is where he shines the brightest." She put her hands on Naishe's shoulders. "I know you don't know him well enough to trust him, and I know you have disdain for his work. But different locks need different keys. We need to turn the people to our way of thinking, but we can't let them know it came from us, because that means letting Elgar know. No one is better at sneaking their thoughts into people's heads without getting caught than a swindler, and you won't find a cleverer swindler than Roger."

"And if we can't find Roger, even that plan is only wishful thinking."

"I can find him," Morgan insisted. "I just might need some extra eyes to look, that's all."

"Well, you'll have them by tomorrow, for all the good it does."

"Thank you. For trusting me, as well as for the rest." She drew back, then seemed to bring herself up short. "I . . . do have a last resort. A new friend, I suppose, who's currently helping in the tunnels. But I really hope I don't have to use him."

SHE DIDN'T, AS it turned out.

Morgan and Braddock had closed the Dragon's Head for the day, but they returned to find the lock open. They drew their weapons, and burst through the door, only to nearly drop them when they saw who was on the other side. It took all Morgan's restraint to make sure the door was fully closed again before laying into him. "You've got to be *joking*. I've been worrying about you for six bloody days, and you just turn up?"

There he was, leaning against the bar—perhaps a touch grimmer than his usual demeanor, but otherwise unchanged. "You should have been worried, and no, I didn't just turn up. My return was calculated very carefully. I left the city, which would have led anyone following me to assume, correctly, that I was lying low. But I made sure to use a lot of my coin, so that my return to Sheath could be seen as simply gathering more resources. I've just broken into your tavern, presumably in response to my financial need, and when you two throw me out in a few minutes, it won't seem odd when we avoid each other in the future. And we really *can't* be in contact after this. We'll have to carry out our parts of the plan separately."

Morgan had so many questions that she had to struggle not to garble the words out of her mouth. "What plan? Why were you lying low? Is someone hunting you? Why didn't you—"

"All right, let me answer those first," Roger said. "My swindling plan, of course. And I was lying low from the person who might or might not be hunting me—who you should really have warned me about, by the way. The others never met him as a child, but you did. I had no idea Len was even back in the west."

"Your cousin Len? I didn't know any more than you. Why, is he back?"

Roger gave her a look. "You saw him yourself. Lord Varalen Oswhent—Oswhent like his stepfather, didn't you remember that?"

"What? No. Lord Oswhent isn't . . ." Morgan had seen Lord Oswhent only once, through the bars of a prison cell, but she tried to think back to that night, to compare her dimly lit memories of that man to the boy she'd occasionally run across in Sheath. "I . . . suppose it's possible. Varalen—is that what Len was short for? He probably told us his given name, but I can't say I really thought about it."

"You certainly didn't tell me," Roger said, though his reproachful tone was easing. "He does look rather different—though only more of an asshole. *And* a traitor, to be throwing himself behind Elgar like that."

"*Oh*. Oh, *shit*." Morgan's heart abruptly started racing. "That's why you had to make sure Sheath was closed to him. But if he'd been making use of old contacts here until then, I can't even imagine what he might know. Your identity, of course, but we shouldn't assume that's the only—"

"He doesn't have much more than that," Roger said. "He called me out to meet him in person. He knows I'm the Fang, or part of the Fang, and he tried to scare me off. But he was fishing, too, and that means he's short on leads. He must have known revealing himself to me was risky—that I might do exactly what I did, and alert our corner of the city to his new allegiance. But he did it anyway. It was quite a gamble, and Len's never been the gambling sort." He caught himself. "Though I suppose I never considered him the evil-abetting sort, either."

Morgan was still trying to map the features of the boy she remembered from Sheath onto the face of the man in the red robes who dwelled in the Citadel. "Do you know why he's helping Elgar?"

"Aye, but does it matter? There's no reason that could possibly justify what he's doing. I hope he changes his mind, but mine is unchangeable, no matter what that means for him."

"He's your cousin," Morgan said.

"He's my least favorite cousin, let me remind you. And he held that title *before* he pulled all this. I need to hide myself away better, and work harder to ensure the moves I make won't be traced back to me, but aside from that, the plan moves forward. The same as ever."

"We should be glad he's so determined," Braddock said. "He'll have to pull every trick he knows to get us through this. Heard what happened in Draven's Square today, swindler?"

"I got a general report of it. Marketing the poison as its own cure—audacious, but not much more than that. Trust me, the man's got no strategy I don't already know, but I have some that have never crossed his mind."

"But is it even still safe to put you at the center of the plan?" Morgan asked. "If you're right, and Len is keeping eyes on you—"

"Len can have me followed, to be sure. I don't know how long he'll consider it worth his while, but to be safe, I'll assume it's perpetual. But now that Sheath's wise to him, he can only use outside help, not inside. Sheath protects its own from outsiders at the worst of times, and given how important I'm about to make myself to them . . ." He grinned crookedly. "I'll wager there's no safer place I can be than in the eye of this particular storm."

"And even though we'll have to put distance between us, you're confident we'll still be able to get word to each other if there's an emergency?"

"Aye, I'll make sure of it."

He was determined, that was clear. And Roger didn't pick fights he couldn't win, not even with the cousin he'd always competed with most. "All right. I'll tell Naishe, then, get her people ready for when their part will be required. And I'll set everyone else on it tomorrow. I just hope you've honed your edges sharper than that sanctimonious little brat's."

Roger nodded, unusually solemn. "He always looked down on you as much as me. He looked down on all of Sheath. So let's show him what a legacy he's given up."

Chapter Thirty-two

Stonespire

THE HARDEST PART of their offensive into Esthrades thus far had been everything that had to happen before they left. There had been endless debates over specific numbers: how many soldiers, how many horses, how many provisions, expenses down to the last copper—the results always somewhat less than Hywel wanted, but never within the realm of what they would consider dangerous. Then Hywel had to twist and turn until he had satisfied every member of his inner circle that he would be adequately protected on the campaign, short of promising to encase himself in metal or go nowhere without being surrounded by a bodyguard on every side. The one thing he refused to do was provide Gerald with definitive conditions for his return. "I'll come back to Araveil once I'm confident Esthrades is free again," he'd said. "As to what that means, I'll figure it out once I see the state of the place."

The state of the place outside of Stonespire, thankfully, turned out to be more confusion than disturbance or harm. The Hallerns' numbers were so limited that they hadn't done anything but fight their way to the capital and capture it—they'd even left Lakeport alone, despite the fortune it represented. It seemed Jill Bridger had been right after all, and Esthrades's greatest prize was its ruler, not any one piece of territory.

Bridger had come with them to Esthrades, and so had Alessa and Hayne, since they said it was only right for them to go wherever Kel went. The rest of Hywel's army contained people Kel didn't know. Gerald had argued he ought to come, quite strenuously, but in the end Hywel had insisted he was needed more in Araveil, to help keep order and establish the new government. Lady Euvalie shone at politics, not warfare; Ithan was still recovering physically, and Ilyn mentally; and Cadfael, his sister, and the *wardrenfell* had all slipped out of Araveil before Kel and Hywel had time to ask for their assistance. He was a little hurt Cadfael had left so abruptly—he'd wanted to catch up with him, and get to know his sister—but he was confident they had good reasons for their departure, whatever they were, and he still hoped to see them again one day.

Speaking of sisters, Kel's own had become significantly scarcer over the past few weeks. At least Hayne was always easy to find, never far from his side. Hywel had been as good as his word about the crutches, so he no longer needed to be carried, but it was still easier to ride in one of the carts. When he did so, Hayne would usually stretch her legs by walking alongside it, always within earshot.

"Have you seen Alessa?" Kel called.

Hayne snorted. "You don't need to ask me, Your Grace. You know where she is."

That meant he definitely did, and he wasn't happy about it.

From the beginning, though only Kel was permitted to be part of his council, Hywel had privately consulted him and Lessa together in certain cases. Kel had been grateful for it then, for the respect it afforded his sister; her lack of royal blood had prevented her from assuming the throne, but she had learned law, politics, and history beside him, and made her own studies into agriculture and medicine. To anyone not put off by her birth, hers was a mind worth consulting.

But as the weeks had passed, she and Hywel had started to meet without Kel, more and more frequently. He had thought nothing of it at first—sometimes Hywel spoke to him alone, too, after all. It would be silly to feel snubbed. But now he felt something much more than snubbed: he felt the greatest anxiety over what might come of this. He couldn't imagine that it would be anything good.

His unhappiness must have shown on his face, because Hayne's tone softened. "You know how sheltered she was at Mist's Edge—how sheltered both of you were. She's never had any real opportunity for infatuations, and she's at a prime age for it. So's the boy, king or no. This sort of thing isn't unusual."

"I know that, but . . ." He trailed off. He didn't know what he meant to say.

". . . but being on the outside is never enjoyable?" Hayne suggested.

"It isn't, but that wasn't what I was going to say. I know how Hywel was raised, but he and Lessa aren't some villagers. Hywel's the *king*. He can't *have* 'infatuations,' any more than I can."

"And yet in the future, Your Grace, it is possible you will also have infatuations, irrespective of whether you are allowed to have them."

Kel made a face. "Ugh, I hope not. It would only complicate things, and you know how that worked for my parents—and for me and Lessa, with a childhood of attempted assassinations over whether or not people thought we were legitimate." He slumped lower in the cart, rubbing his legs. "What about you, Hayne? Have you ever been in love?"

"Not in that way," she said. "But because I am not made for that kind of affection, not because of any rules about my potential offspring and their inheritance."

Kel felt a bit embarrassed, as if he ought to have known that. "Well, at least I know you won't get all swoony over some foreigner and stop paying attention to me, too."

Hayne smiled. "In your sister's defense, unlike me, paying attention to you is not her job."

And on that note, the cart rolled to a stop in front of Hywel's tent. At least he and Lessa weren't loafing around inside it; they both looked all business, deep in conversation with Bridger and a couple of Hywel's soldiers.

Hayne lifted him out of the cart and helped him get the crutches situated, and by then the others had noticed his arrival. "Kelken, perfect timing," Hywel said. "We're still making calculations, but Bridger's just returned, and she thinks we've no need to bother with even the pretense of a siege. We should just make sure everyone's settled and prepared, and then we can launch the attack whenever we choose."

Bridger had gone ahead of them, so she'd have time to slip back into and out of Stonespire before the Hallerns locked it up in the face of the approaching Lanvaldian army. She'd presumably told her fellow disguised guards within the city of their plan, and it was those guards they would count on to open the gates for them when the attack started and help them fight after that. But Kel already knew that the bulk of the manpower would have to come from their own forces—though those forces had themselves been bolstered by volunteers from the militias they'd encountered in Esthradian towns on the way.

"There's one thing I want to be sure of," he said. "Bridger, you and I both believe that your lady risked putting herself in harm's way in order to avoid mass bloodshed within her capital. If we barge in and cause the very same, it would hardly be repaying the favor Hywel and I owe her—we'd be betraying her trust, going directly against her wishes. Are you sure that everything is in place so that won't happen?"

"As sure as I can be, Your Grace," Bridger said. "We couldn't let them lock us into a siege, because then civilians would suffer and starve—another outcome her ladyship wanted to avoid. But having Stonespire opened to us from within should put an end to that possibility. And within the city proper, we'll have them vastly outnumbered. The only question is by how much."

"How many can we count on within the city?" Hywel asked.

Bridger wrinkled her nose, staring at the city walls as if they held the answer. "Hard to say. Besides those I was able to meet with on my brief return, I know of a little over a dozen others who are like me: soldiers disguised as civilians. There are several hundred other guards, but when I left, the most senior among them were still being detained. If they were released in the meantime, or if we can free them, we can use them to swell our ranks. And then there's the people of Stonespire themselves. I'm sure they don't want to be controlled by Hallerns any more than I do, but I couldn't tell you how many of them might actually join forces with us to fight them off. More than zero, but beyond that . . ."

Hywel mopped a hand across his brow. "That's . . . quite the possible range of numbers."

"But it's just noise," Kel reminded him. "The most important thing is whether they'll open the gates for us, and Bridger's already assured us that's true. Beyond that, let's take the most conservative estimate of our numbers and theirs, and plan from there. If we end up being more fortunate than that, even better, but at least we'll know what we're capable of in the worst case."

Hywel's shoulders relaxed, and Lessa gave Kel a grateful smile he wasn't sure how to take. But Bridger cleared her throat. "If the Hallerns have any sense, once they realize we've breached the city walls, they'll retreat up the hill to the hall. There's no decent defensive stronghold in the streets of the city itself; they'd be immediately overrun. So the sooner we can capture the base of the hill, the more of them we can keep cut off. But no matter what, a sizable number of them will probably make it to the hall, because from what I understand, a sizable number have been sheltering there anyway. Now, it's true that Stonespire Hall was intended to be a minor lord's seat, and wasn't built to withstand a concentrated assault from trained and superior numbers. Holding out there, they'll eventually lose. But if our own people are going to take significant casualties, it'd be there."

"If they run into the hall, do we even have to chase them out?" Kel asked. "They'd be more or less imprisoning themselves, and we could take back the city and make sure its people are safe. It could be a sort of miniature siege; if they surrender once they get hungry enough, we won't have to risk harm to any of our own. Although if Arianrod has any rare delicacies, they may be sacrificed in the process."

"I doubt the Hallerns have discovered where any of the most valuable items are kept," Bridger said, "but that's beside the point. The chief problem with your plan, Your Grace, is that the Hallern soldiers are still using Esthradian servants to wait on them, and keeping those of her ladyship's retainers that they deem most dangerous within the hall's prison. They would still suffer, even in a miniature siege."

"Either way," Hywel said, "should we not secure the city proper first? Those in the hall shouldn't start starving immediately, and it will be easier to mount an attack there if we're confident in holding the surrounding area."

"Under normal circumstances, I'd agree," Bridger said. "But there is one more option I'd like to put forward first."

GRAVIS INGRET WAS sitting in a cell he was surpassingly familiar with, though he'd never had quite this view of it until the past several weeks. These were the dungeons in the lowest level of Stonespire Hall, below the level of the hill but still higher than the street at its foot. There simply wasn't much room to make the dungeon very large, and it had always been intended as a last resort, to confine anyone who made it into the hall until they could be transported to a larger jail in the city proper. But their Hallern captors had been afraid that the citizens might assault any of those prisons and turn their occupants loose, so they had stuffed all the Esthradians they considered the most dangerous in here. Gravis supposed he should be flattered, but he knew it was only because he was captain of the guard, not because of anything in particular they knew about him as a person.

The man beside him, on the other hand, had a reputation down in the city that couldn't be stifled. If Gravis had to be confined here, at least it was with such an old friend. "Care to wager on dinner?" he asked. "Watery stew again?"

Dent laughed. "Now, now, don't be so pessimistic. They might give us pickled herring again. I think they mistook it for emergency rations or something."

There were about thirty of them down here, two to a cell. Most of them were other guards, but two were part of the quarter-court Lady Margraine had set to mediate grievances in her absence. Since they were underground, it was impossible to gauge the passage of time, though Dent joked that his and Gravis's new beards provided a rough approximation. And there was no way to check on Bridger's progress, or that of any other of their compatriots who remained free.

"Well," he said quietly, "I suppose this is what she wanted, though I can't say I like it."

Dent tilted his head. "What who wanted? Bridger?"

"No. Her ladyship. The two of us safe and bored in a cell, away from anything of consequence, until we're either released or we die of old age."

"Would you prefer that she had thrown us to the wolves? Commanded us to fight at all costs, until our lives were spent?"

Gravis laughed. "You're still defending her. Just like always."

"And I always will. I gave myself that role a long time ago."

"I remember." He was the one who had gotten the young Arianrod into Zara's care on the day her father had beaten her, but his protection had started long before that. Perhaps as long as she had lived.

"And what about you?" Dent asked. "I might be imagining it, but I think you've loosened up on your veneration of Caius of late."

"Perhaps," Gravis said. It was easier to be honest, somehow, down here in the dark without his armor, even though he knew they weren't alone. "The gratitude I feel for him will never die. He saw potential in me when no one else did. But I can hold on to that feeling just as tightly and still acknowledge he was far from perfect, as no man is. And I can hold on to it and still serve his daughter faithfully—it's what he would have wanted of me, after all."

"Ah," Dent said. "You've found some wisdom in your old age."

"I'm hardly a year and a half older than you."

"Fine, you've found some wisdom in our old age." He leaned back against the cold stone wall. "I should have pushed you more, perhaps. To get along with her, to work with her better, before and after Caius's death. It didn't trouble her, and you seemed so set on holding your grudge, it was too easy for me to take the coward's way out."

"I think we'd have ended up here regardless," Gravis said. "But while we're pointing out regrets . . . it's always been one of my greatest that I misjudged you when we first met. If I hadn't—if I'd been able to see that Lord Caius's disdain for you was unjustified—perhaps I could have served as a bridge between you two, before things got to such a point." When Gravis had first come to Stonespire, a young and eager recruit from a tiny village, he had met Denton Halley almost immediately. Dent had grown up in the capital, and enjoyed the favor of Lord Caius's father, Daven the eleventh, ever since he was in training. It was jealousy that led Lord Caius to frown on him, nothing more. But Gravis had failed to see, in those first few months, what was so special about Dent, and he had let Caius's judgment become his own. By the time he realized he was wrong, it was too late: he had helped Caius push Dent out of favor, where he had remained for years, until Arianrod's fateful tenth birthday. And yet Dent had still become his friend in spite of all that.

"Now I *know* we're old," Dent said, "to be moaning over the regrets of our youth."

"Maybe we're just finally mature enough to admit to them."

"Aye, I like your version better." He wiped his hands on his knees, turning his gaze to the ceiling. "You know, even in the worst case, we'll be all right here."

"What do you perceive to be the worst case?" Gravis asked.

"That Bridger fails somehow, and we can't retake the city. That just means we'll have to sit here until the larger conflict is over. It'll be embarrassing, but we've survived embarrassments before."

"That's not the worst case," Gravis said. "The worst would be if her ladyship fails—if she's killed, and Elgar takes this continent. The terms of the surrender forbid our execution, so we'd probably just be released, deemed irrelevant. And we'd have to live on knowing all the ways we fell short—that we could do nothing to help her, that we were wrong to listen to her. I can't think of anything worse than that."

"That won't happen," Dent insisted. "She's far more than that man's equal, and I know she didn't ask us to surrender this city out of despair. She has a plan, and you know as well as I do what her plans can accomplish. Anything and everything. Things others deemed impossible. She won't lose now, not when she's come so far."

Spoken by any other man, they would have sounded like excuses, but Dent imbued them with painful sincerity, all the long years of his devotion. Gravis knew what it was to believe in a leader too much, but he also knew that in the past he'd doubted Arianrod when he shouldn't have. Now he didn't know what to think.

In the silence that unfolded between the two of them, Gravis faintly heard heavy footsteps on the last few steps leading from the upper floor, then the scraping of the door as it opened. "It can't be time for us to eat yet."

"No," Dent agreed. "Finally. I was starting to think we wouldn't see him again."

Sure enough, the man on the other side of the door was Benwick, one of the hall guards who'd volunteered for Bridger's plan. The Hallerns knew him as Bennett, a supposed servant; they thought the soldier called Benwick Teague had been at Giltgrove for weeks. He couldn't come down here often—the Hallerns were suspicious enough of their Esthradian servants already, and only kept any of them on at all because they liked being waited on and had no servants of their own—so they usually saw him when he'd been ordered to bring food down anyway. But today he was carrying no bowls or trays, and held a finger to his lips as soon as he entered. He headed straight for Dent and Gravis.

"Glad to see you didn't forget about us," Dent whispered when he drew close enough, with a teasing grin.

Benwick grinned back. "To make up for my long absence, I've come bearing a gift I know you'll love." He raised his hand, and twirled a ring of keys around one fingertip, so adeptly it barely made a sound.

Dent and Gravis exchanged a glance, probably not the kind Benwick had hoped for. "You could have stolen those at any time," Gravis said. "That's not the point. There aren't enough of us down here to overpower the Hallerns, and even if we could, that would go against her ladyship's orders."

"Aye," Benwick said, "but her ladyship couldn't have anticipated how the situation would change." He leaned forward, his face nearly touching the bars. "What if I told you that there's a Lanvaldian army sitting outside Stonespire's gates right now, bolstered with the best of our militias? What if I told you those gates will be opened to them in a matter of . . . minutes now, by our fellows within this city, forcing the Hallerns to fall back to this very hall? And what if I told you that they need our help to prevent those same Hallerns from digging in here for days?"

Dent clapped a hand to his forehead. "If you told me that, Benwick, I'd say Jill Bridger is worth her weight in gold, for there can be no one else who made this possible."

"Aye, it's on her word that I know all this, though I haven't seen her." He dangled the keys. "So? What do you say? Surely our orders did not account for such a change of circumstances?"

"It's true," Gravis said. "She ordered us not to rise in rebellion against the Hallerns, or to try to take the city back from them. But she *didn't* order us to stand by and do nothing while others fight for it. The Lanvalds are going to fight the Hallerns anyway, no matter what we do. I'm sure she'd want us to help ensure they win."

"She'd certainly want us to do everything we could to reduce casualties to our own people," Dent agreed. "She didn't spare us Hallern swords only to have us in-advertently killed by Lanvalds. And if we let the Hallerns fortify this place, we're putting everyone here at risk."

With that needle finally threaded, their honor and loyalty both remained in-tact. Gravis sighed. "I do wish I could get my armor back for this part, though."

A handful of minutes later, Benwick had freed everyone from their cells, and they were gathered beside the door to the stairs. "I'll go up first," he said. "Wait for my signal."

Gravis and Dent waited in the stairwell on the other side of the door, so they could hear him better, and everyone else waited back by the cells, staying out of sight. It wasn't long before the echo of Benwick's low whistle came bouncing down the stone walls of the stairwell, and then they all filed into it, following him into the hall above, where they ambushed two Hallerns before they had time to draw their swords. Then they had two swords for the lot of them, which Gravis and Dent laid claim to, but this had been the easiest part. From here, there would be no turning back.

"Remember," Dent muttered to the rest of the group, "we don't have to take the entire hall. In fact, we can't. We just have to make them delay locking it up, or else unlock it from our side. We take the great hall or the wall, and that's all we need."

As long as Bridger and the Lanvalds get here fast enough, Gravis thought. That was the one problem with this plan; even a quarter of an hour more or less could make all the difference. The Lanvalds were fighting their way to the hall at approxi-mately the same time Gravis, Dent, and their party were moving through it. If the Lanvalds arrived at the hall too soon, they'd force all the Hallerns in the city into it ahead of them, and Gravis and the others would be overrun before they could open the gate; if they arrived too late, they gave the Hallerns already stationed here time to assault Gravis's party and slam the gate shut again. "Benwick, do you know the state of the hall doors? Any chance they'll be barred?"

"Not yet. The Hallerns are stockpiling supplies until the very last moment, because they don't know how long they might have to hold out. They have to keep the gate and the hall doors open for that. They'll close them when the Lanvalds get

close, of course, but I don't think hearing the enemy has breached the city walls
will be enough."

"It wouldn't be for me," Dent said. "The hall's on a hill for a reason. They'll be
able to see the enemy approach clearly—I expect they'll lock things up when the
Lanvalds reach the base of the hill."

It was what Gravis would have done, too, but he didn't want to assign their occupiers more familiarity with Stonespire, or even just more cleverness, than they
deserved. "Let's be prepared, even so. The hall door would be easier to defend
than the outer gate, but in order for that to work, we'll have to fight our way out
through the hall doors, get the gate up, then fight back inside the same doorway
and hold it. If the doors are barred to begin with, that plan probably has no chance
of success."

"All I can tell you is they weren't barred when I went down to fetch you," Benwick said. "I don't think they'll have gotten it done so fast."

"We'll try it, then." He glanced at Dent. "One loop beforehand, to pick up as
many weapons as we can?"

"Aye, we daren't risk more than that. Any longer would completely destroy
the element of surprise. What do you think—through the kitchens, stop in at your
study and the small armory, then go all the way around and end up at the great
hall?"

"Just what I was thinking." He nodded at the others. "This is our last chance
to take a breath. Questions?"

A flurry of shaking heads.

"Good. Let's go."

They didn't run into any large groups of Hallerns between there and the small
armory—just a gaggle of servants in the kitchens, but those were Esthradian, and
kept their silence. The small armory only had four men guarding it—dispatched
without much incident, though Benwick took a nick in the shoulder—and then
they finally had enough weapons for everyone, and still no one to sound the alarm.
But their luck shifted once they hit the great hall: they found eight Hallerns there,
and two managed to flee out a side door. If that was as far as surprise could take
them, at least it had been a considerable way.

They left a third of their number on the hall's threshold, while the others, including Gravis and Dent, poured out into the sunlight, intent on the twin winches
that would raise Stonespire Hall's front gate. There were only a couple of soldiers
in the yard, but there were four on the wall above, which unnerved Gravis until he
saw all four of them turn tail and dash back inside. They must have been unarmed
scouts, only intended to keep eyes on the city and the hill, and unprepared to send
arrows down into the yard.

"They'll be back with bows," Dent said, scowling.

"They will, but by that time their fellows will already have engaged us down here. Unless they're famed marksmen, they won't be able to shoot at us without the risk of hitting their comrades." Gravis had time to toss that much over his shoulder, and then they were at the winches. He and Dent each stood guard beside one while two of the others operated them, a few of their number having already peeled off to engage the Hallerns on the ground. "How does the approach down the hill look?" he asked Benwick.

"Not what I'd prefer to see," he replied, squinting through the slowly lifting gate. "The only people making their way up the slope so far are suppliers and their Hallern escorts. They're about to get a great deal more agitated, as soon as they look up and see us on the other side of the gate."

"They'll abandon the civilians and come racing through to attack us," Gravis said. "We've got to let the gate drop again. It's not worth keeping it open until the Lanvalds get here."

"And the hall door?" Benwick asked.

"What do you think, Dent?"

Dent ground his teeth. "Can't tell how many of theirs are going to come up the hill before we get some of ours, but right now I think the threshold's too valuable to give up. Half of you, back to the door."

They were just in time, too; through Gravis's limited field of view, he could see soldiers beginning to gather on the other side of the threshold, coming from within the hall. "Got any ideas about how to handle the bows now, Gravis?" Dent muttered.

"They can't shoot into the hall from that angle. The rest of us need to flatten ourselves as close to the wall as possible. We're harder to hit in its shadow."

"Captain, I think this is it!" Benwick shouted. "The Lanvalds are driving the Hallerns ahead of them up the hill!"

"All right, this is the most crucial moment," Gravis said. "We keep the gate down until the Lanvalds have crushed the enemy against it and cut their way through to the front. Then we open it, and keep it open as long as possible. On my signal!"

And crush them the Lanvalds literally did, catching their foes against the gate in front of them, with the hill dropping away on two sides. By the time the fleeing Hallerns had managed to turn themselves around and put their backs to the gate instead, their opponents had cut any semblance of a formation they had to ribbons, throwing themselves forward and forward without letting up. But the group trying to hold the hall door was having a rough time of it, too. Gravis strained his neck from looking back and forth, waiting for either the moment when there would be more Lanvalds against the gate than Hallerns, or else the moment when the group at the door was in danger of giving out entirely.

Thank the gods, the former condition came to pass first. Even better, Gravis looked out into the crowd and saw Jill Bridger herself gain the ground before the gate, the sword at the end of her long arms clearing a wide swath in front of her. "Now!"

The men on the winches turned them with all haste, and Gravis, Dent, and the others did their best to shield them from any stray arrows. Once again, the gate rose inch by inch, and soldiers on the other side started ducking under it, piling into the yard. At the same time, the line holding the hall door finally broke, and Gravis sucked in a breath. Now would truly come the chaos.

For the next several minutes, everything seemed too fast and too slow at once. At least the arrows stopped falling, but only because the yard was a packed and bloody mess, fighters practically climbing over one another, with no way to see anything more than right in front of their faces. Gravis and Dent stayed as close to the winches as they could, hacking away at anyone who tried to interfere with the men holding them open. The gate was as high as an adult's head now, and Lanvalds were streaming in, though they couldn't stop some Hallerns from following as well. Bridger remained by the gate entrance, picking off foes and covering her allies. Benwick had swapped places with her, taking up a position on the far side of the gate and trying to prevent more of the enemy from coming through. "How many do we need?" he yelled, though Gravis could barely hear him. "We aren't going to be able to keep the gate up forever, Captain. How many do we—"

He cut himself off to close with more approaching foes, but they knew he was just a distraction. They shoved past him, one taking a minor wound for his trouble, and stumbled over and past Dent, spearing the man on the winch next to him in the throat. The gate ground to a halt, suspended with a third left to rise.

"It's all right!" Bridger shouted. "Leave the gate! We have enough to take them!"

Gravis couldn't see enough to ascertain the truth of that for himself, but if she said it, he believed her. He pulled his own man back from the winch, and gave it a swift kick, unspooling the chain and sending the gate back down, scattering all those who had been underneath it. Now the Hallerns caught on the far side had nowhere to retreat, and he expected they'd surrender momentarily. But on their side . . .

Bridger was already driving into the center, her sword a stark horizontal line that beheaded the first man to engage her. Dent rushed up in her wake, now that he didn't have to guard the winch, and Gravis followed them more carefully. He wasn't used to fighting without armor, especially in a big group like this, and he didn't want to be too rash.

He watched Dent parry an assault, then take down the man who'd started it.

"They've got to surrender!" he shouted to Bridger. "They can't possibly win at this point. They can't even keep the hall. We should press them to surrender!"

"I'm trying, sir! It's still so—" She drove her next thrust forward with both arms, burying her sword to the hilt in her opponent's chest. "We can't let up while they're still pushing their attack so aggressively."

It was true. Though the Hallerns kept losing ground, they were fighting more offensively than defensively. Gravis looked for any central figure, someone they would rally around or turn to for commands, but he saw no one. Had they already been cut down?

The three of them were halfway across the yard before Gravis finally felt that the space around them was starting to get less crowded, rather than more. That was partially due to some casualties on both sides, but more to the Hallerns' pulling back inside the hall. Gravis opened his mouth to shout a warning—they didn't want to give the enemy a chance to shut the doors on them—but Bridger understood already, bounding up on her longer legs to occupy the threshold.

She'd gone too fast. There was a man standing in the shadow of the doors, who halted his retreat when she drew alongside him. By the time Bridger saw him in the dim light, he was already within reach, his sword mid-swing before hers could move.

She was going to be struck, dead center, with a naked blade. Dent's protégée, and the pride of the city, where she had refused to apprehend orphan thieves when she was still half a child herself, where she had uncovered even the most hidden nests of the criminals who preyed upon those same children. Even her lady relied on her, though Arianrod Margraine disliked saying such things aloud. She couldn't be cut down like this, by some flailing traitor. But Gravis couldn't parry the blow in time.

His sword was too far away, so he took the hit with his body instead.

Though the pain was searing, there was a part of him that watched it dispassionately, as if it were just another outcome of the countless contests of arms he'd witnessed over the years. The hit tore apart his midsection, not as deep as it might have been, but wide, too wide. The wound couldn't hold itself together, and with it bleeding at this rate . . .

He heard a clattering of metal as Dent's sword hit the ground, the man himself going to his knees at Gravis's side, calling his name. "Sir," Bridger said, as if in shock, though she still managed to stand as a bulwark between the three of them and further harm, dropping back to guard his other side.

"Damn," he said, because perhaps if he treated it casually, it would make things easier for Dent. "Forgot I wasn't wearing my armor, I suppose."

"Do you take me for a fool?" Dent was clutching his sides, as if trying to hold him together. "Gravis—"

"Captain." That was Bridger, lips pressed together in an expression he couldn't read. She stretched a hand out, as if to touch him, but pulled it back at the last second. "Why did you do it? You've never even liked me."

"No, that's—" But he didn't have time to explain how that wasn't true anymore. She deserved an answer to her question. "Because you're the future of Esthrades, and I can only be the past. You—both of you—can see farther down that path she's blazing than I ever could, no matter how I tried. You're the ones she needs at her side when she returns."

When, not if. Because she had to. Arianrod Margraine was many things, and had many faults. But above all else, she was what her father had longed to be his whole life, and never achieved. She was the leader Esthrades needed. And she was not someone who failed, once she had set her mind on something.

"Dent."

He clutched Gravis's hand. "I'm here."

Gravis squeezed back, with what little strength was left to him. "You and I . . . we've already said all there is to say to each other. So tell her . . . when you see her, tell her that I kept the oath I made her to the end. And that I'm . . . sorry about the rest."

"I'll tell her." Dent smiled sadly. "Though she probably won't react the way you're hoping."

"Nonsense. She'll be grandly irritated. I have to get her back at least once." He laughed weakly, more like a sputter. He knew he had said there was nothing left unspoken between them, but this was probably his last chance. "Dent, I'm . . . sorry to you, too. I'm sorry for it all."

And Dent didn't say, "It doesn't matter." He didn't say, "There's nothing to forgive." He knew Gravis, and all their history, far too well for that. Instead, he used the time they had left to say, "I forgive you, Gravis. I forgive you for everything."

He could slip away in peace after that.

CHAPTER THIRTY-THREE

Valyanrend

RUMORS WERE THE lifeblood of Sheath, a collection of streets whose inhabitants prided themselves on being the densest collection of thieves and charlatans per square inch anywhere in the world, yet who had never been through a period of mass arrests. They knew you couldn't afford to have a rumor just out there, substantial, *real,* for anyone to take hold of. Then it was a fact, and *facts* could put you in jail. So the ne'er-do-wells of Sheath had banded together to create a pool of rumors so large, so muddied, so ever-changing, that only the most skilled could successfully wade in and sift truth from falsehood. It had kept them safe for centuries, by keeping them informed as much as by keeping everyone else in the dark.

By essential design, tracking any particular rumor's source was next to impossible. Indeed, asking a purveyor of rumors to reveal their source by name was as good as insulting them—one should simply be grateful to have received the information in the first place, and evaluate its potential veracity on one's own time. And repeating a rumor of any value to a *guard* was like casting a priceless gem into the mud; even a child wouldn't be such a fool.

So it happened that, as the days passed, a series of rumors regarding one particular subject dripped and dripped into Sheath's pool of potential information, like so many rivers running to the same sea. Their origin? Who could say?

"I shouldn't even be telling this to you lot," Marceline said to the gaggle of thieves' apprentices who had gathered near Tom's after supper, "but Tom had a hell of a customer the other day, asking about this supposed protection Elgar's been offering."

She usually found them too childish to associate with, and every one of them was jealous of her proximity to both Roger and Tom, despite never being a proper apprentice. But jealous or not, they were too intrigued not to listen whenever she dropped them scraps.

"This lady," she continued, "said she had serious reason to think these demonstrations with the blood and the steel were all staged. Fake! Said those vials are filled with nothing but pig's blood, and a bit of something to make it smoke when it hits the metal. A reaction of some kind. She wanted him to dig up more proof—

quiet, Brent, you little ass, or I won't tell you anything—but Tom thought it was best to stay clear of that business. Doesn't want Elgar to ever find out, if he should go after this woman. So *I* don't know, but, well, doesn't it seem odd that this marquise seems to have so much blood in her?

"And don't tell your masters I told you, or Tom'll have my hide," she added, ensuring that every last one of them would do exactly that.

"Eh, I'm not sure about it," Morgan said, pouring a refill for a particularly gregarious patron. "Had a fellow sitting right where you are now a few nights ago who said his cousin's a jeweler's apprentice in the Glassway, and she swore her master told her the stuff was just volcanic glass. Expensive and rare, certainly, but not powerful. It's odd, though, for the very reason that it *is* so expensive. No volcanoes in Lantistyne, after all, so most of us have never seen it. What if that's why it's worth the expense, because most of us won't know what it is? And if I follow *that* line of thought . . . well, I'm being cautious. Always best to be cautious, that's what I've learned."

"Oh, I wouldn't gainsay Morgan," Braddock said the next day, after running into a Sheather who'd overheard the conversation. "She's always steered me right in the past. Besides, they're saying in Iron's Den that it's all a part of the war effort anyway, and not the way you'd think. That Elgar wants to know how many potential soldiers he has, and where they live. I say no thanks to that. I'm never fighting for someone else again. Are you?"

And as the rumors swelled, they grew so numerous that even Sheath couldn't contain them. They coursed through neighborhoods one by one, spreading in every direction.

"I'm telling you, I can't pour a single drink at the Dragon's Head anymore without hearing about it," Morgan said to Halvard, buying supplies at his shop in the Fades. "I've always been a skeptic, Hal, you know that. But do you really think there's all this smoke without a little fire?"

"I heard at my job yesterday that people are saying Elgar's protection can't be trusted," Marceline's sister said to her when she dropped in to visit. "Have you heard about this?"

Marceline rolled her eyes. "You mean you *haven't* heard about it? It's damn near everywhere. I'll summarize it for you if you want, but you can really ask anyone."

"I'm all a mess about it, Mrs. Manigault, to be honest," Talia said to one of her most frequent patrons from Goldhalls, weighing and tallying her purchases with practiced efficiency. "I'm the only one in my family who's eligible for it, so I've been thinking about it constantly. But the other day, while I was running errands in the Glassway, I heard people saying that was just the problem—just what makes it so suspicious. Wouldn't the imperator want to protect children more than anyone? Yet children are the ones he says absolutely can't have it. Not the infirm or the injured—even those over a certain age! Is he going to make people give them up as they grow older?"

"Oh dear, do you think I should tell Marjorie not to accept it?" the matron asked, wringing her hands. "She hates the idea of soldiering, but with all her hunting, she's such a good shot . . . a runner, a rider . . . you really think he's looking to poach such people, though she's the heir to a mansion in Goldhalls?"

"I've heard just as bad," Talia's mother said, as Talia masked her surprise. "If this were a matter of science, that would be one thing. But science can be explained. Even magic should work for a *reason,* right? But he asks us to accept that it works because he says it does, on faith. And what good has faith ever done this city? I was saying as much to Mr. Parnell just the other day." She raised her voice, angling it over her shoulder. "Wasn't I, Harold?"

Harold Parnell, slicing meat three counters away, had heard nothing of the conversation beyond the last ten words. But he had an unerring feel for the desired answer to any question his wife asked him, and this one wasn't even particularly challenging. "You certainly were, my dear. And quite right, as always."

"We don't even know what really caused those murderers to do what they did," Talia said, "but I can't help but think it's too convenient that Elgar had his talismans right at the ready so soon afterward."

"It was too soon, wasn't it," the matron muttered, as if to herself. "I told Marjorie as much, or I almost did. Where on earth is she?"

"Thank you for your patronage as always, ma'am!" Talia chirped, tucking her purchases into the crook of her arm before she could leave without them. "Give my regards to your daughter!"

"It's all my mother can talk about," the daughter in question said in the narrow archery range behind Fletcher and Son two days later, testing her bowstring before drawing and lining up her shot. "You heard anything about this, Fletcher?"

Wren brushed his hair out of his eyes with typical nervousness, looking not at her but at the path he knew her arrow would follow. "I've heard about it. Some things that . . . concerned me. But you know me, Miss Manigault—I'm a craftsman, not some kind of authority. I wouldn't want to speak out of turn."

"My mother's no more an authority than you, trust me." The arrow flew beautifully toward the very center of the target and stuck quivering at its heart, and she drew another without pausing. "If you've got anything to say, let's hear it."

"Well, the timing is suspicious, you know? The Issamiri are bearing down on us, and now the Lanvalds are declaring a new king, sowing chaos in the east . . . Elgar will need more soldiers than ever. That it's some kind of draft preparation seems almost certain—or so some of the apprentices are saying. But I heard it could be even worse than that. Get us to accept it, this protection, and then put us in debt to the Citadel. Our labor for his generosity."

"Hmph. Generosity, my foot." She loosed another arrow, and then another, only adding to her little cluster at the bull's-eye. "Damn, but you make fine arrows, Fletcher. I tried to talk to your father about hiring you out to accompany my next hunting party, have you on hand to do repairs and such, but he said he expected you'd be too busy on account of you're likely to get married soon. I suppose congratulations are in or—"

"My father told you *what*?" Wren's voice cracked immediately, so unused to ever reaching that volume and that shrillness.

"Oh. Was he mistaken? He said you were quite in love, and you wouldn't find a better girl who'd have you on the continent."

"Oh gods." Wren covered his eyes with his hand. "I-I mean, I am in love, very much so, b-but we've only just started—I couldn't possibly—if she hears about this—"

"Eh, if she knows your father at all, she'll probably guess the situation pretty quickly." Marjorie Manigault plucked her arrows from the target, oblivious to his distress. "Rotten news about the imperator, though. I'll be sure to tell the hunting party; not a bad shot among them."

"I think that's wise, Miss Manigault. Got to give them the opportunity to make their own decisions, so they should know as much about it as possible. Excuse me a moment." He ducked back inside, and she went back to her shooting, unruffled by the unaccustomed sound of Wren Fletcher yelling, *"Father! What have you been telling people?"*

And at the center of it all was Roger Halfen, who never spread a single rumor. He just went about his business as usual, and if anyone ever asked him for his opinion on the matter, he shrugged and said he figured it was as likely to be true as false. But when he said it, he made sure there was just a little twinkle in his eye, and just a little smile playing about his lips.

WHEN ROGER LEFT his home that evening, the rumors he'd devised still weren't ripe yet, so he wasn't expecting to be popular enough for anyone to be waiting in the shadows alongside his door. So he nearly lost his footing when someone hissed, "Halfen!"

"Who wants to know?" Roger said reflexively, before recognizing the figure hugging close to the corner. "Eh? Londret?"

"I can't stay long," Londret Wapps said. "I left the guard, and I'm leaving the city. But I have some business to conclude with you first."

That did seem to be the case: he had put off his blue-black uniform in favor of a simple traveling cloak, and a bulging pack dangled from one of his hands. The other held something very carefully, but Roger couldn't make it out in the dark. "If you're talking about the drink, I gave it to you in good faith. No interest necessary. What other business do we have?"

"One other thing," Londret insisted. "You were the one who urged me to quit the guard, Halfen, so this is your responsibility now. And I know you'll die before you leave this city, so that makes you an even better person to take charge of it."

He thrust the mysterious item at Roger, and it turned out to be a meticulously folded sheet of parchment. Roger pinched it between two fingers with great skepticism. "What's this?"

"Two days before I left, I saw that sticking out of a pile of papers one of my superiors kept in his room," Londret said. "I nicked it. Open it, and I'll show you why."

Roger did, and saw what was clearly a map of Valyanrend. It was divided into different colored areas, but they weren't the different districts, or any other method of cartographical distinction he'd ever seen used for the city before. "Is there a key?"

"No, but look at this." He tapped one of the colored shapes. "Familiar, isn't it? This is the area where the Silkspoint massacre happened. Precisely the area. All the carnage was confined to that space." He must have taken Roger's silence for doubt, for he continued, "Maybe it's nothing. Maybe I'm just obsessed with what happened. But if not . . . look how many other areas there are. These could be plans for the future, but they could also be realities in the present, already laid down somehow. I know that sounds—"

"It doesn't," Roger said. Here was Draven's Square, for one thing, and a circle around the Glassway, though he knew that one hadn't been used yet. And then, squinting in the dim light, he noticed that each colored area contained precisely one tiny blot of ink. He didn't dare to hope he knew what those represented, but if it was true . . . "I think you're right. It's too convenient for a coincidence. It'll take some time to figure out what precisely these areas are denoting, or why they're arranged this way, but it's worth doing. I'll start work on it immediately."

"Aye, I thought you might say something like that. Either way, I thought you should have it. This city gave me its share of knocks, and I can't say much for its people, either. But they deserve more than"—he nodded at the map—"that."

He saluted sarcastically, and then he was gone, melting into the shadow at the end of the street and leaving only the map Roger held as proof he had ever been there.

Roger turned it over and over, tracing the districts with one finger. It was admittedly a tenuous connection. But if this really was a map of . . . what, potential massacre sites? Groups controlled by the same spell? Something even worse? Then it could be the last piece he needed to make everything fall into place. And it meant he needed to add one more wrinkle to his plan.

As THE DAYS passed, more and more people approached him.

"Look here, Halfen, I know no one's better at sniffing out a swindler than another swindler. And I can't help noticing that you haven't taken our imperator up on his offer. So tell me, what do you know?"

"Don't think I don't know you, Roger. I haven't seen you this smug in years. And I know damn well you'll never rest without bragging about your own cleverness. So let's hear it, then. What's the big scheme this time?"

But Roger didn't give in. He couldn't, not yet. This only worked if he waited until they were truly desperate.

All the while, his friends and compatriots were doing their work. The rumors spread and multiplied, grew in pitch and certainty. And then one night Roger was caught alone by Evie Rhodes, a retired thief and former protégée of his gran's, and he took one look at her face and knew: this was the one.

She told him about her grandchildren—three of them, two who'd already taken the talismans and one who was wavering. She begged him, by the bond between their families, by the respect one thief held for another, to tell her if he knew something, anything, that would suggest her grandchildren were putting themselves in danger. And Roger put on a great show of slowly, slowly being worn down by her pleading, until finally he stretched both hands out in front of him and whispered, "All right, Evie, all right. We'll talk, but not here."

He took her home with him, making a big show of checking to make sure they weren't being followed, and settled her down with a cup of tea. And then, leaning in close to her across the table, he unfurled the most crucial rumor of all. "Look, Evie, between you and me, your instincts are right. These gifts from Elgar aren't what they seem to be; I've uncovered enough proof at this point to be certain of that. But I don't want to take the scrutiny that'll come from saying something like that in the marketplace. Whatever we talk about, it doesn't come back to me, you hear?"

She assured him of her silence, and perhaps she even meant it. But over time, her empathy would be evoked, too. Here and there, she'd let things slip. That was good. That was what he was counting on.

Then it was just up to Roger to do what he did best, and spin a story. And this one, for once, was . . . well, *mostly* true.

"I'll start with something that's hard to swallow, Evie. This magic business?

It's the truth. That's why Elgar's been so keen to capture this marquise, despite the tiny size of her territory: he knew she had the kind of power that's not been seen in this land for centuries. But do you think someone so grasping and ambitious as our imperator just wants to protect us from it? You've got a thief's instincts same as me, so I expect that felt wrong to you from the beginning, too. But as long as instinct was all I had, I kept quiet. Until I was sure. I can tell you now, he wants to use that same power for himself. Against his very people. Those charms aren't meant to protect us from her, they're to put us under *his* spell."

That sentence was completely true, of course, but Roger still searched her face for any signs of disbelief. He didn't find any, which meant the rumors had been doing their job. "To what end?"

"What does he need more than anything else right now, Evie? An army. Enough warm bodies to win him the continent. Once he has it in hand, I can't say what his next priority will be, but even with the advantage of numbers, he'll be fighting for a long time. Anyone snared by his scheme runs the risk of losing themselves for . . . years, perhaps."

She grew very quiet, but he could tell it wasn't out of suspicion. He'd needed a bit of time to swallow such a revelation, too. At last, she said, "But if we're caught between her magic and his, where is there left to turn?"

"I don't think we've got to worry much about her," Roger said. "She may be killed soon, and even if she isn't, she probably just wants him off her land. Not so different from us, really. But as for him, I've done plenty of looking into it these past weeks. It wasn't easy, because nobody wanted to talk to me any more than I wanted to talk to you. Nobody wants to draw his eye. But I did find something. A way to make his little charms work at least partially how he claims they do. A way to avoid the risk of being swept up in his power." He broke off, giving her a serious look. "But that's the one secret you'll never get out of me, so don't try. I need to protect myself, too, and that means I can't have everyone trying to copy me. I won't be blamed if someone messes it up, and I won't have it used to lead Elgar's people to me."

He waited for her assurances before continuing. "If you want my help, the best I can offer is this. Get the charms from your grandchildren, and leave them with me, at a place I'll tell you. One day later, you can return to fetch them, and they'll be there for you, much improved. Now, I know what sort of reputation I have around Sheath, and it's well deserved, but to show I'm not selling empty promises this time, I won't take any coin. Just you and your grandchildren's silence. For I can guarantee you this: if I'm ever exposed, I'll disappear overnight, and everything I know will be gone with me."

In his original plan, that would have been a bluff. But now that Len had been unmasked, Roger had to be prepared to do precisely that, to protect his own life and keep his cousin from connecting him to any of his associates. He'd gone over it repeatedly with Morgan and Naishe both, to ensure any message to run could reach him, no matter who it came from. But right now, that danger only helped him, because it must have added weight to his words he never could have feigned.

Evie nodded. "I'll get them. No matter how I have to."

"Well, you are a thief, even if you've been inactive for a while," Roger said. "I'm sure there are many potential avenues open to you."

ROGER HIMSELF DIDN'T do anything with the talismans, of course. He just brought them to Morgan, and Morgan touched them with the dagger, and that was that. But no one could find out that Morgan had anything to do with the process; the fewer connections anyone could make between them, the better, and they couldn't let the tavern become cluttered with potential supplicants. Much more beneficial to let Evie and those like her assume that there was some complicated process behind it, something they could never hope to replicate.

For there were others like Evie, just as Roger had always wanted. There were people she knew, with loved ones in similar situations, that she couldn't harden her heart to, and there were those who'd made the same judgment she had, and approached Roger on their own. He gave them all variations on the same speech, and made sure Morgan drained the magic from their cursed talismans with the same caution—and Naishe as well, once the numbers became great enough. They'd been hoping, as bad as it felt to say aloud, for another outbreak of violence, for that would have been proof that Roger's methods worked. But Elgar wasn't so foolish as to cast spells on anyone under his "protection" before the time was ripe. Roger suspected there wouldn't be any more incidents—and when it was the Issamiri who were attacked, those who had done it would justify it to themselves as unexpected fervor against a known enemy.

Until then, he chipped away at Elgar's army, in ones and twos and fives and dozens, and prayed it would be enough.

CHAPTER THIRTY-FOUR

Hallarnon

IT WAS THE fourth day straight that Lirien had felt it, this relentless panic, this cry for help. It was alarming not just because of its strength and persistence; it was alarming because asking for help was something Talis did not do. Voltest was the one in pain, and he was more muted, intermittently frustrated and weary and concerned. Talis was a pulse of dread without an end.

At least they were easy to track: together, and moving only within the same small area. Lirien, Rhia, and Cadfael had followed them to a plain east of Valyanrend, only a little out of their way—or perhaps not at all, since it was likely the advancing Issamiri army would have forced them farther north before they could enter the city anyway. There was the beginning of a forest to the west, but their immediate vicinity contained only a single tree and a sea of shin-high grass. Beneath the tree, Voltest crouched, and before it, Talis strode to meet them.

"Thank you for coming," she said to Lirien, which probably wasn't a good sign, either. "I'm not sure what you'll make of this, or what you'll be able to do, but I think it's too dangerous to leave him like this."

Lirien still didn't understand what *this* was, but she thought it would be better to examine Voltest for herself. The thing she immediately noticed was the bandage wrapped around his side, but he didn't seem to be favoring the wound; his knees were drawn up to his chest, his fists were clutching handfuls of grass, and he was rocking ever so slightly back and forth. His face seemed somehow pale and flushed at once, patches of red here and there in a bloodless expanse. He barely looked up when she approached.

"The wound is from a stray arrow," Talis said. "He's been treated, and it's healing—slowly. But surely you must be able to feel that's not the true issue?"

She certainly could. This close, the sense of wrongness was unmistakable. It wasn't like before, when she'd tried to reach out for Talis and found nothing; his magic was still connected to hers, but it was like there was something else running through it, like blood through water. "Voltest, how do you feel?"

"Like I'm tired of being asked that," he muttered, tightening his arms around himself.

Of course. Why had she thought he'd be helpful? "Since I'm here, let me take care of your wound, at lea—"

"No." He shrank back against the tree. "Stay back. Your and Talis's magic is too . . . loud. Just let me be. Just leave me in peace."

"He started saying that yesterday," Talis said, "but before that he didn't want to be alone, even for a moment. I think . . . Lirien, I think it's my fault."

"Why would you say that?" That was Cadfael, of course, only really interested now that Talis was involved.

"I think it might be an aftershock of what happened to me at Sinthil Vlin."

"Then it's Selwyn's fault, not yours."

"All *right*," Lirien said. "No one's blaming her, and you don't need to defend her. Just let her explain so we can fix this."

Talis nodded. "Selwyn kept saying that the steel inhibits magic, but that was never what it felt like to me. If anything, it was like those manacles wanted to steal my magic, to take it out of me. Like the steel had one end of it, and I had the other, and we were pulling in different directions. And the more we pulled, the more the magic . . . warped, I suppose."

Lirien had felt something similar when Jocelyn Selreshe stole her magic, but that had been over in a moment. Talis's struggle had lasted days. "Right, until we couldn't sense you at all, even after you were set free. But that's obviously not the case anymore, for you or Voltest."

"Not *yet*," Talis said, "but I'm afraid that's where it's headed. I think his magic is pulling away from ours—and when it isolates itself completely, I'm afraid he'll lose himself like I did."

Was that why Lirien's sense of Voltest's feelings had been so muted over the past several days? Because his magic was withdrawing? She crouched before him. "Listen, I know that sulking is just what you do, and you can probably barely help it right now. But that wound is one more problem we don't need, on top of all the other problems that'll no doubt be much harder to fix. Can you just let me take care of it, please?"

He took a deep breath, and she could feel how hard it was for him to uncurl himself even a little, to lessen the isolation his magic was trying to inflict upon him. But slowly, gingerly, he released his legs, pushed his knees down, and gave Lirien his hand.

Healing the wound in his side took barely a thought, but she had no sooner done so than she felt something else, something beyond skin and bone. She had never been trained as a healer, so she had no technical knowledge of injuries or diseases; she relied on her magic to tell her what was wrong, and to know how to fix it. But this was different. Her power was telling her something was wrong with Voltest, something that needed healing, but not where or why. It was in every part of him, and at the same time it was nowhere at all.

Lirien tried to concentrate on it, to trust that her magic understood the problem even if she didn't. But Voltest jerked out of her grasp as if she'd hurt him, stumbling to his feet. "How dare you," he hissed, low and venomous. "No. No!"

He lashed out, and the flames that obeyed him sprang to his defense, burning through the air between them and missing Lirien's face only because she summoned her own water to meet him. "Voltest, what the hell? What are you doing?"

"That's what I'm asking you! What, did you think I wouldn't notice until it was too late?" His back was against the trunk of the tree now, one arm curled protectively across his body. "I know you've always considered yourself superior to us, your magic in a purer state. But that doesn't give you the right to decide for me!"

"I didn't—"

"Voltest." Talis cut her off. "What are you talking about? What did she do?"

"I didn't even think it was possible. But if someone outside our group managed it, I suppose I should have assumed it could happen from within." He pointed one trembling finger at Lirien. "She used her power against mine. She tried to steal my magic!"

"No, I—" But she stopped herself there. That was the answer to the riddle. What was in every part of Voltest, and yet nowhere to be found? It was his magic itself that was the injury. "Talis, when I healed him, I found something else, something I perceived as hurting him. I didn't understand it was his magic, but doesn't it make sense? Isn't it in the very nature of this power to be parasitic?"

But Talis's face was drawn in mistrust. "Could you always do this? Steal our magic whenever you wanted?"

"How should I know? I've never felt it like that before. But it wouldn't have been *stolen,* it would just be . . . healed. Gone."

Talis glanced at Voltest. "It sounds like it was an accident."

He shook his head firmly. "That doesn't matter. Don't you see? Now that she knows she can take our magic away, you and I will never be safe. It's unacceptable."

"Gods, spare me from your relentless paranoia." Lirien rolled her eyes. "Neither of you can get rid of *my* magic—even I can't. So you'd best learn to accept it. What other choice do you have?"

In answer, Voltest set the tree afire.

It didn't burn slowly, like logs on a hearth. It was consumed in a moment, from roots to leaves. Though Voltest stood in its shadow without flinching, Lirien could not stand to be so close to such terrible heat and smoke, and backed away from him.

The siblings had been quiet until then, perhaps thinking that such a discussion was beyond their understanding. But now they both drew their swords as one, the reflection of the burning tree glinting off the blades.

It only made Voltest angrier, of course. "You would aid in her scheming? Don't think that you'll receive mercy from me."

He sent another wave of fire their way, but they both deflected it against their swords. "Voltest, leave them out of it!" Talis shouted—brilliant, *now* she was concerned. "They aren't involved with anything Lirien's done."

"They want the same thing!" he insisted. "Those blades would make us powerless as surely as her magic."

The whole time he spoke, he did not stop spreading flame from his fingertips, forcing the rest of them to stay distant. And now the grass had caught it, bright tongues lapping up the tinder in all directions. Lirien pulled more and more liquid water from the air, but she already knew that fighting him this way was a losing proposition. She could protect herself and her immediate surroundings, but she couldn't draw enough moisture to put out all his fires at once. "Voltest, control yourself! You don't want to do this! If those flames reach the forest, who knows how many people you could kill! Not to mention—"

She glanced back at Rhia and Cadfael, already separated from each other by a line of fire and smoke. He could not cast spells at them directly, could not set their bodies afire with just a thought. But the swords made them immune to magic, not to fire itself, and the fire was everywhere. The longer they remained, the less viable ground there was to stand on.

Cadfael was still within arm's reach, so she turned to him first, condensing the water around him so he was completely soaked through. She focused on that water, using her magic to imbue it with more staying power. It wouldn't last forever, but it would shield him from burns while it endured.

But when she tried to do the same for Rhia, a wall of flame reared up between them, too virulent for her to douse. Damn Voltest, he was leaving her no choice. If he wouldn't stop, she really would have to wash his magic away. And Talis was still just standing there, one hand to her head, as if this were some immensely challenging conundrum she had all day to solve instead of an urgent necessity to prevent mass death. But she had never really cared about that sort of thing, had she? Perhaps whatever calculus she was performing only had to do with her own benefit. Lirien couldn't count on her, either, then. And she would have to do this, like it or not.

Patches of moisture fell upon the ground around them, and in places where the grass was already too charred to nurture any more fire, it stayed extinguished. But the rest of the field was a chaotic mess of ever-changing flame, gouts that blazed up and fell back as her power grappled with his. Voltest could not surge beyond her to set the forest alight, but the tree beneath which he still stood was a giant inexhaustible firebrand, blazing bright enough to singe the eyes. Bathed in its glow, Voltest was overshadowed and washed out, even the bright red of his cloak almost impossible to see. But still Lirien struggled toward him with her body and her magic both, pulling on every drop of water that didn't reside within the bodies of those around her.

She heard Rhia scream as flames began eating their way up her limbs, but she was powerless to reach her. She felt the protection she had given Cadfael start to wither and wane, but she had nothing to spare to restore it. And though she knew it was hopeless, Lirien couldn't help shouting as she threw herself against Voltest again and again, an entreaty and a curse at once: "Talis! Talis!"

THE SMOKE AND ash brought tears to Talis's eyes, and she coughed every time she inhaled, though her wind dispersed the worst of it before it reached her lungs. If only it could do the same for the inside of her head, where an even worse storm was raging. She had always been caught between the two of them, but now she could no longer go back and forth. Now each of them was determined to blot out the other, and wherever Talis threw her weight, the other would fall.

But each time she tried to reframe the question, she found another answer. Personally, she cared for Voltest more; he was condescending, full of little habits that irked her, but she could tolerate his company, even when it was only the two of them. Ethically, Lirien's case was damnably clear: she only wished to kill Voltest's magic, while he would have wiped her out entirely. Worse, if his flames were allowed to rage unchecked, many more people could die.

But if Lirien could kill Voltest's magic, she could also kill Talis's. And without him, there would be no one else to help protect her from it. What if Lirien should take it into her head, tomorrow or in ten years, that Talis was too dangerous to keep her power? Would Talis be able to evade her, persuade her? If worse came to worst, could she endure having such a thing stripped from her, or would she rather die?

Worst of all, she had no time to think. She herself was spared from the carnage, floating midair above the burning plain, diverting the ash away from her. But the ground below her looked like some artist's vision of hell. The grass, the air, everything was burning. Only Lirien did not, could not, burn, but Voltest would destroy everything else in the attempt, until she died not of his flames, but of being unable to breathe from the smoke.

He'd destroy everyone else.

She had asked herself if she could live without her magic. But could she live knowing that she had caused their deaths? Could she live knowing that Cadfael had fought through her tempest to reach her, and she had condemned him and the sister he loved so much to die?

But no, it was more than that. Without Lirien, she and Voltest would lose control again, and eventually they would no longer be able to come back to themselves. They would lash out with lethal violence without even knowing why, just as Voltest was doing now. That, not a life without magic, would be worse than death.

In the end, that was the thought uppermost in her mind. That was the edge on which she turned, when she ran out of time to decide.

She gathered the wind, blew the smoke away from Lirien in a great gust, and forbid the rest of the air from feeding the flames, until they starved and died one by one, leaving only the man at their center, cloak charred to ruins, skin stained with ash. He could not freeze any more than Lirien could burn, yet Talis felt the moment when Lirien's magic penetrated him, the first time any one of them had managed that upon another. She touched him not with her cold but with her healing, and melted the magic out of him, just as she had promised. Talis felt it leave through the bond that had connected her to Voltest, until it dissolved entirely, and she knew that severing was every bit as final as Miken's death.

Voltest slumped onto the charred field, and for a moment Talis thought he was dead. But Lirien said, "He's fine," already moving, already grasping Rhia's ruined hand in hers, the blistered skin sloughing away like dirt beneath a spray of water, pristine in a matter of seconds. By the time Rhia drew her first breath without pain, Lirien had moved on again, reaching Cadfael even before Talis, in her dazed state, had taken a step in any direction. His burns were shallower, gone in a single instant, and he dropped his sword from shaking fingers, crouching to take his sister in his arms. She hadn't spoken, though she wet her lips as if she was trying. Talis thought Lirien would go to her, too, but instead she walked back the way she had come, to where Talis stood and Voltest lay.

"Are you all right?" she asked. "Did he burn you, too?"

Talis realized she didn't know the answer to that, and looked herself over. "I . . . seem to be unscathed. Th . . . thank you."

"Thank *you*," Lirien said heavily. "I didn't really think you'd side with me. Or was it because of him?" She tilted her head toward Cadfael.

After all that, she deserved the truth. Talis shook her head. "I didn't want him to die, but even if he hadn't been here, my answer would still have been the same."

Lirien took a deep breath in, letting it out slowly. "Do you feel that?"

Talis closed her eyes, reaching out with her magic. When Miken was still alive, and once she'd taught herself to sense the others, they had always been there slightly, a faint pulse in three directions, more of an idea of a presence than a specific feeling. After his death, her sense of Voltest and Lirien had become primarily characterized by their emotions, and the tug had been much stronger, like an echo of the person it represented, keeping her caught between two poles. But now there was only one direction, as if her power possessed an inner compass pointing north. It was stronger, almost oppressively so when she was fully concentrating on it. But otherwise, it was more like it had been in the beginning—less feeling, more presence. A presence she was capable of ignoring, and didn't feel affected by emotionally at all.

"The magic's in balance again," Lirien said, voicing Talis's thoughts exactly.

"It's just a single line now, one connection between you and me. Maybe we pull in opposite directions so perfectly, we never actually move." She nudged Voltest's unconscious form with the toe of one boot. "He's going to be furious when he wakes up. After all these years . . . I can't imagine what it would be like to go back to how we were before."

"I can," Lirien said. "I did, remember?"

That was true. She hadn't thought much about it until now, but when Jocelyn Selreshe had stolen Lirien's magic, she would have been just like Voltest was now. "What was it like?"

"Nowhere near as miserable as you seem to think. Having it taken away was painful, unfathomably painful, but once the pain faded, I was shocked at how clear my mind was. At how much like *me* I felt. It was as if I had been worn away, molded in a certain direction, the way the cliffs of my hometown have been molded, so gradually I couldn't even see it happening. But when the difference was before me—when I was suddenly restored to my old self—it was unmistakable."

"So then what happened when you got your powers back?"

"Nothing, at first. But I'm sure the same process began again."

"And now?" Talis asked.

"I wouldn't know. My mind feels ordinary, but it has felt so before, and not been. I suspect Voltest is the one seeing most clearly now. Or he will be, when he wakes up." Her eyes drifted to Cadfael and Rhia. "Should we let them be?"

"I want to make sure they're all right, too, but our responsibility is to this one for now." She nudged Voltest with her foot again. "How long can he sleep? He's making me nervous."

Lirien leaned down and shook him gently by the shoulders. "Voltest, wake up. If you're going to be furious at us forever, we've at least had enough of a break from you that we can face it."

Voltest's eyes squeezed shut, and he mumbled something under his breath that Talis didn't catch. "Well, we know he's still in there. Just get up, Voltest, you're not even hurt."

He made a noise that was half groan, half garbled mess of words. "Ugh. Then why does it feel like it? I must be nearly trampled into dust. Everything hurts except my . . . head." He sat up, clapping a hand to his forehead, and gawked at the ruined plain. "Gods! Did I do all this?"

"And nearly killed the four of us in the bargain," Lirien said dryly.

"And to think I can't even remember *why*. Something about . . . no, it's gone. How strange." The timbre of his voice sounded slightly different—less raspy, as if he'd finally cleared his throat and drawn in enough air. "Will everyone be all right?"

"Thanks to Lirien," Talis said. "But as for you . . . you must have sensed . . ."

"Sensed—? Oh." He was still touching his head as if trying to determine its shape, prodding his temples, digging his thumb into the ridge of bone above one eye. Then he suddenly stopped, and sat back on the heels of his hands in the ashes, tipping his head back as if to look at the sky. And Talis, who had been bracing herself for unchecked anger, grief, accusations, had no idea how to handle this.

"What are you thinking about?" Lirien asked, which, yes, did seem to be a logical start.

"That's just it," he said. "Thinking, itself. Back home—in Aurnis, before the war—when I'd finished a particularly good section of a particularly good book, I'd go all tipped back in my chair, just like this, and let my thoughts unspool, as if I had the complete luxury of time. I wonder why I never recalled that before now."

"You've lost your fire," Talis said, "and that's what occurs to you?"

"One of the things. There are many, some so old that they seem new. It's as if the flames took up a space, or walled me off from it. I'm walking through the attic of my own mind, and realizing I'd forgotten how much I left up there."

"Dear gods," Talis muttered, "I hope *this* isn't permanent."

He chuckled, a bit condescending, but that was normal. "Don't worry. I'm entirely sane. If anything, much saner than I was before. I can keep the rest of my thoughts to myself, if they bother you."

"I just . . . was expecting you to be angry. I don't understand why you're not."

"I overused it," Voltest said. "Anger, I mean. It's . . ." He yawned, stretching his arms up straight. "Gods, so exhausting! No wonder I scarcely had time for anything else. But to answer your indirect question, I'm not angry because I understand. What else could you have done? It is the end of something, and I can't help but grieve it, in my own way. But I have survived grief before, and will again. I won't trouble you both with it, to the extent that I can help it."

Talis felt her brow wrinkle, her lips twitch, and felt Lirien notice it. But it was Voltest who said, "That bothers you? You doubt me?"

"No," Talis said, a lie to the first question, though not the second.

"It bothers you that he isn't more bothered," Lirien said, perceiving both.

How could it not? He had once held one of the world's core elements within his flesh, subject to his will, and now he was being told that he never would again. How could he bear such an unfathomable loss? "You know you'll have to be ordinary," she said. "Defenseless. The things you could once do—"

"The things I could once do generally revolved around causing suffering on a large scale," Voltest said. "Which was convenient for someone with so much anger. The other things, such as lighting simple fires, I am content to resume doing the hard way. I could never fly, like you, or heal like Lirien. I—"

"You could see things within your flames," Talis insisted. "The past and present."

"But never the future," he replied. "And that is what concerns me now." He stood up, wobbling a bit. "If you don't mind, I'm going to take a walk. I am and will be fine; I'd just like to be alone."

He took off across the ash before Talis could stop him, scuffing it with his boots with each step. His head was bent slightly, watching the ground he covered.

"Probably best to leave him alone for now," Lirien said. "It is what he wants."

"It's what I want, too," Talis said, turning in the opposite direction from Voltest, toward the still-intact trees. "So you can leave both of us alone."

SHE HAD KNOWN Lirien wouldn't be the one to come after her. She didn't truly enjoy conversing with Talis any more than Talis enjoyed conversing with her; she'd feel responsible enough to come looking if she thought Talis might be in danger, or hurt, or might hurt someone else. But the one who truly wanted to know whether she was all right . . . yes, she knew the only person that could be.

"Shouldn't you be with your sister?" she asked, while he was still an indistinct shape among the trees.

"I was," Cadfael said. "She's still shaken, but after a time she found my constant attention cloying."

"So you've decided to glut me on that cloying attention instead?"

He moved close enough that she could see him clearly, marred with ash and blood from cuts that had healed. Beautiful, still, through all the things of this world that kept trying to make him otherwise. Or perhaps it was that Talis herself could not seem to stop finding him beautiful, despite so many opportunities. "If you wish me to leave, you have only to say so."

That was the problem, wasn't it? If she said she wanted him to leave, he would be gone. "If you stay, you'll ask me why I'm upset. And you'll find the answer stupid, or incomprehensible."

"Lirien already told me why you're upset," Cadfael said. "Because Voltest isn't, despite what he has lost—what you fear so much to lose. And I don't find that stupid or incomprehensible at all. I asked you once before, remember? If you had ever wanted to be rid of the pain your magic caused you? You were affronted by the very idea."

She had forgotten that until now, but he was right. "The magic isn't responsible for what happened the day it came to me, Cadfael. If anything, it saved my life."

"But ever since then, it's afflicted you with sorrow and despair, as surely as Voltest was afflicted by rage."

"So you think I'm a fool not to want to get rid of it."

Cadfael shook his head. "No, I think that's your decision, not mine."

Yet Talis felt certain that, in his heart of hearts, he wished she would become as Voltest was. But he would never say so, because he was convinced it would be presumptuous. She didn't know whether to call that respect or simply cowardice, so she did neither. She just stayed where she was, and he closed the distance between them. He always seemed to do that, these days.

He stood across from her, an arm's length away, but came no farther. "Are you angry?"

"At you?"

"Or in general."

"In general, yes. Or . . . frustrated. All this power, and I haven't changed my situation at all. Lirien used it to achieve her dream, and I never even had a dream to begin with. All I've done is float in place, just surviving."

"Sometimes that's all you can do," Cadfael said. "Sometimes even doing that much is a victory."

She felt a stab of annoyance at him, for always having the perfect nonjudgmental thing to say to her when she was encouraging just the opposite, and a further stab of annoyance when she realized she felt gratitude, too. She lifted her hand, but though he was close enough to touch easily, it felt as if she had to cover a vast distance to reach him. Her fingers felt weak, but still she pushed them forward, until they alighted, trembling, on his forehead, on the seam of the scar she had cut into him more than three years ago.

Cadfael took her wrist in his hand, and pressed her palm more firmly against his skin, her fingertips just brushing his hair. "I would've thought this had taught you from the start," Talis said, "what you can expect if you get tangled up with me. I keep thinking you'll learn to stay away, but you never do."

People had always tended to avoid her, even before these powers. And if any ever ventured close, they had always been easy to frighten off. But Cadfael could not be scared away. She couldn't coax him to leave before she had to decide whether to let him stay. "If you're asking whether I'm worried about what will happen, I'm not," he said. "If you wanted to hurt me like this again, you'd tell me. Even that first time, you gave me a chance to run."

"But what if I can't control myself?" She tried to pull her hand away, but he caught her fingers in his, which was an answer all its own. She shook her head, trying to make him understand. "What if the same thing that happened to Voltest happens to me? It's Lirien who truly saved you and your sister. If she isn't here the next time—"

"She wasn't here the first time." Cadfael took her other hand, closing the circle between them. "It did happen, remember? It happened, and you came back. You can come back again."

"But—" She couldn't say what she really wanted to say. *I came back because of you.* Because that was just another way of saying *I need you,* wasn't it?

She pulled her hands from his, and the disappointment in his face made something twist in her chest. It was too late. The coward's way out wouldn't satisfy her now, either, not after all this.

So she brushed her hands over his shoulders, and bent her head toward him when he tentatively ran his fingers through her hair. It was a minor shift in position, and it arguably left her more vulnerable, not less. But in spite of that or because of it, she could meet his eyes without flinching. She touched his scar again, and then his cheek, and pulled his lips to hers.

She had steeled herself for a variety of responses: shock, confusion, apology, repellence, anger, acceptance, even relief. She had not prepared herself for what he actually did: not content with only her mouth, he pulled the whole line of her body against his, tangled them together everywhere. As if she'd set him free.

Her emotions were a torrent, and she panicked a moment, afraid they'd stir up the wind. But it was quiet, the breeze no rougher than his fingers had been in her hair. "I don't want pity," she warned him. "If you think I'm so fragile—"

"Oh, come on, Talis. You're not that dense." He actually smirked at her. "I'd already asked you for more than enough. I couldn't ask for this, too." He leaned his forehead against hers, the scar rough in some places and unnaturally smooth in others. "Even after you stopped disapproving of me, you still kept your distance. You've always been so careful that we don't misunderstand each other. Haven't you ever thought that we already *do* understand? That we don't need to explain? That that's why we like each other?"

Talis was used to not understanding people, and having people not understand her. But perhaps that was just another thing the two of them had in common. Whatever he seemed to see in her, it hadn't steered him wrong yet. So she didn't explain. She didn't say how humiliating it was for someone so devoted to her own solitude to find herself so in need of one particular person. She didn't say she was grateful to him, or how much they'd both changed, or even that his face didn't irritate her anymore. She just kissed him again, determined, this time, not to pull away unless he did first. And he never did, and that was that.

CHAPTER THIRTY-FIVE

Hallarnon

RHIA AND LIRIEN walked out of earshot of the others, and then kept walking, falling easily into step. Rhia wasn't sure what they were looking for, but she knew they'd recognize it when they found it. And find it they did: a line of willow trees beside a shallow creek, the branches reaching for the water just as the creek curved away. It seemed so private and untouched, as if no other humans had ever set eyes on the place, and no others ever would.

Lirien settled onto the grass in the willows' shade, leaning back against one of the trunks, and Rhia sat beside her, folding her legs beneath her. They were quiet for what felt like a long time, listening to the sound of the water, the wind whistling through the branches of the trees. Rhia yearned to feel at peace, yet her heart was a riot in her chest, her skin still clammy with the echoes of dread. She tried to slow her breathing, to ground her hands in the cool grass. "I'm sorry. I shouldn't be . . . this upset. I don't even have a scratch, but—"

"You were horribly burned," Lirien said. "That's far from nothing. Even if the evidence is gone, your body remembers how it felt." She stared at the water, breathing out long and slow. "Thank the gods Talis made the choice she did. She said it wasn't because of your brother, and I believe her, but I'm sure having him there helped."

Rhia felt a jolt at how casually she said that. "You think they have feelings for each other, too?"

"Oh, I was sure of that from the beginning. All the things she told him about our powers and our pasts, when she barely exchanges greetings with most people? And given that he was spearheading our efforts to free her, it wasn't hard to figure that the feeling was mutual."

"He's never showed this much interest in anyone," Rhia said. "When we lived in Araveil together, he drew people's fascination so effortlessly. There are still many who want nothing to do with illegitimate children, yet even the daughters of wealthy houses wanted him. And none of them moved his heart in the slightest. Now I wonder whether Talis might break it."

"It's probably as likely as him breaking hers." Lirien shrugged. "I'm not much for romance, but I've heard that's the risk you have to take."

She had said that before—that she liked people, but preferred trading them quickly one for another, never putting down roots with anyone. "But then . . ." Rhia fixed her eyes on the water. "Perhaps this is a rude question."

"If it is, I know you enough to know you didn't mean it that way. Go on."

"I just wonder . . . what you want your life to look like. My ties to other people are such a big part of mine. Without them, there's just such a . . . an empty space."

But rather than take offense, Lirien leaned toward her, her face lighting up. "That's it exactly. An empty space. That's the whole point."

"What do you mean?"

"Ugh, how should I explain?" She brushed her hand over the grass. "Do you know of Castle Evenfall?"

"Aye, it's somewhere on the western coast. My father told me it was originally home to the Tournells, before they fell out of favor and Ryvar Radcliffe and his descendants usurped their lands and titles."

"As it happens, you can see it from my village," Lirien said. "It's often foggy along the cliffs, but on a clear day, it looks almost close enough to touch. Even though no one lives there now, for fear of the curse the Radcliffes supposedly brought upon the place, it's still magnificent, massive, the most elegant silhouette. A real castle, as they don't build them anymore. I grew up looking at it, dreaming about it, almost as much as I dreamed about the sea. But though it would have been so easy to get to—an hour or two's walk—I was always forbidden from going."

"Why?" Rhia asked.

"Well, that's the question, isn't it? I don't know that I was ever given a satisfactory answer. Bandits, or crumbling masonry, or that stupid curse still lingering over it after all this time. Everyone else seemed to think it so unnecessary; they couldn't understand why I would even want to go in the first place. Whereas I couldn't understand how you could see a place like that and *not* want to go there."

"I'd want to go there, too," Rhia admitted. "Did you ever manage it?"

"Not yet. Before I was exiled from my village, I'd never been more than a mile or two outside it. And after, I was so angry I wanted to get as far away as possible. I spent years in the south and east, and the next time I came back to Hallarnon, I learned Miken had died there. But I'll go. I'll be able to, whenever I like, because I shrugged off all the ties those villagers wanted to bind me with. If I'd obeyed their wishes for me, I probably would've died without ever going that mile or two beyond the village. I'd be too busy earning money to take care of my parents, dividing chores with my husband around the house, raising my children—everything that encroaches on that beautiful empty space. That freedom, to go anywhere and do anything I like, without any obligations to hold me back. That's what I'll fill my life with, Rhia: the world."

"The world," Rhia repeated. Two little words shouldn't make her heart hurt so much. "That's what I always wanted, too."

"No, you want to be a hero. That's a little different."

"Not the way I imagined it. A hero wasn't just someone who saw the world, she did everything there was to be done in it, every goal, every challenge. She'd see the view from the tops of mountains no one else could climb, the depths of caves no one else had even discovered. Is that so different from what you want?"

Lirien smiled sadly. "Perhaps you're right. Perhaps that is what my dream sounds like, without the gloss of idealism rubbed off it."

"Ah. Am I being foolish again?"

"No, that's not what I meant. Not at all." She bit her lip, and Rhia waited for her to gather the words. "You're so strange to me, precisely because you're not some silly girl who's never experienced anything. You've lost things already. You've known cruelty. What Jocelyn put you through alone would have felled some people, and you'd been surviving on your own for years before that, after you fled Araveil with nothing and no one. I just don't know how you've been through so much, and changed so little. I thought everyone changed." She looked at the grass. "I think I've changed too much."

For someone who claimed to live only for her own whims, she certainly seemed to be hard on herself. But if Rhia said she liked Lirien the way she was, Lirien would just say she didn't understand. "I don't know if I've changed. I've always just tried to do what I thought was right. That and have adventures. But I guess I always thought the one would lead to the other."

Lirien tilted her head to one side and back again, as if weighing two options. "I think it might be my turn to ask an impolite question. Or else . . . a painful one. You told me that being in love ruined your parents. Your parents, but not you and your brother, who would have been treated much more harshly by the common crowd than they were. Were they . . . married to other people?"

"No. Neither of them ever married."

"Then . . . they couldn't be married for some reason?"

"They could have," Rhia said. "But my mother didn't wish to. Her father was still lord of Grayeaves back then. If she'd married my father, he would have expelled her from the castle. I've lived outside of a castle all my life, and been none the worse for it, but apparently, to her, this was an unimaginable fate. But she could no more give up my father than she could her fine things, so it was a grand mess for everyone. Father said they were estranged for a few years after Cadfael was born—Lord Glendower went to great lengths to conceal the pregnancy, and as good as ordered Father to begone with the child. But then *she* begged to be allowed to see her son, so . . ." She shrugged. "Cadfael remembers being with her from time to time, when he was very young. But being with him meant being with my father, too, and . . . well, I'm here, aren't I? That should show you how well they'd learned their lesson."

"Cadfael remembers being with her, but you don't?"

"No, because I wasn't. After I was born, her father summoned mine to Grayeaves for the last time. Lord Glendower gave her a choice: she could leave with me and my father, forever, or she could let us go forever. And she . . ." Her throat closed up, and she swallowed it down, furious with herself.

"Well," Lirien murmured, no more obtrusive than the sound of the water, "I'm guessing she chose to stay with her father."

"No." She forced the words out, trying to remove all sentiment from them. "Rather than make any choice at all, she threw herself from the top of a tower at Grayeaves, and left her father without a legitimate heir. And I went to live with mine." She glanced sidelong at Lirien's face. "Please don't say you're sorry. It was a long time ago, and I never knew her, so there's nothing to miss. Not that I would bother missing a woman who made such a stupid choice. She preferred to destroy herself rather than be with her family, all over a great piece of rock?"

Lirien's eyes were cast down. "Did you ever consider that 'twasn't—" She made a face. "That it wasn't a choice between your father and a castle, but between your father and her father? That it was a choice between one family and another?"

The truth, whatever it was, had died with her mother. So Rhia simply said, "Perhaps."

"Sorry," Lirien said. "My parents didn't say a word to defend me when the village exiled me for a witch; I'd trade them for a hot meal. I'm the last person who would wish you to feel kindly toward your mother if you don't want to."

"It's all right. Whether you hit on the truth or not, that's how my parents were ruined, and Cadfael and I escaped. Despite it all, my brother and I had a happy childhood. But my mother was dead, and my father . . . I know he loved us, but he always missed her. That melancholy never truly faded from his heart."

"Well, I have faith that Talis won't make your brother *that* miserable, at least," Lirien said, with a wry smile. "If this infatuation even lasts."

"If it does last," Rhia said, "I wonder what will become of me."

"How could Talis possibly change that?"

"When we met in Issamira, you pointed out, correctly, that being captain of the guard wasn't what I really wanted. But I thought that what I did want was impossible. I'd been roving the continent for quite some time before that, after Araveil fell. But without my brother at my side, it didn't feel like adventuring; it just felt like being lost. He and I always planned to make our living by the sword, like our father before us. But Talis isn't like that. And if—"

"I see," Lirien said. "If they settle down, and he hangs up his sword, you'll be lost again."

"Perhaps it would be wisest for me to hang up my own. But I've never been good for anything else." She looked down at it, waiting at her side like always. "Does that make me terrible?"

"Why would it?" When Rhia stayed silent, she pressed, "Rhia, why would it?"

She'd never said that part aloud to anyone. With Cadfael, she'd never had to, because she knew he knew. But Lirien had never picked up a sword, and that meant Rhia had to find the words. "I always thought swordplay was beautiful, ever since I was a child. I always wanted to try my hand at it, and I—I *liked* being good at it. But that doesn't mean I never understood." She made her voice firm. "Swords are weapons. And living by the sword, however else you want to dress it up, means looking for a fight. That's fine enough when there's chaos, I suppose—my father made a living defending civilian caravans from bandits, and Cadfael was a soldier. Even when I was wandering, I often came across some trouble or other that needed a sword to put right. But though everything I've been doing has been to create a true and fair peace on this continent . . . if I ever achieve it, I wonder what I'll be like then. If I'll still be able to put more good than bad into the world."

Lirien stared at her, green eyes intent, in a way she had never looked at her before, or never so openly. It was as if she had to figure Rhia out—now, in this instant, or else. But Rhia didn't know the answer, either. She didn't even know the question.

Then Lirien leaned forward and kissed her on the forehead—just one moment, one solid point of contact, and then it was gone. She somehow pulled away and got to her feet in the same movement. "This is why I could only ever be a terrible influence on you. I could never be of help with such weighty questions. In fact, I try to avoid weighty questions as much as possible."

"And yet however you've lived," Rhia said, "you've always tried not to harm people, and been better at it than your fellow *wardrenfell,* as well as countless other people I could think of. So whatever questions you have been able to answer, there must be something in them."

"Perhaps." She tugged on the end of her braid. "It's possible Talis's peevishness has rubbed off on me a bit. I'm going to go wash the soot out of my hair. I'll try to be better company when I return."

Rhia let her go without a word; there was a river right there, so Lirien could have stayed put if she'd truly wished to. She rubbed her fingertips against the spot on her forehead where Lirien had kissed her, trying not to feel irritated over it. She knew the gesture had been meant kindly, not as mockery or condescension. But though Lirien had called herself a terrible influence, Rhia couldn't help feeling that she was the one who had been dismissed, found wanting.

She drew her knees up to her chest, and closed her eyes, listening to the murmur of the river. They'd survived today with their lives, at least, and there'd be tougher battles ahead. She could ponder the direction of her future once she was sure she'd be able to have one.

AFTER FUMBLING HER way back into her clothes, Talis had announced that she was going in search of water. Cadfael knew that what she wanted more than anything was space, so he had stayed where he was for a time, letting her get a sufficient head start. If she was conflicted, he was sorry for it, but he couldn't say he shared the feeling. He didn't know when it had started, or when it had changed, but he had long reconciled himself to the fact that, somewhere along the way, his desire to learn the truth from the woman who had cursed him, and then, once he had, his desire to make things right between them, was now about much more than that. It wasn't even just a desire to help her, though he possessed that as well, much more than he was used to feeling toward people who weren't his family. He simply . . . cared. About her well-being, yes, but also about her thoughts, her opinions. About whether she'd ever manage to break free of the shackles tying her to her past. About how much she did or didn't care about him.

He had gotten dressed again, too, because Rhia was probably going to come find him eventually, and that would have been bad even without Lirien tagging along. He'd half-heartedly followed Talis's trail a little farther into the forest before deciding that he was too pleasantly lethargic to properly get up yet, and then he'd flopped right back down, in a little shower of leaves. He was feeling too content to worry about much of anything. So, of course . . .

"We need to talk," a familiar voice said.

Cadfael threw an arm over his eyes with a groan. "You must be joking. After all this time, you choose *now* to come to me?"

There was a silence, so long he almost wondered if the prideful spirit had disappeared again in a fit of pique. But when he finally opened his eyes and sat up, there Yaelor was, every towering inch of him just as Cadfael remembered. The resemblance to his father was the same, but now that Cadfael knew he was the one who determined how Yaelor appeared to him, he could see bits of Rhia in the spirit as well. Rhia looked like their father, too, after all.

"These are perhaps not the circumstances that either of us would have wished for," Yaelor said. "But I have come to the end of my pondering. If you still wish to know the true nature of the bond between us, I will tell you."

"That easily? All right, go on, then."

"I don't think it will be easy," Yaelor said. "But I'll try my best to help you understand. Have you ever wondered why humans can use magic?"

"I always assumed it was one of those questions that doesn't have an answer."

"In fact, it's quite simple," Yaelor said. "In this world, matter comes in two forms. There is the tangible and finite, and the intangible and infinite. I and those like me are solely comprised of the latter. But humans contain both: the body and the soul. In some humans, the soul is capable of reaching beyond its finite shell. That's all magic is."

Cadfael frowned. He'd always thought of the word *soul* as more of an expression than anything else, a way of denoting the part of a person that was their consciousness, the sum of their thoughts and feelings. "You're saying souls exist after a person dies?"

Yaelor clicked his phantom tongue. "There is something that remains, but not the way it often is in tales, the mind and will disembodied but intact. A human being is a body and a soul, inextricably linked. Take away either, and the spark that makes an individual is gone. And what lingers is imperceptible to mortals, who dwell too much in the world of the tangible and finite."

"But is it . . . painful? Tedious?" Cadfael felt his frown grow deeper. "I'd counted on just being gone. I don't know if I like this idea."

"It wouldn't be like anything you can imagine. You wouldn't have the same kind of consciousness. But no, it is not painful. If anything, it is the absence of pain."

"So not a lamentable fate, you seem to be saying." Cadfael shrugged. "It's hard to believe, but I don't know why you thought I'd be upset. If some echo of me lives on . . . perhaps, at least, I could find the echoes of those I cared about."

"You misunderstand," Yaelor said. "That is what happens to ordinary mortals. It is not what will happen to you." He stared at him, unmoving, unblinking, his chin still tilted slightly upward in that haughty manner that had annoyed Cadfael from the start. "I was permitted to ask you, and only you, to perform a task for me, because you and I are the same. Because we are parts of the same whole."

Cadfael's first reaction wasn't even shock; he was too confused for that. "No. How could that be? You're this . . . spirit that claims to have existed for thousands of years, and I wasn't even born until a few decades ago."

"That's correct. You came into existence less than three decades ago, because a human is a body and a soul, and your body did not exist before then."

"But even if I had your . . . soul, you're standing right in front of me. You told me you had never been human."

"No, I told you that question would take too long to answer. I'm answering it now." He gave a frustrated little sigh. "I must seem so insubstantial to you, so powerless. And in a way, I am. All of the strength I possess is not enough to bend a single blade of that grass beneath your hands. Because I am made of only one thing, and not two. But within my own realm, my equals and I are the strongest beings that exist. We have power that you could never understand, because it is power over a world you cannot ever see or touch. There is so much of me that it is possible for me to lose one soul's worth, and still be as you see me now. That is what I did, to make you as you are." He bowed his proud head, just a bit. "I think that we became more like mortals the longer we spent watching you, speaking with you. And over time, we . . . I suppose we became jealous of you, for you straddled two worlds, while we ruled over only one. We wanted to know what it was like to move through this world as you did. To change it, as we never could. So while I have never been human, I have the memories of human lives within me. As we are now, we are separated by an unbridgeable gulf: the mortal shell that houses your soul, which I could never penetrate. But when your body dies, you and I will become one again, and all you have been and done and lived will be a part of me."

Now the shock was hitting him, as the confusion subsided. "So that's why you didn't want to tell me." He felt his body sag against the earth—it seemed like such a fragile thing now, this temporary vessel that was all that stood between him and being consumed. "Everyone else has some remnant, a soul that lives on, even if it's in a way I can't understand. But I alone will cease to be."

"I didn't want to tell you because I knew you'd see it that way. You will *not* cease to be. You'll simply become . . . more. As will I."

"But we'll only have one consciousness."

"Yes."

"Then that consciousness is *you*."

"It's something larger than either one of us. It's something neither of us can imagine now. You told me you thought you would be nothing after death. Do you truly see this as worse?"

"Yes, because now I know that . . . ." His hands clenched in the grass. "Rhia, and my father . . . everyone I ever cared about, or ever will. Their souls will remain. But mine will never exist beside theirs. Or else it'll just be a single fragment, trapped inside whatever you are." He tore his hands free, letting the blades slip through his fingers. "You changed your mind, to tell me this. Does that mean Lirien was right? Are you doing this now to pull me away from Talis, because you disapprove of how much she matters to me? Is that the only reason you told me to beware of Amerei in the first place?"

"No, that isn't—" Yaelor ground his teeth, but Cadfael thought he saw a flash of guilt in his eyes. That was another thing that made more sense now: how a being who was not human seemed to feel such human emotions. It was because he could remember what it was like to feel them: guilt, pride, anger, loss, love. Things that otherwise would have remained beyond his reach. "You know what I am, and that I can be nothing else. It is valor and its feats that comprise me, not this . . . tenderness of the heart that woman inspires in you. But it was never my intent to interfere with your free will. Your life is your own; you have simply lived it boldly enough to know how it will end. As for Amerei . . . Once, long, long ago, when this world and we were still young, and we still interfered too much in the affairs of mortals, there was one who shone for me above all others. Who lived as if to reach me, along that path that is infinite. And Amerei was jealous, because she wants everyone. She manipulated events in an attempt to draw that mortal toward her and away from me, but her meddling resulted in great suffering, for both the wider world and the one I had so admired. Amerei neither foresaw nor desired such a thing—whatever Lirien Arvel believes, we do not wish to make humans suffer for our own amusement, though I admit we do not always consider their greatest happiness. But I . . . am proud, and I could not forgive her, or stop seeing her as one who brings harm in her wake. No matter how much time has passed, I still wish to protect that soul from her."

"That soul?" Cadfael repeated. "But surely that person is long dead. How could—"

"Cadfael! Did you come this way?" Cadfael tensed, but his sister's voice sounded far off. He didn't think she was in danger of stumbling upon them. "Cadfael? Ugh, where is everyone?" He heard her stomping around among the leaves, and hid a smile.

And then he looked at Yaelor, staring off in the direction of that voice with such longing, such tenderness in his face. "But it . . . it can't possibly be Rhia."

"No, it can't," Yaelor said crossly, "because *Rhia* has never existed before, and never will again. Have you listened to nothing I have said? I'm speaking of a soul, not a person."

"But that would mean . . . a soul can have more than one human life?"

"Most do not," Yaelor said. "It is certainly rare, but sometimes souls retain so strong an attachment to the realm where they once dwelt that they can return to it in a new form. Unbound, a soul is the memory of every life it has ever lived, but, housed in a mortal shell, it can no more remember those lives than you can remember mine. Just like you, she is, in some ways, a fragment of something much greater."

What was it he had said about Rhia to Cadfael, the first time they had met? *So few have walked so far along the path, and borne themselves so well.* He had thought it strange then, for his sister was still so young, and could not truly be said to have walked exceptionally far down any path. He remembered, too, the feeling Rhia had mentioned to him and Lirien, of having lost something she couldn't explain. Yaelor didn't love Rhia—or rather, he didn't love only Rhia. He loved this one particular soul, and had loved it over and over, through every permutation of its existence, every single life it had ever lived.

"Is that why you sent me into this world?" he asked. "You can't tell me it's a coincidence that I ended up her brother. Did you want me here to look after her in your stead?"

To his surprise, Yaelor laughed. "How would I do that? I've already told you that the future is out of my control. How could I have predicted how many children your parents would have? No, I sent a piece of myself into this world on a whim, just as always. And her spirit followed after me, drawing on the age-old bond between us." He smiled with rare softness. "Such a thing is not normally possible. But she would ever surprise me."

Cadfael had at least a dozen more questions, but he held them back, setting his fist against his forehead. He couldn't afford to fall apart now. Rhia would press on to Valyanrend no matter what, and he had to protect her. And if Talis followed them, she might be in danger, too. This was just when he needed to be at his sharpest and best, not chasing thoughts in circles through his head.

"Will you be all right?" Yaelor asked—not exactly sympathetic, but at least he sounded more concerned than condescending.

Cadfael pressed his forehead hard against his fist, focusing on the reality of the pressure. He still had this body, this barrier between him and the all-consuming essence of the spirit. He just had to make sure he kept it intact as long as possible. He could worry about the rest when he was an old man. "I suppose I have to be."

"Should I not have told you?" There, another human emotion: regret.

"I'll let you know," Cadfael said.

Chapter Thirty-six

Valyanrend

TRUE TO HIS word, Elgar had been too cautious to house Arianrod Margraine in the dungeons. Instead, he'd chosen a completely ordinary room in the Citadel, one with dozens just like it, and cleared it of all furnishings. He'd installed an iron ring in the floor, run a length of chain from it, and cuffed the end to one of her ankles. It was long enough that she could pace a tight circle around the room, though she couldn't reach the door or the window, the latter of which had been curtained off, only dim light seeping through. Beyond that, the room contained nothing else.

It was the last place in Valyanrend that Varalen wanted to be—not least because Elgar didn't know he was here. True, he must not have wanted to prevent Varalen from seeing her, or he'd never have been able to get the key from the guards. But letting her know there was even a small way she could help them amounted to announcing a weakness, and he couldn't stand to give her that satisfaction, a window with a much better view than the one Elgar had closed to her.

The other reason he didn't want to do this was that he didn't want to have to look at her, to see the evidence of all she had endured in the past weeks. Elgar had never done anything that would be considered outright torture, but he hadn't treated her like an honored guest, either. Her meals were just barely sufficient, her bed a bare wood floor, her clothes the most threadbare he had been able to find. And though he allowed her to leave the room as often as necessary to accommodate even the smallest issue of hygiene, Varalen suspected he did so at least partially to emphasize her powerlessness. Seren Almasy would've had to be chained hand and foot and watched relentlessly, because Seren Almasy could probably kill a man with a piece of lint. But without her magic, Arianrod Margraine would have lost a fight with the greenest and most inept of the Citadel soldiers. And that collar never came off, even for an instant.

When Varalen entered, she was sitting on the floor, her legs bent beneath her. He remembered how bright and full of life she had been the first time he saw her, and though she smiled at him as confidently as ever, she could not hide how much thinner she had gotten, or the dullness in her skin and hair, that had once so glowed with health.

"I'm here to offer you a deal," he said.

She yawned. "Unfortunately, it's too late for that. I told you I'd destroy you with your master, and I will. You can't bargain your way out of it."

Gods, how could she still possess such certainty? "I meant a bargain not having to do with my ultimate fate, so you might as well listen. It's a simple trade: information you want for information I want."

She cocked her head. "Well, I can't deny I love information. But how are you going to prove that it's both new to me and worth knowing without telling me what it is?"

"Easy," Varalen said. "I know you don't know that Lanvalds tried to liberate Stonespire, because I know you aren't allowed that kind of information in here. I can tell you what happened—I even know some names of people who died. The fighting has stopped, and almost certainly won't continue, so knowing the outcome of that battle is as good as knowing who holds Stonespire now."

As he had hoped, she stiffened at the mention of her city, unable to hide the interest in her eyes. "Stonespire . . . I'd certainly care to know its fate, but from here, I have no way of knowing if anything you tell me is true. There might well have been no battle there at all."

Varalen held up two sheets of parchment. "I thought you'd say that, so I searched through our incoming reports and found one that contains enough detail without being too sensitive for your eyes. I obviously didn't write it, and though I can't prove it's not some fake I had a scribe draw up, that would be rather a lot of effort to go to, don't you think?"

She was quiet, eyes darting from the parchment to his face, mouth twisting as she pondered something. Varalen had thought he would appreciate a version of her that talked a bit less, but so far that had not proven to be the case. "And what do you want from me?"

"Everything you know about vardrath steel," Varalen said. "Everything."

"Why?"

He'd calculated how much to tell her here, just a bit of real meat as a show of good faith. "Because at least one of our rebels in the city has got hold of it. We don't know who, or how, or how much, just that a few spells of Elgar's have been undone by it."

"If all you know is that the spells have been broken, how can you be sure it's not the work of another mage? I was able to break one of Elgar's spells before."

"I suppose we can't be *sure,* but Elgar thinks the steel hypothesis is more likely. His enchantments weren't damaged in any way, just rendered lifeless husks. Only the power was taken from them." Varalen himself wasn't sure what precisely the enchantments were or where, just that the rebels seemed to have a way of locating them that Elgar didn't understand, and that their destruction was setting his plans back at an unacceptable rate.

"Hmm. In that case, I'd suspect vardrath steel, too." As if reminded by the mention of it, she reached for the collar at her throat, shifting it slightly and rubbing the skin where it had been.

"Does it hurt?" Varalen asked.

"No, not really—it's uncomfortable more than anything. It's like having ice around my neck, though ice would eventually make me numb, and this does not. I feel a constant impulse to try to get away from it, even though I know it's impossible. And that's as much as you're going to get out of me without working out some details for this little trade of yours. We can hardly exchange information at exactly the same time, so how do I know I'll get anything at all if I go first?"

Varalen set the report down on the floor between them. "You're definitely going to go first, and I'll be the judge of whether what you know is worth anything. If it is, you can take that, and I'll fill in any gaps myself, within reason. If you'll recall, the last time we made a deal, I honored the terms, and I've no reason to do any differently this time."

"That's supposing you need a reason beyond vindictiveness."

"Again, Your Grace, that's your part, not mine. I don't bear you any vindictiveness. You and I simply couldn't both get what we wanted, that's all."

She rubbed a hand over her face, brushing her hair back from it. It had grown even longer and wilder in here, tangling every time she moved. "What precisely do you want to know? You clearly already know what it does, or you wouldn't have known to use it on me. And if you want to know how to make it, your guess is as good as mine. What else is there?"

"I want to know how it works," Varalen said. "*Why* it works. I've done research, but all I've found is just more concerning the what, not how or why. And if there's anyone whose research will have outstripped my own, it's you."

She paused to think it over, and he did not press her. "Even I don't understand precisely how it works. I expect that if I did, I'd be able to unravel the riddle of how it was made in the first place. But the key point is that vardrath steel is not the opposite of magic, nor does it function by repelling magic. Quite the contrary: it absorbs it. This collar does not prevent me from casting, it simply eats the spell before it can connect with any other target. And yes, that includes any spell I might cast on myself; I've tried. There's no point in my lying to you about that—Elgar could test it himself any time he pleased. But he won't, and I suggest you don't ask him if you don't want to anger him."

Varalen knew Elgar well enough to know that without having to be told. He

didn't even want to be in the same room as the stuff, but would've snarled at anyone who drew his notice to his own fear. "Speaking of tests, Edith Selwyn performed them quite extensively, but the results she gave me were different from
yours: total loss of sight and hearing, and extraordinary pain. How do you explain
this discrepancy?"

"Oh, *that's* easy," she said. "As I understand it, Selwyn tested on a *wardrenfell*.
Their magic . . . think of it like a single mass, a burden they carry that's fused
to them extremely tightly. Think of my magic like my blood, constantly flowing between all parts of me at once, constantly renewing itself. Now think about
something that eats magic, not kills it. It's the difference between trying to take a
biscuit from someone's hand and trying to take one they've digested. The first case
is a matter of whose grip is stronger; the second is simply impossible."

Varalen turned that over in his mind. "So in order to successfully absorb the
magic, the steel would have to break the bond tying it to its host. And that's why
it hurts?"

"Precisely. The magic is welded to . . . well, I don't like this term, but you
might say it's welded to their soul. It's agony beyond what you could ever inflict
with a blade. Does that resolve your curiosity?"

"Not quite. If Elgar wanted to combat this rogue destroying his enchantments,
how would he go about it?"

"He can't," she said. "He's got to be able to create more enchantments faster
than they can be destroyed, or put them in locations the rebel can't reach, or kill
the rebel, or steal their weapon. But he can't create an enchantment that's impervious to the steel's effects. Do you really think it would be so valuable if mages could
just choose not to be affected by it?"

Varalen scoffed. "I suppose if there were a way, you wouldn't want him to
know about it."

"I certainly wouldn't—and *that* knowledge would be far more expensive than
what you're offering me now. But I don't have to lie, because in this case, there
truly isn't a way. It might be different if your master had chosen a different preferred method of casting his spells, but enchantments are uniquely vulnerable to
the steel, because enchantments rely on a finite amount of magic, placed in a separate object. The steel drains the magic, and the enchantment is dead—you have
to start all over again from scratch. On the other hand, we fought a mage in Eldren Cael who was much more of a challenge, even though our party possessed a
vardrath steel blade. Because she relied on herself, and her power, like any mage's,
could not be drained at a stroke."

No, Varalen thought, she really wasn't lying. What she was saying made too much sense, and she had said it with too much conviction. "Damn. He certainly won't be pleased to hear that."

"Well, you don't have to tell him. And I never agreed you'd like what I had to say, only that I'd say it. Have I earned my reward by now?"

Wordlessly, he passed the report across the floor.

As she read, her eyebrows knit together. "A foreign army led by Hywel and Kelken . . . I hadn't anticipated that, but it's in keeping with what I know of both of them. But the rest of this says the citizens of Stonespire rebelled, and opened the gates from the inside."

"That is what it says, yes. It appears some of your guards had the clever idea to pose as civilians, though from your face, it's not an idea they got from you. What about that perplexes you so?"

"It should never have happened," she said. "I specifically ordered them not to rebel."

Varalen shrugged. "Then it seems they didn't listen. Are you really going to punish them for it? It was staggeringly successful. Even on your side, most of the quite minimal casualties fell on the Lanvalds. I don't think more than a couple dozen Esthradians died."

"That's a couple dozen more than ought to have died," she snapped. "If they had just waited for the war to be won in the west, we could have avoided casualties completely. This is *why* I ordered them to surrender in the first place, why I left Adora even though I *knew* what would happen to Seren if we were captured. And they're just getting themselves killed anyway! So they've won back Stonespire—so what? What are they going to do, beyond sitting there and waiting for the outcome of the rest of the war? I thought my guards were smarter than that." She read through the report again. "This mentions Jill Bridger by name, as the one who arranged to let the Lanvalds in. Is she dead?"

Varalen shook his head. "No, that one's definitely alive. My sources were very sure about that."

"What about Dent? Denton Halley?"

"I'm not familiar with that one. I don't remember his name from the list I received, though I admit it wasn't fully comprehensive."

"Is there anyone you *do* remember?"

"That I recognized? Only one. That captain of yours, Gravis Ingret. I make sure to keep apprised of his doings whenever I can, since he once sent me a head in a box and promised that he would kill me. A promise he was unable to keep, it seems."

He was watching her for a reaction, but he couldn't immediately tell what it was. She brought a fist up to her face, leaning her chin against her knuckles. "He's the strangest of that lot. I have so many years of experience with him—I *know* his loyalty, and it has remained constant even when his opinion of me did not. That even he would do this . . . perhaps their national pride was simply so great that they would defy me rather than be conquered by another."

"If that were the case, they would have refused the original order to surrender." Varalen spoke half in spite of himself, but, like her, he couldn't resist a puzzle, a chance to stretch his mental muscles. "I don't think they *were* trying to defy you. In their eyes, something must have changed between when they followed through on your order and when the Lanvalds gave them the opportunity to retake the city. You're right, it makes no sense to fight such a battle for nothing, to risk and even lose their lives. So they must have seen some advantage, some meaning in doing so that even you haven't grasped yet, though I confess I haven't, either."

He saw her face twist in thought—and then he saw all that tension suddenly release, her hand flying to her mouth. *"Oh."* She turned her face down to press her forehead into the heel of her hand, shaking her head slowly. And then her shoulders shook, too, in silent laughter. "Damn. Damn, damn, damn. If those idiots knew the whole time, they could've told me. If their tact was just to spare my pride, I'll really be cross with them."

She didn't look cross. She looked delighted, which was generally not good news for Varalen. "What is it that they know?"

"Nothing you don't, Lord Oswhent. Just who and what I really am, and what I am and am not prepared to do." She smiled. "To get more information than that, you'd have to make me a trade too dear for you to afford. You could tell me more about this Ryam, but you won't, and I've probably guessed all the relevant details anyway. It's got to be an illness, incurable through ordinary methods, but that has a protracted mortality. Deteriorating physical condition, but whose decline is easily measurable, for you to be confident he'll last long enough for Elgar to heal him. Have I gotten anything wrong?"

She could probably tell from his face that she hadn't. "If I had to make a deal with someone over his life, I would have preferred to make it with you," he said quietly. "Even now, if you would agree to heal him, I'd find some way to bring him to you, and some way to sneak you both out of here—out of the whole city, if necessary."

The marquise refocused the majority of her attention on the papers he had given her. "Now, I doubt that's true—even more because you're saying it aloud, in your master's very house. I suspect you just want to see what my abilities are, and if I have any plans to escape, or know any associates nearby who might help me do so."

"Elgar says he'll heal Ryam when the war is won," Varalen said. "But that could be months from now—years, even. If I knew he would be healed *now,* that certainty would be more than worth the increased danger to me."

She didn't laugh in his face and remind him that she'd promised to kill him, which he supposed was something. But she looked solemn, and given how seldom that happened, he knew her answer would not be good. "Unfortunately, no matter the nature of this Ryam's illness or injury, I very much doubt that I would be able to heal him."

That wasn't the rejection he'd expected. "But I thought a true mage was only bound by their imagination. That there would be a limit to the power of spells you could cast, but not their variety."

"You're mostly correct, Lord Oswhent. The issue is that every mage has a unique personality, and some personalities lend themselves more easily to some spells than others. Your master, for example, is better at enchantments than I am— probably better than I will ever be—because his mind is naturally inclined toward them, and in accordance with that inclination, he has been practicing them for decades. I tried some complex enchantments myself not so long ago, and found them quite taxing, but on the other hand, I expect I could do more with fire and other elements than he could, because that's what *I've* spent my life practicing. I never gave much thought to healing after I failed to devise a spell to heal my . . . disfigurement. Until very recently, I did not believe I could do it at all."

"But you did succeed?"

"Only by changing my conception of the spell itself. Normally, it is enough for me to visualize something, to will it, and it happens. I still can't will wounds to heal, but I learned how to take my desire for someone's well-being and put my power behind it. Useful, without question, but I suspect you see the problem?"

Varalen's heart sank. "You can only heal people you hold deep-seated affection for. And knowing you, I'd be surprised if there were five of those on the whole continent."

"I haven't counted. But you're right about the first bit."

There really was no other way, then. He'd have to find another mage who was both charitable and powerful in precisely the right way, and he could pass one on the street tomorrow and never know it. "It seems Elgar is my only chance," he said. "And that you have no chance at all."

"Oh? Is that the deduction you've come to?" She shrugged. "Well, I did tell you I was smarter than you."

"Come on, Your Grace. Is making cryptic prophecies regarding my eventual failure and demise the only enjoyment you can come up with in here?"

"It *is* enjoyable," she said, "but I don't mean to be cryptic. Let me try to clarify. Even if I never escape this prison, Lord Oswhent, you've already given me all the tools I need to destroy you. Not to kill you, but to put you in so much pain you'll wish you were dead. I could do it at this very moment, but I won't. The time doesn't feel . . . ripe."

Varalen snatched the report from her hands and stood up, leaving her in the circle denoted by her little length of chain. "You're assuming that I plan to come back here to chat with you again. Elgar *is* going to kill you, and I need nothing else from you. I don't see why this shouldn't be the last time we meet."

"Oh, if I know you and Elgar, we will definitely meet at least once more." She didn't get up, just stroked the chain idly with one hand. "Try to enjoy your time until then, Lord Oswhent."

THE RESISTANCE AND those who had organized under Morgan had been fully engaged with Roger's plan over the past couple of weeks. Since the rumors were now at a point where they could sustain themselves, even without any further fuel, they had moved their focus to the map of the city Roger had gotten from Londret. Careful reconnaissance and a couple of lucky finds had proven his hunch: the tiny inkblots on the map represented devices like the one Talia had stolen from the warehouse in Silkspoint, anchoring points that sustained Elgar's mindless mobs, controlling whether they were active or dormant. Armed with Naishe's and Morgan's vardrath steel, they'd managed to find and destroy about a dozen of them, though further scouting had discovered two that had already been replaced. But though their work dismantling the talismans had undoubtedly been effective, they couldn't reach the whole city. There were those whose faith in Elgar was strong enough that it couldn't be persuaded away. And then there were those who worked as his soldiers for their livelihood. Wearing the charms on their person wasn't optional for those people, and though Roger had received requests from a few of them, it was a worryingly small number. If they could have rooted out every single inkblot, and been sure they would not be replaced, that would have taken care of the problem. But as it was, it seemed that Elgar would still have an army, just a smaller one than he had hoped.

Marceline needed a reprieve from thinking about it, away from the Ashencourt house, the Dragon's Head, even Tom's. She had decided to spend today like an ordinary day, and turn up some coin in her usual way. It wasn't that she or Tom needed the money; she just wanted to feel like she could still be useful, certain of accomplishing something she set out to do. And pickpocketing, at least, was something everyone agreed she was exceptional at. So she went to Draven's Square and began scanning the crowd for marks, trying to get lost in the search for something much less complicated than revolution.

She discarded two potential marks and found the purse of a third to be drastically lighter than she had hoped. But then she caught sight of a newcomer to the square, a copper-haired woman wearing travel-stained if well-made clothes, taking a leisurely stroll around the stalls. Her pace might be slow, but she was definitely distracted, so absorbed in scanning the multitude of wares set out that she hardly seemed to notice when someone jostled her shoulder. With a target like that around, Marceline's biggest worry was that another thief might beat her to it.

Still, she hadn't earned her reputation through haste or sloppiness, so she didn't immediately strike, just kept track of the woman's movements. After buying a large quantity of herbs (medicinal, not for cooking—Naishe would approve), the woman stopped at a stall Marceline was only barely familiar with, and spoke with its proprietor in a language she thought was Sahaian, sketching idle shapes in the air as if she were trying to recall something she'd seen once. The proprietor eventually nodded and rummaged through a few boxes before brandishing an object Marceline didn't recognize. She wandered casually closer, and made out a slender amalgamation of metal and glass, a long sharp point and a wider body, less than six inches long. She had no idea what it was, but the woman counted out an impressive amount of coin for the thing, and the proprietor wrapped it up carefully.

Marceline would have liked to steal it, just out of curiosity, but it was too big for her to feel confident about her chances. Better to just nick the purse and get out of the square. The woman didn't seem any more alert after making her purchase than she'd been before, and then it was just a matter of executing the same steps she'd danced countless times. She stroked her fingers along the bottom of the purse, feeling for its weight, and discovered it to be even heavier than she had hoped.

Then a hand closed around her wrist.

The last time that had happened, Marceline had been a little child practicing with Tom. She was so utterly taken aback that for a moment she was completely frozen. In the next, she was frantically trying to twist herself free, but the hand wrapped around hers seemed to move with her, keeping her secure without ever tightening enough to truly hurt her.

She was so focused on getting away that she didn't notice the woman wasn't shouting for the guards until she bent her head toward Marceline's and muttered, "Is there a place somewhat more isolated where we could talk? I don't want to inconvenience you more than necessary, but I have some questions."

Then Marceline finally understood: this woman had made herself look like a good mark on purpose. And that meant she knew enough about the craft to know what a good mark looked like.

She went still, mumbling out of the corner of her mouth. "You a thief?"

The woman gave her a tight, brittle smile. "There was an old woman who trained me as a pickpocket for many years. You're quite skilled; I was terrible. But I remember how the game is played."

"Not much to be had around here for a pickpocket without the touch for it," Marceline said. "You couldn't even apprentice."

"I know," the woman said. "I found something else I was good at. Will you let me ask you some questions or not?"

"I guess I don't have a choice, do I? Come this way."

The woman followed her readily enough, though she kept an unyielding grip on Marceline's wrist. When they came to a stop along a dead-end street far enough back from the marketplace, she spared a single glance for the buildings in whose shadows they rested. "I need a way out of the city," she said, without preamble. "As you can probably tell from the purse you tried to steal, I have quite a bit of coin, and I can get even more. Or if you have a different price, simply name it."

Marceline didn't have to feign her shock. "Why do you think I'm the one to ask about something like that?"

"Because no one knows a city better than its thieves and its urchins. You're both."

Half a year ago, Marceline would have proudly admitted that was true and told this woman she was daft if she thought any secret route out of a city as tightly locked as Valyanrend could be found, when thieves had been searching for one for generations upon generations. But now she knew that what the woman wanted was indisputably possible, and that she absolutely could not reveal it to her. The secret of the tunnels was the resistance's greatest weapon; if their security was compromised, the entire mission could be.

She took a deep breath, trying to act as she would have acted, if she had still known nothing. "Miss, I know more than most, it's true. But you're asking for the impossible. I can teach you good ways to almost any district, routes to avoid the guards, places to stay where they won't check. But master thieves five times my age, legends in the flesh, have spent their lives looking for what you ask of me. They haven't found it, and I haven't tried. If that's what you want, though, I'm thinking you won't call for the guards, no matter what I did. Because if you need a secret way out, you're a much worse criminal than me."

She considered herself good at reading faces, sensitive to tells. Yet this woman's face had none; when she did not choose to alter her expression, she looked carved from stone. "I am far worse than you, but like you, my deeds are largely unknown in this city, and I can pass through it as I please. The route I seek is not for me, but for one who is no criminal at all, who is held unjustly by that leader of yours."

"Not of *mine*," Marceline said reflexively. If what she was saying was true, she did feel for the woman; Elgar had certainly caused injustice enough, much more than even Marceline and the resistance knew. But it was because she knew how important their mission was that she couldn't allow it to be put in danger for a single person, no matter how mistreated, or how deserving. And that was only *if* the woman was telling the truth. "Look, I shouldn't even be telling you this much, but if you manage to spring this friend of yours, I could hide the two of you in half a hundred places where Elgar's people would never find you. Just . . . half a hundred places within these walls."

The woman stared at her, searching her up and down for something Marceline could not possibly have guessed. And then she released her hold, twitching her shoulders in a slight shrug. "All right."

Marceline blinked. "That's it?"

"What more do you want me to say? It's clear this conversation has nowhere left to go but in circles, endlessly. Pity."

"But then . . . does that mean . . . I can go?"

"You can go," the woman said. "Turning a thief over to guards is one thing I would never do. But the threat proved a suitable bluff, I suppose."

She bled back into the crowd on the main street, leaving Marceline a little dazed, as if she'd dodged a bolt of lightning. But if she dawdled to question her good fortune for too long, she might lose it. She headed back into the street, too, and looked around to make sure the woman wasn't waiting to see which way she went, only to discover she was already gone. Perhaps she'd thought of another way to help this prisoner friend of hers. Marceline hoped so, at least.

She took a few more useless turns just in case, then headed for the nearest gateway to the tunnels, a staircase in the cellar of an abandoned house a dozen streets away. She didn't often enter the tunnels that way, but after the scare she'd just had, she was through being exposed for the day. She'd head back to Sheath, go to Tom's or the Dragon's Head, and lie low for at least a few hours. Preferably literally; it was early yet, but she could use a bit of sleep.

She pried up the little wooden door in the cellar flooring, feeling her way in the dark for the worn stone steps. Once she got to the tunnels proper, the series of torches would light her way, but they couldn't have any too close to the entrance, lest the light be visible from outside. But when she got a few steps down and tried to pull the door shut behind her, she realized that it had snagged on something— then, to her horror, that that something was a booted foot.

"I don't mean to alarm you," the woman from the square said calmly. "But I expect it's all stone down there, with nowhere to hide. Even I wouldn't be able to muffle my footsteps sufficiently, and I can't afford to let you get too far ahead of me, in case there's a possibility I could get lost. So we might as well get this all over with now."

Marceline felt like she couldn't breathe, something tightening in her throat and around her ribs. "I looked for you," she said. "I—I checked—"

"There's no need to berate yourself," the woman said. "I spent a great deal of my life learning how to track a target unseen. Many with much more experience than you never saw me either, for all their caution."

Her tone was so casual, as if she hadn't just caught Marceline in a blatant lie. By contrast, Marceline fumbled to even form a sentence. "Y-you can't be down here. Listen. You don't even know what you'd ruin, you—"

Rather than press her advantage, the woman held both hands out, palms up. "Don't get upset. I'm not here to ruin anything. Whatever game you're running down here, I don't need to know about it. All I need is a way out of the city. I don't think I could possibly have been any clearer on that point."

"This isn't it," Marceline insisted. "The tunnels are all *within* the city—I told you I could—"

"Perhaps," the woman said. "But now that I'm here, I think I'll just take a look for myself and make sure. You don't have to help me; just stay out of my way, and I'll stay out of yours. It doesn't have to be any more complicated than that."

"There are other people, *my* people, who need to use these ways. Why do you think everything's got to do with you and what you want, just because you grabbed my wrist in the market?" She was babbling, and she knew it, but she had absolutely no idea what else to do. She couldn't overpower this woman, couldn't drag her out of here.

"Because there's one thing I'm sure of," the woman said. "If you hadn't given me anything interesting when I asked you what you knew, I would have let you go, and baited my hook for a different urchin. But you were nervous, and you were lying. I've been taught enough about how to spot a liar to be confident of that. So whatever you know, it must be something useful to me, whether it's in these tunnels or somewhere else. And the best thing you can do, at this point, is tell me what it is quickly, before I ruin anything else."

The last time Marceline had not known what to do so completely had been in the streets of Silkspoint, with an armed guard bearing down on her and nowhere to run. But Naishe had saved her that time, and no one was here to save her now. She could think of all the people whose wit and resourcefulness she admired, but what Roger would do in this situation was different from what Naishe would do, which was different from what Tom would do and what Morgan would do, and around and around it went. There was no way out of this without making a decision for herself, one way or another.

"There is one thing I'd strongly advise you not to do," the woman said quietly, as if following Marceline's thoughts. "Don't ask anyone you care about to fight me for you. Whatever friends you're thinking of talking to about me, of asking to handle me for you, are friends that you're going to get killed. Whoever they are, I'm better than them, and if they try to fight me, I won't show mercy. I don't have time for mercy. I have to succeed, no matter what."

That hadn't been what she was thinking of, but was it possible? Her stomach twisted at the idea of it, but . . . "You've no idea who I might know," she said, thinking of Rask more than anyone. Would Rask really lose?

"It doesn't matter," the woman said. "I am better than anyone you know—better than most people you could ever hope to meet, even if you traveled the world. That's not a bluff—I made a terrible thief, remember? I don't . . . have rhetorical skills. I just have the truth. Please. No one has to die this way, but if you make the wrong decision here, many could."

She looked genuinely sad at that idea—not bigger, as if she were puffing herself up to threaten Marceline more effectively, but smaller, more vulnerable through the emotion she let slip onto her face. That, more than anything, was what convinced her that this woman must possess some truly rare skill, at least as rare as what Rask had. And from there, she knew what she had to do.

"I'll make you a deal," she said. "These tunnels are mazelike—you'd take months to learn them without someone teaching you. If you tell me where your friend's being held, or where you hope to spring them from, I'll teach you the fastest and safest route from there to here, and from here to the other side of Valyanrend's walls. But in exchange, I want something more than just you leaving me and my people alone, though you'd better do that, too."

The woman relaxed, reaching for her purse. "Of course. You'll recall I was perfectly willing to offer you money from the beginning."

"Not coin," Marceline said. "What happened with you aside, I can get as much coin as I want. Here are the rules: if I'm not teaching you or you're not making your escape, you stay *out* of these tunnels. I can't risk you being seen on your own down here; if the wrong people find out about you, they'll try to kill you anyway, no matter what I say. But if you're as talented as you claim, you're going to look after my interests *outside* these tunnels for as long as you stay in this city. That means you help watch the entrances, and handle any guards who get too close. And I might ask you to transport a few things, but only if you prove you can be trusted."

She didn't truly have much leverage to ask for anything; asking was as much about judging the woman's reaction as it was about coming out the victor in this negotiation. But the woman smiled: crooked and dry, but genuine. "You've turned out to be a formidable driver of bargains, but at least you're a wise one. Far better to turn my skills to your own ends than to try to overcome them. I'll do as you say, for as long as I'm here. You have my word, if that's worth anything to you."

"Is it true what you said?" Marceline asked. "Is your friend really Elgar's prisoner, and are they really innocent?"

"I don't like that word," the woman said, "but she doesn't deserve to be jailed or murdered, by him or anyone. And she's not my friend."

"She must be, if you're willing to do so much for her."

The woman shook her head. "I didn't mean she was less than a friend, but much more."

Marceline rolled her eyes. "Oh, it's like *that*. Well, I hope Elgar cares enough about keeping her to make her loss hurt him. He's done enough to this city."

The woman tilted her head, as if trying to read something written on Marceline's face. "You really do want to hurt him, don't you? And these associates of yours . . . they want the same?"

"I thought we just agreed my associates and our goals were not to be your business beyond what you owe me."

The woman smiled again, just as sardonically as before. "Just trust me, then. If this goes well, you and I are going to help each other far more than you realize."

CHAPTER THIRTY-SEVEN

Esthrades

IF ALL YOU did was look at a map, it would be easy to think things were going as well as Kel could have hoped. They had moved on from Stonespire as soon as they could ensure its safety, lest the Esthradians think Hywel's rescue of the city was a ploy to set up his own occupation. It was currently in the hands of Denton Halley and Jill Bridger, who had received the unanimous votes of their peers in the wake of the death of the former captain of the guard. The Hallerns had been well and truly chased out of Esthrades, and they had repaid at least some of the debt they owed Arianrod.

Before they left Araveil, Hywel had told Gerald he would return as soon as their mission was complete, but when that day came, he, Kel, and Alessa all agreed they ought to take a different direction. In a perfect world, they'd have the manpower to liberate Reglay next, but they didn't want to copy the Hallerns and spread themselves too thin. Instead, Hywel had proposed that they station themselves on the border between Esthrades and Reglay. That way, if any Hallerns tried to come stir up trouble in Esthrades again, they'd be ready. And if—when, they hoped—the Issamiri toppled Valyanrend in the west and turned their gaze on Reglay, they'd be able to participate in an attack from two sides.

Yes, all well and good—brilliant, even. But Kel certainly wasn't feeling well and good as he stared down the two people he'd called into his tent—two people who were looking singularly guilty, as if they already knew what he was about to say. They'd better. Here they were acting like children, and *he* was supposed to be the child.

"I hope you both know that this is just as unpleasant for me as it is for you," Kel said. "But at this point, you've really left me no choice."

Alessa and Hywel glanced at each other, and then hastily back at him. "I know," Alessa said. "I've been meaning to apologize to you for a while now. I'm sure it looks as though we've been shutting you out—excluding you from important discussions, or even just from our company. But Kel, I promise Hywel has never made any political or military decision since we've come here without at least asking for your input on the issue. Really, when you're not around we discuss politics very little. But that doesn't excuse—"

"No, no!" Kel shook his head fiercely. "You've got it all wrong. If anything, given the way things are going, the two of you ought to be discussing politics *more*."

Two equally blank stares.

Kel rolled his eyes. "Oh, come *on*. Do you really think I'm so oblivious that I don't know why the two of you have been going off without me? It's obvious that you . . . fancy each other. That's what I want to speak about."

He expected them to go back to looking guilty, but instead Hywel frowned, and Alessa bit her lip. "I won't deny it," Hywel began haltingly. "But is that something you have to look so fierce over? I was under the impression you approved of me."

"As a *person,* of course," Kel said. "But whatever your upbringing, you don't have the freedoms of a commoner. The two of you must decide what you mean by this . . . liaison between you, before popular opinion decides for you. Hywel, your servants and guards are starting to talk of it, which means there's only so long until it becomes a rumor among the common people. What are you going to do when that happens?"

"I've no idea why it shouldn't be known that your sister and I are courting," Hywel said. "If my servants or anyone else ferrets that out, I'll admit to it, and if they characterize it as anything else, I'll correct them."

Kel reeled for a moment, unprepared for that answer. Had matters really progressed so far already? "But . . . but courting is for someone you think you might marry."

"So it is," Hywel agreed, scratching the newly short hair at the back of his neck. "If Alessa and I do reach that step, I was going to ask for your blessing, but . . . I'm getting an inkling you aren't going to give it to me."

"You must be joking. You must absolutely be pulling my leg, or else—or else you've both gone mad. There's no other explanation."

"Kel," his sister said gently, "I know this is sudden, but nothing's been decided yet. We've been spending time together quite properly, just talking and trying to find out whether—"

"That's not the *point!*" Kel spoke so loudly that she fell silent. "Let me tell you what will happen if the two of you wed. It's something Alessa should already know. She was pronounced illegitimate at birth, but she is the child of my mother, born after my mother married my father, and she is older than I am. You, Hywel, are the king of Lanvaldis, and a king, as *you* well know, can legitimize a bastard. If Alessa were ever legitimized as my father's child, her claim, by right of birth, would immediately supersede my own. She would become, in the same instant, the queen of Reglay."

"But, Kelken," Hywel said, "surely you cannot think that I would ever do such a thing, or that your sister would allow it? We have no wish to interfere with your rule—we would do almost anything before that."

"Yes, *I* know that," Kel said. "But I knew that I was my parents' legitimate son, and that my father would have died before he raised Alessa over me. You know who didn't know that? The people of Reglay. Some of our subjects believed that I was a bastard with no right to the throne, and others believed I *did* have the right, but that Alessa would try to usurp me. And so our childhood was rife with danger, every moment. We spent most of it cooped up in the palace, because it was too dangerous for us to be among the people. We had to dodge assassination attempts, and others were harmed trying to protect us. That is the fate the two of you would bring upon yourselves and your children. There *will* be Reglians—and perhaps even Lanvalds—who believe that you intend to legitimize your wife and put some younger child of yours on my throne. And nothing any of us says publicly will be able to assuage those fears completely. You will be in danger from those people for the rest of your lives. Relations between our *countries* will be in danger. I *know* the two of you know this! And still you would be this selfish? I repeat: you're either joking, or you've lost your minds."

He'd thought that would finally chastise them, but it seemed to have the opposite effect. They both stiffened up, faces darkening. "I'm surprised you would say something like that," Alessa said.

"What, that I'd be honest with you about the consequences of your actions?"

"That you'd ask me to give into the demands of the worst sort of people. No matter what you or Hywel or I do, we'll never please everyone, and some people may react violently over it. But we shouldn't let that control our decisions."

"And you're saying this one is that important to you?"

She looked at Hywel as she answered. "I'm coming to believe it might be, yes."

"You're both being so childish," Kel insisted. "You haven't known each other three months! You should know better than to put everything we're working toward in danger just for the sake of an infatuation!"

"That isn't—" Hywel started, but Alessa put a hand on his shoulder, and he broke off. "Fair enough. You tell him."

"Kel," Alessa said, with a look of disappointment and reproach that got immediately under his skin, "I'm willing to put myself in danger, if it ever even comes to that, for the sake of my own happiness. I thought that was something you cared about, too."

"You don't even have to care about mine," Hywel said, as if he couldn't resist. "But care about hers, at least."

And then they just left, as if they'd all decided together that the conversation was over. They didn't even look back. They just walked away.

Kel sank deeper into his chair, quelling the urge to throw something. Screaming impotently was beneath a king, no matter how much of an ass his fellow king was being, so instead he squeezed his eyes shut, clenched his fists on the armrests of his chair, and breathed in and out, trying to steady himself. What had been wrong with his arguments? They made perfect sense, didn't they? So why had the two of them gotten so offended?

He sat there in silence until he heard footsteps approaching. "You can come in, Hayne."

And sure enough, there she was, standing a bit awkwardly at the entrance to his tent. Kel waited for her to come and stand beside him before speaking. "Did you hear all of that?"

"Almost none, but I can guess what happened. How are you feeling?"

"Frustrated," Kel said. "What does she even see in him?"

Hayne hesitated. "Do you want an actual answer?"

"Of course."

"Then . . . I expect she sees that he's a boy of about her age, with a great amount of patience and thoughtfulness and a surpassingly even temper, who desires her company, depends on her advice, and doesn't care about the circumstances of her birth."

Kel's lips cracked in a smile in spite of himself. "All right, fair enough. But those qualities are hardly so rare that she can only find them in Hywel Markham Brionel. And a marriage to him *would* put her in danger. I'm not wrong about that, Hayne."

"No, you aren't," Hayne said. "But Hywel's wife and children will be in danger no matter who he marries. Hywel is popular now, because most of the people both see him as more legitimate than Selwyn and prefer him to her. But his right of succession relies on a scrap of paper—a paper that, as you might say, *we* know is genuine, but the people cannot. Who can say what bad actors might try to inflame the people's doubts about their new king, as soon as he does anything unpopular? Perhaps, irrespective of any romantic feelings he might have, Hywel felt it was wise to court someone who was already familiar with those dangers, rather than someone who would have to become accustomed to them after marrying him."

"Perhaps," Kel said. "But any one of Hywel and Alessa's children, or of their children's children, and so on forever, could try to use their descent from Alessa as a way to lay claim to Reglay's throne. That's not a danger that could come from Hywel marrying someone else."

"Again, Your Grace, I can't help pointing out that a bastard cannot be legitimized after their death, for precisely the purpose of preventing some monarch centuries in the future from upsetting an entire established line of succession. If some hypothetical great-grandchild of Hywel and Alessa tried to use her to lay claim to your throne, they would have no legal standing to do so whatsoever. The law is entirely clear on that point, with no room for debate."

"It doesn't mean they wouldn't try."

"Your Grace, if this hypothetical Lanvaldian lordling—or indeed anyone at all—decided they wanted the throne of Reglay, they would come up with a reason for it, just as Elgar did. Crimes you or your descendants supposedly committed against them, the favor of the gods, anything. But it would be foolish for you and those around you to give undue weight to the potential actions of those people, who may not ever even exist."

"Ah," Kel said, trying not to sulk. "So you're on their side."

The look she gave him was entirely serious, almost solemn. "I am always on your side, Your Grace, whether in matters of life and death or of your own happiness. But I think you would be happier, in the long run, if you examined the one reason behind your actions that you haven't mentioned."

"I've *told* you the reasons," Kel said. "I would never lie about something like that, and to Lessa least of all."

Her tone softened. "I know that. And I know those reasons are sensible and well thought out. I am simply saying that there is another behind them. If Alessa marries the king of Lanvaldis, she must live in Lanvaldis. And she can no longer live with you."

Kel didn't know why hearing that aloud made his chest feel so tight; it wasn't as if it was a surprise. "Hayne, my sister getting married isn't a new concept for me. I've always assumed it was more likely than not to happen, and I would never stand in the way of it."

"You assumed it would happen," Hayne said, "but I suspect you also assumed she would marry someone from Reglay. That she would still be able to serve you in an advisory role, as she has always done, and your relationship would only change a little, not completely."

It would change, wouldn't it? No matter what either of them said. She could love Kel and Hywel both, but no one could serve two kings. He and Hywel were engaged on a joint campaign now, but when it was over, and they both returned home, there would be some state secrets they simply couldn't share with each other. Going too far into Hywel's confidence would mean there was only so far

Alessa could go into Kel's. There would be things he couldn't tell her, and things she couldn't tell him. That had never happened before.

"Is that really what she wants?" he asked Hayne. "To put such distance between us?"

Hayne crouched before his chair, so they were eye to eye. "Your Grace, your sister loves you deeply, but she has always been in your shadow. By marrying Hywel, she wouldn't just be an equal partner in the country and the family they build together—she has the chance to finally be your equal, too. Don't you think that was of paramount importance to her when she considered this match?"

"I don't know," Kel said. "I feel like she's barely considered it at all."

"And that's precisely why she walked away from you, Your Grace. Because you implied that she had not thought it over just as much as you, that she was only acting out of selfishness. But do you really think that's true? A royal marriage should not be made solely for love, but it *should* be made for compatibility, and sometimes love and compatibility go hand in hand. Perhaps you should just . . . think about it. Instead of thinking of all the reasons why it would be a terrible match, see if you can find any reasons why it might be good."

So Kel thought about it. He thought about how Lessa and Hywel were both such shy people, but how they seemed able to carry themselves with more ease when they were together. He thought about the respect Hywel had always shown for her opinions, how calm they were when they disagreed, their tendency to talk through a subject until they'd well and truly exhausted all avenues. He thought about his own parents, how his mother had been considered the best choice for his father from a political standpoint, but how Kel had never known them to endure each other's company for more than half an hour at a time. He thought about the kind of partner he'd want to choose for himself, when the time came: someone who was kind and steadfast, who thought as much about the right thing to do as he did, and was willing to walk that path with him, together.

His face must have changed, because Hayne sat cross-legged beside his chair, putting a gentle hand on his arm. "I know it isn't fair. You have been so brave, and the world meets your bravery by asking more and more of you. You've already endured the loss of your father, having to flee your home, capture and imprisonment, and now you may be asked to give up the person you love most. But whatever happens, I believe you'll have the courage to meet it as well, and make the right choice."

Kel swallowed hard, trying to feel as confident as she was. "And you'll . . . stay with me in Reglay? Whether Lessa does or not?"

She reached up to ruffle his hair. It was treating him like a child, but just this once, Kel didn't mind. "You'd find it difficult to get rid of me, Your Grace."

Chapter Thirty-eight

Hallarnon

ADORA DIDN'T DARE believe the sentry's report, not until she'd seen them in person. And once she had seen them, even she was surprised at the fierce joy she felt, burning through so many layers of sober grimness as if, for just that moment, her troubles had never existed.

Rhia tried to sweep her a simple bow, but Adora was having none of that, and threw her arms around her former captain so tightly she squeaked. "Oof! Your Grace, I couldn't be more pleased at such a reception, but surely . . ."

"Oh, hush. Let custom fall by the wayside for once." Over Rhia's head, she locked eyes with Cadfael, who was standing with Lirien and the woman Adora had met briefly with Voltest, Talis. "It does me such good to see you both well."

"*Both*, not *all*?" Lirien asked, with an arch smile that assured her it was a joke. "Well, not that you asked, but Talis and I are also fine. Though I'm afraid we're the only *wardrenfell* you'll be getting for the foreseeable future. We've parted ways with Voltest, and he won't be doing any more fighting."

"What, just like that?" That was Vespas, come to join the proceedings as lithely as a cat. "Does the man have no conception of what's at stake?"

Lirien could not have known who he was, but she was unperturbed by his sudden interrogation. "I'm sure he does, but you'll have to trust me: he's no longer of any fighting use to anyone. But no danger, either, unless you have a fear of condescension."

"We wanted him to stay with us," Talis said more quietly, not fully looking at Adora or Vespas. "For his own safety, if nothing else. But he claimed that he had already wasted enough time. He's returning to Aurnis, in search of those he knew there many years ago—before he was held captive by Elgar's people, and before he . . . became Voltest, I suppose."

"When he goes back," Lirien finished, "I suspect he'll use a different name. But given that he didn't volunteer it to us, we didn't think we should ask."

Voltest, in Old Lantian, was *ash*. Adora couldn't claim to have even a slender grasp of what had transpired, but if he no longer felt that name was appropriate, that was probably a good thing. "Well, the rest of you have come back at a grand time. We'd of course be delighted to have you with us, but I understand if you believe your group's combination of skills makes you more useful within the enemy's walls than as just a few more soldiers in our army. But if that is your intent, you'll have to leave soon. We're preparing to besiege the city."

Cadfael's eyebrows rose, and Rhia scanned Adora's face in concern. "Is that wise?" he asked.

Vespas gave a bitter laugh. "I wouldn't have said so, under normal circumstances. But it seems these are not normal circumstances."

"My uncle has a contact within the city," Adora explained. "It was she who urged him, in her last missive, to commence a siege without delay."

"She must hold sway with you indeed, then," Cadfael said.

Vespas shook his head. "She's valuable, but it was her argument that left us no choice. The two of you departed Eldren Cael before Adora and I learned the truth of Elgar's plans, but my contact confirmed he has learned to use his magic to bend his subjects' will toward his future conquests. My contact and her associates have discovered his methods, and they've been trying to save her countrymen from him. They are having some success, but Elgar is also accelerating his efforts. She asked us to arrange the siege in case they fail. By sealing the imperator inside, we would ensure that he has to defeat us before he can affect anyone outside the city, and his army would be confined to those he can take within Valyanrend alone."

Rhia and Cadfael accepted the explanation easily, as Adora had known they would. They had seen the effects Jocelyn Selreshe's magic had produced, after all. "We had been aiming for the city regardless," Rhia said, "but this makes me even more confident we should go. Cadfael and I should use our swords in a place where we're more likely to find spells to cut down with them. Maybe we can even help these friends of yours in their work."

Lirien groaned. "Well, I for one would rather stay out here now that I know all that. If a mindless army is massing in Valyanrend and the way out is blocked, we'd be making ourselves ready targets for it."

"That's a surprising amount of cowardice from someone who can heal any injury that's not immediately fatal," Cadfael said.

"It's not cowardice, thank you, it's an aversion to being overworked. And an aversion to being forced into combat with people who aren't in control of themselves. Whether they kill us or we kill them, we're going to feel bad about it. I don't even like to kill those who are trying to kill me on purpose."

"But that's precisely why we should be in there," Rhia said. "To help resolve things without violence."

"That's why *you* should be in there," Lirien corrected. "And your brother. But Talis and I can't break enchantments, unfortunately."

"You can't, Lirien?" Adora frowned, resting her cheek in her hand. "I still know so much less about magic than I'd like. But are you saying your healing has no effect?"

"My . . . oh." Lirien tugged on her braid, as close to embarrassed as Adora had ever seen her. "I suppose I just . . . assumed I couldn't. Until very recently, I had only ever healed physical injuries, and that one exception could have been a special case. But if my magic is capable of perceiving other magic as harmful to the person it's affecting, it might be possible."

After having spent so long with Arianrod, Adora found it strange to hear Lirien talk about her magic as if it were some separate entity with its own will. Arianrod had explained to her already that magic itself wasn't sentient, but for someone who couldn't control what their magic would and wouldn't let them do, it was probably an apt analogy.

With a final tug, Lirien released her braid. "That's something, at least. Worth trying. If I let the three of you drag me along for no better reason than looking after you, I'd have been quite irritated."

"The three of us?" Talis repeated.

"Come on. Don't tell me you're not coming."

Talis tried to keep a stoic expression, but ruined it with a wince and a sheepish smile. "Ah well, unlike you, I don't mind killing people who are trying to kill me."

"That does seem to be a consensus," Cadfael said to Adora. "And from what you've said, that means we have little time to waste, though I do regret we could not stay with you for longer. At the very least, let's make sure we've shared all the information we can think of before we part again."

Adora felt melancholy at the prospect, too, but at least she knew they'd gotten this far safely. She just had to have faith in them one more time. And unlike when she had parted with Arianrod, she didn't think she would be leaving them to more danger than they could handle. "Let's take our leisure together tonight, then. We can celebrate our reunion in whatever small ways are open to us, and you can leave for Valyanrend on the morrow. We won't have a siege in place quite that fast."

"Aye, and a celebration will help take our minds off the fact we're about to besiege a city with its own infinite supply of fresh water," Vespas added, with a grim smile.

Cadfael winced. "It'd take you months. Perhaps even longer."

"The siege is only a stopgap," Adora said. "It's because we agree that Elgar can't be allowed to get his spells out from behind those walls, not because we think it's an effective way to ultimately defeat him."

"Still," Rhia said, "it can't be an easy choice to make. You can't shield civilians from the effects of a siege."

"Yes. I won't even be able to shield you from it, once you're within Valyanrend's walls. I can only hope we succeed in resolving the situation by other means before mass starvation becomes a concern." All this time among her soldiers and subordinates had improved her ability to show a confident demeanor even when she didn't feel it, and she was grateful for that now.

She let the others go ahead of her, toward food and fire and what comfort they could muster this evening. But before she could fall in behind them, her uncle grasped her sleeve. "Your Grace, a word in private?"

She followed him to her tent, taking note of how uncommonly restless he was, glancing through the opening to make sure they were truly alone. "I need not tell you," he said at last, "that we're approaching the same trap that nearly felled Talia Avestri—that's thwarted any army that ever attempted to attack Valyanrend, in one way or another. Our true enemy isn't the aqueduct, it's those damned walls. Without them, everything would be . . . well, not *simple*. But eminently manageable, for an army such as ours."

"You're right, of course," Adora said. "But isn't bemoaning the existence of Valyanrend's walls like arguing with the tides? It's not as if we can break them down."

"No," Vespas agreed. "But I have begun to suspect for some time now that it is possible to move past them. And the more tightly we have clung to the outskirts of the city, the more certain I have become."

"What do you mean?"

"It's this contact of mine. We haven't surrounded the city yet, so most business into and out of Valyanrend still goes on as usual. The one exception is the south—*we* know we would never attack civilians or their caravans, but our foremost camps are close enough to the southern-facing gates that the city deems it too great a risk. That direction alone is closed, and those who were accustomed to use it must go around to other gates if they wish to leave the city. And yet the manner in which my contact's messages reach me remains unchanged. If the messengers were going around to the east or west and then turning back south, they'd approach our camp at an angle, from the southwest or southeast. But they run into my sentries dead-on from the south, every time."

Adora's heart paused a moment too long, then leapt forward in triple-time. But she couldn't tell if it was excitement or foreboding. "You think this messenger has an unsanctioned way of passing through the southern walls. A route Elgar and his people don't know about."

"It's not a certainty," Vespas said, though she could see the eagerness in his eyes. "They could just be taking an odd way around, I suppose. But that's not what my instincts tell me. If we can find the route they're using—"

"You'd be taking a great gamble, Uncle." Adora folded her arms, trying to ward off a chill. "You've earned this woman's trust, though I understand it wasn't easy. If you have your people shadow hers, you may find less than nothing; you may rupture the agreement between you."

"That's only if my people are caught, and they won't be. I'm confident of that."

Adora wished she could feel the same, but she had learned not to bet against her uncle's instincts, honed as they were from decades of experience. "All right. If you think it's worth the resources and the risks, you have my permission to pursue it."

"I don't know why you're looking so glum about it. If this works, we'll solve a puzzle even your glorious ancestor couldn't."

"She did," Adora said. "She just found a different solution. And that's only *if* it works."

Before Vespas could reply, Amali strode into the tent, sending the papers on their strategy table fluttering behind her. "What is it?" Adora asked, when she didn't start in on whatever was on her mind.

Amali bit her lip, her words coming slowly. "Your Grace, we have received dire news from within the city, but I wonder whether now is the time for it. There is nothing to be done about it, and I am told you wished to have a celebration of sorts."

"It's all right," Adora said. "Whatever it is, even if it doesn't affect us directly, I would still prefer to know now. I can veil my feelings from our guests if need be."

Amali still didn't look convinced, but she glanced at Vespas, and he nodded, making his own opinion clear. "Your Grace, it seems . . . the reprieve your friend has been granted is coming to an end."

"Oh." They'd been lucky Elgar had delayed Arianrod's execution even this long, but Adora's chest still tightened with dread she tried not to show. "I see. Has she already . . . ?"

"It took the news some time to reach the camp," Amali said. "The execution has not been carried out, but it has been announced for tomorrow, just past noon." She bowed her head. "I'm sorry."

"That's still more than half a day's time," Adora said to Vespas. "And we didn't have Rhia and the others with us before now. They were going to enter Valyanrend anyway, so if we tell them—"

"I'm sorry," Amali repeated, more firmly. "There's nothing they can do."

"Nothing two *wardrenfell* and two wielders of vardrath steel can do against one mage and a handful of his soldiers?"

"Nothing they can do to get in the city, Your Grace. I'm sure Elgar suspected just such a rescue plan. As I told you, it took the message some time to get here, or it wouldn't have reached us at all. Valyanrend has been entirely closed off since sundown, and will remain so until after the execution tomorrow. No one goes in or out, not for any reason in the world. If your friends were already within the city, that would be one thing. But they won't get there now, I'm afraid."

Again, Adora glanced at Vespas. "And there's no way of finding this alternate route of yours before tomorrow?"

"I wish I could say there were. But it'll be at least a few days until I get any more messages from my contact, so there won't be any messenger to track. And if I sent someone to fumble blindly around in the shadow of the southern wall, I believe I would, as you suggested, do more harm than good."

"But the city will be closed, Vespas. Couldn't you at least have someone there to look, even if they're as cautious as possible? Just in case they find something?"

He sighed. "As you command, Your Grace. Just . . . don't expect too much from it. It's a lot of ground to cover, and I doubt the entrance, if one exists, will simply be out in the open."

He was right. They were both right. Still, it was all Adora could do to keep the angry and bitter thoughts inside her, without giving voice to them. It wasn't fair. If Rhia and the others had arrived a day earlier, even half a day . . . if they'd headed directly for Valyanrend instead of stopping at the Issamiri camp . . . it was almost too much. To be completely powerless was bad enough, but it was even worse to know she *almost* could have saved Arianrod, if things had happened just a little differently. And now this time tomorrow, she would be dead.

Adora swallowed hard, using every trick she knew to maintain her composure. "Please entertain my guests for a while," she said to Vespas and Amali. "They did not know Arianrod well, but I still think it best that we not mention this to them. They wished for a pleasant and heartening evening, and they deserve one. I will be along presently, when I . . . when I feel I can contribute something to that end."

Thankfully, they did not question her, but left her to her thoughts without another word. And Adora sat in silence, in the dim light of her tent, waiting for the moment when she would be able to move without trembling, or speak without pain.

Chapter Thirty-nine

Valyanrend

FROM THE MOMENT the sun rose that day, it fought with heavy clouds, white and silver and dark, brooding gray. Varalen thought it would be only fitting if the skies opened up and poured torrential rain; it would be just like the weather to take Arianrod Margraine's side, and drench the day of her execution to depress turnout and dampen the celebratory mood Elgar was aiming for. But as the early morning hours dripped by, the skies released only the slightest drizzle here and there, and the darkest clouds seemed to pass them by, heading out toward the western coast to empty their multitudes into the sea. By the time they had to get ready to leave the Citadel, there were even weak patches of blue here and there in the sky.

Perhaps that was its own kind of bad luck. If it truly had poured rain, perhaps Elgar would have used it as an excuse to postpone the execution to a later date.

Part of Elgar didn't want to do this, Varalen knew. Not out of any sense of ethics or empathy—if anything, his emotions were what were driving him to see her killed, the satisfaction and relief he'd feel at knowing such a powerful enemy was gone forever. No, it was simply because she was so useful to him alive, a captive mage on whom he was free to experiment, testing out all the ideas he was too cautious to try on himself. But there was nothing for it; the people had gotten too out of hand. They distrusted and picked apart everything he announced these days— not without good reason, Varalen had to admit, but it was interfering with their timeline. He still didn't truly understand, or truly want to understand, Elgar's methods, but the numbers he'd predicted having for his armies by now seemed to only have partially materialized, hampered by the endless torrent of rumors and doubts circulating among the people.

Varalen had tried to figure out where the most pernicious of the rumors had come from, but though he was usually talented at this sort of thing, this time the culprits eluded him utterly. The price of having Sheath closed to him, he supposed. He suspected Roger first—his cousin had claimed he would heed Varalen's warning and stay away from any further resistance business, but he was, after all, a cheater and liar by trade. This was exactly the way he'd choose to fight Elgar, with words and schemes rather than weapons. But when Varalen attempted to put eyes on Roger, he found that his cousin had become relentlessly boring. He rarely left Sheath at all anymore, and even drank less, spending his nights either home alone or cloistered with an old friend or two. As strange as it sounded to think that he of all people might have seen sense, Varalen knew that Roger had always been a coward. Perhaps a guarantee of his own safety was all he had needed to induce him to lay low until the chaos blew right over his head.

But that left Varalen with precisely zero leads. The fact that Roger had immediately cut ties with almost all his acquaintances meant that Varalen had no way of connecting them to him. None of the individuals he had met with at his home had proven suspicious in any way (well, beyond the usual—they were all petty criminals of some sort), and he rarely even conducted business anymore, living on coin he had saved up and windfalls he pickpocketed on very occasional trips to neighboring districts. Varalen was beginning to regret coming on so strongly at their first meeting; he had done it because he had felt honor-bound to try to save his cousin's life, but now he was regretting that a bit, too.

He'd scrubbed his face overzealously in the washbasin that morning, and it still felt raw when Elgar entered his chambers a little before noon. Varalen was surprised to see him in person, and not Quentin or another of his guards, but perhaps Elgar was too tense to sit still. His excitement was evident in the twitch of his mouth, the glint in his eyes, but there was anxiety in the set of his shoulders, too. Varalen couldn't blame him. "That woman does such a good job of advocating for herself," he ventured. "She seems so convinced that the world simply won't allow her to die, I could almost believe it myself."

Elgar laughed. "I envy it, to be honest. How comforting it must be to always have hope, no matter the circumstances. I was petty enough to want to make her suffer, I admit it. But so far I seem to have failed—not that she'd ever give me the satisfaction of seeing it if I'd succeeded. Today will be my last chance. If I fail then, she will leave this world having known only an instant of pain—merely the time it takes to die. We should all be so lucky."

"Your last chance?" Varalen repeated. "Do you have something special planned toward that end?" He had endeavored to learn as little as possible about the execution itself, largely because he had suspected Elgar might make the affair worse, in whatever way, than it needed to be.

"You'll have the chance to see that for yourself," Elgar replied. "Until then, I wouldn't dream of spoiling it. Go and fetch her. I'll send a couple guards after you, but you shouldn't need them; she hardly poses a danger to a child in her current state."

Varalen balked. "If that's the case, Your Eminence, why should I have to go anywhere near her? Just have Quentin do it."

"Quentin is preparing the square and my audience for the execution," Elgar said. "And since you will be at my side throughout it, I might as well gather you and her together."

"Throughout—I'm certain I didn't ask for anything of the sort, and if you knew you intended it, you should've told me." *So I could argue against it at my leisure,* he added inwardly.

"I would have, if it had required any extra preparation on your part. But I'll be doing all the talking today. You simply need to be present, as the one responsible for her capture; it would look odd to the people if I were not seen to honor you. So fetch her, and stand in your assigned place, and I promise I will ask nothing more of you. It *is* intended as a reward, you know."

His manner was so brusque and final that Varalen knew pushing back would be useless. He couldn't help remembering, too, Lady Margraine's prediction that they would meet at least once more. He would not relish having to prove her right.

Sure enough, he opened the door of her room to find her insufferable smugness firmly in place, as if she'd known who it would be before he even opened the door. "Ah, Lord Oswhent. I suppose it's too much to hope for that you might simply be in need of my counsel once again?"

"That would no doubt be less tedious for at least one of us," Varalen said, "but I suspect you already know why I'm here, Your Grace. One might say your death became inevitable the moment you decided to resist His Eminence, but even your remarkable skill at delaying it has finally failed you, I'm afraid."

"Everyone's death is inevitable, Lord Oswhent," she said. "We are merely finding out if mine shall take place today, or at some later time."

Could she still, after all this, hold out some hope? For what? The gods themselves to descend from the heavens and spare her? "I'm too tired to argue with you, Your Grace. I'm going to unlock your chain now. Will you behave, or will I have to drag you after me?"

"I'll walk on my own," she said, "but give me just a few moments of your time first."

Varalen knew why, so he didn't ask. He simply stood still, and waited.

"It seems we are approaching the end," she said. "One way or another. And so, while there is still time, I must keep my promise to you. I must tell you the truth."

"And destroy me," Varalen reminded her. "Wasn't that your boast? Well, I'm no child to plug my fingers in my ears. I'll hear you out—I suspect these may be the last words we say to each other."

Her eyes were fixed on his face. "It's the great wasting illness, isn't it?"

Varalen jumped slightly, then cursed himself. "You'll have to elaborate."

"I'm not sure who he is to you, exactly. Your son? A younger brother? Some other relative? But everything I've heard and intuited about his condition suggests the great wasting illness. And knowing Elgar, I doubt his continued presence at the Citadel is strictly voluntary."

Varalen scratched his cheek, trying to appear bored, though he did not like for her to know anything at all about Ryam, even the most mundane details. "I may be hearing the truth, but it's truth I know well. Do you think to frighten me with the severity of his condition? As learned as you are, there is nothing about that disease you know that I do not. I scoured every source in existence."

"I would expect no less of you, Lord Oswhent. Just as I would expect you to set all your determination toward saving someone you prize so highly. After all, that was what made it so easy to predict what I would do, wasn't it? You, too, were prepared to sacrifice part of yourself to extend the life of one whose presence so enriches your own—only what you sacrificed were your conscience and your peace of mind. What a rare opportunity it must have seemed, to find your services desired by a man who can work miracles! How tirelessly you must have labored to see his dreams fulfilled, all for the beautiful future he promised you!" Her bruised lips smiled, but beneath that smile was the marble stillness he remembered so well from the day of her capture. "What a shame that all that work will prove to have been for nothing in the end."

Before she could take another breath, Varalen surged forward, seizing her by the threadbare cloth at her shoulders. "If you seek to ruin me by attempting some harm against my son, know that I need not wait for Elgar to kill you. If I have so much as a single thought that you could pose even the slightest inconvenience to him, I will wring your neck right here and damn the consequences."

Her mouth frowned, though her eyes still danced with merciless triumph. "The boy is an innocent, Lord Oswhent. Even if I were somehow able to reach him, he would have nothing to fear from me. Besides, nature has devised a more painful end for him than I ever could."

"Well, nature will have to deal with being thwarted this time," Varalen said. "And Elgar will use that power of his for at least one good thing."

"No," she said. "He won't."

Varalen raised an eyebrow. "Oh? Have you had such deep discussions with him that you profess to know his heart?"

She laughed, a little weakly. "Ah, you're right. I misspoke. I should've said: he can't."

Varalen felt his heartbeat pick up speed, slamming painfully against his ribs, the first prickle of sweat on the back of his neck, under the heavy heat of his long hair. But he made himself be still. "I saw Elgar heal with my own eyes. I know it's within his—"

"Yes, of course it is," Lady Margraine said. "And if your son had almost any other illness, no doubt Elgar would be as good as his word. But if you have truly read all extant research on the great wasting illness, you must know that it cannot be transmitted from person to person, nor is it something that forms in the body over time. The only way to contract the great wasting illness is to be *born* with it. And therein lies the problem."

She must have known he could not speak, not to deny her words, not even to ask for clarification. But she provided it anyway. "Healing magic restores things to their proper state. How to say it so you understand . . . ah. Surely you remember Kelken? If those legs of his were bleeding, broken, even cut off entirely, magic could repair them. But a healer's gift could never alter them to work like yours and mine, simply because that is what some people would consider proper. His legs are already in their proper state. And so it is with your son. He was born with a body destined to deteriorate by its very nature. The only way to save him would be to make him a new body entirely and somehow transfer his consciousness into it. And there is no mage who has ever succeeded at that, even in magic's heyday. Elgar can't do it. What's more, he knows he can't do it. But that doesn't matter to him, because he also knows that by the time you learn the truth, he'll already be victorious, and he can do with you as he pleases."

He would have thought the smugness would come back, some vindictive delight at her victory. Instead, she showed him the full scope of her anger for the first time. He had only seen that brutally cold, deathly serious fury once before, when Elgar had mocked her scars at Mist's Edge. This was worse.

"You were the one who took pleasure in outwitting me," she said, as if reprimanding him for his thoughts. "I don't do this for *fun*. I believe the truth should be known, but, more than that, it was because of me that Seren suffered, just as much as because of you. So it was my responsibility to make you pay for it. I am absolutely certain of this, Lord Oswhent: all your efforts and all your schemes and every repulsive thing you did on his behalf because you told yourself it would be worth it when your son was whole . . . all of that, all of it, has been for nothing. Your son will die a protracted, miserable, incredibly painful death, decades before his time. And there is no force on this earth that can save him from that fate." She shrugged. "You would have found out eventually. I just had to make sure you found out from me."

Varalen's bodily functions felt disconnected from each other. He knew he breathed, for he could hear and feel his breath; he knew he stood, because his feet did not give way. But his vision clouded, and his head whirled, and his voice was dead in his throat. She wasn't lying. A lie like that could be easily found out, destroyed by a single word from Elgar. She would only have said such a thing if she knew that all Elgar could do was confirm it.

He opened his mouth, but only silence came out, pierced by the rapping of knuckles against wood. "Lord Oswhent! Is everything all right in there?"

The guards Elgar had promised to send, no doubt, though they had failed to prevent the marquise from doing him harm. Varalen almost opened the door, flung the keys into their faces, and told them to take care of things themselves. What more could Elgar do to him? He'd probably been planning on killing Varalen after the war anyway, when he found out Elgar couldn't make good on his promise—or else he truly believed that Varalen could be pacified some other way. And if Ryam's suffering was truly inescapable, perhaps it would be better for him to meet his end at a single stroke, rather than a thousand cuts.

Even he didn't know why he unlocked the marquise's chain anyway, why he opened the door and followed the soldiers out. Perhaps it was because he'd been on this path for so long, it took less effort to follow it to its conclusion than it would have to turn and walk the other way. Perhaps there was still some tiny part of him that hoped Elgar would reveal some healing method even the marquise hadn't thought of, clear up some terrible misunderstanding. Perhaps he was simply too exhausted to do anything else.

Lady Margraine walked past him to keep up with the soldiers, shaking her head once, as if in disappointment.

Seeing Elgar again was like a blow, everything about him so unchanged—to think they'd parted a handful of minutes ago!—when everything within Varalen had shifted. He smiled, and clasped Varalen's shoulder, and Varalen's stomach roiled at the thought that Elgar had been able to create this feeling in him, this idea that they were on the same side, helping each other in some reciprocal way, *partners,* and not one man draining another dry and casting him out. He had seen that so clearly, once. He'd known who and what Elgar was. And yet, somehow . . .

"It's time to leave, everyone," Elgar said, casting a contented smile over the group at large. To the guards: "Make sure she doesn't make some final effort." To Varalen: "You are about to be praised to the entire city, you know. You could try to enjoy it at least a little."

Does he give me this to make up for his inability to save Ryam's life? Varalen thought dully. *Does he think if he gives me this empty spectacle, it will somehow soften the blow? That when he tells me the truth,* this *will make me forgive him?*

For Arianrod Margraine, Elgar spared less than a look, as if she'd already ceased to be real to him. But she kept watching him for a moment or two after he turned away, scrutinizing the lines of his form. And then she turned to Varalen. She was dirt-smeared, half-starved, bound and chained and disgraced in ways she must once have thought unimaginable, and yet that woman met his gaze and smiled. "Remember what I told you, Lord Oswhent."

BY THE TIME Roger got there, Speaker's Square was packed with people, a slavering crowd that made him sick to his stomach. All his pushing and shoving was to no avail, so he wound up more than halfway to the back of the square, nearly crushed to death. Elgar couldn't hold the promised execution from his accustomed balcony—it wasn't large enough for the level of spectacle he had in mind—so he'd had a raised wooden platform built at the front of the square, about the height of Roger's chest, leaving even less space for spectators. But the platform was otherwise bare: no pillory, no hangman's noose, nothing to give any hint of what punishment he had devised for the marquise of Esthrades, save for the loss of her life.

Roger felt sorry for it, in a way; that, more than anything else, was the reason he was here. The resistance would have stopped it if they could, but Marceline had told him they'd decided they lacked the strength to intervene. It was a shame, given all the marquise had done against Elgar in the past, but they couldn't put the entire resistance in danger on her account. But Roger thought it would be all right if he attended—not to cause trouble, just to see for himself what would happen. Even Len couldn't have begrudged him that.

As trumpets announced their arrival, a line of guardsmen with steel-tipped spears forced the crowd to draw back from the platform, pushing them closer together and increasing the strain on Roger's ribs. They created a circle of empty space for their master to walk through, dragging his captive after him as he mounted the platform. Roger was so far away he could only see the people in front as distant shapes; he couldn't examine the marquise's features or read her expression, so his impression was merely of a thin and drawn woman in worn clothes. He thought she might have been tall, but it was hard to tell; she'd no sooner gained the platform than Elgar forced her to her knees.

Then another figure mounted the platform, and Roger caught his breath. Even from so far away, he'd have known Len's profile anywhere. The guards closed ranks after him, leaving him to take his place at Elgar's side. If he was the only one granted such an honor, then he really must have been as important to Elgar as he'd implied. But he didn't look fierce or grave or determined or whatever a victorious commander should look like when being honored for his deeds; he looked like he was sleepwalking, like he was only half there. Like he'd gotten turned around somewhere, and now he didn't know where he was. What had happened between the last time Roger had seen him and now?

"My people," Elgar began, with that way he had of addressing a crowd, making his voice carry without seeming to shout. "I promised you this day would come, and here it is. I told you that you would see the witch for yourselves, so I have brought her before you. But I did not do so simply to satisfy a demand for blood and vengeance. I mean to show my people what we can overcome."

The marquise's arms were bound behind her back, and Elgar slipped one of his own arms under them, wrenching them toward him. With his other hand, he drew the knife that was always hanging from his belt. "That you may not distrust what I have shown you, you may see the blood flow from the witch's own body."

He cut across her upper arm—Roger could not see how deeply, just that red bloomed over her skin. Elgar caught it in a small bottle of clear glass, filling it up until it gleamed from a distance like the facets of a ruby. "You've seen the effects of vardrath steel upon her blood already, so I won't demonstrate them again now." He couldn't, he meant; he couldn't hold vardrath steel in his own hand, nor cast any spell on her blood while the steel was touching it. "Its only purpose was to prove that she is a witch, in any case. Now, let me show you not only that she is a witch, but that I have learned a way to control her."

He held the bottle high, muttering a few words under his breath repeatedly—nonsense, no doubt. A faint sheen glimmered around the outside of the bottle, like stored sunlight, and the marquise squeezed her eyes shut in pain, curling over on herself, her shoulders shaking. She twisted back and forth, as if trying to throw off a great burden, but to no avail; her shaking only grew worse. "You see?" Elgar said, quickly wiping a trace of sweat from his brow. "I will not tell you she is not to be feared. But just as our ancestors were not defenseless, we need not be, either."

Roger was an expert in brazen lies, but even he was affronted by the size of the one Elgar was coaxing his people to swallow. Couldn't they see he was using a spell of his own, poorly disguised as . . . what, some sort of chant? How was using magic to fight magic comforting?

But the murmurs proliferating around him were approving, even admiring. How he wished people weren't so easy to fool when it was something they already wanted to believe. And they wanted to believe their leader could make them safe. They wanted to believe any threats to their livelihood were that easy to identify, and that easy to destroy.

"But perhaps," Elgar said, walking around the marquise in a slow circle, though his eyes remained on the crowd, "you will come up with a way to deny this, too. Do not think I am unaware of the fears that plague this city, the doubts that would lead you to cast aside help when it is placed into your very hands. Perhaps some among you will mutter behind my back that my captive and I must have devised some scheme to trick you, that perhaps I have offered her mercy if she pretends to be subject to my control. If you knew her as I do, you would know her pride would never permit her to make such a bargain, but I cannot expect you to take my word for it. Look upon her as you wish. See how little she wishes to kneel, how little she is able to hide the pain brought on by my control."

The crowd surged forward, unable to climb up to the platform, but filling the space before it, as much as the guards would allow. Roger was too far back to get much closer, so he wasn't sure what those at the front were seeing. They were certainly shouting, but he couldn't make it out.

Elgar stroked his beard—no doubt pretending to be in thought, when he was actually moving through a series of steps he'd rehearsed beforehand. "There is perhaps one way," he said. "One final test. I hesitated to use it not because it is in any way dangerous, but because it seemed a . . . distasteful thing to inflict upon an already beaten foe. But I had a chance to meet with this woman once, back when she still thought herself a queen. Throughout all our interactions, there was but one thing that aroused her anger and shame: an offhand remark I made concerning the scars her people say line her back, the remnants of her father's great anger from long ago. To be honest, I had thought it merely a legend. But her reaction was such that I knew it could only be real."

Roger could not see the marquise's mouth as anything more than a smudge from this distance, but he noted that she had gone very still. He doubted Elgar was bluffing about this—or that the "offhand remark" he mentioned had been offhand, or innocent, at all.

"What do you say?" Elgar asked the crowd. "Surely this is the last thing her pride would ever permit, not for any price. Look how she seethes even now at the very mention of it! Shall I show these scars to you, in full safety from the terrible retribution of her magic?"

"Gods," Roger muttered. "And you're just going to stand there, Len, aren't you? Aren't you, you coward? How many times in our childhood did I have to listen to you rant about the moral differences between you and me?"

Some members of the crowd looked as sick to their stomachs as Roger felt; some backed away, or made to leave. Some looked uncertain or afraid; some were stoic, simply watching how events played out. But all of those people were silent. The rest of them roared, thundering their affirmation to all four corners of the square. They wanted to behold the sorceress's greatest shame. And then they wanted to see her perish.

Roger would have paid every copper he possessed to avoid seeing either. But there was no gambit he could use, no stirring speech or sleight of hand that could set her free. So he stood there and determined to bear witness, for that was all that was left to him.

VARALEN BOTH WAS and wasn't aware of events unfolding around him. He had always prided himself on his clear-headedness and force of intellect; he had been a planner long before he became a strategist. And now it was as if his utter lack of planning, his complete inability to see a way forward for himself, had hollowed out all that calculation into a vast emptiness. A hole in his head, to match the hole in his heart. In the face of that emptiness, every sight and sensation seemed slow and immense, penetrating through to the depths of his consciousness without drawing any response, like stones thrown down a bottomless well. The chill moisture of the air made his skin prickle and sweat in equal measure. He heard the shouts of the crowd, and idly and half-heartedly tried to pick out individual voices from the chaos. He could make out the deep blue-black of Elgar's clothing, the pale fall of Arianrod Margraine's hair . . . he understood what was happening, but the significance eluded him. There was nothing he could do, nothing he could change. Whether Elgar one day came to rule this land, whether he decided to honor Varalen or kill him, whether they were both overcome and slain by the Issamiri or kept in some prison somewhere . . . he felt no emotion at any of these possibilities. He wondered, in some dim corner of his mind, whether this blankness was momentary, a passing result of shock, or whether he would struggle to feel anything ever again.

But as he floated in too much sensation and too little meaning, at last he saw something that broke through the layers of his apathy enough to trouble him. Something he had heard about, but never thought he'd see. Something he *shouldn't* be seeing. The bare skin of Arianrod Margraine's upper back, and the slender silver lines that crisscrossed one another all over it.

He started out of his stupor, scanning the crowd and the platform to get his bearings. Elgar had the marquise's hair in one fist, the vial of her blood held high in the other. He was holding her hair aside so the onlookers could have no doubt about what they were seeing. The rags he had her in weren't the sturdiest to begin with, and had ripped easily, but at least he'd taken care to only make a small tear, and not strip the woman to the waist in front of a mob.

Perhaps, in this moment, when its taste for blood was up, the crowd would approve of Elgar's actions, or even egg him on. But the events of the day would be repeated over and over, not amidst screaming mobs but in taverns, drawing rooms, kitchens. In the sober telling of it, it would be difficult to find sympathy for Elgar, and difficult not to find it for the tormented marquise, even if she was an enemy. Elgar might succeed in persuading the people that his control over her was real, and that they should trust his methods. But he'd only gain in their esteem as much as he lost, by showing himself so eager to debase a conquered foe.

He didn't know why he acted. Elgar's success or failure, in public opinion or otherwise, meant less than nothing to him. The blankness within him prevented him from feeling true rage and hate, the burning desire for revenge that might have caused him to come up with a plan of sabotage, or even just to delight in realizing Elgar was making a mistake. But perhaps the routine of pulling the man he was forced to serve back from his worst impulses had become reflexive. Or perhaps he simply didn't wish this vulgar show to continue, while he had to stand here as if he were part of it.

Whatever the reason, he moved almost before he realized it. Three long strides put him within Elgar's reach, and then he placed a hand on his forearm, grip too weak to truly restrain him. Elgar glanced back at him in surprise, arm lifting and head turning slightly. He did not speak, but the irritation in his eyes conveyed both the question and its tone perfectly: *What the hell is it, Varalen?*

"You're in excess," Varalen said, not caring how loud his voice was or who did or didn't hear it. "You'll only appear garish now, the more this goes on. Have you truly not realized that?"

Elgar waved impatiently at the crowd. "Is that what you see out there? Do you think they want restraint? They've lived in fear of this one for ages, and now I'm granting them the ability to put that fear to rest forever. What they want is a show."

"Oh, they'll get one," someone said quietly—Arianrod Margraine, whom Varalen had forgotten at Elgar's feet. She delicately extracted her hair from his fist, as if he'd grabbed it without thinking and she wanted to spare him the embarrassment. "At long last." With no further warning than that, she worked two fingers into the space between the inside of the collar and the skin of her neck, and gave one good sharp pull.

The collar sloughed off as if it had been made of dust, flaking into pieces that littered the platform around her. From this angle, Varalen could see the true state of the weapon he'd thought had rendered her impotent: the outside of the collar maintained the thinnest layer of its former glimmering sheen, but the rest of it was dull and tarnished all the way down. How could that be possible? How could she have overcome this, after what Edith Selwyn had achieved with the same steel in Lanvaldis, after Elgar himself had confirmed its effects?

Perhaps similar thoughts had stunned Elgar as well, but he recovered faster.

He raised the vial over her, but Lady Margraine laughed, a harsh, rasping sound. "You really seek to control a mage with her own blood? Do you know nothing?"

The vial shattered, the liquid it had contained spattering Elgar's face and neck. A few stray drops landed on Varalen's left sleeve, staining the cloth a darker red and just dampening the skin beneath.

In that first moment, he thought she meant to cut Elgar with the broken glass. She'd managed a couple shallow slices to his cheeks, but the vial was so small there wasn't much to work with. But as Elgar staggered back, the blood on his face began to darken and smoke, spreading across his skin like a bruise. When he put a hand to his face, the stain spread to his fingers; he snatched them away, but it was too late. It overtook half his face, the top of his neck, three fingers, and a sliver of his palm before the edges of the discoloration started to shimmer; was Elgar fighting it with his own magic?

That was when the pain in Varalen's arm became so urgent that it pierced through even his shock, and with a jolt of horror, he remembered the drops that had fallen onto his sleeve. He ripped the ruined cloth free with his right hand— and screamed as his skin came away with it, stuck to the cloth like melted wax. Underneath, his flesh was raw and scabrous, burning with pain, as if fire ran in his veins instead of blood. But no, it wasn't fire: *I'll turn the blood in your veins to poison,* Arianrod Margraine had said. *I will obliterate you along with your master.*

That was what she had wished him to remember. That she did not bluff.

Elgar was still staggering around the platform, forcibly holding his hands away from his body so as not to spread the contagion, screaming as he fought its effects on his face, where most of her blood had landed. The skin bubbled and popped like hot tar, melting and reforming and melting again, one mage's power warring with another's. One eyeball burst in its socket, wrenching a gasp from the stunned and terrified crowd, kept in place only by Quentin and his men. Surely they could fix this, Varalen thought desperately. She was one unarmed woman. All someone had to do, anyone, was draw near and slit her throat.

Though his vision was starting to swim, he could still see her clearly. Her body was curled in a semicircle on the platform, her hands clenched into fists. He knew what her expression meant: those fierce eyes, the gritted teeth. She was a pred- ator who'd gotten her jaws around the prize. She would hold on until it killed her.

Varalen meant to do just that, but his legs wouldn't work properly. When he tried to take a step, he fell to his knees instead, the pain of the impact a distant echo compared to the acidic burning of his own skin, the relentless creep of the corrup- tion, taking him apart bit by bit. If someone cut his arm off now, could they save him? Did he dare ask?

He couldn't tell who was screaming anymore, him or Elgar, or if perhaps the spell had melded them together, merged them into one great beast that howled its protestations into the encroaching black—

TRY AS HE might, Roger couldn't get an inch closer to the platform. The members of the erstwhile mob, panicked by such a display of power from an enemy they had been assured was powerless, were trying their best to disperse, like rats scurrying back to their holes. The captain, desperate to prevent the injuries that would surely result from a stampede, had ordered his guards to encircle the crowd and hold them still. No one, guard or onlooker, had yet dared to climb onto the platform where Elgar and Len screamed in agony. Elgar was still standing, but Len had collapsed on the planks, limbs jerking in repeated spasms. Roger couldn't tell if he was conscious. The marquise lay between them, not speaking a word or making a single movement, intent on the devastation she was causing. Though Roger was no longer too stunned to move, he had no idea what on earth he could do, or who he could do it for: Len? The marquise? Himself?

But there was one in the crowd who did not share his trepidation. A figure moved ahead of him, struggling toward the platform. Though she must have been crushed by the same press of bodies as Roger, she still slipped inexorably forward, like water seeping through cracks. Her copper hair glinted in the sunlight like a beacon.

She moved with such singular purpose that her destination must have been clear, to Quentin and his men as well as Roger. When he saw how many of them stood between her and her goal, he thought she'd never have a chance. But that was before the soldiers tried to close in on her.

They began to advance through the crowd in a semicircle, no doubt hoping to block her path forward and then complete the circle behind her. But at their approach, she did not break into a sprint, as Roger would've tried to do. She didn't change pace or direction, and only paused to shrug off the hand of a spectator who'd tried to grab her as she went by. But when she drew within a couple yards of the soldiers, she seemed to switch places with a man standing to her left, and he suddenly lost his footing, sprawling across a trio of others and taking one down with him. The crowd stirred with agitation, like reeds bending in the breeze, but the people closest to the fallen citizens stood well back to keep them from being trampled until they could stand up. The soldiers had to keep their distance, too, circling around those who had fallen while keeping their eyes on the original woman.

Many more people tried to lay hands on her now, but though Roger never saw her lash out at them, and she never drew a weapon, not a single one ever achieved more than a momentary fistful of her clothing. Some she simply evaded; some she tripped up, rearranging the crowd at her whim and leaving carefully controlled disorder in her wake for the soldiers to avoid. They were probably realizing that spears were an excellent weapon for corralling an unruly crowd, but they were terrible at hitting one single person within that crowd, provided you weren't allowed to hit anybody else. The woman didn't have to hurt the guards or the civilians; she just had to ensure they stayed in each other's way. Some of the spectators seemed to have realized that as well, and they struggled out of her path, wary of being skewered by a misaiming spearman or thrown to the ground to be stepped on.

But the rising panic of individuals within it inflamed the crowd as a whole, and they surged against the guards with renewed force, trying desperately to disperse. Though Roger only sought to keep still and upright, even he was unnerved by the jostling all around him. *"Hold!"* the captain shouted to his men—a plea for restraint, not a show of force. Despite Elgar's plight, the captain was prioritizing the safety of the crowd over that of his master, unwilling to pursue the woman too aggressively if it meant causing a massacre or a stampede.

But then, as she gained the very shadow of the platform, one guard saw his chance. Everyone who wasn't armed had drawn back from the disastrously botched execution, and when the woman stepped forward into that gap, there was enough space, finally, for him to let loose with a full thrust, sending the spear as far forward as it would go.

As quickly as he'd moved, as flawless as his form was, he was attacking someone who was no longer there. The moment he'd stepped forward to lunge, the woman sprang into the air, gaining a truly impressive height, and the spear point, aimed at her stomach, whistled past beneath the soles of her feet. But she had to come down, and now there was a spear shaft where she needed to stand. Roger couldn't see how she wouldn't end up tangled around the thing.

But that wasn't what happened, either. As she descended, one foot landed on the shaft of the spear, weight balanced for a fraction of an instant; the other struck the shoulder of the guard who held it and stuck there for a breath longer. And from there she vaulted onto the platform itself, where Elgar and Len were still screaming in the grip of whatever the marquise had done to them. Despite the horrifying sight they made, the woman paid them no mind. She was at the marquise's side in two strides, threading one arm under hers to help her to her feet.

And then they disappeared.

Chapter Forty

Valyanrend

"Seren, run!" Arianrod's voice rang clear and vital over the receding shouts of the guards, the pounding of feet against the cobblestones, the pressure of Seren's heartbeat in her ears. "Don't slow down! Just get to somewhere we can hide!"

She would have been happy to run as fast as she could, but it was Arianrod who was slowing them down, so much so that Seren was practically dragging her along. Her relief at seeing her again was marred by heartache at the state of her, so thin and pale, what passed for her clothing dirty and torn. But she had planned for the possibility that Arianrod might be weakened or injured. The entrance to the tunnels was so close; she just had to take enough turns to leave the guards behind. If the two of them were spotted at the entrance, they would never make it out.

Yet that seemed strangely easier than she had imagined. She risked a glance over her shoulder, but saw no pursuers. Could she and Arianrod possibly have shaken them off that quickly? Surely they could run fast enough to keep pace?

She didn't have time to think about it. The entrance was a single turn away, and they were out of sight. It would be all right. They would make it.

Arianrod tripped as they descended the cellar stairs, catching herself on Seren's arm. "What's down here?"

"A place to hide, like you said. And much more. We've just got to get this door open." She let Arianrod lean on her while she fumbled with the latch, then quickly pulled her through, shutting it behind them. The flare of torchlight dazzled her for a moment after the darkness of the cellar, but it was another comfort. She had already memorized the way.

Even racked by exhaustion, Arianrod wouldn't have been Arianrod if the sight of the tunnels hadn't aroused her curiosity. "Do these go all the way through the city? They can't be common knowledge."

"They definitely aren't, but you have admired my resourcefulness in the past, my lady. And they do go through the city, or most of it."

"Do you know where you're going down here? Do you have a way out?"

"Yes," Seren said, to both questions. "There's one passage that goes under Valyanrend's walls, and comes out aboveground on the other side. We'll make it to the Issamiri army, and everything will be fine."

"You really did think of everything, didn't you? Outside the city . . . just like that day, only . . ."

The lack of pursuit and the extreme unlikelihood of being found here had finally given Seren the chance to take more detailed stock of her surroundings. For the first time, she noticed something strange. Though she was no longer running, Arianrod's panting breaths were coming faster, not slower, as if she were still in the throes of exertion. "What's wrong?" she asked. "Are you in pain?"

Arianrod winced, pressing a hand to her chest. "It does . . . hurt, somewhat. It's all catching up to me now. Creating such a reaction—like the one Adora and I read about—it was no simple thing. I had to burn such a mass of power . . . and then to keep fighting him . . ." She shook her head. "I'd thought I would just . . . die there, drag him down with me, but then . . . there you were. Finally paying back your mythical debt so poetically."

She broke off, overcome by a noise so hoarse it took Seren a moment to recognize it. "Why are you laughing?"

Arianrod leaned against the wall, but still her breathing was more labored, still growing faster. "I just thought, can you imagine? Two people both get sentenced to death, fifteen years apart, and foil each other's executions? I'd say you and I have got to stop living so dangerously, but . . ." She sagged into the stone, giving it more of her weight. "Gods, even . . . that same spell . . ."

And then Seren understood. That was why no one had followed them in their desperate flight from the scaffold. It had seemed preposterous that they had managed to outrun the guards, but they hadn't needed to. Arianrod had veiled them both from detection, just as she had the day she'd first saved Seren's life. To the onlookers, they must simply have disappeared.

Arianrod shifted, slipping down against the wall, and then Seren saw it: she tried to clutch at the stone to steady herself, but her fingers were too weak even for an action as simple as that. They fluttered ineffectually, unable to grip.

I think this is as far as I can go, the girl of ten had said, with the same melancholy, almost rueful smile, the same ink stains on her smaller fingers.

"No," Seren said. "No. What did you do?"

Arianrod just laughed, though Seren knew she couldn't spare the breath to do it. "It's not as if you left me a lot of options, charging up there the way you did. I can't even say for sure if Elgar's going to die now, because I had to use the last bit of power I had to get us off the platform without being skewered."

Seren's heart felt like there was a fist around it. "To protect me. You did it to protect me. Again."

"Well, to protect us both, of course. Don't look so aghast." They stared at each other in silence for a moment, and then Arianrod closed her eyes. "Seren. Come on. It's no fun at all if you look at me like that."

How could she still talk like this? Seren had planned out everything, everything but this. "What can we do? How can I help you?"

Arianrod's eyes fluttered half-open. "I . . . don't know, to be honest. In the past, I would simply rest until I felt better, but . . . I don't think that's going to be an option this time."

She shifted against the wall again, trying to push herself higher, but instead her legs buckled beneath her. Seren rushed to catch her, and Arianrod landed heavily against her arms, incapable of slowing her own fall even a little. Seren eased her to the ground, keeping her upper body supported, and realized in despair how light and insubstantial she felt, as if she were crumbling away. "Please," she said. "You have to tell me what to do. I can't come up with plans like you can, I—I've tried and tried, but it always ends with you hurting yourself to save me, and I can't—"

Arianrod shook her head with a sharp jerk, her cheek brushing weakly against Seren's arm. "Seren, don't. Isn't this enough? Haven't I asked enough of you already?"

"What do you mean?"

Arianrod swallowed once, then twice, still, *still* unable to catch her breath. "I . . . never knew how to fix it. The more I tried to give you the freedom to do as you willed, the more you subjected yourself to all my goals, instead of seeking your own. If I couldn't convince you, after all this time, that I wanted a person and not a tool, at least I should've been able to . . . give you some piece of what you always sought from me." Her eyes clenched shut, and she seemed to force them open again with difficulty. "You thought I didn't understand, but I do. The kind of words you wanted most to hear, that I've never known how to say. Kindness, or tenderness . . . you deserve that. You must know it."

She probably meant it to be comforting, to offer some kind of acknowledgment. But all Seren felt was fear, because she knew Arianrod would only admit such things if she was certain this was the end.

She held Arianrod close to her chest, as if she could prevent her from slipping away. "I don't need any of those things. I don't care about those things. Just, Arianrod, please get up, please don't—" Her voice caught in her throat on something dangerously like a sob, and she struggled to speak past it. "You can't leave me with all these people I can't understand, who could never understand me. No one could ever get as close to me as you. If I have to be alone like that again . . . anything but that. Please, Arianrod, anything but that."

Arianrod strained to lift one hand, as if to cup Seren's cheek, but it fell limp before crossing even half the distance. "I'm so sorry," she said, and she sounded it, as Seren had never heard her before. "I wish I could—"

"You can do anything," Seren insisted. "You told me that. You can do anything you want."

Arianrod's lips curved weakly in the flickering torchlight. This must be what sadness looked like on her, the only smile Seren had ever seen that did not reach her eyes. "I say so many things, Seren. Why do you always remember the most embarrassing ones?"

"You have to," Seren said. "You have to get up, because if you don't leave this place, I won't ever be able to, either."

Arianrod winced, and when her eyes shut, this time they fluttered, but didn't open again. "That isn't fair."

"I don't care about that, either. When has anything ever been fair?" She gritted her teeth to keep her voice from going shrill, and pressed her forehead to Arianrod's, proving to herself that she was still warm. She was still here, still breathing. "Try," she said. "Just try. For me. Because I'm asking you."

In the silence that followed, Seren squeezed her eyes shut. Arianrod's breathing grew so faint that, even as close as they were, she couldn't tell if it was still there, or if she only wanted to imagine that it was. She couldn't bear to open her eyes, in case they would tell her that Arianrod had already gone. She would just stay like this, she told herself. As long as she could feel the warmth of Arianrod's skin against hers, she could still hope. And if it ever faded, she would never need to do anything again.

But then she did hear something, loud enough that she couldn't have imagined it: a sigh. "I suppose you're right about one thing. Lying down for death just isn't like me. But . . . Seren, I can't move my legs. I can't even feel them."

"That's fine. That doesn't matter. I can carry you." She was more or less carrying her already, so she carefully got to her feet. With the torches blazing along the path, she didn't need to feel her way, and there shouldn't be any need to fight down here. She would get them out of the city, to the Issamiri army, and then . . . something. As long as they kept going, as long as they were still together, there had to be something.

She put one foot in front of the other.

"OH GODS, WHAT now?" Morgan asked. It was Roger in the doorway, as disheveled as Marceline had ever seen him; he looked like he'd barely escaped a stampede, hair plastered every which way and one shirtsleeve torn. At least, what with all the excitement in the city, they were the only three people in the Dragon's Head; this was clearly not going to be a conversation just anyone could overhear.

"I need you two to round up your resistance friends, as quickly as possible," Roger said, as soon as he'd drawn a full breath. "The marquise escaped her execution. Every guard in the city's going to be looking for her, and we've got to find her first."

Morgan buried her face in her palm with a groan. "So it's going to be one of those days."

"I don't understand," Marceline said to Roger. "I thought everyone decided the marquise wasn't their concern."

"Aye, when the work of rescuing her fell on *us*. But now that she's freed herself, we'd be fools to let her drop right back into their clutches. You should've *seen* the spell she loosed on Elgar and Len, Morgan. Damn, but *that's* magic, not Elgar's little trinkets." He paused, mouth twisting. "Oh. Also, Len might be dead. I'd rather not deal with that at the moment, so pour me some ale, please."

"You're not getting so much as a drop of water until this is resolved to my satisfaction," Morgan said. "Is *Elgar* dead?"

Roger laughed. "That'd be convenient, wouldn't it? But I doubt we'll have such luck. His people carted him off afterward, and he was definitely moving. Won't be very happy the next time he looks in a mirror, though."

"The whole thing will have rebounded on him, then," Marceline said. "He staged that performance with such care, all to show the people the extent of his control over her, and instead she attacked him and fled. If the people weren't worried she was too strong for him before, I can't imagine they aren't now."

"Oh, aye, that's inevitable, with the way she hurt him. I'm telling you, you should've seen it. I can't imagine what'll be harder to fix—his face or his reputation."

"And what about her?" Morgan asked. "How the hell did she get away from that many guards? And what about the vardrath steel?"

Roger's grin faded a bit. "Well, that's the thing. As far as I can tell, she . . . broke the steel. Tore the collar from her neck with her bare hands, and it just crumbled away. Which is rather alarming, because we all thought that wasn't possible. Even Elgar was caught completely off guard. As for what happened after, she had a compatriot in the crowd. I thought the woman was going to try to fight the guards for her, but instead they just vanished. I couldn't tell you whether they only hid themselves from view or actually went somewhere else, but I couldn't track them either way. Neither can any of the guards; they're in an absolute uproar. And I don't think Elgar or my traitorous cousin are conscious enough to give them orders. That's why I came straight here, so we wouldn't miss this chance."

Those were some tough revelations to digest. Morgan recovered first, clutching the hilt of her dagger. "She destroyed the steel? She didn't just cast in spite of it, she physically ruined it?"

"Aye. Completely. And before you ask, I haven't the faintest idea how she did it. I'm as good as anyone at sleight of hand, but that was no trick." He shrugged. "Another reason we need to be the ones to find her, I suppose. Though if she doesn't want to be found, I'd hate to run afoul of either of them, let alone both together."

Marceline had been half distracted, wondering what Naishe would say. "Either of what?"

"The marquise or her associate. Absurdly agile woman, appeared out of practically nowhere. No one in the crowd could lay a finger on her. I don't even know where she came from, but since the city's been closed off, she must have arrived in Valyanrend before then."

Marceline had an acute suspicion she knew more than a little about this woman, but before she could ask for more details, Morgan smacked herself in the forehead. "Oh gods, the city! It was supposed to open up again after the execution! What the hell's going to happen now?"

"Well, like I said, Elgar and Len aren't in any state to give orders. I can't imagine any of the gates will be opened before at least one of them regains consciousness."

"But what if they don't?" Morgan insisted. "What if they both die of their wounds?"

"Then we'll have chaos," Roger said, matter-of-factly. "And we'll have many, many more problems to worry about than whether the gates are open or shut. Although I'll point out that Elgar's death has been rather the point, so a certain amount of chaos is inevitable."

Marceline shook her head. "I think most of us would take Elgar's death any way we could get it, but the advantage of having the resistance do it is that they could take charge of things afterward, at least in the beginning. Without them, we run the risk of one of Elgar's subordinates taking over, the way Norverian did after Gerde Selte died. True, that subordinate wouldn't be a mage, but I'd still rather not face that situation if we don't have to."

Morgan did not look in any way mollified. "I don't truly like the idea of handing power to anyone—even Naishe, and I'm pretty sure I like her. Do you even know what she'd do with it if she did get it?"

"Naishe has a plan," Marceline said brusquely, because she didn't want to admit she had never asked what that plan was. "And what else do you want us to do, run the place ourselves?" She took Morgan's silence as an end to that thread of discussion. "But Roger, there's something else I need to ask you. This woman who rescued the marquise—"

"I really can't tell you much more than I've said, monkey. Copper hair, fighter's build, spectacular ability to not get hit, didn't say a word."

Marceline didn't need to hear another word, either. She stood up. "I've got to go out."

"No you don't," Roger said. "Didn't you hear me? I need you to fetch as many of your resistance friends as possible, right now."

"Morgan can do that," Marceline said, already heading for the door. "I'm busy, and it can't wait."

"What the hell is more important than this?" Marceline couldn't answer that, so she didn't, and pressed on out the door. "Gods damn it, monkey, I'm talking to you!"

CHAPTER FORTY-ONE

Valyanrend

THEY MADE THREE turns before Arianrod reacted at all, three turns after long stretches of walking in silence, guided by Seren's memory and the flickering torchlight. She had to fight the urge to look down at Arianrod every moment, for fear that she might slip away between one step and the next. Her breathing was so soft it made no sound, or else was swallowed up by Seren's own. She knew from experience that the tunnels were long, but those first three turns still felt like they spanned a million miles.

Then, at the fourth turn, Arianrod moved.

Just as Seren stepped to the right, she raised her head as if it took all her strength to do it, and made a movement so slight Seren strained to recognize it: a shake of the head. "Go left," she said, in a whisper as fragile as glass.

Seren frowned. Arianrod had never been to the tunnels before, and it was doubtful she had known of them—had she not asked Seren, a handful of minutes ago, if she knew where she was going? "Did you not wish me to take the path out of the city? It's this way."

But Arianrod made that tiny twitch of the head again, even weaker than before. "Go left," she repeated—she who was so eloquent, who laughingly admitted to loving the sound of her own voice. "Ser—" But then even that whisper died in her throat, and she could say no more.

Seren took only a moment to choose. There were torches down both pathways, so she wouldn't be stumbling blindly. And even if they escaped the city, it wasn't as if she knew of anything out there that could do any good. If Arianrod wanted to wander down these tunnels forever, Seren would do it gladly, as long as it meant she would stay.

The next fork wasn't so lucky, the right lit with torches but the left pitch dark. Seren paused when she reached it, wondering if Arianrod would choose again—if she even could, with her voice so weak. But with only a slight clearing of her throat, she managed, "Right."

It was "left" at the next fork, and then "left" again—still in the torchlight, though Seren couldn't tell if that was coincidental or on purpose. The next turn had two lit pathways again, but this time Arianrod slung one arm around Seren's neck, anchoring herself, and stretched the other out into the empty space in front of them, as if reaching for something just beyond her grasp. "What *is* that? Seren, it's . . . right, this time."

And Seren still didn't understand, but her heart clenched with barely restrained hope, because not only had Arianrod moved both arms, her voice had sounded like her voice.

They walked without turning for a long stretch, Arianrod's hand still raised before them as if feeling for the wind, and the quality of the light ahead of them began to change. Once they got close enough, Seren saw that it was because the tunnels opened up into a wide, vaguely circular chamber, dotted with braziers all over. "Watch out," Arianrod said, before she could enter it, and Seren realized there was a step cut into the floor, the only one she'd ever seen in the tunnels. She carried Arianrod over the threshold, and found herself standing before a semicircle of nine statues of clearly sophisticated make. None of them meant anything to Seren, artistically or otherwise, but they must have had some significance, for these revolutionaries to bother lighting the way to them.

Arianrod said, "Seren, put me down."

Seren blinked, scanning the room for any spot that might possibly be suitable. "On the . . . floor?"

"On my feet." To prove it, she bent her knees, closing them around Seren's arm. "I might still need . . . assistance, but I think I can manage it."

"Already? How can that be?" She had never been this severely weakened before, and her previous close calls had taken her days to recover from.

Arianrod looked up at her, searching her face. "You really don't feel *anything*? I'm practically choking on it."

"On what?"

"Magic." She turned her outstretched hand in the air, as if examining something she had never seen before. "I can feel it seeping into my skin. I draw it in every time I breathe. I don't know how this is *possible*. Where is it all coming from?"

Seren could feel nothing, not even a draft. But even if she didn't already trust Arianrod, what else could be responsible for such a sudden change in her condition? "And this magic is . . . healing you? Replacing what you lost?"

"More the latter than the former, I think. I still feel like I've been trampled by a horse, but that's an improvement over barely being able to feel anything at all. Speaking of which, are you actually going to put me down, or have you become overfond of carrying me?"

"If I said yes, would you let me continue?" It took her a moment to realize she'd actually said the words aloud, and then it was all she could do not to audibly sputter.

But Arianrod just laughed. "Another time, perhaps. Unfortunately, this place so piques my curiosity that I must insist on being allowed to explore it on my own two feet. We shall have to hope they've recovered enough to carry me."

Seren eased her gently down, setting her on her feet and giving her her own weight a little bit at a time. She had to lean on Seren for a minute, taking in deep breaths of this miraculous air Seren couldn't feel, and then she was finally able to walk, slowly but steadily. She examined each of the nine statues in turn, bending low to read the characters carved into their bases.

"Are the statues doing . . . whatever it is?" Seren asked.

Arianrod shook her head. "If anything, I suspect it is the opposite—that the statues were built here because of the special nature of the place. As a way to mark it, perhaps, or to exalt the beings they depict."

"The beings they depict?"

"Old Lantian virtues." She waved a careless hand at them, starting with the woman on the far left. "*Asariel*: both wisdom and its pursuit, the passion for knowledge. *Tethantys,* usually translated as *ambition,* though it only means the determination to see one's dreams to fruition. And I think you heard Adora tell Cadfael about *Yaelor*: courage, but generally courage in some noble enterprise. And so forth." She walked over to the sixth statue, a ragged man offering a crust of bread in his outstretched hand. "Speaking of Adora, this would be her favorite. *Gilmarion*—compassion."

"Then surely Asariel must be your favorite," Seren said.

"Of this lot? I can't deny it. And yours would be . . ." She pointed at the seventh statue, a lutist with her instrument. "That one. *Telfair*."

"A musician? How do you make that leap?"

"That's not what it means. It's any craft, anything that takes great skill to master. The refinement of an art. Though most would consider your art unsavory, none could deny you have reached the pinnacle of it."

Seren considered her words, surveying each of the statues. Then she nodded at the fifth one, in the very center of the semicircle: a mother holding her sleeping child. "If they're all virtues, that one must be love, or something like it."

"I don't know that I would call love a virtue, but our distant ancestors clearly did," Arianrod said. "You're right, of course."

"Then it's that one," Seren said quietly. "That's the one for me."

Arianrod looked at the statue, and then at Seren, pursing her lips as if practicing words before she spoke them. "Seren," she said at last, "you don't have to stand on ceremony with me." Her best attempt, Seren knew, to offer her permission to say and do whatever she needed to.

But even given that permission, she could not bring herself to fully close the distance between them; if she clutched at Arianrod now, she was not sure if she could ever let her go. "You're really here," she said, part question and part statement. "You . . . aren't going to leave."

"The danger of that has passed. I'm sure of it." Seren thought that would be all. But then Arianrod moved, taking Seren's face in her hands. She held it as if it were dangerously breakable, though it was she who had felt that way only a handful of minutes ago. "Seren. You saved my life."

She swallowed before her voice could break. "No, I failed, I—"

"That isn't true. Listen. If even I could think of no way to save myself, I thought it was better to accept it than to struggle fruitlessly against it. But because I was too proud to fight for my life, I nearly lost it. Without you, I would have died mere steps from my salvation. What an ignominious end that would have been."

Seren felt herself trembling, too many emotions clamoring to be expressed. She was so used to shoving them down, but now she simply couldn't. She slipped her arms around Arianrod's neck, buried her face in her shoulder, trying to convince herself that this was real, not some dream she had fled into to escape the truth. She hadn't failed, and Arianrod wasn't gone. They had been given another chance.

She had been expecting Arianrod to step back, to disentangle herself from such cloying sentimentality. But instead, she wrapped one arm around Seren's shoulders, drawing her close and holding her there. Her other hand stroked Seren's hair, as if testing out the movement. "It's all right," she said. "I'm still here."

They had been close before, of course, but had Arianrod ever simply held her like this? Had anyone? "I'm sorry," she said, though she couldn't bring herself to move. "I know you wanted to examine the room."

"Those statues look like they've stood here for hundreds of years," Arianrod said. "I doubt they'll crumble to dust in the next ten minutes." She sighed against Seren's hair. "I know you must've been very frightened, and it would be absurd to expect you to recover from that so quickly. You don't have to pretend you're not upset."

And somehow, those felt like the kindest words anyone had ever said to her.

MARCELINE PELTED DOWN the tunnels as fast as she dared, taking the turns she knew by heart. The torches flickered reassuringly exactly where they should be, lighting all the right paths. She'd already turned onto the route she'd taught the woman to take, from the closest tunnel entrance to Speaker's Square to the one outside the walls. The woman had a head start, but the marquise would be slow, tired and weak from her imprisonment. That was the only chance Marceline had to catch up to them.

That said, she didn't know what she'd do if she found them; stopping to think about it would have meant letting them slip away. She was now even more certain that the woman hadn't been bluffing about her talents, and Marceline was no fighter; if she tried to delay them by force, she'd just get herself killed. But the woman had known her as an ally, and shouldn't attack her on sight. If Marceline could just talk to them . . .

She narrowly avoided tripping over a brazier. She'd what, convince them to stay in a city where they'd be in danger every moment, rather than running to their allies outside its walls? It sounded foolish even in her head, but she couldn't stop thinking about what Roger had said, how easily the marquise had wounded Elgar, even with his soldiers all around him. Even she couldn't strike at him from the other side of Valyanrend's walls, could she?

As she neared the end of the tunnel with no sign of them, Marceline swore under her breath. If only she'd asked more questions, weaseled enough out of the woman to guess the true nature of the prisoner she'd been so desperate to free. If she hadn't run into them by now, either they'd been able to move a lot faster than she'd expected, or they never made it out in the first place. She wasn't sure which option she preferred. If they'd joined the Issamiri, Elgar's greatest foe would be safe, but also permanently beyond her reach. But if they weren't in the tunnels and they weren't outside, they were probably dead.

Finally, she reached the lip of the tunnel entrance. The Issamiri were still massed in the south, and hadn't yet laid siege to the city, but she still shouldn't venture too far in that direction, lest they have some outlying scouts that could catch sight of her. She would just take a vantage from outside the entrance, and if the two of them were nowhere to be seen, she would give up and leave them to their fate, whatever it might be.

The view directly outside the tunnel, in the shadow of Valyanrend's walls, showed her nothing but empty plain, and a great line of tents erected at the edge of the forest in the distance. Damn. Perhaps the magic Roger had seen really had transported those two somewhere else, though if that had been the case, Marceline didn't know why that woman had gone to such effort securing an escape route.

She turned to go back the way she had come—and hit the ground hard as someone tackled her, leaning their knees against her shoulders and twisting her arms behind her back.

ARIANROD NEVER RUSHED her, but waited until she had settled, until her breathing and the beat of her heart had finally quieted down. Only then did she finally begin to explore the room, pacing a slow circuit of it, glancing from the floor to the faces of the statues and back again. She scuffed at the floor with one foot, but when she attempted to bend down to look at it she swayed on her feet, seizing gratefully on Seren's outstretched arm. "I suppose I haven't recovered as completely as I had hoped. Will you tell me if you see anything carved into the ground?"

Seren shifted the dust with her boot as well, but when she bent down, she saw nothing. "All I can make out is stone."

"Hmm. Well, I definitely see something, but it's quite faded. Perhaps it's like the power filling this room—one may need some facility with magic to see it."

"What is it?" Seren asked.

"I think it's more runic? But the runes on these statues are ones I know well, whereas the ones on the floor . . ." She kept moving around the room, turning her head this way and that as if the correct angle would reveal everything to her. "They're arranged in some kind of diagram or pattern, but the words . . . *confinement* but also *open, protection* but also *disarmed . . . weakened, healthy, possibility, forbidden . . .*" She put her hand out, tracing invisible lines in the air. "Just give me a moment. I feel I am so close to it."

It took her many moments, pacing back and forth and muttering to herself, but Seren was in no hurry, and only mourned the fact that she could do nothing to help. Then, just as she began to think Arianrod would wear a groove into the floor in the shape of this diagram she was puzzling over, she suddenly stopped, pulling herself up short in the center of the room. She snapped her fingers, but instead of smugness, her face showed intense shock. "Great gods."

"What on earth is it?"

Arianrod raked a hand through her hair, clenching her fingers around the strands as if she needed something to hold on to. "It's . . . what I have been searching for, after a fashion. But it's also proof of just how wrong I have been all this time. We were all wrong: Elgar and I, Jocelyn, and who knows how many other mages before us. We all made the same assumption—that the problem was within us, with mages themselves. We thought that mages must have come back weaker than we had been hundreds of years ago, that we were . . . maimed, damaged, imperfect somehow. But we are the same as we ever were. It is the world itself that has changed.

"I searched old books of magic in the hope they could tell me what I was doing wrong. But I didn't find it for the same reason I've never found any manuals on how to speak or walk—those long-ago mages could never have imagined it would ever *need* explaining." She smiled wryly. "When Adora and I were going through her library back in Eldren Cael, I found a journal in which an instructor of magic noted that his students kept having difficulty with their spells at the *end* of the day. And I was so preoccupied with the time, I didn't realize that the true problem was the environment. A large group of mages spent a full day casting spell after spell in the same place, and the magic in the world around them eventually grew thin, replenishing itself only while they slept. That was the answer to the riddle all along.

"We thought we had to reach within ourselves for the magic, to rely on that alone—we assumed that was what the mages of old had always done. But what they had actually done was reach *out*: into the world itself, dipping their fingers into a wellspring too deep to exhaust. Like this." She turned her hand over, and light flickered in her palm, a delicate dancing sphere.

Seren grabbed her wrist. "What are you doing? You're far too weak to—"

"That's just it. Like this, the spell costs me nothing. I need magic of my own only to forge the initial connection, and then the world's magic flows into me, far more than I could ever lose. This is how they did it, Seren. This is how it's supposed to be. We were each so proud of our little sparks, unaware that we stood in the ashes of a fire greater than anything we could have imagined."

She fell silent, and Seren leaned against her shoulder. She knew this was a moment of unrivaled importance, even emotion, for Arianrod, who had sought this answer for so long. But she still understood magic as little as she ever had, and was not sure what to say. "To go from the kind of wellspring you're talking about to the remnants of today . . . it's more than monumental. It's as if the world itself were turned on its head. What could possibly have caused it?"

"I couldn't say for sure, but the Curse might have played some role. We know it eats magic, and it's huge. The puzzling thing is, the Curse used to be growing, but now it's retreating. That implies that at one point, it was absorbing magic faster than the world could produce it, but now the reverse is true. We know *when* that change happened, but not why—with all due respect to Adora, I can't believe that the Rebel Queen simply brought magic back through an effort of will."

Seren scuffed at the floor, frustrated that she couldn't see whatever was drawn there. "And what does this have to do with it?"

Arianrod looked at the floor, too, but Seren knew she was tracing hidden runes with her eyes. "I think it's a spell. A truly immense one—it must have required more power to cast than I can fathom. Whoever conceived it was a true genius."

Seren knew she didn't use that word lightly for anyone except herself. "What does it do?"

"I'm still trying to figure that out, but I think I know the reason for all these contradictions in the runic. The spell's a sort of lock that can be opened or unopened at will."

"And is it open or closed right now?" Seren asked.

"That's the intriguing thing. It's open. The spell is inert."

"Then could the spell be to blame? For magic dying out, and its resurgence?"

Arianrod shook her head. "I don't think a single spell has the ability to do that, no matter how powerful the caster. If anything, I think this spell was put here *because* magic was dying. Once the dearth of power became too severe, it would become exhausting for mages to exist at all, even without casting any spells. You remember how Voltest and I felt on the Curse, with that yawning magical vacuum always pulling at us? I don't think it would have gotten quite that severe, but it might have been close. And yet there was never any outbreak of unexplained illness or fatigue, as might have been expected. I think this spell was meant to protect mages from that fate, to . . . cut them off from their magic somehow, until the world was safe for them again. It *is* safe now, with magic expanding, which is why the lock's open. But in all the generations since, mages forgot how to cast."

"But you can only cast like that in this room," Seren said. "Isn't that right?"

"Well, for the most part. Now that I know the trick, I can reach out to the world's magic in a limited way, but it won't be as effective as in here."

"So why is it different in here?"

"That's certainly the question. If the Curse is a force that pulls magic out, that implies there's another force that puts magic in. But that force isn't constant, and the Curse is. What could it be?"

She hadn't expected an answer, of course; if she couldn't solve it, there was no way Seren could. But a new voice slipped seamlessly into the silence at the end of her question, as if the three of them had been conversing together all along: "It's up to me to answer that, I think."

Seren leapt toward Arianrod, snatching a dagger free. There was a woman standing in the center of the semicircle of statues, and she hadn't been there a moment ago. At least she didn't look like a fighter: she had a tall and willowy frame, with almost spindly arms, and her pale hair was long and loose. But in a place full of so much magic, she wasn't about to take any chances.

The woman's eyes flicked to Seren, and she sighed. "Oh, Amerei's going to be so insufferable about this. I suppose I ought to thank you, though."

"Thank me?" Seren repeated.

The woman nodded at Arianrod. "For saving this one, so she could make it here. I don't know of any other mage with the intellect and the knowledge of Old Lantian required to decipher this spell."

Arianrod stepped up beside Seren, as if providing reinforcement. "If you know so much about it, wouldn't that mean you've already deciphered it?"

"In fact, I never needed to," the woman said. "I was simply there when it was made."

Arianrod swallowed that without surprise, though the spell must have been created centuries ago. "Well, drat. You're the missing piece, aren't you? I was hoping it wouldn't be something like this."

"Oh? And why is that?"

"You knew she would appear?" Seren asked, at the same time.

"Not as such." Arianrod fluttered a hand at the woman, and then swept it at the statues behind her. "But look around you. The people who lived here in the distant past knew this place was special, and when it came to depicting why, they created these statues. That's how they understood the magic of this place—as something that could speak to them, that had a will." She turned back to the woman. "And it's tiresome because if the magic of this place were simply controlled by a mechanism, I'd just have to figure out how it works. But *you* control it, don't you? And that means you're going to want something."

The woman smiled at her, but not with any smugness; there was such fondness in it that Seren could almost feel it in the air. Arianrod must have felt it, too, for she took a step back, a frown creasing her face. "What is it?"

"I've waited a long time to speak to you face-to-face," the woman said. "The right was denied me until now, until you had done all of this and arrived at this answer. The rest, you could not know without being told. So I was permitted to tell you, lest that knowledge be lost from the mortal world forever."

"You wanted to speak to me? Why?"

"Why," the woman repeated, as if savoring the syllable. She nodded at the statue on the semicircle's leftmost edge, the woman with scrolls gathered up in her arms. Asariel. "That question, and all those who ask it most ardently, are mine. Why should I not wish to converse with them?"

"I'm sure you won't mind some more complicated questions, then," Arianrod said. "First things first: you don't have a human form. You're presenting one to my eyes and ears, but your body, such as it is, is comprised entirely of magic. Is it so concentrated here because this is your domain?"

"You have it backward a bit," the woman said. "We exist everywhere equally. But this place is where we first made contact with the mortals of this land—hence why they constructed these statues, to mark it. And so this place became more magical than other places, because the stone itself remembers that long-distant day. When magic was plentiful, there would hardly be a difference between this place and anywhere else. But as magic drained away from the world, it lingered here, like a coastal pool when the tide goes out."

"You say 'drained away,' but it was intentional, wasn't it? Was it not you, and those eight compatriots of yours, who drained it?"

"Yes and no." The woman—Asariel—turned, gazing upon her own stone likeness. "Mortals are a contradiction—the infinite, cloaked in a finite shell. Though your outward form must inevitably decay and die, still something within you reaches for eternity. We are what reaches back, and that connection results in what you call magic in some of you. But the connection requires two halves—from us, and from you."

"Why in the world would humans ever decide they didn't want magic?"

"Because they forgot where magic came from," Asariel said. "In the beginning, we spoke to humans often, with all the excitement and impetuousness of youth. They gave us names, helped us to understand ourselves, to speak as they did. But they venerated us too highly, and gave us too much influence. They would risk death in half a hundred ways to fulfill our passing whims, or fight each other when we disagreed. They would demand things we could not give, or require certainty where we could provide only possibility. There are those of us who lie at times, but none of us have ever lied about what we can and cannot do. Yet still they would go on, asking Yaelor to protect their children in battle or praying to Telfair for victory in contests of skill. I remember one, so long ago, who fasted before Amerei's likeness for a full turn of the moon, beseeching her to grant him the love of a beautiful woman. But even if she had possessed the power to change hearts, what could Amerei tell him? To her all mortals are beautiful.

"We agreed that we had been too present, that we needed to retreat. It took some doing, and many mistakes, but we eventually arrived at the compromise we maintain to this day. But though we explained, or tried to, what we were doing and why, still the mortals felt abandoned. As generations passed, and those who had seen us no longer lived, many doubted that we had ever existed, or chose to bestow the worship they had once piled ineffectually onto us on fanciful beings dreamed up by their fellows. We did not mind; we had never wished to be worshipped, and did not even need to be acknowledged. As long as mortals continue to ask why, to seek the truth no matter how obscurely it is hidden from them, my power will never wane. Magic did lessen, since there were those who persecuted the ones who bore it, and weakened the connection between us and them. It wouldn't have been enough to extinguish it, had those circumstances remained.

"But then came . . . that empire."

"Elesthene," Arianrod said.

Asariel's face grew stormy, the anger of centuries past made fresh and new. "In that empire, no one was encouraged to ask why. They were given lies for answers, and punished if they questioned them. The zealots in charge of religious dogma even tried to erase what had gone before—not just to stop any new learning, but to destroy knowledge that had already been gathered, to make future generations more ignorant than those before them. And then . . . then they attacked the University."

"The University?" Seren asked.

"A place of learning modeled after the *zarasaing* in Sahai," Arianrod said. "It used to be in southern Selindwyr. But when the Ninists moved their armies into Selindwyr—"

"They sought to burn the University's books," Asariel said. "But the library was built of ashencast, an enchanted stone that protected the contents within from damp or flame. So the soldiers pulled all the books out, and dismantled the library, stone by stone. They housed the books inside another building, made of wood, and for kindling they used every student and every teacher currently living at the University. They burned them alive, for wondering what the stars were made of, for trying to trace the lineage of kings. For remembering that magic was so much more glorious once. And though I stayed with them until the very end, I could do nothing to save them. I could not douse even the smallest flame of that fire." There was raw pain in her voice, and Seren realized that for a being that had lived for millennia, this grief was not far distant at all. "But there was one thing I could do. I could withdraw my blessing from a land whose people would commit such atrocities. And so I did.

"I wasn't alone; in time, every one of us turned our faces away from that empire. That was when this spell was cast, to protect, as you have surmised, the mages that remained. It severed them from the world, so they could not feel its magic, or cast any spells—doing so even once would have drained them dangerously."

"So mages never died out and came back," Arianrod said. "We've always been the same. It's the world that's been different. That's why things changed with Talia Avestri, isn't it? Because she proved the people could break free of Elesthene."

Asariel glanced at the far end of the semicircle, where a hooded statue stood. "It was Irein who most greatly loved the Rebel Queen, and poured all their power back into this world, so that her dream of halting the Curse might become a reality."

"That would make sense, if you like those who are like you," Arianrod said. To Seren, she added, "*Irein* is . . . strength of will. The ability to persevere, even when all hope seems gone."

"Irein was the first, but we all followed eventually," Asariel said. "And we were right to hope, for Elesthene fell."

"And magic's been slowly returning ever since," Arianrod finished. "Faster than the Curse can eat away at it. Were you responsible for that, too?"

Asariel actually snorted. "Mortals are so amusing. They call it the *Gods' Curse*, yet it was mortals who created it. You've already stumbled upon how—you recreated it for yourself not long ago."

"You mean what I did to Elgar? What I read about in Adora's book?" To Seren, she explained, "It talked about a kind of corruption, when two mages' powers oppose each other with sufficient strength and persistence. I assumed it would happen when I tried to harm Elgar with my blood, just as he tried to use it to control me. The corrosion that ate away at him was the result. But you saw how small it was. In order to create something like the Curse, there'd have to be—"

"Armies of mages, set against each other," Asariel said. "Precisely."

Arianrod swore under her breath. "You're telling me a magical conflict of that scale changed the face of the continent, and I've never encountered it in any book of history? If something like that could be hidden, I can't even imagine what other monumental events have been lost to us." She glared at Asariel. "But *you* know. You've hoarded all the world's knowledge, for all this time."

The spirit nodded gravely. "Because I could not bear for it to be forgotten, any more than you."

"Then tell me," Arianrod said. Perhaps she had not fully recovered, but her fingers were trembling.

"Tell you what?"

"Everything!" She clenched her hands into fists, trying to keep them steady. "Please."

Asariel's face bore the same tenderness she must have felt for those long-ago University researchers. "If I were to tell you that, we would be speaking for all your life, and still we would not finish it. Don't you think that a waste of all you have still to live, and all you might find? It is my hope that you may discover things even I don't know, because they are things no one yet knows." She bowed her head. "But I am not indifferent to your desire—indeed, perhaps no one understands it better than I do. So ask me three things. Any three you like, and I shall tell you all I know of them."

Arianrod caught her breath, and Seren almost did, too; how could anyone faced with such an opportunity possibly choose? "Three?" she repeated, as off balance as Seren had ever seen her. "And I have to decide right now?"

The spirit laughed. "Let's say three for this conversation. We can talk more if we win a more leisurely future."

Arianrod twirled her hair around one finger, pacing back and forth. "Now that the question of magic has been answered . . . that was what I wanted to know most for such a long time. I didn't exactly have an immediate replacement lined up. Let's start with a simple one, then—very easy for you to know, and very difficult for me to find out. Is the Endless Sea empty of life? Does it simply stretch the long way around to eastern Inkei?"

"No," Asariel said. "It is very, very wide. But there is a landmass on the other side, though between the length of the journey and the roughness of the seas, very few have ever survived a voyage even in one direction."

"And you exist there, too? You exist there right now, just as you exist here and in Sahai and Akozuchi and everywhere else?"

"Yes, but we are not precisely the same everywhere. We change as people change." She smiled. "I'll count that as part of the first question."

"All right, I'll move on." She tapped her chin. "Next should be . . . my family's ancestral sword. Not the Vandrith one that Lord Oswhent used to bind me—Silverthorn, the sword of the Margraines. In my family, the story goes that it was lost when Gwendolen Margraine fell in battle against the armies of Elesthene, after she left her homeland to fight alongside the people of Selindwyr. But I don't even know if that's true, let alone what became of the sword afterward."

"It is true," Asariel said. "And she must have fought bravely, for Yaelor was well pleased. As for the sword, it fell into the snow beside her when she succumbed to her wounds at last, and was picked up by a retreating Selindwyri soldier who had lost his own, and had no idea of its true origin. He took it with him when he deserted the army, and he fled deep into the north, past the Howling Gate, lest he be tracked down. He lived a quiet life, and his descendants never left that village. The sword hangs over the mantel there still."

"My ancestors will be disappointed; many of them imagined all kinds of adventures for that blade. But at least it wasn't melted down. I couldn't get you to mark it on a map, could I?"

Another smile. "I already told you it was a village north of the Howling Gate. You're perfectly capable of discovering the rest for yourself."

"Yes, I've already figured out your game. You like to answer questions, but only in ways that will lead to more questions. Here's my last one." She tapped the floor with the toe of one boot. "Who created this spell? It's the most incredible thing I've ever seen. I'm almost irritated thinking of the intellect that must have given rise to it."

"Ah." The spirit sighed, relishing the question. "Truly a rare mortal indeed. But it's a more complicated question than you might think, because there are many ways to answer it, many ways to describe a single person. I could give you a name, but it would mean nothing to you. So I suppose it is most correct to say that this spell was created by the one who would be immortalized in this land as the Magician."

"The Ninists' Magician?" Arianrod looked down at the floor again, tracing some curve of the spell with her foot that Seren couldn't see. "Is that how it happened? Knowing how magic had deteriorated, some magical genius devised this spell to protect mages, and the Ninists made up a story about a naïve youth led into disaster by some comically evil woman?"

"Many of the specifics of that story are wrong," Asariel said. "Most, I would say. But you're right that the only purpose of this spell was ever to protect mages from harm, and the Magician was not swayed by the advice or entreaty of anyone else. The story was devised—"

"To shift the blame for magic's extinction onto convenient scapegoats, and leave the empire blameless," Arianrod said. "That much is obvious."

"Just so. To blame the kinds of people they wanted to blame."

Seren looked down the row of statues, stopping at the one in the center. "I'm a little disappointed there was no love story, though."

"Seren," Arianrod said. "The story is that she seduced and deceived him; it's hardly the romance of Irjan Spear-Thrower."

Asariel shrugged. "There was a romance. But it had nothing to do with this spell, or with anything that befell magic. And if you want to know about it, you should ask Amerei."

"I suppose that means my questions are all used up." Arianrod sighed. "Just when I'd really gotten started, too. What a pity."

The spirit laughed admiringly. "You mean you don't have enough to think about?"

"If you know me, you should know I can never have too much to think about." She gave Asariel a wary nod. "Until we meet again, then."

"Until then, Arianrod Margraine." And she was gone, as abruptly as she'd shown herself in the first place. Or rather, if she existed everywhere, she must not truly be gone completely, but returned to whatever veiled state from which she watched over this world.

Arianrod sagged a bit, eyes fluttering down to the spell on the floor. "Gods, I should hope that's enough for one day. I'm not done with this room yet, but . . ."

She was utterly exhausted, of course, though she was too stubborn to say it aloud. "I understand," Seren said. "Let's withdraw for now. It'll keep perfectly well until your return."

Arianrod brushed her hands down her arms, as if making sure they were still there. "I know you had a way out for us, Seren, but I'm not sure tramping around in search of the Issamiri army is wise for me in this state. There's no longer anything magically wrong with me, but physically I'm still . . . annoyingly vulnerable. Perhaps we can risk one night in the city—or at least a few hours' nap—and strike out again tomorrow?"

"I'd love to," Seren said. "But . . . well. We're lost, aren't we?"

"What do you mean? We're in tunnels beneath Valyanrend."

"Of course, but they're a maze, and I don't have the whole layout memorized. I was never shown how to get here, so I can't get us from here to anywhere else. I don't even remember the turns we made to reach this chamber in the first place. Well, I remember the first one was left, and the second was right, but after that . . ."

"Oh, is that all?" Arianrod waved a dismissive hand. "You forget how good my memory is, Seren. I recall the commands I gave you at the turns; we just have to reverse them, and you can lead us from there."

"There's no way you remember *that*. With the state you were in——"

"Shall we wager on it?" Arianrod beamed at her. "Loser has to do the laundry when we finally get to wash these damned clothes?"

Seren laughed. "I'll name myself the loser preemptively. You have many talents, but I doubt you've ever done laundry. But there's another problem. I only know how to get to three exits. One was where we went in, the one closest to Speaker's Square, and I wouldn't risk that one; I bet most of Elgar's soldiers are still searching that area. The second is the escape route I wanted to use, the one that leads outside the city, and you need to rest before we can venture that way. But the only other pathway . . . it's the one my teacher used most often for herself, and it comes out in Sheath. That's no place for you, especially not now."

"Sheath Alleys?" Arianrod perked up, a hunter sensing prey. "The fabled haunt of the most talented thieves and rogues on the continent? Come now, Seren, I deserve a lark, after the weeks I've had. I wouldn't miss a tour of that place for anything." She turned toward the tunnel entrance without waiting to hear more.

"No, my lady——" Seren hurried to catch up with her. "If you go through Sheath unarmed, obviously a foreigner who doesn't know her way around . . . they'll scent weakness, even if that's not the truth. More people than not in that neighborhood would rob a stranger of every coin they owned, given the slightest chance. And you'd be lucky if that's all you lost."

"Then we'll never find a better time to visit," Arianrod said, already striding confidently down the tunnel. "For once in my life, I haven't a copper on me."

CHAPTER FORTY-TWO

Valyanrend

VESPAS LOOKED HAPPIER than Adora had seen him in weeks, which was rather at odds with the hissing, scratching tangle of limbs he deposited at her feet. The tangle rolled itself the right way up and resolved into a sitting position, revealing that it was not a cat, but a scrawny redheaded girl, as furiously disgruntled as he was self-satisfied. "It's . . . a child?" Adora asked.

"A child, Your Grace, whom one of our people found emerging from a tunnel beneath the walls of Valyanrend. I admit, I'd thought your urging that I send someone up to the southern wall to investigate was done solely out of sentiment. I've never been happier to be wrong."

That certainly explained his euphoria, but gave rise to half a dozen more questions. Adora struggled to untangle them in her mind so she could ask them in the right order. "This scout saw the tunnel with their own eyes?"

"She did, Your Grace."

"And she's absolutely certain it leads to Valyanrend's interior?"

"Well, she didn't see that with her own eyes, no. I only had one soldier out that far; she couldn't explore the tunnel and keep hold of this little hellion at the same time. But that's where it goes, Adora. I'd bet my life on it. We can have it explored as soon as you like, but what else is out there for it to lead to, if not the city?"

Adora suspected he was right about that, so her next order of business was to examine this "hellion" more closely. Though she was slightly built, she didn't look malnourished or impoverished, and she was older than Adora had thought at first glance—fifteen or sixteen, perhaps. Her mouth was still twisted in anger, but her eyes were clever and calculating. A child, to be sure, but far from guileless or naïve. "And what was one such as you doing in such an obscure and sought-after place as those tunnels?"

"Helping you as much as me, if you lot weren't too stupid to heed me," the girl snapped. Adora wasn't sure if she didn't know she was in the presence of a foreign queen or was simply too angry to care, but either way, she was impressed. "His soldiers called him Lord Vespas, so he knows Morgan Imrick, and she's been helping him this whole time, just like he wanted. Well, I say I'm a friend of Morgan's, and I don't deserve to be treated so poorly by you and yours."

Adora raised an eyebrow at Vespas. "She's not wrong."

He smiled. "Not in theory. I will point out, my young friend, that any discomfort you sustained was purely the result of your own struggling, and no one here intends you any harm. I simply couldn't let you scamper away before our curiosity was satisfied."

"It's Morgan who tells you things," the girl insisted. "I didn't make any deal with you, and I didn't get taken captive and hauled out here just to docilely answer questions."

"True, again," Adora said. "Let me see if I can smooth things over here. We can't undiscover the tunnel, so it's useless expecting us to pretend we don't know it's there. Given how useful—even indispensable—it would be to our aims here, I think it's reasonable for us to at least explore it enough to confirm it leads to the city—"

"You won't find where it leads to," the girl said. "It's all a mess of tunnels on the inside, going every which way. You wouldn't be able to get anywhere without a great deal of practice."

Adora glanced at Vespas, but he shook his head, unperturbed. "If there are many tunnels, that suggests there are many entrances. I'm sure it's very difficult to find a route to any particular place, but we don't need a particular place. Any place at all will do, so long as it's solid ground within the walls of Valyanrend. And to find that, I expect, would be much less trouble."

The girl fell silent, unwillingly conceding the point, and Adora vacillated between one opinion and the other. On the one hand, the girl was clearly upset, and had undeniably been hard done by. She didn't want to keep her in captivity here, but if they released her, she could potentially alert the wrong people back in Valyanrend. Wouldn't it be better to try to get her on their side before doing anything else? But on the other hand . . . "Do you think we should explore the tunnels as soon as possible, before the gates are opened up again?" With a sudden ache, she remembered the reason why they'd been closed in the first place. "Do you . . . have any of you heard anything from inside the city? Do you know how it . . . how the execution was carried out?"

Before Vespas could answer, the girl scoffed. "You really don't know anything, do you? It's chaos behind those walls. No one knows when the gates will be opened. And you were just going to charge into it unprepared?"

The barely veiled shock in Vespas's face matched the twist Adora felt in her stomach. How strange to hear the word *chaos,* when those walls looked so tranquil and steadfast. "What happened? Did something go wrong at the execution?"

The girl pressed her lips together. "If I'm a prisoner, I don't much feel like talking."

"Please." Adora's heart fluttered like a trapped bird. "The woman who was going to be killed today is my friend. If there's a chance she's still alive . . . can you not tell me even that much?"

"Damn, who knew that lady had so many people concerned for her? You aren't in love with her, too, are you?" Before Adora had time to react to the implications of *too*, she added, "If you care about her that much, you ought to've left me to my business. If I hadn't been trying to make sure she was all right, I'd never have gotten myself snatched by your lackeys in the first place."

"You were following Arianrod?"

"Ugh, *maybe*. I'm not sure. I can't think what that woman was playing at." She must have seen something in Adora's face, for she elaborated at last. "There was a woman I agreed to help, who wanted to get one of Elgar's prisoners out of the city. When I heard that same woman had snatched the marquise herself from the jaws of Elgar and his men, I rushed to the tunnels to try to find them. But they weren't there, and if you know what she looks like but haven't seen her, and that sentry of yours didn't catch them, they must not have come out this way. I can't understand it. I didn't teach that woman how to go anywhere else, but the city guard's been turning Valyanrend upside down and hasn't found them. So . . . maybe she's alive. But Elgar didn't kill her."

Adora's chest felt like it had opened up, like she hadn't been able to draw a full breath before now and hadn't even realized it. She couldn't think what it might be, but she was certain Arianrod had a plan. Even she might have resigned herself to death, when faced with such a hopeless situation—or perhaps she always knew Seren (for it could have been no one else) was going to rescue her. But once she *had* been rescued, she'd have a plan, or make one as she went. Arianrod wouldn't escape her own execution just to die of carelessness in some back alley. They might yet be reunited.

She pressed a hand to her heart, as if she could slow its beating. "Uncle, we need to summon Rhia and the others. They'll—"

"Not yet, Your Grace, if you please," Vespas said. "We have other business to discuss first, that that little group would only complicate. And while I am relieved that your friend and fellow queen lives still, may I remind you that we have much larger considerations than her survival."

He was right, of course, on both counts. Adora pushed her curls back from her face, and bent toward the girl. "What's your name?"

She hesitated, but said, "You can call me Marceline."

"Well, Marceline, I owe you for helping Arianrod, and I don't wish to subject you to any further discomfort. But for the sake of my country and my people, I must win this war. I must make certain decisions in order to prevent the weakening of my position. Can you understand that, if we let you go and you try to sabotage that tunnel entrance somehow, or array your friends against us . . . can't you see how I can't allow that? What a position that puts me in?"

The girl tilted her head, pensiveness taking some of the fury out of her face, so she must either be pondering Adora's question or her own answer. "And if you were me," she said at last, "what would you do? I know your uncle and Morgan are supposedly working together, but even Morgan admits they don't want exactly the same things. I know you've brought this great army all the way up here to fight against people who are my enemies, too. I just don't know who *else* you might have come to fight. And not knowing that, how can I know you know a way into Valyanrend and *not* warn anyone?"

"We haven't come to fight anyone who isn't Elgar or his underlings," Adora said. "I swear to you. My ancestor turned back from this city, once it had become clear that its people had freed themselves. I have no wish to cross the line she left behind her."

"But you would cross it," the girl said. "She never entered this city, and you would. If you think Valyanrend should be freed by its own people, why do you even care about such a passage? What reason do you have to make use of it?"

"I should think it's obvious," Vespas said, "that Elgar isn't going to simply walk out of Valyanrend and come meet us. It should also be obvious that your little group cannot defeat him without help, or I wouldn't have just received a missive from your associate begging me to contain the city. Our first priority is not allowing you to fight him on your own terms, it's making sure he doesn't survive to ruin this continent. And at this point, it seems any strategy that accomplishes that is going to involve going in there to get him."

His words were true, but harsh enough to make even Adora cover a wince. Still, Marceline raised her chin bravely, meeting his eyes. "Listen. I'm not stupid. You must think those tunnels have handed you the surprise attack of your dreams. This whole army could pour into Valyanrend like bees from a hive, at any time and in a dozen places, without warning. But while you have good numbers and good odds against Elgar's *army,* this is the largest city on the continent, and many of its citizens already believe you're coming here to slaughter them. If you do what I've just said, the common people of Valyanrend will get involved, because they'll believe they have to fight for their lives. Hell, for all I know, maybe they do. They'll have you outnumbered, and you'll have them out-armed and out-trained. I can't say who would win in the end, but either way, more people will die than I want to imagine."

"You misunderstand our intent," Adora said, before Vespas could snap back and make things worse. "We have no plans to sneak our entire army into Valyanrend, for exactly that reason. Any move we make against Elgar within the city would be targeted, precise. I have a handful of associates with particular talents that lend themselves to fighting magic. All I need is for you to let them go back into the city with you. They have the greatest chance of killing Elgar directly, which is what we both want. As long as you won't interfere with that, or with their safe return, you're free to go."

"You'll never keep to *that*," Marceline scoffed.

"That's my concern. Will you do as I've asked or not?"

The girl squinted at her, incredulous. "I would, but . . ."

"Your Grace," Vespas interrupted, "a word in private, if you please?"

Marceline smirked, her eyes cold. "Aye, there it is. Just like I thought."

Shunting the girl out of the conversation would increase her distrust in them, but they couldn't simply let her stand privy to all their discussions, especially when it seemed they weren't yet in agreement. Adora dragged a hand through her curls, only to feel her fingers snag on a tangle. A fitting outcome. "All right," she said to Vespas. "Let's be quick."

She and her uncle closed themselves off in her tent, and Adora finally let her posture relax, wiping her forehead. "What is it that you couldn't say out there?"

Unlike her, Vespas still held himself tight and stiff; she could tell he was choosing his words carefully. "That child wasn't entirely wrong. There's a non-negligible possibility that a surprise attack through those tunnels would lose us the war, rather than win it. The population of the continent's largest city obviously dwarfs even our army, and if even half of them decided to fight us with everything they had, we'd simply be overwhelmed. But I very much doubt that half, or a quarter, or even one in ten, would do such a thing. People behave and react according to their habits, and the people of Valyanrend are not martial by nature. The arts of war are not popular pastimes for those coming of age there, as in Kaiferi and Araveil and Eldren Cael; they are taught trades, the arts of the pen and the ledger. If we attack fast enough, and secure the right locations right away, I don't think they'll fight back. I think they'll consider the conquest of their city a feat already accomplished, or else something that will play out between us and their imperator's soldiers, not them. They'll wait for the dust to settle, and petition the victors for favors. That is their custom."

Adora eased herself into a chair and folded her hands in her lap, practicing the composure she maintained for her people. Her voice sounded strange to her own ears, but at least it sounded steady. "If we did that, I suspect it would play out as you've described, yes. But that is not why we're here. Even if we did take Valyanrend, what on earth would we do with it? We'd just have to hand it back to its people anyway."

"No, we don't have to do that," Vespas said quietly. "In fact, I believe that would be greatly unwise." He sat in the chair opposite hers—more heavily than she had, his head hanging low. "Adora, I would never presume to teach you history; you know more of it than I do. But I have lived nearly twice as long as you have, and I can offer you the experience of that life. I see the dread and care this war has exacted from you, and I feel the same. But for me, these emotions are all too familiar. This is the second war I've had to fight to protect our country and our people from the ambitions of our northwestern neighbors—two different leaders, two different plans for the continent, but for us, the result was the same. Fighting and death, even in the best scenario, and so much worse if we lose. Our people have watched this happen over and over, and every time they have suffered for it. I know you know how many times it has been repeated, generation after generation. How much more evidence do we need to realize that these people are never going to stop coming for us?"

"Before the war you fought with my father," Adora said, "we hadn't had more than a border skirmish with the Hallerns in a hundred years."

"And I know that seems like a long time to you, but it isn't, not really. A handful of generations. Would you truly be content passing the struggle on to your grandchildren, condemning them to go through the same thing you are right now? We have a chance even Talia Avestri was denied, to get within Valyanrend's walls at last. Do you not want to end this cycle forever?"

Adora pressed a hand to her forehead, but hurriedly let it drop. She had to be able to see his eyes for this. "And how do you wish us to accomplish that, Uncle? If you truly believe a desire to conquer us is in their very nature, we could only end it by slaughtering the inhabitants of that city down to the last. We could not even spare the children, lest they grow up to seek revenge. And then what? Should we pull the city itself apart, stone by stone? Should we salt the earth where it once stood, that weeds may not even grow there?"

"You know that's not what I meant, Adora."

"No, I don't, Uncle. I truly don't know what you mean. Even if we tried to be merciful, and merely claimed the city for ourselves, how would we hold on to it, without doing all the things that were once done to us? We would still be fighting the Hallerns, only this time it would be a constant struggle to hold our dominion over them, to keep them from rebelling as we once did. And it would never end." She shook her head. "When Talia Avestri struck Valyanrend the most grievous blow it had ever received, she could have pressed her attack—the city was in chaos, much more than we could ever hope to cause. I am sure she could have entered the city if she'd truly wished to, tunnel or no tunnel. But she did not. She left things as they were, and turned her army homeward, to nurture and rebuild in a time of peace. Would you do any less than she did? The greatest leader in our history?"

"It is true," Vespas said slowly, "that we prospered under Talia Avestri as we had not prospered in centuries. But what if she could have done even more? Had she pressed her attack, had she subdued Valyanrend forever, what would the place called Hallarnon be like now? Would Elgar have ever reigned there, or Norverian, or Gerde Selte? Would its people suffer as they do now, or would they be living in a better world?"

"Perhaps it would be better for them," Adora said. "Perhaps Hallarnon, in that alternate future, would be a glorious place. But what would have become of Issamira?"

Her uncle frowned. "What do you mean?"

"We both love our country, Uncle, but our reasons are not the same. You love it *because* it is yours, where your family and your people live. But I love Issamira because of what it is: a place where no one's conscience is compelled, where children are born perfect as they are, and never already disgraced. Where monarchs and nobles exist to serve the people, rather than to enrich themselves at their expense. Such a place could never conquer outside territory and hold it in bondage, not while still calling itself a kingdom of the free. To do that, it would have to change, to become a country I have no desire to fight for. As far as I'm concerned, if Issamira loses what makes it great, it might as well cease to exist."

Vespas was silent. Adora waited for him to speak, but he did not. He merely sat there, head slightly bent, face stony. Was it frustration that had him so frozen? Was it that he was certain he was right, but he would not turn traitor against her, and so he felt powerless? Or was it something else?

Either way, she had no time to waste, and if he would not speak, she would have to continue anyway. "Here is what will happen, Uncle. We will summon Rhia and the others, and we'll explain everything to them. And presuming they agree to follow Marceline through the tunnels and into the city, I will accompany them."

"No," Vespas said immediately.

"I'm afraid I've decided," Adora said. "In order to determine what to do, I need to see the state of Valyanrend for myself."

"If you are set upon this—"

She held up a hand. "No, Uncle, you cannot go with me. If anything truly went wrong in there, you alone would not be able to make a difference. And if I were to be lost, our people could not lose you, too. I need you here where you belong, at the head of our army. I need you to oversee the siege, and make sure Elgar and his enslaved army are contained. And if you come to believe something has happened to me, though my brother will become my successor, I give you full sanction to act as you see fit."

His jaw tightened. "Full sanction?"

"That's what I said. But keep one thing in mind, lest you be tempted to mount your conquest prematurely in my absence. You are my general, and I am your queen. Do not forget what that truly means. Your actions are my actions, the lives you take snuffed out by my hand as well. And any injustice you commit falls upon my head, and I must pay its price."

Vespas pushed himself to his feet with a shaky laugh. "You have learned much in a short time. I used to think it a pity that Jotun never knew you would succeed him, and never taught you how to rule according to his fashion. But now I think if he had, you might have been too formidable. I pity instead that he will never know all you've become. But you have my word: I will take no action that would bring shame upon your head, or his." He gave a crooked smile. "And I suppose . . . I was not looking forward to having to betray the trust of Miss Imrick, who told me when last we spoke that her people and ours were not destined to be enemies. Whatever else happens, at least I won't have that on my conscience."

They returned to Marceline, and Adora felt a pinch of satisfaction at the girl's surprise; perhaps she had not imagined she would actually have an audience with Adora or Vespas ever again. "My terms remain the same, provided my associates agree, with one addition," Adora said. "I will be accompanying them as well."

Marceline's eyes went wide, while her mouth shrank to a pursed line. "You? What on earth would you want to do that for?"

"Not to invade your city, as I think should be clear," Adora said. "Beyond that, my reasons are my own. Though if I do find my friend in addition, I shall be truly grateful."

Marceline groaned. "Oh, all right, then. But you follow me, and you come out of the tunnels where I show you, with no nonsense in between. And you stay out of my people's way. Agreed?"

"Of course," Adora said, with her most diplomatic smile. "You won't even know we're here."

THE AFTERNOON, AS Morgan could have predicted, had been a disaster. She'd alerted Naishe, all right, but all the resistance's searching had turned up no marquises, and no accomplices. Morgan herself had pitched in where she could, leaving Sheath to ask around the Fades, but to no avail. When she trudged back to the Dragon's Head, tired and footsore, she was hardly expecting or wanting company.

Roger was the only member of their band inside the tavern—Marceline was still on her mysterious errand, then—but he wasn't alone. He was sitting at the bar, and on the stool next to his was a young woman Morgan had never seen before, her long limbs curled over the bar, her shabby clothes and long pale hair in a frightful state of disarray, but her blue-gray eyes so sharp and clear that she could not be some drunkard. She was wearing a long, faded gray coat that might once have been black, and that was peculiarly too big and too small for her at once; her torso was swallowed up in a sea of fabric, but her arms poked out of the sleeves. Still, from what Morgan could tell from her limited view, the rest of what she was wearing was in even worse shape.

They were so deep in conversation that neither noticed Morgan's entrance, heads bent close together like two conspirators trading priceless secrets. Only that was definitely not what they were doing, because Morgan recognized snatches of what Roger was saying. This was one of his seemingly infinite well of inconsequential and mundane family stories. She'd been subjected to them about as many times as anyone, and, like everyone else she knew, found it nearly impossible to sit through even a single one in its entirety.

But this woman wasn't looking at Roger like she wanted to strangle him to free herself from the boredom he was inflicting on her. She was looking at him with something almost like greed, as if he were a priceless gem that had suddenly fallen within reach of her fingers. "That's so fascinating," she said, with not the faintest trace of irony. "This cousin of yours was right to be suspicious. A fishwife in Valyanrend whose primary trade was mackerel? It's quite peculiar."

Roger was looking a little stunned; doubtless no one had given that story such a level of scrutiny before. "Aye, that's—that's what I've been *trying* to say to people. Any fishwife worth the salt on her wares would know that cured mackerel sells for a pitiful fraction of what you can get for it fresh."

"Only because you westerners don't know how to preserve fish without ruining it, but I digress. Forgoing the sale of fresh mackerel closer to the coast to bring it all the way to Valyanrend and reduce its price by half? It'd be financially ruinous. Either this woman was a true imbecile, or the fish was merely a prop to keep her inconspicuous while she went about her true business."

"A diversion!" Roger slapped his thigh. "That's *just* what I've been saying, miss. And given the events that took place between the first and last times Cousin Ayne saw this supposed fishwife—"

"I'm glad you seem to have finally found your perfect audience, Roger," Morgan interrupted, "but I'd like to remind you that you aren't allowed to run any jobs at my bar."

He gave her a wounded look. "I'm not trying to *swindle* her, Morgan, just look at the state of her! And she's already had all her money stolen anyway."

"If she doesn't have any *money,*" Morgan asked through gritted teeth, "then what is she doing in the Dragon's Head, which is not a shelter for the destitute but, in fact, an establishment whose services all *require* money?" On second glance, the woman truly did seem to be in a bad way: she was unhealthily thin, and there were stains and even a few tears in her threadbare clothing. "She hasn't been begging, has she?"

"I've never tried, but I don't think I'd be particularly good at it," the woman said, tapping her chin thoughtfully. "People don't tend to find me sympathetic." She smiled at Morgan, and though it was genuine, there was something intimidating about it all the same. "There's no need to worry. Though it's true all my coin has been stolen, my . . . associate has already come to my aid, and she has enough for the both of us. She is currently procuring me some suitable clothes, but as I was too fatigued to make the walk with her, I am resting here. This gentleman has served me neither food nor drink, so I owe you nothing as yet, and merely ask for your patience until her return."

"I promise you, there's no gentlemen in here," Morgan said, raising an eyebrow at Roger. "Are you going to tell me your clothes were stolen, too?"

"I'm sure it must be hard to believe," the woman said, "but, in fact, they were." She tugged at the sleeve of her coat. "This is merely a temporary measure, and we drastically overpaid for it. Though I have longed for years to visit this city, I must admit I never anticipated my entry would be under such . . . difficult circumstances."

She shouldn't have, but Morgan felt herself soften a bit; she loved her city, and couldn't help feeling pleased that someone else understood its importance. "Well, perhaps this will teach you to keep a firmer hand on your belongings while in Sheath. The . . . skill of our denizens can be quite shocking to newcomers."

"Oh, on the contrary, the people here were very helpful. We asked where to find lodging, and they pointed us here straightaway. They said the Dragon's Head was the most honest establishment in Sheath—though not, I confess, in a way that suggested it was a compliment."

"Aye, they look down on me for it," Morgan admitted. "Always have. They probably sniggered to send you to me, too; I wouldn't be surprised if they snuck a search of pockets to ensure you had nothing to pay me with. Either way, it's early for most customers to come by yet, so I'll let you stay here unless space becomes a problem. But no food, drink, or lodging until I see some coin."

The woman looked untroubled at that, so she was either telling the truth or a very good liar. She turned back to Roger. "In the meantime, if you aren't otherwise occupied, I believe you were telling me you had many stories of that sort?"

Morgan rolled her eyes. "She cannot be serious."

"You're the one who's mistaken," the woman said calmly. "This man is a treasure. I haven't heard this many obscure details about this city and its people in entire works of scholarship."

Roger leaned back smugly against the bar. "Did you hear that, Morgan? A *treasure*. And you said those stories were useless."

"Because I'm not some scholar, or whatever the hell she is. I know how not to get robbed in this city, and that's more than she does."

The woman yawned; she really did look exhausted. "In my defense, I had drawn the ire of some rather powerful men."

"That's not a defense, it's an indictment," Morgan said. "Someone in as poor shape as you shouldn't go around making enemies of cold winds, let alone men of influence."

"Mm," the woman mumbled. "It must be something about my face."

Morgan suspected it had more to do with her obvious strangeness and imperturbable humor, but before she could say anything to that effect, the door swung open. It admitted a woman Morgan had seen only once, months ago, but whose face and form she could never forget.

She was reaching for her dagger in an instant, but Seren Almasy was faster. Morgan was saved only by the fact that the bar stood between them. Seren could probably have vaulted over it, but she didn't, choosing instead to stand, knife drawn from somewhere, at the other woman's side, as if to ward her from attacks from Morgan and Roger both.

The woman flashed a lazy smile at Roger. "Do you also feel that we missed something?"

"Morgan," Roger said, a warning and a demand for clarification at once.

"It's her." She waved at Seren with the hand that held the dagger. "That's Seren Almasy." She didn't have the dexterity to vault the bar, but she edged around it, planning to lunge as soon as she got an opening.

Roger was still stunned in his seat, but the woman stood up. She was taller than all of them, and somehow she didn't look quite so weak anymore. "Whatever is going on, following through with that attack would be a huge—"

Morgan ignored her, and lunged.

She got about five inches before her shoulder slammed into a barrier she couldn't see, wrenching her whole body sideways. "I *said*," the woman continued, "that would be a mistake. You aren't going to hurt Seren, and you aren't—"

Morgan didn't waste time on surprise; the coldness of the dagger's blade told her that barrier was a spell. She sliced through the space where her shoulder had been, and felt the obstacle melt away, the blade gleaming in the light.

The next thing she knew, Seren had leapt at her, a movement that should've impaled her on Morgan's knife. But somehow she flowed around it, and in the next moment she had Morgan's wrist in her grip and slammed it down on the bar. "You keep that away from her," she growled, leaning enough weight on Morgan's spine to bow her back. "Drop it or lose the hand."

The dagger was Morgan's best defense, but when she kept her grip on it, Seren did something with her free hand, some stab of her fingers in just the right spot, that sent pain and numbness shooting down her arm. Her hand opened involuntarily, the dagger clattering to the floor.

Poor Roger stared at it helplessly, no doubt wondering whether he should dive for it. But he was a talker, not a fighter, and he knew it. "She's no threat to you anymore," he told the woman instead. "If you want to leave Sheath and this city untroubled, killing her would be—"

"Seren's not going to kill her," the woman said dismissively, though Morgan wouldn't have bet on that. "But your side *did* attack us first, and it *is* curious that a tavern owner in Sheath would possess a weapon as expensive as I happen to know that one is, so . . . perhaps you might offer us an explanation?"

"Ask *her* for an explanation," Morgan snarled, struggling uselessly to throw even one punch. "She knows what she did. She knows what she took from me. If she hadn't played us false back then—!"

Perhaps she had landed just one punch after all, for though she could not see Seren's expression, she felt her tense, as if she had been struck. "The others told you what happened."

"Aye, I had the whole story from them. Seth wouldn't even have been on that half of the continent if it wasn't for you."

The woman prodded the dagger with her foot, pinning it against the base of the bar where no one could get at it, but there was less urgency to the movement. She was looking not at Morgan, but at her companion's face. "Ah," she said quietly. "I understand now. You must have known that boy."

Had Seren talked about Seth to this woman? Why? "I more than knew him," she said. "He lived here. I was the closest thing to family he had."

The woman shrugged that off easily. "Well, if you truly know everything as you claim, then you must know that your associates behaved quite dishonorably in my city, and Seren put her own life and safety at risk ensuring they continued to possess theirs. Whatever debt of suffering she might owe you is paid."

Morgan sagged against the bartop. "I know." She hadn't been able to do anything for him, not even to grieve in the way he deserved. The idea of having someone to fight on his behalf, something she could still do for him, had been so tempting. But it wasn't the truth, any more than it was what he would have wanted.

The woman seemed to realize that the hostility had gone out of her. "Are we all finished? That's a relief. I owe that boy my gratitude, too, in a way; he did save Seren's life, after all. Having to harm his friends would be a pity. I'm still curious about how you got that dagger, though."

"Well, I'm curious about half a hundred things about you," Morgan retorted. "If *she's* traveling with you, you must be more than you seem. Were you ever even robbed in the first place?"

"I was, but not through the methods you must be used to. Elgar took all my possessions when he locked me in the Citadel." She sprawled back onto her barstool, though her foot never moved from the dagger. "I might've come up with a decent façade if I were only dealing with you, but this one"—she tilted her head toward Roger—"is surely perceptive enough to figure it out on his own before long. So I may as well simply tell you the truth; it is long and winding, but I will swear to every word of it. First, an introduction: I am Arianrod Margraine, the first of that name to rule Esthrades. And, as promised, I am now possessed of at least enough coin for a night in this place."

Chapter Forty-three

Valyanrend

"I CAN'T BELIEVE it," Morgan groaned, grinding her teeth together. "You just saw her!"

"I told you, I was too far back! I never got a good look at her! As far as I knew, she could've been any blond woman in the city!" Roger just kept gesticulating at the marquise, as if his arcane hand movements strengthened his point. "Besides, when I saw her, she looked half dead. I wasn't expecting her to come sauntering into the Dragon's Head, wearing somebody else's coat and apparently not on the run in the slightest."

"I am still on the run, to be strictly accurate," the marquise said, already chewing her way through a third biscuit. "I was just hoping to get a quick nap in before resuming the literal running part."

"I can't argue with your obvious need for rest," Morgan said, "and for once, an interloper in my establishment has actually provided proper payment. You can stay the night here, and perhaps more nights in the future if it becomes absolutely necessary. But you'd be safer in the tunnels beneath Valyanrend, and even safer with your Issamiri friends."

"I'd undoubtedly be safest with Adora, but now that I know the situation here, I think I'd also be useless. But it's no hardship for me to return to the tunnels; there's much more I have to do there anyway."

Morgan and Roger exchanged a look. "Return?" Morgan repeated.

The marquise blinked at them. "Oh, right. You mentioned them so casually, I almost forgot they were a secret. It's Seren that found out about them, not me."

Before Morgan could ask how, Roger said, "What is it you have to do down there that's so important?"

She took her time chewing and swallowing before responding. "It's that room with the statues. There's a very complicated spell there that I want to study with fresh eyes, with the benefit of rest."

Roger frowned, and Morgan glanced down at the dagger that was once again sheathed at her side. "But there can't be," he said. "Morgan took vardrath steel into those tunnels, into that very room. And she felt nothing."

The marquise's eyes lit up, eagerness cutting through her exhaustion. "Now *that* is interesting, and definitely warrants further examination. Perhaps I can convince you and that dagger to return to the tunnels with me, Miss Imrick. But I can assure you I'm not mistaken. There is an immense quantity of magic in that room, and a very powerful spell."

Morgan put a hand on the dagger. "I want to know the answer to that riddle, too. I'll go with you, but only if you solve another riddle for me first. Roger says you were able to overcome vardrath steel—to tarnish and crumble it into dust. How is that possible? Is it something Elgar could imitate?"

She smiled. "Ah yes, that was quite the oversight on Elgar's and Lord Oswhent's part. Unusual, for them: Elgar is generally cautious and thorough, and Lord Oswhent is certainly clever. But as far as I can tell, they both got their information on vardrath steel from research performed by former Administrator Edith Selwyn, and as Edith Selwyn is not a mage, she could only observe the effects of the steel on others, not feel it herself. She never understood that it doesn't function like a lid on a jar, keeping magic contained. It absorbs magic altogether."

"Aye, we've seen evidence of that ourselves," Roger said. "That's why Morgan could break Elgar's enchantments, because the steel absorbed the magic he'd put into those objects."

"Exactly so. But if the magic is being absorbed, Mr. Halfen, then it has to *go* somewhere. Objects that absorb heat become hot; different objects melt at different temperatures, but even the sturdiest material cannot absorb heat endlessly and remain unaffected. Vardrath steel's absorption ability works brilliantly on a single spell, because a spell uses a relatively small amount of magic. Edith Selwyn ran her tests on a *wardrenfell,* a person who comes to possess magic in a sort of parasitic relationship, and thought herself successful because she rendered her subject effectively harmless. But true success would have made the *wardrenfell* like one of Elgar's stones after you had drained them—devoid of magic entirely. Because that didn't happen, the steel must have a limit. It can exert enough of a pull on a *wardrenfell*'s magic to cause them intense pain, but it lacks the power to absorb so much at once. My magic, on the other hand, is not separate from me; having it suppressed makes me feel weak and sick, but as long as I don't cast, there's nothing to absorb. But what, I wondered, would happen if I *did* cast? Could I possibly reach that limit that I knew existed?

"It was just a theory. I had no guarantee it would work, and no alternative plan if it didn't. But I was a captive, after all—it wasn't as if I had anything else to do but try it out. I was in that collar for weeks, and it wasn't removed for a moment. If I was conscious and had the slightest bit of energy to spare, I poured my magic into it—a little bit at a time, of course, so as not to deplete myself too dangerously. And over time, I felt the collar begin to weaken. It wasn't just that it made me feel less ill, although that did happen; even its physical properties changed. I could feel it growing more brittle and fragile, and the surface of it where it touched my skin felt rough. Eventually, after long weeks of effort, it became weak enough that I could pull it apart with my hands, without using magic at all. I had fed it morsel by morsel until its stomach burst."

She sat back, a bit weary after having talked for so long, but she still beamed at them with undimmed brightness. "To answer your second question, yes and no. Yes, Elgar could hypothetically ruin the steel through the same method I did, presuming he's able to figure out how I did it, but it would take him weeks at a minimum. So no, it's not a skill he's going to be able to use in battle—or even a skill that I could, for that matter. Your weapons will still be effective."

Thank the gods for that, at least. Morgan was satisfied, but Roger still scratched his chin. "So was that why you delayed before you attacked? Why you went through all that humiliation first, at the execution? Because you needed more time to decay the steel?"

"Oh no, I had accomplished that a couple days earlier," she said. "I had actually stopped putting magic into it, lest the steel dissolve entirely, because I needed Elgar to think I was still helpless. I was saving up my magic instead, though there wasn't time to reach full strength before the fated day came. During the execution itself, I waited because I was hoping I could get Elgar and Oswhent to clump close together, and hit them both with a single spell." She glanced at her retainer. "I owed Oswhent that, for the suffering he put Seren through during my capture."

Morgan saw Roger flinch, but his expression was one of sadness, not anger. Given what she already knew about the person Len had become, she assumed Roger felt the marquise's anger was probably justified. "So are . . . are they dead?"

"Alas, probably not," the marquise said with a sigh, propping her chin on her hand. "As I said, I wasn't at full strength. I was planning to use all my remaining power to ensure the spell destroyed him, but then Seren showed up, and I had to use it to get us out of there instead. Elgar is a talented mage in his own right; he was most likely able to save himself in my absence. Either way, the spell I cast doesn't work like a normal wound; they can't die of complications after the fact. If they're still alive by now, they'll stay that way. Still, the wounds I caused are also permanent. Elgar fought the spell's casting, but now that it's taken hold, he can't heal it away. I definitely damaged him. That's not nothing."

And damaged Len, too, Morgan thought, but Roger only said, "You're right.

That's good news." He pushed himself to his feet. "I'll leave you ladies to your rest, but don't you run those experiments in the tunnels without me. Meantime, I'll see if I can turn up where the hell Marceline ran off to. What does she think is more important than this?"

THE ROOM MORGAN Imrick had provided was probably the best she had, though that wasn't exactly saying much. Seren had certainly had much, much worse in her time, but it was several steps down from Arianrod's customary accommodations. "Will you be comfortable enough, my lady?"

Arianrod glanced around the room in confusion. "What's the matter? It's quite clean."

It was, Seren realized. She had been preoccupied with the facts that the bed was narrow and the blanket thin, that the little table only had one rickety chair, and that there didn't seem to be any way to heat the water in the basin, supposing it had actually contained water to start with. "You do remember that I was very recently imprisoned, yes?" Arianrod sank onto the bed with a yawn. "I predict I'm about to have the best nap of my life."

"I'm sure you need it. I'll guard the door."

"You'll do no such thing," Arianrod said. "When was the last time *you* had a decent night's sleep? Don't bother answering, I already know it's too long. No one knows we're here, the room's locked, and you sleep like a cat anyway. Leave the door to take care of itself and replenish your own energies."

"But—"

"That was an order, and I'm too tired to argue it further. Come here and take off your godsdamned boots while you can still feel your feet."

Only half reluctantly, Seren checked that the door was latched one last time and then abandoned it. She sat at the foot of the bed and obediently pulled her boots off, and was forced to admit Arianrod was right: her feet *were* terribly stiff.

Arianrod must have been able to tell from her face. "You see? I did you a favor."

She was smiling, relaxed, but though Seren knew she was just tired, seeing her lying on her back like that, so perfectly still, sent a stab of fear through her. Before she knew what she was doing, she had twisted around and leaned forward, bending over her in search of any sign of undue weakness. She laid the back of her hand against Arianrod's forehead, but there was no difference in temperature.

Then she caught herself. She drew back a little, but couldn't seem to make herself move more than that. "Forgive me."

"It's all right." She raised herself up on her elbows, as if to prove she wasn't paralyzed. "I wouldn't lie about my physical state—that wouldn't do either of us any good. So believe me when I say I'm conclusively out of danger. There won't be a relapse, and I shouldn't even have a long recovery period the way I did at Stonespire and Eldren Cael. No more than the mages of old did."

It was heartening to hear that tone of calm certainty again, and it soothed her as it always did. Arianrod moved to one side of the bed to make room, and then they lay side by side, staring up at the bare ceiling. Though Seren was exhausted down to her bones, still sleep proved surprisingly elusive, as if darting just out of reach. "If you truly have recovered so quickly," she murmured, "you have no excuse for not eating like it, starting first thing tomorrow. And I know some stretches you can use to strengthen your muscles, which I'm sure are in a dreadful state. Your magic may be in order, but your body has a long way to go."

"Oh my." She felt Arianrod smile in the dark. "If I don't keep a close eye on you, I may end up with a nursemaid instead of a bodyguard."

"And when I don't keep a close eye on *you*, my lady, you read through lunch in the best of circumstances."

Arianrod hummed slightly, just on the verge of hearing. "That's not what you called me before."

Seren frowned, shifting on the thin mattress. "It isn't? When? It's what I always call you."

"When we were first in the tunnels," Arianrod said. "You . . . called me by name."

"Did I?" She cast her thoughts back to that terrible time, but she honestly couldn't remember what she had said. Still, Arianrod's memory was nearly infallible. "I apologize, then. I must have been too distracted by everything that was happening."

"Why would that change what you call me?"

Seren felt her face heat, and was grateful for the darkness of the room. "Because it's how I think of you. How I used to think of you, when I was a child who knew nothing about titles, and before I ever imagined I would come into your service. But I *am* in your service, and a servant should not take such liberties."

Arianrod considered her words. "I suppose you're right. Servants are expected to adhere to certain forms of address, and it wouldn't do to throw all that into chaos in public." She yawned again. "But when there's no one else around, I should think it wouldn't matter what you call me. Or . . . no. In situations where there's no chance of causing an incident of manners, it would be . . . nice. For you to use my name."

"Nice," Seren repeated.

"That's what I said, Seren." And that seemed to settle the matter, as far as she was concerned.

Seren was the one left chewing it over in her mind, not quite content to swallow it just yet. Try as she might, she couldn't seem to subtract enough weight from the word to feel natural saying it casually. Not yet, at least. She sighed. "I think I shall have to work up to it, my lady."

"You're free to be as ridiculous as you'd like," Arianrod replied. "Good night."

Chapter Forty-four

Valyanrend

VARALEN WAS AMBIVALENT about the prospect of ever waking up again—and that was before he tried to move and felt stabbing pains all along his left arm. They probably hadn't cut it off, then. He cracked his eyes open, and found himself in bed, a sheet over him and a familiar face bent toward his bedside. It was one of the only faces left on this earth he was actually glad to see.

"Quentin," he breathed. "Dare I ask what's happened?"

The captain hung his head. "It would be easier to tell you what hasn't happened, my lord. His Eminence has been awake for the better part of a day—he did ask me to send you to him once you rejoined us, though no one has been able to do much for you, I'm afraid. The marquise is still in the wind, despite all our best efforts, and His Eminence is refusing to allow the gates to be opened again, lest that aid in her escape. But if she continues not to be found, we'll effectively besiege ourselves even without the Issamiri, though it seems they're poised to cut us off further. The people are, naturally, rather alarmed, but His Eminence has refused to address them, leaving it to me and mine to come up with what to say to them. And we, as you know, are no orators."

Poor Quentin. Always so steadfast and loyal, always just trying to do what was best. Before Arianrod Margraine had told him the truth, Varalen would have leapt up in a panic, desperate to assuage Elgar, to salvage the situation. But now? He could almost have laughed, if the thing in his heart that made him capable of mirth did not seem to have been cut out. It was a crisis, to be sure, but he couldn't care less.

He shifted again, a reflex after so long in one position, and again he suffered a thousand pinpricks. "What happened to my arm?"

"None of the healers we consulted knew what to do about it, my lord. It seems to have stopped spreading, but it isn't receding, either. And no salve they put on it made a whit of difference."

Seeing it for himself, Varalen wasn't surprised the healers had been baffled. From his shoulder to the tips of his fingers, the skin of his arm had gone a mottled purple-black, as if it were charred and bruised at the same time. He touched it with the fingers of his right hand, and it felt charred, too, peeling and rough. He felt the sensation of his fingertips only dimly, and not without pain. "Is it . . . infected?"

"They don't think so. You aren't feverish, and there's no inflammation or pus. But as for what it actually is . . ." He shrugged helplessly.

"Magic, I suppose," Varalen said. "Some infernal offspring of that woman's imagination. Is Elgar still wounded?"

Quentin raised a reproachful eyebrow at the lack of title, but let it pass. "He is, my lord, and quite . . . visibly. He's much like you, in that he's in no danger anymore, but the marks won't recede, and they still cause pain. It's one of the reasons he's so agitated, and one of the reasons why he won't go before the people."

"I wonder what he'd even say to them. If it were me, I'd be quite out of ideas. I suppose he could tell them she's dead, but that only works if she doesn't turn up again, and I wouldn't bet on that."

"Still, my lord, I'm sure whatever help you can provide His Eminence will be most welcome."

Again, Varalen felt that absence where humor would have been. "I'm not sure of that, Quentin. But we shall never know, I'm afraid. Where is my son?"

"In his chambers, where he's always been." The captain scratched his side-whiskers anxiously. "What do you mean, we'll never know?"

"Quentin." Varalen hauled himself up in bed, trying to use only his torso and his right arm, though the action still sent pain all along his left side. "I have long noted your loyalty and dedication. That is not always remarkable, or worthy of praise—every despot has his lackeys, and following orders is often the simpler choice. But I've noted it in you because you have always seemed decent and just to me as well. Can I ask you why such a person has devoted himself to Elgar?"

Quentin was still watching him with wary confusion, but Varalen knew honesty came naturally to him. "I believe you know that I first served under Norverian. He was . . . unsuited to leadership, because he had only ever concerned himself with himself. Any coin he could get his hands on went toward his own comfort and luxury, and he neither knew nor cared how anyone else would get by. His Eminence was put in charge of the treasury back then, largely because no one else wanted the job, I think. But he knew Norverian was too foolish to understand the reports he compiled, so before long he began to simply falsify them, lowering the totals and hiding money away. But rather than keeping it for himself, he poured that money into the projects that Norverian had let languish, that the people so desperately needed: repairs to city roads and the cisterns beneath the aqueduct, imports of medicine . . . he averted quite a few disasters, and went to great pains to ensure his master never learned of what he had done. But the rest of us, those who lived in neighborhoods he had improved, could hardly fail to notice. So we learned that we had, in effect, two leaders: a child to appease, and a man who actually did the work. And when, in time, he killed Noverian and deposed him, there were those ready to support him from the beginning. I was one of those people, my lord, and have been ever since."

"I see." Varalen had known how Elgar had come to power, of course, but he had never heard the rest of it. Had Elgar been skilled at manipulating others from the start, or had he actually possessed a few scruples back then? He remembered what Arianrod Margraine had said about Elgar back when he had first brought her to the Citadel. "It's true that Elgar is devoid of the vices and appetites many others possess. Power has not corrupted him in that way. And that is no small thing."

"And yet I do not think you are about to praise him to me, my lord," Quentin said.

To his surprise, Varalen discovered he had a single laugh left in him, bitter though it was. "I'm not like you, Captain. I've never thought Elgar was a good person—I know quite well he isn't. There was a time when I thought he'd be . . . if not good for this city, then at least neutral, certainly no worse than many others. But now I know the truth of that as well. I've only ever served him because it benefited me—even just to keep me and Ryam from being harmed. But as soon as I believed he could truly help my son . . . there is nothing I would not have done, even though I knew who Elgar was. You, at least, are innocent of that."

Quentin's bushy eyebrows drew together, a frown creasing his weathered face. "You're frightening me, my lord."

"Good. You should be frightened—of Elgar, more than you've ever been frightened of anyone. He's a mage, Quentin. Arianrod Margraine is, too—he didn't lie about that—but the battle you witnessed the other day was nothing less than magic against magic. He has no cure, no shield, no godsdamn prayer; he has his own power, the same as hers. And he would use it to enslave this entire city—this entire continent, if he could.

"I can't make you believe me. If the evidence of your own eyes can't do that, I expect you're a lost cause. But unlike me, you're still a good man. You can still get out of this with your conscience intact—hell, maybe even with your life. You just have to see him for what he is. And then you have to leave, immediately, before he can catch on. If he knows he can't keep you willingly, he has ways to keep you without your consent. I wish I could tell you more about them, but . . . I didn't truly want to know. But I know they're as real as this mark on my arm." He swallowed hard. "And if this warning has been any use to you at all, I can only beg that you will take my son with you when you go. I could not secure a future for him, but he shouldn't have to die Elgar's captive. If you could take him to

Sheath Alleys . . . no one there trusts me anymore, nor should they, but Ryam is blameless, and he's still a Halfen. With both her husbands dead, my mother goes by Rheila Halfen again now. If you could just get him to her, I would be more grateful than I could possibly say."

Quentin stared at him, stone-faced. He ran a thumb and forefinger down each of his side-whiskers, mouth perfectly still until the moment he spoke. "If you think it wise—if you think it essential—to leave now, why are you not following your own advice?"

Varalen smiled bleakly. "They would never let *me* go, Captain."

"They would if I were escorting you."

"Not with my son."

Quentin fell silent. He must have known he couldn't deny it. "It's not only that," Varalen said. "It'll be safer for you if I stay behind to distract him. My chances of remaining inconspicuous with this arm are next to none, after all. People would probably accuse me of being cursed. And who knows, perhaps they'd be right."

Quentin gave him a mournful look. "It sounds to me like you're just making excuses."

"Of course I am," Varalen said. "You see, I'm still being selfish. I want my son to live as long as he can, but I don't want to have to watch him die."

"And that is truly your answer, my lord?"

"I've never been a lord," Varalen said. "They used to call me Len Varsten, of Sheath." He stood up from the bed. "Goodbye, Captain."

Quentin sat there a moment longer, as if he were still seeing some afterimage of Varalen. But then he stood up, too, head still bent. "I'm sorry. It should've been . . . Forgive me."

And then he was gone. Gods willing, to get Ryam and get the hell out, but Varalen probably wouldn't ever know. In a kinder world, he would have gotten to see his son one last time. But he needed to move quickly now; he couldn't give sentimentality the chance to ruin his plan. Ryam would understand, he hoped. And if not, he'd just have one more reason to add to the pile of his resentments in the future.

"Well," he said, to no one in particular. "Let's get this over with."

He asked a passing servant to direct him to Elgar, and found him shut up in the map room, alone, both hands braced against the table. Varalen could immediately see why he didn't wish to face the people like this—if it had been him, he wouldn't want to face his own mirror. The side of Elgar's face had received the same treatment as Varalen's arm, disfigured by a purple-black blotch of peeling skin. He had apparently not been able to reconstitute the eye the marquise had burst, but he hadn't had time to have something made to cover it, either, and the socket gaped repulsively, its interior the same unnatural color and texture as the rest. Tinier spots extended down his jaw and neck, and across the bridge of his nose.

He turned the better half of his face toward Varalen, casting the other into shadow. Thank the gods for small mercies. "There you are," he said, rubbing his good eye. "You certainly took your time."

"Yes, I was rather unconscious," Varalen said. "Having nearly died and all."

Elgar scoffed. "My injuries make yours look trifling. You didn't even lose the arm."

"Somehow. I expected worse from her, after all the anger she clearly bore me. I wonder if she was determined to get you first, or if the sudden appearance of Seren Almasy ruined her focus." *Or perhaps she thought I was as good as dead already,* he thought. "Have you figured out what spell she used? Is there any way to reverse it?"

"No, and I don't know. Whatever she did, it consumed the magic I tried to use to counter it, and just made the resulting spell worse. And I haven't been able to heal it beyond what I managed at the time." He pushed off the table and faced Varalen fully. "But there's a much bigger question. What the hell happened with the steel? I thought Selwyn assured you it was foolproof."

"She never actually said *that*. She just said she was certain it worked on true mages, because it had been used that way in the past. But I do wonder if Arianrod knew she could do that from the start." She had certainly not told him everything she knew about vardrath steel, though he could hardly blame her for playing him false. No wonder she had been so relieved that Elgar didn't want to experiment with the steel himself.

"We'll just have to assume it may not work in the future," Elgar said. "I suspect she needed time to wear away at it, though I suppose she could have waited until the execution on purpose, to damage me as publicly as possible. No matter. Next time, she'll be killed on sight, and the body charred to ash. Perhaps I'll bury the ashes in a pit for good measure."

"You still have enough optimism to expect there's going to *be* a next time," Varalen said. "That's . . . certainly one way of looking at it."

If Elgar recognized the sarcasm, he ignored it. "There's just too damned much to do. That woman's gotten loose in an entire city, and without the damned steel, who knows what spells she's devised to hide herself? I've got to assume my guards will be useless at finding her, so I'm going to have to devise something myself, some spell to reveal her, or counter her magic in some other way. There's the matter of the people, who need to be placated anew—more speeches and assurances, especially now that I've confined them to the city. And then there's the bloody resistance, always keeping my plans behind schedule. It would be enough for twenty of me, and no one is any bloody use!"

"Ah," Varalen said. "Are we perhaps having an unpleasant time of it?"

Elgar squinted at him, not even crossly, but in confusion. And that was almost worse, that he couldn't even fathom Varalen defying him anymore. "What on earth is the matter with you?"

"That's the question, isn't it?" He folded his arms, keeping both his eyes fixed on Elgar's one. "Why don't you consider it, and think about what reason I might possibly have for this sudden shift in behavior?"

"Are you blaming me for that injury? Do you think I should've protected you better? My face should be proof enough that I could barely protect myself. And if anyone should've known about the flaw in the steel, it should've been you, not me."

Was he truly that oblivious, or was he doing this on purpose? Had he forgotten about Ryam completely—that Ryam was the only reason Varalen had worked so tirelessly on his behalf? Or did he think feigning ignorance would make him more sympathetic somehow? Varalen couldn't tell—not from Elgar's face, nor from what he knew of the man. Perhaps that was proof he had never known him much at all.

"Arianrod told me," he said. "That you lied to me. That you can't heal my son."

He watched Elgar's half-ruined face closely, curious, despite it all, whether guilt would cross it, or regret. But once confusion gave way to realization, the only emotion he saw was calm, even contentment. Elgar was secure in the knowledge that he once again understood what was happening, and nothing more. "Ah. That. Well, to be fair, I don't *know* I can't. I'm certainly prepared to try my hardest. But yes, it probably won't work."

Was that what his plan had been, rather than simply killing Varalen once the war was over? Would he have tried to heal Ryam, and then feigned shock and horror when it didn't work? Would he have genuinely tried everything he could, merely hiding the fact that he'd known beforehand that it would be useless? And if he had done that, would Varalen have believed him? Would he have been sympathetic—would he even have forgiven him?

"I can't believe it." He stared down at his ruined hand, opening and closing his fingers despite the pain. "I can't believe that even I was so thoroughly taken in by you."

"What's so hard to believe?" Elgar asked. "Your vision was clouded by your own self-interest, as everyone's is. You presented yourself to me as a man of principle, who was too good for my employ, but in actual fact, I was the one whose dream always encompassed the world and its betterment, whereas yours never extended further than your own progeny."

He had prided himself on his intellect and perception, his understanding of others, but it seemed that Elgar was the one who had deciphered him, while keeping himself opaque. What an embarrassment for a strategist. "You're right. What a cruel twist of fate indeed, in every way. If Ryam had been healthy, and my vision less clouded, I could have used my talents against you."

Elgar laughed. "No, Varalen, if I'd left you to your own devices you'd have stayed out of this war entirely. You'd be off in some far-flung corner of the world chasing a cure for your son, perhaps, or trading in silk and porcelain in Lakeport, soothing your grief with the coin that lined your pockets. And if he'd been well, and you'd never suffered any ill fortune? Gods, you'd have been even more insufferable, even more self-absorbed. Don't fool and flatter yourself into thinking that you'd have been some rebel, sacrificing it all for some flawed concept of justice. You don't know the meaning of sacrifice. You know grief, and loss, but you're not giving up your son, he's being torn from your grasp bit by bit, while you do everything you can to hold on to him. I'm sure it's miserable in a way I can't imagine, but it doesn't make you virtuous, just unlucky."

Varalen thought of Roger, the one person, besides his father, he'd always held up as the pinnacle of selfishness. And yet, somehow, in all the years since they'd lived in Sheath together, his cousin had become someone capable of risking his life in rebellion. Having to think that, at the end of it all, he'd end up losing to that craven little weasel . . . that was truly adding insult to injury. "You're right, again. I've never sacrificed anything. And I never will. Even now, I'm not being magnanimous; I'm simply surrendering something I no longer want." He took a deep breath, gathering himself. "But even a man as selfish as I am can still do a bit of good if he truly sets his mind to it."

He gripped Elgar's slightly bent head by the ear, and slammed the wounded side of his face into the strategy table with all his strength.

He'd used their initial conversation to take stock of the room, identifying all potential weapons and complications. Elgar must still have been recovering, because while he was otherwise fully dressed, the sword and knife he always wore were absent. There was nothing else in the room that was expressly intended for use as a weapon, but that meant there was nothing for Elgar to take hold of, either, and increased the importance of the element of surprise. Varalen's immediate surroundings, besides the table he'd just made use of, were maps, which were useless, and chairs, which were too heavy for him to wield against Elgar, especially with one damaged arm. The only object light enough for him to lift but heavy enough to cause damage was a glass inkwell near one corner of the table, and Varalen had maneuvered himself halfway between it and Elgar. If the pain that coursed through his arm when he so much as brushed it against something was any indication, having his entire wounded face bashed against solid wood would be debilitating for Elgar, and his strangled scream and the way he buckled against the table seemed to support that hypothesis.

Seizing the opening, Varalen snatched up the inkwell while Elgar was still curled around the edge of the table. The drawback of making sure the sightless half of his face hit the tabletop was that he was now out of Elgar's blind spot, fully in view. So he brought the inkwell down on the uninjured half, landing a blow on the edge of Elgar's cheekbone. He knew he lacked the strength to shatter the thick glass, but even if he couldn't cut Elgar, it still served as an efficient bludgeon.

But perhaps he was too weak after his injury, or perhaps the inkwell was lighter than it seemed, or perhaps he was simply unused to bludgeoning people in general. After two blows, he still hadn't managed to beat Elgar into unconsciousness, and on the third try, Elgar grabbed his wrist, wrenching his arm to the side and causing him to drop the inkwell to the floor.

Before he could do anything else, Varalen stomped on the inside of his ankle, making his legs give out. As Elgar fell forward, Varalen grabbed him around the throat with both hands and thrust him against the table, squeezing as tight as he could and digging both thumbs into his windpipe.

Every moment he kept his left hand clenched as tight as it could go was agony, but Varalen ground his jaw shut and held his whole body taut, devoting every inch of consciousness to maintaining the pressure. Elgar's face started turning additional colors, and a strange noise came from his blocked throat. He struggled, trying to push off from his feet, but Varalen kept the whole weight of his body pushing down, keeping Elgar's head and back flat against the table.

Then the edge of Elgar's flailing hand, a ridge of bone just beneath the skin, struck the side of Varalen's wounded arm, and he flinched, his grip slackening just a little.

Elgar surged forward and kicked him in the leg, while his hand took another shot at Varalen's arm. They both fell to the floor in a heap, limbs pinwheeling, each trying to swipe at the other first.

They were both exhausted and hurt, but that just meant they were evenly matched. It was no valiant contest of fists, just a sluggish and pathetic struggle, yet they were fighting for their lives all the same. He tried to rain blows on Elgar's face, but every one he landed with his left hand hurt him just as much. Then he felt a shift in the air, like a weight pressing down on him, restricting his movement and his breathing, though there was nothing there. It lasted only a handful of moments before fading away—it had probably been difficult enough for Elgar to muster the concentration for a spell in this state, and he must have been drained from his fight with the marquise. But the spell did its job, for those few seconds, and Elgar slipped from his grasp, wrenching Varalen's injured arm to the side so hard he thought it was about to tear from his body. His good arm was too far away, and he couldn't stop Elgar from kicking him in the ribs, a crushing pain that was repeated over and over until he could hardly see, black and red bursting behind his eyelids.

Elgar stood over him, gasping, sweating, hair mussed, flushed in the half of his face that still changed color. But unharmed, beyond some bruises-to-be. Not even scratched. He opened his mouth as he caught his breath, flashing his teeth. "Oh, good show, Varalen. As valiant and pathetic as I would have expected of you. How far you must think I have fallen, to be undone by such a simple ploy, from such a ruined man!"

"Worth . . . the effort, I thought," Varalen panted, gripping Elgar's ankle with both hands. But he couldn't budge that foot. "One ruined man can take on another at least, right?"

"Is that how you see me?" Elgar scoffed. "Did you think I was defeated? Did you think that, after a single attack from that woman, I retreated here merely to curl up in surrender?" He traced a hand delicately down his ravaged cheek. "Or did you think it was this that had undone me? Varalen, I don't care about my face. It may cause some difficulties for me with the people, and I shall have to ponder how to confront them with it, or how it may be cleaned up. But unlike you, I understand sacrifice. I would give up far more than this, to achieve the world I wish for."

He idly leaned his weight on Varalen's ribs, pressing down until he wheezed. "I'll tell you what. Before you die, I'll show you just one thing. I wouldn't want you to depart this world thinking that I'm destined to lose, after all. Then you might die with some consolation, or even hope." He straightened up. "Do you remember another great failure of yours, many months ago now? Do you remember the object I asked you to procure for me from Hornoak that ended up in my greatest enemy's hands?"

"How could I forget? Oh, wait, I've forgotten. What was it called again? A *wardrenholt*? Not that I ever understood its significance, because you took great pains to tell me as little as possible."

"So I did. And how right I was to suspect you."

"Yes, well, that's the problem with retainers you have to compel into service, isn't it?"

"Then let me make up for it by telling you now." Elgar reached into his pocket, and produced a glass sphere with a cloudy interior, as if it were filled with smoke. "Here it is."

Varalen was so caught off guard he actually stopped struggling for a moment.

"That can't be. Arianrod insisted that whatever she had done to that thing made it impossible for anyone to recover it."

"And I'm sure she's right," Elgar said, turning the stone over contemplatively. "I made this one myself." He grinned at Varalen's confusion, and the right side of his mouth wrinkled oddly, the skin too stiff. "I'd hoped to find one that already existed, because it's not as if I ever came across specific instructions, and magic is a dangerous thing to play around with. But with limited options remaining to me, I thought it worth the risk. The idea certainly sounded simple enough that any mage could do it—you just put your magic into a receptacle, a little bit at a time. The one I sought to recover was a stone, but I used glass, because I wanted a physical representation of how much I had generated. I guessed that for a mage used to enchantments, it would be fairly easy to pick up. And the image within has grown thicker as I've progressed, so I seem to be doing it right." He rubbed the side of his face. "It was no more than a curiosity at first, to make up for the loss I suffered because of your incompetence and Arianrod's plotting. But with the resistance able to kill my spells, I thought about what you said: if I had any hope of success, I had to place my enchantments somewhere no one could get to them." He tossed the sphere and caught it again. "This is my answer."

Varalen glared at it. It was so close, but even if he could dash it from Elgar's hands, he suspected the glass wouldn't break. "So you figured if you could put enough power into that thing, you wouldn't have to control your army with dozens of spells anchored in specific neighborhoods. You could just use one."

"Insightful as always. If the rebels want to unmake my army now, they'll have to storm the Citadel and take it from me. And to have a hope of doing that, they'll have to come out of the shadows at last." He stared into the depths of the sphere, then down at Varalen's face. "What do you think, my strategist? Am I a doomed and cornered man now?"

He must have seen the answer in Varalen's silence, in the glib reply he couldn't give. "See, that's much better. A bit of humility at the last. The Ninists believed their Lord of Heaven looked kindly on humility above all else."

Varalen coughed. "That was just a lie the religious hierarchy told to curry favor with the nobles, by urging the poor not to aspire beyond their station."

"Sadly true. But since the Lord of Heaven himself never existed, what's one more lie?" He raised the sphere, his humor fading into seriousness. "You did much for me—much more than you ought to have, given that I was never able to offer you anything you truly wanted in return. So I will make sure this is painless for you."

But Varalen still knew one vital thing Elgar didn't. He knew that Roger was the Fang. And he knew withholding that information had saved at least Roger's life, and probably several of his associates' as well, who might have been too easily discovered through their connection with him. He couldn't gloat over the knowledge, not like Elgar showing off his little sphere—he didn't particularly want to be tortured into revealing it. But he could die knowing it, at least. "If you could read the thoughts in my head at this moment, you'd regret your lenience."

"I can live with that," Elgar said. "You, on the other hand . . ."

Chapter Forty-five

Valyanrend

WHEN THE HAMMERING on her door forced Naishe into wakefulness, she opened her eyes to darkness, the dim light of barely dawn still too weak to properly illuminate the room. Beside her, Wren turned over, mumbling sleepily, "Who's that?"

"I'm quite certain I know," Naishe said, getting dressed as quickly as she could while the banging continued without a pause. She adjusted the blanket back over Wren. "Don't bother getting up; this'll be over with quickly. Though once it's properly morning, I'm going to have a stern talk with Mr. Redding about who, precisely, pays the rent on this room."

She flung the door open so abruptly her father nearly stumbled over the threshold, his fist flailing through empty space. "Oh, this had *better* be good. And if you even *start* another argument about me leaving—"

"It's the opposite," her father said, his face stony. "It's very, very bad. So bad that *everyone* ought to leave, but since you won't, you'd at least better be prepared to hide." He pushed past her into the room, then stopped short when he saw Wren, helplessly sitting up in bed, the blanket pooled around his waist and his clothes folded on a chair five feet away. "Does the boy not have his own lodgings?"

"He's a man, not a boy, and these are *my* lodgings, that I can do with as I please. If matters have deteriorated as far as you implied, surely you have no time to criticize?"

Her father actually seemed to accept that. "Fine. Shut the door. You need to hear this."

Naishe felt, privately, that *he* could have shut the door, since he was the one to walk through it, but she had more pressing concerns. "All right. What is it?"

"Wallward Heights has been surrounded. The entire district. The city guard have gone in there and demanded all able-bodied and unwounded adults to come out of doors. All those chosen have to accept one of those infernal talismans, and if they refuse, they're arrested. The *whole* district, Naishe."

Naishe sat down heavily on the edge of the bed, trying to think this through. "But only that one district? Isn't that odd?"

"It has no significant strategic meaning to the resistance," Wren said. "We would know."

"I suspect Elgar's testing how it goes over," her father said. "He doesn't have the manpower to do this to the entire city at once, and it might provoke a revolt. But if they prove mostly tractable, he'll probably move to other districts in the coming days. Perhaps the relative lack of resistance presence is why he chose Wall-ward; he felt they were likely to obey, and if nothing catastrophic happens to them for obeying, the rest of the city may feel that's the wisest course."

"Still, after what happened at the execution, I can't imagine confidence in the imperator is at a high."

"It isn't, but they don't need it to be. In a way, it helps his people's arguments. Since the marquise is on the loose in the city, and they haven't been able to lo-cate her, they suspect some Valyanrenders may be helping her. They're acceler-ating their distribution of the talismans to try to combat her influence, and they won't allow people to refuse for fear of how far that influence may have already spread."

"None of that is true," Naishe said. "Well, the first sentence, perhaps."

"Of course none of it is true. But they're using it as an excuse, and people are believing it. We thought that her escape would make Elgar seem weaker and less creditable in the eyes of the people, and perhaps that's true for some. But it also makes them more afraid of magic, and more eager for protection."

Naishe stood up, locking eyes with Wren. "It's useless to sit here speculating right now. We can speculate to our hearts' content *after* we make sure the rest of the resistance knows about this. And Morgan and her people, though I suspect the guard will be loath to tackle Sheath anytime soon. I'll take Rask; I'm sure he'll want to help spread the word, too, and he's efficient at that sort of thing."

"Good thinking. I'll alert the Iron's Den lot, and send them in different directions."

Naishe was about to grab her bow and storm out of the room, but her father caught her by the elbow. "Vanaishendi. You're not listening to me. We don't know how fast this is going to spread, or to which neighborhoods. You—and even this whelp—are exactly the fighters Elgar's people are looking for. You've got to hide yourself before you have to decide whether to be arrested or accept one of those cursed things."

"*You* can hide, if you like," Naishe said. "I'm not going to use this information to save myself and leave my friends and compatriots to fend for themselves—my subordinates, who trust me to lead and protect them. The vast majority of them are as at risk as I am, and deserve the same choice you've given me. I thank you for the information, Father—and even for the warning, truly. But I have work to do, and I cannot put it off to argue with you."

She tried to push past him, but he took hold of her elbow again, gently. "Wait. I can move through this city, too. Let me help. Three will get the job done much more quickly than two."

Naishe stood still, searching his face. "Are you sure?"

"Why wouldn't I be? If I can't convince you to keep yourself out of danger, I can at least lessen the danger that reaches you. Why do you think I've been keeping my ear to the ground in the first place?"

Naishe didn't know what to say, and in a different time and place, she would have waited to untangle it, to say precisely what she wanted and meant. But in this time and place, people were counting on her. "All right. In that case, ask for Talia at the Parnell Grocery and tell her everything you told me. There aren't as many of us near her, but she can identify the ones there are and send you where you need to be. And, well . . . thank you."

"Don't mention it." He grinned crookedly, more like the father she remembered from her youth. "You're not the only one who knows how to do what must be done."

"I'm glad we're all in agreement for once," Wren said. "But, um. Could I trouble you both to go out ahead of me?" He glanced meaningfully at his clothes, still just out of reach on the chair.

"Great gods," her father said, and lunged for the door.

Arianrod Margraine's "nap" ended up lasting the rest of the daylight hours, and extended far into the night. She woke up just before dawn, and she and her retainer gave Braddock a terrific shock when he wandered down to the first floor to find them rummaging around in near-darkness in search of water. But after her ladyship had drunk her fill, cleaned herself up, outfitted herself in the clothes Seren had bought, and eaten another meal, the early morning daylight revealed a vast improvement. The unearthly pallor of the previous day was gone, and she moved without the slowness of an invalid. She was still thinner than she ought to be, but that was not something that could be fixed overnight.

It felt more than a little strange to be trotting down the tunnels with her, even with all the time Morgan had spent with Lord Vespas. Braddock was minding the tavern, so it was just the four of them. Seren tended not to speak unless spoken to first, and the marquise seemed entirely preoccupied with Roger, so Morgan was left to awkwardly bring up the rear in silence. She couldn't imagine how Roger must be feeling over Len, but perhaps the knowledge that Lady Margraine's spell almost certainly hadn't killed his cousin had lifted his spirits, for he answered all her questions—and her requests for more of his damned stories—with his usual charm. Morgan still couldn't believe he'd actually found someone who wanted to listen to them, let alone that that person was a foreign queen.

Besides the nine statues in its center, the chamber looked as empty to Morgan as it always had, but Lady Margraine insisted she could see a great spell inscribed on the floor. Morgan unsheathed her dagger and waved it around, but she felt no more than she had the last time she'd been here. She extended the blade toward the statues, but the marquise grabbed her arm. "I wouldn't do that if I were you. I can't say exactly what would happen, but I don't think it would be good. Probably the blade would come out the worse for it. And please don't try to undo the spell on the floor, either—it's practically a work of art, besides potentially still having some future use."

"But why is none of all this magic getting through?" Morgan asked. "Is it like what you said about the *wardrenfell*—the steel's trying to absorb more than it can take?"

"No, the sword we used still went cold when a *wardrenfell* touched it. I can only conclude that the steel simply isn't reacting to the magic in here, but I have no idea why that would be. That's what's so fascinating about it. Will you bring it over here for a moment?"

Morgan did, and the marquise touched the blade with a wince. "Well, it definitely hasn't become inert." She held out her hand, and a ball of light coalesced in her palm. "Can you try to destroy this?"

Morgan slashed the blade across the sphere, and the light dissipated. "Hmm," the marquise said. "So the steel can still absorb spells just fine even when I create them from the magic in this room. And it can still detect *me,* even though, from my point of view, I'm practically drowning in all the magic in here."

"What *I* want to know," Roger said, "is why the dagger is so different from that ruby I found. I couldn't even get it in here."

Morgan had heard this story before, but the marquise raised an eyebrow. "The ruby?"

"I found it, left behind by a long-dead thief. It could detect magic, too, or I think it could. It was the opposite of the steel—light, and heat. And it didn't absorb the magic, just indicated it was there. But when I tried to bring it down the tunnel to this room, it exploded. And whatever caused it to work broke; the pieces are useless."

The marquise pondered that in a brief silence. "Seren and I . . . we have reason to believe that, once, the whole continent was like this room, suffused with this much magic. But vardrath steel is ancient; all of it that exists is from centuries upon centuries in the past, so long ago that the method of its creation has been lost to time. What would happen if you created vardrath steel in a world where this much magic was everywhere? If the steel were constantly absorbing it right out of the air, before long it would decay simply by existing. I ruined my collar in a matter of weeks; who would pay for a weapon that would crumble to dust in that time? But because the steel hasn't crumbled to dust—on the contrary, has lasted hundreds of years—those who created it must have found some way to prevent it from feeding on . . . how to define it? Magic that would be useless to its purpose? Though it's not as if an object can determine such a thing."

"What if it created a sort of base measurement?" Roger asked. "Where anything above the typical saturation level of magic becomes a target? If the ruby was made centuries later, when magic was much scarcer, that would explain the difference. It wasn't built to measure something so immense."

"I think that's right for the ruby," the marquise said, "but it doesn't fully explain the steel. One mage or one spell in a world with little magic would register far below this base measurement, yet the steel still functions perfectly."

"But, well . . ." Seren said, from slightly over Morgan's shoulder, and she jumped. That woman was better at veiling her presence than Marceline in the middle of a crowd. "Don't we already have an example of the steel failing to absorb magic when it could have? My lady, you keep saying that nothing happens unless you cast, because your magic is part of you. But why couldn't the steel just take it anyway, like draining the juice from a fruit? It would kill you, because you can't live without your magic. But shouldn't it be . . . possible?"

The marquise frowned, winding her hair around her fingers. "That's a good point. You're right, I had overlooked that."

"Here's what I want explained," Morgan said. "Does the steel eat magic, or does it only eat spells?"

"What's the difference?" Roger asked.

"No, she's right," Lady Margraine said, pointing at Morgan. "The magic in this room is just passively existing. And my magic, when I'm not using it, could be said to be passively existing, too. A spell is actively trying to *do* something. Perhaps that makes the quality or the concentration of the magic change." She tapped her chin. "It's not a full explanation—it doesn't cover why the steel reacts to me and not to the room, among other things. But I think it's the right direction. If I ever solve it entirely, perhaps I'll understand how the steel was created." She glanced down at the floor. "In the meantime, shall we move on to this?"

Morgan scuffed at the stone uneasily, disturbed by the fact that something so monumental could be so completely hidden from her. "So this controls whether *every* mage can use magic or not?"

"Not precisely. It's more that it puts a barrier in place, that you'd have to overcome in order to cast. That's what all the runic is for, to allow a workaround for emergencies."

"But that could be a fix to our problem, right?" Roger asked. "Elgar doesn't even know this place exists. If you can invoke the spell again—"

"No," the marquise said firmly.

"Why not?"

She gave a little huff. "It is irritating in the extreme to have to say this, but the intellect responsible for this spell was truly exceptional. I'm still just trying to understand it. If I tinker around with it impetuously, I risk—"

They were cut off by the sound of rapid footsteps in the corridor just outside. Seren put her hand on her wrist, but Roger shook his head. "Footfalls that light must be the monkey's. Took her long enough."

Before Seren and the marquise could do more than look confused, Marceline burst into the room. "You won't believe the night I've had. I only just got back to Sheath, and Braddock said you two had come down . . ." She trailed off, apparently realizing there were four of them. Then she laid eyes on Seren, and her entire affect changed.

"*You!*" She pointed one finger at the center of Seren's chest, heedless of their difference in height. "How the hell did you—why didn't you just—do you know what I've *been* through because of you?"

Seren Almasy, who had so ferociously knocked a knife from Morgan's hand not a day earlier, quailed apologetically before the anger of a scrawny child. "That's what I get for being concerned, I suppose," Marceline continued, buoyed on by her own momentum. "Did you have a nice tea with my friends while I was being dragged all over creation by yours? And you didn't give a thought to the *very clear instructions* I gave you—lucky you didn't run into bloody Rask or Ritsu or Gods know who down here. But I expect as long as you got your lady out, you don't care about anything else, do you?"

"Seren," the marquise said, "how could you have failed to mention making the acquaintance of such a marvelous young person? And you must be the monkey, though I'm not sure why. Seren is my retainer, so I take full responsibility for any inconvenience she might have caused you, the full extent of which I hope you'll relate without any abridgement whatsoever."

"Oh, aye, I know all about you," Marceline said. "It seems everyone I meet is going into fits over you, and it's never any good news for me." She braced her hands on her knees, taking a much-needed breath. "And to think I just got the lot of them settled well away from us, too. I'll have to go right back there and fetch them."

"Monkey," Roger said, "I think I understood every third word of what you just said. Who is it you've got to go and fetch?"

"You wouldn't believe me if I told you, Roger, so you'll just have to wait and see for yourself." Marceline turned on her heel. "Oh, and I'll tell Braddock he's got to close the tavern for the day, so you can all come meet us there when you're finished with . . . whatever this is. I can't imagine what this is doing to your profits, Morgan. Half of Sheath thinks you're pregnant."

And then she was gone, before Morgan had time to say a word. "*I* can't imagine what that one will be like when she's grown," she muttered to Roger. "What do you think? Are we done here?"

"We can always come back. Whatever Marceline's up to, it sounds more urgent. But, ah, your ladyship? Could I have a quick word? In private?"

"THIS IS WHAT I wanted to show you," Roger said, pausing in front of the only door he'd ever found within the tunnels. "But before we go in, I need to ask you not to mention this place to anyone else. I discovered it, and I haven't shared it. I'm only showing you now because you may need any resource you can get if you're to understand that spell, and I won't throw away any advantage it could give us in the fight ahead."

Lady Margraine nodded, and Roger opened the door.

There wasn't much to see at first; this room was out of the way of the lines of braziers Naishe's people had constructed, so Roger had to follow her in with his old friend the candlestick. Lady Margraine drew close to the shelves, squinting in the dim light. "A library? I admit, that's not what I expected. Can you even read Old Lantian?"

"No, but—"

She caught her breath, as if he'd punched her. "Does that say *A History of Castles and the Ruins of Stone*? It can't be. That book is lost. There've been books *written* about the search for it."

"I'm not surprised," Roger said. "This library is from before the fall of Ninism. When I found it—"

She snatched the candlestick from his grasp with surprising strength, cupping her hand around the flame to protect the books. "*The Death of the Forest Clans*—my ancestor wrote about the loss of this one. The first Daven. It had already been purged from libraries in his day. The rest of this shelf I've never even heard of, except . . ." She pulled out a thick stack of parchment, loosely bound in dark blue leather. "There's no title. What's this one?"

She propped it on the little desk and flipped it open, but when she got to the first page, she froze. Roger peered over her shoulder to see words in a tight, irregular script, with a gentle line through them as if they'd been crossed out: *On the Aberrant and Medicinal Uses of Obscure Herbaceous Species.* Beneath them, in a thinner, more swooping hand, was written, *Darling, no one's going to read a book called that, no matter how well researched it is. Try this.* Beneath *that,* in careful block letters, was written, *One Hundred and One Dangerous Plants.*

Roger frowned. "But even I know that one. It's incredibly common."

"It's the original," Lady Margraine said quietly. "The notes that comprised the first draft of that book. For all its popularity, nothing about the author has ever been known." She stepped back, turning in a slow circle, keeping careful control of the candlestick. "This entire place . . . every single book here is . . ."

She had weathered imprisonment and the near-loss of her life with equanimity, but she stared at those books as if they were long-dead friends, miraculously restored to life before her eyes. "They're all books the Ninists wanted to destroy," Roger said. "But there were those who . . ." *Who felt the way you do about them,* he thought.

"The things that are here could . . . the lost knowledge contained in this single room . . ." She put a hand to her head, as if she was dizzy. "But Seren will worry if we take too long. And if I start looking through these now, I don't think I'd be able to stop. I'll do a thorough search later, if you have no objections."

"That was the point, after all." He held out his hand. "Can I have my candlestick back?"

"Oh!" She struck her forehead. "I can't believe I forgot I don't need one." In the blink of an eye, the whole room was suffused with light, and the marquise drank in the sight of the library afresh, eyes roving eagerly over title after title. "There's still enough lingering magic, this close to the statue chamber, that I don't need to use any of my own to do something like this," she told Roger. "But on the surface, I'm afraid I've still got to conserve it as much as possible. I'm not in danger, but I'm not . . . recovered. Please don't harp on that in front of Seren."

"Of course." He took the candlestick when she offered it to him. "Shall we rejoin the others?"

"Just give me a moment," she said. "Just one more moment."

So he stood by the door and waited until she could bear to leave. He remembered standing outside that same door, contemplating the infinite possibility of what might be contained within. He had been a bit disappointed, back then—it was far from the worst outcome he could have imagined, but there had been a part of him that had dreamed of some thief's grand treasure hoard. But a room full of gold and jewels would have meant nothing to her. This was the greatest treasure she could possibly conceive.

Back in the corridor, she put a hand on his arm. "Thank you," she said. "For showing me this. You didn't have to."

Roger thought of the nameless scribe, the last one who remained protecting the room. It must have been the greatest treasure that person could imagine, too. "In a way, I did," he said.

CHAPTER FORTY-SIX

Valyanrend

THE QUEEN OF Issamira, who was loitering in Morgan's bar when they entered as if she spent her mornings in such places all the time, had no sooner seen Arianrod Margraine than she clamped herself around the marquise's body like a vise, even though she only came up to her shoulder. "Oh, thank the gods it's really you! Didn't I tell you this would happen? Do you even understand how close you came to death, or how worried you had everyone? Ugh, I can't even be properly angry when I'm so relieved . . ."

The marquise's attempts to gently pry herself free were to no avail. "Yes, Adora, you were right. It was a thoroughly reckless scheme, and I've definitely suffered for it. Now can you please detach yourself, this is . . . deeply embarrassing."

It seemed the queen had brought a whole group with her, as there were four others in the tavern along with Braddock and Marceline—and Ritsu, whom the latter had fetched out of his hiding place in the tunnels on the way. "You invited him, but not Naishe?" Morgan asked.

"Oh, Naishe is coming. There's just something she has to tend to first. She said she'd explain."

From behind the bar, Braddock cleared his throat. "Er, Roger?" And that was ominous, because Braddock called Roger *Halfen* or *swindler* on a good day, and far worse things on a bad one. "I had a message from your aunt, before the monkey came back. Should I give it to you now, or would you rather . . . ?" He glanced around the crowded tavern uncertainly.

Roger collapsed onto his usual barstool. "If it's from my aunt, I bet it's about Len. And if it's making even you use delicacy, it's got to be atrocious. Let's just get it over with."

Braddock passed over a folded sheet of parchment, and Roger examined it suspiciously. "You didn't read it, did you?"

Braddock scowled. "Of course not. But your aunt delivered it in person—said she didn't trust messengers, and didn't want to leave it at your house with no one there. And she looked properly distraught. So I made some inferences."

Roger was already bent over the parchment, brow furrowed and mouth twist-ing. "Well, this isn't what I thought I was going to read. My aunt says she was visited by Elgar's captain of the guard—former captain of the guard, it must be, because I can't imagine the man's going to have a job after this. *He brought me my grandson, whom I had hardly expected to see again, and passed on a warning he said came from my son: to stay as far away from Elgar and his people as I could.*" He hesitated, drawing in a breath. "Elgar's captain said Len was alive when he left him, and no longer in danger from the spell cast against him, though it left him wounded. But he also said . . . that he expected Elgar would kill Len, and blame it on Arianrod Mar-graine."

"On me?" the marquise asked. "Have I even met your cousin?"

"You have," Roger said flatly. "His name is Varalen Varsten, but he goes by Oswhent these days. Or . . . went, I suppose."

"Ah. Well. That's a bit awkward." She shrugged. "I'm not going to apologize for my part in it, I'm afraid. If anything, I treated him gently, considering all he had done to me and mine."

"I wasn't looking for an apology," Roger said, still in the same tone. "He's done more than nothing to me and mine, if we're counting offenses."

Before she could respond to that, Naishe came through the door—and since she was the last one they were expecting, Braddock locked it behind her. "I'm the only one who can be spared for strategizing; the others are busy across the city, spreading word and making preparations. I have much to tell. Who are all this lot?"

"The issue, as it happens," Roger said, "is that everyone has much to tell, and now it seems time is of the essence. So how about we take turns imparting new information, and we can make the introductions as we go?"

IN THE END, to prevent things from becoming more chaotic than they already un-avoidably were, the main meeting took place in Morgan's bedroom, with only a very select group—one that Morgan would have found unimaginable only a day earlier. It was herself; Roger; Naishe; Ritsu; a woman named Lirien Arvel, who was apparently a *wardrenfell*; the marquise of Esthrades; and the queen of Issamira. Seren had agreed to budge no farther than the door of Morgan's room, which she was guarding, and the rest of them were on the first floor of the firmly closed tav-ern with Braddock and Marceline.

When everyone, finally, had no more words to speak, and no news to impart, the seven of them sat there in taut silence, the weight of everything slowly settling over them like a blanket of ash. As Morgan sifted through it, one truth stood out most starkly, and as she glanced around at the circle of faces, she thought she could see them realize it, too.

Roger spoke first. "It seems that, if we hope to defeat Elgar, we'll see the odds further stacked against us the more time passes. An immediate attack isn't possible, but given all we now know, it would be to our advantage to strike as close to immediately as we can."

Naishe nodded. "From what my father said, it seems clear that hunting his little stones down piecemeal isn't going to work anymore. Our efforts in that area have done much more than nothing—they have delayed his plans, and shrunk his armies, but those strategies alone merely postpone his supremacy. We have to cut off the head of the serpent, and that is not any stone; it is Elgar himself."

"I agree, but he must know you will come to that conclusion," Arianrod Margraine said. "I suspect he will confine himself to the Citadel as much as possible; we shouldn't pin our hopes on waiting for him to leave it. We'll have to storm it, and slay him within it."

"Then you should be the heart of our offensive," Naishe said. "We have a handful of pieces of vardrath steel among us, but they need close proximity to work. You can pit your power against his from much farther away. And the spells you can cast aren't limited, like Talis's and Lirien's are."

The marquise shook her head. "Perhaps before the events of the last few weeks, that might have been possible. But both my body and my magic have been significantly drained over that time; I had to keep myself constantly on the edge of exhaustion to destroy that collar quickly enough, and after that I nearly died. I will be well again in time, but I could not match Elgar spell for spell as I am now. Besides, I've found something else I can do that may be even more vital to our cause."

"Let me guess," Morgan said. "It involves that spell in the statue room. We never actually finished discussing it, but you told Roger you didn't think you could use it."

"I told Mr. Halfen that I would not use it to seal magic up again, even if I could figure out how to do so, which I haven't yet. We have to look to the future of this world after Elgar is gone, and I refuse to sacrifice the place that magic and mages will have in that future out of worry that we won't be able to defeat Elgar otherwise. The original spell must have allowed for some way to cast around the barrier it creates, or the lock could never be opened again once it's closed. But I don't know what that way is, nor am I confident I could replicate it even if I did. I can't risk locking that door again, not when it might be forever this time."

The rest of them gave each other sober looks, but no one objected. "I suppose we could put Talis at the head of the offensive instead, then," Lirien ventured; Talis herself was not present, by her own choice, and had given Lirien the right to speak in her stead, as the only other *wardrenfell*. "Her winds work very well on crowds. Perhaps she can even modify them to move people out of the way without crushing them."

"Are you saying you aren't good at handling crowds?" Morgan asked.

Lirien winced. "It's difficult for me to attack without killing; ice in the blood isn't something most survive. I would much rather devote myself to healing our own people, but I'm prepared to fight, too, if it comes to that."

"And I, Rask, Talia, and the rest of our recruits that are fit to fight will support you," Naishe said. "And . . . perhaps my father as well."

"I'm sure Braddock will want to join the fight, too," Morgan said. "I'll give him my dagger. Roger and I aren't fighters, so we and Marceline will have to do what we can to help outside of that."

"I'm not a fighter, either, and I don't know the city like the rest of you do," Queen Adora said. "I can bring a few dozen of my best soldiers through the tunnels from outside, but I think the bulk of my forces should remain where they are, keeping Valyanrend cut off until Elgar is dead. But perhaps I can command them myself, and send my uncle to assist you instead."

"No, Adora, you're with me," the marquise said.

"With you where?"

"Deciphering the spell Seren and I found. We're short on time, so we need as many informed opinions as we can get if we're to glean all we can from it. You're the only person here whose grasp of Old Lantian equals mine—except perhaps Voltest, but as I understand it, he's no longer available. And you were right, back in Eldren Cael." She traced her finger through the air, as if writing out a word. "That book we found, that talked about a spell reacting against an opposing spell? I tried it for myself—that's how I was able to hurt Elgar. But the results left no room for doubt; your interpretation of the runic was the intended one. *Corruption* is the correct translation."

"But I can't read the spell," the queen said. "It seems that those without magic can't even see it's there."

"So I'll have to transcribe it for you, which will take time and effort, because the positioning of the runes is as important as what they say. But I still believe it is the most effective use for both of us, unless you can provide a convincing alternative."

"No, I . . ." The queen shrugged. "If you think it's worth going through all that just to have me take a look at it, I won't gainsay you. At least my translations of Old Lantian are something I have extreme confidence in."

"All right, so that puts you and me in the tunnels. I'll ask Seren whether she would prefer to be with us or fight at the Citadel; she is the best judge of where she would be most useful. Naishe's forces are also all committed to the Citadel, and we'll have Adora's elite soldiers, Rhia and Cadfael, Talis and Lirien, and this companion of Morgan's who will be wielding her vardrath steel. Miss Imrick, Mr. Halfen, and the formidable monkey will not be fighting and will most likely be useless at translating runes, so we'll have to ponder the best place for them. That just leaves . . ." She glanced at Ritsu, who had been maintaining a polite silence when not asked a direct question. "Do you know where you ought to be placed?"

"Oh! Yes. Forgive me, I had thought it was obvious." He smiled apologetically.

"I actually don't know what you mean, either, Ritsu," Morgan said. "I thought you said that, without your enchanted sword, your skills with a weapon were limited."

"That's true, I'm afraid. But I have other skills—or perhaps I should say other advantages—that it would be selfish of me to squander." He pressed a hand to his chest. "As I said to you before, it's possible I could pass as Shinsei once, but not more than that. I said we should use that one chance judiciously, perhaps to steal some item or piece of information that would be of great value to Elgar. But what better time for me to use that chance than now? What better item to steal than his life?"

There was a brief silence; perhaps the others, like Morgan, needed a moment to contemplate the full ramifications of what Ritsu had proposed. Arianrod Margraine spoke first. "You . . . understand that he is a mage, yes? And you have no magic, no vardrath steel, and no natural fighting prowess beyond a bit of sword-play? You'd be relying wholly on the element of surprise. He doesn't seem like someone who lets his guard down in the best of circumstances, and I did just deal him a severe wound at what he thought was his moment of victory. If he isn't willing to let you close enough to strike—if he's suspicious of your long absence—even if you simply couldn't kill him fast enough, or wounded him instead—you'd have no defense. He'd kill you easily."

"Yes," Ritsu said. "But if it *did* work, the war would end in that instant, and all of you would be spared. Isn't that great a reward worth that great a risk?" He met their scrutiny with a melancholy shrug. "I am only one person, after all, and I have no real use beyond this. It would be selfish not to try, I think."

Damn, Morgan wished Deinol were here, or even Lucius. They were both better at this sort of thing than she was. She only knew how to appeal to someone's logic and practicality, not their emotions. And if Ritsu was talking like this, willing to sacrifice his life, he'd already left the first two behind. "You don't have to have a use. All I've ever done is run this tavern, but that doesn't mean I'm just going to throw my life away, either."

"It will not be thrown away," he said gently. "It will be wagered on the hope of peace. And I think many people, including me, would say you have done far more than run a tavern."

"We can make sure you aren't defenseless, at least," the queen said. "My uncle emptied his armory of vardrath steel before we headed north. It was only a handful of pieces' worth; I was just going to distribute them among the soldiers I brought through the tunnels, but we can certainly spare one for you, if you're determined to attempt something so dangerous."

Ritsu shook his head. "I thank you for the offer, truly. But I am afraid it cannot be. Elgar is intimately familiar with the sword I was accustomed to bear as Shinsei; he enchanted it, after all. That sword is lost to me forever, and I will already be slightly suspicious for returning without it, even though I have a perfectly true and reasonable explanation. But if I come bearing a vardrath steel weapon, he will know immediately that the curse is broken, for I could not have touched the steel without removing it. Even Morgan's dagger is too big to conceal. I'll have to do without its protection."

"Not so," Naishe said. "There is one more option open to you." She reached beneath her shirt, and revealed the steel pendant. "This is small enough to conceal. It is not a weapon on its own, but it can still protect you."

Ritsu hesitated, but finally nodded. "I suppose that would be all right. He'll notice right away if he tries to cast a spell on me, of course, but if he were to succeed, that would probably be the end of me anyway. And I'll also need a uniform in his blue-black, as much as I don't want to wear it. I got rid of mine back in Araveil."

Morgan turned to Roger, and they shared a grin. "We've got that more than handled," she said. "You can have your pick. Anything else?"

"A sword, to actually do the deed. Just the ordinary kind."

"Done," the queen said. "What's next?"

"There's something I can't help but notice," Lady Margraine said. "Something still troubles you, Mr. Halfen, but you haven't spoken of it. You don't wish to have your concerns addressed?"

Roger smiled ruefully. "Still trying to sort out what I think myself, before I put the question to anybody else. I just wonder what the common people will do once the fighting starts. They'll see our side's got magic—that's unavoidable. But Elgar's been stirring them up against magic every chance he gets, and some of that fear's taken root. We've roused suspicion against him in return—not that he hasn't done a bit of that himself, especially with this new edict. But if we start fighting him, and the people come out on his side because they think mages are trying to destroy the city, that could ruin everything."

"That's a concern I have as well," Lirien said. "I know too well what fear of magic can drive people to do against those who possess it. And that was merely in a small village. If a vengeful mob should form in a city of this size . . ."

"Agreed," the marquise said. "That is an outcome we must take all possible care to avoid. Mr. Halfen, as I understand it, Elgar made Valyanrenders afraid of what I might do with magic, and you made them afraid of what *he* might do with it. What if we gave them something to hope for instead?"

"I'm all for it," Roger said, "but I don't know enough about magic to pull that off myself. And even if I did, I suspect the plan would have needed someone like you before it could work anyway."

She shook her head, then nodded it at Lirien Arvel. "Not me. Her."

Lirien drew back a little, wary. "Me?"

"If we're going to combat people's fear of magic, we need to show them that it's simply the power of potential," the marquise said. "It runs in both directions equally: ruin or salvation, creation or destruction. No one has more raw ability when it comes to healing than you do. If you used your power at its greatest scale—"

Lirien threw up her hands. "No, no, no, thank you. This is just what I've spent my life trying to avoid. If I showed myself to the world, even if they didn't persecute and exile me like my fellow villagers, it would be almost worse. I'd never be able to be free or anonymous again; word of me would always spread, and everywhere I went, I'd be besieged by requests to heal every last ache and pain of every soul in the area. And the moment I refused even one, or sought to live for myself a little, I'd be right back to being a cursed witch. No, my lady. This plan of yours may work, but if you think I'm going to walk among the people like some miraculous healer out of legend, you will find even your stubbornness has a limit to what it can accomplish."

"*You* will find," the marquise said, "that my stubbornness is matched by my adaptability. If you wish to remain anonymous, I can try to accommodate that. I know the scope of your magic is limited in ways mine is not, but you can manipulate water, and you can heal. Do you think you might be able to combine those spells? Could you use water to heal, instead of your hands?"

Lirien sat down heavily in Morgan's chair, winding and unwinding her braid around her hand. "So, imbue some water with that power, and scatter it over people? Like pouring out a jug?"

"I was thinking of something on a much bigger scale, but that's the basic premise, yes."

"I . . . think I can do that? Washing something clean, purifying it, is the connection that allowed me to heal in the first place. It's just asking physical and magical purification to mirror each other." She thumbed the end of her braid. "So that's your idea for me to stay anonymous? I allow the water to do the healing for me, and its beneficiaries have no idea it came from me?"

"Does that sound feasible?"

"In theory, but we'd need both a large amount of water and a way to transport it. I couldn't just dump buckets over people's heads. I suppose I could wring water from the air, but that's a difficult process, so the scale would be limited. If we could guarantee rain, that would solve things, but even I can't do that."

"We can't afford to sacrifice scale," the marquise said. "But we *can* get you rain on command. Or as good as, anyway."

"I don't follow," Lirien said.

"Mr. Halfen knows what I mean, I'm sure. This has to be a truly grand gesture. We need symbolism."

"Water and symbolism?" Roger asked. "Then there's only one place that could possibly suit. The Precipitate."

"The aqueduct? Well . . . yes, I suppose that could work. The water's already falling from high up; I'd just adjust the trajectory. And there's certainly plenty of it to spare. The only problem is, it might be *too* much. I've never tried to control that much water at once before."

"So is that a no, or a maybe?" Lady Margraine asked. "Because we are in rather a tight spot, and most of us may indeed be called upon to do things we've never tried before."

"You make it sound like I can simply decide whether it works or not."

"That's because you can," the marquise said. "Your magic is restricted in direction only, not degree. Within the parameters it's set for you, you can do anything. So long as you can see your way to it, you can make it a reality."

Lirien pressed her forehead into her palm, as if gathering herself. "All right, fine. If I do this, I won't have to kill anyone, just heal them. I'd rather that anyway, even if it's difficult."

"Good, then. There will, unavoidably, be fighting, and that means there will be wounds. You can demonstrate magic's beneficence and provide our forces with a tactical advantage."

But something about that sentence seemed to strike Lirien oddly; she sat up straight and stiff, putting a hand to her mouth. "No," she said. "No, wait. I still can't say with complete certainty that I can bend the Precipitate to my will. But if I can, I should be able to help much more than healing wounds."

She leaned forward toward the rest of them, spreading her hands out before her. "Stopping Voltest was the first time I realized my magic could dissolve other magic, as long as that magic poses a threat or causes damage to the one affected by it. I could heal it away, like sealing a physical wound. The queen reminded me recently that it's the same with Elgar's spells. They're causing harm to those who bear them; they're warping their minds. If I'm raining my magic down over the city anyway, I can use it to destroy those bonds. Surely the people will notice, when they come back to themselves, that something was done to them. And it should be obvious at that point that Elgar is behind it—especially when those whose talismans have been altered by Roger and the rest of you are spared any compulsion."

The rest of them were silent, but it was a different sort of silence this time, a slowly growing excitement. "But then this could be it," Roger said. "The whole army he worked so hard to build, destroyed with a single spell!"

"Not quite," Lirien said. "The water from the Precipitate can only rain down in the open. How many of his mindless soldiers I can hit with it depends on how many are out of doors to be hit. So I'll have to rely on the rest of you to lure out as many as you can before I cast that spell. I doubt I'll be able to do it more than once."

"And don't forget, not all of Elgar's army is composed of the unwilling," Lady Margraine said. "There are those who have remained loyal to him and fought for him until now, and we cannot assume that they will ever desert him. Our fight within the Citadel will be relatively unchanged, but it should be much easier to gain entry, at least."

Roger nodded, taking in those caveats. "So we bait Elgar's soldiers out of the Citadel, Lirien rains the Precipitate down on them, they become confused and harmless, and it opens the way for us to gain the Citadel interior with far fewer soldiers to fight through. We've got the tunnels, so we've got the advantage of positioning, and Talis can scatter any blockades they try to put up. Then it's just . . ." He looked askance at Ritsu. "If you're truly determined to do this, you'll have first shot; the soldiers at the Citadel should recognize you and let you through to see Elgar. But if . . ."

"If I fail," Ritsu said, "it will be up to you. And you'll have to fight through to him the ordinary way."

"In which case Talis and those armed with vardrath steel will have the best chance," the marquise finished. "We can further sew up the details once we rejoin the rest downstairs. But are we agreed on the essential shape of the plan?"

One final silence meant that there were no objections.

The seven of them filed back downstairs, picking up a wordless Seren on the way. Marceline and Rhia jumped to their feet when they entered, and the rest of them looked as if they wanted to. But Morgan went right to Braddock, and he looped an arm around her shoulders, gently taking her weight. "You all right? You're trembling a little."

"Aye." She rested her head on his shoulder. "I'm fine. It went better than I thought it would, honestly. It's just . . . it's really happening. No more picking at him from the shadows. This is the time."

Braddock opened his mouth, but he was interrupted by an exuberant hammering on the tavern door. He rolled his eyes. "If that fool can't tell we're closed, they're already too drunk to have need of anything we provide."

But the barrage of knocks persisted, and he disentangled himself from Morgan with a sigh. "Quicker to just take care of it." He unlocked the door and swung it open, already upbraiding the person on the other side. "You daft idiot, no customers means no—"

"Braddock, you magnificent ass!" yelled a cheerful voice Morgan knew in her bones, a strong arm clapping Braddock on the back. "Don't be a stranger, man, it's been ages. Ahh, but it's good to see the old place again. You lot wouldn't believe the journey I've had!"

He had breezed past Braddock before he could utter a word, and nearly ran right into Morgan. "Deinol—" she started, but he couldn't be stopped.

"Morgan, there you are!" He threw both arms around her, though he was oddly delicate with the left one, just patting her with the heel of his hand. "I'm . . . sorry about the mess I caused—everything we told you of in our letter. Lucius is here, too, he's just outside with the, ah, rest. He wanted to . . . give me space, and let me explain things to you first. We've got a lot to discuss, that's for sure! And you won't believe who we brought back with us." He tried unsuccessfully to peer around Morgan and Braddock to see the rest of the room. "Rather crowded for an early closing, isn't it? You having a party or something?"

"Deinol," Morgan said again, more heavily, though she couldn't help tightening an arm around him in return, to make sure he was really there.

"What?" he asked, wide-eyed and guileless. "What? Did I miss something?"

CHAPTER FORTY-SEVEN

Valyanrend

THE MATTER-OF-FACT INTRODUCTION of the supposedly long-dead prince of Aurnis had thrown the tavern into a temporary uproar, but in the end, the strategy they'd devised remained unchanged. Ryo Serenin would change the shape of the continent after Elgar was defeated and he returned to reclaim his kingdom, but he was unmagical, and had no soldiers to command beyond the two royal guards he'd brought with him, only one of whom could actually fight. So, in practice, they'd added a couple swords to their number, and nothing more. Still, Adora was heartened to know of it. It helped her picture a better future, the potential for reconstruction and flourishing after this war's end.

Besides the prince's arrival, it seemed the tavern owner and her friends had some personal business to sort through with the new guests, so Adora had gratefully taken Arianrod's invitation to follow her and Seren into their room to hold their own discussion. Arianrod sat down on the bed, and addressed Seren first. "So. How much did you overhear?"

"Enough, I believe, my lady. I know you are to be out of direct combat, and though it is perhaps not what you would have wished, I must admit I am relieved."

Arianrod sighed. "I simply can't do two things at once, and I'm more suited to one than the other. It is what it is." She tilted her head, asking a question before she even said the words. "What about you? You're suited to combat, not magic and runic. But there will be no fighting where I am, and if you wish to use your skills to their best effect, you will have to forego serving as my bodyguard for a time. I won't order you to do one thing or the other, but I hope you will consider it carefully."

"As it happens, I've already considered it," Seren said, avoiding Arianrod's eyes. "And if the choice is truly left to me, I'm afraid I choose neither. Forgive me, my lady, but I must beg your permission to attend to another matter. I suppose it is . . . somewhat more personal, but it will help us in the battle nevertheless—so much so, in fact, that I believe it must be done. And I am the only one who can do it."

Arianrod fell silent, and Adora knew she was turning that over in her mind, holding her response until she had fully analyzed every angle of it. "This thing you have to do," she said at last. "I know what it is, don't I?"

Seren smiled as if in spite of herself. "Only you would know that, my lady. But, knowing you, I would not be surprised if you had guessed."

But Arianrod did not smile back. "Have you found him so quickly?"

"It was not precisely quick, my lady. You were, of course, always my priority, but your location was never a mystery. Once I had my escape route secured, it was only a matter of waiting for the day you would be brought out of the Citadel. In the meantime, I searched for him—primarily to ensure he would not complicate our escape, but also . . . in case a chance presented itself."

"And you want to keep him from getting involved on Elgar's behalf?"

"Among other things."

Arianrod could not hide her displeasure, but her tone was measured and even. "I understand an impulse toward revenge. I wouldn't mind killing him myself. But you were given a second chance, to heal from the wounds he caused you without even a scar. Don't chase him so recklessly that you throw that away."

"Your warning is wise, but you needn't worry. I'm well aware." She stepped closer, face-to-face with her once more. "You asked me once, correctly, to have faith in you. To believe that you knew what you were doing, and that you were equal to the challenge set before you, no matter how daunting it might seem. I ask you for the same favor now. Destroying a chosen target is what I trained for, and what I do best. Gauging risk accurately and dispassionately is part of that. I can and will defeat him. And then I will return to you. I promise you that."

Arianrod huffed a dissatisfied breath out through her nose, but she said, "You've promised, so I'll hold you to it. I suppose there's nothing else to say."

But they both looked like they wanted to regardless, and Adora tried to sidle away, hoping to give them space. But Seren's attention shifted to her the moment she moved. "Your Grace."

"Ah, yes? Did you need me for something?"

"I will not be able to accompany my lady while the two of you do your work," Seren said. "But I know too well that, many times, she has exerted her magic until she has lost consciousness, or even drifted close to death. In my stead, you must watch over her, and ensure she does not attempt such a thing again. Especially now that even she admits she is not yet at full strength."

Adora nodded firmly, before Arianrod had a chance to interrupt. "I still regret that I was unable to keep her from leaving Eldren Cael, and unable to help rescue her from Valyanrend. I had to rely on you for that. But you can rely on me now. I won't let her go too far."

"As much as I love being treated like a misbehaving infant," Arianrod said, "I'll point out that the very chamber we'll be occupying is a magical wellspring. Still, I have every intention of being careful. Even I know that I can't treat myself too roughly if I want to continue my recovery."

And non-mages had no inkling of the room's magical saturation, apparently. "Arianrod, are you really sure that's the best place for me during the battle? Or for you, for that matter?"

"Where you're concerned, I don't know why you find it so hard to believe," Arianrod said. "You yourself said you had more confidence in your translations of Old Lantian than in your battle strategies, and your people won't *need* a battle strategy; all they have to do is keep Valyanrend surrounded. And our forces on the inside will have their pick of more capable commanders, including the prince who just showed up. Perhaps you think the spell I found is of merely academic interest, but that room has done more to help me understand magic than all the books I have ever read on the subject combined, and magic is the weapon Elgar wields. Just because I refuse to seal it off, that doesn't mean we couldn't find some way to . . . I don't know, dampen or otherwise alter his use of it. That's the point, that I won't even know what is or isn't possible until I've explored it thoroughly. By myself, I'm sure I could unravel all its secrets eventually, but we don't have time for eventually. That's why I need you."

The confirmation was reassuring, especially from Arianrod, who would never say something untrue just to make someone else feel better. "And where you're concerned?"

She smiled wryly. "In my case, I suppose you're surprised that I'm not insisting on leading the charge into the Citadel and killing Elgar myself, or something like that. Unlike Seren here, I am content to know that he is dead, without needing my hand to be the one behind it. I did already deal him an injury he won't soon forget, and if we're talking about those who have the greatest claim to revenge against him, I would hardly be first in line."

"I don't *need* to be the one to kill Ghilan," Seren insisted. "But there are few who have a hope of killing him, and I'm one of them. And I need to be sure."

"And you'll feel better if it's you."

Seren's mouth twitched. "Perhaps."

"Who is Ghilan?" Adora asked, wondering if she wanted to know.

Arianrod shrugged. "Who cares? Someone who will be dead soon, anyway."

Seren smiled, pleased by her confidence. And Adora smiled, too, to herself. Arianrod would never say something untrue just to make someone else feel better, but there was a time when she would never have said anything reassuring at all, because she wouldn't have known how. "Well, if you insist, I shall take your word for it. But from what you both have said, I assume he is deadly in some way. I hope you have a suitably thorough plan, Seren."

"My occupation once consisted of devising such plans, Your Grace," Seren said. "And though it lacks humility to say so, I believe this is one of my best."

KAITAN ENREI WAS sitting at the bar of the tavern where he'd rented a room for years, and yet he still had to shake himself every so often to make sure he wasn't dreaming. It was such a strange and surreal meeting of worlds he had always assumed would be forever separate. Here was the window where Braddock always used to seat himself, keeping one eye on those passing by on the street outside, only Rana was standing there now, leaning against the pane. Gao, not Deinol or Roger, was seated beside him at the bar, drinking his customary tankard of water. And in the middle of the room, in conversation with a sea of people who were mostly strangers to him (the only one he knew was Cadfael; his sister, not so dead after all, still wore the *tsunshin* Cadfael had said she favored, but she seemed to have disappeared) was Ryo himself. He looked so at home in the place where Kaitan had only ever been *Lucius*; he had easily grasped the proposed plan of attack, and offered no objections or amendments, only his help. And now, it seemed, he was getting to know the others, with the same sincerity and acceptance that had won him so many loyal subjects and friends back in Kaiferi. Watching him was bittersweet, because Kaitan knew he'd never be counted among either again.

The last time he had been truly alone, he had found acceptance in this very place. But now not just Deinol, but Morgan, Roger, even Braddock knew who he was, what he'd done. The others at the tavern were still in the dark; out of some sense of courtesy, Deinol had confined his full explanation to those three. He probably would have told Ritsu as well, but the young Aurnian had always known who Kaitan truly was. He and Deinol were so relieved and overjoyed to see each other again, their meeting so unfraught, that Kaitan almost felt as if he had been replaced. He had also realized that Deinol had known about this curse of Ritsu's back in Araveil, and had kept it from him. So he had been losing his friend's trust even then.

As for the others, it was probably too early to tell how they would treat him going forward. They'd had to contend with so many conflicting emotions: shock at his and Deinol's unexpected return, relief that they'd even managed to come back safely after everything they'd gone through, concern over Deinol's injury, and shock again when he detailed how he'd come by it and what had resulted from it. As angry as Deinol had been when he'd first asked Kaitan for the truth, he had shown none of it before their friends; he had explained everything concisely, dispassionately, and, Kaitan had to admit, more fairly than he deserved, without laying explicit blame on anyone. Yet as those who knew Deinol best, they must have noticed the coldness he constantly emanated in Kaitan's direction—even more noticeable in one who was normally so free with his attachments. They must have noticed that Deinol had been hurt on his behalf, and that Deinol had not forgiven him. Who could blame them if they felt the same?

So here he was, avoiding the question. The four of them were cloistered together in Morgan's room, and he had not even tried to join them. He might have spoken to Seren, but she was with the queen and the marquise, or Cadfael, but he was in the corner with the other Lanvald, Talis, their heads close together in a way that suggested they did not wish to be interrupted. He'd never been particularly close to Marceline, but even if he had been, she'd already left to tell Tom Kratchet the news, and Ritsu seemed to have disappeared as well—not that he'd ever liked Kaitan anyway. Naishe, a stranger to him, was still deep in conversation with Ryo. That left only one other stranger, the Hallern *wardrenfell* called Lirien Arvel.

Well, he'd always hated being alone most of all. He'd try anything.

She was sitting at a table by herself, neither visibly discontented nor visibly preoccupied. Kaitan leaned on the table next to hers, not wanting to presume too far into her space. "Will you be staying here tonight as well, Miss Arvel?"

She shook her head, her long braid snapping back and forth. "No, the queen already took rooms for the lot of us in a different district. I'm just waiting for the rest of them. The queen herself is still in discussion with the marquise, and Rhia took a walk with that young man, Ritsu; I believe they know each other. Cadfael's waiting for Rhia, Talis is waiting for Cadfael, and I'm waiting here. I do hope they come back soon, though; if I'm to climb the Precipitate and harness its full force in the coming days, I'll need to be rested."

"Do you . . . really think you can do it?"

"Her ladyship certainly thinks so, no matter what I say." She wound her braid around her hand. "I suppose it's no different from anything else I've had to do before now. I don't want to do it, but it has to be done, so . . . I always seem to let myself be dragged into things like that, one way or another."

Kaitan scarcely knew how to talk to her about such an undertaking. It had become clear, in the course of the hurried explanations he and the others had been given, that just about everyone else in the Dragon's Head had seen some tangible proof of magic before, and was comfortable believing in it. Morgan, Roger, Braddock, Marceline, Seren, Cadfael and his sister, even Ritsu—he'd had dealings with all of them in the past, yet somehow along the way they'd slipped into a different world.

"I'm still trying to understand how magic works," he admitted to Lirien. "Or trying to understand that it works at all, really. Though I suppose it must be true—the last time I saw Seren, she was close to death. Nothing but magic could have brought her back from that."

"Again?" Lirien asked. "I had to patch that one up recently myself. She really must make a habit of courting harm."

"So you can . . . you can truly heal any wound?"

"As long as it can properly be called a wound, yes. Most diseases, too. But don't spread that around, all right? I've worked hard to remain unknown, and I want it to stay that way."

"Of course. I wouldn't tell anyone, especially not with the city in the stormy mood toward mages that it seems to be. And I wouldn't try to call upon your gift lightly. But if it was a matter of someone here at the tavern, someone who knows everything already and would be a help in the coming fight—"

"If you're injured, I don't mind fixing it," she said. "But if you are, you're hiding it very well."

"It's not for me," Kaitan said. "Did you see what happened to Deinol?"

"Oh, right. That one. I don't suppose you still have the fingers?"

Evidently Kaitan was still adjusting, because the question nearly knocked him flat. "Ah . . . no, I'm afraid not."

"Then, unfortunately, there's nothing I can do."

"Why did I suspect you'd say something like that?" He ran his fingers over his scalp. "I suppose otherwise it would have been too easy."

She smiled sympathetically. "If there's one thing I've learned about magic, it's that it's never easy. But at least if you lose any pieces during the battle that you'd prefer stayed attached, you can bring them to me. That's a better offer than most get."

"Are the two of you discussing your particular . . . magic?" Kaitan struggled not to jump, still surprised, after all this time, at hearing that voice again. It seemed that Naishe had left without his noticing—and Cadfael and Talis as well, now that he scanned the room—and there was no one left to shield him from Ryo's attention. Even so, the prince only looked at him directly for an instant, then kept his gaze trained on Lirien. "Is that an offer you extend to everyone?"

"What, the offer to heal you if needed? As long as it's someone who knows about me already, I'm content to help with whatever I can."

"What about the wounds my companions and I bear now?"

"I wasn't aware you had any," she said. "The lot of you look fine to me."

"Perhaps that might be the case for me and Rana, even though for her the appearance belies the reality," Ryo said stiffly. "But Gao could not more obviously be missing an eye."

"Oh, I see. That's your misunderstanding." She pointed at Gao's patch. "That's an old injury, already healed. And because it's already healed, my power won't heal it again. On top of that, the eye in question is gone. I can restore a bit of blood and skin, but I can't grow him another appendage. As for the two of you, who seem to have two eyes, two ears, and four limbs, I assume your injuries are scars. If you were willing to cut those scars out, I could heal the skin flawlessly where they had been. But I doubt you'll find that worth the pain and effort."

"Certainly not," Ryo said. "There's no shame for me in that scar; I earned it defending my home. Though I hope to reclaim it one day, the mark can serve as a reminder of all I suffered, and all I survived."

Rana lifted her sleeve, brushing the thumb of her left hand over the little silver scar on her arm. "The look of the thing isn't the problem, I'm afraid."

Lirien stepped closer, peering down at it. "Why, what happened?"

Rana tried to make a fist, showing her how little she could do. "It's been like this ever since the cut was made. But that was five years ago, so it isn't a new wound by any standards."

Lirien pulled Rana's wrist toward her, testing the skin on and around the scar with her fingertips. "This is your problem? No, this I can fix."

Kaitan felt a burning ache in his chest, and then immediately felt guilty. Rana must be feeling much more, and he was hardly entitled to feel anything on her behalf. She controlled her face well, as she always had—he had learned it from somewhere, after all—but she couldn't quite mask the widening of her eyes, the tremor down both arms. "What? But you just said—"

"I did, and I stand by it. I can't heal this scar in its current state. But you're not missing anything in there. It's just that the . . ." Her nose wrinkled. "I'm no student of the medical arts; I know magic, not science. So don't ask me to explain it to you from that perspective. The cut you received, it severed the part of you that connects muscle to bone. But it's not *gone,* it just didn't heal right. If we cut in the same place again, to the same depth, I can heal it the right way."

Now even Ryo and Gao looked stunned, as if they were trying not to hope too hard. But they stayed just as silent as Kaitan was, doubtless not wishing to interfere in such a significant moment any more than he did. Rana's throat worked as she swallowed again and again, struggling to clear it enough to speak. "And if you do this, I'll be able to wield a sword again? I'll be as I was before?"

Lirien bit her lip. "Well . . . probably not exactly. And certainly not right away. There are muscles you haven't exercised in ages, and my magic can't restore the strength that you once had. You'd have to train yourself up to it, bit by bit. And, of course, you'd have to endure the pain of cutting into your arm again—into that precise spot, or it won't work."

"Please don't insult me by suggesting that any amount of pain could possibly deter me from this," Rana said. "I will endure whatever I must endure, as long as I can be sure of the result."

"And I wish I could be sure myself, miss, but 'tis not something I've ever attempted, you understand. If you didn't think it was worth the pain, that would be one thing. But if the pain doesn't scare you, I can certainly assure you it won't make your hand *worse*. As for how much better, I couldn't say. We'd simply have to do it and see."

Rana turned to the three of them, and Kaitan couldn't help but feel gratified that he was still included in that number. "Will you help me?"

"Of course," Ryo said. "Whatever you need."

Gao snorted. "That was rhetorical, right? Shall we get you drunk first so you feel it less?"

"Gao, don't joke," Kaitan said.

"Who's joking? She really would feel it less."

Rana shook her head. "No, I want to retain all my focus, just in case . . . just in case." And then she looked right at Kaitan, dark eyes boring into his. "And you. I have one favor to ask you in particular."

"I owe you anything you could ask," Kaitan said. "But even if I didn't, I would do it anyway."

She held out her right arm. "Of the three of them, your hand has always been the steadiest, your cuts the most precise. I can hardly cut into my arm myself, and I don't think Lirien has any experience holding a blade—"

"Correct," Lirien interrupted.

"So if someone else has to do it, I suspect you will be the best choice. Can I trust you with that?"

Kaitan bowed his head. "Whenever you wish."

"Now, then." She glanced back at Lirien. "Unless you need something else?"

"I'd love at least one decent sleep in between crises, but that won't help me do this any better," Lirien said. "Let's go."

They borrowed the knife from Morgan, and used Kaitan's room. Rana lay down on the bed, and Gao held her steady, so she wouldn't start squirming when the knife went in. Ryo pinned her right arm on either side of the scar, and Kaitan prepared himself to make the cut. "Whether you want to slice or stab is up to you, but you need to go precisely as deep, at precisely the same angle," Lirien said. "You have to get everything affected by the original injury."

Kaitan swallowed his nausea, thinking it through. Though the original cut had been a slice, stabbing might be better; he could be more accurate without risking greater harm, and he could go as deep as he needed to at once, without repeated slices if the first ones were too shallow. "Everyone else ready?"

They nodded—Rana couldn't speak, because she was biting a scrap of leather, but no one else said a word, either.

Kaitan raised the blade, and slowly began to press it down into the meat of Rana's arm, waiting for Lirien to tell him to stop. Rana was proud and disciplined, but pain was pain, and she couldn't keep her arm from shaking a little, though Ryo did his best to hold on to it. Lirien hooked her fingers around Rana's wrist; she seemed to be able to sense the nature of the injury. "You're not quite there yet. Just a little deeper. You've got to keep the angle of the blade steady. Now can you widen it a little at the deepest point, to make sure I don't miss anything?"

Kaitan felt like he was sweating all over, like he'd have to lose his grip, but in the next instant, Lirien put a hand on his arm. "It's done. Take the knife out."

Kaitan pulled it free, heard Rana's muffled grunt of pain, and braced himself for the welling blood, but there was nothing. Her arm was pristine, markless, and the only blood was on the knife. He heard his shaky indrawn breath. "How is it? Do you feel any different?"

Rana sat up, spitting the leather into her left palm. "I'm not sure. I never lost any feeling in the hand, I just couldn't . . ." She lifted her other arm, bringing her right hand alongside her left, the fingers curled slightly. She tried to make a fist, and grimaced. "Gods, they really are weak. But . . ." She clenched her fingers again, and this time, she folded them into a fist: shaking and unsteady, but drawn all the way in to her palm. "There . . . there it is."

The lot of them, excepting Lirien, sagged where they were, as if the same tense thread had held them up, and it had finally snapped. They swayed, and for a moment Kaitan thought he, Ryo, and Gao would all fall to their knees at once. But they righted themselves, and caught each other's eyes half-nervously, half-exuberantly, laughing as if they were tipsy. Rana smiled, too, and they all politely pretended not to notice there were tears in her eyes.

"Damn," Gao said. "After that, I'm getting everyone a drink. Water for me, mead if they have it for Rana, the palest ale possible for the princeling, and—"

He cut himself off, hissing a breath through his teeth. But before any of the rest of them could say anything, Rana held up her restored right hand. "Kaitan made the cut, and this is my celebration. Let him have one drink with us. It's a small thing."

They all looked at each other again, but the ease they'd fallen into without thinking was gone. Now it was as if they were locked in a four-way draw, standing off against one another. But before Kaitan could offer to leave, Gao bent his head. "Fine. I'll get it."

"I'll just have water with you, Gao," Kaitan said, but Gao refused him with a twitch of his shoulder.

"It's bad luck," he muttered. "I'll get you ale."

"And I will remove myself," Lirien added, "from whatever this is, thank you very much."

"We are," Ryo said, "indebted—"

"Oh no, I don't think so. We're all square. Just leave me out of it. Good night, everyone."

And she slipped out of the room ahead of Gao, who was just a touch slower, leaving Kaitan alone with Rana and Ryo. "Well, sit down then," the prince said. "It is your room, after all. For the duration of this evening, I'll let Rana have her will."

But it doesn't change anything, he meant. Kaitan could hear that part underneath, as clear as the words he spoke.

THE STREETS WERE dark, fitfully lamp-lit; a light rain had fallen while they strategized, but had ceased long since, leaving only a slight glimmering where the flames caught in puddles that had not yet dried. Ritsu walked through the city, still so new to him despite his memories of it, and thought of walking through a different city for the first time, when he had been a different man. He remembered the snow that had blanketed those streets, and the blood. He remembered how terrifyingly certain he had been then.

The young woman at his side both did and did not look like the girl he had met in that other city, more than three years ago. The golden hair was the same, even about the same length. The sword was the same, though Ritsu now remembered it as a *tsunshin,* the sword he and Sebastian had both trained in. Her eyes were the same shape and color, to be sure, but he couldn't quite say they were the same. He wondered what she thought had changed, when she looked at him.

Morgan had explained to the newcomers that Ritsu had been subject to a different variety of Elgar's magic, a curse that she had healed with vardrath steel. But that was all. She had not said that he had once been Shinsei, or named anything that he had done. But the girl—Rhia; he finally knew her name—had seen him in Araveil. She could have exposed him, if she'd wanted to, but she had stayed silent. And when, nervous and trembling, he had asked if she would take a walk with him, she had agreed without hesitation. "I know him," was all she had said, when her brother questioned her.

And now here they were, step falling into step. Ritsu tried to think what he could possibly say to her. But in the end, she was the one who broke the silence. "Back then. When my sword touched you, and you screamed . . . that was because the curse had broken, wasn't it?"

"Yes," Ritsu said. He was glad Shinsei had hesitated, at least, to fight the girl who had been so justifiably angry at all the death he had already dealt to her people. Still, he had nearly killed her with his first strike, and would probably have killed her with his second, if her vardrath steel blade hadn't destroyed the enchantment Elgar had placed on his sword to improve his fighting skill. Without it, she was clearly a prodigy, and he had never been anything close. The outcome should have been a sure thing, but when she decided to knock him out instead of killing him, she had saved his life and set him free at once.

"But it wasn't permanent? Or you wouldn't have needed Morgan to do it again."

"It would have been. It's just that Elgar found me, and cast it again. It never worked as well the second time, but I wasn't able to shake it off completely. I'm . . . glad that I'm finally able to thank you for that. I almost killed you, and you still showed me mercy, even after all I had done."

"Oh," Rhia said, scratching the hair at the back of her neck. "That's . . . not what I thought this—I mean, I'm sorry. I abandoned you there and ran away. If I hadn't, perhaps you would have been free much sooner."

"N-no," Ritsu stammered, "no, please don't apologize. You had every reason to be afraid of me—to hate me, even. And I don't know if, in the state that I was in, I would even have been capable of fleeing. You probably would only have been killed by Elgar's men."

"Perhaps." She stopped in the middle of the street, and Ritsu stopped with her, skirting around a puddle. "I feel as if there's something else you want to ask me, though. Am I wrong?"

"I just . . . don't understand why you didn't kill me. It was clear you had contempt for what I'd done—the people I'd killed."

"But that wasn't your fault," she said gently.

"Yes, but you didn't know that."

"That's true." She bit the corner of her mouth, staring off down the street, as if picturing that scene again in her mind. "I wish I had an answer for you. You deserve that. But I really couldn't say. I have a habit of doing things that feel right to me at the time, and killing you just . . . didn't feel right. Maybe it was only because I'd never killed anyone before, or maybe there was something deeper to it. But despite how angry I was at the deaths of all those people, I couldn't put my heart into it. That's the truth." She shrugged. "I was only seventeen, after all. A child more than not. Though I'm sure that answer is unsatisfying."

"Not really. It is the truth, and that's what I wanted. Thank you for telling me."

Rhia was still gnawing on her lip. "I meant to ask you. About the battle to come, and the role you've chosen for yourself within it. Are you . . . sure?"

Ritsu smiled. "Are you?"

She ducked her head. "Well, aye, but mine is . . ."

"I hope you're not going to say it's less dangerous than mine. All of us could die in that struggle; I don't view myself as exceptional."

"Sure, but I, and most of the others, we can still fight our way out. We can rely on the skills that have kept us alive this far. That's why I'm not afraid." She tapped the hilt of the sword she wore, the same sword that had broken and healed him on that long-ago night. "I've faced death before, but this, and my own skills, have protected me. And that was even without my brother at my side, and he'll be with me for this. But all you have is the hope that Elgar won't see who you really are. That seems awfully slim to me."

"Honestly, I don't know how slim it is or isn't. I can remember how it felt to be Shinsei, even if I can't replicate the odd ways in which his mind worked. I remember I got lost once before—or perhaps I should say I got found?—and spent some time as myself, or almost myself, before falling under that curse again. But when I returned, he wasn't suspicious of me, even though I'd been gone for so long without a word. Why shouldn't it be the same a second time?" He shrugged. "But even if it isn't, I want to try it because, if it *does* work, the prize is too great. Because if I didn't try it, and we failed, I would never forgive myself. It's the same for you, isn't it? You have that sword, but even if you didn't, you'd be fighting. So you aren't fighting *because* you have it; you're fighting because you want to do something, anything, to help."

"Well," Rhia said, mouth twisting in something that was almost a smile, though her eyes remained melancholy. "You're right, I suppose."

"But?"

"But have you thought that, if he finds you out, he may not kill you? He may put you under that curse again instead?"

He had thought about it, torturously. But he had come to the only conclusion he could. "If it comes to that," he said, "I'll have to make him kill me first."

"I'M SURE SHE'S all right," Talis said, venturing a hand on Cadfael's arm. "And if she knew you were trying to spy on her from the shadows, I don't think she'd be pleased."

He smiled, not pulling away. "I know. I'm not actually trying to go after her. I don't know where she is, and that's . . . fine. She can take walks with mysterious youths unsupervised if she insists."

"Then why did you leave the tavern?"

"I couldn't really think of a reason to stay, could you? I don't want Adora to have to head back to our inn alone, so I can't retire, but that doesn't mean I can't stretch my legs outside." His smile took on a certain teasing edge, an expression that still looked so new on him. "Why did you follow me, then? To make sure I didn't do something stupid and embarrass myself in front of my sister?"

"Something like that." In truth, she just preferred to be around him over anyone else in the tavern, but she couldn't say that. He probably already knew, anyway. "I . . ." She fisted one hand in the cloth at her hip. "Never mind."

"No, what?"

"You already told me once that I explain things too much," Talis muttered. "I'm trying to restrain myself."

"That's not what I said." He turned slightly, catching her by the sleeve. "Just because you don't always need to doesn't mean you can't. And it certainly doesn't mean I find it tedious. What is it?"

"I just . . . I'm not sure . . ." Gods, this was irritating. Why couldn't she just speak to him as usual, and not care what he thought? "I'm not sure where I stand with you. It might just be my imagination, but I feel like you've been distant since . . ."

"Oh!" He clapped a hand to his forehead. "No, it's not your imagination, but it wasn't that. Yaelor finally appeared to me again, long after I'd ceased expecting to see him. I've just been . . . preoccupied with what he had to say."

Talis hadn't been expecting that, either. "Does that mean he said something unpleasant?"

"I'm not sure *unpleasant* is the word. Certainly unwelcome. I've been trying to put it out of my mind, but I'm not having as much success as I'd like." Talis must not have been able to keep the curiosity off her face, because he added, "I don't mean to be evasive. I don't want to keep it from you, but I would feel guilty if I told you and not my sister, since it concerns her far more closely. But *because* it concerns her more closely, I'm at a loss for how to broach it with her—or if I even should. Learning all this has brought me no peace of mind, so why should I inflict that on her?"

"Because you suspect she'd want to know, and she wouldn't appreciate you making decisions for her to coddle her?"

That smile came with a wince. "Right. Exactly. So I've got to tell her. Eventually." He sighed. "As if we all didn't have enough on our minds."

"Well, what about using me to practice, then?" Talis asked. "I know you don't want to tell me the whole of it yet, but what about some hint, or some adjacent conversation?"

"That . . . might be good, actually. Thank you." He brushed his hair back. "Let's see, how should I start? What if . . . what if you knew . . . there was a way you could be forced to become someone else?"

Talis thought about it honestly, because he deserved that. "I don't know. I don't always think I've done the best job with the life that's been given to me. Being someone else might not be so bad."

"But then the people you loved wouldn't be able to recognize you."

Ah. So that was the real problem. He had already been separated from his family once, for the three years he believed them all dead. No doubt he dreaded returning to any version of that.

"It wouldn't come to that," someone said—Lirien, damn it, interrupting before Talis could speak. "Your sister said something to me once: *I know my brother the way sailors know the stars.* And I believed her, then and now. You could never become so different that she couldn't find you again."

Talis was irritated first because it was a good response, and second because she hadn't thought of a better one first. "Do you always like to eavesdrop on private conversations?"

"If it's private, you shouldn't have it in the middle of the street. I've simply been standing here; it's not my fault you didn't notice me."

"Is everything all right inside?" Cadfael asked.

"Entirely. I just sought to avoid a weighty conversation. And walked right into another, it seems, but I suppose that's to be expected on a night like this. I'm sure Rhia's having yet another." She yawned. "I just want to go back to the comforts of the inn, but I'm uneasy about separating our group. Since you two clearly want to be alone, I guess I'll check on the queen."

After she had left, Talis and Cadfael turned to each other sheepishly. "It was good advice," he said. "I . . . didn't know Rhia saw me that way. I should have thanked her."

"She'll live," Talis said.

"Well, what about you, then? What do you think? Besides that you might not mind being someone else."

"I think that . . ." She scrubbed a hand over her face. "Ugh, I don't know. It's just so hard to think of what it would really mean, to be someone else. You don't seem to mean that someone else would take your place, exactly, or kill you in order to live. But any other way I think of it, becoming someone else just means changing, and that doesn't frighten me. You and I have done so much of that already. The girl I was when I lived in those mountains has been gone a long time, but even the person who met you in that meadow, who carved that scar, no longer exists. I *did* become a different person, but at the same time, I've always been me. And it didn't take a god, either."

Cadfael thought it over, tracing the line of his scar back and forth. "I think . . . that's what Yaelor was trying to tell me, too."

"Does that mean it's good advice or bad?"

"In this case, it means it helps. Thank you. And . . . thank you for being at my side, and Rhia's, in the fight to come."

"Of course. If anything, I should thank you for being at mine, given what you did for me in Araveil." She still hadn't exactly thanked him for that the way he deserved, but he didn't seem to mind.

The street was still a little damp, but the sky had cleared enough to see the moon. Cadfael tilted his head up to look at it, then glanced back at Talis with a smile, as if he'd spied some mutual friend. "I wouldn't be anywhere else."

THE TAVERN WAS quiet, and the moon was high, casting a faint silver outline through Morgan's bedroom window. All of their unexpected guests had either left or gone to sleep, but the stillness didn't calm her. Her head felt hot, as if the thoughts inside it were moving too fast; when she twisted restlessly, her cheek brushed against Braddock's, his skin cooler beneath the stubble.

"You aren't sleeping," he said.

"Neither are you."

"Because I'm waiting for you to tell me what's bothering you."

She had known she couldn't hide it from him. "We're used to taking things on together. Our imprisonment at the Citadel, all our travels in Issamira, even the decision to resist Elgar. But I can't fight the way you can. I trust my fists to bring anyone causing trouble in my bar to their knees, but I've never killed people. So when you take the front lines this time, you'll be going somewhere I can't follow you. Somewhere the outcome isn't up to me."

"So you're worried because you can't make sure I won't botch it without you?"

Morgan turned to face him. "I'm worried because I don't like giving fate the chance to deal us different hands."

Neither of them liked to lead with sentiment, but she could always count on him to answer her frankness with his own. "I wouldn't like it, either, if you were the one taking a greater risk. I'd probably try to put my foot down and forbid you from it—I'm a little surprised you haven't."

"I haven't tried because I don't like failure. I don't need you to tell me you're set on this." She sat up in bed, and he moved with her, grabbing the blanket to keep it from falling to the floor. "Are *you* not concerned for yourself? Or would you even tell me if you were?"

"Of course I'd tell you. And . . . a little. Not as much as when we ventured into Lord and Lady Selreshe's estate, but I suppose I know more about magic now than I did then. And I'll have far from the riskiest position—more of a diversion than anything. I'll keep my guard up, as I always do, but I'm not planning any great sacrifice." He put an arm around her shoulders, and she leaned into him, letting her spine soften. "Fate's not more stubborn than you. And even you see things my way every once in a while."

"I'll allow that," Morgan said, "because you're comforting me."

He laughed. "See? What did I tell you?"

But then it was his turn to fall silent, and she couldn't let him stay that way, not after he'd helped her. "What is it?"

"I just wondered . . . what'll happen after this. Between us, I mean."

"Won't things be the same? Is there something you wish was different?"

"It's not like that."

"Well, just spit whatever it is out, then."

He brushed his chin against her forehead. "Do you see me staying here . . . more permanently?"

"That was my hope, but it's rather up to you."

"You already know my answer." And she supposed she did. *I tied myself to you a long time ago,* he'd told her in Issamira. "Do you think . . . we might get married someday?"

Morgan put both hands over her face. "You're asking me that *now*? After you just calmed me down?"

"It's not something you have to decide now. I just want to know if it's possible or not."

"Of course it's *possible,* I just . . . I didn't know it was something you cared about. I don't know that it's something *I* care about. A way for rich folks to make alliances and transfer property, more than anything."

"Well, don't you have property you'd like to transfer? To ensure I can take care of this place in your stead if need be, or that any children we might have hold an undisputed claim to it?"

Gods, children were a whole other question. Morgan sagged against his chest. "I'll tell you what. You come back to me safe once the fighting's done, and I'll finish this conversation with you."

He smiled, that open and unguarded one he'd started giving her and nobody else, what seemed a long time ago now. "I'll make that bargain."

But though they'd agreed, and though Morgan felt certain she'd be able to sleep now, she couldn't resist turning the matter over in her mind just a little more. "You don't have a surname. You'd have to become an Imrick."

Braddock laughed again. "Oh, I'd become an Imrick no matter what. I'd be a fool to think you'd ever be anything else."

Chapter Forty-eight

Valyanrend

THREE DAYS.

That was how long it had taken them to pull everything together. A couple weeks, as Morgan kept saying, would have been ideal, but they didn't have that kind of time. Yet Marceline found herself feeling optimistic more than concerned. They had made their tasks fit the time they had. Perhaps there were things they could have done more thoroughly in more leisurely circumstances, but there was nothing essential they had left undone. And, most crucially for her and the others without enough fighting skill to take on Elgar's soldiers in the streets or at the Citadel, they had found a way that they could help.

Morgan had been in the tunnels since before the sun rose, walking every pathway they'd need to use and making sure there weren't any unlit braziers or supplies blocking the way. Their initial assault would be a series of strike-and-retreats all across the city, intended to inflate the enemy's estimation of their numbers and draw as many soldiers out of the Citadel as possible. They would use half a dozen tunnel entrances into half a dozen neighborhoods to make it seem as if they'd appeared from nowhere, and to disappear just as quickly when they were no longer needed. Eventually, every fighter they could spare would aid the vanguard at the Citadel, so they couldn't afford to let anyone get pinned down once the distraction had run its course. There were enough medical supplies in the tunnels to do preliminary patch-ups on the injured, and food and water to keep their strength up. Any noncombatants who weren't distributing those would be running messages between divisions and keeping track of the information coming in from all corners of the city—of the battlefield, as it would be before long. "Is everyone in position?" she asked Marceline.

"Aye. We have Naishe reporting from Edgewise, Braddock from Silkspoint, Talia from Draven's Square. Rask went with the prince and Lu—Kaitan, or whatever his name is—so we won't have any more contact with them for a while. Talis and the siblings are ready to lead the push into the Citadel as soon as they get the signal, and Ritsu's with them. The queen just finished giving orders to her soldiers, and I passed her and the marquise on their way to the statue chamber. I couldn't find that troublemaker Seren Almasy anywhere, but the marquise told me not to worry about it. And as soon as I'm finished here to your satisfaction, I'm going to leave for the Precipitate with Lirien. Anything I left out?"

Morgan smiled. "Not at all. Well done." She put a hand on Marceline's shoulder, and lowered her voice. "How are you feeling?"

Marceline took a moment to check. "Strange. Not excited, but . . . expectant? And not frightened. I don't really understand it."

"Some people get that way, before events of great moment," Morgan said. "They're eager just to get on with it, no matter how dangerous actually getting on with it might be."

"Well, not for us," Marceline pointed out. "We're not the fighters. We're mostly going to be down here the whole time."

"But we still have our parts to play. Don't forget that."

"Of course. I've *been* playing my part in this whole enterprise for a long time. From before I even really knew that's what I was doing."

Morgan looked at her more keenly, and gave her a firm nod. "Yes, you have. You've done more than many twice your age, and shown resourcefulness to make any Sheather proud. You can hold your head high, whatever comes after this."

Marceline grinned, only blushing a little. "I'll be glad to finally get to what I was *meant* to be doing, and honing my craft as a thief. Though maybe that'll feel a little shabby, after all this."

"Nonsense," Morgan said. "With the way you're going, I'm sure you'll become a thief of legend."

"Just make sure they don't call me the monkey," Marceline called over her shoulder, before setting off to find Lirien.

ANOTHER MEETING OF two worlds confronted Kaitan, on this most momentous of days. He had been in this tunnel before, on a night that seemed simultaneously far distant and close enough to touch. He had come, back then, on a much more personal errand, though it had seemed no less significant to him. And he had been with a nervous Morgan, a taciturn Braddock . . . and Deinol, full of purpose and hope and urgency, driving them all on to rescue Seth. That man still existed— even more fiercely, in some ways—but Kaitan wondered if he would ever catch a glimpse of him again.

"You truly used this route before?" Ryo asked, as if reading his thoughts. "All the way to the Citadel?"

"That's right," Kaitan said. "Roger was the one who found it—he likes to go skulking in Ninist vestries looking for hidden treasures and secrets like this. He didn't go with us, though; it was just us four."

They were more than that today, here for a much more complicated purpose. They had no reason to believe that Roger's tunnel had been discovered, but no proof that it hadn't been. If it was simply sealed up, that would be one thing, but there was the possibility those in the Citadel had left it open in order to lure potential intruders into a trap. It provided a perfect opportunity to attack the Citadel from within, but they had taken only a relatively small group so their losses wouldn't be catastrophic if they guessed wrong. Besides, they were trying to get as many charmed soldiers as they could outside so Lirien could douse them; alerting them here prematurely instead could prove disastrous.

Since it was such a dangerous task, Ryo, by all rights, should not have been permitted to undertake it. But when Braddock had volunteered, Ryo had insisted on taking his place, saying he'd promised Deinol that Morgan, Roger, and Braddock would all be under his protection, and he wouldn't have anyone making him a liar. His declaration had prompted an uproar, and not just among his *kaishinrian*; Lady Margraine in particular had been furious that the only heir to the Aurnian throne, so recently rediscovered, might be about to throw his life away once again. But her proposal to tie Ryo up and leave him in a storeroom until the battle was over had been outvoted, so here they all were.

"I still wish we could have taken our tunnels here," Rask grumbled, and Kaitan had to suppress a smile at the *our*.

"Those tunnels do lead here," he said, "but they come out within a prison cell. We could attempt to crack the lock on the door, I suppose, but then we'd have multiple floors of dungeons to navigate, likely populated with a dozen guards or more. This one will put us much closer to our goal, with the potential for far fewer complications."

Rask had volunteered himself along with twenty fighters under his command, so the only ones here who weren't resistance members were Ryo, Kaitan, and Gao, whom no force on earth could have kept from accompanying his prince. Rana's hand was growing stronger by the day, but it had not yet had enough days to permit her to take the battlefield; Ryo had informed her that if she tried, he would exile her from Aurnis. A grave threat, and probably one he'd hated to make, but it was the only one she had a chance of listening to. Instead, she had joined Morgan, Roger, Marceline, and the other noncombatants, who had set themselves to being go-betweens. The maze of tunnels would let them move quickly and discreetly to almost any location in Valyanrend, but the one place it wouldn't get them was down this very passage, a small and separate affair that only led to the Ninist vestry where they'd entered it, and the door they were camped below now. Unless and until they could successfully open the Citadel to their friends, they were completely cut off. So they'd had to resort to other means of keeping themselves on schedule.

The oil lamp had been Naishe's idea, and she'd measured it precisely. When the oil ran out, they'd know it was time to press their attack. But the wick still blazed merrily behind the glass shutter of the lantern Rask was holding. He paced over to the orderly line of his subordinates and sat down, but Ryo and Kaitan stayed where they were, within arm's reach of the passage door. Perhaps he'd wanted to give them some space.

"It was a rescue you staged, was it?" Ryo asked. "A prison break?"

"So it was, *kaihen*. Morgan's kitchen boy had been poached off the street for deserting and thievery, and we couldn't let that stand."

"Deinol told me about him," Ryo said. "A boy who was wise beyond his years, and kinder than some men ever come to be."

"And a loss that I'm sure grieves him still, even more than it grieves me," Kaitan said. "Why do you marvel over these details so, *kaihen*? Are they that hard to believe?"

"That's just it." He ran a hand over his chin. "I'm trying to picture it, but every part of it seems incredible to me. You must have taken such a great risk, and all for a boy you didn't truly know very well."

"I knew he was important to Deinol, and he didn't deserve to be imprisoned. I might not have been Seth's closest friend, but I never saw him treat anyone unfairly, or even utter a harsh word. And he was too delicate for Elgar's dungeons."

Ryo fell silent, and for once, Kaitan understood what he was thinking perfectly. "*Kaihen,* when will you stop taking my act of cowardice as some indictment of your own character, or of my regard for you? What happened at the palace— what I did—you could never have changed it. It was due to my own weakness. And if, in the years since that terrible day, I have been able to show more courage than I did then, it is not because anyone else ever reached higher in my esteem than you. It is because I had already learned the consequences—the misery and wretchedness and regret—of cowardice. That's how I understood it would be better to die than to make that mistake again. Isn't that what mistakes are for, that we might learn from them?"

"It . . . is so," Ryo said, clearing his throat. Perhaps he felt embarrassed to be having this conversation within earshot of so many others, though Kaitan did not care who overheard. At least the prince had accepted his words at all. Ryo glanced at Gao. "You look like you have something to say. Don't hold back on my account."

Gao tilted his chin, pointing it at Kaitan. "It just isn't fair. That *he's* here, and Rana isn't."

Kaitan would have expected Ryo to agree, but his answer was fierce and unhesitating. "Do not allow yourself to lose sight of who our true enemy is. We may no longer count Kaitan among our comrades, but he is an Aurnian, born and raised. Elgar destroyed and captured his home as surely as he did ours, and his claim to vengeance is no lesser. And never forget, beside Elgar's crimes, Kaitan's cowardice is as dust on the wind. Today we fight in common cause, and you will think him as much your ally as you do me. Our victory may depend on it."

Gao scratched the leather over his missing eye, mouth twisting in a disgruntled way Kaitan remembered. He lifted his shoulders, then dropped them again. "Never say I couldn't follow a command when necessity demanded it, *kaihen.*"

"Well, I'm bloody glad *that's* settled," Rask said, and their heads all turned as one to where he sat with the still-flickering lamp. "Let's keep our heads on properly, shall we, boys? We've only minutes left. No falling apart at the crucial moment, eh?"

A SPINDLY OLD man stood immortalized in stone, barely dressed in ragged, threadbare clothes. But though his limbs were shriveled, his lined face was kind. In his outstretched hand lay a single crust of bread, proffered without hesitation, though it be all he owned.

"I knew you would like that one," Arianrod said, already arranging sheets of parchment on the chamber floor.

Adora glanced at the statue's base, where there were inscribed the runes for *self, without, care.* Gilmarion—the Old Lantian spirit of compassion. "They're all beautiful," she said. "And interesting. I like the challenge the artist set themselves, to capture each one visually."

On the left side of Gilmarion were Asariel, wisdom and the pursuit of knowledge; Tethantys, ambition and inspiration; Yaelor, valor; Isedra, justice; and Amerei, the spirit of love. The right side was given to three virtues that were harder to translate. *Telfair* was often rendered in modern Lantian as *craft* or *artistry,* the diligent refinement of a skill until it approached perfection. *Sareseth* was even harder, comprised of the runes for *loyalty* and *conviction. Fidelity,* perhaps: the unwavering championing of a person or cause, no matter the adversity it brought—as the statue of the martyr standing serene atop his pyre demonstrated. And the last . . .

"That's the one who helped your ancestor with the Curse," Arianrod said, nodding at the runes for *soul* and *strength*: Irein, or perseverance, will.

Adora examined the statue, a cloaked and hooded figure pressing on despite an arrow wound in the side. "So she didn't do it alone after all."

Arianrod looked up from her work. "Does that really bother you? You must have guessed it was something like that—that either she had some unknown power she'd successfully kept hidden from everyone, or some other entity helped her. Or did you really think she'd turned the Curse back by wanting it very intensely, and nothing more?"

"I . . . couldn't say for sure, of course. No one ever knew the reason—I wonder if she herself did. But it seems as if we really ought to credit this spirit with the deed, and not the Rebel Queen."

"Nonsense," Arianrod said. "Asariel told me Irein only acted in response to Talia's wish, moved by the strength of her will. If it weren't for her, it would never have happened. The credit is no less than she deserves." She laid the last sheet and stood up, taking in the scene as a whole. "All right, we're out of time. We've got to crack this today."

"I've been trying my best," Adora said, walking a slow circle so she could read each sheet of parchment in turn. She hadn't spent as much time here as Arianrod had, because she had to cross in and out of Valyanrend to fetch her best soldiers and give instructions to Vespas and Amali. They were, of course, deeply unhappy that she was going to remain within the city for the duration of the battle, but she was only just able to convince them not to follow her back by assuring them that she wouldn't be anywhere near the actual fighting, and in the company of a mage at least as powerful as Elgar.

But there was one person who wasn't accompanying them for the first time today, and Adora couldn't help asking, "Are you worried about her?"

Arianrod shook her head once to the side, not *no,* just a sign of irritation at the question. "I told her I would put my faith in her, as she always puts hers in me. And she is the best at what she does, it's true."

"And every time she believed in you, I'm sure she still worried for you anyway," Adora said. "You're not betraying her by feeling concern."

"But I *would* be betraying the cause, if I let anything distract me today. And the less I think about it, the sooner she'll return. Now, no more delaying. Let's set to it."

Because Adora couldn't see the runes that comprised the spell, Arianrod had drawn them on parchment and placed the parchment on the floor to mark the corresponding positions of each rune. She'd also drawn the whole thing on another sheet in miniature, so it was easier to take in as a single piece. They had made progress, even if they didn't yet have a tangible advantage to show for it, and most of that progress involved the realization that the spell was made up of a series of concentric rings, with runes lining up at specific points within all the circles at once. But there were other runes that were confined to a single circle, without making any additional connections. The spell's primary function—to cut mages off from the world's magic, or to release that barrier—was something Arianrod had deciphered before Adora had ever arrived, but they both felt certain there was something else hidden in the runes, some other purpose. "I don't understand why this Asariel isn't helping us," Adora said. "Doesn't she want to see Elgar fall as much as anyone?"

"These spirits don't seem to have the flexibility of humans," Arianrod said. "They can't change what they are to suit the situation. They want people to follow their paths, so to speak. The spirit of knowledge doesn't want to just tell us things, she wants us to discover them through our own intellect. She only told me as much as she did because otherwise that knowledge would have been lost, and that's the last thing she could allow to happen."

"So as long as it's possible to figure this out, no matter how difficult it might be, we're on our own?"

Arianrod smirked. "Eager for gods to solve all our problems already, are we? Honestly, I'd rather she stay out of it. I don't want all my victories handed to me, either."

"Well, if you and I manage to solve this, we'll be worthy of only the highest scholarly distinction," Adora said. "Can you pass me that quill?"

DESPITE HERSELF, AND even though she'd seen it before, Lirien couldn't help feeling a breath of awe as she gazed up and down the full length of the Precipitate. They had told stories of it in Sundercliff, but because no one there had ever actually seen it, that had only added to its mystique. An architectural achievement that had no equal, a man-made river funneling enough water to quench the thirst of the continent's largest city. Though she had learned to dull the constant awareness of nearby water at the back of her mind, when presented with this much, her senses were still a bit overwhelmed. But she couldn't afford to be awed by it now. She had come to master it, after all, and if what Arianrod Margraine had said was true, she'd only be making things more difficult for herself by fixating on how powerful it was.

She followed the water with her eyes until it disappeared beneath the earth, then turned to the girl at her side. "I've heard tell that the combined web of underground cisterns that catches the water here is almost as large as Valyanrend's smallest district."

Marceline nodded. "Aye, almost a whole neighborhood. The other cisterns it flows to from there are much smaller—they'd have to be, to disperse it around the city more or less evenly. Why?"

"I was just thinking that all of this only works because of the people who live here. I'm told the cisterns are built larger than they strictly need to be, so they're never filled to the brim, even during heavy rains. But even so, their construction still relies on having people to drink the water, to open up more room. If most of the city's population died or left, the cisterns would overflow, and Valyanrend would be flooded."

"Aye, that's true enough, though I can't say I find it a possibility that frets me much. It's not as if it's likely to happen." Marceline shrugged. "Perhaps that's as much as to say that a city would die without its people. If only someone could have gotten the imperator to understand that."

"It's hardly the gravest of his crimes," Lirien said, glancing up and down the nearest pillar of the aqueduct. "You really just climb these things?"

"Not that one," Marceline said, walking past it. "You have to start with this one, and only this one. I'll show you where all the right indentations are, and how to space yourself out, but once you start, you'll be on your own."

"And people do this for fun? Just risk falling to their deaths when they don't have to, for no good reason at all?"

"You aren't paying attention," the girl snapped. "This is serious. If you don't know the hand- and toeholds to use, you're more or less guaranteed to slip, and I'm not going to be able to catch you if you do."

She was so authoritative, like a tiny general. Lirien smiled faintly, then stepped beneath the shadow of the pillar, resting her palm against the stone. It came away wet, soaked in the spray that hissed into the air with the falling water. "I didn't realize it would be like this—that the water had spread this far."

"That's what I've been *saying*. It would be challenging just to climb this dry, but we don't even have that luxury."

"You misunderstand," Lirien said calmly. "If I'd known it was going to be this wet, I wouldn't even have bothered calling you all the way out here. I can climb this on my own."

"And break your neck before you're halfway," Marceline insisted. "You haven't the skill for it. Trust me. If you slip—"

"The water won't let me slip," Lirien said. "But you're free to watch for yourself, if you like."

She kicked off her boots, and approached the pillar Marceline had indicated—no need to make things needlessly harder for herself just for the sake of showing off. She placed her toes upon the first indentation in the pillar's side, and the water running down it froze around her foot, solid enough that even all her weight couldn't crack it. It probably wouldn't hold for too long, but the point was to keep moving anyway. "It would've been too tiring if I had to condense the water out of the air first," she said. "But with so much all around me, getting it to do this becomes easy. Now, are you going to show me the best route or not?"

Marceline looked a bit put out, but she was as good as her word. And then there was only the climb, the ice serving as a safeguard in case her feet slipped on the wet stone. Even with the help, it was still arduous going, putting a strain on her limbs she knew she'd feel in the coming days. When she finally hauled herself over the lip of the aqueduct, she almost flopped right into the water. It was rushing by with surprising speed, the one dangling arm she dipped into it buffeted by the current and painfully wrenched downstream at the shoulder.

Then she had gained the top at last, and the roofs of the city spread out below her, gray shapes looming in the mist. She stepped into the center of the aqueduct, and the water surged and roared all around her, swirling up to her shins and nearly knocking her over. She knew large bodies of water, of course; she had grown up on the very shores of the Endless Sea, the largest body of water in the world. But because she had lived by the sea, the workings of rivers still remained a bit mysterious to her, and here was a river made by human hands, the size and scope of which had never been duplicated. Seas went back and forth, tides in and out, sustaining themselves on cycles; lakes caught and held, shivering in crystalline repose. But rivers were change, constant and unrelenting. Rivers could not wait, could not rest, never and always the same thing. Again, she had to stifle a sense of awe at it, and to push down her trepidation. She'd already almost exhausted herself before the real work had even begun.

But it was one thing for Arianrod Margraine to propose such a thing in theory, and another for Lirien to carry it out. She was used to working with a little water at a time, pulling it from the air or freezing it in a human body or around a fish. Even just to *move* this much at once would be something she had never done before. And then she had to add this healing business on top of it, making it affect people that the water touched even if she couldn't see them from here. It was giving her a headache just thinking about it. But the trouble was, she was the only person in the world who could do it. She had to figure it out, because there wasn't another option.

So she stood barefoot in the midst of the aqueduct and closed her eyes, feeling the weight of the water rushing past, moment by moment. She reached out to it, which was easy enough, and tried to comprehend what it was, the simple will that consumed it to flow ever forward, the same path over hundreds and hundreds of years. And then she tried to move it.

The strain was immediate, a white-hot flash of pain that burst through the center of her forehead. Everything this man-made river was resisted what she wanted it to do. It possessed such volume, such force, such centuries of habit; it had existed like this long before she had ever come to be, and her whole life would comprise only the smallest fragment of its continued existence. In her mind, it rose up like a great wave to crush her, flattening her intent into nothing.

But she couldn't let it end there. *Think,* Arianrod Margraine had instructed her. *Objects are static, but people can reshape their conceptions of themselves endlessly. Think yourself into mastery over it, and the magic will make it a reality.*

For Lirien was not small, not really. Not anymore. She carried the ocean inside her, everywhere she went. The Endless Sea, the greatest thing in the known world, large enough to swallow every continent on their maps. The sea had chosen her, alone out of everyone. Even now, she could picture those waters perfectly, in every setting, set afire by sunset or silvered under the moon or shattered by pelting rain. She swam untouched among waves that had dashed others upon the rocks. That was how she would cast this spell—by bringing the sea itself to this landlocked city.

There is no difference between us anymore, she thought at the river. *It gave itself to me, that its yearnings might hold true even in the driest desert. Though the sea lies forever beyond your reach, even you must have felt that yearning.*

And the river yielded to her, for no river could resist the call of the sea.

CHAPTER FORTY-NINE

Valyanrend

THE MAN BEFORE Naishe fell back, taken by an arrow in the shoulder that seemed to sprout from nowhere. Whatever she could say about her father, his aim was as unerring as ever. She returned the favor by firing at another soldier attempting to breach the protective wall the other members of the resistance had formed in front of the two of them, the only two archers in their group. She felt a bit uneasy about allowing herself to be protected even in a small way, but Wren had assured her that she'd be better able to protect everyone else like this.

"This isn't going to work," her father said softly at her ear, even as he nocked another arrow. "I don't want to kill them any more than you, but injuries aren't stopping them. Eventually, we'll be overwhelmed."

"Eventually, Lirien will cast her spell," Naishe said. "We just have to hold out until then. And the injuries aren't stopping them, but they're certainly slowing them down."

He proved her point, guiding an arrow into a soldier's leg that dropped her right to the cobblestones. She wouldn't be walking on that. "What if Lirien isn't able to cast that spell after all?"

"Let's hope it doesn't come to that," Naishe said.

"But what if it does? Will we even know if the spell fails? You've got to have a plan, Naishe."

She ground her teeth at his condescension, but at least he'd called her Naishe, if only because a single syllable was more efficient in a situation like this. "We'll know. Marceline is with her, and she'll get the news to us if things go badly at the Precipitate. And if that happens . . . we'll have to be more aggressive here. I don't like it, but we have to get to the Citadel, or it's all over. And at least some of these people threw their lot in with Elgar willingly."

"It's proving harder to tell which is which than I thought," her father said. "I'd assumed those he controlled would be . . . I don't know, like sleepwalkers. But these people seem perfectly ordinary. If I didn't know from all I've heard that there was dark magic at work here, I'd never have believed it."

He wasn't wrong. She didn't like to think about that terrible day in Silkspoint, but she could remember it clearly. It hadn't occurred to her at the time because she'd been so focused on simply surviving, but when she recalled it later, the soldiers' behavior was noticeably odd. They didn't merely take little heed of injuries, as these did; they never spoke a word, never changed facial expressions beyond rage and neutrality, and seemed completely unaware any of their fellows existed. But these called encouragement and strategy to one another, and though they did their best to fight through their injuries, their uninjured allies supported and protected them. "I don't understand it, either. Something must have changed—in Elgar, in his chosen targets, in the spell itself. But I don't know enough about magic to guess what he could have done to alter the spell so fundamentally in such a short amount of time. The marquise insists that such widespread control can only work with the simplest of commands, but perhaps the command was changed?"

Two more arrows left her father's bow in quick succession, and Naishe hurried to attend to her own. "Could it be possible that no soldiers under Elgar's spell were sent to this location?" he asked. "That they're all willing volunteers, and those who aren't were sent somewhere else? You said those altered in Silkspoint could not distinguish between foes and noncombatants. Perhaps any voluntary recruits would likewise be cut down, so he has to divide his forces into all one or all the other."

Before Naishe could explain why that was highly impractical, something hit her arm. At first she thought it was a spray of blood; then, for just a moment, she thought it was raining. She looked up reflexively, but no storm clouds met her view; the sky was open and clear, a perfect blue. Then there could be only one answer. These were the waters of the Precipitate.

Though a battle raged around her, something within her could not resist closing her eyes, leaving her head tilted up toward the sky and letting the water wash over her. It was cool but not cold, rinsing the sweat from her body and soothing her weary muscles. Then her father grabbed her elbow. "Look."

Naishe looked, and saw Elgar's army thrown into confusion. Some soldiers stood blinking in the middle of the street as if they'd caught themselves daydreaming; others had a hand to their heads, seemingly struck by sudden dizziness. Still others watched their comrades drop out of the fight with puzzlement or anger, and arguments were already breaking out between those demanding they continue to press the attack and those demanding to know what had just happened. Soon the whole contingent would be in chaos, more preoccupied with one another than any external foe.

"Now there can be no doubt," her father said. "There were those whose minds were altered among this crowd, and yet . . ."

"It does confirm it," Naishe agreed. "But it's a mystery that will have to wait, I'm afraid. Lirien came through with her part of the plan, so it's time for us to keep to ours." She lowered her bow, and cupped a hand around her mouth. "To me, everyone! Fall back!"

They knew what she meant, though Elgar's guards, both willing and compelled, had no idea. They would fall back only to the tunnels. From there, they would join the march to the Citadel.

RASK STOOD UP, holding the lamp protectively against his chest, and showed them the last fitful flickers of the flame. "It's time. Let's get the passage open before it dies completely, or we'll never see what we're doing."

Kaitan nodded, pressing his ear to the hidden door. "I don't hear anything. Let me look first."

He eased it open a crack, but saw only dimly lit darkness on the other side, and the bottom edges of a few barrels and shelving. But no feet, and still no sound. "All right. I don't think we'll get a better opening."

They heaved the false floor up together, and helped one another climb up into the kitchen stores, more or less unchanged from the last time Kaitan had come this way. Someone had left a candlestick on the edge of a crate, but it was unlit, the wick burned down to less than a stub. Between that and the thin layer of dust over everything, it was probably safe to assume no one had been in this room for some time. "Good for Roger," he muttered. "His secret remains undiscovered."

"Careful," Ryo warned. "This seems like a distant storeroom, but we'll have to get through the kitchens to get anywhere, and there might be cooks or servants about."

As it turned out, there were, but the Citadel kitchens were cavernous, and almost all of the people working within them were confined to one room, clustered around an immense stewpot or carefully slicing a roast. The latter for Elgar, the former for his people, if Kaitan had to guess, but either way, the they were able to go around that particular chamber and creep into the entryway unobserved, the slight sounds of their footsteps drowned out by the violently boiling pot and the head cook's shouted instructions. But it was there that their unobstructed path ended.

Ryo reached the entryway first. "Five in the corridor. Haven't seen us yet; no time to delay."

They surged into the corridor like a wave, overwhelming the soldiers before they even had time to shout. Kaitan, Ryo, and Gao plunged into the center of the knot of men, while Rask and his people fanned out around them in a circle, hemming them in. The fight was flawless. Whatever might have come between them in other ways, the way they fought together was unchanged, their bodies trained and tested by the countless times they had been shoulder to shoulder or back to back against uneven odds. And for as long as the combat lasted, it was possible to pretend they could ever go back to that time.

Then it was over, and Ryo sheathed his sword, with a glance only for Gao, as if Kaitan had never existed. "Well done. Let's hurry. Without a map of this place, we have no idea how long it will take to get to the entrance. We can only pray everything went off properly outside."

They followed the corridor until it opened up abruptly into a high-ceilinged dining hall, scattered with trestle tables over a slightly dusty checkered marble floor. Seated at various tables were about thirty soldiers, who more or less all looked up at once when their party rounded the bend. A flurry of hands snatched up their weapons; chairs screeched across the marble as their occupants hastily pushed them back. And then, for a moment, their two groups simply stared at each other.

"Ah," Gao said. "I was wondering when we'd get to this part."

THE RAIN SEEMED to linger in the air, to catch the sun more deeply than Rhia had ever seen before. It blanketed the city in every direction for as far as she could see, purifying everything it touched. From here, the Precipitate was merely a shape on the horizon; Lirien herself was too far away to see. Yet it seemed to Rhia as if she could feel her intent anyway, the ghost of her presence urging them on. So many times when she had seen magic, it had been violent, frightening. This was just as majestic, just as awe-inspiringly impossible, but in a way that seemed to draw you in, rather than to warn you away. Marveling at its beauty, she felt confident that Arianrod Margraine had been right. If anything could convince people of the good magic could do, the scale of it, it would be this.

Brushing against her side as he drew near, Cadfael squeezed her shoulder. "Ready?"

"I'm trying to be." She shook herself. "So much depends on this."

"That just means there's no need to hold back. We're equal to this, I'm sure of it. Remember, I've helped take down a mage who stepped too far once before. They're not as invincible as they'd have you believe."

They both turned to look at Talis, who was staring at the raindrops that had landed on her bare forearm, as if reading a message written there. "Everything all right?" Cadfael asked.

"What? Fine." She shook herself, too, much more fiercely than Rhia had, wiping the rain roughly from her arm. "Tired of waiting, though. This means we can finally begin, right?"

Cadfael glanced at the far end of the long avenue, where Elgar's soldiers were bickering amongst themselves. "I'd say it's working, so . . ."

Rhia gave a whistle to alert the others, and then she, Cadfael, and Talis set off down the avenue. Their group was waiting closest to the Citadel, tucked away in various alleys and side streets so they wouldn't draw attention when everyone else lured Elgar's soldiers away. They would never have found the Citadel completely undefended, but Rhia was confident they could take a group this size, especially when a third of its members were either clutching their heads or insisting on going home.

Talis pulled ahead of them, taking a deep breath. "All right, a gentle touch," she muttered. "Let's hope this bloody works."

With no further warning, a gale erupted in the midst of the squabbling soldiers, pulling dozens into the air. Though they screamed and flailed, they seemed to fall too slowly, and when they hit the ground, all they did was roll; there was no blood, no broken bones. It was as if they were merely being picked up and set down somewhere else.

Cadfael grinned. "Knew you could do it."

Perhaps Talis was trying to remain stoic, but she still let a twitch of her mouth slip through. "That was one of us. Come on, the stragglers are your responsibility; I'm taking a page from Lirien's book today." Not fighting to kill, Rhia realized.

Once they recovered their feet, the soldiers Talis had scattered did one of two things: they either turned on their heel and ran without looking back, or did their best to form up and cover the entrance to the Citadel once more. "Well, well," Cadfael said. "Nice of them to sort themselves into groups for us."

By then, their allies had reached them, including the soldiers Adora had handpicked from among her ranks. Rhia and Cadfael fought with them, cutting through those defenders who refused to be dissuaded by Talis's repeated gales. The waters of the Precipitate continued to fall, soaking into Rhia's hair and clothes, but she never felt weighed down by it. And though her sword was cold, somehow it didn't bother her this time.

For a while, it went as well as they could have hoped, their side almost completely insulated from casualties and most of their foes simply brushed out of the way. But then Rhia looked up at the sound of a massive groaning of wood and screeching of metal. Those watching from within the Citadel must have seen what was happening, and they were lifting the bridge that spanned the moat and abandoning their comrades on the other side.

"Oh, no, you don't," Talis said, lifting herself into the air.

Arrows flew toward her, but her winds flung them all aside. She lifted herself over the lip of the retreating bridge and immediately started blowing soldiers into the moat. When there were none left on ground level, her winds snaked up the walls and dislodged archers from their posts, making them fall with that same unnatural slowness so they hit the waters below without injury.

"Take me over there, too!" Cadfael shouted.

"I can't, remember?" she called back. "Not while you carry that."

The swords Rhia and Cadfael bore didn't distinguish between beneficial and harmful magic; none of it could touch vardrath steel, no matter its intent. She remembered the day by Lake Rovere when Lirien, unbeknownst to her, had kicked her sword aside in order to save her from certain death. Strange that the falling rain still felt so special to her, distinct in some way from ordinary precipitation. Could there be some slight magical quality in it that was still able to touch her skin, before the steel's pull snuffed it out?

Cadfael tried to shove his sword into Rhia's hands, but she shook her head. "Don't be ridiculous. What good are you going to do her over there without a weapon?"

"Then I'll trade weapons with—"

"No. Come on. Isn't this the opposite of our usual roles?"

He laughed. "You've got me there. I suppose that was . . . overly impulsive."

"She's doing well," Rhia said. "Once she finishes with the walls, there will be no one left to shoot at her, and no one else high enough to reach her. I think the group going through the Citadel from the inside will be the most help to her, not us. But perhaps"—she glanced behind them, where the allies who were bringing up the rear were beginning to clash with those few soldiers who had picked themselves up again multiple times or struggled out of the moat—"we might see to others who aren't Talis, who need our help instead?"

ADORA TAPPED THE point of her quill against the parchment. "Seems to me you've figured out the locking and unlocking portion of the spell by yourself. Everything you've shown me just builds on the same thing. It's a series of dualities, and lining them all up in one direction goes to *open,* and all in the other direction goes to *closed.*"

"Right, although I wouldn't want to actually attempt to use it that way, lest I missed something."

"But look here." She held out Arianrod's sketch of the spell in miniature. "We've seen how the runes form rings nested inside each other, and that makes sense for a lock. But if you look at it like this, from the center going out, doesn't it also look like four lines extending at right angles from each other?"

"I . . . suppose it does," Arianrod said. "Why is that significant?"

"You know, like an Old Lantian quarter-lyric?"

"I'm not familiar."

"Really? Well, it's a kind of love poetry that was popular back then, especially if you didn't want just anyone to be able to read the full contents of your message. Old Lantian poets were very fond of them, as you might imagine, but the form lived on through scholars even into the days of modern Lantian. You have to understand runic to read it, and they're intended to be puzzles, so both the writer and reader of the message would have to be highly educated—"

"So, strictly love poetry for academics," Arianrod said. "And given that's a subject I've never been curious about, I'm not surprised I've never heard of it."

"But our Magician, if that's who really made this spell, obviously had heard of it, so we're going to have to solve one. Each line forms a line—that is, a line of poetry—but the runes are out of order. You have to unscramble them to decipher the message. Then when you have all four lines, you have to put *them* in the right order to read the poem as it was meant to be read."

Arianrod traced the four lines on the parchment. "I doubt our Magician actually left a love note of any sort here, but if he was familiar with the form, perhaps he used it to hide a message of a different kind. How about you take these two lines and I'll take those two, and we'll see who finishes first?"

"You would make a competition out of it," Adora said, readying her quill.

Arianrod grinned, unrepentant. "I have to make it fun somehow, don't I?"

In the end, they were each too busy offering suggestions on the other's work to keep score, and graciously agreed it was a tie. Because runes could have different pronunciations and meanings depending on context, the solution was not a series of opposing nouns, but rather two complete sentences. In Old Lantian they rhymed, but she and Arianrod didn't bother trying to carry that over into their translation. The four lines, deciphered and set in order, read roughly:

In flowers undying
I buried my first act of love.
But this, my last,
I hold out as a hand to you.

Arianrod clicked her tongue, getting restlessly to her feet and beginning to pace. "Well, that's useless."

"Do you think we got it wrong somewhere?" Adora asked, falling into step with her.

"No, that's the only solution that makes sense. But it just sounds like another riddle, not an answer. And if it's a riddle that takes any great amount of time to solve, that's time we don't have. Are we supposed to go off in search of whatever these undying flowers are supposed to be? The battle would be over."

Adora looked at the four lines again. "Would the creator of such a complex riddle really be so foolish? He must have known it might be centuries before anyone was able to solve it. Hiding something anywhere at all, and trusting it to still be there after hundreds of years, seems too ridiculous to me."

Arianrod brushed her hair back from her face. "Then the only thing I can think of is that the words themselves are meaningless. There has to be a solution, because it's a test, and we had to prove we could pass it. But beyond that, the runes could say anything. Still, if that were the case, solving it should have accomplished something. But nothing has changed."

"No, I think you've hit on it," Adora said. "Maybe we have to . . . I don't know how to put it. Let the spell know we solved it. It's not as if it has eyes to see what we wrote down."

Arianrod picked up the parchment with a sigh. *"In flowers undying I buried my first act of love. But this, my last, I hold out as a hand to you."* She waited, tilting her head to the side. "Nothing. Was I not sufficiently dramatic?"

Adora felt a stab of disappointment, but then she remembered. "No, this is just our translation. It's not actually the solution."

Arianrod raised an eyebrow. "So you want me to, what, read it in the original Old Lantian?"

"No, it's . . ." She made a small noise of frustration in the back of her throat. "It's about the runes, I know it. Not the pronunciation, the runes."

"Perhaps, but we can't exactly recite the runes aloud. And I'd be wary of engraving them in the floor, even if I had the tools. I wouldn't want to damage the spell."

The *we* snagged in Adora's mind, and she remembered the final line of the translation. "Not *we*. *You*. 'I hold out my hand to *you*.'"

"That's not exactly how it—"

"I mean to say, the words aren't completely meaningless, but it *is* a test—it's two tests. One is the solution to the puzzle, but the other is being able to see the puzzle at all. Arianrod, this was never meant for me. It's a message left by a mage for a mage, and no one else. There has to be a way you can present the solution magically. It won't work otherwise. I'm sure of it."

"Magically and runically, eh? This room certainly has enough magic in it for me to cast any spell I please. Let's see . . ." She raised a hand, and traced their solution in the air with one finger. As she did so, the runes appeared shimmering before her, as if she'd written them upon the fabric of the world. She finished, and they hung in the air for a moment, four distinct lines of light.

Then that light exploded outward, engulfing the room.

IT HAD BEEN a while since she had done it, but Seren was quite used to waiting in the rafters. She had never taken contracts as an assassin of the Inxia Morain, but no trainee could become a full-fledged member without offering her superiors proof that she could track and execute a target of her own devising without getting caught. Some of her fellows had chosen targets based on their level of influence or protection, in order to show off, but all of Seren's targets had only one thing in common: they were those who, as in her native city, sought to buy and sell orphaned or unwanted children. Many of those deals had taken place in warehouses like this one, though seldom in the middle of the day. She'd learned it was far better to already be in position than to try to infiltrate a crowded room— less important, admittedly, with a potential audience of one, but old habits were easy to fall into.

At least she didn't have to perch on a beam like a nesting bird, a position that would inevitably have made her legs stiff if she had to keep it up for long. The warehouse was expansive, built on an open floor plan so that even though it was technically two stories, the second floor was more like a giant's shelving, wooden planks jutting out from the walls in three directions to fit more barrels of dried foodstuffs—mostly fruit, but with some salted meat in a particularly cool and dry corner. Not especially flammable, and there was enough space on the upper level for her to jump down without landing on a barrel. There were four slender wooden pillars that ran from the ground to the ceiling of the second floor, supporting the roof; good to keep in mind to help her avoid her foe once a fight broke out.

Ghilan hadn't been particularly discreet since his arrival in Valyanrend; in fact, he'd made himself all the easier to find by becoming a neighborhood nuisance. She had no way of knowing what specifically had happened, but it seemed that he'd either been turned down by Elgar or Lord Oswhent when he offered his services, or else he'd learned something about the imperator in the meantime that had given him pause. Either way, a monetary windfall had not presented itself, and he'd taken to living in the warehouse in secret, dining on its various offerings so he could save his coin for the local taverns and brothels. It had worked well for a time, but apparently a subordinate of the warehouse's owner had discovered him when she came to take inventory. Ghilan had resisted the woman's attempts to run him off, and she, not being a fighter, had retreated and reported the matter to her employer. He had hired a couple more combative individuals to finish the job, but Ghilan had sent them on their way with several broken bones between them. They'd tried to report the matter to the city guard, but Elgar's guards were far too preoccupied with Arianrod, the Issamiri, and Elgar's various whims, so until now no resolution had been forthcoming. Little did they know, Seren was about to take care of this problem for them, for no other recompense than her personal satisfaction.

Ghilan certainly entered the warehouse like a man returning home; he didn't even look around before plopping himself down on a folded cloak on the warehouse floor. But he must have been more aware than he seemed, for after a few moments he called, "Well, come out of hiding, then. Did the promise of coin tempt you to forget how I handled the last lot, or did that useless oaf simply not tell you?"

"Oh, I'm not hiding," Seren said, pausing so she could hear his sudden intake of breath in the stillness. "If I had been hiding, you would already be dead. I was simply waiting. But I have to say, I'm rather disappointed." She jumped down from the rafters, landing in the spot she'd chosen before, and then leapt from there to the ground floor; Ghilan was already back on his feet. "You could do worse, certainly. But surely you dreamed of more for yourself in this city than a hostile residence in someone else's drafty warehouse?"

She was gratified, she had to admit, to see shock and even fear in his face. She had never seen them before, and suspected he was not a man who often felt them. A promising start, as she intended to make him feel much more than that. "What's the matter? I thought you'd be delighted. Didn't you bemoan the fact that you'd never get a chance to truly match yourself against me?" She spread her hands, allowing him to see how completely they had healed, and stood up straight to show the full mobility of her once-broken leg. "Well, here I am. Good as new—better, even, because now I actually want to fight you."

Ghilan was recovering gamely from his initial shock, but his usual glee was still nowhere to be found, replaced by a stormy frown etched deep into his face. "Forgive me if I'm skeptical, Miss Almasy. I'm quite sure of the injuries I inflicted. If you have some way to heal from even that much damage so perfectly, how could anyone hope to stand against you? I love a challenge, but not a rigged contest."

"Is that your only issue? You've seen magic before—thwarted magic, even, if what I hear is true. So why be unnerved by it?" She bent her arm, watching the muscles flex as she stretched her fingers one by one. "The power that healed me isn't mine—if it had been, I would have used it much earlier. And the one who helped me is long gone."

He finally started to relax, once more on ground that felt familiar to him. "And now you want revenge, is that it?"

"Precisely. That, and the security of knowing you won't be around to ruin my lady's plans anymore. If you were another man, I'd have had to approach you unseen—I'm very good at that, but it's tedious." Besides, even though she knew it was childish, part of her wanted him to have time to realize she was the one who'd killed him. "But you won't run away from a fight, will you? I'll even let you fetch the hammer and everything."

Ghilan laughed, not a little snicker but a big booming guffaw, his head thrown back. "Ah, how unfortunate for you, Miss Almasy. When we first met, it pleased you to seem so far above me that nothing I said could touch you. I proved you wrong then, when I evoked your anger, and while I can't truly say I proved my strength near Lakeport, I at least proved that you ignored me at your peril. Can you survive being proved wrong a third time?"

"Yes," Seren said, "I admit it. You turned out to be powerful enough to earn my notice—to make me regret not killing you at Stonespire. Congratulations. Enjoy it while you can."

"Oh, I intend to." He straightened up to his full height, taking the time to survey their surroundings. "Do you mean us to fight here?"

"It suits my purposes well enough. Do you have some objection?"

"Not at all. But I do have to correct you on one thing." He tapped the weapons at his side, a shortsword at each hip, one slightly longer than the other. Had he taken them from two different opponents? "I lost the hammer back in Araveil, as it happens. I suppose I could've replaced it, but I thought it was time for a change. I'll be fighting with these now."

Seren kept her face impassive, but that was a bit of a complication. In all the extensive scenarios she'd played out in her mind while preparing to face him, he'd always been wielding a hammer. This would be a different sort of fight altogether—with such lighter weapons, he'd be much faster, and his reach would have a smaller radius but be far more accurate within it. Her strategy relied on getting in close, but if he overreached with one blade, he still had the other. She'd never seen him fight with the hammer before, so at least she wasn't losing the advantage of experience—when it came to fights against other opponents, she had trained against every set of weapons imaginable. Still . . . her muscles tensed uncomfortably, and she fought to loosen them again. She had already decided on this path. If she backed down now, he'd never consider her worth his time again. And if she wanted to get rid of him then, she'd really have to hunt him down. Better to do it now, this way, for efficiency's sake as well as for her pride.

She was one of the best fighters her teacher had ever trained, and he'd trained hundreds. Many of them had gone on to become infamous assassins in the guild, whose stories would be told and retold for generations. But Seren was the only one who'd gotten away. And now, finally, she knew what the source of her strength really was.

She drew her favorite knife, whose precise shape and weight she would have known even in dreams. "We've no one else to start us off, so let's begin."

They leapt toward each other.

Ghilan had already drawn both his swords before the distance between them could close, but he didn't have a chance to get them into position. Seren moved not in front of him, but past him, skimming her knife along the side of his arm as she went. It was a trivial wound, not enough to truly slow him down, but it was still a good start, to bolster her confidence and rattle his own. Ghilan shook his arm out, heedless of the blood that spattered the floor between them. "Come on. A little scratch like that is beneath you."

"Come on yourself. I'm sure you've engaged in testing the waters at the start of a battle countless times before." She didn't often banter during a fight—she didn't see the point—but it served a purpose this time. He already believed they were the same, and it would be beneficial for Seren to encourage that. She remembered how Arianrod had handled Jocelyn—by inducing her to underestimate Arianrod's true abilities. That was crucial here as well. If he guessed he was facing off against a fighter with over ten years of specialized training, he might suspect some part of what she planned.

She didn't manage to draw blood again on the next few passes; they were still feeling each other out, testing speed and reflexes, poking around for weaknesses. He was, after all, an experienced fighter, so he didn't make the mistake of trying to land a killing blow right away. That was one of the central lessons Gan Senrian had taught her: the most important part of a fight is not discovering your opponent's weakness, or setting up the perfect strike. The most important part of a fight is that you yourself don't make a mistake. If you can ensure your opponent makes one first, the killing blow creates itself.

But Ghilan was disciplined, too, despite his eagerness for the fight. So they flowed around and around each other, drawing close without ever touching, as if moving through the steps of a dance they knew by heart. With every pass, Seren tested his movements anew, whether and how closely he'd follow her in one direction or another, how confident he had to be before he'd risk a lunge, his preferred ways to block or avoid each of her strikes. The mismatched lengths of the two swords complicated matters, for she had to judge them as two different weapons, and not mirror images of each other; the longer one nearly nicked her a few times. But she had a flexibility that he lacked; the crowded nature of the warehouse was nothing but a hindrance to him, while Seren could dodge around one of the wooden pillars without taking her eyes off him, or half-scale a pile of crates to put her closer to his eye level.

"You do love to jump about, Miss Almasy," Ghilan said. No doubt he missed the hammer now; it would have let him clear out more space, but he wasn't going to smash any barrels with those swords. "Are you a fighter, or an acrobat?"

"Must I choose only one? It's natural for me to lean on the expertise I possess. You don't hear me calling that absurd strength of yours an unfair advantage." His slashes came faster, one after another after another; perhaps he was showing off. But Seren dodged each one easily, and the next round, and the next. He kept adding one more slash to his flurry of attacks each time, as if hoping to catch her by surprise. But she wasn't some novice, to be taken in by such an elementary trick.

He put up both swords, taking a step back. "Perhaps I should give myself a rest and wait until you're actually ready to face me, then."

"And drop your guard? I wouldn't advise it." She held up the knife. "I'm very good at throwing this, too, you know."

He laughed. "If you were that good at it, you wouldn't tell me, you'd just do it."

Normally, that would've been true. But she had something specific in mind this time.

When he swung at her again, she made him bend around a staggered stack of crates, while she used them as stepping stones. She leapt around and down, lashing out with the knife as she drew near and opening a wound in his upper back. So close. But not where she wanted to hit him, not yet.

Three passes after that, he slashed open the side of her left arm, and she carved across his left hand with her right. He dropped the sword, and she kicked it away. But he was too smart to glance after it, and merely gripped his remaining one with both hands. She hadn't expected him to use it like a club, and couldn't quite dodge clear. But stunningly, he managed to only hit her with the flat: a blow that set her ears ringing, but drew not a drop of blood. And judging by the way he swore, it hadn't been intentional.

Still, he expected the blow to leave her dazed, so when he got in close, she buried the knife to the hilt in his shoulder. She drew it out to stab again, but he got the sword between them, and her knife dragged along its edge with a harsh screech of metal. She stood where she was a moment, untangling their blades so she wouldn't be disarmed—but it was a moment he seized. He dropped the other sword and took both her shoulders in his huge hands, and then he threw her against one of the wooden pillars holding up the roof.

The pillar was thin, so it mostly hit Seren's right shoulder, only getting a sliver of her back. But Ghilan's strength was still formidable, and the impact shuddered down her arm, pain shooting all the way to her fingertips. He hurled her against it once more, and this time Seren heard the joint give way, her right arm wrenched out of its socket. Her knife slipped from her fingers, dropping uselessly to the floor.

Though Lirien had healed the wounds Ghilan had inflicted on her outside Lakeport until no physical traces remained, her memories of that time were not so easily wiped clean. She could remember the sound and feeling of splintering bone with sickening clarity, and she had to force down a wave of nausea. But this was not the first unpleasant memory she'd had to carry—far from it. She had spent a lifetime forcing them down, pushing them away. That had done her no good; she knew that now. But she could delay dealing with it just once more. This would be the last time.

Ghilan still had her by the upper arms, and he pulled her close to him, leaning his face down to hers. "You were right, Miss Almasy," he rumbled, that hateful eagerness in his eyes. "Once you put your acrobatics aside, your body is so fragile."

"Unfortunately for you," Seren panted, "you seem to have forgotten how to count since our last meeting. You of all people should know I have two hands."

She had palmed it before he even touched her, knowing exactly what he planned to do. She lashed out with one foot, surprise and pain caused him to loosen his grip on her arms, and she struck with her left hand, stabbing him at the base of his neck—not with the knife, but with the needle she'd bought at the Night Market. It was hollow, and the glass cylinder attached to it could hold liquid. Sahaian healers used them to get medicine directly into patients' blood, though not as frequently as they would've liked, as the things were still expensive to craft. And one of Seren's peers in the Inxia Morain had used them to unleash poison on her targets, so that even a small prick could be fatal.

This particular needle did not hold poison; having had too many unpleasant experiences with various toxins during her training, Seren had never liked to use them, even with the protection Arianrod's blood apples provided. Or, to be strictly accurate, it wasn't poison at this dosage. It was common knowledge that snow's down could kill you if you ingested it—its numbing qualities turned paralytic at high concentrations, eventually causing the body's vital processes to fail. But no assassin she knew of had ever used it to kill, because of the sheer amount you'd have to take to ensure death. If your target was so oblivious that you could get them to drink a pint of it without noticing, there was probably a much simpler way to kill them. Still, most healers deemed snow's down far too dangerous to let inside the body in any quantity at all, lest it provoke a fluke reaction. Seren had measured this particular dose with great precision, to ensure that the effects would be rapid, but not fatal. But the small dose was also the reason she couldn't just stick Ghilan in the arm and be done with it. She needed to hit the spot on his spine that controlled everything below it.

Ghilan reached up with one hand to touch the back of his neck. "Did you stick me?"

That was all he had time for. He abruptly fell to the ground, rigid as a tree, with a terrific crash that disturbed a cloud of sawdust from the warehouse floor.

Seren crouched by his head, watching his beady little eyes flick around and around. "Don't worry, you aren't permanently injured. I didn't sever anything, the snow's down has just numbed your nerves. I measured it quite conservatively, though I had to estimate your weight. You aren't going to be able to move for at least five minutes—I was aiming for seven, but I can afford to be off by a little."

He stared at her blankly, wetting his lips with his tongue. "I don't get it. If you were close enough to stick me, you could've slit my throat."

"I'm glad you realized that," Seren said. "If I'd said it, it would've sounded like gloating. I considered slitting your throat, when I thought through how best to dispose of you. But if I'd done that, you would've died too quickly, without having enough time to comprehend that you'd lost to me. I know I should be above petti-ness like that, but it just wasn't good enough."

Ghilan gave a wheezing laugh. "I knew we were the same. I would've had to savor it, too."

"No," Seren said. "No matter how much you try to graft your shallow desires and meaningless way of life onto me, we are not the same. I don't kill for the sake of killing, and that's never why I wanted to be strong. I wanted to be able to make choices for myself, without having anyone else force my hand."

"Pfft. And that's different from me how? Are you saying I *don't* want to be able to make choices for myself?"

"Fair enough. Perhaps I should say instead that the choices you make are un-inspired." She rested her chin in her hand. "There was a time when I believed that carving out a place for myself in this world meant ridding it of all those who might threaten me. I sharpened my skills in Sahai by hunting those who bought and sold children. I ventured back across the sea to take revenge on those who'd harmed me there. But none of those deaths ever satisfied me. That was our greatest similarity, I suppose. You sought excitement, and I sought . . . meaning. But neither of us would ever have been satisfied. That road has no end."

"Aye. Because those who live by the blade can't set it down. It would be like leaving your heart somewhere. How else would we achieve anything?"

Loath as she was to admit it, he had a point. She had no talent for anything else. And she *had* changed things. She had removed those who caused too much harm, and made others afraid of following in their footsteps. And she had protected Arianrod, when she had once feared she would never be strong enough to help her at all. "I have walked the path of the sword, as my old teacher wished—or perhaps I should call it the path of the knife. And I'm sure I'll continue to rely on those skills in the future, to bring me closer to what I want. But now I can look forward to the day when I can put the knife down. When I won't need it anymore."

Ghilan wheeze-laughed again, more derision than delight. "Looking *forward* to it? You? Don't be absurd. What would you even be without the knife?"

"That question used to frighten me, too," Seren said. "It doesn't anymore. There is one last thing I should tell you, though."

"And what's that, Seren Almasy?"

"I was trained," she said, "by people who know more about killing than I ever will. I once aspired to reach their heights; now I think it's just as well I don't. But I was taught that, sometimes, the manner of a killing matters. That's why I lied about the dosage."

"The . . . dosage?"

"It's for two minutes shorter than I said. That's why you've slowly been getting feeling back in your limbs, and you probably thought I miscalculated. It's why you've been keeping me talking, so you can take me unawares. So you could have that last little flicker of hope, and then see it snuffed out. Weren't you the one who wanted to see my best?"

Ghilan lurched to a sitting position, but Seren had snatched her knife off the floor before they even started speaking. She stabbed him in the throat, and he fell right back down, stirring up enough sawdust to make her sneeze.

She checked her right arm—definitely dislocated. Arianrod wasn't going to be happy about that. "You were right," she said. "We should've done that to start with. I feel much better now."

She left the warehouse, shutting the door behind her. Time to keep the other half of her promise.

CHAPTER FIFTY

Valyanrend

THE LIGHT BLINDED Adora for a moment, and she stumbled backward, flailing with both arms and catching hold of something with her left hand that she couldn't see. But as spots danced before her eyes, the light gradually settled, forming an uneven coating on the floor and a shimmering block in the air where Arianrod's runes had been. There was another message there now, written not in runic, or even in Old Lantian at all, but in their modern tongue.

Please don't misunderstand, it said. *I did this not out of shame at our gift, but only to protect our people, that we might not suffer even more than we have already. I know one day we, and magic, will rise again; you must surely be proof of that. Not everyone who is well-studied is wise, but if you have solved my riddle, you must have a great intellect, and a great desire to know. Such a person is bound to discover that it is possible for one mage to use this spell against another, or against many others—an unavoidable consequence, and never my intent. Please, do not let fear or lust for power lead you down that road. Magic should be free to all who can wield it, not hoarded like a miser's gold. I am sorry I could not be there to meet you, but know that I have imagined you through all these long years. I have imagined the future that could be. With this, I entrust it to you.*

Adora felt odd reading those words, almost guilty; they had not been meant for her eyes. But she could not tell what emotion they evoked in Arianrod, the mage this long-ago genius had waited for; her expression was closed, and she kept her thoughts to herself. But then she glanced at Adora, and blinked. "What happened to your hand?"

Adora had no more idea than she did, but, now that she considered it, her left hand did sting a bit. She realized the thing she had grabbed to stop her fall was the crown held in the statue of Tethantys's fist. There must have been some sharp edge to the stone, for it had sliced open her palm, and blood dripped down her wrist.

"Are you all right?" Arianrod asked.

"I . . . yes. It's bloody, but it's not deep. How clumsy of me."

"Just be careful you don't bleed on the parchment. Those runes took a long time to draw."

"Speaking of runes . . ."

As one, they turned to look at the floor, still glowing with that unearthly light. Arianrod clicked her tongue. "So that's the secret." A completely different set of runes was inscribed in the light, not in a series of nested circles but in one continuous spiral. "I can't believe that little bastard set us *another* puzzle. At this point I think he just liked them. Could all his wisdom not have foreseen that we might need to use this thing *quickly*?"

"I'm surprised I can see this one at all," Adora said, "but at least that means you won't have to copy it for me. Is it another sealing spell?"

"I'm still figuring that out, but I don't think so. The other one had a very clear duality—open or closed. But this . . . there's no contradiction, no push and pull. Can't you tell that just by reading it?"

Adora tried, but though there were runes, they didn't form sentences, or even coherent thoughts, just strands of maybe-phrases. "I don't understand it," she admitted.

"Yes you do. Start at the center, here." She pointed. "*The golden heart.* Or *a golden heart.* Unclear."

"*Silver* is over here, but I'm not sure if it's directly related. And . . . why the rune for *to fall*? *Falling silver*? Or else *buried silver,* but that's not strictly the right rune, and our learned friend would never make that mistake. But see, they're just—"

"I thought of something," Arianrod said. "Considering where we are. *Silverfall* is the name of a district in Valyanrend—it's where we sent Lirien. Named for the Precipitate."

"You think they're named after districts in Valyanrend?" Rather than ask why that could be, Adora tried to test the hypothesis, looking for more phrases that could fit. Those runes could be *Silkspoint,* and *to fade* and *location* could be the Fades. The more she looked, the more she thought Arianrod was right.

Arianrod scuffed one foot at the center of the spiral. "But the one sequence I don't understand is *golden heart*. It's not Goldhalls, that's clearly over here. And what other district could it be?"

"None," Adora said, after only a moment. "It must be the Citadel. It's at the heart of the city, and though its walls are black now, you can still find historical texts and songs that describe them as golden."

"Though we still don't know exactly how that changed." Arianrod paced in front of the statues. "So. A map of Valyanrend. Why do I need a map of Valyanrend? What the hell is that supposed to help me accomplish?" As she turned to stride in the other direction, she abruptly stopped, gaze caught by the blood that still dripped down Adora's arm. She touched her wrist, careful not to stain her fingers. "Of course. That's the answer."

"My hand?"

"Blood, Adora. Blood flows through the body in veins; that's how it can go where it's needed. When Asariel talked about the magic in this room, she said it was like a tide pool: a place where magic collected, when once it used to flow everywhere freely. Magic doesn't literally flow through veins, of course, but this map is like the 'body' where that magic dwells. I think I'm supposed to connect to it, and then I'll be able to use it to sense other places where magic has gathered."

"Connect to it how?"

"We're going to have to find out. I think I've got the right idea, so the only thing left is to try it." She sat cross-legged in the center of the spiral, closing her eyes. "I should warn you, I'll be opening myself up to a lot of magic at once, and a lot of information. It may be overwhelming."

"Then why are you warning me?"

"Because if it gets to be too much, you may think I need to be pulled out of it. In which case . . . I trust your instincts."

"Pull you out *how*?" Adora protested, nearly splattering Arianrod with drops of blood from her hand as she sliced it wildly through the air.

"I'm sure you'll figure something out. We're out of time to discuss it further." She grinned, eyes still closed. "Let's see how well I understand his little spell."

The light on the floor flickered and then flared slightly; perhaps it was Adora's imagination, but the color seemed warmer. Arianrod's brow creased, her face tense with concentration. "Gods. Right. That's about what I . . . thought."

"Say something," Adora said. "Something else. How is it?"

"A lot of . . . information. But I can understand the map—the distribution of magic throughout the city. Mages in eras past must have used this to measure how severe the magical drought had become. I can only imagine what it must have felt like once—how much magic there must have been everywhere."

"Can you see where Elgar is?"

"We know he's in the Citadel, but no, I can't see individuals, just relative magical levels. Perhaps I'll find more of Asariel's 'tide pools,' though I think it's not very . . ." As she trailed off, her eyes squeezed shut even tighter, and her hands balled into fists. "Oh, no," she said. "Oh shit."

"What is it? Do you need to be pulled out?" Adora still had no idea how to do that, but she was at least prepared to shake Arianrod as hard as she could.

But Arianrod relaxed slightly, as if trying to prove to Adora that she was fine. "No, there's no need to worry about that. But Elgar . . . he's not acting the way we thought. I think . . . I think our people might be walking into a trap."

By THE TIME the lot of them gained the Citadel entrance, things had come off more or less like Rhia had predicted. Prince Ryo's contingent had fought their way through the halls of the Citadel until they reached Talis's position. She had been having a grand time sending every foe who got within ten yards of her into the moat, and was unscathed when the others arrived. They got all the gates open and the bridge restored, and Rhia and Cadfael raced inside with the rest. After satisfying himself that Talis was all right, Cadfael turned to Kaitan, whom he'd apparently met briefly on his earlier travels. "What's the situation here?"

"I'd say the distraction definitely worked. The guard presence is a lot lighter than you'd expect in this kind of situation. We always knew we were going to be fighting through superior numbers to reach you, but it was the difference between a challenge and an impossibility."

"What about Ritsu?" Rhia asked. "Has anyone seen him?" Ritsu hadn't been able to wait outside the Citadel with them, because they couldn't risk any of Elgar's soldiers seeing them together and getting suspicious. According to the plan they'd all discussed, he was also supposed to wait until their diversions drew manpower outside the Citadel, because if he showed up too early, someone might have tried to send him to handle one of those very diversions. He was supposed to enter the Citadel ahead of the rest of them, but Rhia hadn't seen him do it, and hadn't seen him anywhere else.

"No sign of him, but that's not necessarily a bad thing," Kaitan said. "There's been no sign of Elgar, either, and Ritsu is supposed to be with him, after all."

"Isn't that a little odd?" Rhia asked. "Of course we would never have expected him to take the front lines, but he should at least want to keep communication open between himself and his subordinates, and to know they have him protected if things go sour."

"She's right," the prince said. "I've been thinking that the behavior of those we've encountered has been strange as well. If they have evidence that their stronghold has been breached—and I think we've provided more than enough—they should be falling back to his location, protecting him at all costs. But I haven't seen even one soldier flee in search of him. They just keep coming at us. It doesn't make sense."

"Remember, Lirien's magic can't reach us in here," Talis said. "Could it be some effect of the spell Elgar used on them?"

"He wants them to not defend him? Or you think they lack the mental capacity to fall back?" Ryo scrubbed a hand over his face. "Either way, I suppose we've no choice but to press on. The enemy hasn't given us any indication of where their leader might be, so we'll just have to search until we find him."

"He probably won't be on the ground floor," Kaitan said. "He was wounded, remember? The last time I was here, I was brought for a brief audience with him, not that I had any choice in the matter. I don't remember exactly how to get to that room, but I remember roughly where it was. We could try searching that area first."

"It's as good a plan as any," Cadfael said. "Any objections?"

No one spoke.

"Then lead the way, Lu—ah, Kaitan."

"The route I took to the second floor is through here," Kaitan said. He started walking, and the rest of them filed after him. "There's this huge room—a stage for grand celebrations or affairs of state at one point, perhaps, but mostly standing empty when I saw it. The grand staircase that curls around its outer edge will take us to the second floor." He frowned as a sequence of multiple doors appeared before him. "Let's see. I remember we were outside for a brief time, before we ascended the stairs. A hallway that led to some courtyard—a large space, but without any way to reach the higher levels. And then we passed from there into the room I spoke of."

His first choice led to a dead end, with nothing for their pains but another group of soldiers to subdue (though Rhia couldn't help thinking they must be stretched thin). He realized halfway down that his second choice wasn't right, and turned them back around. But his third choice revealed sunlight streaming through a small window set above a heavy wooden door. "Yes, this is definitely it. It was night when I went up there; I'd forgotten that window until now."

"Let's hurry," the prince said. "The longer Ritsu goes without success, the less likely it is he'll achieve it. We have to assume things will still be up to us."

They plunged through the door—and stopped dead in their tracks.

The courtyard was ringed with soldiers, in so many lines that the far side of it wasn't visible. Sinthil Vlin's courtyard was a back-alley lot compared to this one: carefully trimmed hedges lining shady paths covered by rose arbors, orchards full of fruit trees, a man-made pool in one corner swimming with ornamental fish. It was so lush that the soldiers appeared crammed in haphazardly, as if some giant had arranged them wherever they would fit. They hadn't been talking amongst themselves, or debating strategy. They had simply been standing there, waiting.

"So this is where everyone's been hiding," Gao said.

"I don't understand why, though." Rask drew his sword. "Elgar clearly isn't here."

"Neither is anything else of value that I can see," Rhia said. "It's just soldiers, and trees, and fish."

"Perhaps it's what's past here," Ryo said. "The second floor. In which case, our guess was right."

"Well, they're not waiting for us to figure it out." Talis summoned a wall of wind in front of them, forcing the attacking soldiers back before they got too close. "Shall we perhaps ponder it after we take care of them?" She glanced over at Rhia and Cadfael. "We're about to be short on space, so those with vardrath steel should remember that if you get too close to me, you'll dampen my wind."

"Understood." Cadfael stepped up beside Rhia. "Cover each other?"

"Always," she said.

RITSU HAD BEEN on tenterhooks since coming into contact with the first soldier. He didn't know which or how many of Elgar's people might remember him; Shinsei had possessed no interest in anyone that wasn't his master or someone his master had told him to pay attention to. He remembered Captain Gardener, but he'd already fled the Citadel with Lord Oswhent's son. He remembered Lord Oswhent, too, and the strange mixture of kindness, condescension, and nerves he'd always brought to their interactions, but Captain Gardener had said Lord Oswhent was most likely dead. Aside from those two and Elgar himself, he had no idea who might have authority within the army. But though it seemed the initial soldiers he encountered had no knowledge of him, they did not turn him away, but brought him to one of their superiors at the gate. She apparently recognized him, though Ritsu couldn't have picked her out of a crowd. When she waved him in to the Citadel, no one objected.

But once within the Citadel, Ritsu was faced with his next challenge. He remembered how to get to certain places: the chambers he always used, the kitchens, the barracks, Elgar's strategy room and his private study. But if Elgar wasn't in any of those places, he doubted his memories would be of any use. "Why is the Citadel so empty?" he asked the soldier who'd escorted him inside.

"You mean besides those we sent to subdue the attacking rebels in the city, Commander? I'm afraid you've missed quite a bit while you've been . . ." His face paled as he realized he had no idea how to finish that sentence. ". . . away. His Eminence's greatest threat is no longer the rebels or the Issamiri. It's the vile magic that woman, the marquise, brought with her into this city. His Eminence ordered us to protect his warding stone, so we can keep at least this place safe from her influence. The vast majority of those who are left are barring the way to it."

"Warding stone?" Ritsu repeated.

"Aye, the result of all his research into magic. Our best hope of protection. Perhaps we ought to set you to guarding it, too, Commander."

It was easy, too easy, to give Shinsei's reply to that. "I take orders only from my master's own lips, unless he tells me otherwise." He hated calling Elgar that, but it was the only thing Shinsei had ever called him; to say anything else would raise suspicion. "The only other person he had me heed was Lord Oswhent, and we were . . . separated. In Araveil, after I lost my sword."

The soldier winced. "The lord strategist perished of his wounds, I'm afraid. Another casualty of that foul magic."

That was true, though not in the way he believed. "Then take me to my master. He'll tell me what I need to do next."

The soldier glanced nervously back at him. "He, ah . . . His Eminence said he was not to be disturbed, Commander."

There was one other advantage to Shinsei's reputation: everyone knew he was a prodigious swordsman, and many soldiers who had never fought alongside him would still have heard tales of the carnage he wreaked on battlefields. None of those soldiers would know that all that skill had dwelt in the enchanted sword Ritsu no longer possessed, and that without it his skills could only generously be called mediocre. And most of those soldiers would probably want to avoid opposing a man with that kind of reputation, especially if he also had a reputation for being unstable. "There is no one else who can command me. I can't help without direction." He let a distressed edge seep into his voice, not quite a whine, but with a hint of rising upset. "Don't prevent me from seeing him."

"N-no, I wasn't—I wouldn't—prevent . . ." The soldier swallowed hard, his hands a flurry before his face. "I was just . . . reporting what His Eminence said, Commander. I wouldn't judge . . . that is, of course you know best what you should do. His Eminence will be relieved to know you've returned to us, I'm sure."

Would he really? That was the important question, whose answer would most likely determine the success or failure of Ritsu's mission. But he couldn't let any of that trepidation show in his face. "Where has he gone?"

"He's resting in his private study, sir. The wound from the witch tired him exceedingly, and his recovery will take time. But he was able to finish his work on the warding stone, and he said as long as we protect it, it'll protect us."

Since this warding stone could not actually be a device to defend against magic, Ritsu was curious what it actually was, but he'd have to leave that mystery to the others. "Then I will go to him."

"Of course, sir. I'll just . . ." The soldier backed away slowly, utterly failing to look casual. "I'll be on my way. Good to have you back, sir."

Left alone in the corridor, Ritsu took a shaky breath, wiping his sweaty palms on the blue-black uniform shirt Morgan had found for him. Naishe's pendant was a comforting weight beneath it, slightly cool against his skin. Elgar wouldn't be able to cast at him without warning. Confronting him didn't mean he'd be forced to become Shinsei again.

He adjusted his uniform, and checked the sword at his side. He stood there taking deep gulping breaths for a little while longer, until he felt like he could at least appear calm. And then he made his familiar way up a side stair to the Citadel's upper floors, heading for Elgar's private study. He had to pause just outside, to compose himself one last time, before reminding himself that he owed it to the others not to delay this any longer. He pushed the door open without knocking, and walked into the center of the room.

And there he was.

He wore no armor, and had no bodyguards to defend him. He was just sitting there, alone, sunk into a richly upholstered chair, the deep blue-black of his clothes making him look like a stain on the bright and busy fabric. He had with him the same sword and knife Ritsu remembered, the knife still on his belt, the sword leaning, unsheathed, against one arm of the chair, easy to hand. Though his face was as ruined as Ritsu had heard, he did not seem to be in any pain; his eyes were heavy-lidded, as if he were in a doze, but as Ritsu crossed the threshold they fluttered open, one sharp and alert, the other gaping empty. "Ah," he said. "You're a bit late."

Seeing him again—fully understanding who he was, without any enchantments between them—made Ritsu feel sick. In his mind, he had composed so many speeches, so many crimes of which to accuse this man, so many questions to ask him. But now they all seemed to slip through his fingers, leaving him as blank and empty as when he had used to stand before Elgar, with all his memories washed away.

Elgar glanced around the room. "I hope you don't misunderstand this arrangement as laziness on my part. I am helping my soldiers, much more efficiently than if I were to remain on the front lines with them. The device I've created needs to reside in a very specific place, so as to keep it as safe as possible from interlopers like you, who might all too easily force it from my hands and destroy it that way. But though I cast my best enchantment on it, to ensure I could draw upon its strength even without having to touch it directly, that connection still requires focus. So while you see only one man alone in a room, the truth is that I am sustaining an entire web of spells, with a bit of concentration left over to cast a couple more. And to converse as necessary, of course, though I shall have to be careful not to overdo it."

Despite himself, Ritsu felt overwhelmed. Though they had exchanged words countless times over those five years, Elgar had never spoken to him in this way—as someone, Ritsu realized, who could form his own opinion. Who could truly answer back, not merely trot along like a pet. And then he realized something else. "Interlopers . . . like me?"

"Do you not find it an apt description? You are here to disrupt my plans, aren't you?" He smiled at Ritsu's surprise. "Did you truly think I wouldn't recognize your deceit? I'm sure you fooled the soldiers out there, who never knew what to make of you to begin with. But I made you, boy." He caught himself, twitching one shoulder in a shrug. "Well, I made Shinsei. And I know you're not him. You're . . . whoever you were before."

It was so strange to remember that Elgar had no idea who that was. He had asked Ritsu for his name, no doubt to ensure that he gave him a different one. But that had been five years ago; he must have forgotten it. Beyond that, he knew nothing of Ritsu's life, save that Sebastian had been his friend. He had controlled him down to his very marrow without ever knowing more about him than a passing traveler on the street.

"Why?" he asked. "Why was I the one who didn't die? Why was I the only one who had to endure all this?"

Elgar shrugged again. "I'd like to know, too. I never got that spell to work again. Of course, I did stop trying, eventually—it was such a waste of manpower, to cause that much death. I did think, if the day came when you ever managed to slip the leash completely, at least then I'd be able to ask *you*."

So there was no answer, then, no grand secret, at least not of Elgar's design. Ritsu didn't know if that made things better or worse. Had he really wanted there to be a reason? "*How* could you do it? How could you subject me to such suffering?"

"Actually, the whole idea was that you *wouldn't* suffer," Elgar said calmly. "In fact, I would say that Shinsei suffered less than anyone—certainly less than I, or any other of my soldiers. I did my best to strip you of guilt, sadness, uncertainty, anger—anything I could think of that might trouble your mind. As you know, those things did eventually seep in anyway, despite my efforts, but even then you still felt them less than any ordinary person would have. And it wasn't only the absence of emotions, either. I gave you contentment and satisfaction, a sense of purpose and belonging. And when I'd achieved my new world, you could have retired from service, and been free to bask in it—the world, and the knowledge that you'd succeeded in your mission to help create it. Who could hope for a sunnier fate than that?"

Ritsu stared at him in shock. "Do you even understand the things I felt when I woke up and realized what I had done—everything I had done? When I was finally able to experience the full horror of it?"

"Ah, well, I can't fully be blamed for that," Elgar said. "If things had gone according to plan, you never would have woken up at all, and the hypothetical pain you'd have felt on doing so would have been irrelevant."

"But I did," Ritsu said. "I did wake up, that night in Araveil, when I touched vardrath steel. And you put me back under again anyway, even though you must have seen the torment I was in!"

"Do you even remember that night?" Elgar asked. "Really remember it, not just flashes? When I found you, you were in hysterics. *Torment* didn't begin to describe it. You could barely speak. You wouldn't move from the spot where that girl left you. If I hadn't intervened, your mind might have shattered. True, I could never re-create the full breadth of the stillness and calm I'd been able to imbue you with the first time. But I made your pain manageable, even if I couldn't negate it in its entirety."

"It's pain *you* caused!" Ritsu shouted. "Is this truly how you seek to justify yourself?"

Elgar raised an eyebrow, as if at an obstreperous child. "No. That would imply I bothered with such things. But I'm not a man who's ever felt troubled by the need to justify myself. I'm simply answering a question that you asked me—that you shouldn't have asked, if there was a chance the answer might upset you." He brushed some dust from his sleeve with the knuckles of the opposite hand. "It's time for me to ask you a question. Now that we've come to this, what's your plan? Are you just here to kill me? Or are you after some more complicated form of revenge?"

Perhaps he guessed that Ritsu himself wasn't entirely sure. Elgar's death was the end goal, of course, but before getting there, perhaps he had let himself imagine some kind of greater meaning, some absolution. Justice for Sebastian, even though he knew in his heart that was impossible. Sebastian was gone, and nothing that happened in this room would change that.

Elgar tilted his head slightly, as if straining to hear something. "Hmm. Do you have vardrath steel on you? My magic can't seem to find purchase."

Ritsu couldn't help his flinch. "Again? Already?"

"Perhaps you've noticed, but I'm in the middle of something rather crucial," Elgar said. "I can't afford to waste unnecessary time and energy, and I certainly can't give you the opportunity to ruin things. But I wasn't going to hurt you, just subdue you. I am indebted to you, after all."

"Indebted?" He hated how shaky his voice sounded, that he could only repeat Elgar's own words back at him. "For . . . the things I did before? For the Lanvaldian war, and King Eira, and everything else?"

"Well, that, certainly. But I was actually referring to the fact that it was your performance as Shinsei that gave me the inspiration for the spell I used to create my army in its current form. If it weren't for that, I would have had to use my original formulation—so much cruder and more cumbersome." He braced his arms on his knees so he could lean forward. "When I control multiple people at once, the commands I use have to be simple, or they won't work. That's why I relied on *kill*—the simplest command there is. But it was always unwieldy, because I had to come up with ways to prevent my soldiers from killing each other or any random passerby who might happen to show up, and I obviously had to put that command to rest whenever I didn't want to use it immediately. You were the one who caused me to think of a different command—because, after all, I never actually controlled you. I changed the things that you believed were true, but your actions while under those beliefs were all your own. That was my inspiration. I replaced the compulsion to slaughter with an injunction for the members of my army to *act in the way I would wish them to act*. To act, if you will, in my best interests. Any actions that are neutral in that regard remain unaffected."

"I . . . don't understand."

"Simply put, they can't do things I wouldn't approve of, and if there's a meaningful way for them to help me—say, disposing of my enemies—they have to take it. But otherwise, they're the same as they were before." He leaned back in the chair, utterly satisfied with himself. "It was undeniably a more difficult spell—I needed the power of the *wardrenholt* to cast it. But the results! Incredible! No one's personality changes; no one takes on the aspect of a deranged beast or a lifeless puppet. Their own friends and family wouldn't even suspect anything was different, beyond perhaps a sudden shift in political views. And I don't have to worry about them going out of control, either. I just . . . change their priorities a bit, and leave it to their own judgment to figure out the best way to help me." He smiled. "You were always so good at that, weren't you?"

Ritsu jerked reflexively away from him, his heart beating so wildly in his chest it was almost difficult to breathe. His hand went to his sword, driven by some stomach-roiling mixture of anger and fear.

Elgar didn't flinch, and didn't reach for the sword at his side. "Oh, come now, don't bluff. What do you think you're going to do with that? You and I both know the only talent with a weapon you ever had came from my magic. To be honest, I was a bit disappointed. I finally got that spell to work, and the servant it brought me wasn't even an *average* swordsman."

"I know how to kill you with it," Ritsu said. "That's all the expertise I need. Without the aid of magic to stop me, are you any better skilled?"

Elgar still didn't get up. "I wonder. I did go through some training, back in the village where I was born. My father was a mercenary, and thought it essential for his son to know his trade. But he died when I was young, and by then I already knew where my real power came from. I'm not sure how much of it I even remember. Shall we find out?"

He wouldn't have been so unconcerned if he were truly in a tight spot—or was he simply that arrogant, that he believed there was nothing his former servant could do to harm him? Ritsu knew he was protected from spells by the pendant he

THE RISEN CITY   455

wore, so that couldn't be Elgar's plan. And without magic, there was only so much
he could do to try to escape his situation. Ritsu just had to make sure he failed.

He drew his sword, and approached the chair where Elgar sat. But when he
tried to slash down at it, his blade met another midswing, the two swords sliding
against each other with a whisper of metal. Elgar was standing, and his sword was
in his hand.

"I might have undersold myself a bit," he said.

CHAPTER FIFTY-ONE

Valyanrend

"ACCORDING TO WHAT the Valyanrenders told us," Arianrod said, "Elgar was controlling his army by placing objects he'd enchanted throughout the city's neighborhoods—splitting it up so that each object controlled people in a specific location. But if that were truly the case, the magic should feel uniform, relatively unchanged from one district to the next. Instead, it's all concentrated"—she tapped the stone at her feet—"here. At the Citadel."

"And the Citadel can't be one of Asariel's tide pools?" Adora asked.

"No, because . . ." She frowned. "It's hard to explain how I see things when I'm connected to the spell. But as far as I can tell, the magic at the Citadel is abnormal—swollen, almost. What the hell did he do?"

Adora was out of her depth when it came to questions of magic, but she tried to think it through logically. "Well, he must have noticed that the resistance kept destroying his enchantments when he spread them out. It makes sense that he'd want to keep them close, to keep them protected."

"Of course that's the smarter move," Arianrod said. "It's so obviously the smarter move that the only possible reason he could've had for not doing it to start with is because he couldn't. So why can he do it now? What changed?"

"You're making it hard for me to follow you," Adora said. "I'm still not sure how these things work. Magic isn't the same thing as physical strength, but can you make it stronger by training it, by practicing? Or do you have to augment it in some other way?"

Arianrod took an audible breath, her face going paler. "Shit."

"What?"

"There was something I stole from him months ago—I'd almost forgotten about it. An object from centuries past that was often harnessed by those without magic, usually to disastrous effect. But they were originally made and used by mages themselves, as just what you said—a way to augment their power. They were called *wardrenholt.*"

Spell-holder, more or less. Apt enough. "But I thought you said you stole it from him."

"Strictly speaking, Seren stole it," Arianrod said. "That's not the problem. The problem is, since every *wardrenholt* that ever existed was made by a mage . . . there's no reason, beyond common sense, why a mage couldn't make one again."

WITHOUT HER BROTHER'S grounding presence at her back, Rhia would have lost the thread of the fight by now. She had never been a soldier in a war, and the last time she had seen this many people fighting each other in one place was the night she fled Araveil three years ago; even their struggle with Selwyn's forces at Sinthil Vlin was nothing compared to this. She knew that even the chaos of this courtyard, that seemed so unimaginable to her, would be dwarfed by many a proper battlefield. Yet the scene before her stretched the limits of her comprehension; she could only seem to focus on a few people at a time, while the full crowd slipped from her view.

There were the Aurnians, guarding one another's blind spots as if it were habit; there was Rask, carving out a circle around himself with his sword, and striking down all who dared enter it; there was Talis, struggling to find enough empty space into which to drop the soldiers her winds caught up. In here, without Lirien's magic, they could not tell which of the soldiers had been spelled; some wore their talismans openly, but that wasn't a perfect distinction. Still, they couldn't allow themselves to be killed without making sure Elgar was destroyed first, and that meant pushing through with more force if they had to, as much as it pained her.

"Gods damn it, we need a new plan!" Rask shouted. "We're not making any progress here. We're just pinned in place!"

"We're not going to be able to get our whole group past them," Talis said calmly, her wind easily carrying her words to their ears. "Not without killing many, many more than we have already. But if we split our forces, some of us can keep them distracted until our reinforcements arrive."

"Wouldn't that weaken the group that stays behind too severely?" Rhia asked.

"We can't split them evenly, but we could lose one or two," Rask said. "So let's choose carefully."

"It's no difficult choice at all." Kaitan disarmed an opponent and kicked him backward, landing him in a hedge. He risked a glance at Rhia and Cadfael. "You two have to go. There's no telling how long this fight's going to drag on. You have the best chance of defeating Elgar if Ritsu fails."

"He's right," Ryo called to them. "The best we can do is keep them occupied here, but we'll clear a path for you."

Cadfael was looking up at Talis, hovering above their heads. "Talis—"

"The second we can spare someone else, I'll join you," she said. "But right now, I have to stay and keep them corralled. Our efforts would collapse without me here."

He must have known how true that was, because he didn't object further. He simply asked Rhia, "Agreed?"

"Let's go," she said.

Kaitan had already pointed out the door they needed to take, at the far side of the courtyard from where they'd entered, and Talis scattered the soldiers standing closest to it, dropping them in a heap in the fishpond. But they'd tried that before, and as had happened then, more soldiers saw what they were doing and rushed in to fill the gap. This time, however, Rask and half a dozen of his supporters were already there, pushing everyone back from the doorway so Rhia and Cadfael could draw closer.

And then they were through, with Rask slamming the door behind them. The corridor on the other side could hardly be called that, just a dozen paces and a tall stone archway. And then she and Cadfael stood frozen to the spot once more, for an entirely different reason than last time.

The cavernous room and the winding grand staircase were there, just as Kaitan had said. The floor was tiled marble, silver-white; the staircase was dark wood, with a carved balustrade along the inner edge. And that was all—or so very nearly all that the empty space was dizzying. There was not a single other person in the room, no furniture, not even a layer of dust. There was only one object, a glass sphere about the size of an infant's head. It was floating in the air in the center of the room, far above their heads, on a level with the top of the staircase. Yet despite the distance, as she and Cadfael drew underneath it, Rhia felt a muted kind of pulse, as if the air around the sphere were trying to push her away from it.

Cadfael raised his sword, keeping the blade between him and the object. "Be careful. Whatever that is, it can't touch the sword, but it can still touch us around it."

Like Voltest's fire, then. Rhia shuddered, remembering the burns. "Do you think it can hurt us?"

"I'm not sure. I'll go first." He put an experimental foot on the bottom stair, leaned his weight on it, then slowly started to climb. After about ten steps, he said, "It makes me feel a little queasy every time that thing . . . pulses, but I don't think it can do more than that."

So Rhia followed behind him, and nothing of note happened until Cadfael gained the upper landing, which jutted out into the grand room like half a balcony before giving way to another archway that led to the upper floors. But when he tried to move past the landing, he ran into something, like an invisible wall. He reached out, testing it, and Rhia saw his hand go completely flat in midair, as if he were pressing it against something smooth and hard. There must have been some kind of spell in place, to keep anyone from getting to Elgar.

Cadfael thrust his sword at the barrier, and it passed right through. But when he tried to follow, he found his body blocked. He waved the sword around horizontally, tried holding it close to his chest, but he still couldn't pass through. "What the hell?" he panted. "Why isn't the sword dissolving the magic?"

"I think it's because the source of the spell is somewhere else," Rhia said. "So it just keeps flaring back up again. Like if you doused only the top of a fire."

"Somewhere else?" Cadfael repeated.

"Yes. There." Rhia pointed at the sphere, still pulsing away far out of reach. "*That's* what we're going to have to touch with the sword."

"So what should we do?" Adora asked, pacing helplessly back and forth between Arianrod and the statues. "Should we try to warn our forces at the Citadel? Pull them back?"

"What would be the point? We still need to defeat Elgar, and we still won't have a better opportunity. Besides, for all we know, they've discovered the *wardrenholt* for themselves already. It *is* physically at the Citadel; I'm sure of that."

"Then is this as far as we can go? Is there nothing else we can do to help?"

"Calm down." Arianrod said that, but she looked a touch less than calm herself; the pallor in her face hadn't faded. "There is, at least, something I can try to do."

"If it's dangerous, then no," Adora said. "I promised Seren—"

"It's not that." She smiled wryly. "I forget you're so . . . annoyingly good at reading me. If you detect any uneasiness in me, it's not because I'd be putting myself at risk. There is enough magic in this room to sustain any spell I could ever cast. And with this spell our puzzle-loving friend left us, I could try to force the magic to level out, to disperse it more evenly across the city. It wouldn't destroy Elgar's *wardrenholt,* but it would lessen the amount of power he's able to draw from it. Perhaps that might make the difference."

"It can't do anything but help," Adora said. "But why do you keep saying *try?* That isn't like you at all."

Arianrod's face was tight, tense; she ran a hand through her already-disheveled hair. "It's not dangerous, but it's still . . . difficult. I'd be a fool not to admit that. Free-floating magic, the kind suffusing this room right now, doesn't have a will, so it can't resist me. But it's still immense, much more than my body could ever contain. The difference may simply be too great. And as if that weren't enough . . ." She ground her teeth. "I'm not at my full strength. I will be, before long—I'll be stronger than I ever was—but right now . . . right now I'm . . ."

Adora understood perfectly, perhaps more perfectly than Arianrod knew, because she had seen her at less than her full strength before. The only reason she knew about Arianrod's scars, about what her father had done to her, was because Adora and her father had been scheduled for a diplomatic visit only a couple weeks after Arianrod's tenth birthday. Caius had seemed singularly displeased to see them, but that hadn't particularly bothered Adora, who well knew how he and her father hated each other. He claimed that Arianrod wasn't feeling well and had chosen to take her meals in her room, but after a full day without a single glimpse of her, Adora's father had grown suspicious. "If the girl is truly that ill, Caius, you ought to have healers attend to her. In their absence, I wonder if you are not trying to bait me with a show of disrespect. Why did I bring my daughter, if not out of courtesy to yours?"

Caius had grumbled noncommittally, but with no clear argument against it, he eventually gave in and summoned Arianrod to take dinner with them. Seeing her, Adora hadn't known what to think. She was slower and less vibrant than she remembered, but all her movements were careful rather than sluggish, and she didn't look sick in any other way. She ate almost as much as the rest of them, and invited Adora up to her room afterward to look at whatever books had caught her interest lately, the way she usually did. But just as Adora was starting to think that perhaps Arianrod really was just tired, she saw several lines of blood seeping through the cloth at her back.

Adora's involuntary shriek had summoned Dent; Arianrod gave him a tight but reassuring smile. "If Zara is still down in the city, perhaps you could convince her to come up to the hall for a bit?"

The healer had tried to bustle Adora out of the room, but Arianrod had objected. "She's too smart for that," she said. "She's already guessed; there's no point in trying to hide it now."

Adora had, in fact, already guessed. An assassination attempt would have been one precise and brutal strike; any killer close enough to make so many cuts would have succeeded in their aim. Barring that, there was only one person who could strike the marquis's daughter with impunity.

Dent had guarded the door while Zara restitched the wounds that had come open and Arianrod lay stoically on her stomach. "It won't be like last time," the healer said. "Most of these are scabbed over already. It's blood from the burst stitches more than anything."

Arianrod caught Adora's eye warily. "I was only just starting to be able to do things. At first I had to lie on my stomach all the time. Dent had to feed me soup, because I wasn't allowed to sit up and move my arm to eat it myself."

"But you listened to me, for once, and did everything I asked," Zara said. "It's because of that you're alive now."

So it had been that dire. Adora, who back then was only ten herself, with both brothers and both parents, had never come that close to death, or loved anyone who had. At the thought of what had almost happened—what *had* happened—to Arianrod, she couldn't suppress a shudder.

Arianrod's keen eyes caught it right away, narrowing slightly. She pressed her lips together, then said, "I'll be fine now, but . . . Zara says the scars won't ever fade completely. That they'll . . . that they'll last forever. I wonder . . . what someone would think, if they saw them."

It was an indirect question, of course, and Arianrod looked as vulnerable as Adora had ever seen her, exposed in her moment of weakness. As sorry as she felt, she knew she couldn't say that part of it; Arianrod hated pity, and would have closed herself off from Adora forever if she'd attempted to make her swallow it. So instead she said the rest. "I'm sure they would think that you were very strong. And brave."

Arianrod frowned, as if she sensed a trick. "Why?"

"Because of how you're able to talk to me right now. Because of how you've been since I've seen you. It must have been hurting so much, but you ate and conversed with us for hours as if nothing was wrong. I could never have done that. It must have been so hard—harder than I can imagine."

She knew she had said the right thing, because the tension in Arianrod's body eased, revealing the exhaustion she had felt she had to hide. "It was," she admitted quietly, "a little difficult."

So Arianrod had not closed herself off from Adora that day, or any day since. And now, so many years later, Arianrod was letting her see that moment of doubt again.

"You're the one who told me," Adora said. "Over and over, until it finally sank in. Magic isn't of the body, it's of the mind. It doesn't matter how strong your body is or isn't; it doesn't matter what it contains. If you can think your way to doing it, you can do it." She glanced at the statue of Irein, the mysterious figure in the cloak, pressing on despite everything. "Now I know my ancestor had no special trick, no secret knowledge. And she must have known she didn't. I can't imagine what she felt when she marked the edge of the Curse with her sword and declared she would turn it back. But whether or not she was certain she could do it, or whether she was afraid she couldn't, she must have been determined that she *would* do it, no matter what. Because if she hadn't been, that spirit over there would never have worked her will upon the world. It had power on the Curse, and if it has power anywhere, it must surely be in this room."

And again, that must have been the right thing, because again Arianrod relaxed and smiled as if they were whiling away the hours in her study and Adora had told some joke. "So you're saying you think I'm as stubborn as Talia Avestri, eh?"

"*As* stubborn?" Adora feigned shock. "When have you ever been content with a tie?"

RITSU AND ELGAR circled each other, careful footwork bringing them close but not too close. Had they both been veteran swordsmen of great talent, their steps and swordstrokes would have been much more complex, an intricate variety of lunges, slashes, dodges, parries, ripostes, feints. Instead, they had to be content with knowledge of the basics, and a duel between those who had practice on their side rather than talent. Ritsu knew all too well that, had Kaitan Enrei or the prince been here in his place, Elgar would already be dead—as he himself would have been, against any of Elgar's favored subordinates.

Ritsu's father, too, had made him learn a set of fundamental sword forms by heart, whether he wanted to or not. And he was young enough to be the imperator's son, so he had a certain physical advantage. But the forms his father had taught him had been for the *tsunshin,* and he'd just spent five years fighting with a Lantian one-hander. He kept having to shake off moments of confusion, reminding himself he held a sword Adora had provided him, that there were some forms from his youth that would translate and others that would not, and that he no longer had Shinsei's unnatural strength and speed to assist him. Still, he did not feel that he was hopelessly outmatched. As long as he stayed careful, he could win this.

But Elgar must have concluded the same, or better—or else he was very good at feigning nonchalance, and Ritsu had never noticed that in him. "You should have just run away, you know. I kept you captive for five years—I'm sure I might have kept you forever, and that it is a curious series of happenstances that set you free. You would really throw away all that luck just to die here?"

"It wasn't luck," Ritsu said, lashing out at Elgar's thigh only to be parried. So he knew that one, too. "It was the kindness of those who owed me nothing."

"In that case, you're even more fortunate than I had guessed, and with more to lose. Is your thirst for vengeance that great?"

"It's justice, not—" Elgar slashed high, but Ritsu knew *that* one, and slid their swords together in a tangle. A twist of his wrist would almost have disarmed Elgar, but he disengaged at the last moment. "—not vengeance. It's justice for the whole continent."

"Is that what you tell yourself? It's mere pettiness." Block high, block low, disengage, dodge to the side, parry-riposte. "What do you think would happen to this continent without me? It was chaos before I came, and it'll be chaos if I fall. The other countries aren't strong enough to keep Hallarnon at bay; I proved that. And you have no idea what this city was like under the greed of my predecessors."

"And what will happen to this continent with you?" Ritsu asked. "Other tyrants sought to usurp the people's livelihoods, their freedom of action, but you would steal their very minds."

"Not *steal*. Just adjust, slightly. I know you found your own experience unpleasant, but you were, I'm sorry to say, an experiment—and clearly one that had its flaws. But I wouldn't be taking anything away from them. They can live their lives in peace, just as they did before—indeed, that's what I *want*. A whole continent, in peace and order and prosperity. And to ensure that peace and order and prosperity, its residents won't want to rebel. That's the only difference."

Ritsu tried not to flinch at the reference to his past, or the word *experiment*. "It's still unforgivable. They should have the right to rebel if they choose—the right to think you're wrong, no matter how infallible *you* believe yourself to be."

"Why should they have the right?" Elgar asked. "If it only causes misery?"

Their swords clashed again, but without as much force as before. They were both tiring from the strain of using unaccustomed muscles. But it was no effort to answer him. "Free will is the birthright of every human."

Elgar stepped back, head slightly cocked, giving himself room. "Oh? Then what does that make you?"

It was so predictable of him, but Ritsu lunged.

The wound he caused was trivial, a shallow gouge to Elgar's forearm. But the wound he took in return, as recompense for leaving himself unguarded, opened up the soft flesh of his hip, right beneath his rib cage. He staggered, and Elgar shoved down on his shoulder with his free hand, forcing him to either go to one knee or fall outright.

Elgar pointed his sword at Ritsu's throat. "My father did tell me—did yours?— that one should leave one's emotions behind before starting a swordfight. One of the few useful bits of advice he ever gave me." He twitched the sword slightly, and it clinked against metal: the chain holding up Naishe's pendant. "Ah," he said, as Ritsu's blood chilled. "There it is."

THREE TIMES RHIA and Cadfael had thrown their swords at the floating glass sphere, and three times neither of them had come within a foot of it. Three times they had had to run all the way down and back up the stairs to fetch the swords from the ground floor and try again. And each time they failed, she could see in his eyes that they both knew they were wasting time, that Ritsu might be dying or dead or worse, that their friends back in the courtyard were putting their lives on the line to give them this chance they were pathetically squandering.

"This isn't working," she said.

"Gods, I know! I'm no fucking dartsman. If we had infinite time, one of us would be bound to get a lucky shot eventually, but it takes us minutes to try even once. But what else can we do? Even if we had a ladder, it wouldn't be tall enough to reach that thing. Tying the swords to a rope and swinging them at it might do it, but I don't have a rope, and I don't know where to get one. Perhaps under different circumstances one of us could use the other as an anchor and lean out over the edge, but the railing's too thin; even one of us could barely stand on it, and if the person leaning fell, they'd probably pull the other down after them. Then we'd both be dead for nothing." He put his face in both hands, muffling a growl of frustration. "This must have been the point. He knew we were coming for him with vardrath steel, so he created a puzzle even vardrath steel couldn't solve."

Rhia took a breath. "There is one way to solve it."

"What? I'll try practically anything at this point."

At a time like this, she would have wanted to be steadfast, serene. Instead, it was all she could do to keep from trembling. But all the nerves in the world couldn't change what she knew, or what she intended. "We jump. That is, I'll . . . I'll do it. I'll jump."

Cadfael didn't erupt at her, as she'd feared. He just stared blankly, as if she'd spoken in a different language. "Rhia, what are you saying?"

"You're right, the rail on the landing is too flimsy. So . . ." Rhia started kicking the balustrade, the ancient wood already bending with the first strike. On the fifth, it broke, several banisters and their attached railing falling to the ground floor below and leaving empty space at the edge of the landing. "There. Like this, with a running start, it would be easy. I jump, and I hit that thing with my sword with room to spare."

"And then you fall to your death," Cadfael said.

"We don't . . . know that for sure. It would be bad, but we know the most talented healer on the continent."

Cadfael pointed at the floor. "Rhia, that's solid marble. You'd be in pieces. Ten to one you'd die on contact." He shook his head. "Look, we have to find another route. This can't be the only way up to the higher floors."

"I'm sure it isn't," Rhia said. "Otherwise we'd have found Ritsu stuck out here, too, unless Elgar's soldiers know some trick to take the barrier down. But do you have any idea where those alternate stairways are, or who we might have to fight to get to them? We already had to leave the rest of our allies behind. That barrier is where it is because Elgar's close. That thing is still floating up there because Elgar's still alive, because Ritsu hasn't succeeded. I'm sure we could find a dozen different solutions if we had the time, but we don't. We're out of time, Cadfael. Even if it's small, I just have to take the chance that I'll survive it. And if not . . . that's how it has to be."

Cadfael said nothing. His face was haggard, as if in his mind, he'd lost her already. Maybe he was right. But even so, she had to press forward.

"Please," she said. "Please understand. I don't *want* to do it, but I have to. It's the only way."

Again, Cadfael didn't scold her. And he didn't beg, which would have been worst of all. Instead, his expression closed off completely, as if he were made of stone. "If you do this, you're only going to have one chance. Every advantage counts."

"I know," Rhia said.

He drew his sword from its sheath, presenting it to her hilt-first. "Then use this one instead. I'm sure you're attached to yours, but mine is longer and wider. Better chance to hit."

There wasn't much of a chance she would miss at that distance, but he was right; any advantage might matter. Rhia stepped forward to take it—and Cadfael lunged.

ARIANROD'S EYES HADN'T opened for a moment. Her breathing was measured but shallow, audible in the total silence of the room. Adora had to remind herself, about every ten seconds, that even though she couldn't see it, magic was everywhere around her, keeping Arianrod from danger or pain. No matter how much it looked like pain when her face twisted, or her fists clenched, it was merely concentration, effort. Effort she had to believe would pay off, because there was nothing more she could do.

Well. Perhaps there was one thing.

She was not Talia Avestri, any more than she was her father, no matter how much she admired both of them. She could not lead her troops into battle, and she could not believe in her own strength enough to move a god. Her life had been guided, would always be guided, by a different star.

She glanced back at the silent statues, at the one that twisted her heart every time she looked at it. The old man surrendering his last mouthful of food to someone else. The strength of that, no less than that of the wounded figure pressing forward, the warrior with her broken sword. That god was here, too. Their equal.

So Adora sat down next to Arianrod, and clutched her friend's hand. And the next time she made a fist, Arianrod's hand wound unconsciously around hers, like ivy tracing its way up stone.

She murmured, "It's working."

OF COURSE CADFAEL had known, from the very moment they left Eldren Cael together, that he and Rhia were bound to end up in this sort of situation eventually. Honestly, the most surprising thing was that it had taken this long.

He had practiced it on the road, at times when she was asleep or off somewhere with Lirien. His sister was fast, always just a little bit faster than you were expecting, and he'd only have the advantage of surprise for the duration of one movement. So now, when he did what he'd practiced, it came out perfectly assured, as smooth as butter. He lunged, tapping the pommel of the sword hard against her abdomen in just the right spot.

Rhia dropped like a stone, doubled over in pain as all the breath was knocked out of her. She lay in a heap on her knees, curled around the injury, making uneven little gasps as she struggled to inhale. Speaking and standing wouldn't come back to her for a good minute or two, and he needed that time.

He turned his sword back around, directing the point at where the sphere lay suspended in the air. "Still so trusting, Rhia. How could you possibly think I'd let you do this? I already lost you once."

Rhia wheezed indignantly at him from her little heap, but she still wasn't capable of drawing a full breath, let alone speaking a full sentence. Her body still bent toward her target, but for once her stubbornness was to no avail.

Cadfael walked to the edge of the landing, eyeing the glass sphere. Rhia had been right: it was plenty close enough to jump. Even easier for him, since he was significantly taller. The only thing making him hesitate was the way it was pulsing; if the force of it was strong enough to push him back in midair, that could ruin everything. But as he watched, something within the sphere seemed to flicker, like a guttering candle, and the pulsing eased. He checked the barrier on the landing, but no such luck there. Still, he suspected he had one or another of his allies to thank for this, wherever they were.

He wasn't like her; he held no hope and no illusions about what would happen to him if he made the leap. That floor would be the end of him, however he landed on it. But at least, if what Yaelor had said was true, he could still watch over Rhia, even if he wouldn't be himself. Thanks to Talis, he didn't feel as afraid of that out-come anymore. Even Lirien had helped: *You could never be so different that she couldn't find you again.*

He wished he could have the chance to say a proper goodbye to her, to say . . . so many things. But that hit wouldn't keep her down for much longer, and if he kept looking at her face, the tears already spilling from her eyes, he'd never go through with it.

"I'm sorry," he said. "I love you. I'm so sorry."

Then, before she could say or do anything else, before he could lose his nerve, he took a running start and leapt from the landing.

The edge of his sword struck the sphere, and it shattered, the sudden, ferocious impact so jarring that it knocked the sword right out of his hands. And then he was falling, the wind deafening in his ears. He thought someone was shouting some-thing from below, but before he could turn his head to look, the floor rose up and crushed him, and he saw nothing more.

"PLEASE," RITSU SAID, hating himself for it. "Please, just kill me. Don't do that to me again."

Elgar still had the point of his sword looped just under the chain at Ritsu's throat. One good tug would snap it. But his expression wasn't gloating, or trium-phant. His brow was furrowed, a slight twitch in his jaw. Ritsu saw sweat beading heavily on his forehead. "Don't be rash. If you just behave, you can save yourself. Why waste that?"

"Not myself," Ritsu said. He tried to push himself up off his knees, but the blade of the sword was too close. He'd have slit his own throat.

"No, that spell is useless to me now. You already broke it twice; I'd be mad to trust it a third time. But it *did* work on you, when it failed on everyone else. It'd be a pity to give up such a resource if I don't have to."

"So you'd spare me so I could go back to being your experiment again." He glared into Elgar's eyes, so he'd know how serious he was. "Never."

"You're so eager to die?"

"At least I'll die as me."

Elgar rolled his single eye, as if this were the most inane, trivial conversation he'd ever had. "I was almost looking forward to it. To seeing who was underneath the only one ever to survive. But it turns out you're just a petulant child. Perhaps your mind was merely too simple, devoid of anything grand, anything aspiring." He sighed, untangling his sword from the chain around Ritsu's neck. "Very well then, if you'd rather die as . . . what was it?"

But before Ritsu could answer, Elgar swayed on his feet, his sword sliding against Ritsu's jaw too lightly to draw blood. There was something different about his face, his posture, as if strength and vitality had drained out of him. "No. What the hell did they do? They couldn't have reached it."

Ritsu didn't know what *it* was, but he didn't have to; it was enough that Elgar was unbalanced, and probably wouldn't be again. It was enough that, as he staggered back, Ritsu saw the knife Elgar wore on his belt, unprotected.

Still kneeling, he drew it, and stabbed up into Elgar's stomach with all his strength.

Elgar dropped his sword, and lurched forward. Ritsu caught him with his body, Elgar's chest landing on top of his shoulder. He drew the dagger out before Elgar could reach for it, stabbed him again; he knew his only chance was to keep him too distracted and in pain to save himself with a spell. "My dream is far bigger than you," Elgar said, unable to hide the weakness in his voice. "I cannot let you put an end to it."

Ritsu shifted, and Elgar fell to the floor, the impact wrenching a groan from him as it agitated both his wounds. "For once, it isn't up to you. Not a pleasant feeling, is it?" He brought his knee down hard on Elgar's wrist, and raised the dagger once more. "This is for Sebastian, but my name is Ritsu. You'll never take it from me again."

Then his next strike found the heart.

"Oh," Arianrod said.

"What happened?"

"It's . . . gone. All that magic I was holding back—some of it dispersed throughout the city, like I wanted, but the rest of it just dissipated. As if it had never been."

Adora hardly dared speak the words. "Does that mean . . ."

"That's what it means," Arianrod said. "He must be gone. Dead. However they did it, they succeeded."

Adora couldn't help it—she closed her arms around Arianrod, just as she had done when she first saw her again after her failed execution. But this time it wasn't out of concern for her well-being; she, Adora, simply needed someone to hold on to, to reassure her that they had come at last to the end, and she could return to her home without even another day of the strife of war.

"All right," Arianrod said, "I'm allowing this just this once. You were, after all, very helpful." She looked down at her hands. "Why did you bleed on me?"

"Sorry," Adora said. "I forgot I was still bleeding when I grabbed your hand. I just wanted to make sure you were all right."

"Well, I'm fine. Probably better than you, to be honest. Only you could sustain a battle wound in a place with no foes to fight."

Adora opened her mouth to reply, but then shut it when she heard footsteps echoing off the stone walls of the corridor outside the statue room. It sounded like only one person, so at least they weren't about to be overwhelmed. But she still tensed in readiness until Arianrod said, "If anything does happen, *I'm* the one who's going to take care of it, you know."

But it turned out all was well—better than well, for the one who appeared in the entryway was Seren Almasy, more bloodstained than Adora and with one arm swinging at an unhealthy angle, but otherwise in one piece. When she saw the two of them, she smiled, and Adora was taken aback by how relieved and content she showed herself to be. "You're all right," she said. "We both upheld our promises, then."

"You look dreadful," Arianrod said.

"Do I? I feel fairly well satisfied."

"Yes, yes, good for you. Now come here so I can fix that." When Seren hesitated, she rolled her eyes. "This room is full of magic, remember? You'd do me more harm by forcing me to keep looking at that thing."

Seren obligingly stepped forward, and Arianrod placed her hand beneath Seren's clothing to grip her bare shoulder. She paused to concentrate, and Adora liked the way her face looked in that moment, its sharper edges softened just a bit. And then Seren's arm shuddered and realigned itself, her cuts melting slowly away.

Arianrod gave a satisfied smile, then held out her hand. "You, too, Adora. Let me see it."

Adora laid her hand in Arianrod's, and she brushed her thumb over the cut on her palm, as if trying to smooth out a wrinkle in some fabric. But as she did so, the cut itself was smoothed away, leaving only a tiny scab, already mostly healed.

Seren tilted her head toward Adora, though her eyes remained on Arianrod. "You're getting better at that. Have you been using it since you helped me at Stonespire?"

"Only on Dent, and I didn't tell him. I was, as you say, less adept at it then, but I was still able to make that wound on his arm heal a little faster." She tapped the scab on Adora's hand with her thumb. "It doesn't hurt anymore, right?"

"Not at all. It looks days old already. When did you come up with that?"

"Not that long ago," Arianrod said, "but I'm definitely not prepared to get into the intricacies of it now." She looked from Seren to Adora and back again, and Adora liked that expression, too: pleased but not smug, as if she had seen the two of them on either side of her, well and mostly undamaged, and confirmed that everything was as it was supposed to be. "Well, according to the plan we all agreed on, it's Naishe's show now. Everyone Elgar controlled will be released, and with him dead, she shouldn't have any trouble getting the rest of his people to surrender."

Adora caught Seren's eye over Arianrod's shoulder. "Do you want to say it or should I?"

"We all know you won't be satisfied unless you see it happen for yourself," Seren said to Arianrod.

"I guess we're heading for the Citadel, then," Adora finished. "Let's see if I still remember what sunlight is like."

NOW THAT CADFAEL knew what fate awaited him after death, he wasn't as surprised as he might have been to discover he still had a consciousness. It was just that it felt . . . small. Surely the mind of a god had more to it than this? And he'd thought he'd have some divine awareness of all the world at once, but all he saw was blackness.

Then he realized the blackness was because his eyes were closed.

He pulled them open with an effort, but the world looked upside . . . oh. He was lying down, his head pillowed on something. His limbs felt as if they'd been beaten for an hour or two, but he *could* feel them, which was probably something. He blinked, struggling to pull everything into focus, and realized someone was bending over him.

"Am I dead?" Cadfael asked.

"Alive, more's the pity." He knew that voice.

"Talis?" And yes, of course it was her, her sharp gray eyes and disheveled brown-blond hair, her disapproving mouth. "I . . . fell, didn't I?"

"You certainly did, you idiot. If you'd just waited another minute for me we could have accomplished everything a lot less dramatically." Her voice softened a hair. "Though I suppose you had no way of knowing I was coming."

Cadfael tried to think back to the moments before he hit the ground, but all he could remember was falling. "What did you do?"

"I couldn't quite catch you," Talis said, "but I slowed your fall enough that it didn't shatter you. I don't think you have any broken bones at all, in fact, though you'll probably have quite a collection of bruises tomorrow. Thank the gods you dropped the sword, or there wouldn't have been anything I could do."

That had been her voice, then. "You saved me."

"I did. Even though I tried to kill you once already. I know what you're going to say—I've really got to make up my mind."

"That wasn't what I was going to say at all." He stared at her. "Why did you save me?"

She pressed her lips together. "Because I wanted to see you again."

"So it was selfish. Is that what you're saying?"

"Of course," Talis said. "What, did you think it was out of concern for you?"

"Good. I'm . . . relieved."

She frowned. "Why?"

"I'd hate to think I put you out in this rescue attempt. I'm glad to know that you'll always do as you please, even in the direst circumstances."

"If that was a joke," Talis said, "I'm going to drop your head this moment."

"No, I—"

"Cadfael!" someone shouted. "Cadfael, gods damn it!"

Cadfael smiled. He knew that voice, too. "I'm here, Rhia. I'm all right."

Rhia came running up to him like a miniature hurricane, limbs flailing every which way. "Do you have any idea how angry I am at you right now? I don't even know what to start with, that you almost died, or that you lied to me, *again*!" She smoothed her hands over his shoulders, as if she were checking for cracks.

"Sorry," Cadfael said. "I'd say it won't happen again, but . . . well. I'm always going to put your life over following your principles."

"And that almost got *you* killed!"

"Then I count myself very lucky." He tried to sit up, but he felt a little dizzy, and Talis steadied him with an arm around his shoulders. "Talis, I'm assuming if you're here, things must not be going terribly with the others?"

"You assume correctly," she said. "There were two reasons I was able to get away to come see how you were faring. One: the teams we set to cause distractions throughout the city are finally starting to make it inside the Citadel, including Naishe and her people. And second, something happened to the spell Elgar was using to control part of his army. It wasn't totally broken, not like what Lirien did, but it was like the spell was wavering. Some of the soldiers on the other side started getting confused, or scared, or drifting in and out of awareness. But since it didn't stop entirely, we figured Elgar wasn't dead. The others covered me so I could come help you."

"Oh, no!" Rhia bolted back to her feet. "Elgar! Ritsu! We have to get back up there! We have to help—"

"You've already helped," someone said. Cadfael was still sore, but he craned his neck enough to see that Ritsu Hanae had come out onto the landing, swordless, with a hand pressed against his bleeding side. "It's over. He's dead."

Rhia immediately bounded up the stairs, meeting Ritsu on his way down and letting him lean against her for the rest of the descent. "How bad is it?" he asked her warily.

"What, your wound? It's not . . . spectacular, but that's why we have Lirien. You won't die before we can get you to her."

"And the rest of the city?"

"I expect Naishe will have control of it within the next couple hours," Talis said.

Ritsu all but collapsed against Rhia's side; he looked like he could've slept for an age. "Then my part is done."

"All of us in this room have seen our parts come to an end now," Cadfael said, finally sitting up without light-headedness. "We'll have to leave the rest of it to the new administrators."

"But *I* am just getting started with *you*," Rhia said. "Once I get back from making sure Ritsu gets to Lirien all right, you are going to listen to a detailed account of every single negative emotion you caused me to feel over the past ten minutes."

"Wouldn't miss it," Cadfael said, as she steered Ritsu carefully down the corridor. He leaned back against Talis, and ventured a grin at her.

But she didn't smile back. "I have to tell you something."

"Something I won't like?"

"Something *I* don't like. But it's still true."

Cadfael sat back on his hands so he could see her face better. "Whatever it is, you can tell me."

"When Lirien made that rain fall on the city, I felt it. That . . . corruption in me, the way it was for Voltest. It's been quiet now, since he lost his power, but it won't stay quiet forever. One day—I don't know when, weeks, years—it'll get stronger than I can control. And when I feel like that's about to happen, I'm going to ask Lirien to do what she did for Voltest. To take it away."

Cadfael was quiet for a while, trying to let her know he took it as seriously as she did. "I think that's wise."

"I won't be able to fly again," she said, voice breaking just a bit. "Or defend myself. I'll be just as helpless as I was when . . ." She didn't have to finish it.

"But you said yourself, that could be years away."

"Still. One day."

"Well, no matter what happens, you won't have to be defenseless," Cadfael said. "I know I'm good with a sword, and it turns out I'm not as bad a teacher as I thought. If you want to learn your way around a weapon, I can help you. That's a start. As for the rest . . . I'm sure you'll be sadder in some ways, and you'll miss things. But you'll be happier in others."

"And I'll gain things? Like what?"

"Freedom," Cadfael said. "Freedom from the past, to the extent that's possible."

Talis uncurled her body, rested her hands on the marble floor, and leaned forward where he was leaning back until he straightened to meet her. "And you?" she asked, as if she had to be that close, to say it that softly.

"No," Cadfael said. He brushed her messy hair behind her ear. "You have me already."

Chapter Fifty-two

Valyanrend

MARCELINE HAD ONLY gone to the Citadel in the first place because she'd assumed there would be celebrating, and she didn't want to miss it. As it turned out, she couldn't even get across the moat. Naishe's people, led by a Rask who was scowling even more inhospitably than usual, had blocked it. And rather than cries of victory, she heard voices raised in argument.

As she pushed through the crowd, a hand caught her sleeve. "Careful," Wren said. "Better to leave them to it."

"Who's *them*? What's going on?"

"It appears that the marquise of Esthrades doesn't approve of Naishe's plans for the city going forward. So they're having it out, and the queen . . . well, she's participating, though I can't honestly tell what side she's on." He glanced down at Marceline's face, and gave her a reassuring smile. "Don't worry. The marquise has no real power here. She can object all she likes, but it won't change the result."

Still, Marceline wanted to hear it for herself, so she gently disentangled herself from Wren and stepped forward until the three of them were in full view.

The marquise was the one who looked most different; Marceline had only ever seen her calm and composed, but now she was just noticeably harried, the faintest flush in her pale face. "If you do this, you will ruin everything we accomplished today," she was saying. "Indeed, had I known this was the end you envisioned, I doubt I would have risked my life for it. You told us you would take control of the city!"

By contrast, Naishe looked precisely the same, cloaked in the stoicism that she prized. "And so I have. If I did not mention that it would be temporary, I don't see how that is the business of foreign rulers. If anything, it was presumptuous of you to assume that I would ever accept a crown. The people will be ruled by representatives that they choose—one person for every district in the city. I have already put out the word for each district to nominate one individual, and they will be brought here to determine Valyanrend's new government."

"You're saying Valyanrend will be ruled by thirty-seven random people?"

"Perhaps your hearing is damaged," Naishe said calmly. "I said Valyanrend would be ruled by thirty-seven individuals chosen by its people."

The marquise folded her arms. "It is your memory that is damaged, Miss Kadife. Since the fall of Elesthene, no government of the people in Hallarnon has even lasted a decade before being overturned. You are far from the first revolutionary to lead this city in revolt, and far from the first to hold such naïve ideals. Those ideals have ended in despotism *every single time*. Still, that would all be your business and not mine, if Hallarnon's tyrants did not refuse to limit their bullying to their own people. How soon after your new government falters can I expect to be invaded and imprisoned again, do you think?"

"If the government falters," Naishe said, "I shall be here to fight any tyrants that arise, just as I fought this one."

"You needed our help to defeat this one."

"And I am grateful for it, but that does not give you any sway over what happens here. Be content that I save the ideals you so scorn for my countrymen alone, and do not seek to wield them against you and the legacy of the pack of opportunists who gave you that throne—or against your friend there, whose ancestor betrayed her fellow revolutionaries by accepting a crown."

Marceline felt Wren tense behind her, and even she held back a wince at hearing such combative words. But if Naishe had intended them to cause anger, she failed: the marquise burst out laughing. "Miss Kadife, if my people wanted to overthrow me, they could do so tomorrow, and they know it. I keep them from doing so not by forcing them to live in constant terror, but by being better at my office than they would be in my place. They prefer to have me labor on their behalf than to do all that work themselves. Adora is still a new queen, but I would be shocked if her people did not come to the same conclusion as mine; they would be fools not to see that all she does is for them."

"Then your people have exercised their will, after a fashion," Naishe said. "I merely wish to give mine that opportunity outright."

The marquise made a frustrated noise in the back of her throat. "Adora, either disagree with me or support me, but don't just stand there."

The queen bit her lip. "No country has suffered more than mine at Hallarnon's hands, since long before it assumed that name. I have already been warned against making a mistake here, lest I doom my children or grandchildren to more warfare in my stead. On the other hand, we should not let fear make us too cynical. There is no established royal lineage in Hallarnon, and there is now no shred of government at all. There are no better circumstances under which to try to bestow the right of rule on the people than we see before us now. So perhaps . . . perhaps I might suggest a compromise?"

The marquise said nothing, but tilted her head curiously. "I'll hear it," Naishe said.

"Then, Miss Kadife, out of respect for all you are and all you have done, we shall trust your judgment of your own people, and leave you and them to establish a government as you see fit. But in light of all our nations have suffered when Hallarnon is mismanaged, and all we have sacrificed to help it back to the correct path, I promise you this: if your people prove unworthy of the faith you place in them, and my friend and I are forced to return here once more under the banner of war, we will appoint a government as *we* see fit, and you shall not be part of it." She turned to the marquise. "And I promise *you* that, if we are ever forced to do this again, I shall demand of you only your counsel and such magic as it will not endanger you to provide, and the troops and coin shall only be Issamira's own. Can we agree on this much?"

Naishe considered it. "If I live to see you two attempt to determine Valyanrend's government, for any reason, I'll resist you."

"Then you'll lose," the queen said. "But you agree?"

"To the rest of it, yes."

"That's hardly agreeing to anything at all, but as I agree with Adora that you would lose, I won't pursue it," the marquise said. "Her assurances mean more to me than yours, anyway." She glanced at the queen. "Since our presence is unwanted, shall we withdraw and leave them to it? And perhaps you can try to convince me on the way to be more optimistic than I currently am."

The queen smiled. "I shall treasure so rare a request from you, Arianrod."

Once they were out of sight, Marceline saw Naishe sag a bit, just a dip in the line of her shoulders, a slight retreating of her posture. "Don't hold back," she told Wren. "If I've just made a terrible mistake, I want to know about it as soon as possible."

"My primary concern is your happiness," Wren said. "And you'd be miserable as a queen. But even if that weren't the case, I don't think you made a mistake. The queen was right; Hallarnon is different from the rest of Lantistyne. Despite all our changing regimes, we haven't had a monarchy since before Elesthene. Even if we crowned you, it would probably be as likely to fail as anything else we could do."

"It is still true," Naishe said, "that most of our tyrants have either died in their beds or only been deposed by those even worse than they are, but every elected government has started failing nearly as soon as it existed."

"And the day I made my first arrow, I'd ruined every single one I'd ever attempted. Proving that we could make a government of the people work, after buckling to so many despots . . . that would mean something. And if we're going to try it, best to try it when the other nations are all strong. So they can stop us if it goes bad." He shrugged. "I can't tell you it's definitely going to work, Naishe. But there's more than *no* chance, and I think it's worth the risk. Isn't that why you did it?"

"Mostly." She leaned on his shoulder. "I didn't want to say so in front of the rest of them, but there's another reason I couldn't accept it."

"Because if you claimed a crown," Wren said gently, "people now and in ages to come would say that's the only reason you did any of this, to take power for yourself. That you stirred up a rebellion not because of injustice, but because you saw an opportunity to become queen."

"Maybe Talia Avestri could live with that, but I couldn't. Besides, I want to keep protecting the interests of the people, the way I only can if I'm one of them." She glanced at Marceline. "What do you think, monkey? Whose side are you on?"

"I don't know about sides," Marceline said, "but I know Hallarnon's brought a great deal of strife to the rest of the continent. They deserve to see that we can be trusted this time. And if we can't be, *we'll* deserve whatever happens."

"Hmm. So this country has to earn your loyalty, too. There's wisdom in that. But you don't have to wait at the Citadel just because we are. Surely there's somewhere else you'd like to be?"

Marceline nodded, her feet already twitching southward, wanting to carry her away. "Aye, Tom'll be waiting at . . . well, at home. He'll want to hear all the details from me before Roger can embellish it. And then I'm going right to the Dragon's Head. I can't remember Morgan ever throwing a party before. I wouldn't miss it."

Naishe grinned. "Now that we're law-abiding citizens, don't let me catch you stealing."

"*You're* a law-abiding citizen," Marceline said. "And that's the thing—you'd have to catch me."

"Halvard?" Morgan asked. "Oh, thank the gods."

Halvard lived in the Fades, the district next to Sheath, and she'd been buying supplies for the tavern exclusively from his shop for years. It was a great relief to encounter someone she knew in this situation, but it was also surreal—to be in this situation herself, and to find him in it. They were standing in a corridor of the Citadel, where Morgan's friends and allies had just waged a life-or-death struggle. And they were apparently going to decide Valyanrend's future.

Halvard's bushy eyebrows rose, but then he laughed. "How'd you get picked for this? We weren't entirely sure the chosen ones weren't just going to be hostages, and it seemed like the crowd was going to coalesce around either me or a friend of mine with four children—we're about the same size, a head or two above everybody else. I persuaded them to make it me."

"Oh, Sheath *definitely* thinks this is hostage-taking in disguise," Morgan said.

"So they think you can take it? Or they just hate you that much?"

"I don't think it's either, exactly. I always had a reputation for being honest, in a place where people take pride in being the opposite. In a way, I think my fellow Sheathers thought this was what I deserved—whether it turns out to be good or bad."

He thumped his chest. "Ahh, the justice of a bunch of reprobates."

"If it helps, I don't think Naishe means us harm," Morgan said. "The one leading them, I mean. I don't know her well, but I think I know her enough for that."

"Of course she doesn't," another familiar, albeit less familiar voice declared. "My Talia thinks the world of that girl, and she inherited her ability to judge character from me. Well, mostly."

Morgan turned, startled twice in as many minutes. "Mrs. Parnell? Did the resistance actually ask for grocers, not representatives?"

"Ideally, they were asking for those with expertise in management," Talia's mother said. "Which is my forte, you understand. And you can call me Sarine. We are supposed to be equals, after all." She jerked her head at Halvard. "I think the rest of them are already in there. I was hoping to just talk to you, but if you trust him, he can stay."

"I trust him," Morgan said. "What's on your mind?"

Sarine leaned forward, and Morgan was surprised to realize the other woman was a couple inches shorter than she was. "We have a rare opportunity here. Under ordinary circumstances, the representatives from the five richest districts would band together to bully everybody else. But that can't happen this time, because two of the five are precisely who their respective districts *wouldn't* have sent if they could have been certain that this was actually a call to governance and not a clever way to take hostages. The representative from Westfall is, of course, me."

"What?" Morgan asked. "Don't you live in Basket Hill?"

"When we choose to go out," Sarine said, "we generally do it in Basket Hill. But the grocery, strictly speaking, is just over the line between it and Westfall. We can't quite live like our customers, but we have to live where they are."

"Fair enough. So we have you and . . . ?"

"And Goldhalls itself, the crown jewel of wealth in this city. They are going to be absolutely furious up there when they find out Naishe's offer was meant in good faith, but because they weren't sure, they have given us the gift of sending Marjorie Manigault, whose head is full of archery and hunting, rather than her neighbors' blinding greed. We can trust her to yield to common sense and common interest, but don't waste time on the other three misers."

"Good advice," Morgan said. "It's practically a given that we'll choose to settle things by majority vote. The richest districts can't have the majority, but they can intimidate the rest. Keeping them from voting all together is essential."

"Agreed," Halvard said. "I'm no politician, but I'll follow your lead, ma'am."

They passed through the corridor into another strange sight: a broad open room two stories high, with a marble floor and a winding outer staircase, though the wooden railing at the top appeared to be broken. And in the center, a giant table had been set down as if it had fallen there, with mismatched chairs scattered around it.

"We dragged it down from upstairs," said a sinewy young woman, her riding boots propped up on the table. ("That's the Manigault girl," Sarine whispered.) "There's so many of us that we needed the space, and this was the biggest room we could find on short notice. You three the last of us?"

Morgan did a quick count. There were thirty-seven districts in Valyanrend, and thirty-seven people in this room, so that did seem to be the case. "We're ready to get started."

"May I just say," said a tall man in an elaborately embroidered cloak, "that this is all *highly* irregular."

"Indeed it is," Sarine said. "When one tyrant is deposed in this city, we usually get another in short order. This is a refreshing change."

Laughter chimed from a dozen throats, and the man in the cloak scowled; he was probably one of the three Sarine had warned them against. Morgan pulled out one of the few empty chairs, though there did appear to be more than thirty-seven. "Well, I'd like to stay stuck here no longer than we have to. Shall we start putting proposals to votes? A simple majority?"

"There's nothing simple about it," the man in the cloak said. "The districts aren't equal in terms of population size, and they *certainly* aren't equal in terms of tax revenue—"

"I *am* a tax collector, actually," said the woman directly across the table from Morgan. "Since even Valyanrend's largest district is not twice the size of its smallest, I don't think anyone should be allowed two votes. As for the average wealth of the inhabitants, I think we can agree that's irrelevant."

"But—"

Marjorie Manigault raised her arm across his chest, as if setting a barrier between him and everyone else. "Hugo," she said. "Don't be difficult. Majority vote is logical. If we can't even agree on that, we'll be here forever."

When he fell silent, Halvard stepped in. "All right, it's settled. Nineteen votes to pass, anything with eighteen or less fails."

"But what if someone abstains?" someone else asked.

A delicate clearing of the throat drew their attention to a young man in a much less elaborate cloak, notable only for its deep green hue. "Any abstentions shall be removed from the final vote tally, unless the final result is a tie, in which case they shall be counted as votes against. So it's only nineteen votes to pass if everybody votes. That's standard procedure. Do the lot of you not even know that much?"

"And what basis do you have for declaring that?" Hugo asked.

The young man gave him a withering glare. "I'm a legal scholar, of course. Why the hell were the rest of you chosen?"

"You must have plenty of ideas, then," Morgan said, ignoring the question. "If you're so confident, why don't you start us off?"

He sighed. "The first thing to do is to protect this government itself. To throw up as many shields around it as we can. So, for example, any vote to disband the government, or to change the manner of elections in any way, after today, will require a unanimous vote. No abstentions."

"Then shouldn't we also prevent people from putting themselves in contention in districts where they don't actually live? There should be a requirement to either own property or reside in a family residence in the district in question—"

"No, they'll dodge that," the legal scholar said. "Anyone with the coin will simply buy a second house in a different district. So we prohibit them from owning noncommercial property outside the district they wish to represent, and institute a residency requirement for . . . eighty percent of the year? Seventy? Let's say seventy-five."

"We'll need to set an appropriate yearly salary," Sarine said. "Something low enough that no one would be tempted to take this job for the money, but high enough that no one's going to take bribes just to feed their family."

"And we'll need to decide what to do about the guard," Halvard said. At least a dozen people groaned.

"We could adapt the rules of the guard in Esthrades," the scholar said. "They've been in place since Stonespire became a city, and they're quite popular with the people. The guard's primary function is to protect the populace, not to halt crime. They aren't permitted to draw their swords on citizens unless blood has already been shed. And they're given the authority to mediate disputes, but any actual crimes, as well as grievances they couldn't resolve, are addressed by the current ruler—which would be us, in this case, I suppose."

"And we could make Naishe the new captain," Morgan said. "If she'll accept, that is."

"But if we're putting ourselves in charge of grievances," the tax collector said, "won't that be . . . unimaginably time-consuming? Do all of us have to be present to render a verdict, or can we take it in shifts—but then what happens if someone who wasn't there objects to the way a grievance was handled?"

The scholar opened his mouth, but he was preempted by two fists slamming down on the table. They belonged to a red-faced woman about Sarine's age, her hair tied back with a tattered scarf. "I won't be participating in any votes until we get what we deserve. You've all just been talking away, and you haven't mentioned us once."

"Oh, this should be good," Hugo said, managing to fit a truly astounding amount of snide into just five words.

Morgan ignored him. "Who's *us*?"

The woman gestured to her right, where a thin and pale young man of about twenty was sitting, all but putting his head down on the table. "I was chosen from Rat's Tail, and he's from the Bowels. The two districts the lot of you like to pretend don't exist. But if my vote's truly as good as yours, then I want aid for our people. All the food and medicine we petitioned Elgar for, only to be denied. And until we get it, we won't be voting for anything."

The young man nodded mournfully. "Our need has long since passed the luxury of waiting."

"But not the luxury of threats, it seems," Hugo said. "You overestimate yourselves. Two votes won't make the difference in any of these proposals."

"Hold on," Morgan said. "They did interrupt the proceedings, but I'm sure their need *is* great, and we can address it with a single vote."

"Why?" Hugo asked peevishly. "Do you want to set the precedent of allowing one or two belligerent representatives to take the entire governing body hostage? If we prove that such a tactic works, we invite everyone to start clamoring for their own special interests."

Morgan felt in her bones that this man spent his every waking moment consumed with his own special interests, but his point, as stated, wasn't wholly without merit, and more than a few voices murmured their agreement. Trouble was, now that they'd veered from their original course, the momentum they'd been building threatened to dissipate. Everyone suddenly thought of their own particular proposals, or started arguing with their neighbors. The legal scholar attempted to wade into the fray, offering his opinions on what was and wasn't feasible, but he was either ignored or shouted down for his condescension. Sarine was trying unsuccessfully to extricate herself from a debate with Hugo, and Halvard just glanced at Morgan helplessly, both hands raised as if in defeat.

"All right," she said, and then again, in the voice she used to tell gathered drunks the tavern was closing: "All *right*!"

Well, at least she still knew how to grab attention. "I know that most of us feel like we shouldn't even be here. I'm sure that once each district is able to properly vote on who they want, a lot of us will be swept out. But right now, we're here. We can be the reason this experiment succeeds or fails. Aren't you tired of all the imperators and the lord protectors and the grand duchesses? Don't you find it embarrassing that this city existed for centuries before Stonespire was even a dream, and now they've so passed us by that we're stealing their ideas? I don't care about golden walls or lavish parties or anything the wreckage of Ninism tells us about how magnificent that bloody empire used to be. But this city was a beacon once, long, long ago. It showed the rest of the continent, the rest of the world, how things could be. Don't you want to do that again?"

Sarine Parnell gave her a beaming smile. "Personally speaking, I wouldn't half mind it."

"Damn right," Halvard said, thumping one great fist on the table.

"And there *are* ways," the legal scholar insisted. "It's not as if the project's doomed. Our choices here matter."

Marjorie Manigault finally took her boots off the table, and leaned forward over it toward Morgan. "And you would be . . . ?"

"Morgan Imrick."

"Well then, Miss Imrick, since you were the one to administer the kick this gathering needed, why don't you decide the order in which we take up all these various issues?"

Morgan waited for voices of dissent, but though a few people looked as if they wanted to object, no one actually dared to. "In that case, we'll start with the proposal about sending aid to Rat's Tail and the Bowels—not because anyone's been bullied into it, but because it ought to have been done a long time ago. Then we'll run through the essential safeguards our scholarly friend proposed: elections, residency requirements, salaries, the guard. After that, we'll go around this table, and each person will put forward one proposal for debate, which we'll vote on as they're presented. We won't all be guaranteed to get what we want, but we'll each have an equal chance to be heard. That's fair, isn't it?"

Again, some visible discontent, but no actual argument.

"Then let's get to it. Oh, and we'll need to write all this down. Does anyone have . . . ?"

The legal scholar withdrew a gigantic roll of parchment from the depths of his cloak, then dropped a quill on the table with a clatter, setting an inkwell delicately after it. "Honestly, I'm amazed the rest of you arrived with your boots on."

CHAPTER FIFTY-THREE

Valyanrend

THAT NIGHT, NAISHE found herself appointed not queen, not grand duchess, but captain of the city guard. She'd be lying if she claimed to have no misgivings, but she could at least say that she had no regrets.

Valyanrend's new governing body, whose members were still not in agreement about what to call themselves, had given her a copy of their proposed changes to the way the guard was run, while still offering her the chance to make additional improvements as she saw fit. It was a good start. She hadn't imagined taking any official position at all, but this one she could work with. It was, in largest part, just giving her sanction to protect the people and hear their grievances, which she had been doing unofficially already.

And she'd thought that would be the end of it, but she was in for a surprise. As she and Wren left the Citadel, she was surrounded by dozens upon dozens of her former subordinates. At first, listening to their excited chatter, she thought they merely wanted to celebrate, but then their mood settled over her, seriousness layered under the joy.

"We were thinking," Rask said, as the others quieted down and let him speak, "that as of this moment, the resistance is most likely disbanded."

Naishe struggled to exchange a glance with Wren, who'd been nearly swallowed up by the crowd. "I suppose that's true. Did you wish me to declare it?"

"No need," Rask said, tapping the hilt of his sword. "But the city guard is probably going to have to be disbanded as well. We know better than anyone what a lot of corrupt cowards and ruffians most of them were under Elgar; rather than try to weed the good from the bad, it would probably be simpler to throw the whole lot over and start recruiting again from nothing."

"That was my thinking, aye," Naishe said. "Is that what you wanted to ensure?"

"No. We wanted to put ourselves forward." And then Rask, of all people, went to one knee before her. "Everyone here, Captain, presents themselves as a candidate. We're prepared to swear loyalty to you, just as we did before."

"Rask," Naishe said gently. "You're *volunteering* to keep following my orders? Right when you could have been free of me?"

He scowled, so yes, he was still Rask. "Are you trying to make this as difficult for me as possible? I'm on my bloody knees already."

"Well, there's no need for that," Naishe said, offering him her hand. "You won't be swearing any oaths to me. If anything, you're promising yourself to the people of this city."

"Aye," Rask said, with that rusty grin of his that always looked like he didn't use it enough. "I can live with that."

Talia was second behind Rask, with her perfectly opposite grin that always saw the light of day. Naishe glanced at the spot on her stomach where they both knew the scar lay. "Haven't you sacrificed enough for this city already?"

"What, and go back to my parents and become a grocer? Don't condemn me to that, Naishe."

Naishe shook her head, but she didn't protest further.

She went through all of them, right there in the street. It was easy to approve the ones she knew personally; as for those she wasn't confident she had the measure of, she deferred them to another day, when things were settled enough that she could test and interview them at her leisure. But then, just when she thought she was done, one final candidate stepped forward.

"I do hope all the places aren't filled already," her father said.

Naishe stared at him, dumbfounded, and also absurdly on the edge of tears. "Father, don't joke."

"Who's joking? If anything, I thought I was apologizing. This moment needed you, and you were more than its equal. And if I had dragged you away from it as I'd hoped, I would have done a great wrong to you and the continent both."

Damn it, now she really *was* going to cry. But Wren squeezed her hand, and she pulled herself together. "What will Mother say?"

"That it's long past time I found an occupation for myself that wasn't mercenary work, I expect. And that I should have trusted you to know yourself from the start." He eyed Wren dubiously. "I couldn't say how she'll feel about him."

"Best to quit while you're ahead, I think," Naishe said.

So she confirmed her own father to the guard, right there for everyone to see. And then, once it was truly over, as touched as she was, she still felt relief that she could finally be alone with the one person she wanted at her side right now.

She and Wren walked the streets of Valyanrend together, as they had done so many times. "You must know I would confirm you in an instant," she said, "but I figured you wanted to wait until we were alone."

Wren winced a little, but he looked her in the eye. Had he cut his hair? She could see both of his eyes more clearly than usual. "No, actually."

"No?"

"I'm sorry," he said. "It suits you, perfectly. And I wish I could stand beside you in everything, but I don't think I can take up a weapon again. I'm already haunted by what happened to Zack, and . . . I know it's weak of me, but . . ."

"It isn't weak," Naishe said firmly. "You're suited to many things, and brilliant at them. This doesn't have to be one of them."

"Thank you," he said, taking both of her hands. "Really. I . . . did actually have something I wanted to ask you."

"I can't wait to hear it."

He smiled shyly, still not looking away. "I've been making good money work-ing with my father. I've saved a lot. And I can keep working with him, whether or not I live with him. So I was thinking . . . what if I pooled my coin with yours, and went half with you on a place a bit bigger than the room above Mr. Redding's?"

Naishe laughed. "What, you don't like being woken up by my father in the morning?"

"Naishe, I'm serious."

"So am I." She squeezed his hands. "We were practically living together there anyway. Doing it while going halves on a bigger place can only be an improve-ment. No promises about my father, though."

"About that." Wren's gaze turned thoughtful. "I actually had an idea."

"Oh, this I have to hear."

"I thought we could introduce him to my father."

"What for? You know I'm fond of your father, but mine is going to hate him on principle, just because he's related to you."

"He's certainly going to try," Wren said. "But what do we know about your father? He thinks the world of you, and he thinks you're far too good for me. Whereas my father . . ."

". . . thinks the world of me, and is always saying I'm the best woman likely to have you," Naishe said, trying not to sound like she was boasting. "Oh gods, it's perfect, isn't it?"

She could picture it now, Wren's father taking any opportunity to wax on about Naishe's many sterling qualities, how lucky Wren was, and her own father fumbling desperately for a way to disagree with him. With any luck, after enough of it, he'd be forced to admit he liked the man.

"You're brilliant," she said, kissing Wren at the next street corner.

He leaned his forehead against hers. "Don't praise me too much prematurely. But it's worth a try, at least." He glanced up and down the street. "So. I hear they'll be celebrating at the Ashencourt house, and at the Dragon's Head in Sheath. Which one should we go to?"

Naishe only had to think about it for a moment. "Neither," she said. "Right now, I'm walking the streets of a free city with the man I love. Changing anything would only be a step down."

"Agreed," Wren said. "I'll walk until sunrise if you will."

QUEEN ADORA WAS still with them when Seren and Arianrod set out for the Dragon's Head, but they ran into a slight wrinkle before they could reach it. The queen's uncle had been ordered to remain outside Valyanrend's walls during the battle, and he had done so. But once Adora's soldiers started coming back to report the day was won, he couldn't contain himself, and snuck within the city to see her. Adora was put out with him for a bit, but Seren suspected it was mostly perfunctory, and it ended with her inviting him back to the tavern with the rest of them.

By the time they arrived, the celebration was already well underway. Morgan and Braddock were taking turns behind the bar, Roger Halfen was having a drinking contest with Deinol and half a dozen resistance members, and Rhia was sitting at a corner table with the Aurnian prince and his royal guards, drinking water and having an animated conversation about swordplay. Ritsu had apparently fallen asleep on his feet, and Cadfael and Talis were in the process of carrying him to bed. Arianrod walked past them up the stairs, and Seren and Adora followed her into her room and shut the door behind them.

Arianrod perched on a corner of the bed. "It seems our part is well and truly over. What do you say, Adora, are you going to linger in the city for a few days and see how it all turns out?"

"I'm afraid not," the queen said. "My army has been rendered unnecessary, and its presence is no doubt causing a lot of fear and unease. I have a responsibility to remove it as soon as possible. We'll depart for Issamira at first light tomorrow morning."

"All right, if you insist." She brushed her palms over her knees. "I should also ask . . . I believe I shall have occasion to acquire a great deal of Old Lantian texts in the near future. I presume you would help me translate them, if I sent some to you in Eldren Cael?"

"Well, of course. But where would you get them?"

"That's . . . probably best kept to myself."

"All right, if *you* insist. I'd rather get to read them than know where they came from, anyway." She looked Arianrod over. "Have you thought about how you're going to get home?"

Arianrod blinked. "Walk east until I hit Stonespire?"

"She means," Seren said, "how are you going to ensure you get home *safely*. I'm the only retainer you have on this side of the continent right now."

"Bah. Do I need retainers to get home? Who wants to kill me at this point?"

"That *is* the point," Seren said. "We can't be certain."

"All right, what's your suggestion, then?"

Seren turned to Adora. "Could we ask . . .?"

"Oh, of course. Think nothing of it. I'd rather know you were safe, too. I'll have them report to you here."

"Tomorrow afternoon," Arianrod said.

"Right. You must be tired, after everything."

"I'm not any more tired than I've been, I just want to leave at my own pace. There's no telling when I may be able to come back, after all."

"I'd like to come back again, too," Adora said. "There's so much history here."

Seren was silent, because she did not feel about history the way those two did; it was a passion that was simply beyond her. But Arianrod looked at her, and then kept looking, as if her gaze had gotten stuck on something.

"And, well, perhaps it's too soon to ask . . ." Adora was saying.

"What?" Arianrod asked, without moving her eyes from Seren.

"Now that Issamira is no longer in crisis, will you start lending me your books again?"

"If you promise to return them in a timely manner for once, I don't see why not. Though I maintain you don't want the Gorrin. If I could un-read it, I would."

"See, that just makes me curious."

"Well, three of his sentences will cure you of that."

"Then perhaps instead . . . let me think . . ."

"It's useless for you to decide now," Arianrod said. "I won't even be home for some time, and you'll have changed your mind by then."

But the queen seemed to have entered a world of her own devising. "There's an obvious link between those statues in the tunnels and the Ninists' Nine, but I want to revisit some scholarship about the historical roots of Ninism. Now that we know some version of the Magician was real, it might be easier to reexamine the reigns of certain kings and queens for . . . Oh, but I think I've already read something to that effect . . ."

"Adora," Arianrod said, with great seriousness. "You know I am terribly, and indeed quite infuriatingly fond of you."

"Ah," the queen said, as at a loss at being on the receiving end of that as Seren would have been. ". . . But?"

"But perhaps you might contrive to be somewhere else for the better part of an hour," Arianrod said, with a slight tilt of her head in Seren's direction.

"Right." Adora backed away immediately, hand to her cheek as if it could hide her embarrassment. "Have a good—that is, ah . . . hm. Well then." She slammed the door so hard behind her it was a wonder it didn't shake the building.

"Huh," Arianrod said, in the sudden silence. "Did I do that badly?"

"I think you did it about as well as the circumstances allowed," Seren said. "And certainly in your particular way. I'm glad to have some time alone with you. Especially after today."

"Why? Were you worried something might happen to me? Or that it might happen to you, despite your claims?"

"Not really," Seren said. "And no. I just feel . . . as if certain burdens have been lifted from me. So I wanted to see you, so that I could . . ."

"So that you could be happy with me," Arianrod finished, as if it was obvious.

"Yes."

"Then is there a reason you're standing on the opposite side of the room from me?"

Because she wasn't sure what she might say or do if she were any closer. But she only shook her head, and sat next to Arianrod, their knees brushing.

She moved before Seren did or said anything. She turned to face her, and draped her arms around Seren's neck. "Unless you have an objection," she said, "I'm going to kiss you."

"I want you to," Seren said. "I want you to do everything you want to me."

"Everything?" But her smirk was interrupted by a glance at the closed door. "You don't think Adora's going to take that bit about an hour too literally, do you?"

"I think," Seren said, "that unless this tavern goes up in flames, nothing could induce her to open that door until you open it first."

KAITAN LEANED AGAINST the windowsill next to Braddock's accustomed seat, taking stock of the room. Cadfael and Talis were drinking alone at a small table, but he couldn't find Rhia anywhere. Which was a shame, since he wanted a chance to talk to her now that she wasn't occupied with Gao. Seren and the marquise had finally come downstairs again, too, and were currently engaged in a minor debate at the bar over whether they might be able to get drunk, since they had both gone much longer than usual without eating any blood apples. (Seren argued no, but the marquise remained optimistic; having apparently never been drunk, she was quite curious.)

He was about to venture a walk outside when an arm threaded through his—an arm he would have known anywhere. "Rana," he said. "To what do I owe such an unexpected pleasure?"

"Oh, don't be so formal, Kaitan. It feels odd." She wiggled the fingers of her right hand at him. "Let's just say I'm feeling better tonight than I have in some time, and I need someone to celebrate with me. You didn't seem like you were up to anything without me."

"I wasn't, but what about the other two?"

"Ryo and Gao? From the sound of it, the prince and Queen Adora will be talking for an hour, and Gao is—"

"Here," he said, stepping up beside them, with the same lightness that kept his foes from noticing him until it was too late. "What are we talking about?"

"We're celebrating."

"Ah, are we now? I'm glad you told me. Is there a particular reason that one is invited?"

"Come on. If he'd acquitted himself badly in the fight today, you'd already have said so. So can you give him a reprieve for one evening?"

"At your request, I could do much more." He threw an arm around Kaitan's shoulders, and Kaitan flinched, expecting some trick. But there was nothing. It was just Gao being as good as his word. "All right, Kaitan. You're the regular here. You can help me learn what's what. That big fellow behind the bar, he has an understanding with the proprietress of the place, yes?"

Oh, of course. He wanted gossip. No matter how many eyes he had, or how many years he'd been wandering away from home, Gao was still Gao. "Morgan and Braddock, despite their mutual gruffness, have a solid and long-standing companionship, yes."

"But whatever's going on with that scarred fellow and the windcaller does not appear to be long-standing."

"Cadfael and Talis? Aye, I don't know when that came about. Certainly not when I first met him."

Gao's eye brightened with curiosity. "You met him before all this?"

"Aye, in the east. We nearly killed each other over a mutual mistake, actually."

He laughed, that delighted and unrestrained laugh of his, his head thrown back. "That's exactly like you, Kaitan. Getting yourself into something like that, and then getting out without any bloodshed."

Kaitan waited to feel the sting, the sense of an insult lurking below the words. But there was still nothing.

"Do you remember," Rana said, "when Ryo wanted to tour the Howling Gate, and that mouth of yours got us into trouble in that fishing village—"

"I maintain," Gao said, "that if that mariner couldn't stomach being defeated in a contest of insults, he shouldn't have started one."

"And Ryo was going to have the two of you duel to settle it before Kaitan stepped in."

"Aye, by the time that one was done, we had a pound of free cod in the bargain." Gao smiled fondly, remembering, and this time he didn't catch himself and stop.

"And then the rest of you made me cook it all myself, even though you know I can't cook," Kaitan said.

"Aye, and after three bites Gao announced that he'd rather have had the duel."

They all laughed at that, even Kaitan, some of the tension in his body finally easing. Then Gao leaned close to him and said, "This is important, now. Who's that fellow that's been so deep in conversation with your friend Morgan?"

Kaitan knew Gao, so he immediately guessed where this was going. "Oh, Gao, don't."

"It's a simple question!"

"It won't end simply for you, you can bet on that. He's Queen Adora's own uncle. He's a nobleman *and* a general."

"You're not exactly dissuading me." He grinned at them, pure mischief. "I'm going to go introduce myself."

And he was off, leaving Kaitan to exchange a look with Rana. "That flirt is going to get himself in trouble."

"When," Rana replied, "have you ever known that flirt to get himself in any trouble but precisely the kind he was looking for?"

"A fair point. Good to know that hasn't changed."

They stood close together, shoulders nearly touching. It was somehow achingly familiar and entirely uncharted, all at once.

"I tried to fill in for you, you know," she said. "To be the one who talks everyone else back to reason, to view violence as a last resort *because* of how easy it would be to win. But you were always best at that."

He didn't feel best at it at the moment. He felt as if he'd almost forgotten how to speak at all. "So you're saying you missed me?"

"Could you doubt that? It's clear you missed us. And it's only natural. We were good together."

"I don't understand," he said. "You haven't forgiven me. You don't trust me. Why are you even speaking to me?"

Rana sighed. "Forgiveness is a difficult business, Kaitan. For me, the hardest part of your flight was the absence of answers. I had no idea why you had done it; I just knew that the Kaitan I thought I knew could never have done such a thing. It made me fear that perhaps I had never known you at all. But that wasn't true. Now that I understand the reasons behind what you did, I believe you're still, mostly, who I thought you were. That's more important than forgiveness, at least to me."

She glanced across the room at Ryo, still deep in conversation with Adora. "As for trust, the prince and Gao act as if, once broken, it's too complicated to ever repair. But it's just forging links in a chain. The more times someone proves they can be trusted, the more you'll trust them. That chain was broken between us, but there's no reason it can't be forged anew in the same way. I understand why the others might not want to try. But that doesn't mean it's not possible."

It would have been possible, Kaitan thought. Perhaps. With Rana, specifically. That alone was much more than he could ever have hoped for, but it would never be. Rana would be returning to Aurnis with the prince she served, who would need her more than ever in the time to come. And exiling Kaitan from Aurnis was the least of what Ryo would do. After tonight, they'd likely never see each other again.

But he didn't say that. He resolved to enjoy this one night with her, as if it were some beautiful dream of the past. He'd save the regret for when he woke up.

As much as Rhia wanted to stay by her brother's side, she sensed that he and Talis had things to discuss that she would only have intruded on. Instead, she'd entertained herself for some time with the man she'd met in Araveil, Gao, though she'd never have dreamed then that he was royal guard to a prince. The prince himself was only too happy to enfold Rhia in their conversation; upon seeing the *tsunshin* that she wore, he peppered her with questions about her training, and explained the methods and philosophy behind the two great sword schools in Aurnis. Rhia's teacher hadn't had more than middling mastery of the blade himself, and many of the movements in her repertoire were self-invented, or created with Cadfael's help. But none of them seemed to look down on her for that; if anything, it only made them more interested.

But the more time she spent without a glimpse of Lirien, the more she grew worried. This should have been the kind of gathering Lirien loved: light and festive, full of laughter and mostly empty of weighty conversation. So why wasn't she here enjoying it?

It was highly likely that if Lirien was alone, it was because she wanted to be. Still, Rhia couldn't help wanting to put her worries to rest. She decided she'd just find out where Lirien was. If she didn't want to share her thoughts, that was up to her.

She didn't have to look far. Lirien was only a little ways down the street from the bustling tavern, angled so that she could still see its brightly lit windows, but couldn't be seen from them. Her hands were empty.

"Sorry," Rhia said, when Lirien caught sight of her. "Should I leave you to . . . whatever you're doing?"

"I don't mind if it's you," Lirien said. "How is it in there?"

"It suits me quite well, to be honest. Satisfaction for a job rightly done, and celebration with those we care for."

"Then why did you leave?"

"I was worried about you."

"Well, don't be."

"All right," Rhia said. "But you didn't ask me to leave, either, so . . ."

Lirien smiled, like ice melting. "And unlike most people, you'd actually leave upon being asked. I'll tell you, because I would've had to tell you anyway, or else be more furtive and churlish than I'd like. After this, I'm finally going to resume my wandering. And I'm going to resume it alone."

"Ah." Rhia couldn't say she wasn't sad to hear it, even though she'd known, deep down, that it was unrealistic to hope Lirien might want to continue traveling with them once "them" included Cadfael *and* Talis.

"It's not just because of those two," Lirien said, as if reading her thoughts. "Getting away from them will undeniably be a relief, I won't lie. But even if they didn't exist, it would still be the right decision."

"If you're confident it's the right decision, why are you brooding so uncharacteristically over it?"

"Ugh." She tugged at her braid. "Because I knew I'd have to tell you, and I knew you'd make that disappointed face."

"Hey," Rhia said. "You don't have to worry about me, either."

Lirien smiled, a bit gentle, a bit sad, a bit self-deprecating. "But I do."

"I'll be with my brother," Rhia said. "I'll be happier than I've been in a long time."

"But you don't understand why I'm doing this," Lirien said. "Do you?"

"Do you need some big and complicated reason? You've always wanted to travel the world on your own. You don't have to justify it to me. But if you have something you *want* to say, of course I'll listen."

"When I met you in Issamira," Lirien said, "you'd already spent so long living for other people. People you loved, and people who loved you, but still. If things had been just a little different, you might still be there, twisting yourself into the shape of the captain of the guard, because that's who they needed you to be."

"That's true," Rhia admitted. "But I don't regret the time I spent in Eldren Cael."

"Even so, if you allow that to keep happening over and over, you'll never figure out what you want for yourself. You'll never find the answers to those questions you asked me when we sat by that river."

"And you're so sure you would stand in the way of that?"

Lirien put a hand on her shoulder. "If I only had to worry about me, it'd be all right. I'm good at holding onto people loosely, for a little while, and then letting them go. But that's not something you can do. And I . . . can't let you hold on to me that tightly. Not as we both are now. So you have to let me go."

Rhia looked down at the cobblestones. She couldn't truly say she thought Lirien was wrong. Not completely. But either way, it was what she'd decided. "All right. If that's what you want."

And it must have been, because Lirien's posture relaxed. "Thank you. And . . . I'm sorry. I think, given enough time, you'll agree it was better this way."

"There's one thing I have to know," Rhia said. "If, one day, after I've answered those questions to my satisfaction, I decided I felt more hopeful about it than you—if I ended up coming to find you—what would you do? Would you be angry? Because if you never want to see me again, you should tell me so now, and I'll abide by it."

Lirien turned away, running her thumb along the edge of her jaw as she looked off down the street. "If you ended up coming to find me . . . well, if you did that, Rhia, I'd think that it was very like you."

CHAPTER FIFTY-FOUR

Valyanrend

DEINOL WOKE UP in the alley that ran alongside the Dragon's Head, which was more or less where he'd expected to find himself. After weeks of repentance, recovery, and a very limited budget, he considered himself entitled to overindulge a little, and wasn't even particularly bothered by the headache or the pain of the brightness against his eyes. What *did* shock him was the realization, as his vision swam into focus, that Ryo Serenin was standing in the alley beside him, as if waiting for him to wake up.

Deinol scrubbed his good hand over his face. He had no idea what he must look like. "How long have you been standing there?"

"I don't know. A handful of minutes. It seemed rude to wake you." He said that without embarrassment, as if waiting there indefinitely were not the much stranger decision. "Are you well?"

"That depends. Well enough for what?" He rolled to the side, pushing himself to his feet with the assistance of his good hand and testing his ability to take his own weight. "I'm well enough for standing, possibly for walking. Undecided on eating, and definitely not well enough for sparring, though"—he shook the other hand—"I expect I'm finished with that for good."

Ryo frowned. "There are methods—"

"Oh, I know. I've still got the thumb and most of the first finger, and I could use a wood or metal brace for the rest—not very dexterous, but enough to provide the support I'd need to wield a sword the weight of mine. Or I could learn to fight one-handed, with a saber or rapier or something. But I'm not like you and your sworn swords, Ryo. I'm choosing to go a different way."

If Ryo objected to the use of his name, it didn't show on his face. "What do you mean?"

"To be honest, I've never been *that* good at swordplay," Deinol said. "It's always irritated me. I've spent my whole life trying to push past my limits, to be as good as someone like Lucius. But I don't think it was ever going to happen for me, even with two hands." He spread the left one out, flexing the fingers that remained to him. "But it's more than that. I think that always focusing on my swordsman-ship prevented me from realizing I'm better at other things, and it's those things I should rely on to make my way in the world, not brute force. I didn't use swords-manship to rescue Seth, but I did endanger him with it, by running after Seren even when I knew I wasn't her equal. I didn't use it to help Ritsu, or to win Lu-cius's friendship. And I didn't use it to convince you to set aside your revenge for the time being and help the people of this city. So instead of taking this hand as a challenge for my swordsmanship to overcome, I'm going to take it as freedom—permission to set it aside for good."

Ryo nodded decisively. "I agree. In fact, that's a large part of what I came to discuss with you. Will you take a walk with me?"

Deinol groaned. "You really are unfailingly serious, wanting to talk business even at a time meant for celebrating. But all right. You paid back the debt you owed me faithfully, so I suppose I can grant you this much of my morning."

They left the alley side by side, turning into the gentle brightness of the street, and Deinol realized it was still early. There weren't many people up and about yet, and such a busy neighborhood looked unusually peaceful, almost serene.

"I'm told that you were once a thief, but no longer," Ryo said, conversation-ally. "Is that true?"

Deinol had originally decided to leave thieving behind out of friendship with Lucius, who had decided he couldn't do it anymore. That condition was no longer relevant, but he still knew what his answer would be. "It's true," he said. "Thiev-ery wasn't my best skill, either."

"Do you know what you'll do instead?"

Deinol had no idea why a foreign prince was so interested in his employment prospects, but he couldn't see why he shouldn't answer truthfully. "I'm not sure. I don't have a lot of experience with honest work. But I'm determined not to make that an excuse. I'll find my way eventually."

The prince fell silent, and Deinol didn't push him, just kept matching him stride for stride. He presumably hadn't come here just to talk to Deinol about triv-ialities, so there was no need to rush him.

"I have to thank you," he said abruptly, surprising Deinol with both his words and their meaning. "Were it not for your criticism, I might not have ever come to this city, and I would have missed the opportunity to be a part of this fight. Even worse, I might have continued to make worthless decisions with regard to Kaitan."

Deinol had no idea how to respond to that. Were you supposed to handle a prince's gratitude delicately, or as if you'd received a priceless gift? "Well, I . . . if it worked out, I'm glad. I don't need any more thanks than that."

"Perhaps not, but I wanted to ask you . . ." Here it was. "I'll have to go back to

Kaiferi soon, to prepare for my coronation. And I wanted to ask you if you would come with me."

Thank the gods Deinol had held off on eating breakfast—he would have spat it in Ryo's face. "W . . . what the hell for?"

"Because it appears that you are at loose ends in this place," Ryo said mildly. "And because you gave me good counsel in the past, and would not fear to do so in the future. Because all this travel I've had to do over the last five years has shown me the blind spots in my upbringing, and I wish to correct them. And because I thought you might say yes. If all goes well, I might one day have heirs, and perhaps you would tell them, too, the story of the kitchen boy I did not get to know, who was wiser than a prince."

Deinol leaned against the wall of the nearest building, blinking the morning sunlight out of his eyes. In moments like this, when it was quiet and the scent on the air was familiar, he could almost feel Seth's presence. "Well," he said. "When you put it like that."

"That's . . . not quite a yes, I don't think."

"Because it's not something I can decide in an instant. Or without conditions." He rubbed his chin. "You'd need to pay me wages, for one thing."

"I thought that was implied," Ryo said.

"And I need something else from you, too. Something you're going to like a lot less." He pushed off from the wall and stood straight, so he and Ryo were the same height. "I need you to let Lucius come back to Aurnis."

Ryo bristled, though he tried to hide it. "Why?"

"Because keeping him from it is just being cruel, without helping anyone else. He's not a danger to anyone there. And because being there will help him grow, and if you don't like the person he's been, you should want that, too." He held up his hands. "I'm not asking you to change your attitude toward him. He's not entitled to your presence in his life. I'm just asking you to let him come home."

Ryo looked up and down the street. "I thought this was his home."

"I used to think that, too. But the truth should be obvious by now, even to me."

Ryo brushed his hand along his left side, where Deinol knew his scar still lay. "Though it wasn't your intent, it's advice that will help me as much as him. I . . . don't want to be someone who lets go of the past, exactly, but I want to be someone who isn't bound by it. I suppose it wouldn't do to seek your service and then deny the first request you ever made of me."

"Does that mean you'll do it?"

"I'll do it. Does that mean you'll come?"

"I told you, I'll think about it."

"And how long is it going to take you to think about it?"

"I figured we could stand here and find out. Why, were you going somewhere? It's a fine morning."

Ryo smiled slightly, and inclined his head just a bit. The silence spread out between them, punctured only by a lone bird. But it wasn't awkward or heavy.

He might have been a prince, but beneath that, he was just an imperfect person who was trying to put more good into the world than bad. And that was all Deinol had ever wanted to be, too.

ROGER AWOKE SLUMPED over the bar, with a brutal crick in his neck letting him know what a bad idea that had been. He rubbed his jaw, then stretched out both arms and arched his back, taking an inventory of his physical condition. At least he knew his own limits, and had only a slight headache after the night's indulgence— nothing enough water wouldn't fix. And a cursory glance of the bar's ground floor told him that he was alone, at least for now.

But he'd hardly fixed himself the drink of water in question when he heard someone else coming down the stairs. He'd expected Morgan, but it was the marquise who greeted him, hiding a tiny yawn behind her hand. He wondered if he should tell her that her long hair was sticking up a bit in the back.

Instead, he toasted her with the water. "Surprised to catch you alone these days, Your Grace. You look none the worse for wear, which I'll wager is more than most of our fellows from last night can say."

"It was difficult to come down here alone, I'll tell you that much," she said, with a slight smile. "Seren sleeps like a cat; I've had to learn to be nearly as light-footed as one to get up without drawing her after me. If she's not woken up on her own, she must need the rest."

"Well, the bar's not open, and I don't think I have Morgan's authority to offer you some breakfast. A fellow Sheather in a tight spot might get a free meal, but someone with your means is going to have to pay for every crumb she eats here."

"As it should be. I'm not here for sustenance anyway. There's something I need to talk to you about before I leave." She inclined her head toward the stairs. "Privately."

Roger obligingly followed her upstairs, to the room he'd rented from Morgan for the night but hadn't precisely used. He wondered if he could get his coin back, but he wouldn't hold his breath. The marquise shut the door behind him, and looked him dead in the eye, with an expression of such unaccustomed seriousness that he knew no joking would be permitted in this conversation. "As I understand it, the tunnels under Valyanrend were first discovered by you and your people, and only offered to the resistance later, to help them in their efforts. Is that true?"

"More or less," Roger allowed, still without any clue where she was going with this. "Morgan and Braddock were the first to find them, and the ones who enlightened me. But I'm the one who's explored and mapped them most extensively, and still the one who knows them best."

"So you're the one who discovered the library?"

Ah. Now he had it. "Aye, Your Grace. And the only one who's been in there, save a little assistant of mine." Marceline would hate being called that, but she never had to know.

"Good," the marquise said. "I'm sure I don't have to tell you that the legal provenance of those books is absolutely impossible to determine, but you'd have no more lawful right to them than you would to the moon. But I also know you're a thief by trade, who can't be expected to swear by legality, and I've no desire to be on bad terms with you. I am taking those books, one way or another—every last tome and every last page. If you try to hide them from me, I will find them, and you'll have made an enemy of me—and you don't want that, Mr. Halfen. So I strongly suggest that you simply make me an offer. Not per book, because I don't want to waste time counting them. Make me an offer for the library itself—and consider that while I have very deep pockets, I won't be made a fool of, even at the hands of a swindler."

Gods, but she could be intimidating when she wanted. And Roger didn't want to be on bad terms with her, either. "How long do I have to come up with a price?"

"I'm prepared to stand here and wait until you have it." So, in other words, she wasn't going to give him time to consult experts or rehearse elaborate arguments. Well, fine. If she was forcing him to go with his instincts, at least he knew clearly what they were.

He took several breaths in and out, just to make sure no sense of regret washed over him. But if anything, he only became more resolved. Good. That was as much as he could hope for.

"Fifty gold pieces," he said.

He could see her surprise. It would be a staggering sum for any private citizen, though not so much for a royal. But the library was theoretically priceless. It was certainly at the lower end of what he could have demanded. "And what else?" she asked.

"The last person to watch over that library," Roger said, "had only the highest hopes for it. As far as I can tell, you are exactly the person they would have most wanted to find it. You know the languages that will allow you to decipher books I can't even read, and the history to put any lost knowledge in its proper context. And no matter what you find, I can't imagine you would ever destroy even a single page, for any reason. You're someone who wants to hear the truth, not what pleases you. And you don't wish to deny the truth to others."

"All true," she said, smiling, "but I doubt you're that charitable."

"I'm not, Your Grace, though I'm not lying when I say it made up part of my considerations. You have a great undertaking ahead of you, to absorb all that knowledge. But among the many, many things you learn, there will undoubtedly be some tidbits that would be of great use to a swindler of Valyanrend. I want those detailed and sent to me, by your own hand." He grinned back at her. "You may think all a thief wants is to make a pile of gold large enough to let him live luxuriously for the rest of his days, but I'm aiming far higher than that. Thanks to everything that's happened in Valyanrend, I've already ensured my name will be remembered as a revolutionary. But before all that—always—my goal has been to immortalize myself as a thief. And in pursuit of that goal, I'll use every tool at my disposal." He paused. "One last thing. The person I mentioned, who stewarded the library, left a note behind. I'm happy to let you read it, but it's the one thing you can't have. They addressed it to the person who found the books, and that's me." He extended a hand to her. "So? Is that deal acceptable to you?"

"I was prepared to promise more, if necessary," she said. "I obviously don't have that much coin on me at the moment—even Seren doesn't—but you must know I'm good for it. If it makes you feel more secure, I won't start reading the books yet, but I'd like access to them. Many of them must be falling apart, and I suspect I can use magic to preserve them, though it'll be an arduous process."

Roger surprised himself with the relief he felt at that; the ancient letter-writer truly couldn't have found a better inheritor for their books, armed with the kind of magic they must have thought was forever out of reach. "So, with your magic, the books might never decay?"

"I . . . actually don't know. The spells might wear thin after a while, or after I die, or . . . who knows. But it should prevent any immediate disintegration that would come about simply from handling them. And if any are in truly terrible condition, I can always have them copied, though of course it would be best to preserve the originals if at all possible."

"Good." He hadn't been able to put a name to it until now, but ever since he'd found the books, he'd felt . . . guilty. Guilty, because he wasn't the person that steward had yearned for in their letter, who could cherish and protect those books as they'd wanted. *But you see,* he thought, *I got them where they needed to go in the end, even if it was mostly an accident. So now you can truly rest in peace.*

He finished the rest of the water he'd brought with him, and tucked the empty tankard under his arm. "I can go with you to the library now, if you like. No time like the present for this preserving business, and though I'm sure you're good for the coin, you understand I'm going to take certain precautions until it's in my hands, right?"

"I'd be suspicious if you didn't," she said. "But we should probably wake Seren first. If she comes to consciousness and can't find me, your friends will have a very stressful morning."

KAITAN HAD LEFT the Dragon's Head early, because in the morning, with everyone asleep around him, it was easy to pretend he still belonged there, and he did not want to see that illusion shattered when they awoke. He had taken an aimless walk around Sheath, not intending to go anywhere in particular, but as his legs grew tired and he began circling back toward the tavern, he crossed paths with Ryo, also walking alone. Kaitan turned away, but Ryo said, "Wait. We should talk."

Kaitan turned back, and fell into step with him. "You know my position," Ryo said. "It remains broadly unchanged. But that doesn't mean I don't still owe you an apology for how I acted when we met. It was beneath me, and it caused great harm. But even if it hadn't, or if I had only harmed you, I still would have been in the wrong. So I'm sorry."

"The fault is as much mine as yours," Kaitan said. "Everything I said then was the truth, but in the way I said it, I still provoked you on purpose. I wanted you to pass judgment on me, *kaihen,* but I sought it in a cowardly manner, by encouraging your anger against me. That only added to my shame. So let me ask you again, properly and without subterfuge. If you wish to take my life as punishment for the oath I broke and the friendship I betrayed, I will surrender it willingly."

Ryo stared at him, but Kaitan still had not regained the ability to read his face. Was it pity there, or anger? Or were those just the things he feared to see there?

Finally, Ryo shook his head. "If nothing else, I know that if I took your life, that friend of yours would track me down and badger me to death, wherever I might run."

"He does seem to have developed a talent for that," Kaitan admitted.

"More than that, he's right, Kaitan. In judging you, I should not consider my anger at the past, my desire for vengeance, or even some idea of balancing the scales. I should think of how to create something better in the future. Killing you would accomplish nothing, besides giving you an unearned sense of peace. Gao was right after all—your cowardice should be its own punishment. But it can only pain you while you live. If you truly wish to change, that pain will spur you forward on the path. And if you don't, you will never be able to outrun the knowledge of what you truly are."

Kaitan knew how true those words were, but they did not feel as hopeless as they would have in the past. He did not feel that Ryo was pronouncing an immutable sentence on him, but extending him a challenge to overcome.

"When are the three of you going to leave?" he asked.

Ryo wrinkled his nose. "Honestly, I'd prefer to stay in Valyanrend a bit longer; I feel I'm witnessing history being made here. But Gao and Rana remind me that, now that Elgar has fallen, Aurnis will soon descend into chaos with no clear leader. I have to return ahead of that. It would help to get official recognition that I am the true prince of Aurnis from Valyanrend's new governing body, so I've already petitioned them for that. But if I don't receive it by the end of the week, I'll have to leave without it." He cleared his throat. "Also, you're mistaken about one thing. It's the four of us that will be leaving. I offered Deinol a place at the palace once I'm crowned, and he's accepted it."

Kaitan was less surprised that Ryo had offered than that Deinol had accepted; the prince had become famous in Kaiferi for promoting candidates the wider world considered unlikely. "It'll be no small thing for him, to leave behind everything he's ever known. But I'm proud of him for taking the leap. Though I'll miss him, of course."

Ryo cleared his throat again, more awkwardly. "Whether you miss him or not . . . that's up to you. He's asked me not to exile you from Kaiferi or Aurnis, and, upon reflection, I've agreed."

For a moment, Kaitan couldn't believe what he was hearing. Then his heart leapt in his chest, and he fought to keep from grinning stupidly. "I . . . I don't have the words to thank you for that, *kaihen*. I can only hope for the chance to show you my gratitude in the future."

"Don't celebrate prematurely," Ryo said. "If you do decide to return, it won't be easy for you. The people will learn what you've done, and many who once venerated you will likely turn against you. I will forbid any violence toward you, but I won't lie to protect you from their judgment. You've lived freely and anonymously here for all these years, and you could continue to do so. But there you will have to bear up under the full weight of your shame."

Kaitan did risk smiling at him then. "Wouldn't you say that's as it should be?"

"I just don't understand what you see in it. I know there are things that are important to you here, things you'll be sad to leave. So why not stay?"

"Because unlike you, *kaihen,* it's people, not ideas, that mean the most to me. With you, Rana, Gao, and Deinol in one place, I could not possibly live anywhere else. Whatever I have to endure, I'll endure it. If there are people whose forgiveness I can win, I'll attempt it. Otherwise, I'll accept their censure as my due. I can't really argue the point, after all."

Ryo fell silent again. But in some small way, that silence echoed the silences they had once shared, that had been easy instead of fraught. "I meant what I said, Kaitan. I don't know if I'll ever be able to forgive you, not in the depths of my heart. And though it's supposed to be a title that lasts for life, I can't let you rejoin the ranks of my *kaishinrian*. But I don't want you to think . . . that I wish for you to fail, or to suffer. I was angry at you for a long time, but I'm trying to set it aside. And my offer to you is made genuinely. If you ever become the person you dreamed of, or achieve the absolution you crave, you will have deserved it. And I'll never say otherwise."

He was always like that, in the end. He was as vulnerable to tempests of emotion as anyone, but those storms always passed, and the foundation underneath was unshakable. He would always act in accordance with his principles. And Kaitan, as ever, felt grateful to be the subject of his consideration, no matter how fleetingly. "I understand, *kaihen*. It will be just like the duel we fought all those years ago. You couldn't just hand me the victory, for then it would have been meaningless. And you fought against me with everything you had, skill and conviction both. You wanted to give me the chance to overcome you. And when I did, though you had given everything, you were the first to congratulate me." He bowed his head. "That remains one of the days of my life that I treasure most. And if the day ever comes when I earn your congratulations a second time, I can't imagine how much it would mean to me."

Ryo nodded, acknowledging him. "I think I would like to see that—someone who lives for people, rather than ideals. I wish I had understood that in you earlier. And . . . I saw the way you fought yesterday. There was nothing cowardly in it. This place has done you good." He smiled, a small smile, but rich with sincerity. "Or I should say, it's the people who have."

"Yes," Kaitan said, watching the streets pass by, tracing the route in his mind that would lead him back to the Dragon's Head. "They have."

IT WAS STILL early morning when Ritsu awoke, and the Dragon's Head was wreathed in stillness. The members of the resistance had slipped away late in the night, and Morgan had sent Marceline home to Tom's (despite her bitter protests) before things got too raucous. The queen of Issamira had left the city as she'd promised, though he could not have said whether she'd been able to find her uncle first. And it seemed Kaitan Enrei had awoken even earlier than Ritsu, for he had fallen asleep by the window last night but was not there now. Roger Halfen was slumped over the bar and snoring, and a quick check outside revealed Deinol passed out in the alley. Morgan and Braddock had returned to their room eventually, and so, he assumed, had the marquise and her bodyguard, though they had still been drinking (and still, to the marquise's disappointment, utterly failing to get drunk) when Ritsu had gone to bed the second time.

He cleaned up a bit at the bar, careful not to disturb Roger, and tried to bring some water out to Deinol, only to find he'd up and left in the meantime. He made use of the now-empty alley to wash up, and when he returned, Roger was gone, too. So he prepared himself some bread and cheese, and was still eating it at the bar when Morgan came down.

She smiled at him, looking refreshed and only slightly disheveled from her rest. "It's nice not to be the first one up for a change. Have you been protecting the place from this group of louts?"

"It hardly needed my protection," Ritsu replied. "And they all left peacefully, as far as I know."

"Well, thank the gods for small favors. I've never hosted such a celebration before; I have to admit I was a little nervous." And she could say that with such sincerity, she who'd been part of Valyanrend's resistance and just been roped into deciding her country's future. Ritsu didn't understand her, but he thought it would be worthwhile to try, no matter how long it took. Perhaps it would help him decide what he wanted to do from now on.

As if reading his thoughts, she leaned over the bar toward him. "Things will probably become less lively around here in the coming days. The Issamiri troops will leave, and I expect our Esthradian guest and her entourage will be going home, too. As for Lucius—or whatever I should call him—I honestly haven't a clue what he'll do now. I've never done well trying to predict that one's actions." She stole a bite of his cheese. "And what about you, Ritsu? Will you go back to Aurnis, now that it's free again?"

"I don't know," Ritsu said. "Before Elgar and his curse, I lived my whole life in Kaiferi. But perhaps that's the very reason why I shouldn't return. My parents were killed during the war, and I . . . lost my best friend as well. The city I knew so well will undoubtedly seem much smaller and sadder without them." He chewed his next bite thoughtfully. "Then there's the matter of how I'll earn a living. In Kaiferi I trained to be a swordsman—not that I was ever very good at it—but I've no desire to hold a weapon again. But I know no other trade, and the only coin I have is what you gave me."

Morgan braced both hands against the bar, stretching her arms out as she pondered the question. "You could always stay here, if you wanted. Valyanrend boasts more trades than any city on this continent, and between us, our motley group has more connections than you'd think. Once you decide what you'd like to learn, one of us could probably put in a word for you and get you apprenticed. You're a bit older than apprentices usually run, but you'd be far from the only person who ever wanted to switch trades at your age."

It was as generous as he'd come to expect from her: offering help not in the expectation of receiving anything specific in return, just with the general understanding that it would be decent of him to return the favor one day, if he ever got the opportunity. Ritsu resolved to make sure of it. "Thank you. This city . . . I thought it would have too many terrible memories for me, because when I lived here I wasn't myself. But if anything, I'm finding the opposite is true. It's because this is my first time living here as me that I want to make it my own, to write over those memories with new ones. So your suggestion makes a lot of sense. But I'm afraid that, if I take you up on it, I might have to impose on you even further, at least for a while. Perhaps you'll let me continue to run errands for you in exchange for lodging until I've earned enough to live someplace else? Though I'd need your help to discover where that might be."

Morgan was quiet for a bit, her gaze floating off to focus on something over his shoulder. "When I said you could stay here, I meant *here,* at the Dragon's Head. You've been very helpful so far—you've done more than what's been asked of you—so if you wanted a more permanent position, I could offer you a room, meals, and a daily wage. It wouldn't be much, but you could save the coin until you find something you might like better. Or even if you never do, and just stay here, it won't be a problem. Truth be told . . ." She was quiet again, wetting her lips with a fretfulness that was unlike her. There was clearly something turbulent beneath her simple words, but Ritsu couldn't think what it might be. "I had a hired hand not so long ago," she said at last. "A kitchen boy. I didn't want to fill his place, but at the same time, I liked it when he was here. I didn't think I needed help when Deinol convinced me to take him on, but it turned out to be more than welcome."

"Ah," Ritsu said, with a pang of remembrance and sadness at once. "You mean Seth."

"You knew him?"

He hadn't touched those memories in a while, but they were still there, the boy with golden hair that Ritsu, in his confused state, had originally mistaken for Sebastian, but who had turned out to be much gentler and quieter than his old friend. "Only briefly. When I first met Deinol, he was still alive. I'm sorry that I wasn't able to help him, but he was always kind to me, though I was a stranger. If he hadn't convinced Deinol to bring me along, I'm sure I'd be in a much worse position now."

"That sounds like him," she agreed, with a bittersweet smile. "Well, either way, the job was his, once. But it can be yours now, if you want it. For as long as you want it."

Ritsu remembered the stories that Seth had told him, of his contentment with his life in Valyanrend. And he remembered Seth's kindness toward him, when the curse had been looped so much tighter around him, and he had so much less of himself. *After we find Seren, let's go after whatever it is you want. You'll never find out what it is if you don't try, will you?*

Trying could start from anywhere. But it was better to start with not wanting to be alone, and not having to be.

"You don't have to fret so about it," Morgan said gently. "It's not a limited offer, and you don't have to decide now."

"I would like to," Ritsu said. "Decide now, and take the job. If you'll have me."

"Wouldn't have offered if I had any doubts." She cast a wistful eye around the room. "So many friends are leaving the place, or have already left it. It'll be nice to start filling it up again. Even Seth was a new face here, once."

And he had made this city his own, regardless of how he came to it. That was comforting, too. "There's one more thing." He pulled Naishe's pendant from beneath his shirt. It was slightly warm from his skin, no trace of magic to be found. "I forgot to give this back. Can you get it to Naishe for me?"

"I can try if you like," Morgan said, "but I bet she'll just tell you to keep it. So you'll know that as long as you wear it, you're still you."

"Ryo says you're coming with him to Aurnis."

"Aye," Deinol said.

It was the first time Kaitan had spoken to him directly, without being spoken to first, since Deinol had asked to be left alone back in Lanvaldis. But he didn't look angry about it. "Don't give me that look," he said. "You must know it wasn't for you."

"But asking Ryo not to exile me was."

Deinol ran his good hand through his hair. "Aye. I suppose I can't really argue with that."

"Deinol, I—"

"Don't. My head hurts too much for the kind of conversation I know you want to have. And I already had one of those with that prince of yours. We're doing this one my way."

He held out his other hand, the left hand, the one Ryo had truncated, though it was really Kaitan's fault. Kaitan flinched reflexively, but caught himself, and didn't look away. He wasn't about to fail this test in the first moment.

He knew the stubs of Deinol's fingers were still tender, not yet entirely healed. So he took his hand carefully, gave it a gentle up-and-down shake.

"You hurt Ryo worse than you hurt me," Deinol said. "You never betrayed me, not really. You lied to me, but you never let me come to harm if you could do anything about it. You would never have run away if I was in trouble. And asking you to choose between me and Ryo wasn't fair. So if he can still give you a chance, it would be petty of me to do less."

"And what does that mean for us?" Kaitan asked.

"It means it's nice to meet you," Deinol said. "I don't really know Kaitan En-rei that well, but I promise not to judge him by how close he is or isn't to Lucius Aquila."

"It's my hope," Kaitan said, "that you'll find you know him better than you think. But we have time."

"So we do." He opened the tavern door and called, "You about ready, Morgan?"

"We're waiting on you two," she called back.

Deinol turned to him. "Breakfast? We think Roger's gone off somewhere with Seren and the marquise, but everyone else is accounted for."

And as Kaitan walked through the doorway, he saw that they were: Morgan and Braddock and Ritsu, Ryo and Rana and even a smirking Gao, who was no doubt about to launch into a full account of his evening as soon as Kaitan sat down. Whatever the future might bring, right now, in this moment, he didn't have to choose between two worlds. They were both already here.

"I wouldn't miss it," he said.

CHAPTER FIFTY-FIVE

Reglay

FINALLY, KEL WAS returning to Second Hearth again.

It was strange to think that this castle was where he had spent more than eleven of the twelve years of his life. He had left it shortly after his father died, to make a secret journey to Mist's Edge, and from there he'd devised the plan that had destroyed Mist's Edge, fled to Esthrades under Arianrod's protection, been captured in Lanvaldis, seen Hywel crowned, taken back Stonespire . . . so many things, and all of those things seemed to hang between him and his former home, making it feel strange to him. It was so much smaller than he remembered.

He'd been a mess of nerves all morning. This was the first time he'd publicly address the people of Reglay since leaving it. *He* knew that he hadn't done it out of cowardice or selfishness; there had been nothing he could do for Reglay then, but Arianrod had convinced him he could still help Lantistyne as a whole. But that didn't mean Reglians would see it that way. If they believed he had abandoned them in their hour of need, could he blame them?

There was one other thing he was nervous about doing, something he'd wondered about for a long time. But when it finally happened, it was so quick and unexpected he didn't have any time to prepare. The first room he had wanted to see upon returning to Second Hearth was his father's study—*his* study, now. He had headed there as soon as they'd arrived at the castle, assuming he could attend to more official duties after he'd had some time to himself. But when he nudged the door aside with his elbow, he found someone already there, standing beside the massive ebony desk that still seemed far too big for him.

He almost thought she was someone else, some servant or official. She didn't wear a crown, or any other finery, and her hair was a wayward mass of black curls, impossible to tame. But there was only one woman that Kel didn't already know who could look so at ease in the home of another monarch.

"Oh," Adora Avestri said. "Kelken, I presume? I apologize—news of your return hadn't reached me yet, which means some poor messenger must be rushing around the castle looking for me. I meant to greet you immediately upon your arrival, but I seem to have become held up here longer than I realized."

She somehow both was and wasn't the person Kel had imagined, the person who had written to him so long ago, *May the crown rest lightly on your brow all the days that you wear it, and may those days be long.* Perhaps she had changed as much since then as he had. "I'm glad to finally meet you, Adora. Thank you for holding Second Hearth in my absence."

"Not at all. The Hallerns surrendered it without a fight. I just wanted to ensure things remained orderly within for your return, but I am glad of it; I fear my continued residence here was making some of your people nervous."

"What are you looking for?" Kel asked, maneuvering himself carefully behind the desk.

She had a book in her hand, and waved it at a stack of half a dozen more at her elbow. "I was . . . well, I hope this isn't presumptuous of me, but your library has gotten somewhat disorganized, so I've been spending most of my time here setting it to rights. I recalled seeing some books left in the study, so I went to fetch them, but this one caught my interest and . . . I'm afraid I lost track of the time."

"Not to worry," Kel said. "Arianrod told me once that you'd been borrowing her books since you were eight years old. I can certainly lend you that one, if you'd like." He took a quick glance at the title—something about dramatists during the First Empire, so not a resource he thought he'd miss. "Thank you for seeing to the library. It's one less thing I'll have to sort out for myself now that I'm back."

"I'm glad you've taken my meddling so well." She smiled, an expression, like most of hers so far, that was more eyes than mouth, but to Kel that made it feel more genuine. She pulled out the chair for him questioningly, and when he moved into it, she helped him get settled, leaning his crutches carefully against it. "There must be other questions you have for me, no?"

"As many as you have time for, I'm sure," Kel said. "How close did you come to Mist's Edge on your way here?"

"Oh, we quartered there overnight. It will need very extensive repairs, but the part of it that's still standing remains capable of housing visitors. An elderly gentleman I encountered asked me to give you his regards—the Hallerns had been keeping him imprisoned when we found him, and not feeding him well, so he was still recovering when I left, but he means to travel here as soon as he can."

"Eirnwin?" It was all Kel could do to keep his voice from cracking. Though he'd known it was a possibility, he hadn't dared hope Eirnwin would survive the destruction of Mist's Edge.

"I'm certain that was his name, yes."

"So we're both harder to kill than we appear. Thank you, you've eased my mind a great deal."

"Yet you still seem troubled," she said, with a gentleness and delicacy he admired. "Is there anything else I can ease your mind about?"

Kel hesitated, but he couldn't think of a good reason not to tell her. Perhaps one monarch ought to project strength and confidence in front of another, but she had only appeared like a human being to him, so he didn't see why he shouldn't do the same. "I'm going to address my people, for the first time since I left them. I know what I'm going to say, but I can't help but feel anxious when I wonder how they'll take it. I fear that I . . . that I may be destined to be unpopular with them."

He saw surprise on Adora's face, and then he saw her catch herself. "I suppose that kind of anxiety is only to be expected. I also assumed my people were bound to view me negatively, until I was confronted with proof that the opposite was true. But perhaps I can assuage your fears, as others once did for me. As far as I can tell, your people have been greatly awaiting your return. It is not strange—tales of your heroics have been spreading up and down the east, and many have reached this far. You are the youngest of Lantistyne's monarchs, with the smallest kingdom, and no doubt some of your citizens fear that Reglay might be swallowed up, Elgar or no Elgar, or that you might not have learned enough to be equal to the task of ruling it. But with all you have already done—the feats you've accomplished and the misfortunes you've survived—I think whatever you say today will be a formality more than anything. It is your deeds that will convince them, and in that sense, the hardest part is behind you already."

When he thought about it as if he were someone else, it did make sense. A boy king who had endured such setbacks only to help restore his fellow nations . . . he'd probably imagine that such a person was honorable, brave, even wise. "I just worry that when they actually see and hear me, they'll be disappointed. That they'll doubt what they think they know of me."

"I used to fear the same," Adora said. "When I started to give commands, I mimicked my father, whose rule I had admired. But I thought the immense gulf between us would be laughably apparent to everyone. It turns out, it wasn't. Sometimes people see things within us that we struggle to see in ourselves, yet overlook the things that seem most obvious to us."

Kel wondered which monarch he would most want to model his own rule after. Though he had loved his own father, he did not wish to emulate him;

he had been plagued by indecision through all the years of his kingship, vacillating from one position to another, often too vulnerable to outside influence. He admired Arianrod deeply, but she could never be imitated—only she could possibly be anything like herself. But now that he knew how much effort it took to be her, when she appeared so effortless to the world, he thought, could he not be the same in only that way? Could he create the version of himself he most wished to be, and devote himself to making that person real, even if only in the eyes of his subjects?

"What about you, then?" he asked. "Does this mean the crown rests more lightly upon your brow than it used to?"

"Ah, do you still remember that? I'm afraid I should've written, *May the crown be a burden that you choose, and not a weight forced on you.*"

Kel nodded. "Yes, that's a lesson I had to learn, too."

"Then you've learned it much earlier than I have."

"Not at all. If you think about it, I'm actually your senior. I've been an heir to the throne my whole life, and you've only had three years. And my coronation was before yours, if I'm not mistaken."

She laughed, and he was pleased with himself for having caused it; she didn't seem like someone who laughed out of politeness. "I hope to speak with you at much greater length before you leave," he said, "but I intend to address the people before the day is out, and . . . there is something I must discuss with my sister before that can take place."

"I'll look forward to it, then." She inclined her head toward the book she still held. "If I may . . . ?"

"By all means, take it with you." She bowed herself out, and Kel used the remaining minutes before Alessa's arrival to gather himself. It wasn't usual for him to be so nervous before a conversation with his sister, but he wanted to be sure he said the right things.

She slid the door open and shut without ever making a sound, a technique she'd mastered when his father was still alive. "Thank you for hearing me out," she said.

"Of course. I'm your brother. It would be a sad day if I couldn't hear you out." He rested his hands on the desk. "What's troubling you?" He thought he knew, but best to let her tell him in her own words.

"I wanted to know," she said, "if . . . if Hywel and I were to declare our betrothal, today or any other day, if you would be able to accept it, or if you intend to fight it in any way you can. If your primary concern is that our heirs may become a danger to yours, Hywel thought of a potential solution to that. Bastards cannot inherit both their parents' names and titles, so if I were naturalized as my mother's child, I could never inherit anything of your father's, no matter what anyone in the future might plot. If it will change your mind, I'm happy to do it. But if your mind cannot be changed, no matter what Hywel or I do or say . . . then I will not marry him." She swallowed hard, but did not look away for a moment, letting him know how serious she was about this. "Hywel is kind and admirable and . . . so many things, but I can't promise our match would be successful. Perhaps my feelings will fade with time, or I'll one day meet someone else I like more. But even if I never did, I could not risk being at odds with you for the rest of our lives."

Hayne had been right, then, though Kel had already come to that realization himself long ago. Lessa had never stopped thinking of him, and of what might be best for them as siblings. And now he could honestly say he had thought about it, too—putting his own feelings aside, just as she had. "You know," he said, "I did spend quite some time getting to know Hywel back when we were in prison together. Even though I haven't known him all that long, I suppose I know him more thoroughly than I could hope to know almost anyone else you might marry."

"I . . . suppose you're right," Alessa said, "but you already said—"

"I regret what I said." He wrinkled his nose. "No, what I mean is . . . I regret that I said it in that way. I would always want to know that you're aware of the risks of being his wife, but I shouldn't have assumed that you weren't. It's not for me to tell you what's good for you, or weigh risks on your behalf. If *you've* decided that marrying him, living with him, will make you happier than not doing those things, that's what matters most. All I want is for you to be sure, so if you need more time to decide, then take it. But if you *are* sure, then . . . as your brother, I couldn't let you *not* marry him."

Alessa was stunned, and then deeply, unguardedly happy. Kel knew for certain, then, how much this meant to her, and how much she had been willing to give up for him. "This is . . . I'm overjoyed to hear it, of course, and grateful, but it's . . . quite the reversal."

"I know. I grew up a bit. Hayne helped."

Alessa laughed, but it was a little watery. "Are you . . . are you really sure?"

"I'll miss you," he said. "How could I not miss you? But I'm sure. So long as you are." He took a breath, and made his tone breezier, lest they both dissolve into tears. "As for this plan to give you our mother's name, you and Hywel can decide whether you want to go through with it. Either way, I'll declare the betrothal when the time comes; I'm the first person my people will look to in order to determine how they feel about it, and if I seem happy and confident, it may help." He winced. "Speaking of Hywel, I've got to apologize to him, too, don't I?"

"I wouldn't worry about him," Alessa said. "He always said he was certain you would give your blessing in the end."

"Because he's just that compelling a brother-in-law, eh?"

"No. Because, he told me, you were someone who would always put other people's happiness above your own, and mine most of all." She smiled, a welcome flash of levity. "So it seems he learned a few things about you in that prison cell, too." But then, just as quickly, she was serious again. "Kel, I need you to promise me something. It's important."

He put a hand to his chest in mock outrage. "What? You're asking me for another favor? I thought I just gave you one."

"You gave me one for me," she said. "But now I need you to give me one for you."

"All right, let's hear it, then."

She put her hands over his, on the desk that had once been his father's. "As you grow, as you make this place your own, people are going to flock to you. Some of them will just be after some scrap of your power, something they think you can do for them. But I know you, and when you meet those people I'm sure you'll see them for who they really are. But there will be other people, who want to be near you simply because they love you. There will be, Kel, because there are so many things to love about you, and I won't be the only one who sees it. And when you meet those people, I want you to promise me you won't be too afraid to open your heart to them. I know what this place was like when our parents lived here—little more than a dreary prison, full of danger and discord. But I know you're going to change it, to bring back all the color and liveliness we never had as children. I know one day I'll come back here, and I won't even recognize it. But you have to promise me that you'll believe in it. That you'll believe you deserve all the good that will come to you, all the good that will come *because* of you."

"If you ask me to believe it," Kel said, "I will."

"Good," she said. "That's fine for now. Until the day you can believe it for you."

He left her to go out onto the balcony on the second story of Second Hearth, a place he and Lessa had been forbidden to play when his father was alive, lest they make themselves a target for assassins. A high and cushioned chair had been placed there, so Kel could say everything he wanted to say without fear of tiring. Before crossing the balcony threshold, he looked out at the crowd, more people than he had ever had to contend with at once. But they didn't look restless, or riled up;

the prevailing mood was one of expectation, a subtle energy thrumming through them. Most kept their eyes trained on the balcony.

Kel gripped his crutches tightly, and made his way into the open air to meet them. And as the sunlight fell on him, a great roar went up, a cheer that echoed from hundreds of throats at once, reverberating from the very walls of Second Hearth.

And then they all fell silent, and waited for him to speak.

EPILOGUE

THE WIND HAD a mid-autumn snap to it as Roger made his way through the familiar streets of Sheath Alleys, gold weighing heavy in his pocket. He couldn't remember ever carrying that much on him at once, and, truth be told, he was a bit nervous about it. He was an accomplished pickpocket himself, though he hadn't made a living with it since he was Marceline's age. But even the greatest taker could be taken from, if he wasn't careful.

Come late afternoon, the Dragon's Head would be packed to bursting, but that was exactly why Roger was coming here now, when the neighborhood was just waking up. Braddock was behind the bar, bent over it and sanding out a splinter; Ritsu sidled out from the back, arms full of groceries he'd no doubt just bought. "Good morning, Roger. We can't serve anything yet, but give me five minutes."

"Good to see you, Ritsu. I actually didn't come to eat. I have some news." Roger was surprised Halvard's had even been open at this hour, but since Halvard himself spent his days at the Citadel now, he'd given the day-to-day running of his business over to his apprentice, who happened to be Marceline's sister. Cerise had always been the industrious sort, it was true.

As for Morgan, she kept saying she'd bow out of politics and take the bar back from Braddock "once things are settled," and every time she said so, Braddock hummed noncommittally and kept up the job. He must have known as well as Roger did that she'd keep going back to the Citadel as long as the people of Sheath would have her. Absolutely all the representatives agreed that making the trek to the Citadel every morning was a bother, but absolutely none of them could agree on a district where their hypothetical headquarters should be located instead, so nothing had changed on that front. Morgan said they were working on getting the Citadel libraries open to the public, though, as soon as they hammered out the security details with Naishe's people.

"What's the news, then?" Braddock asked, finally looking up from the bar.

Roger jingled the coins in his pocket. "The marquise's delivery arrived this morning. The rest of it, I should say."

The deal they had made was this: she would send him ten of the fifty gold pieces, he would hand the library over to the subordinates who paid it, and she would send the rest of the coin upon final receipt of the books. It wasn't, perhaps, the most careful arrangement on either side, but Roger trusted her not to stiff him, as he imagined she trusted him not to try to withhold a book or two. He'd already given the original ten, as well as whatever else he could spare, to his aunt Rheila, so she could take Ryam across the sea to Sahai and pay for him to see the best healers there. There would be no miraculous cure, but the Sahaians had done the most research on the great wasting illness, and with the proper care and instruction, Ryam might extend his projected lifespan by years, even a decade. His life would never be easy, but he might still win himself enough time to fill it with things that mattered to him.

"That's not news," Braddock grumbled. "You just want to gloat about your windfall."

"You underestimate me, my friend. In fact, I've come to *share* my windfall." He stepped up to the bar, and spread twenty gleaming gold coins across it with practiced sleight of hand. "There you are."

Braddock made no move to touch them. "What's the joke?"

"There's no joke. Half for you, and half for Morgan. Though you'll both probably just put the money into the tavern anyway."

"That's half of what you have left, swindler."

"Aye, I can count. It's more than I need, so I'm thinking of my friends. Better that than spending it all on drink or gambling it away, no?"

"I . . . suppose." Braddock scratched his stubble awkwardly. "Damn, between this and what we got from Prince Hephestion when we were in Issamira, we could really change the place. No room to make it any bigger, of course, but even after the repairs are done . . ."

While he was pondering that, Roger snatched a coin off the bar and tossed it to Ritsu, who had just set down enough items to catch it. "I'm taking this away from his share for doubting me. Perhaps you can put it to better use."

Ritsu stared at it, not with Braddock's suspicion, but as if he couldn't believe his luck. "Are you . . . sure?"

"Of course! Anyone stuck working for Morgan needs to have a bit of fun now and again, and anyone this good at working for Morgan deserves the extra." He winked. "Got to run. Make sure he's not broken over there. Oh, anything new from Deinol?"

"Not since his last, but since his last was such good news, I think he's just busy."

"I'm amazed that prince hasn't gotten sick of him yet."

"I'm not," Ritsu said. "He saved my life, in a way. Him and Seth, even before Morgan broke the curse."

Roger slapped Braddock on the shoulder. "You see? It's good to show gratitude to your friends. He understands."

And then he was off again, before Braddock thought of any more questions or the mood got any heavier. This was a light day, meant for light things. And he had one more of those left to see to.

He'd been walking toward Tom's, but he ran into Marceline on the street about halfway there. "Roger? Tell me *you* aren't on your way to see the old man." She had stopped protesting that he wasn't *her* old man, but hadn't quite adopted it herself yet, so it seemed this was her compromise in the meantime.

"Actually, I was on my way to see you. I was going to ask Tom's permission, too, and I still can if you like. And look, this isn't exactly easy for me to say. I've never wanted an apprentice, and never thought I'd have one. But with all your tricks and all your resourcefulness, with the resistance and everything that followed, I'd be a fool if I let you join up with anyone else."

"Ah," she said. "Thanks, but I'm done with apprenticeships. You weren't the only one who offered, after everything—though you're the one I'd have been most likely to accept, I'll admit that much. But I'm not even quite sixteen, and I've done things some thieves never accomplish in their whole lives. To go from that to being some swindler's apprentice, even a swindler such as you . . . I'm sure you can see how I'm beyond all that now. From now on, I'm just a thief in my own right."

Roger knew she wasn't being contrary or trying to get him to pursue her—the words were mature and polite, without any gloating. He supposed he only had himself to blame. A different thief, perhaps a better one, would have been able to see the potential in her before it became obvious to everyone. "I understand. It's not the done thing, as I'm sure you know, and perhaps there are those who will spurn you for not being properly apprenticed, but I won't be one of them. And maybe I can still do one thing for you." He reached into his pocket. "Got my due from the marquise at last, and I thought I'd give you a cut. You are the only other one who knew about the books before I sold them, after all, and I never consulted you."

"Aye, but you did the right thing anyway." She raised an eyebrow. "Wasn't expecting to get anything from you."

"Well, that's the best kind of coin, then, isn't it?" He held it out to her: ten coins, half of what he had left. "Come on, don't you be difficult with me, too."

Marceline laughed. "Roger, do you think I don't know why you're going around giving so much of that away? Do you think Tom never told me that a thief who gets too comfortable too early in her career will never make a name for herself? Do you think I want to be weighed down any more than you do?"

"I'm not giving away *all* of it," Roger said. "Ten is as much as I'm keeping for myself."

"Well, I weigh considerably less than you, so I need to be lighter still. I will take one, though. Thank you."

"One?"

"Aye." She held up a hand, a single gold coin caught between two of her fingers. "This one."

"What the—" He reached into his pocket again. Fuck it all. Nine. "Monkey, when did you—"

"You see, twenty was definitely too heavy for you." She laughed again, dancing out of reach, just as light as she claimed to be. "See you around, Roger."

Damn. Maybe the girl was right, and apprenticing would just be an insult to her. Either way, it was a good reminder not to let his own skills dull—and a reminder that she'd be formidable competition, if she ever decided to compete with him.

He really was going to keep ten coins for himself, but now that left him with a surplus of nine. He thought about it for a bit, but only for a bit, and then he set off for Wallward Heights, for a Ninist vestry he'd last been in one sleepy afternoon many months ago, with a gentle and impressionable kitchen boy. That kitchen boy was only a memory now, like the gods of Ninism and the empire of Elesthene. But it was a more precious memory to Roger than the nine pieces of gold he was about to give away.

He put them in the hidden compartment beneath the Traitor's feet, where he'd once found the ruby that had led him to nine very different statues, and a truth that these lies were built upon. He should write something, later, to put in here with them, something to set any enterprising young thief who knew how to read finger-signs on the path to finding that truth for themselves, without just giving the whole game away. Roger was a thief, but he was also a storyteller, and you didn't start a story with the end.

He stepped back out into the gentle autumn sunlight, pondering a visit to the true Nine, not that any of them would acknowledge him. He suspected that they'd poke their noses into mortal affairs again, here and there—never enough to upset their precious balance, but with whatever little nudges they chose to allow one another. That much, at least, didn't bother him. Hell, that meant *Morgan,* who he'd played with in the streets of Sheath as a child, would probably have more power over Lantistyne's future than they would. And thinking about that made Roger feel as light as Marceline had seemed. That was how things should be.

The wind picked up, chilling the edges of his ears. Perhaps there wasn't much of the autumn season left after all. It'd be a far different end to the year than the last one—half of their original group of six wouldn't be at the Dragon's Head to bid it farewell. But they'd have Ritsu, and probably Marceline, and who knew who else that wind might blow into town?

He wondered if, perhaps, it would snow in Valyanrend this winter.

THOUGH IT WAS the seventh day, the day the throne rested from judgments, Stonespire Hall was busier than it had been all week. Alone out of everyone, Seren had nothing much to do, so she had spent the previous days evaluating the progress of one task after another and pitching in wherever her help was most sorely needed. The hall had been cleaned top to bottom, the first of the supplies for a fortnight of grand dinners had arrived, and the guest rooms had been laid out. And now a very familiar figure stooped to get her full height under the doorway to Arianrod's study, sweeping into an efficient bow. "Lieutenant Jill Bridger from down in the city, your ladyship, having recently been assigned the position by your ladyship's own hand."

Arianrod stood up from her desk. "Yes, Bridger, I know who you are. And I was there. I'm sure none of my guards have ever deserved a promotion more. What news do you have for me?"

"Your guests have arrived," Bridger said, to the point as ever. "I escorted them from the city gates, and they await you in the great hall. The captain said to tell you he'll be there soon; he's finishing up his weekly review."

Seren didn't miss the extra note of satisfaction with which she said the words *the captain*. After Gravis had been commemorated, Dent had been Arianrod's only choice to succeed him—and, indeed, no one else had so much as put themselves forward. He finally had the position Arianrod's grandfather had started grooming him for so long ago. As for Bridger, Arianrod had decided that the city needed its own leadership, since the captain of the guard was almost always at the hall and wouldn't have as comprehensive an understanding of the streets as those who always lived and patrolled there. Bridger had been serving in that sort of role unofficially anyway, and others before her; Arianrod had just made it clear.

"I suppose it's not good form to keep family waiting," Arianrod said, making a face as if the word tasted odd. She glanced at Seren. "Shall we go meet them? If they prove to be terrible bores, I can always ask you to entertain them for me."

The two people standing beside the great oaken throne were both shorter than Arianrod, but they had the same pale hair, and the woman's features looked so much like the way Arianrod's might in several decades that even Seren was surprised. The young man had her eyes, and a bit of her jaw, though none of her expressions. He wore a sword at his side, but Seren suspected it was largely ceremonial; she had heard how severely his leg had been shattered, and he still walked with a cane. He brightened when he saw Arianrod, an easy smile crossing his face. But the woman stood very still, with an expression Seren could not read.

"Your Grace," her cousin said, making a slight bow that adroitly left the weight off his bad foot. "What a marvelous city. I've long wanted to visit Stonespire."

"It is at that," Arianrod said, as immodest about her city as she was about herself. "I've arranged for my captain to give you a more thorough tour in a bit; I'd take you myself, but I'm afraid there is simply too much left to do, so I'll have to join you for dinner instead. But we can always move it to another time if you'd rather rest after your journey first."

"Not at all." He tapped his cane against the side of his foot. "I've quite gotten the hang of it. Taken plenty of long walks around Araveil already. But perhaps you're a bit weary, Aunt? You're . . . unusually untalkative."

The woman in question cleared her throat, as if coming back to herself. "I beg your pardon. I had been warned, but even so, it's . . . quite extraordinary."

"The resemblance," Arianrod said. Not a question. "I'm not her twin, of course, but I'm told I inherited much of her. You and my mother were identical?"

"We were certainly born that way, though of course we acquired minor differences as we grew. You never saw a portrait of her?"

"My father was having one finished for her, but then she died, and he destroyed it. A choice I'm told he regretted, but he was ever like that."

"A stubborn man in all respects," her aunt said. "But he did love her—and, as strange as it seemed to me, he made her happy. I never doubted that. There's a portrait of her as a young woman at our manor in Araveil I shall send to you. I have others of the two of us that I treasure more, and you should have a likeness of your mother."

Arianrod shrugged. "If you say so." Her eyes flicked to Seren. "This is Seren Almasy, my self-appointed bodyguard. Seren, my cousin Ithan Vandrith, and our aunt, Lady Euvalie."

Seren inclined her head, untroubled by the Vandriths' curious looks; she was used to them. "Self-appointed?" Ithan repeated.

"Yes, she's quite concerned for my well-being. Though I am grateful, of course." She grinned, and Ithan smiled back; though their temperaments seemed quite different, Seren guessed that they both appreciated a wry joke. That was better than nothing to build on, she supposed. "Before we get into more trivial matters, I believe I owe you two an apology. It seems I quite destroyed House Vandrith's ancestral sword. I can't say it was accidental, but it was the best choice open to me at the time. And I'm unfortunately unable to replace it."

"Think nothing of it," Lady Euvalie said. "If what I hear is true, that sword caused you a great deal of suffering. Perhaps it is we who should apologize."

"And it's not as if I could wield the thing anyway," Ithan said. "I used to be the best fighter in our family; I haven't the faintest idea where it would go now. Count it an acceptable loss, cousin."

"And where will you go now?" Arianrod asked. "I'm told you used to be something of a wanderer, to use your skills where they were needed."

"Well, that is the question." He shrugged. "I'm the youngest son of a youngest son, so nothing much for me to inherit, and swordplay's the only thing I've ever been good at. My family's tightly knit enough that I can bother them for a while, but that won't last forever. I'm sure the king would give me a position if I wanted one—or even if I didn't—out of gratitude or pity or something, but that's not the right way to go about it. Positions should be offered to those suited for them."

"So you would be suited for the knowledge of swordplay, but not for fighting yourself. What about a master of swords, making sure greener recruits learn all their forms? I'm told they're respectable positions, and in demand."

Ithan exchanged a glance with his aunt. "Yes, she's been telling me much the same thing. Perhaps the lord of some castle in the Lanvaldian countryside will take me on, though hopefully not as a favor to my family."

"No," Arianrod said, "when I said they were in demand, I meant *here*. Dent has asked me to hire one, and I haven't gotten around to it. Apparently Gravis was better at that part of captaining than he is. You'd have to live here at the hall, or else down in the city nearby, but if you think it's a position you'd want, you can talk it over with Dent. I've no idea what makes a good master of swords, so if he recommends you, that's good enough for me."

Another glance at his aunt, this one much more incredulous. "I . . . wouldn't want to burden your captain with having to judge his lady's relative."

"Why would it be a burden?" Arianrod asked. "I don't care if he hires you or not. He would know that. It would do me the advantage of having the search done with, but if you aren't a good fit, we'll find someone else."

Ithan laughed, cupping his chin in one hand. "Your frankness is refreshing, cousin. I shall certainly speak with the captain about it. It would be nice to live among family without being an imposition."

Seren could tell Arianrod wanted to ask him what precisely would be nice about it, but she refrained, and soon their conversation was concluded until dinner. Dent came to collect the Vandriths, and Seren and Arianrod returned to the study, the latter breathing a theatrical sigh of relief. "That was all right, I suppose. I might have known seeing me would give Euvalie too many thoughts of my mother, but she did *want* to see me. Hopefully it does not cast too great a pall over her visit."

"I don't think it will at all," Seren said. "I think, if anything, she'll be glad to know her sister's daughter is well." When Arianrod seemed to accept that, she added, "If Ithan takes that position, it means you'll have family at the hall again."

"Yes, though I can always dismiss him if he proves irksome. If there's something to be had in keeping family close by, I may as well discover it."

"I suspect Dent is more your family than anyone named Vandrith will ever be, but I agree it's a worthwhile experiment."

Arianrod rolled her eyes. "If you claim that family ought to be important to people, and then redefine *family* to mean *people who are important to you,* you've actually proven nothing at all. How tedious." She sat back down at her desk, spreading the papers out. "Dent suspects he shall be able to keep them busy for a couple hours, so let's see how much work we can complete in that time. It may not seem like it, but we are making progress."

Only she could say something like that. To anyone else, the progress would be unmistakable. She had handled all the work created by the brief occupation already: all damage to the city had been catalogued and reconstruction efforts fully funded, the victims commemorated, disrupted trade routes restored, militias honored and disbanded, annual taxes reassessed, and an impressive array of grievances that had piled up in her absence resolved. Esthrades still prospered, despite all that had happened, and Seren had no doubt that it would flourish even more in the future. She could not say what would happen in any of the other nations; she did not have the political skill or historical knowledge for that. But she knew that Arianrod had already proven herself more than equal to any challenge that might arise in the lands she governed.

"My lady," Seren said.

"Mm." Her head was already bent over some piece of paperwork.

"Compared to the war you've just won, all of this will be simple for you to accomplish—it takes time, but no great intellectual effort on your part. Once it's finished, how will you occupy yourself? I know you well enough to know that your mind requires a challenge, but since I don't think you're willing to start another war just to create one, I do wonder what you'll do instead."

"Oh, so many things." She sat back in her chair, a contemplative smile playing about her lips. "In fact, it feels a luxury to have so many choices. Reading and translating the books I got from Valyanrend makes a decent starting point; who knows what lost knowledge I might glean from them, or what endeavors that knowledge might inspire? I want to undertake diplomatic missions to all of Lantistyne's other countries—to see them for myself, and make sure their rulers aren't engaged in anything too stupid, but don't worry, I won't tell them that part. While you may think it's a bit silly, I'd like to recover Silverthorn, the Margraines' ancestral sword, if I can; I don't fight with blades, but it is a part of my family's history. And you already know the most important task I'm going to set myself."

"I do?"

"Of course. What else could it be but ensuring that magic returns to this land as it once was?"

Despite what she'd said, Seren did feel a jolt of surprise. "But if that . . . god, or spirit, or whatever it was is to be believed, that's a task that must involve far more than just us."

"So be it, then."

"And . . . it's a task that would prove impossible to complete in your lifetime."

Arianrod laughed. "When I was small, they called magic itself impossible. The first Daven Margraine said that he would be a lord one day, and they told him that was impossible. They told the sixth Daven he could never survive the fall of Elesthene, and his daughter that the numbers in her head were just delusions. They told me I could never defeat Elgar, and here we all are. A genius needs an impossible task, Seren. Otherwise it's just boring."

Yes. That was how she should always be. The girl who believed, *knew,* that she could do anything she wanted, and proved to everyone else that they had been fools to doubt her.

Arianrod drew a finger across a sheet of parchment on her desk. "Things might be very different, in the future. If this peace holds, I might be able to leave Esthrades for longer periods of time, to travel to places I never could before. Perhaps even across the sea. I might see the Palace of Memory with my own eyes one day." Sahai's greatest repository of information, full of works by only the country's most distinguished scholars, chosen by the most rigorous methods anywhere in the world. "If I did all that . . . would you still wish to come with me?"

Seren bit her lip. "Of course. Always. But you should know, the training of the Inxia Morain is . . . complicated, and mine more so than most. It is common for us to make enemies, and sometimes those enemies are very powerful, or grow to be. If you go to Sahai, and I go with you, I may bring additional danger on our heads. Any assassination attempts aimed at me may expand to include you as well."

Arianrod rested her chin in her hand, her face serious. "Ah. So you're saying, if we go to Sahai together, a whole lot of people might try to kill us."

"Precisely."

"And that's different from our life at home . . . how, exactly?"

Seren's laughter burst from her chest so forcefully she could never have contained it. It sounded strange to her, because she was still unused to laughing so freely. But Arianrod was looking very pleased with herself, and Seren didn't cover her mouth, or try to keep her shoulders from shaking. She hadn't considered it before, but it was nice to have someone try to make you laugh on purpose.

She inclined her head. "All right. You win. If you wish to go to Sahai, my lady, I will see to it that you get there."

Arianrod was silent for a bit, still resting her chin on her hand. When she did speak, her voice was as soft as Seren had ever heard it. "What is it that you wish for?"

She tried to think of how to say it, as she always did, and, as always, the perfect words eluded her. "Only . . . that we might not be parted."

Arianrod pushed her chair away from the desk, standing to meet her eyes. "Seren, you know I am not skilled at sentiment. The extravagant promises people make one another in tales, the stuff of vows and protestations . . . these things are more incomprehensible to me than any foreign tongue could ever be. So I cannot swear to you that we will remain together forever, that no circumstances or changes wrought by time will ever alter the way we feel at this moment. But I can say . . . when you and I come to the end of our lives, we might find we have spent them, more often than not, in each other's company. And if that should come to pass . . . I would be well content." Her mouth twisted—betraying, perhaps, the slightest scrap of vulnerability. "Can that be enough for you?"

Seren swallowed a lump in her throat. "I could never ask for anything more."

That earned her a glower. "That's *not* an answer."

"Ah. No. Sorry. I meant—that sounds . . ." She struggled vainly for the right word, and settled on, "Wonderful."

She only noticed the tension in the set of Arianrod's shoulders when it dissipated. She ran a hand through her hair, with a smile that was . . . relieved, perhaps? Though maybe a bit self-satisfied, as well. Seren had certainly never minded that she was vain, or ever doubted it. "Good, then. And I can promise we won't leave the continent for another few months, at the very least. As for the more immediate future, I'm going to try to finish the rest of this book"—she tapped one of the ancient tomes on her desk, with a title Seren assumed was written in Old Lantian—"and then we shall probably have to prepare for dinner with the Vandriths. But after they've retired for the evening, I'll give Benwick and Dent the night off, and we can have the orchard to ourselves for a while. You know very well that you won't relax unless I make you."

"I would never deny it," Seren said. "Shall I leave you to your reading until dinner?"

"Might as well—oh, drat." She stared at an empty spot on her desk where something was clearly supposed to be that was not. "I noticed some interesting runic combinations in that book yesterday, and I meant to see if any of them had made it into Hodge's *Irregular Runic*. But if the book's not here, I must have left it in the library. Can you go check? It should be on the desk with the new arrivals."

The book was easy to find, a smallish tome with a well-preserved cover. But as she walked back through the study doorway, opening her mouth to speak, she fell silent.

She had felt no alarm, not even in the first instant. Though Arianrod was slumped in her chair, the regular rise and fall of her breathing was clearly visible even from the doorway. Seren crossed to her on silent feet, and rested the back of her hand lightly against Arianrod's forehead. There was only the slight warmth of her skin, no feverish flush or alarming coldness. She had not been casting spells, but had fallen into an entirely ordinary nap.

Seren would never have dreamed of waking her; whatever Arianrod said, she had to be made to relax, too, and there was no one in Esthrades who deserved it more. But it would not do for a bodyguard to nap just because her mistress did, so she retreated to the broad windowsill looking out on the orchard and took a seat, pulling her legs up after her. She rested her chin on her knees, and settled in to watch over Arianrod until she awoke.

And if she let herself smile, well, no one was there to see it.

THE MESSENGER FROM Esthrades had delivered three things: a heavy and slightly misshapen lump wrapped carefully in cloth and twine, a rectangular wooden box about the width of Adora's two hands, very tightly sealed, and a letter, sealed in wax. The Margraines had given up the sigil of their house hundreds of years ago, when the sixth Daven and his children had rebelled against Elesthene, so Arianrod's letters always came with only a simple *M* pressed into the wax.

Adora knew exactly what the carefully wrapped lump was, but she hadn't a clue what could be in the box, so she put off her impatience and excitement for a few minutes more, and opened the letter first:

Adora,
There are five books here, all of a good length. I'm afraid that since I'm the one preserving them, I have given priority to those that seem the most valuable to me. But I have also included one that, to you, will surely seem beyond price. I'm sure you'll know immediately which one I mean.

As for the rest, I've saved the books on magic for myself, since I assume you'll find them rather less compelling than I will. But I've given you some works of history and biography that seem promising, and relatively untouched in our mutual studies thus far. I look forward to inevitably debating the merits of their scholarship with you, and trust you'll pass on any truly earthshattering revelations sooner rather than later.

The box has also been spelled—a new trick I've been working on. It came off flawlessly in my tests at home, but if something's gone wrong on the journey and the contents are unpleasant, I can only apologize. But no matter what, it will certainly not be dangerous, and the spell will dissipate once the box is opened. If it does work, consider it my first repayment for all the gifts of cinnamon you've delivered to me over the years.

I've considered your request to visit you in Eldren Cael for the midwinter celebrations, and I think it remains feasible. I shall have to consult with Dent closer to the date, but he is optimistic. I suppose I shall also have to thank Kelken and Hywel for ensuring that my lands were as undamaged by the Hallerns' pathetic invasion as possible. Perhaps you will advise me as to how to seem appropriately grateful in writing, as it is very troublesome.

I don't know what you mean by asking how "things" are with Seren, but she remains in good health, and says she is drafting a list of questions and requirements for you regarding midwinter security in Eldren Cael. I am sure it will be astoundingly dull, and I give you permission to disregard it, but she will sulk if I don't send it.

I hope to receive your thoughts on the books soon. Give my regards to your mother, but not to Hephestion.

A signature was not necessary, as no one else on earth could have written such a letter. But Adora did not have time to give it more than a fond smile, because she couldn't wait to get a look at the books a second longer.

They were, as Arianrod had promised, largely works of history and biography, any one of which would have been a stunning addition to even the most comprehensive libraries on the continent. But it was the fifth one that stopped Adora's breath, bringing her heart into her throat. Her mind translated the Old Lantian title reflexively: *Betrayal on the Plains,* by Valter Lisianthus.

Not only had she never read this book, she had never even *heard* of this book. Many scholars of Lisianthus speculated that some of his works had been lost to time, judging by references and quotations found in journals and letters written by his readers from many centuries ago. But they were thought to be merely a handful of shorter poems, perhaps several hundred lines each. She had never read anything suggesting an entire lost epic.

She was desperate to get started, but she knew that once she began reading, she wouldn't be able to tear herself away. And there was one more thing she was too curious to let sit. It took all ten of her fingernails and the edge of a penknife, but she finally managed to pry the lid of the mysterious box open.

When she saw the contents, she couldn't believe she hadn't guessed.

Pillowed on a folded handkerchief was a generous pile of blueberries, not dried but mouthwateringly fresh, and glistening as if they'd just been washed. Adora brushed her fingers over them, and found them slightly cool to the touch, despite all the hard riding over hot plains they must have taken to get here. If it was a spell that was broken upon opening the box, she could probably guess what it was: it preserved the contents precisely as they were when the box was closed. It was the only method Adora could think of to get fresh Esthradian blueberries to Eldren Cael without spoiling them on the way.

There were half a hundred things waiting to be done, of course. There were laws to amend and architectural proposals to review, budgets to balance, acts of valor to reward. Now that the war was done, her mother wanted her to force Vespas to retire from the army again, whereas Vespas had arrived to argue that his exemplary performance in a second Hallern war merited freedom from any and all demands his sister might attempt to lay on him. The latest scouting reports from the border had arrived from Amali Selreshe, as exquisitely detailed as Adora had come to expect, and Hephestion had pronounced himself well enough to travel again, so she had to decide where to send him. Now that Rhia would definitely not be returning to her former position, Eldren Cael needed a new captain of the guard. And she really should, at least tentatively, begin looking at the field of potential marriage candidates and determining which she was positive she could exclude; it wouldn't do to give anyone false hope, especially since the negotiations could ultimately take years.

But even a queen could claim an hour or two for herself now and then, especially in peacetime. The work would still be there when she was finished.

Adora gently flipped the book open with one hand and reached inside the box with the other. She hadn't forgotten the horrors Jocelyn Selreshe had inflicted on her family. But magic could do things like this, too. Magic was the reason the blighted lands of the Gods' Curse were slowly returning to life. And most importantly, she had promised her oldest friend that mages would never be feared in Issamira as long as she was its queen. At this moment, it wasn't a promise that felt hard to keep.

She turned her eyes to the first line, and let the story carry her away.

FROM THE EDGE of Sundercliff, Castle Evenfall had looked slender and delicate. Up close, it was monumental, a hulking mass of stone that was nearly as tall again as the cliff on which it sat. Ivy had wound its way up those proud walls, weeds and daffodils choking the paths where travelers had once trod. The only sound, beyond the faint and lonely cry of a gull, was the crash of waves against the cliffs, not so different from the way they had sounded from the edge of Lirien's village.

She could see Sundercliff from here—little more than a boring brown smudge. She had thought briefly about stopping there first, trying to negotiate for the lifting of her exile: *I'm sure you haven't heard any news from outside of a ten-mile radius, but*

I actually helped save the continent from a despot. And magic's only going to get more common from now on, so your attempts to brand me as some demonic anomaly won't fare so well in the future—just letting you know! But she didn't want to provoke any violence, and, after all, she didn't actually want to return. Better to let them think whatever they were going to think of her, and be on her way. But there was one place she *was* determined to go, no matter what. And now that she was here, she wasn't disappointed.

She was still deciding whether to go inside. It wasn't some superstitious fear of the unquiet ghosts that were said to haunt this place; she simply wasn't sure whether it was fair to invade other people's privacy like that, no matter how long dead they were. It was *probably* safe—this castle was renowned as a miracle of construction once—but she hardly wanted to survive a continent-wide upheaval just to be taken out by falling masonry. Still, she might have a rare window into the lives of First Empire aristocrats and their Elesthenian replacements, or even find a surviving relic or two from the days of the Tournells. When she thought of it that way, it seemed an excursion worth making.

But until she was sure, one way or another, there was nothing stopping her from sitting out here on the cliff, tasting the salt wind off the Endless Sea, and kicking her legs out into empty space.

Was it so bad to live for yourself? That, in truth, was the sin that had gotten her expelled from Sundercliff. She had refused to care about the things the other villagers had decided were most important: family, community, nation. She had never felt that desire that so preoccupied them, to belong to something greater than yourself. To find a worthy husband, to nurture their children, to work for the good of the village, to live for the glory of Hallarnon . . . no. As far as she was concerned, someone consumed by that might as well be dead.

And for that they called her proud. But what had she really asked for? To find shelter of an evening; to eat a few fish. To walk down a road that changed, whose every bend held the promise of the unexpected. To see strange horizons, and distant cities, and oceans not her own.

To see this world, and know it, and live joyously within it—and then one day to die, and leave dust where she had been, careless of any kind of legacy. Was that desire truly a mistake—an arrogant presumption, lodged too deeply in her heart to be torn out? Even now, after all this, she couldn't truly think so. Even now she still wanted it, and damn what anyone else might say.

She turned her head slightly, just enough to acknowledge the presence of the figure sitting beside her on the cliff. A slip of a girl, long hair tangled by the wind. She looked a bit younger than Lirien, though that might have just been the guileless expression on her face—and besides, the being that looked out from behind those innocent eyes was doubtless older than Lirien could guess.

"You look different," she said.

Amerei shifted toward her, without disturbing a single blade of grass. "You must already know that's your fault, not mine. It means your opinion of me has changed."

"I suppose, now that you mention it, I can stand you a little more than before." She looked out over the water. "Just tell me one thing. It's bothered me from the moment I first found her by that lake. And now that, thanks to Cadfael, I know something of this business of bodies and souls, I think I know what it is. She and I . . . we met once before, didn't we?"

The spirit smiled. "Once?"

"You're saying it's more than that?"

"It would have to be, for you to have even an inkling of it as you are now. Many times, in many lives. Most souls are still too young for that. Even we were surprised when it started happening."

"Ah," Lirien said. "So it's like that, is it?" She tilted her head back, filling her gaze with the sky. "Does that mean . . . that everything has been decided already? What I'll make of my life, whether I'll help or hurt her?"

"No," Amerei said. "It has always been your choice to make. For all those times, they were all different."

"And what about you, who bore witness to all those times? What makes *you* keep coming back?"

"Even mortals journey in search of themselves, don't they? So it is with us. But since we are much larger, we have much farther to travel, and countless destinations to reach. Through all the lands of this world . . . through the ages, through the abyss of memory . . . still we search, to understand what we truly are." She glanced up at the castle towering above them. "Do you know the story of the last lady of this place?"

"Aravain Tournell. Aye, I've heard it. She was a general in the First Empire, but she betrayed her country rather than fight against her lover, who had rebelled against the last of the Fortindair emperors. And she lost everything."

"That is not why," Amerei said. "She was always a kind girl, but shy, doubtful of her own judgment, no matter how high she rose. It took the one she loved and trusted most to show her that the doubts she held, the injustices she feared existed, were graver and more deeply rooted than she had guessed. That is the true reason she turned against her former masters, though I was certainly blamed for it. And though she lost more than some ever possess, I believe she would say it was the right choice." She smiled. "Yaelor is so stubborn. For him, our paths are always separate, always in competition. But sometimes love can *make* you brave. Sometimes you find the strength to stand only when you know you are not alone."

"Huh," Lirien said. "I'm surprised. To hear you, out of everyone, say something so idealistic."

"You shouldn't be," the spirit said. "I, out of everyone, dwell most poorly with cynicism."

"I suppose that's true." She leaned back on her hands, burying them in the long grass. "Now that I've had my question answered, what did you come here for? Not to ask me for another favor, I hope?"

"No," Amerei said, with an unrepentant smile. "I really would be testing my luck with the others to try that again. I simply wanted to let you know I'll be watching over you. I'm curious to see what path you end up walking."

"And if it ends up being yours or not, you mean?" She shook her head. "You just can't let a single person go, can you?"

"Throughout the centuries upon centuries of my existence," Amerei said, "mortals have shaped my being as much as I theirs. So if I believe in my own importance, if I put myself at the center of everything, it is because mortals have placed me there, too."

"I can't argue with that. I've heard the stories and songs, too, after all." She got to her feet. "Here's something they don't say. Sometimes, you have to put yourself at the center of everything. I've tried everything I know how to get her to do that, because I think it's what she needs. That's a kind of caring, too—a different kind than if I'd stayed with her, but that doesn't mean it doesn't count. Now, with any luck, she'll figure out who she's meant to be. And maybe she'll meet someone else, and maybe she'll forget about me, and maybe she'll realize we would never have been any good together. And maybe she won't. What would be the point of the future if you knew everything that was going to happen?"

Amerei laughed, clear and bell-like, her green eyes closed. And then she was gone.

"That was a bit rude," Lirien said. "I know you're still there. You were the one who told me that."

But she was smiling as she looked out at the sea.

It was a fitfully sunny morning in southeastern Esthrades, patches of golden light dappling the grass as they broke through the clouds. They had finally found a significant enough clearing in the forest for a rest, such a rare thing in this area that Cadfael stopped to admire it. It was more or less a full circle, with only grass within, and a couple rocks along one of the outer edges that could serve as seats. He and Rhia made use of them, but Kaitan was restless, pacing across the clearing and back. He hadn't even put down the large and mysterious wrapped bundle he'd been carrying for the duration of their journey, and Cadfael was no closer to knowing what was in it.

Apparently Kaitan's ultimate destination was Kaiferi, where he'd rejoin his friend Deinol and Prince Ryo in time for the latter's coronation. There had been quite the stir in Aurnis over the miraculous return of their heir after five years, and some had doubted his identity, but between the palace servants who had helped hide him while he recovered from his wounds, the testimony of his surviving royal guards, the unanimous support of Lantistyne's remaining rulers, and the tales of the bravery he'd shown during the fight for Valyanrend, his reinstatement was barreling on at a good pace.

As for Cadfael and Rhia, they planned to eventually swing north. Talis was visiting the remains of her village, all the way up in the mountains of southeastern Lanvaldis, as a way of paying her respects and trying to move on from that part of her life. Cadfael would have accompanied her, but she insisted it was something she had to do alone. So he and Rhia would meet her afterward, head to Araveil to ensure their house was still in good standing, and from there, the three of them would go wherever their whims took them—just as he and his sister had talked about doing so many years ago, though he could hardly have imagined Talis then.

In the meantime, Rhia had wanted to go to Lakeport, so that's where they were going. They were glad for the chance to reunite with Kaitan, but Cadfael wasn't entirely sure why he was still traveling with them, since they'd gone out of his way some time ago. No doubt he would talk about it when he was ready. And he remained a surprisingly decent travel companion, even though he still couldn't cook.

Kaitan tilted his head, as if listening to something carried on the wind. "It's strange to say, but the forest feels more peaceful than the last time I was here. Though perhaps that only goes to show that I've let the tales of the Esthradian forests affect me too deeply."

"I haven't heard those, but I think I feel it, too," Rhia said. "We're well into autumn, but it's such a mild day. Hardly any leaves have fallen."

"Will you stay here long, do you think?" Kaitan asked. "In all your traveling?"

"A scene like this makes it easy to say so. And I'd like to see the way Esthrades thrives, now that its rightful ruler has returned." She smiled, her gaze going far away. "But that's the possibility of it all, isn't it? Every nation has a chance to change now. It's not just what Arianrod Margraine will do with Esthrades, but what the new Kelken will do with Reglay, what Hywel will do with Lanvaldis—even what your prince will do with Aurnis. And who knows how fundamentally Hallarnon might change, for better or worse?" Her smile turned fond. "And Adora will finally have full control of Issamira, of course, but that's the one place we're sure we aren't going to go for a while, since I spent so long there already. But we'll see her again one day. And you? I suppose you'll stay in Aurnis for the foreseeable future?"

"Indeed, I'm not sure if I'll ever leave it again," Kaitan said, only half joking. "I've missed it—the true Aurnis, not some territory on a map. After five years of occupation, it will finally belong to its people again."

"And Lanvaldis as well," Rhia said, "though I can't say I have the same attachment to it." She stretched her arms over her head. "What do you say, Cadfael? Should we stop to eat now, or press on for Lakeport?"

"Before we get into all that," Cadfael said, "Rhia, I've been waiting for us to be alone, but it's been a week already, and we haven't been alone for more than a couple minutes at a time. And we aren't likely to be alone much in the future, either. So I know it's a bit casual, but you should just take this. I can't stand to hold on to it any longer."

He handed Rhia a sheet of parchment, but she kept looking at him, not at what was written on it. "What's this?"

"A present from the king. There's one for me, too. Just read it, and you'll understand."

Once everything had settled down, Hywel had invited him to Second Hearth, where he'd been staying with Kelken and Alessa. It was about as different as could be from the feeling of being summoned by Eira, but Cadfael still hadn't wanted to take any chances. He'd come with his guard up and his excuses prepared: he had resolved never to serve a monarch again; helping Kelken and Hywel escape Selwyn's clutches was a special case, since he didn't do it under orders; now that Lanvaldis was relatively peaceful again, he was determined to stick to his original goal of freely traveling the continent with his sister; and so forth until Hywel hopefully got sick of him. But the subject Hywel had broached was one he hadn't been prepared for: "I've been considering how best to reward you for all you've done."

Please don't say with a position among your guardsmen, Cadfael prayed. "Well, if you're struggling, Your Grace, there is the matter of our house—Rhia's and mine, where we lived with our father. It's still vacant, which is a stroke of luck, but since the two of us were both presumed dead, I expect we'll struggle to lay claim to it. And there's the matter of the three years of taxes we didn't pay, of course."

Hywel had smiled. "I'll have a deed to the place drawn up. And you can consider the taxes forgiven; it's the very least I can do. But I had something else in mind—I hope you're not offended that I consulted Kelken and Alessa, though I confess their advice mostly confirmed my own inclinations."

That was good news, actually; those two knew precisely where he stood when it came to serving kings. "And what did you decide?"

"Well, there's a slight snag. You know my mother was illegitimate, and never held a surname till she married my father. So I know the laws well. Only a monarch can legitimize a bastard, and only to one name. Once it is done, it can never be changed. So I hope you will think as long as you need to about this decision."

He produced a piece of parchment, though he did not unroll it. "It has come to my attention that your mother was Maia Glendower, heir to House Glendower and the castle of Grayeaves. I'm not sure if you know that the most recent Lord Glendower, your grandfather, died half a year ago, but the castle and lordship have been trapped in a struggle between three distant relatives ever since. If you and your sister were legitimized under the Glendower name, you would immediately become the next Lord Glendower, and the castle would be yours by right. You would—"

"I know what you're trying to do, Your Grace," Cadfael said. "I thank you, but it's unnecessary. Or . . . no. Strange as it may seem, it is unwanted. Please bestow the castle and the lordship on whomever you deem fittest to possess it. But I do not and have never wanted that name. You can ask my sister as well, if you like—I would happily surrender it to her—but I am as confident as I have ever been in anything that her answer will be the same as my own."

"Kelken and Alessa were confident in it, too," Hywel had said, and it was only then that Cadfael noticed he had never looked surprised. "They convinced me to go a different way."

He finally unrolled the parchment—which turned out to be two sheets, not one—and handed him one of them. As he read it, Cadfael's fingers started to shake, and his vision swam. He could hardly believe what he held in his hands.

"Your Grace, I underestimated you," he said. "I did not expect to receive any reward I cared for. But this is the best gift you could possibly have given me."

Now, as Rhia read her own parchment, she pressed a hand to her mouth, her eyes filling with tears. "Oh, Cadfael, this is . . . after all this time . . ."

The parchment was covered with line after line of self-important official language, but the essential part was clear: *From this day forward into eternity, the undersigned known as Rhia will possess undisputed right to and inheritance of the surname, lands, titles, and other significant property of Hafter Llewellyn, a resident of Araveil . . .*

"He'd probably say it's unnecessary," Cadfael said, trying to break the solemn pall that hung over them. "He always wanted us to use his name anyway, legal right or not." He said that, but half his mind was focused elsewhere, musing on the adjustment of having to introduce himself with an altered name. Cadfael Llewellyn. He tried it out silently: *I'm Cadfael Llewellyn, and this is my sister.* Two things he had thought lost to him forever, finally where they should be.

Rhia wiped the tears from her face. "I should beg your pardon, Kaitan."

"Oh, not at all. I feel privileged to witness a moment that brought you so much joy," he said, as courteous as ever. "But if it's not too forward of me, perhaps I might propose an additional way to celebrate."

He finally produced the package from under his arm, and unwrapped it carefully, setting its contents on the grass. Rhia frowned down at a pair of *tsunshin.* "Swords? But we already have our own. And these . . . well, pardon me for saying so, but they don't look particularly exemplary."

"They're dueling swords," Kaitan said. "The edges have been blunted. It's true that some duels between *shinrian* are fought with live steel, but I'm fairly certain your brother would kill me if I suggested that."

"That's correct," Cadfael said.

Rhia still looked troubled. "I don't understand. You want to duel me? But we don't have any grievance, do we?"

"No, of course not." He gave her a reassuring smile, then sat cross-legged on the grass, unsheathing one of the dueling swords and examining the blade. "I just thought it was the one thing I might be able to do properly."

"What do you mean?"

He laid the blade across his knees and reached for the second one. "*Shinrian,* as I'm sure you know, is a mark of skill, not virtue. That's why a *shinrian* can never be unmade, no matter how dishonorable his actions. There was a point in my life when I wanted that title more than anything, but I almost didn't get it, because no one wanted to have to lose to me. But then someone I admired—that I admired more than anyone—finally accepted my challenge. He didn't hand me a victory; he simply gave me a chance to earn one."

He looked up at her. "In so many ways, I'll always fall short of what he was and is. But there is one thing he did for me that I can pass on. If the title of *shinrian* holds any interest for you, I can give you a chance, too."

Rhia rocked back on her heels, crumpling the grass. "I . . . haven't thought about it in so long. When I was a child it all seemed great fun—I just assumed I'd win it eventually as a matter of course. And by the time I'd matured enough to know it was all a lot more complicated than that, I already had other things on my mind. You don't think it would be presumptuous of me to aspire to that title now? I'm not even Aurnian, after all."

"I'm only half Aurnian myself," Kaitan said. "And there is no requirement of nationality, which I think would be as absurd as the requirement that once stood against women. The only rules are these: you must fight a known *shinrian, tsun-*

shin against *tsunshin,* and you must have a witness declare that you won fairly and honorably. But the witness can be anyone—your brother will do. And there is no particular solemnity attached to the act. One of the *shinrian* I admire most earned the title while drunk, and plenty of people with no other noble qualities have possessed it. You don't have to worry about being the worthiest candidate, and I assure you that you'll be far from the unworthiest."

Rhia was still biting her lip, though her gaze was less clouded. "What happens if I lose?"

"Nothing," Kaitan said. "I'll let you challenge me as many times as you like. Though you may have to come to Aurnis for at least some of them."

She turned to Cadfael. "And you're all right with this?"

"I don't really understand it," he admitted. "But as long as you fight with those blunt blades, and your opponent promises to behave himself, I don't see why I should object. I certainly consider myself qualified to judge a mock duel."

Rhia brushed herself off and held out her hand. "Then I accept. I'm honored to have the chance, especially from you."

"I feel the same," Kaitan said, smiling. "As for the rest, I'll let my sword speak for me."

They marked out an arena in the clearing, and took up positions on either side of it, waiting for Cadfael's signal. And Cadfael himself stole a moment to take everything in, letting the wind and the scent of the forest wash over him.

He hadn't seen Yaelor again, but that didn't trouble him. If anything, he admired the spirit's restraint. Now he had a sister, and a name. He had Talis, who already yearned to see again. He had a rare and beautiful sword that would never mean any kind of destiny to him, only the proof of his father's love. And beyond that, he was unfettered, free. Yaelor must have wanted to make sure he knew that.

The spirit would always be connected to him, of course. He would always know everything Cadfael did, and no doubt he'd pass silent judgment in that haughty way of his. But that didn't bother him as it once had. If anything, it was a challenge he could choose to meet. *Maybe I'll make myself worth watching yet.*

He raised a hand and said, "Begin."

ACKNOWLEDGMENTS

When I first started writing what would become *The Empire's Ghost*, I didn't know if I could even finish a novel. Three door stoppers later, I owe thanks first to Pete Wolverton, my editor, who understood what I was trying to do from the beginning and kept me on track to the end. Thank you to Sarah Bonamino, Sara Beth Haring, and everyone at St. Martin's Press, with an extra helping of gratitude for Young Jin Lim, who created three covers I love and incorporated all my tweaks. And thanks once again to my brother, whose homemade computer is still going strong all these years later, planned obsolescence be damned.

Finally, thank you to my readers. To my parents, my first and most loyal fans, who always took me seriously when I said I wanted to be a writer, even when I was five and my backup plan was "Narnia explorer." To every relative, friend, friend of friend, and online reviewer who let me know they enjoyed the series, including those who insisted they don't "normally" like fantasy (I think you might be surprised!). And to everyone who followed these characters to the end: I hope I gave them a send-off that lets you imagine many more adventures for them. I know I will.